UNREMEMBERED

MURDER

Carroll John Daly

THE COLLECTED

OF RACE WILLIAMS

INTRODUCTION BY

STEEGER BOOKS

2022

UNREMEM-

HARD-BOILED STORIES

BERED

VOLUME 7

MURDER

BROOKS E. HEFNER

CARROLL JOHN DALY

ASSOCIATE EDITOR

Ray Riethmeier

ACKNOWLEDGEMENTS

Walter Behnke, the Estate of Carroll John Daly, and Brooks E. Hefner

Cover photo © Mark Krajnak | JerseyStyle Photography

ISBN

978-1-61827-653-7

Introduction

BY BROOKS E. HEFNER

HISTORIES OF HARD-BOILED detective fiction—that American blend of tough-guy action, vernacular narration, and a hint of deduction—love to celebrate the genre's founding figures. Dashiell Hammett provided the sophisticated model; his Continental Op stories showed a world filled with corruption and violence, a world managed only by the efforts of a laconic, slangy, wise-cracking, and nameless narrator. Raymond Chandler provided the world-weary polish, first in his finely wrought Carmady and John Dalmas stories in the pulps, and then in his renowned Philip Marlowe novels. Marlowe's private detective loner—one deeply indebted to Hammett's other pulp creation, Sam Spade—combined the right amount of weariness and wit, of dangerous dames and colorful metaphors, perfect for a world where surety appeared to be slipping away and powerful forces—for Chandler, usually the wealthy and elite—seemed to be pulling everyone's strings. This genre—or perhaps this style or attitude within a genre—has had such an influence on crime fiction that it is difficult to find any example of the genre in contemporary American culture that doesn't exhibit some trace of the hard-boiled. Innumerable adaptations since Chandler's heyday have included such diverse variations as the work of Chester Himes and Mickey Spillane, James Ellroy and Sara Paretsky, not to mention countless film noirs modeled on the attitudes and postures of hard-boiled fiction. For all intents and purposes, American detective fiction is almost inevitably hard-boiled.

Such truisms about the genre nevertheless obscure a more complicated truth. Hammett's first hard-boiled stories appeared, as many crime fiction fans know, in a pulp magazine named *Black Mask*. Chandler's first stories appeared there as well. From the mid-1920s through the mid-1930s, editor Joseph T. Shaw all but made the hard-boiled style the house style of *Black Mask,* emphasizing action over deduction and spare narration over gratuitous detail, placing the magazine in contrast with the classic detective fiction of the Arthur Conan Doyle and S.S. Van Dine model. During Shaw's sometimes tumultuous tenure as editor, he introduced a number of other talented purveyors of the hard-boiled style: Paul Cain, Frederick Nebel, Raoul Whitfield, Horace McCoy, Lester Dent, George

Harmon Coxe, and others. In 1946 he collected these writers in the first anthology devoted to hard-boiled fiction, *The Hard-Boiled Omnibus*. If anything, *The Hard-Boiled Omnibus* both created the first canon of hard-boiled writers and emphasized the collective nature of the enterprise. After all, many writers worked together to produce the style of these stories in *Black Mask,* and, with Shaw's editorial suggestions, the "hard, brittle style" associated with the hard-boiled became a product of the publishing culture that was *Black Mask.*[1] A glaring absence from Shaw's volume, however, was a wildly popular *Black Mask* writer named Carroll John Daly. There are many reasons Shaw may have excluded Daly: Daly's star had fallen by the mid-1940s, Shaw never really liked Daly's cruder style, and Shaw had not really "discovered" or cultivated Daly the way he had done for so many of these other writers. In fact, Daly began publishing in *Black Mask* four years before Shaw entered its editorial offices. And Shaw's omission is a crucial one, for if any one writer can claim to be the originator of the hard-boiled style, it is Carroll John Daly.

Daly presents a curious problem for historians of the hard-boiled. His name is briefly mentioned in many of the standard narratives of the genre's emergence, and he is often credited with originating the style, but then quickly dismissed as some kind of evolutionary Neanderthal, a writer who somehow invented something without realizing what he was doing and went on to see others perfect it while he remained in a state of arrested development. For example, William F. Nolan, in his excellent collection *The Black Mask Boys*, called Daly "an artificial, awkward, self-conscious pulpster" and described his writing as "impossibly crude, the plotting labored and ridiculous."[2] Ron Goulart called him "a somewhat embarrassing founding father."[3] Others have made equally broad judgments. In one of only a couple of academic articles on Daly, Michael S. Barson called him "a third-rate word-spinner who hatched a second-rate protagonist who did his thing in these fourth-rate productions best left on the broom-closet's top shelf in the back."[4] One must, however, balance these harsh words with praise for Daly, and such praise often came from *Black Mask* readers and writers. Daly's greatest champion was Erle Stanley Gardner—fellow *Black Mask* contributor and creator of the Perry Mason series of novels that began in 1933. Nearly every significant effort to write Daly out of hard-boiled history was met by a Gardner response. Not long after Raymond Chandler published his famous homage to Hammett, "The Simple Art of Murder," in *The Atlantic Monthly* in 1944, and when Shaw was about to present his canon in *The Hard-Boiled Omnibus*, Gardner lauded Daly in Howard Haycraft's *The Art of the Mystery Story*, a documentary volume by one

---

1   Joseph T. Shaw, *The Hard-Boiled Omnibus* (New York: Simon and Schuster, 1946), vii.

2   William F. Nolan, *The Black Mask Boys* (New York: Mysterious Press, 1987), 35.

3   Ron Goulart, *The Dime Detectives* (New York: Mysterious Press, 1988), 32.

4   Michael S. Barson, "'There's No Sex in Crime': The Two-Fisted Homilies of Race Williams," *Clues: A Journal of Detection* 2.2 (Fall–Winter 1981), 110.

of the great historians of mystery fiction. Gardner's contribution, "The Case of the Early Beginning," argued that "Daly did as much, or more, than any other author to develop the *type*" of what he called the "action" detective story.[5] Throughout his career and even after Daly's death, Gardner was insistent on the importance of Daly as a foundational figure for *Black Mask* and for the hard-boiled model of writing. In a 1965 contribution to *The Atlantic Monthly*, Gardner resolutely claimed, "Carroll John Daly helped to originate the hard-boiled school of detective writers when, some forty-odd years ago, he created the character of Race Williams."[6]

Despite the efforts of writers like Gardner, traces of Daly have remained scant; he still appears a kind of ghostly forbearer, unseen and unheard, rather than one of the most successful and popular *Black Mask* writers of the 1920s and 1930s and one of the best known writers of pulp crime fiction in his heyday. His work has only occasionally appeared in crime fiction anthologies, often with headnotes and introductions apologizing for his inclusion, but by and large Daly's short fiction and serialized novels remain hidden away in the pages of rare pulp magazines. This volume—the final in a series chronicling the adventures of Daly's most successful character, Race Williams—seeks to correct that by providing a definitive edition of Daly's work, documenting the untold history of the emergence of the hard-boiled detective. For the first time, readers will be able to assess Daly on his own terms and to read the stories that captivated pulp magazine readers and provided the basis for Hammett, Chandler, and the rest of the American crime fiction canon. Of course, the stories here show Daly's innovations in language and action, as well as his penchant for pulp melodrama. But one thing is sure: with Race's two guns blazing, this is hard-boiled history.

As is the case with his fiction, Daly's biography also remains little documented; a handful of sketches present just a few (occasionally contradictory) details about him. Daly's grandparents emigrated from Ireland in the wake of the 1840s Irish Potato Famine; his paternal grandfather, William Daly, set up as blacksmith in Manhattan, living in the diverse Ward 20 on West 34th Street. His maternal grandfather, a liquor dealer, settled in Yonkers, New York, just north of the city in Westchester County. Daly's father, Joseph Daly, studied law at Cooper Union and soon moved to Yonkers to set up practice with John F. Brennan, a classmate. After rooming with the Brennans for a time, Joseph would soon marry John's sister, Mary. With a successful law practice and a strong connection to the Tammany Hall political machine, Joseph Daly would soon build an enormous Queen Anne style home in Yonkers, which the society pages took great notice of in 1894. Carroll

---

5   Erle Stanley Gardner, "The Case of the Early Beginning," in *The Art of the Mystery Story: A Collection of Critical Essays*, ed. Howard Haycraft (New York: Simon and Schuster, 1946), 205.

6   Erle Stanley Gardner, "Getting Away With Murder," *The Atlantic*, January 1965, 72.

would have been about five when his family moved into this mansion. Seven years later, on June 27, 1901, tragedy struck the family as both of Daly's parents died of heart failure on the same day, a freak occurrence that garnered significant attention from *The New York Times*, given Joseph's prominence in New York Democratic politics.[7]

Daly spent the rest of his youth living with his uncle John Brennan, who willed Daly nearly $40,000 on his death in 1925.[8] For the years between his parents' death in 1901 and his emergence as one of the most popular writers in *Black Mask*, most of the details we have appear in an autobiographical statement in *Black Mask* from 1924:

> I was born in Yonkers, Sept. 14, 1889; attended half the prep schools in the country with a fling at the American Academy of Dramatic Arts; a little known school devoted to the study of the human body; a short period at the study of law and a longer one in stenography.

> My first business venture was the opening, with another chap, of the first moving picture show on the boardwalk at Atlantic City—came theatres at Asbury Park, Arverne, and a stock company at Yonkers. After that the deluge—stock salesman, real estate salesman, manager of a fire-alarm company, and a dozen or more other jobs.

Daly was quite honest about his peripatetic working life: his first business venture was The Criterion Theater in Atlantic City, which Daly briefly owned with John Child in 1911 before selling his interest in the theater back to Child within six months.[9] In 1916, he took over the Warburton, a theater in Yonkers, and recruited a stock company before shutting it down within a month.[10] Despite his patchy work history, he did manage to settle down in one respect. Daly married Margaret G. Blakely—known familiarly as Marge—in 1913, and their first and only child John Russell Daly was born in 1914. Daly's World War I draft card shows that he was then serving as a law clerk in his uncle's law office, but by 1920 he was working as an independent real estate broker, possibly following in the footsteps of his father-in-law Samuel Blakely. It's clear, however, that this was around the time he began to seek publication of his fiction.

Daly began writing in earnest in the early 1920s, publishing in a handful of general fiction pulps like *Brief Stories*, *10 Story Book*, and *People's Story Magazine* before breaking into the pages of *Black Mask* in 1922. This relationship became absolutely central to Daly's success over the next decade. While he continued publishing in other pulps—includ-

---

7   "Died Almost Together," *New York Times*, June 28, 1901, 5.

8   "John F. Brennan Left $174,150.82 Estate," *New York Times*, May 13, 1925, 23.

9   I.B. Pulaski, "Atlantic City," *Variety*, March 18, 1911, 24. I.B. Pulaski, "Atlantic City," *Variety*, October 21, 1911, 30.

10   "With the Press Agents," *Variety*, October 20, 1916, 10. "Shows Closing," *Variety*, November 24, 1916, 13. "Stock Repertoire," *The New York Clipper*, December 6, 1916, 13.

Carroll John Daly

ing *Argosy All-Story Weekly*, *Top-Notch*, *Action Stories*, and others—Daly's strongest affiliation was with *Black Mask*. Above all, Daly's creation in 1923 of the first undeniably hard-boiled detective series character, Race Williams, is his greatest legacy as a writer of pulp fiction. This new style of detective fiction, however, wasn't a sure thing; the *Black Mask* publication of Daly's first hard-boiled stories was nearly an accident. As he reflects in "The Ambulating Lady," a piece published in the *Writers Digest* in 1947, *Black Mask* editor George Sutton was on vacation when these stories were submitted and associate editor Harry North accepted them. On Sutton's return he expressed his dislike for Daly's hard-boiled characters, but the characters drove circulation numbers up. North became a central figure in the direction of *Black Mask* during the years he was associate editor—cultivating Daly, Gardner, and Hammett—before taking a position at the newly founded magazine *The New Yorker* in 1925. Daly and Race Williams quickly became synonymous with *Black Mask*, and his name on the cover— especially in the early years—could mean "a 15 percent rise in sales for that issue"; a 1924 Readers' Poll listed Daly and Hammett as the two reader favorites.[11] By the time Joseph T. Shaw arrived at the magazine in 1926, Daly was central to the magazine's identity; indeed, at that point his name had appeared on more covers than any other contributor. It was also around this time that Daly started to move toward longer novelettes, producing his first Race Williams novel-length serial, *The Snarl of the Beast*, in 1927.

As Daly's pulp successes increased, he found himself both settled and established. After living far uptown in Manhattan (at 620 West 190th Street) following his marriage, he purchased a newly constructed home at 37 Concord Avenue in White Plains in 1923. Three years later, in November 1926, he was the subject of a brief news sensation when he was mistaken for a swindler named John J. Daly, arrested by U.S. Marshals, and imprisoned in Manhattan's notorious Tombs for a night before clearing things up.[12] Despite this case of mistaken identity, Daly was at his professional peak. As the pulps thrived, so did Daly, and

---

11 Nolan, 39. *Black Mask*, October 1924, 40.

12 "Innocent Novelist Jailed as Swindler," *New York Times*, November 11, 1926, 1.

his greatest successes occurred between the introduction of Race Williams in 1923, and the beginning of the decline of the first generation of the pulps in the late 1930s. His Race Williams serials began to be collected in book form in 1927, supplementing his primary income from the pulps. And when magazine pay rates were cut—sometimes in half or more—in the early 1930s as a result of the Depression, Daly responded by churning out more fiction and new characters, tripling his published output from 1931 to 1933, and still receiving top rates for his work. During the 1930s, Daly introduced new characters— Satan Hall (1931), Vee Brown (1932), and Clay Holt (1934) were the most popular—and published regularly not only in *Black Mask*, but also in *Dime Detective*, *Detective Fiction Weekly*, and other crime fiction magazines. Race Williams continued to sell at high rates, even after Daly left *Black Mask* over a shakeup in editorial strategy under Joseph Shaw in 1934. In the late 1930s, the popularity of Daly's characters almost translated into film—a transition that other *Black Mask* writers like Hammett and Gardner had made—as he had a couple of contracts for the film rights to the Race Williams character nearly executed.[13]

For a number of reasons—possibly including the Hollywood potential of his characters and his son Jack's interest in an acting career—Daly and his family decided to relocate to the west coast, and, after a brief stay with Erle Stanley Gardner at his Temecula ranch in 1938, rented a house in Santa Monica in 1939. Like many other pulp writers, Daly was chasing new forms of entertainment in the face of declining pulp sales: film, radio, and, later, television. However, he never broke into the business and continued writing for the pulps as they declined precipitously throughout the 1940s. As the decade wore on, Daly found it harder to place stories in a contracting pulp market that demanded shorter stories, not the serials and novelettes that had been his bread and butter. When he was able to place these shorter pieces, the rates were among the lowest he had ever been paid. Squeezed out by a real estate boom in Santa Monica, the Dalys soon moved, first to a desert home in Coachella in 1944, then to a small house in Montrose, California in the Crescenta Valley north of Los Angeles in 1948. When he wasn't writing or reading mystery fiction, Daly was pursuing two of his beloved pastimes: mentoring teenagers and young adults in the neighborhood, and studying and practicing hypnotism, a hobby that only turned up in one of his late stories. Meanwhile, Daly's son Jack, back from the war, pursued a career as an actor, and by 1950, began receiving work in both motion pictures and television. Daly would publish through the mid-1950s, but by then most of the magazines in which he'd regularly appeared would be long gone. While pulp writer and historian Frank Gruber writes that "[t]oward the end of his career he had become reduced to writing for the comic books," there's only evidence in his correspondence with Erle Stanley Gardner that Daly tried his hand at comic strips, and that, as Stephen Mertz describes, his focus in the later

---

13 See David Wilt, *Hardboiled in Hollywood: Five* Black Mask *Writers and the Movies* (Bowling Green, OH: Bowling Green State University Popular Press, 1991).

years was on attempting to sell to television.[14] After his move to California, and especially by the late 1940s, Daly regularly touched his friend and admirer Erle Stanley Gardner for loans to carry him over between increasingly rare and small payments from magazines and Marge's inconsistent work opportunities. Meanwhile, as pocket paperback novels filled with ever more sensational content began replacing pulp magazines as escapist reading material, Daly was eclipsed by writers like Mickey Spillane, who found astonishing success, in part, by introducing heavy doses of sex and sadistic violence into the hard-boiled pulp formula. As many critics have noted, Spillane was a huge fan of Daly's work and wrote a well-known fan letter to him in 1952, admitting that "Race was the model for Mike" Hammer.[15] Such praise troubled Daly, who remained conservative about sex and felt distraught over Spillane's astonishing success, considering his own virtual poverty in the early 1950s. The final pulp publication under Daly's own name—fittingly, a Race Williams story billed on the cover—appeared in *Smashing Detective Stories* in May 1955, just two months after Marge died.[16]

The final trace of Daly is a bit of cruel irony. His obituary notice, published January 15, 1958 in *The New York Times*, begins, "Carroll John Daly, who wrote the 'Race Williams' series for The Saturday Evening Post, died Monday in Los Angeles."[17] Neither Daly nor Race Williams ever got close to the pages of the high-paying, culturally-authorized *Saturday Evening Post*. If Daly had not spent the last fifteen years of his writing career attempting to get published in a magazine, any magazine, such a mistake on the *Times*'s part might be merely funny. But to glance over Daly's record of submissions and rejections, a copy of which is held by UCLA, is to witness Daly's desperation as he sent dozens and dozens of stories to one magazine after another, only to see the vast majority of them rejected. He would almost always start with the high-paying slicks, like *The Saturday Evening Post* or *Collier's*, but the rejection notices from these magazines came far quicker than those from the numerous pulps he would submit to afterwards. This evidence makes it clear that Daly's moment had passed, that both he and Race Williams were—for a time at least—relegated to the literary historical dustbin.

Unlike Hammett, who shifted to the slicks in 1932 with his Sam Spade series, or Gardner, who transitioned to *Liberty* in 1934 and *The Saturday Evening Post* in 1937, or Chandler, who reluctantly published one of his last short stories in *The Saturday Evening Post* in

---

14   Frank Gruber, *The Pulp Jungle* (Los Angeles,: Sherbourne Press, 1967), 141. Stephen Mertz, "Carroll John Daly: The Post War Years," *Race Williams' Double Date and Other Stories* (Normal, IL: Black Dog Books, 2014), 14.

15   Mickey Spillane, *Byline: Mickey Spillane* (Norfolk, VA: Crippen & Landru, 2004), 215.

16   Daly's final pulp appearance was under the pseudonym John D. Carroll in *Double-Action Detective Stories* #4 in 1956.

17   "Carroll J. Daly, Wrote Mysteries," *New York Times*, January 17, 1958, 25.

1939, Daly never quite managed to straddle the cultural divide between the low-paying pulps and the high-paying slicks, even if he routinely tried to sell (or "slant" in writers' slang) his work to outlets like *The Saturday Evening Post* and *Collier's*. Had he done so, his name might be better remembered today. But in some ways, the case of Daly's disappearance from the critical and historical radar makes collections like this more exciting: to read Daly's Race Williams stories is to follow a long obscured path of hard-boiled history, winding through the desolate highways of Westchester County and the dark alleys of New York City, surrounded by tough-talking figures and explosive action. Few writers embody the energy of the pulps like Carroll John Daly, and this republication of his Race Williams stories, in the signature two-column format of the pulps, is the first time most of these stories have been available since their original publication. It is a long overdue triumph for one of the most influential and successful figures of the pulp era.

THIS VOLUME CONTAINS the final published adventures of Carroll John Daly's Race Williams, stories that range across more than a decade of Daly's life. Devoted fans of Daly's "confidential investigator"—a title he usually preferred over "private detective"—might have worried about the fate of Race during the Second World War. Race disappeared from the pages of the pulps between March 1941 (in "Too Dead to Pay," *Clues*) and October 1944 ("Body, Body—Who's Got the Body"), his longest absence to this point. Pulp readers of hard-boiled fiction had no doubt gotten used to seeing Race a few times a year: *Black Mask* published Williams stories regularly from 1923 through 1934, and *Dime Detective* featured the character from 1935 through the beginning of 1940. Indeed, the first six volumes of this series feature stories published over an 18-year period. However, once *Dime* severed their relationship with the character, Race had no consistent home for the remainder of his time in print. Two stories presumably rejected by *Dime* ended up appearing in *Clues* before Race's long hiatus during the war. Daly, too, ceased regular publishing during this time: between May 1941 and March 1944, he published just one story; it did not include his most famous detective character.

Daly shifted away from pulp publishing at this time for several reasons. Letters to Erle Stanley Gardner reveal his increasing frustration with the pulp market: lower rates, lower (from his perspective) standards, and a radical new sensationalism were particularly discouraging. This also meant that Daly and Race both seemed a tad bit too Victorian for the current generation of pulp readers. At the same time, Daly—having relocated to the west coast only a few years before—was closely following the war. During this period, Daly was also consumed with family life: his son, Jack Daly, enlisted in the army, was married (in 1942) and the couple had their first child in 1943. Jack was also in the midst of pursing an acting career, something Daly wrote proudly about to Gardner. The years that followed, however, were not especially good to Daly in any professional sense. His struggle to find outlets for his work was a recurring theme in this correspondence, and he found it difficult to believe that a legendary character like Race Williams no longer had value in the pulp marketplace. His pay rates were cut by more than half and his stories seemed increasingly out of sync with pulp readers. He was especially discouraged when Mickey Spillane debuted Mike Hammer in 1947; Spillane's tough-talking, action-first private detective was simply a version of Race Williams, updated with additional sex and violence thrown in for a readership looking for mid-century sensationalism.

The slow decline of Daly's career, however, tracks with the fate of the pulp magazine market as a whole. While Race first appeared in the pioneering *Black Mask,* part of the first generation of genre-specific pulps founded in 1920, in the mid-1930s he moved to *Dime Detective,* founded in 1931 as part of Harry Steeger's Popular Publications. In the mid-1940s, Race began appearing in a host of titles, no longer identified solely with a single magazine or publisher. These included Street & Smith's *Detective Story Magazine, Thrilling Detective* and *Popular Detective* (both part of the Thrilling Group), along with *Smashing Detective Stories,* and a couple of return appearances in *Dime Detective.* With each new generation of magazines attempting to supplant its predecessor, the cost of individual issues dropped, and so did the pay to writers. Daly and Gardner both felt that this resulted in inferior work, and they looked back on their heyday of the 1920s as a golden age for pulp writers.

Nevertheless, Daly's Race Williams soldiered on in characteristic fashion through this decade of adventures. Longtime fans would no doubt be delighted to see Race in a host of familiar situations and settings. Many of these stories feature Race ranging across Manhattan and Westchester County, encountering blackmail schemes, inheritance scams, suspicious guardians, helpless young heiresses, and racketeers aiming for respectability at any cost. When Race leaves his native New York, the destinations are notable. "A Corpse Loses Its Head" (July 1945) opens in Florida, a setting Daly had used a few times before, notably in the novel *The Hidden Hand* (1928). "Unremembered Murder" (March 1947) has Race visit a rural town named Norton to sort out the details of the murder of a local judge; this trip to investigate corruption in small town America recalls earlier stories like "The Death Drop" (1933) and Race's first appearance in "Knights of the Open Palm" (1923). Of particular interest is "This Corpse on Me" (June 1947), Race's first appearance in *Thrilling Detective.* This story has Race tangled up in a war-related spy story around Indio, California, near where Daly and his wife moved in mid-1944 after they had to leave Santa Monica when their landlord sold the house they were renting there. After moving in, Daly wrote to Gardner, "I have two articles I am thinking of writing[:] one of them, The [*sic*] first is… IS COACHELLA VALLEY THE GARDEN SPOT OF AMERICA. The second is IS COACHELLA VALLEY THE HELL HOLE OF THE EARTH." [18] Despite Daly's difficulty in adapting from New York City to the rural desert, "This Corpse on Me" makes an intriguing use of this unusual setting: "Open and legal card rooms in Indio. Like an

18   Carroll John Daly to Erle Stanley Gardner, 28 September 1944, Erle Stanley Gardner Papers, Box 143, Harry Ransom Center, The University of Texas at Austin.

old-time Western thriller." While the story tantalizes with the idea of Race himself relocating to the west coast for a different brand of adventures, the stories that follow see him back in the comfortably dark and crowded streets of New York.

Beyond its mirroring of Daly's own relocation, "This Corpse on Me" also injects what appears to be some degree of self-consciousness into Race's fictional world. One character, Addison Howe, is an artist whose best days are behind him. He tells Race, "I could make a few thousand dollars in a morning, not so far back, but the touch, you know, the divine spark—it burnt out suddenly. Just like that. I couldn't make a nickel with my brush now." Howe's struggles cause Race to meditate on the artist's former success: "I recalled Addison Howe's paintings. None of this arty stuff. His simple desert scenes. What color! He must have made a fortune. In all the national magazines—double page spreads too and often paid for by some big advertiser. They said he could name his own figure." A dried-up artist with a history of success in the "national magazines," an artist who "could name his own figure" for his superior, but not pretentious work ("None of this arty stuff."): Howe sounds a lot like a late-career Carroll John Daly confronting a pulp market that was no longer clamoring for his work. But because Daly is writing this story, he can craft his own conclusion to this crisis, leaving some hope for an artist who feels he has lost his touch.

One of Daly's more interesting experiments in the stories collected here reflects his growing personal interest in pop psychology. "Race Williams' Double Date" (August 1948) has Race's head spinning as he quickly discovers that the two young women he had encountered early in the story are merely two personalities of the same woman. He was excited when this story was accepted, though it still necessitated some compromise, writing to Gardner, "Dime Detective has bought my first dual personality story—Race Williams—and even so I had to bow to the publics [sic] ignorance and have it turn out a fake at the end. Up until then it is all true." [19] This story features Race consulting psychiatrists and specialists in personality disorders in an unusual investigation for a detective who never enjoyed the brainwork of detection. Given Race's background, it's certainly notable to have him say, "Then I got mixed up in the scientific world myself"!

Across his career, Race—typically a loner—had a few companions. One figure that remains consistent from the early stories is Jerry, who Race calls "my boy—anyway my assistant if you are one to quibble over calling a forty-one year old 'boy,'" and who continues to offer the occasionally insightful quip at opportune moments. In "Head Over Homicide" (May 1955), the final published Race Williams story, Jerry seems concerned that Race is veering a little close to the sensational detective fiction Daly hated: "A half-naked girl— Ain't we getting just like the dicks in the racy fiction?" And while in earlier adventures Race had often dangerous romantic interests like the Flame and Jane Blake/Iris Parsons, here

---

19 Carroll John Daly to Erle Stanley Gardner, no date "Saturday" (late November/early December 1947), Erle Stanley Gardner Papers, Box 143, Harry Ransom Center, The University of Texas at Austin.

Race is a bit more free and easy with his attractions. He's no lothario, but his early insistence that "there's no sex in crime" no longer seems quite so clear in these late stories. These stories, however, do see the introduction of one new recurring figure, the dandy informant Reginald Riley, formerly "a hardened criminal." First appearing in "I'll Feel Better When You're Dead" (December 1947), Riley shows up in another four stories after that, always providing Race with a tantalizing bit of information—sometimes for a price—and always affecting the accent of culture and refinement. Riley's importance in these later stories suggests that the post-war traffic in information might be just as important—if not more so—than Race's signature brute force.

Nevertheless, fans of Race Williams will still find plenty of that force across these stories. While they feature a bit more brainwork than usual—Race insists that "There are times when I use more than my brawn and my trigger finger, and do more than talk through the side of my mouth"—he still cracks more than his share of heads, and his aim remains impeccable. However, his final adventure ("Head Over Homicide") ends in a fashion more characteristic of the generation of detectives that followed him: asking for payment after having foolishly returned a check to his client, shaking his head over the inscrutability of human nature, and apparently a little bit drunk. "I have always said my business is a rough business, no place for clever thinking and keen character analysis": The final words of this, his final adventure, remind us that Race would always put action over deduction, and this transformation of detective fiction remains the core of the powerful legacy of both Race and his creator, Carroll John Daly.

Body, Body— Who's Got the Body?

CHAPTER 1

I WAS ENDING up a case and I didn't like it. Larry Lapeno was a tall slender grease-ball with thin sneering lips that some women called smiling ones. His eyes were shrewd and foggy. His black hair the kind that first caused white towels to be placed over the back of Pullman chairs. I didn't like Larry Lapeno and I liked him even less now as I sat beside his desk and counted out five hundred dollars in black-mail money.

"Really, Williams"—he ran a hand through the shiny blackness above his oily forehead—"the damned letter isn't worth five dollars to the girl. I suggested she use you, and I set the price at five grand so you could pull me down and pose as a clever man to the— Miss Cole is the name, isn't it?"

"There's the money." I bit the words off sharp. "If I don't get the letter, I'll blow a hole in your forehead."

"You know, I think I cut my price because I like you, Williams, You're so forthright. At first, it was simply business. Now I like to send clients to you. You are not a time waster." He was slowly counting the money while he talked. "And don't think I underestimate you. Many people have threatened me and I have laughed. But I haven't laughed at you. There are times when I believe you shoot men for the simple pleasure of it."

"Get through with the deal or it will be more than a simple pleasure."

"Two hundred and twenty dollars," he murmured, then in his usual voice which was soft and oily like his hair and skin: "I could notify the police to pick you up if anything happened to me."

It almost turned my stomach to sit there and look at him and realize the suffering the man had caused—broken homes, broken health, children tossed about from one divorced parent to another, suicides. How he did it with those brains or lack of brains of his I don't know. The cops had watched him for years now, but no one ever saw him buy a letter, let alone steal one.

"Five hundred dollars," he said finally, as he slipped a rubber band around the stack of small bills and tucked them into an envelope. Then he lifted a slot in the wall behind him, shot the envelope into it. "How naïve I was the first time I did business with you, Race Williams. I gave you the letters, you gave me the money, and then you stuck a gun in my stomach and took both. Now you see the money drops into a safe a few stories below and makes of you an honest man. There, don't be impatient." He leaned forward and looked at me eagerly. His eyes grew bright through the mist. His words lost their softness or at least took on a sharp edge when he spoke.

"Williams," he said, "we all reach our peak in business at one time or another. Yes, even in blackmail. I am about to reach mine and retire. I will complete one final deal. It will involve a half million dollars. Perhaps more, certainly not less. Your fee will… can be enormous." And after a long pause and leaning far over the desk: "If you work for me, for me instead of your client, I will add out of my own pocket exactly fifty—"

That was as far as he got. Maybe I didn't mean to do it. Certainly, I didn't think about it before I did. And I couldn't know if he was offering me fifty dollars or fifty thousand or fifty million for that matter and I never would know. My right hand simply snapped up from my side and smacked across his left cheek. It was an open slap, but I must have had my heart in it for he fell along the flat desk, catching his feet in the chair and crashing to the floor. When he got to his feet, I could plainly see the marks of my fingers. His face was livid.

"Williams," he said, slowly and with viciousness, "Race Williams, you are the first person ever to… to knock me off my feet."

"You've had breaks then," I told him. "Give me that letter—now."

A shaking hand went below the desk, trembling fingers came up and handed the envelope to me. I took my reading glass out and compared the handwriting I had with the letter inside. It was what I wanted all right, so I pocketed it and turned toward the door. He spoke then, and the same quiet viciousness was in his voice.

"I'll never forget," he said. "Never. I have seen people grovel at my feet. I've known a woman to jump from a hotel window. You will come crawling and—"

I turned, crossed the room and put both my hands around his throat.

"Out with it, greaseball." I forced him to his knees. "I've done business with you because it saved other people from being blackmailed first by you and then by some private detective. Now it's me, eh? Well, you've got nothing to lay over my head but death. All the sins on the calendar wouldn't make me cough up a nickel to you, let alone grovel at your feet. As for personal, bodily harm from a rot like you—that's a laugh. But you might hire someone—" I stopped then and let go of his throat. His lips were blue, his tongue was sticking out. Hell, I had nearly strangled him, though why that should bother me I don't know.

But it bothered him all right. He was kneeling there blubbering out words. I had misunderstood him. He intended me no harm. He didn't know why he spoke as he did. It was right for me to strike him. He had nothing but the kindest intentions regarding me. Certainly, he thought I intended to kill him and maybe at that he was right.

I went whistling down the stairs and out the front door. It had to come sometime, of course. I knew that now. I always knew that. Some day I was just going to up and shoot Larry Lapeno deader than all hell. Not a nice thought. But maybe I'm a lad who doesn't have nice thoughts.

I went to meet the girl. Her name was Avery Coles and she was a cute trick in a sophisticated way. She said she was twenty-three and that could be. She had been around and had lots of personality, but I don't think you could lay a finger on that thing called charm. If you wanted looks and clothes, carriage and plain class, she could furnish all that. It was simply that the soft grayness of her fine direct eyes could go hard and cold and suspicious at times. Her teeth gave you the impression of being sharp. But not pointed. Yet fitted into her face and looked good there. Her hair was black and stiff and as severe as an Egyptian goddess'. Pretty? Sure. Beautiful? Well, I think her face was too finely chiseled for that unless you were a sculptor. Striking is the word. You liked to be seen with her, but never felt fully at ease. Her long fingers with their vivid nails were something to see when she held the long white ivory cigarette holder in them. She gave the appearance of one who wouldn't unbend to a Greek god.

Why so much of this Ivory Lady who wouldn't unbend? Well, she was unbending to me and I— Damn it, I didn't know if I liked it.

I met her in one of those small restaurants off Park Avenue where five dollars leaves you both hungry. It was called the Golden Shepherd and the tiny shaded lights on the tables were needed even at midday. She was holding the cigarette and looking toward me when I came in. If she were worried, she didn't show it. But I thought her face lit up a bit. I slid into the chair opposite her.

"There is your letter, Miss Coles." I put it down before her. "I took two thousand dollars with me, bought it for five hundred.

You have fifteen hundred dollars coming to you less my commission of ten percent of five hundred, that leaves fourteen hundred and fifty. You won't want it here?"

Her laugh was like light opera in a penny arcade. Good but low.

"How businesslike." She picked up the letter and glanced over it. Then, stretching forth the hand that was free of the cigarette she laid it on my right wrist. "Why the Miss Coles?" she asked.

"Still business." I smiled and when she handed the letter back to me, nodded at my question if it was the right one, I struck a match to it, holding it over the ash tray.

"Oh," she exclaimed, half stretched a hand toward it, but as the flames licked up thought better of it. "I wanted you to read it. I like so few people and those I like I want to like me, not because of the good things they know about me but despite the bad things they know. Don't you feel that way?"

"No." I could be emphatic on that as I let the letter burn out in the tray, jamming it to bits with a knife. "They might not like my sins."

"Of omission or commission?"

"Commission." I took a laugh. "I nearly killed this Larry Lapeno today."

"So that is his name." Her shoulders moved, which you could take for a shudder or not as you pleased. "But let us forget that unpleasant bit of business."

Avery Coles took the fourteen hundred and fifty bucks, assuring me easily that she often carried that much money around with her. Then she invited me to a party that evening.

"In your honor," she told me over the cream of tomato. "And you will be my only guest," she finished over the dessert. What she might have told me over the demitasse, I don't know. We didn't have a demitasse and besides I already had told her I couldn't come. Which was true enough. I had another case, a client I was to serve that night. A client who sent me two one-hundred-dollar bills.

"You know, Race," she said, when I had paid the check for what would have been a free lunch in the good old days, "I think you are afraid of me. You needn't be. You can dismiss from your mind all questions of should you see less of me. If I decided to see more of you, it wouldn't make any difference what you thought. I am turning into a woman who gets what she goes after."

"I'm flattered," I told her.

"And a bit relieved, although you probably would call it amused. But I won't play with your emotions." And putting those strange gray eyes on me: "At least, I don't think I will." And suddenly: "I would go a long way for you, Race. Much farther than you think."

And that was that. I put her into a taxi and went back to my office. Another pleasant surprise there. A Mr. Harrington Grover Wainwright requested me by mail to call at his house on a matter of "vital importance" on Wednesday evening. Since it was now Tuesday night, business certainly was picking up.

Fifty dollars less the luncheon larceny that afternoon. Two hundred dollars in advance for me to be at an uptown entrance to Central Park from twelve until two on Wednesday morning, plus whatever would develop from that. And now on the same Wednesday an invitation to visit Mr. Harrington Grover Wainwright on a matter of vital importance. Vital to him or to me? Well, vital to me meant money for me. And vital to him meant money for me, too. So I couldn't lose, any way you looked at it.

The twelve to two arrangement I didn't like any too well. But the note was anonymous and the two hundred was good and if the letter was sincere someone would count on my being there. If it wasn't sincere, it was a trap to kill me by any one of a hundred criminals I had displeased one time or another. If any murderer was willing to bet two hundred to nothing that he could shoot me to death at Central Park West between midnight and two in the morning, why I'd take that bet any time. The note said there would be more money coming if my services were required. If they weren't, I was two hundred to the good. I'd be there all right.

As for Avery Coles. She did bother me a bit. If it had not been for her eyes, I would simply have put it down to a young girl over dramatizing the service I had done her. As a matter of fact, I should have got that letter back for nothing. I had got more than one letter back from Lapeno that way and more than once just missed the chance to expose him. Sometimes I thought there was someone behind him and that he was only the front for the business. He was that dumb. Yes, Avery Coles did bother me.

I had saved a young girl of seventeen from kidnapers once and the way she went on about me you'd think I was Frank Sinatra. Her family had to send her across the country to school and I got love letters from her that would knock you silly until she suddenly up and married the undergardener at the exclusive school for girls. At that, I think the family still blamed me for it, though when I put it up straight to her old man he seemed to prefer the undergardener.

But I couldn't see Avery Coles in that light.

An hour later I had the lowdown on Harrington Grover Wainwright. He was big stuff with lots of dough, middle-aged, and gave plenty to charity. In fact, he was nationally known as the chairman of many charity institutions. A bachelor, too. What that lad would need with a private investigator in a matter of vital importance I didn't know. Probably wanted me to shoot up a joint to break a lease. Still, guys like that lose a two-dollar portrait of their grandfather and spend ten grand to get it back.

I went out and ate a big dinner that was five times as large and one half the price of the Golden Shepherd. At seven o'clock I was home in bed with the alarm clock set for eleven and a penetrating coldness creeping into the air. A gentle touch of rain against the window panes that was beginning to lose that soft patter and pound like sleet.

It did pound like sleet while I leaned against the stone wall right at the edge of the park from five minutes of twelve until after two. Oh, there was atmosphere to the waiting, all right, but the swaying shadow of rain-swept trees in the darkness never sent chills up and down my spine. It was dark, gloomy and cold. My right hand deep in my jacket pocket caressed the butt of a gun, my mind caressed the thought of the two hundred bucks.

Nothing happened. No, I wasn't mad. A hundred dollars an hour is not a bad price for doing nothing. If I thought of anything in particular it was that the job I was waiting for might interfere with the one that was coming up later that same day.

I went home and went to bed. I won't say it was the easiest money I ever earned for I had picked up twenty-five hundred dollars once and a trip to Havana for a case that never broke at all.

No word from that anonymous client the next day and, of course, no demand for the return of the two centuries. No cold in the head either, just waking to a nice winter day.

The day of great wealth may be passing, but it didn't seem to be at the house of Harrington Grover Wainwright. Wainwright let me in himself. I won't go so far as to say there was anything secretive about his manner, but certainly he spoke in a low voice. Still, most people needing a private investigator for the first time act that way. In fact, even a hard-boiled lad like I am likes it better. But it's easier with those baggy-eyed sporty money gents who say, "Come in, boy, have a drink, have a cigar. I'm in trouble with a woman again and want to get out of it as cheaply as possible."

Wainwright was in trouble, all right. He didn't especially show it in his looks, but it was in his manner, the hesitancy of his speech and his approach to the matter in hand. Besides which, people don't send for me unless they are in trouble.

He was a white-haired, sanctimonious-looking gent. The sort I don't fancy, but, then, everyone to his own taste and I've known dozens of them that were far better men than I ever hope to be. But these God's gifts to humanity who never let their right hand know what their left is doing, generally let everyone else in the community find it out anyway. He muttered something about it being beastly weather outside and that he had dismissed the servants for the evening in the same breath and led me to the library. He carefully closed the door, spun the key in the lock and sat down behind the flat desk in the center of the room.

I could see him better now in the light and he looked more like a blessing to the community than ever. Immaculately dressed, so closely shaved—and it now after eight in the evening—that the blue veins stood out through the powder on his face. But at that it was a good face as the books tell us. Free from wrinkles and that look in his eyes of the man who is always feeding stray cats. But successful confidence men look the same, so what?

Yes, the day of great wealth was lingering around. The library was big. Too big. It looked as if it should have signs on the wall reading "Quiet Please." But there were little ladders on wheels running along the shelves of books. A half dozen or more small desks and tables and filing cabinets tucked here and there. There

CARROLL JOHN DALY

were easy-chairs, too, a huge fireplace and a great thick animal rug of some kind.

And there sitting across from me was Harrington Grover Wainwright, all of him. And all of him was plenty. Tall, heavy, round of face with red cheeks and merry sort of eyes that looked as if they were doubtful about being merry at the present moment.

"Sit down, sit down there." He nodded at me, although I was already seated. "You're the man from the agency, I take it, the private detective."

Now that was a bad start and maybe I frowned. I don't like being called a private detective, the name smells slightly. I leaned forward and told him how it was with me—and with him, too.

"Mr. Wainwright," I said, "I have a license to operate as a private detective. I have an office, yes, and I have a smart boy to take care of things there for me. But I am not a detective. I am a private investigator, a personal agent. No one sends me, no one ever sends me anywhere. You wrote to me, asked me to call. Remember?"

"Of course. To be sure, Mr. Williams. Certainly." He shoved a box of cigarettes across to me, took one himself, lighted it.

I remember thinking how tiny it looked sticking out of that great face. Like a child's whistle on top of a locomotive. "Personal agent, private investigator to be sure, personal and private, like a layman and his lawyer or his doctor. That's the way I want it. A man and his lawyer. A man and his doctor. Almost a man and his spiritual adviser. I am slightly confused and bewildered, Mr. Williams. My life has

been so—shall I say even. Serene perhaps, charities you know, other people's troubles, and now when trouble besets me—well, I am at a loss. I who—"

"Suppose, Mr. Wainwright," I broke in, "suppose you tell me just what is on your mind."

"Don't get the idea that I condemn my fellow man," he was going right on anyway. "We who are seldom tempted seldom sin, you know. We who have money so often fail to understand the viewpoint of those who lack it. We who have warmth and shelter and food— But there, I'm getting away from things. So often I must admonish my colleagues in our charitable work that they must put themselves in the other man's place, sit across the table from themselves, so to speak."

I wished he'd sit across the table from himself now and see how he liked the blast.

"Well," I said, "you were tempted and sinned and now you want to get straightened out. That's my business."

He seemed shocked and surprised and then he wasn't. He sat back and laughed. It was not an unpleasant laugh, but there was something wrong with it. It didn't sound real.

"Perhaps you are right," he said. "I have been tempted and I have sinned, you say. Well, yes, I was sorely tempted, but it is sometimes difficult to distinguish justice and righteousness from sin. Or are you of the school of adages—'two wrongs do not make a right?' Or in this case perhaps I should say one wrong."

I gave it to him straight then. "To be

perfectly frank, Mr. Wainwright, I don't know what you are talking about."

He moved his thin lips and the cigarette seemed to cross quickly from one side to the other, then back to the middle again. It isn't often today, at least in the best circles, that you meet a cigarette smoker who keeps the butt in his mouth while he smokes and talks, too, for that matter. For he said, and his enunciation was perfect despite the fact that the cigarette remained in place:

"I suppose, Mr. Williams, I am trying to say that the confidence of a man and his personal agent are sacred. Yet the law doesn't recognize it as such."

"But I do. The law can't take letters out of a man's mouth and put them together to spell words. At least out of my mouth they can't."

"Ah, yes, very well put." He gave a little nervous laugh this time. "Now how much should a man tell you and show you?"

"He should tell me as much as I need to know and I will be the judge of that. He doesn't have to show me anything."

The nervous laugh came again.

"Peculiarly, Mr. Williams, I was thinking of reversing the proceedings. Show you everything and tell you very little."

"That," I said, "would hardly work in your case."

"Really." His eyes opened wide and his face creased and uncreased much as if dough were being kneaded by invisible hands. "You know what my trouble is?"

"Hardly." I wanted to get down to facts. "But my guess is that your trouble is blackmail." And before he could break in again, I explained, "You are a man of wealth and position and as you say, temptation has passed you by. Many esteemed, many really great men, have committed in youth slight indiscretions that have pursued them in later life. Even a kindness in a charitable way that can be misconstrued by a hastily written letter. A thing so trivial in itself that it is forgotten, then out of a clear sky it pops up on you, looks pretty bad presented as a blackmailer presents it. You pay and you pay and you—well, you finally come to me."

"Yes, of course. You have been highly recommended to me as a man who never has let a client down. A man who never broke a confidence. So you pass your word to me to never disclose anything I show you tonight, for I shall tell you very little."

"That," I said, "is understood."

"And you will accept my little commission without question and at your fee."

"I will accept it or refuse it," I told him, "and keep my mouth shut."

"No matter what it is?"

"No matter if you had walked into a saloon and shot up the entire establishment."

He laughed at that one, the nervous little laugh.

"I see you know that I have strongly advocated the abolishment of strong drink, but not that drastic." He came to his feet. "However, come with me." And as I followed him across the room to a curtain in the corner that he tossed back disclosing a small door: "This room is too big for work that demands my entire concentration. So I have a small den, here." He put a key in the lock, spun it and pushed open the door. The best and easiest description of that room for either one of us is that it was a pocket edition of the outer room, a little more class to the desk perhaps, a little more color to the curtains at the windows, iron shutters before them, too. A little more homey, too, for there was a huge coat tossed carelessly between two chairs.

Wainwright snapped on an overhead light and closed the iron shutters of the windows. Then he walked over to the two chairs and turned on a lamp behind one of them. He reached down and gripped the coat.

"Perhaps," he said, "this will be self-explanatory."

I knew he was prepared to startle me so I prepared myself not to be startled when he jerked up the coat to disclose the homey bit of atmosphere beneath it. But I was wrong. I was startled. The homey touch was a dead body, a glassy-eyed, black-haired corpse that sat grotesquely against the wall.

CHAPTER 2

I WAS WRONG about another thing, too. I was wrong about my hunch, that almost certainty of feeling that some day I was going to shoot Larry Lapeno to death. That's right. I wouldn't shoot him to death now. There he sat before me, the sneering greaseball.

Wainwright was watching me closely. This little bit of drama was not quite up his alley. Then it struck me funny and I laughed. The dead skunk and live reformer.

"Larry Lapeno?" I muttered. "He threatened you, pulled a gun on you and, just like that, you did him in."

"No... no," Wainwright said very slowly. "I am not going to lie to you. He talked about—he talked well. It was real, it was horrible. He told me of the people he had ruined. He described homes he had broken. He went into detail on a suicide, a young mother I believe. I was a frightened, shocked man when he started in to talk. After that I am not quite sure. The drawer of my desk was open, there was a gun lying in it. He was telling me I think of how the woman looked when she hit the sidewalk. I was not a desperate, half-crazed man, Mr. Williams. I seemed to be the avenging hand of outraged justice. There was something horrible in the room with me. Something horrible in the world with other people. It was my duty to destroy it. I lifted the gun out of the drawer. He was turning. I think he saw, but I am not sure. The bullet went through the side of his head. He turned a little more and sat down—like that—like he is now."

Mr. Harrington Grover Wainwright sat down, too, and put his head on his arms. I was looking straight at his back, but it didn't shake. His body was very still, no sobs came.

I tossed the coat back over the dead Lapeno. Murder? Yes, if it is murder to kill a rat. I was not thinking of ethics then, at least spiritually or morally. I was thinking of it legally. Homicide was the word for it, no two ways about that. I went around the desk and sat down and lighted a cigarette. Wainwright didn't move. I didn't disturb him. I blew smoke toward the ceiling. He wanted advice, of course. Justifiable homicide. Certainly. But that was my opinion only. I knew that Larry Lapeno was a blackmailer. I knew he had wrecked homes and lives and caused people's death. The police knew it, too; that is, the big cops knew it. Everyone he had blackmailed—and there must have been plenty—knew it. Yet no one could prove it. There was no evidence that would convict him before, why should there be any now that he was dead?

There wouldn't be much trouble to get the district attorney to accept a plea of second degree, maybe manslaughter. At that, Joe Gorton, the criminal lawyer, might get Wainwright off altogether. Wainwright was a big man. A wealthy man. A charitable man. But it would wreck his life. The institutions for good that he headed. It would shake the confidence of those who respected him. At that moment I had a great deal of respect for him myself. Looked at fair and honest, the only reason I hadn't killed Lapeno was because I didn't have the courage. It took a long-nosed, black-ribboned, glasses-wearing, sanctimonious old coot to blast him right through the gates of hell.

Wainwright sat up. He sat up very slowly, but kept his arms bracing himself on the desk.

"We who are seldom tempted seldom fall, Mr. Williams," he said slowly. "It wasn't money. It wasn't passion. I hope it wasn't fear and I am sure it wasn't hate. I have tried to tell myself it was a public duty, but I am afraid I am trying to make a martyr out of a criminal."

"Well," I said briskly, "Larry Lapeno was blackmailing you. You refused to pay. He came to the house, forced his way in. He threatened you, pulled a gun. You told him to get out. He struck and cursed you and struck you again. You remember little—the desk—the gun there and then the shot and you were holding the smoking gun and he was dead." And suddenly: "Where's the phone? You need Joe Gorton. He'll make the story stick."

He was shaking his head at me.

"That isn't the way it happened, Mr. Williams. I… I… this Lapeno telephoned me and came over and made demands and I shot him." And when I would have cut in with that was what he thought happened, he held up his hand and said, "I won't pretend not to know what you mean. I won't say I am above going on the stand and lying. But I am not going on the stand. I… my work couldn't afford it. I am chairman of a great many charitable boards. I give freely, I hope, but I also influence others to give. So much work in my charitable field depends upon the man himself, his character. Maybe I am overestimating my own importance and really trying to protect myself from the shame and publicity of a trial, but I hope not."

"Well"—I stiffened slightly and looked at him—"why did you send for me? Do you… you want me to take the blame for killing him? You want me to say I did it?"

"No." He shook his head. "I don't want that. If anyone else is accused of the crime and there is a danger of a miscarriage of justice I will talk, of course. He must have had many enemies."

"Plenty," I admitted. "There must be hundreds of respected people who had the motive. But the trouble, Mr. Wainwright, is that he was killed in your house and his body is here to prove it."

"That's it." Wainwright nodded his head slowly. "I don't want the body here, as you say, to prove it. I want it found somewhere else."

"But—" And I stopped. As a rule I don't need a brick wall to fall on me, but I was slow on the trigger this time. I didn't come right out with it. I asked him again, "Just why did you send for me?"

"To dispose of the body," he answered, and I thought his voice shook a bit this time. "To take the body off my hands. To charge me one fee and then for us both to forget the… the incident."

" 'Incident' is good." I sat back and tried to make smoke rings, but I never was much at that. I was thinking. In my long and highly colored career I had done most everything. But when I shot guys I let them lie. I didn't play "Body, body, who's got the body?"

Mr. Wainwright was talking. "Let me say that I don't want you to do anything against your own better judgment. I have your word that you will not break my confidence. And I have a hope that if your ethics forbid this, you might suggest someone else."

"I couldn't," I told him flat. "You'd have killed one blackmailer only to perhaps take on another for life." Suddenly remembering what Lapeno had told me about his great peak being reached: "Tell me, Mr. Wainwright, did this blackmail involve any great sum of money?"

"It would depend on what you would call a great sum."

"A hundred thousand dollars, a half million even?"

He didn't laugh, but I think he would have if he had been in a laughing mood. He said simply:

"No such sum, of course. That would be ridiculous. I am a well-to-do man, my charities are far lower than the newspapers lead people to believe. You see, I often give as the head of some foundation or through people who wish to remain anonymous. The sum mentioned was ten thousand dollars. The blackmailer immediately cut it to five thousand and I think less would have covered it."

"And you paid?"

"I paid nothing. Things came to a head before that—I mean, I shot him."

"You got the letter?"

"I got, as you call it, the letter. It has been destroyed."

"And just what did you intend to do, if the body was not removed?"

"I don't know. I don't—" He squinted his eyes up then. "Well, I have many filing cabinets. I ship them around at times. I thought of sending one to my summer home in Maine, but it is a little early for that."

"You have been reading too many detective stories," I told him, with a grin. "You'd have the body on your hands again in Maine. What did you expect to pay me?"

"Five thousand dollars and my assurance that I would admit the shooting if you were… er… inconvenienced dangerously."

"That," I said, "is a delicate way of putting it. You mean if there was a possibility of me burning for the crime. Well, Mr. Wainwright, when I work for a client I work all the way for him. I'll take your body for ten thousand dollars and take all the risks that go with it."

"No... no, I couldn't."

"Too much?"

"Not the money, but the other. I couldn't have a man suffer for my wrong. I wouldn't—"

I got up, leaned over and gripped his hand.

"We'll do it my way. Don't worry. They never burned me for guys I pushed over and they'll never get me for a lad I didn't kill. Ten thousand in cash."

And cash was right. He had it there in his safe and counted it out to me. He told me he had got it out of the bank to pay Lapeno and said, too, when I asked him if his taking so much money out would not excite comment, that he often drew larger sums of cash, "anonymous gifts" he explained.

I stuffed the money into my pocket. It took a lot of stuffing since they were none too large bills—Larry Lapeno's suggestion, I presumed. Then I asked Wainwright to give me a few minutes alone in the smaller library while I thought things out. He went into the other room and I closed the door, lifted up the coat and sat down facing Larry Lapeno. Gruesome, I don't think so. I said, half aloud and half to myself, "I didn't have the pleasure of killing you, Larry, but it looks like I'll bury you—and for ten thousand cash at that."

I pushed back one of the steel shutters, found it well oiled or at least that it moved silently, lifted the window and looked out into a narrow alley. I even stuck my head out and saw the street beyond, the big iron gate that gave onto the sidewalk. I looked the other way. A shorter alley, then a back fence, and another alley to the street behind.

I sat down and thought some more. Maybe I don't think well. Maybe I'm a great artist at heart, for the simplest things always appeal to me and win out at the end. Of course, I wandered and had visions of a wagon backing up with Murphy Office Supplies on it and all that stuff. But what if it were ever discovered that Lapeno visited Wainwright the last time he was seen alive.

I went out then and tossed it smack in the face of Wainwright who was slowly pacing the room. I said:

"Things are settled. Go to bed at ten tonight, leave the window in the small study unlatched and raised a quarter inch, also draw back the inside iron shutter or curtain or whatever you call it." And with a grin for he seemed worried: "Your body will be gone in the morning. If the police find it out, have me arrested for burglary."

"I appreciate your kindly humor," he said, very seriously. "What are the chances of my being involved?"

Involved was a nice word you've got to admit, but for ten thousand dollars he was entitled to use it.

"Well," I told the truth, "your chances of never hearing about the matter again are good. The cops will hardly trace him here. Blackmailers do not confide their business transactions to others. Anyway, deny he was here. And don't think of your sacred honor in that, think of mine. I'll leave your friend in a place where any of a hundred might have left him. Professional crimes are duck soup for the cops, amateur ones plenty tough. They've got to have a motive and if they find people Lapeno has blackmailed they'll have plenty with motives. Cops can't go around arresting them in dozen lots. Every victim might have killed Lapeno, but only one did. It will be like trying to find who stole a dress in a bargain basement on Dollar Day. Good luck."

He wanted to say more, but I didn't wait. I gave him a reassuring handshake and walked out the front door and down the steps.

It was going to be a nice clean job. Ten thousand for disposing of a guy I would have killed and buried for nothing. Sure, I felt good. Ten thousand is a lot of money outside the movies or even inside, for that matter.

JERRY WAS AT my apartment when I got there. I went whistling in. Jerry, my boy—who was no longer a boy except that he was as fresh as ever—I had picked up some years before when he was headed straight for Sing Sing. He might be yet for that matter. But I could trust him with anything.

"What's the joke?" he asked, when I started to laugh.

"Larry Lapeno," I told him. "He won't be making me irritable any more."

"No?" Jerry opened big eyes and his large mouth widened. "You bumped him, boss? I knew you would—" He rubbed his hands together. "He's been in your hair for months and you've been in my hair. Why you didn't—" He looked hard at me. "Don't tell me he isn't dead?"

"He is." I nodded. "No kidding, Jerry. I'm going to let you help bury him tonight."

Ten o'clock that night was the big moment. It's a dead hour on that residential street of Wainwright's. Later you get the homecoming theatre crowd and later still the night-club or party crowd, and later—well, I wanted to run a bit with traffic, not drive through the night alone.

We came from the street behind Wainwright's house, parked the car and I hopped out and made smack for the alley and down it to the fence. If anyone saw me or anyone in that house came out, Jerry was to toot the horn, drive around the block and pick me up on the other side.

There was no toot from Jerry as I hopped the six-foot fence, dropped on rubber soles to the walk behind and hot-footed it for the study window. One quick look up and down and I jumped, got hold of the broad window sill, armed myself up on it and had a finger under the window. I dropped inside, clicked my flash once, then picked up the coat and, placing it neatly over a chair, reached down and lifted Lapeno up in my arms. He wasn't too heavy, just awkward. I slid him feet first out the window, let my hands slip from under his shoulders to along his arms, almost to the wrists before his feet reached the stone below, then I let him go. It was a good job, a silent job. Quickly, I closed the window and let myself down beside him.

No moon and the alley was pretty dark. I tossed the body over my shoulder and reached the fence half-way down the alley. Rigor mortis had set in and Larry was a little on the stiff side which made it fairly easy getting him up but hard dropping him over the fence. He balanced nicely then and I was over the fence and had him on my back again.

A man, a single man passed on the sidewalk. I gave him a full minute, let my flash go once and waited. I heard the motor pur across the street and shortly after that Jerry swung the car around and drove up before the alley.

We work fast, Jerry and I. We are alive to prove that. He was out of the car, had swung the rear door open and was across the sidewalk and into the alley. We didn't talk. We just pulled Larry up between us, swung an arm of the dead man over each of our shoulders and hustled him out to the car like any stiff, no pun intended.

A quick glance to see if we were observed. A hoarse laugh from me when I saw that the approaching man was watching us and then I was sitting in the back seat with the corpse.

The man didn't glance back at us when Jerry jumped behind the wheel and drove away. It was just another drunk to him.

After that we crisscrossed a few streets for safety and turned onto Broadway. By this time Lapeno was on the floor and I was on the front seat beside Jerry.

"How much speed?" Jerry asked.

"Fast enough to get the thing over with, but not fast enough to get us a ticket. We have a body to deliver."

"Within the city limits, eh?"

"Sure," I told him. "Westchester is a nice county, besides, our own police are entitled to this corpse."

Straight up Broadway, down the hill at 181st Street, under the elevator pillars, over the bridge at Kingsbridge and so straight ahead to 242nd Street. There a swing right along Van Courtland Park, under the tunnel to the left skirting to the right of the lake. Then, as we reached the hill up to Central Avenue, we swung left and along the golf course, counted two parked cars.

"Easy does it, Jerry," I told him, as I climbed over the seat to the back and folded Larry Lapeno up like a ball. Hard against the rear door he was. Jerry slowed down and waited. Then he said, "It's clear to the curve, boss. I can swing to the bank. You say when."

"Bushes," I said.

Ten seconds later Jerry's whisper.

"Bushes it is."

The car swung sharply, the wheels going down in the slight incline. I threw open the door, raised my foot and sent Larry flying out. I jerked the door closed, climbed back into the front seat and we were hitting it up.

This time we turned right and up the hill to Central Avenue. So to Jerome and more elevator pillars and away toward the city, Just a single stop on a dark side street while Jerry took off the phony license plates and put our own back on. Sure, that's right. It's foolish to take chances. I knew of a case once where an old lady said, "I wasn't doing nothin' in particular. I just seen the license number and remembered it."

So home, but not to bed. We were hardly in the apartment when the bell rang and up came Sergeant O'Rourke. Now Sergeant O'Rourke and I are good friends. I'd helped him more than once because he was regular and I liked him. And he has helped me many times. I guess because he liked me, maybe envied the red tape I so often cut with a revolver.

It was nothing for Sergeant O'Rourke to walk in on me at all hours of the day or night. Sometimes with a problem, sometimes to give me a tip. Sometimes just to trip me.

"Lucky to catch you in," he said indifferently, as he sat down and put his hat on the floor beside him. "Just spending a quiet evening at home, I take it?"

I grinned at that. Of course, he had been watching from across the street. Guys, especially cops, don't pop in on you right after you arrive unless they were waiting or unless it's a very lucky break. Then they don't mention it.

"Now, now, O'Rourke." I wagged a finger at him. "You probably spent the best part of an hour across the street. Wouldn't trip up a friend, would you? I got home this minute. Bring the sergeant a drink, Jerry."

"I wanted to see if you had any reason to lie, Race," O'Rourke said, with a smile as Jerry came in and planted a bottle and a glass beside him. "I guess it's just the cop in me."

He poured himself a stiff drink, lifted it to his nose and put the glass down again. Then he pushed the bottle away.

"Private stock, Jerry!" I bellowed at that damned boy of mine. His hatred of cops was still so strong that he couldn't even take O'Rourke, and no matter how often I told him he always brought out the cheap liquor. "That bottle," I added, "is reserved for Inspector Nelson."

O'Rourke's smile became a chuckle when Jerry arrived with the good stuff. He took a quick smell, downed it straight, shook his head once, took out a huge handkerchief, wiped off his mouth, filled up the glass again but let it stand and said:

"Got a report. Larry Lapeno is missing."

"Dead?" I showed surprise and satisfaction.

"Just missing." O'Rourke raised the full glass and juggled it slightly, but didn't drink any of it. "But when a guy like that is missing alive he turns up dead. His old aunt called. She said he left word with her if she didn't hear from him to call the police."

"Wasn't he ever missing before?"

"No," said O'Rourke. "Guys like that are missing once, just once."

"I wouldn't think a guy like that would walk the streets of New York without a bodyguard."

"He generally has two men with him. They slept in his house, downstairs. This time he got a call and went out alone, Tuesday night, just before midnight."

"How would I be interested?"

"I don't know." O'Rourke came to his feet, knocked off the glass of whiskey, shook his head again, but didn't refill the glass. He picked up his hat and stuck it on his head and walked toward the door. "If you didn't know, I thought maybe you'd like to know. You've threatened to kill him."

"I've threatened to kill half the crooks in New York, for that matter." I shrugged my shoulders. "You think I did it?"

"No." O'Rourke shook his head. "Guys you get aren't missing over ten minutes, then they're found dead. My guess is that someone is holding him, torturing him, maybe he has some letters he can't get his hands on and wishes he could. Blackmail is such an easy racket, until you blackmail the wrong man. I knew a doctor once who went wacky and cut out a blackmailer's heart and—"

"Better look up the doctor then, if Larry's got a heart." And as O'Rourke swung open the door: "Thanks, old sock, but I'm in the clear. Not that I wouldn't have killed him if I'd thought of it, but—"

The door had opened and closed. O'Rourke was gone. I never was a lad to talk to myself.

I slept like a baby, that is, if you believe that a baby never wakes and hollers during the night. When I got up about ten o'clock, Jerry had left for the office. I glanced over the headlines as I dressed. It was not surprising that Larry Lapeno had not been found, at least when the paper went to press. It was surprising that no passing car had sighted the body if no passing car had. New York people are not too dumb. Certainly, I'd never report a strange body myself. Are the cops thankful? I should say not. They want to know what you were doing at that particular spot at that time of day or night. Where you had been, probably everything you did since you first fell out of your baby carriage. A dozen different dicks ask you a dozen different times how the body was

lying and they accuse you of lying more than the body. You're lucky if you aren't arrested for making false statements and impeding the course of justice. A lot of people know that. So if anyone did see the body it was a lad who knew enough to let sleeping dogs lie, with apologies to all canines.

I had a good breakfast at Jake's and went down to my office. Jerry screwed up his face and clutched his nose when I came in. So I knew that not only was I having a visit from the cops, but a particularly nasty cop at that. So I was not surprised to walk into my private office and find Iron Man Nelson. Inspector Nelson of the Homicide squad, standing looking out the window. There were two other plain clothes men with him, a thick-headed, bull-neck lad called Stein and a round, red-faced giant whom I knew only by sight.

Nelson swung from the window, pushed out his stomach under the impression it was his chest, tried to make his iron chin come out the same way but without much success. He was the terror of the evil doer. He didn't speak, just glared at me. I walked over to my desk and said in passing:

"Why don't you rent that face out to the comic papers? They could use it to frighten women and children."

I sat down at the desk and he walked over and leaned on it and glared some more. The two dicks turned and stared at me rather blankly, not knowing how things were going to break. Then Nelson spoke.

"We picked up Larry Lapeno this

morning. He was dead. Murdered. Know how he died?"

"Sure," I said. "He was shot through the head."

Nelson stiffened. "What part of the head?" he asked.

"Straight between the eyes," I told him.

"So you are not going to admit killing him?"

"Claim killing him, you mean."

"What made you think he was shot straight between the eyes?"

"Because every time a lad gets shot straight between the eyes you come running to me. Haven't you found any other good shots in the city?"

"It's like that, eh?" Nelson took a cigar from his pocket, bit off the end of it, rocked a bit on his heels, and actually lighted it. That lighting it was a bad sign. Nelson never smoked except when he was sure of his ground, had a real break in a case.

"Race"—Nelson jarred up and down confidently now—"I want to give you a break. Larry Lapeno was an unsavory character. A jury would listen to reason. The D.A. would listen to reason. You threatened to kill him, you know."

"So I shot him and get twenty years because he had it coming to him. Is that it? And I threatened to kill him. Well, I bet I can produce fifty people who threatened to kill him, but they all couldn't have or could they? How many slugs did you find in his body?" And when he remained cockey: "Come on, Nelson, take yourself and your gallery out of here."

"And you, too?"

"Got a warrant?" I wasn't alarmed, but I wasn't pleased either. I didn't like Nelson and he didn't like me, but he wasn't the dumb cop I liked to paint him and I knew it. And I wasn't the dumb dick he liked to paint me and he knew it.

He looked at his two men, nodded confidently. They nodded back. Then he said to me:

"Do you think I need a warrant?"

It was my turn to lean forward now and do the chin-and-glaring-eye act. Also I let my coat fall open and my right hand creep up above the desk and not too far from my left armpit. I've got a reputation to uphold and part of that reputation is that I won't be shoved around by the cops. I know my rights. And what's more I know the lawyer to get who'll see that I get those rights.

"Yes," I said slowly, "I think you need a warrant. In fact, I know you need a warrant." And I tossed it all in now. "Unless you want to formally charge me with murder."

"Suppose," he said, "I just intend to take you out of here by force? Then what?"

"Then," I said, "you'll take me out in a cloud of smoke."

"Like that, eh?" He wasn't as sure of himself.

"Just like that," I told him.

He thought that over a long time. No, he wasn't afraid. Not Nelson.

"Well, suppose you put your coat on and we'll walk down and see the commissioner."

"No," I said, "I don't have to do that either. A citizen doesn't have to call on the commissioner any more than the commissioner has to call on a citizen."

The two big dicks were shuffling uneasily. Nelson wasn't doing so good with his hard-boiled stuff. He tried being a little persuasive in a nasty way.

"O.K., Race," he told me. "It wasn't my idea, but the commissioner wants to give you a break. We've got some stuff on you, boy, or I wouldn't be here. I'll give you a few facts and then if you won't come down to see the commissioner I'll—" He paused and turned. O'Rourke had walked in the door. "What are you doing here, Sergeant?" Nelson demanded.

"Commissioner asked me to come up and suggest that Race visit him at once. Go on talking, Inspector. I won't disturb you."

Nelson didn't like that, but there wasn't anything he could do about it. O'Rourke was only a sergeant, to be sure, but he could easily have been an inspector. Yet he didn't want it. He felt that by being a sergeant he was closer to the man on the beat, the backbone of the force, the closest connection between the citizen and the authorities and so in everyday contact with the pulse of the people— and the criminal, of course. I don't know how O'Rourke rated on the pay end of it, but I did know that he had the confidence of the commissioner and the ear of the commissioner. Nelson didn't like it. Most of the big-shot cops didn't like it. But that's how it was just the same. Nelson went on talking.

"I'll give you a few facts and then if you won't come down, I'll get that warrant you're so anxious to see. Listen. No. 1: Larry Lapeno left his house just before midnight on Tuesday last. We'd like to know where you were at that time. No. 2: It's not simply gossip, but an established fact that you threatened Larry Lapeno. No. 3: You visited Larry Lapeno and threatened his life Tuesday afternoon at three o'clock. What business you visited him on we don't know in a legal sense. But we know his business and we can assume, though not prove, that you aided and abetted in a crime of blackmail by purchasing letters for some client. No. 4: On Wednesday morning, in a letter postmarked Tuesday evening 7 P.M., I personally received a letter unsigned, but written by hand, that if the writer should be found dead, you, Race Williams, would be responsible and the letter requested me to trace your every movement at the time of the murder."

"If it was unsigned how do you know Lapeno wrote it?" I asked.

"Because," said Nelson, smacking his lips, "when I went to his house today and told his aunt of the finding of his body by Motorcycle Patrolman John Drake she gave me a letter Lapeno had requested her to give me if he died an unnatural death. Well, he did."

"And why do you think Lapeno honored you with all this correspondence? Not a personal friend, I presume."

"No." Nelson didn't flush. He wasn't built that way. "I don't know why."

"I do," I told him, and meant it. "He knew you hated me and would do everything to lay the killing on me."

"He knew perhaps," Nelson corrected, "that I hated your methods of abetting criminals, no doubt." And turning to O'Rourke: "It might interest you to know that your... this man Williams actually threatened us with violence a few minutes before you came into the office."

"I threatened nothing. I—" I started and stopped.

O'Rourke said: "Tush, tush, no blood was spilled. Go on, Inspector, I am sure Williams will see the reasonableness of your presence here and your request that he visit and talk with the commissioner."

"All right," Nelson snapped. "Just where were you from 11:30 P.M. on Tuesday until 2:35 A.M. on Wednesday."

"I don't know." I shrugged my shoulders. "Offhand, I might say I was home in bed, but really I can't remember." But I didn't feel the ease I tried to show. Those hours and even minutes were familiar ones to me.

"Well," Nelson went on, "I want to be quite frank with you. I happen to know that you left your apartment at 11:30 P.M. and returned to it at 2:35 A.M. the following morning."

"Oh, yes," I nodded. "It was some business of a confidential nature with a client." But I had a new respect for Iron Man Nelson. Here it was scarcely noon and Nelson sure had been around. But I said, with great indifference, "What difference does it make since Lapeno was killed at five this morning?"

"How did you know when he was killed?"

"You just said so."

"I said he was found dead at five o'clock."

"Oh, well, what has that got to do with my little business of Tuesday night and Wednesday morning?"

"Because"—Nelson poured it on heavy now—"Larry Lapeno was killed between twelve midnight and two o'clock Wednesday morning."

"Medical examiner's findings?"

"His opinion," Nelson replied.

"Doc Walgrine?"

"Yes."

I tossed back my head and laughed. I knew old Doc Walgrine.

"Baloney, Nelson," I told him. "Walgrine wouldn't make a guess even before an autopsy and don't tell me he performed one already."

"What he means," O'Rourke put in, "is that Dr. Walgrine said it was quite possible, even very likely, that he was killed about that time."

"You mean it could happen?" I asked O'Rourke.

"Well," said Nelson, "will I get that bit of paper or will you come and have a talk with the commissioner?"

I reached for the phone.

"You better get the paper," I told him. And when he said nothing, I gripped the receiver. "Get the paper. I'm calling my lawyer, Joe Gorton. He'll have me sprung in no time. You'll have to charge me with murder, Nelson, and you'll have to make it stick."

Nelson set his jaw tight and I lifted the receiver.

O'Rourke said: "Just a minute, Race. Conceding all that you say is true, that Gorton can spring you, that you have your laugh on the inspector, Joe Gorton will charge you a thousand dollars at least, maybe twenty-five hundred."

I let the phone rest a minute. O'Rourke had appealed to my baser nature. Joe Gorton would lay it on all right. I knew that.

"It's a lot of money for an innocent man to spend just for a laugh," Nelson said sarcastically, but I could see that he was thinking, "Maybe I'll get Williams his little bit of paper, anyway. Yes, by God—"

"But the commissioner suggested Race come and see him," O'Rourke put in, and then to me: "You could call your lawyer from there, Race, just as well as here." And when I looked at O'Rourke: "You could talk to the commissioner on the phone first, if you won't take Nelson's word for it."

"I didn't give him any word," snapped Nelson. "He don't want to come. He has his rights. He don't have to. I would be breaking the law. A guy must have a funny sense of humor who spends all that dough for a laugh."

"Oh—" I started to shrug my shoulders again, then thought better of it. A lad can overdo indifference. But I said, "I might get some good advice from Joe. He might see my client, the one I visited during those so important hours. I might find it ethical to disclose where I was and so have an alibi, surprise the inspector."

Which crack set Nelson thinking. Suppose I did have an alibi, suppose Joe Gorton sprung it just after the papers carried the arrest? Nelson wouldn't like that. Yes, I guess those were the thoughts I read in his face, for he said gruffly:

"Well, make up your mind. Call the commissioner if you like, O'Rourke."

Which if it appeared weakness was good common sense on Nelson's part.

If the commissioner decided I should be held, Nelson would get the credit. If things went wrong and I blasted out with an ironclad alibi, Nelson wouldn't get the blame.

CHAPTER 3

THE COMMISSIONER DOESN'T like my methods when they interfere with police matters. Maybe he doesn't like me. But unlike Nelson, he's too big a man to dislike me. Also he respects a man who I won't take guff from anyone. Still, at that, I was a little bothered. Nelson might have enough evidence to throw a warrant at me.

Riding downtown after O'Rourke had called the commissioner, I could picture Joe Gorton sitting there pounding the ends of his fingers together and saying:

"It's evidence, yes—circumstantial evidence, of course—perhaps enough to get an indictment, but unless they can produce something more tangible, a witness to the shooting, why, no jury will convict you."

And my saying: "But I didn't shoot him, Joe. I was standing in the rain. I got an unsigned letter to prove it."

"Of course, dear boy," Joe would say, "of course you didn't shoot him. It'll cost a bit to prove it, though, say five thousand dollars now."

When I walked into the commissioner's office I was still thinking and trying to decide if I'd tread the light and graceful or stampede all over his office. Different attitudes at different times and with different men. And certainly Commissioner Blake was a far different man than Inspector Nelson. Nothing rough about him, not even around the edges. He was so smooth at times that you could easily slip on his words—and often did and found yourself out cold on your back.

He was in one of those affable moods now when I came into his office. He didn't get up, but he did stretch out a hand and let me shake it.

"Sit down, Race. Sit down. Let us see if we can't straighten out this thing for the best interests of us all."

"Which means I'm the goat, eh?"

His laugh was short. "Always suspicious, Race. Sit down too, Inspector, and you, O'Rourke. Nothing formal. I know, Race, that O'Rourke is a great admirer of yours at times—not your methods I can assure you, but your results. Take this Larry Lapeno. I quite agree with you that he was a slimy customer at best and the community is better served if he is dead. But we do have laws, you know. And I suppose Nelson has laid his cards on the table—most of them, anyway."

"All the big ones." I smiled.

"To be sure. To be sure." The commissioner caressed a chin and I mean a chin, for he had more than one. "I suppose Larry wanted more money than your client could raise, one word led to another, your temper and— Why, it might even be self-defense."

"You think a man should plead self-defense for the killing of that snake?"

The commissioner spread his arms far apart.

"We have to have laws and judges to enforce them, lawyers to interpret them and a jury to decide the facts. No individual can have the right to decide the fate for another individual. Do you want to tell the story of that fatal night, the death of Larry Lapeno?"

"I don't know it." I didn't shrug my shoulders with the commissioner. "But I do know that a hundred, perhaps a thousand people had good reason for killing him."

"Those people—for I presume you are referring to the victims of his blackmail—are amateurs. This was a professional job. Lapeno was killed by a man who was not afraid of killing, was not alarmed afterward."

"What makes you think it was professional?"

"What amateur, what person unused to death by violence and the methods of crime and criminal would cart a body around for close to twenty-four hours? Maybe less, maybe more. As we see it now, Race, he was killed sometime between midnight on Tuesday and two-thirty Wednesday morning. He wasn't concealed from view, so the body couldn't have been there in the bushes long. Now will you tell me where you were between the hours of twelve midnight and two A.M.—in confidence?" he added, and the smile was not on his face.

I thought it over. It was not a good story. I was simply standing in the rain. So I shook my head and stuck to my original story. I said simply, "I never break the confidence of a client."

"All right," said the commissioner, rising. "I'll leave you here for ten minutes to decide if you'll give me that information. If you won't, you had better get in touch with your attorney"—he pointed to his telephone.

Then he turned and walked out of the room.

Nelson seemed pleased. O'Rourke seemed worried. And me—I was figuring just how much Joe Gorton would shake out of me. Why didn't I have an alibi for that night? Why didn't a guy in my position make a business of having alibis, but how could I? I was trotting around all hours of the day and night. Of course, I remember talking to the cop on the corner when I left the apartment and when I went back. Besides there was the doorman and— All right, I'd spend the money. I'd tell Joe it was a little trouble that didn't amount to anything in case the commissioner was bluffing. I was picking up the phone when the commissioner came back.

"Come with me, Race," he said, and I followed him across the hall into a small library. There was a young girl sitting by a desk. She was quietly but neatly dressed and almost shy of manner. I wouldn't have known her at first if it hadn't been for her eyes. It was Avery Coles, no mistake about that. She stretched out a hand and I took it.

"Your client, Race, and your alibi." The commissioner didn't seem displeased. "You see the young lady is more than glad to account for your missing hours. You're an odd chap, Race. After all, the truth would not have hurt your client's interests. At least, that is her belief."

I said: "It is very nice of you, Miss—"

"Avery," she cut in quickly, "just Avery, Race, please."

It sort of made me look at the commissioner, but he was smiling blandly, so I said, "It was quite unnecessary, Avery."

"But why shouldn't I tell? How absurd for you to think for a single minute that I would mind your saying you were with me. When your boy at the office—Jerry it was—called me on the phone and told me, why I came down at once."

"There is yet," said the commissioner, "the question of time, Avery. You could be mistaken."

"No, I couldn't." She clutched her hands together over her heart like a school girl. "I couldn't—I— But the diary won't be mistaken, will it? And you won't show it to anyone?"

The commissioner said: "I suppose not. I mean, I suppose it won't be mistaken. And I won't show it to anyone. I'll leave you two alone until it comes. I have to talk to Nelson."

She started to talk as soon as we were alone in the room, but I shushed her up. A dictograph or even an intercommunication system could pick up our conversation. So I took her over to the window and, tossing it open, let the cold air come in. Then we leaned out and talked in whispers.

"What's this about my being with you? And Jerry calling you? He— Why, he didn't know."

"He knows now." She placed a slender hand on my big one. "I came into your office and heard them talking. When you and the officers left, I told Jerry that I was coming here and for him to say he knew and telephoned me. It's murder or something, isn't it? And if you were with me, you couldn't have done it, could you? And when the commissioner—he's really an old dear, he knew my father—when he questioned me as to how I knew the exact time I threw in the diary."

"But when he sends for it and you say it got lost?"

"But my maid will give it to him."

"You… you— But he'll have an expert examine it, be able to tell when it was written or approximately." And then it striking me: "How could you have written you were with me in it, if you came right from my office and the diary's at your apartment?"

"Race"—she turned and put both hands on my shoulders and I was glad we were far above the street—"I did write it that night. Don't look at me so blankly. I wanted you there, you know, and you wouldn't… couldn't come. So I pretended you did come. Other girls do the same thing I guess, and I wrote it in the diary just as if you and I were alone and— You're not mad?"

"Mad." I thought of the money she'd saved me. "Of course, I'm not. But you don't mean to say you wrote it as if I really were there?"

"Yes. I used to do it at school, too, silly things about the holidays that other girls would find and read and become jealous. You see, I guess I haven't really grown up."

Looking at her then and listening to her, I guess she hadn't, too. All but her eyes. Oh, not at first glance. But if you looked at them long and hard it was there, tragedy and sorrow and a certain worldly knowledge far beyond a simple sophistication. And I wondered— Was there a touch of evil? But, no, there couldn't be. But the thought was there for I said, "You'll want something in return for this?"

She seemed shocked. At least, she drew herself up suddenly, then she said: "Perhaps—" She paused and the music was in her laugh. "Yes, I will. I think it's only right that we should have a date together, just like it was in the diary. I'll send for you and you'll come. Promise."

"I promise," I told her. "I'll be there."

"Your word. You'll play the part of the diary."

"My word," I grinned at her.

The commissioner came in shortly after that. He held the diary in his hand and he gave it to her very seriously.

"I wish to talk to you a minute, Avery," he said. "Remember I haven't seen you since you were a very little girl. That is all, Race." He didn't stretch out his hand to me, just looked at me. "I can understand, if not appreciate and admire, your reluctance to disclose the name of your… your client, I believe was the expression. Good-day." And when I reached the door: "The matter seems cleaned up, but as you pointed out so clearly yourself the final examination of the body will hardly point out the time of death with such accuracy."

I went. I had thanked the girl. It would only embarrass her if I waited outside. But I was surprised at Commissioner Blake. Nelson, now, I could understand, but I really thought the commissioner would be glad an innocent man was above suspicion, even me. I shrugged my shoulders as I sought the elevators. After all, things would not be too pleasant for him. He could probably trace down a hundred people who had reason enough to kill Larry Lapeno and he'd know, too, that there were several hundred more he never even had heard of. He'd have a tough job solving that crime—and I wasn't going to help him.

Back at the office Jerry told me.

"A dame, boss," he said, his eyes glowing, "something like a hophead's dream, a slim bit of passion from the Arabian Nights. She must have come in on a draft. I was listening to the cops and never saw her until she was standing there beside me, listening, too. She put her fingers to lips that were like… like to burn you up and hid behind the screen where we hang our coats. Then you went and she came out. She told me—"

I cut him dead there and got the information. The same as she gave me. I didn't dismiss her with a shrug. She had saved me from an embarrassing position to say nothing of a piece of change. I suppose girls do write things in their diaries when they think they are in love and I suppose, somehow, I'd pay for it later. Well, that was all right. I'm a lad who pays his debts. And for once, me, a lad who never believes in coincidence had to believe in it now, for she sure had knocked off that bit of fiction in her diary at the right time. A gift from the girl and a gift from fate and I let it go at that.

O'ROURKE WALKED THROUGH the outer room into my private office and closed the door behind him.

"Well?" I took a good look at his somber gray eyes. "That has been cleared up. How's old Iron Man?"

"But is it cleared up?"

"What do you mean?" I stiffened a bit now. O'Rourke was my friend, but O'Rourke was an honest man, and I don't know who I'd less rather have on my tail if he really meant business. "Didn't the commissioner tell you—I mean about the girl?"

"Oh, sure. That." He nodded. "I wasn't thinking of that. I was thinking of your idea, that there was someone else behind Larry Lapeno. I never agreed with you that Larry was dumb, but we've searched his house with a fine tooth comb, investigating, you know. A few letters that could be used for blackmail, but nothing like the business we expected."

"What did you do with the letters?"

"Oh, the commissioner is a stickler on that. They are being sent back to their original owners, telling them that if they had come to the police in the first place they would have been protected and their names never discovered."

"Did you make copies of the letters?"

"Why, what for?"

"So you did." I nodded. "That's why blackmail prospers."

"Just for the record." O'Rourke bristled slightly, but he reddened, too. "Of course, those that concerned past unsolved crimes will have to be investigated, the others—" He just spread his arms far apart.

"The others," I told him, for I held strong views on blackmail, "no doubt, will pop up twenty years from now to haunt some relative. Oh, I know, just routine questioning because someone's father or

CARROLL JOHN DALY

mother went with a woman who— Damn it, O'Rourke, you fellows encourage the filthiest traffic in the world!"

"Do you suggest that we condone crime?" He put on his official dignity.

"Hell!" I went after him. "You know my views on that. You ride a few criminals and tens of thousands all over the country are paying out blackmail every day. Indiscretions of youth, sudden moments of passion, a family row, a few drinks too many, a woman of easy virtue and some upright citizen pays all his life. For what? Because you guys don't condone crime. You know my views. There's a homicide bureau, the pickpocket squad, the narcotic, chemical, ballistics, but what have you got in the way of a blackmail bureau? A couple of roughnecks who go through a victim's past life until what the blackmailer knows is insignificant in comparison. Then—"

"You've been doing pretty good tor yourself as an in-between," O'Rourke cut in.

"That's what riles me," I told him. "Someone has to protect those unfortunate people. And you can't prove that either. You know I meet a blackmailer. You know I pay him money, but you can't prove even that. What do you do? Hire a few frowsy dames to park in a hotel room with a frowsy detective and hope a still frowsier blackmailer will try to cash in on it."

O'Rourke had the grace at least to flush.

"That was Nelson's idea," he said.

"Yeah, I know. They had someone call up Lapeno and tip him off to some easy dough, even told him I could be the go-between. Lapeno laughed himself sick and that's all the good it did. He demands police protection and gets it, and his victims—blah."

"That's right," O'Rourke finally agreed with me with a sigh, which always made me madder than when he argued. "So how about helping out a bit. Who do you think was behind Lapeno?"

"It was only a hunch," I told him. "And if I knew what? No proof without betraying the confidence of a client. Or," I added, "I might shoot him to death between twelve midnight and two-thirty some nice winter morning."

"Atta boy!" said a voice from the doorway, and I looked up to see Marty Gibbs of the *Star* parked in the doorway. "So they tried to frame you for the death of Lapeno, Race, and— Oh, hello, Sergeant."

O'Rourke said, coming to his feet, "You publish a story like that, Marty, and—"

"Like what?" Marty was all innocence. He winked at me.

"That the police tried to frame Williams."

"Police?" Marty Gibbs seemed shocked. "I was thinking of the blackmail gang. They fear Race. They know he suspects. They put him on the spot. The cops fall for it and then—Girl of Love Nest Saves Famous Detective—" And when I turned on the scowl: "I mean Noted Personal Agent."

O'Rourke stamped out of the office and Marty came over and sat down on my desk, swinging his legs back and forth.

"The love nest story will be a new one for you, Race," he said.

"It won't be, because you won't publish it." And when he just grinned: "Because it isn't true."

"No." Marty looked shocked again. He could look shocked very easily. "The crime was committed between twelve and two-thirty or so a noted inspector police claims. A girl walks in and alibis you." And when I would have spoken: "I know. With you, it's simply business. But when a sensational murder takes place— Boy, it's a love nest. A sparkling, bewitching piece the girl, too?"

"Know who she is?" I didn't raise my voice.

"No, but I have ways of finding her."

Which I doubted, but didn't like, anyway. "Look at that," he said, placing a late edition of the *Star* before me. The first picture I wasn't sure of. It was a couple of feet sticking up in the air and a body crumpled in leafless bushes. But the picture beside it was Larry Lapeno— cane, gloves, smiling face, white, even teeth, greasy hair and the captions below the pictures. BEFORE AND AFTER. HE PUT THE FINGER ON THOUSANDS—WHO PUT THE FINGER ON HIM?

"His heirs," I said, "can sue you on that."

"You can call spirits from the very deep," grinned Marty, "but do they come? Besides, he had two suits pending against the paper already. I'm holding your love nest story for the morning edition. It's an exclusive."

"And why," I asked, "are you holding it?"

"I thought maybe you wouldn't like it."

"I don't," I told him flat.

"You haven't knocked me around."

"That," I said, "can come later."

He still grinned, but he moved off the desk.

"You know, Race," he spoke confidentially, "you know what would make a good story? A better story than the love nest one? That you know who was behind Larry Lapeno, that you threaten vengeance because this lad tried to frame you." And growing enthusiastic: "Better still, you swear to get him because of the lives he has ruined, the suffering he has caused. That's it. Race Williams in a new light. The great humanitarian. People will eat it up. Nelson will turn a pasty yellow."

"And what good will it do?"

"Hell," said Marty, "you don't think as much of yourself as I do, as any crook does. This master blackmailer suspects that you know him, fear enters his heart, fear of death by violence. He's a coward and a rat and we picture him crouching over the letters that bring suicide and poverty, and then like a cornered rat he decides to strike, strike you before you strike him."

"But I don't have any idea who he is."

"That's it. He comes after you, you meet and bang, bang, you kill him. Hot stuff?"

"Marty," I told him, "you're nuts. I haven't any reason to suspect that there was a master hand behind Lapeno. It was simply a hunch and not a very strong hunch at that."

"But in one little slip this master blackmailer gave you the clue. With that single clue—"

"What clue, what slip? Damn it, I don't even think there was anyone behind Lapeno."

"What difference does that make?" Marty exploded. "The story will be dead in a couple of days, anyway. The clue and the slip will be enough for the reader. We don't have to explain it. It sells papers. It's a good story. I want a good story. If the blackmailer shows up and you kill him or he kills you, it's another good story. If there isn't any other blackmailer, this is still a good story. Is it my fault if you were wrong?" When I smiled at him, lighted a cigarette and leaned back in my chair, he said, "Of course, if you give me that story I won't print the love nest one."

"So that's how it is?" I wasn't leaning back in the chair now. "You haven't forgotten the knocking around?"

He moved toward the door before he spoke.

"That, as you say, Race, is to come later." His eyes narrowed and he watched me closely. "They're both good stories, take your choice."

"Marty," I said, slowly, "you are somewhat of a rat. And not a very healthy rat, at that. If you publish that love nest story you won't be nearly so healthy." Reading in his face the swell story he thought he would have if he were picked up and sent to the hospital or the morgue and thinking myself of the influence of the press and the circulation of the *Star*, I added, "If you can interpret anything from my conversation that would lead you to believe that I claimed to know who this master blackmailer is, why go ahead, but I won't confirm it."

"Nor deny it?" His eyes opened wide, sparkled, his tongue licked at thin, broken lips.

"Nor deny it," I told him.

And he was gone. The story would be good for the paper, of course. The by-line would be good for Marty Gibbs and the publicity would not be bad for me.

The next morning Jerry brought me in the *Star*. His face was alive with enthusiasm. There was my pan across the front page. The heading was not bad. INNOCENT DETECTIVE QUESTIONED IN LAPENO MURDER SWEARS VENGEANCE. PERSONAL INVESTIGATOR AWAITS SECRET INFORMATION WHICH WILL DISCLOSE HIDEOUS HAND BEHIND MURDERED BLACKMAILER.

If you liked the sensational, Marty Gibbs was a great feature writer. The slip and the clue were cleverly hinted at in his "exclusive interview." He didn't say it exactly, in fact, he didn't say it at all, but you were left strongly with the impression that I would know "like a bolt from the blue from an undisclosed source." Then the question: How would I act? Would I disclose my information to the police who had suspected me of the crime and blundered continually in the disgraceful way they handled the blackmail situation in "our great city" or would I, Race Williams, man of action, drag the sniveling rat from his hole? Or would the rat, desperate, creep out into the night and attempt my destruction in the darkness "of our great city?"

Jerry loved it. And I—well, he had remembered personal investigator and—sure, I took a laugh. But I suppose at that I did like it.

CHAPTER 4

I GUESS IT was about an hour after I had admired my picture in the *Star* that Jerry stuck his head in the door and said a party with a snazzy male voice who wouldn't give his name wanted to speak to me. Would I take the call and would he listen in from the outer office?

I told him I'd take the call, but he wasn't to listen in.

I recognized the voice. It was my sanctimonious friend. That's right, Harrington Grover Wainwright.

A nervousness had crept into his voice and also a hesitancy. He wanted to know if what the paper said were true about my knowing the name of the man behind Larry Lapeno. And when I told him that it wasn't, he wanted to know in a most tremulous voice when I would know.

I said that I didn't know when I'd know and maybe led him to believe that I would know very shortly.

"Is it true, Mr. Williams, that you'll... you'll dispose of him?"

I grinned to myself and replied: "That is a reasonable assumption, if you don't dispose of him first."

That seemed to shock him so I asked him what was on his mind.

"I have been a foolish man, Mr. Williams," he told me. "My little personal business with the party now deceased is not a closed matter. Someone else has taken it up. I received a telephone call—I'm afraid he suspects—well, the truth."

"Good Lord!" I said. "But how?"

"He... he said he sent Larry Lapeno to me and has not seen him since.... No, he

didn't accuse me, but he is coming to see me tonight alone. I thought you might—"

"Dispose of another one?" I almost shouted into the phone. It struck me suddenly that I was going to have a steady job getting rid of a philanthropist's corpses.

"No... no—" He fairly gasped the words. "I wouldn't. I couldn't. I haven't slept. I— God help me, Mr. Williams, I am shocked beyond words. I think... I feel almost certain that I recognized the man's voice on the phone."

"Who was he?" It was my turn to gasp.

"I can't— It is too horrible to think of. Even contemplate. Yet I must believe. He's coming at ten tonight. I was thinking, if you could be here... no servants... come unannounced and unseen. I—"

His voice was broken now. There was the weirdest rattle, like a dying Frankenstein monster, over the phone, right out of the movies. So I put on the brakes and said calmly. "There is nothing that can't be fixed up. I'll come—" And after a pause: "As I came last time, I mean when you didn't receive me."

"The study window you mean and—"

"Exactly, now forget it. Say nine o'clock."

"You think... you won't— It is horrible to think of and—"

"Sit tight," I advised him. "Read yourself a good book. We'll handle it one way or another."

"Thank God for your calm, assuring voice," he said, almost as if reciting a prayer. "I am a worried, broken man. You may name your own fee."

Which last line was not a bad one to

hang up on. So what? So I sat down to think. Marty Gibbs had cast my bread upon the waters and it was floating home cream puffs.

My first thought was one of satisfaction that I had guessed there was another blackmailer. My second thought was one of satisfaction that this blackmailer didn't know I had carted the body away from Mr. Wainwright's house. How did I arrive at that conclusion? Certainly, he wouldn't go to a house where I might also cart him away, just as dead.

Then the question: Did this blackmailer believe I knew or would shortly know who he was? There were two schools of thought on that. The first that he didn't or he wouldn't go nonchalantly on plying his trade. The second that he did and he wanted to clean up all he could and make a get-away before I put the finger on him. And Harrington Grover Wainwright would be big business to start with.

That this blackmailer suspected Mr. Wainwright of killing his partner, I doubted. He would be a foolish man, indeed, if he chanced walking into his death also. That he was a common gunman or a well-known crook seemed out of the question also. Otherwise, would Wainwright have recognized his voice on the phone? It must have been a business acquaintance or a social one that so shocked him. Or again it didn't need to be someone he knew at all. Nice people don't kill without unpleasant reactions and Wainwright was certainly nice people—which I am not and will admit right now.

But why would a master criminal, a blackmailer who had hidden himself away for years, suddenly walk right out and do his own business? There was an answer to that—the first school of thought. Panic at my knowing him shortly and a final stab at heavy cash before his get-away.

I quit thinking. I am not the deducting, deducing book type of detective. I'm a hard working, plugging sort of guy who can recognize a break when he sees it and act at that same minute, at that same second or even split second if guns are brought into it.

I called Jerry and prepared him for the worst or the best, according to how you look at it. I told him simply to be where I could get him on the phone, that we might have to repeat the body act.

"Again, boss?" He opened those expressive eyes very wide. "Not that I mind, understand. But it always seemed more convenient to let 'em lie where you—" And when I did the staring act: "You know, let 'em just lay. I... I think you're over dramatizing it."

Whatever I did was right with Jerry, but juggling the corpse around afterward struck him as an anticlimax.

That afternoon O'Rourke called on me. I thought it was about the baloney in the paper and he was a long time coming around to it. But it seemed he took the article for just what it was, baloney, and finally approached his real reason for his visit.

"Race," he said, looking off into space, "you never was a ladies' man, sort of felt it would interfere with your business. Now, you're not in love, are you, not thinking of getting married?"

I leaned back and took a long laugh. O'Rourke looked so serious.

"What put that into your head?" I asked.

"The commissioner," he said. "You see, he feels a sort of obligation toward that girl. Was a great friend of her father. I didn't know he could be personal in matters, but I guess he can. Since you are not serious and she quite evidently is and believes you are— Well, forget her." And in a sudden burst of his old-time friendship: "Oh, I suppose you were just kidding around, but she's young, unsophisticated and—"

"Just," I cut in then, "who are you talking about?"

"The Spellman girl, of course. I—"

He stopped there. I stopped, too. The voice in the outer office was loud and demanding. The knob turned, the door was flung open and Inspector Nelson stormed into the room.

"I want to talk to you, Williams," he said. "I want to talk to you now. I want you to know exactly where I stand before you start making a mess of things. I know enough to make trouble for you, real trouble, but if you are willing to play ball, why I am— A-ah! Sergeant—"

O'Rourke walked toward the door. "I was just leaving, Inspector," he said.

"Me, too." I reached for my hat on the costumer across from the desk.

"No," said Nelson. "I speak to you now or—" He put one of those big hands of his on my shoulder.

"Nelson"—I looked at him coldly—"you're very fortunate I got a new rug, paid for, too." And when he looked at me dumbly: "If I didn't think you'd mess up the rug I'd shoot that hand off my shoulder at the wrist." With that I knocked his hand from my shoulder and pounded out after O'Rourke.

The elevator door closed almost in my face and I missed O'Rourke. Another elevator door two flights down closed in Nelson's face and he missed me. I didn't catch O'Rourke on the ground floor. Nor did Nelson catch me on the ground floor. I took a walk in the park, had dinner and loitered over my coffee.

What Nelson had to say to me didn't matter. What O'Rourke had said to me probably didn't matter either. But I was of a curious turn of mind and I couldn't locate the Spellman girl. At least by name, I couldn't. A couple of women had been in love with me, yes. Some young girls, too. That happens to lads who throw their weight around, though not as much as to a lad who croons. I was trying to think of the name of the girl who eloped with the school gardener. I couldn't remember it. But I didn't think it was Spellman. Yet, the name was familiar. Still all names are. I was wondering if she had turned up in the city again minus her gardener but with the same childlike romance in her heart.

I tried to think what the girl's name was who had run away from home with a bum last summer. Her father was a big shot and knew Commissioner Blake. But then all big shots knew the commissioner. The kid was seventeen. And the bum was a second-rate swindler with a first-class line, at least for kids. They were going to be married and I had dragged her out and

30   CARROLL JOHN DALY

her hero sort of lay on the floor after my first wallop and she changed her affections to me. She had written me letters and tried to see me. Let me see. Her first name was Gladys. Her last name. Her father's name. Was it Spellman? I didn't know. I'd find out the next time I saw O'Rourke.

I was glad now I hadn't caught up with him. I was glad, too, that Nelson hadn't caught up with me. This was one night when I certainly didn't want a bunch of cops in my hair.

So nine o'clock found me once again back at the window of Wainwright's study. I had come by the same way, too, through the alley behind and over the fence. This time no Jerry waited with a car. There would be nothing outside Wainwright's house to identify me with the inside of it until I sent for Jerry. Nothing, unless a pistol shot in the night. I wondered a bit about that.

Nothing happened as I reached the window, chinned myself for a moment, then swung up onto the broad sill. A flip of my finger beneath the slightly raised window, an easy push and I was in the room.

I closed the window and felt my way across the room to the strip of light that came from under the door to the big library.

In absolute quiet I pulled the door open and peered out into the lighted but silent library. Almost at once I saw Wainwright. He was sitting at the desk looking straight at the huge fireplace in which big logs were burning brightly. His face was lined, more deeply lined than when

I had seen him there a few nights before. There seemed to be shadows under his eyes, and if his steady glare at the fire was what people call day-dreaming he was having a daymare. He raised his eyes once and looked toward the ceiling and half shook his head. For a moment his eyes cleared and he clasped his hands in front of him. Then his lips moved. He looked like a man in prayer.

I remember thinking while I watched him that if a man's life is written on his face then here had been a good life. Giving unstintedly to the poor.

He turned his head and saw me. If he was surprised it was a very mild surprise. When he smiled at me I wondered what there could be in his life that would make him fear blackmail. Something stupid, no doubt. Something you or I—well, that I, anyway, would laugh off if a blackmailer threatened me with it.

"Ah, Mr. Williams," he said, motioning me to a seat across the desk from him. "Rather, Race Williams." And when I sat down opposite him: "I must look on you now as a good and trusted friend."

"You paid for what you got," I told him. "You paid well. Now your—" I started to say "conscience" but didn't. I said, instead, "Now, it is difficult to kill a man no matter how justifiable the act and it worried you."

"No." His head was slightly down and he raised it and let mild blue eyes meet mine directly. "I didn't tell you the truth the other night. I didn't kill the man." He raised his voice slightly. "The child, the grown child of a very dear friend of mine killed him."

"A young man?" I didn't know whether to believe him or not.

"A young woman," he told me. "A charming young woman. You see, Mr. Williams… Race, I was a very foolish man. I dabbled with something I did not understand. I had the girl bring the blackmailer here, to reason with him, to plead with him and pay him, of course. He had what she wanted or at least she thought he did. I was an old man and she was a young girl and he was strong and powerful and had nothing to fear. So she killed him. You understand?"

"No, I don't. You told me quite a different story, the description of what was in your mind and your heart and in your soul when you pulled the gun from your drawer and shot him."

"I did. Yes, I suppose I did. At school I was known for my histrionics and—"

I wasn't listening to him. I guess he knew it for his eyes turned and followed mine. I wasn't sure at first. The thing that I was looking at was in the shadows and the thing I saw might not have been a shoe, a shoe with a foot in it, perhaps a dead foot. I could have sworn it was not there a few minutes ago, a few seconds for that matter. But it was there, and then it was gone, as if a shadow crossed it or a door closed softly. I turned back to face Wainwright and to crack wise about another body, but thoughts were racing madly through my head. I think I knew and yet I didn't know, but certainly I knew part of it before I saw the gun he held so tightly in his right hand. He was leaning across the desk, pointing the gun directly at me, and believe it or not, I could feel rather than see his finger pressing on the trigger.

There was no kindliness in the man's eyes now. No sudden change from good to evil either. Just a cold, calculating sort of viciousness, and perhaps a bit of satisfaction.

Then a voice spoke behind me. "Don't shoot yet, Mr. Wainwright. Until we know who he is going to get his information from. Put them up, Race Williams, both of them, high."

I put them up high. And so would you. There is not much chance to draw, aim and fire when one gun is a few feet from your stomach and the other hard against your back.

The girl was the girl of my alibi, the girl who had written in her diary about me. I knew then why she had written in the diary and given the date and the time. It was no coincidence, And if it wasn't a coincidence, what was it? It was knowledge. She knew, then, in advance, the exact time that Larry Lapeno was going to die. But she knew more than that. She knew that I would not have an alibi for that time. She knew that I would be standing in the dark and the sleet and the rain. She could only know that in one way or maybe two ways. Either she herself had mailed me the two hundred dollars that sent me to the entrance of the park or someone she knew had sent them. Sure. I suddenly became a deducting, deducing detective of fiction, but it took two guns to do it.

"I don't believe his silly story," Wainwright said, impatiently, as his gun steadied and I thought he was going to shoot. But he didn't. "He couldn't have information coming or— Search him, my dear. You should relieve him of at least two guns. He carries them under his armpits I believe." She got both of them out all right and laid them on the far end of the desk from me. "Nothing in his hip-pockets?" Wainwright watched her closely as she searched me. "Good." And when I felt a sudden satisfaction that some hunch had told me to carry my tiny automatic sleeve gun that night, Wainwright of the honest face spiked that satisfaction.

"Both his arms, my dear little Avery," he said. "Our intrepid Mr. Williams is noted for his concealment, yes and use, too, of a sleeve gun. It doesn't show." And as she ran a hand along my arms: "Deeper, my dear. Back near the shoulders."

He waited and I waited, too, as the girl settled her hand directly on the tiny automatic, hesitated a moment and took it off again.

"Not a thing," she said, and I thought I detected a nervousness in her voice, a nervousness that must have been in her hands, too, since she did not recognize the feel of the gun.

"So you are the blackmailer?" I said at last.

"Ah, a Sherlock Holmes." Wainwright smiled at me. "The wisdom of a second Solomon. Yes, my dear Mr. Williams— Mr. for we can hardly be called trusted friends now. A rather unique set-up, isn't it? But, then, charity is part of my business. It gives me a good name and costs me nothing. Indeed, I cash in on it. It is so easy to take a little kitty from each pot. And since so many people insist upon anonymity—oh, not from altruistic purposes, but through a fear that others will pounce on them for donations—I often take the credit for the donations. The technique of my avocation is not much different from that of my vocation, blackmail. In blackmail we threaten exposure or prison if possible. In charity, the fear of being known as a mean man, spoken about in hushed shame by those we wish for social or business reasons to respect us. I have aided the poor by the weakness rather than the strength of the rich, and made myself rich on that same weakness. Always man fears exposure. But let us talk about you, Mr. Williams. What was this story in the paper that you were to receive information of the identity of the blackmailer behind the dear, departed Lapeno?"

"What good would it do to tell you?" I asked. "You intend to kill me, anyway."

"It would be useless to pretend differently," he said easily. "Still, there are many ways to die. Larry Lapeno died easily with a bullet through the side of his head. A bullet in the stomach now—I am told can be quite lingering and very painful. I had a client once who— But you would not be interested."

"I would be interested in knowing just why you picked me out for the body... the disposal of the body. And why you killed Lapeno."

"Not me, the little lady behind you," he corrected mildly. "Lapeno had fallen prey to the greatest of all human frailties. And that, Mr. Williams, is not women nor liquor nor even drugs. It is the one incurable vice that doctors can do nothing about. It is gambling. Despite the huge, untaxable income I permitted him, he was in need of money. Again he had become lazy, look how often he directed clients to you." And leaning forward and the gun coming even closer to my stomach: "He hinted at something once, Mr. Williams, once when I refused him money, money which I gave him after the hint. And immediately I began to plan for his death."

"But where would I fit into the picture?" I was still sparring for time. Trying to figure out where the girl stood behind me, how close was her body to the gun that was pressed against my back. If I could pitch over backward in that chair I'd come up with the tiny sleeve gun in my hand. Yes, I knew if I came up it would be in my hand all right, but would I come up again? A .25 automatic against a .45 revolver, one hidden in the sleeve, one facing my stomach. And a girl behind me with another gun.

Two shots would be all I could have and they must be perfect ones. A .25 is not a deadly weapon unless your aim is good. Was I thinking of actually killing a girl? Of course, I was. I didn't paint any romantic picture of disarming the girl and killing the man all in one single sweep. One plan only, at least one hope only. To get out of there alive if possible. Who else died didn't bother me then.

"Where do you fit into the picture?" Wainwright was saying. "Can't you guess what Lapeno's hint to me was?"

"By God, yes!" I said, without thinking. "His half-million-dollar blackmail scheme."

"Ah—" His eyes widened. "So I was

right and it had reached that stage. You see, I never actually feared Lapeno. He was a coward at heart and he was deadly afraid of me."

"Which he had reason to be," I put in.

"Which he had reason to be," he repeated. "But I feared you, Mr. Williams. A half million dollars is a lot of money."

"Which I turned down."

"Really? Well, it didn't matter. A man might be so noble, of course. Still you could have pretended to accept the proposition and got him to talk. No, Mr. Williams, I feared you so I killed Lapeno. It tickled my fancy to have you dispose of the body for me. It amused me to send you a couple of hundred dollars to stand alone in the rain and be without an alibi. I am a wealthy man. I am ready to retire. It would be convenient to keep you busy while I wound up my affairs." And with a shrug and a raise of the gun which I felt might pop off any second he said, "Now, who could possibly have been able to disclose to you my identity?"

And it struck me all at once. I might start things moving. I might not be alive to see the end of that movement, but I had an idea one of them would be dead, too. I said: "Well, the young lady behind me knew."

"Nonsense. I have evidence right here in this house, evidence that made her work with me, evidence that caused her to toss away all her upbringing and work with"—a pause—"a blackmailer."

"Well—" I guess I cleared my throat for my position was not a pleasant one. "Who do you think alibied me?" And when he looked at me blankly: "Did she know or didn't she know about the two hundred bucks you sent me?" And as his face paled a little: "And why do you think she did it. Because she—"

The girl broke in. "He lies! I—" And swinging suddenly to one side of me: "His leg, boss! There might be a gun strapped to his leg."

"No," Wainwright snapped. "I'd kill him before he could ever bend forward."

"He'd go down and up," the girl said, and then cried out, "I can see the outline of a gun strapped to his leg!"

Wainwright cursed. Even then the words seemed strange coming from his lips. The girl swung in front of me just before she ducked down at my legs. For a split second I was out of range of the man's gun. The girl's gun I could see dangling in her hand as she started to bend. In that split second I did it. I threw my weight back and kicked up with my foot. Maybe the toe of my shoe striking the girl's gun delayed my backward plunge slightly. Maybe if it hadn't been a glancing kick I would have been killed.

Wainwright fired. I could see the yellow-blue flame. Then the sudden pain in my head as if I had been hit. But I hadn't, for I heard a picture crash to the floor behind me. My head must have hit the edge of one of the filing cabinets. Maybe it helped save my life. Maybe it didn't. Certainly I was spinning in the chair when I crashed and certainly my head was spinning when I came up. But I came up with the gun in my hand and death in my heart. He fired again and I think skinned the lower part of my leg. That is, I thought that then, later I knew he didn't.

He fired once more after that, but I wasn't afraid then. There was fear in his eyes, beads of perspiration on his forehead, terror perhaps in the gaping hole in his face, for his mouth hung open.

We fired together, but I knew he was going to miss. And I think he knew I wasn't. And if that was the truth we were both right. I shot for the wide open spaces and since no mark appeared on his lily-white face I guess I hit the bull's eye or the bull's mouth if you want to be literal. Smack in the gaping hole it went and he slid back into the chair. Sat down for all the world like a man at ease. Then he began to disappear slowly. He was gone, quietly and softly but for a slight scraping of the chair along the waxed surface as he hit the floor.

The girl, of all things, was smiling as I crossed to the desk and peered down at the blackmailer.

He was dead all right.

CHAPTER 5

I TURNED TO keep an eye on the girl and got my first good look at her. Was she too heavily made-up? Well, I shouldn't say that, exactly; I might say she was made up to be the girl I knew and not the demure little miss of the commissioner's office. Had she fainted? Was she staring wildly at me with frightened, unseeing eyes? She was not. She had one of the filing cabinets open and was going rapidly through it. She finally got what she wanted and turned toward the fireplace.

I crossed the room, had her by the arm

and swung her around. Both her hands were behind her back, but she wasn't near enough to the open fire to chuck in what she held.

"Give me those letters or whatever you are concealing," I ordered.

"No," she said. "I sold my mind to that devil on earth and my soul to the devil in hell for these. I'm going to burn them now, as you advised in the restaurant." She looked at my gun. "You could kill me, but I'd burn them."

"That," I said grimly, "it not a bad suggestion. But hardly necessary." I held her tightly to me and put my hand around her, trying to get what she held.

"I gave you life tonight, Race Williams," she said coldly. "In return, won't you give me these two bits of paper to destroy? They are not mine, they are—" She hesitated a long time. "One is not mine."

"Gave me life?" I laughed.

"Yes. I held tightly for a full second to the gun in your sleeve." She put her eyes straight on mine and I'll admit my grip on her loosened. "Then I risked my own life by stepping in front of you when you so stupidly tried to compromise me by disclosing the alibi."

"That I don't believe," I told her, and then added honestly, "Though it looks as though I'll have to swallow the gun story." And suddenly: "Why did you do it?"

She looked at me. "Because—maybe I wanted you alive. Certainly, I wanted him dead."

It jarred me a bit if anything can jar me.

"You had a gun of your own," I said. "Why didn't you use that on him?"

"A lady never kills a gentleman, at least in cold blood." And damned if even then it wasn't a nice smile she gave me. "Besides, he took the gun from my bag tonight and replaced the live shells with blanks. I discovered that."

"Why tonight?"

"Because of the two bits of paper I hold behind my back. He promised to show one of them to me tonight. He never had it here before. I guess he was afraid I would kill him to get it."

"And was his fear correct?"

"I don't know," she replied, slowly and rather thoughtfully. "I might say that I have gone through hell to keep what one of those sheets contains from being made public; that is, another girl who has taken my place has gone through hell. That girl is myself, of course. But such a different person. I suppose I'm sort of a Dr. Jekyll and Miss Hyde." Her laugh was not good now. "But sometimes I'm afraid I'll never slip back to being the girl I was. A convent-bred, demure little thing, like in the commissioner's office. At first the person I am now didn't seem too real to me, it was as though I were acting a part. Now, the person that I was doesn't seem real to me."

"You are not very clear."

"No, I'm not," she said. "You see, Mr. Wainwright was my father's friend. He bled my father white, bankrupted him by blackmail through Larry Lapeno, even loaned father the money to pay him, took mortgages on father's property. I never knew what it was until my father just folded up and died. He was delirious then and he told me, just me. My mother's an invalid, you know."

"No." I watched her closely to see if she were lying. "I didn't know."

"May I destroy these papers?"

"What's in them?"

"I saved your— Well, if I tell you what is in one of them will you let me destroy it now?"

"Maybe. If I like the story."

She looked at me a long moment, said abruptly: "My mother shot a man to death before I was born. Another woman knew it, saw it, but she protected my mother. But to protect this woman, my mother had signed a statement that she herself had killed him. Somehow, this statement came into the hands of Mr. Wainwright and he blackmailed my father through Larry Lapeno. My mother never knew. She doesn't know now. It would kill her, of course. Do you want to read it?"

"No," I said gruffly. "If you didn't save my life, at least you gave me a chance to save it myself. Toss the papers into the fire." And when she did: "If you knew just where that document was, and worked for this man, why didn't you get it before?"

"It was never here before. You see, he had twisted my mind and warped my soul, but he wanted my body. He was a shrewd man. He read the truth there. Somehow, I wasn't big enough for that. He promised to show me my mother's statement tonight. He did. I saw where he put it. He was retiring from business. We were to be married. The day we were married he would give me the statement to destroy."

"Did you believe that?"

"No, but I believed and hoped that if I once knew where it was for so short a time I could get it—and I did. He read the

newspaper about your finding the man behind the blackmailer. He didn't believe it, but he wondered. He was a careful man. He decided to kill you tonight. He wanted to involve me in your death, as he wanted to involve me in the death of Larry Lapeno."

"He said you killed Lapeno."

"Yes, but I didn't."

"What was the other document you burned?"

She didn't hesitate. She said simply, "A signed statement that I killed Lapeno."

"And you didn't?"

"Why, no." The smile was there and this time it was not too bad. "You remember, I have an alibi. You and I were together when Lapeno died." And when I just stared at her: "Yes, I worked with Mr. Wainwright. I went down to the very depths to protect my mother. At first, he pretended to be an old friend giving me a position as secretary. Then he found out what I was after. And he made me work with him. Maybe I fooled him. Maybe I didn't. But he was changing my personality to suit himself. Anyway, that is what he thought and I certainly did change. You see, he was the only man in the world who could pull Larry Lapeno out into the night unescorted. The night he killed him he simply sent for him. You wonder about my being blackmailed by Lapeno. Well, I sent Lapeno the very letter you paid to get for me. He had met me as Mr. Wainwright's secretary. But he didn't know I was the girl he was blackmailing. Because, as you know, he never saw her."

"What," I said, "could possibly be the purpose of that?"

"Because I wanted to meet you. I wanted to get to know you. I wanted—"

"You wanted me to kill Wainwright and get your mother's document, so you tried to make me fall for you?"

"That's right," she nodded. "At least I wanted that document."

"You didn't fool me," I said, with some pride, for she was a damned fascinating girl.

"No," she said. "I fooled myself. I played a game." She put both her hands on my shoulders. "Look at me, Race. I liked you. I told myself that I only liked you and would use you. But tonight—" She was getting pretty close and her breath was warm against my face. "I guess I have loved you for some time, but tonight I knew it."

I took both her hands from my shoulders. I smiled at her. At least, I twisted up my lips as I looked into those hard, calculating eyes. But they weren't hard and calculating now. They were soft and appealing, maybe like the girl's she had been. Then I shook my head and laughed. She was a damned smart girl.

"You want me to let you go," I said, "to walk out into the night free, absolutely free from all that you have been, for your mother."

"That's right," she said. "I won't offer you money, though I will shortly have a great deal to offer you. But I know that wouldn't do any good."

"No," I said, and my voice was hard and cold, "that wouldn't do any good."

"You won't let me go?"

"Lady," I said, "no. This dead guy had a big game. This dead guy—"

She cut in. "The filing cabinets are all the proof you need that he was the blackmailer. They are full of letters." And when I gave her the cold and stony stare: "I suppose I could prove to you that—well, I have proved to myself that I love you, love you better than anything on earth. Anything—" And the hands were working again. I gripped them tightly and said brutally:

"Better than your dying mother, I suppose?"

"Yes, yes." She barely whispered the word. "It is terrible, isn't it? But it must be true. You see, if I had... had died without getting that signed statement of mother's—well, I threw myself between you and his gun. Why—" She was fighting to get her hands free now. "So that you might live even if I died."

She broke loose then and walked across the room toward the door. When I called to her to stop she threw the words back over her shoulder.

"Think it over, Race," she said, "or shoot me in the back if you wish. Anyway, you'll know where to find me or tell the police where to find me if you want it that way."

The library door to the hall opened and closed and I was alone. Alone with a corpse.

With a corpse? And it suddenly struck me. There was another corpse or had I really seen that foot? And didn't the girl know about that or— I went to one of the filing cabinets and jerked it open, shuffled through the files. Letters, letters, letters! All pertaining to charitable work. And then I found it. The drawer did not come out far enough. I didn't jerk the thing off its hinges. I found the little spring and snapped it back and there were some real letters. Love letters, threatening letters, a copy of a page from a hotel register, a snapshot of a man and a girl on a beach. Another one of a room which was not too nice.

I banged shut the drawer, took my handkerchief and wiped off any prints. What should I do? Walk out and let the police find the whole business? Or should I call up O'Rourke and let him get the commissioner? There was the dead man with the gun in his hand. There was the picture on the floor and the bullet-holes in the floor and the one in the wall. There were the letters to prove the great philanthropist was a common crook, the most vicious of all crooks, a blackmailer. There was—

I crossed over to where I thought I had seen the foot. It was in semi-darkness. I pulled out my flash and found a closet door. I gripped the knob and jerked open the door. I didn't need my flash. It was one of those closets where a light snaps on when you open the door.

Yes, I saw the foot all right, two feet bound tightly together. Hands, too, bound behind the man's back and a coat tossed over his head. Was this torture? Was the man bound before he was killed? I leaned down and jerked back the coat to look at the dead man's face.

Surprised again? Yes, I was surprised. Then it hit me and I threw back my head and laughed. I couldn't help it. No, the man propped up against the wall in that closet wasn't dead. He wasn't even unconscious. Eyes that were wide and staring and uncertain had suddenly taken on a hopeful look. Now that I laughed they took on a threatening look, an angry look that was fast turning to a doubtful, maybe an embarrassed look. Certainly, the man was red in the face. And suddenly I realized that perhaps it was not entirely from embarrassment or even anger. For the gag was tight across his lips, a handkerchief evidently first being shoved between his teeth.

I leaned down and tore loose the knot that held the gag in place and jerked the handkerchief free from his mouth. He tried to talk, tried to talk and suck in air at the same time. He was not very successful. He choked, gasped, coughed and began to come back to life.

You know who he was? Or maybe you don't. Well, he was Inspector Nelson. Old Iron Man Nelson himself. In person.

After a while he began to talk. All of it was abusive. Most of it profane. Some of it obscene. And the end of it was what would happen to me the minute he was untied.

"What makes you think I'm going to untie you?" I asked him.

He blew up then. Went off again and finally settled down.

"You came in a different window," he told me. "You hit me on the head. Rolled me in here, bound and gagged me. And Mr. Wainwright, despite his prestige and standing and wealth, isn't entirely free of blame. He hired you, I know."

"So!" The truth dawned on me. "And I was giving you credit for tracing down the blackmailer. And what did you do? Break the law. Tap my telephone wire and come here to meet the blackmailer and steal my show."

"I came to your office to give you your chance to disclose what you were hiding from the police." And when I just stared at him: "Cut me loose," he ordered. "There will be others, the police will be here any minute."

"No, they won't." I shook my head. "An inspector of police doesn't take men into his confidence when he breaks the law and taps a telephone wire. Besides, when the other cops come, won't you be a pretty picture?"

At that, I didn't know what to do with him. A less kindly man would have shot him through the head and called it a day. I talked to him a bit, sort of felt him out. Sure, I got his story. Oh, he didn't actually admit that he tapped the wire, but he said he came there, was talking to Wainwright when someone hit him on the head. But the truth was that he thought he had bluffed Wainwright into hiding him in the closet until I came, evidently to horn in on the deal. But one thing was sure; he was certain I had cracked him down. He didn't know Wainwright had done it. He didn't know there had been a girl in the house, and he didn't have any idea that Wainwright was the real blackmailer. I guessed I'd never be able to prove he'd tapped the wire. But I scared hell out of him, anyway, before I went to telephone O'Rourke.

"One more foul peep out of that big mouth of yours, Nelson," I said, "and I'll telephone Marty Gibbs of the *Star* to come and take pictures. The readers of the *Star* might enjoy a little light comedy with

their tragedy. A dead blackmailer outside and Iron Man Nelson trussed up in the closet. Anything for a laugh these days. But it won't inspire public confidence."

I went to the phone and called O'Rourke. I told him nothing, except that it was important—and how!

Ten minutes later I let O'Rourke in the front door. I showed him the corpse and the evidence in the way of blackmail letters, pointed out the shots in the floor and the one in the wall where the picture had crashed. I didn't mention the girl at all. And sort of slid in Nelson. I entirely forgot to tell him about the body of Lapeno I had carried out a few nights before. I told him that the *Star* story was to throw fear into the blackmailer so he would try to trap me, that Wainwright called me up. That he said he was being blackmailed and that he thought he knew who the blackmailer was and so I came to see him. I repeated the telephone conversation, for I felt Nelson had heard it, anyway. I said Wainwright had taken my guns from me, was about to kill me when I tossed over backward and produced my sleeve gun and did him in.

O'Rourke was a thoughtful and very wise man, a good politician, too. He walked up and down a minute before he spoke.

"It'll rock the city," he said. "It will wreck institutions that have been doing a great deal of good. Big names will refuse to be associated on stationery that bore and still bears the name of Harrington Grover Wainwright. Thousands—well, tens of thousands of people will refuse to donate to worthy causes that this man has wrecked. I'll call the commissioner, Race." And as he reached for the phone: "No one need know what happened—maybe."

Only Nelson. I got ready to deliver the punch.

He dropped the phone back in its cradle.

"He's an honest man," he said, after a bit, "but he thinks of only one person, Nelson. He'll talk his head off if—"

"He's in an embarrassing position," I cut in, and I went into detail about Nelson and his tapping my wire and his being bound up in that closet.

O'Rourke smiled and lifted the telephone.

"Strange, Race"—he winked at me—"that you forgot to mention Nelson until after the commissioner arrived. Or I would have untied him, of course. If you had, I would have done my duty."

Commissioner Blake came and looked at me, looked at the body, looked at the letters in the cabinet, listened to me, stuck his face close to O'Rourke's and then said to me, "What did you say, what about Nelson?"

That was all right with me and I led the commissioner and O'Rourke to Nelson.

"Nelson frightened me, commissioner," I said, with a broad grin and in a loud voice. "Threatened me bodily harm. I was afraid to untie him until you came. There seems something wrong with him."

The commissioner did his stuff well. His dignity and displeasure were grand to behold. That is to me, not to Nelson.

"And you," the commissioner was saying when O'Rourke and I went back into the library by the fire, "you, Inspec-

tor Nelson, whom I trusted above all men, permit yourself to be bundled up like… like something you would never condone in a rookie. And outside in that room an ordinary citizen, Williams, fights for his life to rid the city of—"

That was all I heard. O'Rourke was soft-soaping me.

"You have done a great service to the community, Race. You may be asked to do a greater one."

"It's to be a hush-hush affair, eh?"

"The commissioner would have nothing to gain by hushing it up, except to benefit the community. It would drive him out of his job if the truth ever came out. He… he'll want to talk to the district attorney or the mayor—or both perhaps."

"They are elected to office," I said. "The truth would be hair on their chests."

"It never helps a public official to expose a righteous and respected citizen, especially when it makes other righteous, respected and influential citizens look ridiculous, if not feel slightly tainted."

That was the way they worked it. I didn't see the mayor or the district attorney who had to run for office. I didn't even know if the commissioner talked to them. But I did know he used another phone in the house, and I did know that the commissioner gooed all over me. And I did know that for once I got my way in a blackmail case. My silence was the price of returning every letter to the original owner without making a copy.

"What are you guys doing for the good of the community that I don't do?" I asked. "Look at the newspaper notoriety, look at the business I lose. The story is not simply national, it's international. Why—"

Nelson whispered something to the commissioner then and he threw it at me.

"What about the body here before, what about 'You're expecting another body?'"

And that, of course, was part of my telephone conversation. Did it throw me? It did not. I said easily:

"What's a body to you gentlemen? Does one more or less make a difference?"

It didn't. I had my way about the letters going back. And that is the real story behind the death of "The greatly beloved and esteemed philanthropist, Harrington Grover Wainwright" as the papers called him. "Murdered by an unknown friend while he was thinking only of the welfare of his fellow man."

But it wasn't that bit of flowery writing that tossed me for a loop in the papers next day. It was the picture alongside the "kindly" old coot Wainwright. The picture of a young and beautiful girl. The daughter of the "beloved philanthropist's best friend now departed." The caption read:

INHERITS GREAT FORTUNE OF BRUTALLY
MURDERED BENEFACTOR

And the name was the name of Miss Avery Spellman but the face was the face of Avery Coles.

I knew then what O'Rourke meant when he spoke of the commissioner's concern over Miss Spellman. And later I knew why the commissioner had treated me so coldly that day in his office when he left me with Avery.

How did I know later? It was the day after the funeral of Harrington Grover Wainwright, which I didn't attend, that I got the note from Avery. It read simply:

Come and see me tonight and keep your promise. Remember—we were to live the few hours that I imagined in my diary.

And with it was the page from the diary itself. The alibi page. It was rather a startling bit of writing.

"Most of those few short hours," some of it read, "Race Williams held me in his arms and told me he loved me. Now I know—I know—"

So the commissioner had reason to believe that I played fast and loose with sweet young womanhood.

Did I keep my promise? Sure I did. What had I to lose? Besides, I was armed when I walked into her apartment.

CARROLL JOHN DALY

A Corpse Loses Its Head

It was Florida in all its glory. Too early in the season for crooks, but late enough in the fall to avoid the murky chill of New York. The Casa Manana Hotel was big and as free from a crowd as a blue fish is from wings. You could run a foot race in the hall without bumping into anyone. I ran the foot race, but I did bump into someone.

"Hi, Feller," she said. "I'll race you to the stairs."

With that she cut loose and I after her. She was about twelve or thirteen, I thought, and she made those slack-clad legs fly over the soft, luxurious runner.

It was pretty close to the stairs when I passed the kid and a woman opened a door on my left. My shoulder brushed her arm; the handbag she held was knocked from her grasp and flew across the hall. I skidded to a stop, grinned sheepishly, and reached for the bag.

I didn't make it. The woman grabbed for the bag ahead of me, muttering a curse that didn't fit in with the climate, the hotel, or her apparent position in life. She snatched up the open bag. But she didn't snatch it up before I saw the thing that protruded from it. It was black, it was squat, and it had a stubbed nose. It was a high-caliber automatic pistol. My first thought was a natural one. The lady was no lady.

The kid laughed, and the lady who wasn't a lady snorted and said:

"How dare you act like a little hoodlum?" Then she glared at me, and I got a good look at her face. She wasn't so old, and she wasn't so young. She wasn't so bad-looking, either. Her face was sharp, her lips thin and her nose straight. Her face was white like marble, smooth and hard. But inside her I didn't know. There had been the curse on her lips and a coldness in her eyes when she retrieved the gun. One thing was certain. She didn't know I had seen it. But I always see a gun, can even sense one. If I couldn't, I wouldn't be alive today.

Then the woman spoke to me. She said stiffly:

"Peggy's guardian is rather particular as to her associates. Please do not annoy the child again."

The child winked at me. When the woman turned her head, I winked back. And that was the beginning of my friendship with Peggy. I knew that the woman looked me up, for I found out she made inquiries at the desk. But I wasn't registered under my own name.

It was at lunch while the woman was called to the phone that I got the note. The head waiter brought it to me.

"From a lady, Mr. Richards," he smiled as he addressed me by the name I was registered under. Not that I'm ashamed of my right moniker, but I was away for a

rest and didn't want to invite trouble. And my name always invites trouble.

The note was in a clear, round scrawl. It read:

Hi, Feller:

You don't seem to have anyone to talk to, and I certainly don't.

I go in swimming at the Cameo Beach Club every morning at eleven. Aunt Clarice doesn't get into a bathing suit.

I beat you racing.

Peggy.

Then a P.S. that was as snappy as the letter and to the point. It said:

P.S. If you are staying at this hotel you can swim at the Cameo Beach Club free of charge if you pay a dollar a day.

Which statement wasn't any more naïve then the simple larceny this playground of America practices on the Northern visitors free for nothing, gratis.

So that morning found me on the beach at the Cameo Club, the dollar paid. Why not? She was a cute kid. I like kids. Besides, I was a bit curious as to why an apparent lady of means, with a child, staying at a high-priced hotel, cursed under her breath and carried artillery in her purse.

Peggy spotted me first. Just came up to me in the water when I had about given her up, grabbed my hand, and said:

"Let's swim out and talk it over. Aunt Clarice is off her feed today."

She could swim, too, and we lay out on the Atlantic while she blew water up into the air and talked. She was an odd kid, sophisticated in some things and simple in others. She was reserved when she wanted to be, too, and wide open along other lines. There were times when I thought she was a child of pampered wealth, of middle class, and once she surprised me into placing her as the lower East Side. It was about her swimming, and it slipped out.

"No"—she had just finished demonstrating a bit of crawl that had me moving to keep abreast of her—"I didn't learn to swim at any swanky club. I picked up what I know from some rough going in the East River." And then she added, "It's dirty but cool in hot weather."

Later she pulled this one:

"It was a swell club, all I can remember of it. But I wasn't old enough to swim then."

"Is Aunt Clarice your mother's or your father's sister?" I tried a bit of pumping.

She turned over on her back then, shook a finger at me, and said:

"Naughty, naughty. Curiosity killed the cat."

That was the beginning. We talked in the water, separated on the beach and occasionally we had confabs at the hotel. But not often. Aunt Clarice had an eye like a vulture, and one afternoon when I was coming up the steps I was pretty certain that she snapped my picture.

Now the kid was all right, and I got quite a kick out of her. Still things were getting a little difficult. Twice Aunt Clarice tramped down the porch and snatched Peggy away when she was talking to me.

The sun deck on the second floor was all right for those who like the sun dished out to them through a glass roof, but me, I had formed the habit of making a moon deck out of it. When things got quiet and I got tired of listening to the night clerk run down the management of the hotel, I'd laze in its deserted grandeur.

So it was about a quarter to twelve one moonlight night that I lay off in a deck chair watching the smoke from my butt curl up toward the moon. I was alone, with row on row of deck chairs laid out for the early-morning sunners.

And the kid came. I heard the door open and her slippered feet cross the concrete. Then I saw her in the moonlight. The fur around her tiny ankles, the pajamas showing beneath her blue padded bathrobe, her brown hair all rumpled up and catching lights from the Florida moon. She looked as if she'd been in bed and decided it was too nice to stay there. And she had a grin from there to Key West that wrinkled up her nose. She climbed into the chair beside me, leaned far back, stuck her feet straight up in the air, and put her two hands back behind her head.

"You shouldn't come out here, Peggy," I said. "You should be in bed. Your aunt will be furious, and you'll get punished. Do you want to tell me something?"

"I want to tell you a lot of things," she said, "but I'd catch hell if I did."

"Peggy," I said, "you shouldn't use such words."

"Why not?"

And there you were. Why not, indeed? I just said:

"I don't like it."

"All right, Feller, then I won't say it. I want to please you, because I like you." And suddenly: "My mother died when I was three, but I remember her. She was very beautiful and very sweet. My father—"

"Yes?" I said. "Your father?"

"My father was drunk most of the time. But I liked him. He was like you."

Funny, but that was a compliment. Not in the words she used, but in the way she said them. Finally, she went on:

"You'll let me talk, Feller, won't you, and when I don't feel like talking any more or maybe cry, why it'll be O.K.? And you won't tell anyone?"

"No, kid," I said seriously, "I won't tell anyone."

"Good. It ain't anything much, but you're the first person I ever felt like talking to. Some of the things my father wished and dreamed for me and told me about are coming true. This hotel, running around the country in a car, having nice clothes. Father kept saying he'd get his money back. But he was always afraid. Often he'd go out and say, 'Peggy, when I come back tonight we'll be rich and I'll take you around the world.' Then he'd stand up stiff and jerk his vest down before the mirror, and out he'd go."

"And?" I tried when she took a long time.

"And he'd just come home drunk." A long pause and finally: "The last time he said it, he... he—"

She stood up then, leaned forward and put both hands on my shoulders. Her eyes were moist. She kept those eyes right on me.

"They brought him home dead," she said, and when I simply squeezed her hand: "Killed."

She turned suddenly and ran from the deck: I sat a long time after that and smoked. I wondered. Of course, she had said, "Killed," but, somehow, it was as if she had said, "Murdered."

KIDS ARE FUNNY. The next day she met me on the beach and she was all gay. The night before was forgotten.

"Saturday night, Feller," she told me, "and a dance at the hotel. Aunt Clarice said I can sit up and watch the dancing. We'll sit by the window, you and me, and watch." And suddenly: "We'll dance, too."

"I don't think your Aunt Clarice would ever stand for that."

"No. Well, we'll pretend to anyway."

And that was that. It was a small figure to blot out the Florida sun, and the Chamber of Commerce should have done something about it. It was Aunt Clarice. She still had the bag in her hand, and I wondered if she were going to open it and pop me off right on the beach. But she didn't. She gave me a look that should have had the same effect, grabbed the kid's wrist, and said:

"I told you, Peggy, that I don't want you speaking to people, especially that man." And as they started toward the clubhouse: "Now there will be no watching the dancing tonight."

So the dance was off, but that evening I wandered around to the place the kid had picked out and sat down in one of the big porch rockers and watched the dance. An hour later two hands went around my face and covered my eyes and a quick, excited voice said:

"Guess who?"

I was wrong in my guess, but I could have been right. I said:

"Aunt Clarice." And we both had a laugh. Strange the things you'll laugh at when a kid's around. Peggy had slipped down while Clarice was telephoning New York.

I was just putting the kid off the arm of my chair and standing up and telling her that she had better go back when the old—or rather young battle-axe swung along the porch and spotted me with my arm around the kid's shoulder almost under a light.

All right, I thought, this is the showdown. If she lays a hand on the kid I'll open up and make her wish she had a machine gun in that bag. But Aunt Clarice floored me. She said:

"Oh, Mr. Richards, I was worried about dear Peggy. But now that she's with you it's all right." She stretched out her hand and the granite cracked up and her face looked almost human.

The kid recovered first. She said: "We were going to dance, Aunt Clarice."

And Aunt Clarice chirped—yes, there was a bird-like note in her voice, and I don't mean vulture, either:

"Of course if Mr. Richards wishes to be so kind and isn't afraid of making himself ridiculous. You're fond of children I take it, Mr. Richards."

Maybe I said that I was. I don't know. But we were on the floor moving about, Peggy and me, before I had a chance to know what I did say. We had a swell time for the next hour. Of course, the kid couldn't dance, but neither could I, so we were even.

From then on I saw a lot of Peggy. We went to the movies, and Aunt Clarice explained that Peggy's guardian was very particular, but she had got permission for Peggy to be friendly with me. And what did I think? Aunt Clarice didn't tell me who the guardian was, but to my way of thinking she had snapped my picture, mailed it to New York, and this guardian had looked me up. Then he had telephoned Clarice that I was O.K. And what's more, if that kid needed protection, he came out ahead on the deal. I'm a man who not only carries one gun but two, and I've been known to use both of them at times. Also I get good pay for my services. So the kid was getting the highest-class service for nothing. But it suited me.

That was a week! That kid and I went everywhere. She didn't break down and confess any more, and all I found out was that Aunt Clarice was not a real aunt but a pick-me-up of her guardian's. Who the guardian was the kid didn't tell me, and there were times when I thought that she didn't know herself.

I didn't meet her on the sun deck for a "moon burn" as she called it any more. I told her I went right to bed at night, though, as a matter of fact, I still slipped out there when everyone else was asleep. That night, feeling certain that she had gone to bed, I went out on the deck. I slipped open the glass doors quietly and was just going to cross to one of the front chairs when I heard the sound.

So Peggy was there, waiting for me. I

was actually pleased, but I put on a severe look, straightened—and stopped dead close by the stone pillar. A voice came to me. It was not Peggy's voice. It was a husky voice. The man was saying:

"She called me 'Feller' and then damn near kicked all my teeth down my throat."

I quickly stepped out from behind the pillar and walked toward the two figures that bent over one of the steamer chairs. One of them was trying to lift something in his arms; the other, whose back was clearly visible in the moonlight, had a gun dangling in his right hand. I won't pretend I didn't know what that burden was that they were trying to lift. I crossed the hard cement and my feet must have pounded out the hammering that was going on inside me. The man with the gun turned quickly, jerked up his gun, and spoke without any nervousness.

"Stay out of what doesn't concern you, brother," he told me. "Sit right down in that chair or I'll blast your—"

What he'd blast, I never knew. My gun was in my hand before I started across the floor, and my hand was in the air when he turned. It was coming down, too. Just a single thud and he hit that cement like a thousand of brick. His companion swung then—not because he was quick, but because I had jerked a hand under his chin, fastened it on his coat lapels, and pulled him around. He was facing death, but he didn't know it.

It was the kid all right. She was breathing rather loud, sort of pulling, gasping breaths, and I was seeing red inside. The man didn't try to struggle. He was too surprised for that. But when

he got over his surprise, he started to threaten me. And then the girl started to cough and sob a little, and finally called out faintly:

"Feller— Feller—"

"It's all right, Peggy," I said. "I'm here now, and no one is going to harm you."

The lad I held cursed again and my hand tightened on his throat. Peggy was on her feet when a voice spoke from behind me. It was Aunt Clarice.

"What happened? Peggy, are you all right?"

That was the first time I ever heard real feeling in her voice or at least real interest. I said:

"It looks like an attempted snatch. Get the police. I'll keep this lad here."

The man I held struggled to get free; at least, he twisted himself so he could talk clearly. He said:

"No cops in on this, sister, or I'll blow the works." And to me: "You've butted into something, stranger, that don't concern you. It's a private affair."

"Let them go," Aunt Clarice said to me in a stifled voice. "You must—for the child's sake. Please. Come on, Peggy."

And there she was, taking the kid and leading her from the deck. I could see the girl's uncertain feet going across the cement; could hear, too, her quick gasp as she nearly tripped over the leg of the man on the floor. Then they were gone and I was standing there holding a hood tightly by the throat. The door closed and the man grew bolder.

"See what you get for being a smart guy. Take your hands off me."

I dropped my hand and stood looking

CARROLL JOHN DALY

at him. It was surprising, of course, but there is nothing new in my line.

"Cops, eh?" He started in to straighten his tie as he put mean, slit-like eyes on me. "A fine mess you'd be in. Someone's got to make a complaint, and if there's no complaint you can't get very far, stranger, because you saw a couple of men talking to a kid. We was wondering what she was doing out here so late at night. Now take yourself off and consider yourself lucky you haven't got a belly full of lead."

I gave it a few minutes' thought and decided to call it a day or a night, if you want it that way. Of course, all along I knew there was something fishy about the kid, the Aunt Clarice set-up, and the gun in the bag. I'm not one to call the cops. After all, I make my living from people who for some reason or other don't want to call the cops. Somewhere, somehow, this was my kind of job. I'd find out about it and see what I could do to help the kid. So I half turned as I started toward the door. No sense in getting Peggy into trouble.

Now some people are never satisfied. This lad was that sort. He was tough; he was hard. He'd show me where I got off. He reached out a hand, grabbed me by the shoulder, and swung me around. Then he pushed his flat face close to mine and let himself out.

"I'm taking a good look at you, buddy," he said. "I'm marking you down for the future. I want to remember you."

"All right." Things exploded inside of me. "Remember me by this!"

My right hand turned into a fist and cracked against his chin. He picked

himself up off the floor like a champion doing a back dive, missed the low footrest of the chair behind him, and laid himself out on the floor almost gracefully. I stepped over the other man as I went into the hall.

Aunt Clarice opened her door finally and stood blocking my entrance. I had pushed her aside and stepped into the room before I said:

"I want to see the kid."

"She's… she's all right. I just put her to bed."

"I want to see her."

"You can't."

"Lady," I said, and meant it, "you can be nice about it or nasty about it. But I'm going to see her now."

Aunt Clarice looked at me steadily for a long minute. Then she said:

"All right." She led me across the room, through a bathroom and into the room beyond. Peggy was sitting up in bed. She looked sort of pale, but she smiled and held out her arms to me. Then she put her hand down quickly and pulled the blanket over something she had in bed.

"Hello, Feller," she said. "Some fun, eh?"

"Miss Clarice," I said to Aunt Clarice, "I want to talk to Peggy alone."

She bit her lip, started to put up an argument, took a good look at me, then left the room and closed the door.

"All right, Peggy." I went to the bed and sat down. "Now you tell me things. I am going to watch over you. You needn't be afraid to trust me."

"Of course," she said. "You sure put the heat on Clarice. I was scared, yes, but I don't know very much. Listen, Feller, I'm like a princess out of a fairy story. There's money in me some place." She put her tiny arms around my neck and pulled my head down. "I'll tell it to you like a story, for I don't really know much about myself. Once there was a little girl who had everything, and then suddenly she had nothing and lived with awful people in an awful place. There was a wicked ogre who came to see her and complained about the money that was spent on her, and she didn't dress very well or eat very much. Then after a long time this same wicked man came and he took her away and she met Clarice. After that, money and clothes, trips and running from hotel to hotel and a place in the mountains by the lake. And a fear that someone was watching her. But I don't know, really." And when I just looked at her, "That's all. You'd fight for me, wouldn't you, Feller?"

"Any time, Peggy. Now. Aunt Clarice— Have you reason to be afraid of her? Would she harm you?"

"Hell, no, she— I mean, dear me, no. She's paid to watch over me, I think. This man told me that some day I was to have a lot of money because… because of my father."

She told me lots more, but when I'd get to questioning her, she'd smile and run her hands through my hair and admit that it was all rather mixed up because she lived so much alone and that she made a story out of it.

"Sometimes I get mixed up and don't know what's real and what I just made up."

"One thing else, Peggy," I said. "I want to see what you hid under the blanket when I came into the room."

Two red spots came up on either cheek. She said:

"No, I can't show you that. It's part of the dream, like what I make up." She shook her head when I insisted and said, "No, you won't like me any more. You'll think I'm just a baby."

But I made her show it to me, and it put a lump in my throat. I just looked at it and couldn't speak. It was a doll—yes, a dirty doll. Why I should be surprised, I don't know. I won't try to explain it, but I wouldn't have been more surprised if it had turned out to be a Thompson sub-machine gun.

She threw her arms around me when I was leaving.

"Good-bye, Feller," she said. "I'll always remember you, Race."

I was gone and back to my own room before I realized what her last word had been. She had called me by name, my real name. She, too, knew then.

I didn't sleep very well that night and was up and downstairs the next morning by seven o'clock. But eight came, nine, and then ten, and neither Aunt Clarice nor Peggy showed up. So I called their room and got a real shock. Aunt Clarice had telephoned down for an early breakfast, and they had left the hotel suddenly before six o'clock.

CHAPTER 2

SOMEHOW, AFTER THAT the sun didn't seem so warm or the moon so bright or the cold chill of a New York winter so hard to take. I waited around the hotel for a few days with the hope that I'd hear from the kid. Then I went back north.

Business was not so good. Then the check came in the mail. It was made out to me and was for one thousand dollars. The letter read pretty nice.

Enclosed check for one thousand dollars. Will you kindly call on me at my home at eight o'clock tonight? You may consider this sum in payment for a few minutes of your time even if you do not accept the business which I offer you. Very truly yours,

Joseph P. Mack.

Sure, the check was good, undoubtedly. I had known Joe Mack ever since he started up from the gutter right through his bootlegging days and into his trucking business and political racketeering. Mack, Sheider, and Carlson were the three lads who exploded the adage that there's honor among thieves. The government indicted them first. Mack evidently had paid up, squared himself with the other powers, and let his two associates go to jail.

All three of them went back to the gutter from which they started; that is, figuratively speaking they did. Mack was reputed to be living on the money he had held out. Lately it was assumed that Sneider and Carlson had been shaking Mack down with a threat of exposing his past. And that would take in everything, I imagine, up to and including murder, yet, he never had been dragged before a city magistrate.

So you see how I felt about that damned check. I'm not too particular, but I do draw the line some place. I hunt skunks; and I don't protect them. If I had to name one man who never had a good mark on his record or one bit of human kindness in his whole body, I would unhesitatingly name Joe Mack. The thing was an insult. I had helped to expose Joe Mack. He even had threatened me. That he didn't make good, I'm alive to testify to. That he tried to have me killed I can prove. The two lads who had a go at my life didn't live long enough to explain.

But at eight o'clock that night I rang the doorbell of the quiet, respectable old brownstone front in the Fifties and was let in by the seedy-looking servant, Manuel. My eyes opened a bit wide when I was shown into the library. There was a lawyer there.

Charles Phillip Parsons was well known in the city. He was an estate lawyer and had a name and a reputation, both of which he risked by showing his pince-nez-adorned Roman nose in the house of Joe Mack. Mack himself was something to look at. He wasn't young; he wasn't old. Long, gaunt, thin of face, with a beak-like nose and round, small eyes. He was dressed entirely in black and always put on a sanctimonious air and spoke in a low voice.

"Sit down, Williams," he said. "Sit down, Race, boy. Have a cigar, a drink. What's mine is yours."

"And what's yours belongs to the people." I remained standing. "I'm not going to do business with you, Joe Mack. So you can save yourself the embarrassment of talking to me."

"There, boy, there. A lot of water has gone under the bridge since we last met. A lot of it. This is Mr. Parsons, here, Mr. Charles Phillip Parsons. You've heard of him, of course."

"Yes," I said. And when Parsons started to speak: "Don't bother to apologize for being here. I'm here myself, but it's just to return the big crook's check."

"Now, now, now!" The man's round eyes snapped. "For your own interest, Race, listen to me for a few minutes. I have led a hard life. I have made mistakes. It is to correct some of those mistakes that I have sent for you. Our esteemed fellow citizen, Mr. Parsons here, will assure you that the purpose behind your visit tonight is a laudable one, even a noble one." His voice broke then, and if I didn't know the man I'd almost think he was going to burst out crying. "Perhaps the final act of a man who is trying to right a great wrong."

He did it so well I was tempted to applaud. But I got another look at his face, thought of the kind of man he really was, and didn't feel like kidding around. Parsons said, a bit dramatically I thought:

"The man speaks the truth, Mr. Williams." And when I just stared at him: "Good God, you don't think I'd be here unless I felt it my duty, I might even say a sacred trust?"

I'll admit I was impressed. Parsons was class. What's more I thought he would be hard to fool. Our best-moneyed people trusted him. So I said:

"All right. I'll listen. Tell me about it."

Mack coughed behind his hand. He cleared his throat again. Then: "I can't tell you my full purpose, Race. I'll put it this way, and my check tonight will back it up. Twenty-five hundred dollars now, smack on the line, for your attention for a month, a single month. Then your decision if you'll take over a trust—as Mr. Parsons says, a sacred trust."

"And in the meantime what will I have to do?"

And the joker came out.

"Simply protect my life. Stay here with me and see that no one takes my life. Nothing more."

It was then that I laughed, tore up his check and tossed it onto his desk.

"Here's wishing the boys who want to get you luck," I said and walked out of the library.

Charles Phillip Parsons caught me before I got into my car.

"I didn't know that he was going to ask you that, Mr. Williams. But please reconsider your action. Think of my position. Think of my reputation."

"You'd better think of that."

"I mean," he stammered, "that I wouldn't be here if I did not feel that justice was being served. I can't tell you—a confidence, you know, between lawyer and client."

"Joe Mack is your client then?" I just looked at him. "Has he got any money to pay you? I understand you come high."

He stiffened.

"In a way, I suppose, he is my client, but let me assure you that he is paying me nothing."

"So it is blackmail then." And when his eyes just popped and his glasses looked as if they'd fall off: "If he gets killed, he can't expose you."

I thought he was going to have a stroke, so I smiled to let him know I was only kidding. He said, and his dignity was pretty good and genuine, too, I thought:

"Your levity is ill-timed, Mr. Williams. He is paying me nothing because I refused to accept any money, despite his offer of a very handsome fee. May I ask you to reconsider your decision?"

"Sure," I said.

"Ah, you will take this… this case?"

"No." I shook my head and jerked the car into gear. "I simply said you might ask me." And with a grin as he stepped back: "You can call spirits from the vasty deep, but will they come?"

Back at my apartment, I felt pretty good. Though I admit it wasn't a lot of satisfaction for a thousand dollars. I should have poked Joe Mack in the nose. So I spent a good part of the evening telling Jerry, my assistant, that money wasn't everything in life. Jerry looked sour, but I was just being human. If there was no one else to pat me on the back, why I'd do it myself.

That was Wednesday. It was the following Monday night when a cop came tapping on my door. Sergeant O'Rourke wanted to see me. He wouldn't tell me any more, but he looked very serious, so I went along with him. Besides, Sergeant O'Rourke was a good scout.

Of course, I had a feeling that something was wrong when the scout car drew up before Joe Mack's house and I spotted the two harness bulls and a couple of plain clothes men on the steps. But it wasn't O'Rourke who met me in the front hall of that house. It was Inspector Nelson.

"Come in, Williams," he said. "How well do you know Joseph P. Mack?"

"Well, enough not to like him," I told him.

"Fine. Good. Dislike him well enough to kill him?"

I saw Sergeant O'Rourke across the room. I saw Lieutenant Hathaway from Homicide. I saw a couple of boys setting up a camera, and I saw little Bilkie from the fingerprint department.

I said: "So he's dead, eh?"

"Dead!" Nelson gave a theatrical gasp. "How did you know that?"

"I'm psychic." I nodded at him and walked over to the small trunk with the lid up that was the center of attention by the couch. I looked in. It was not a pretty sight. There was a body with its legs drawn up shoved into that trunk. But the body had no head.

"Know who it is?" Nelson asked.

I shrugged my shoulders. "How can I tell?"

"Who do you think it is?"

"Joe Mack," I guessed.

"Right," said Nelson. "It's his house. He was here alone. Besides there's his watch and letters, keys and stuff in his pocket and a card on which was written, 'I want your head.' Know why he was killed?"

"You mean a reason?"

"Of course I do."

"Hell," I said, "I know a thousand reasons, a hundred motives. And so do you. If you were half the cop you pretended to be you'd have found out long ago that Joe Mack— Oh, hello." I had raised my eyes suddenly and for the first time saw Charles Phillip Parsons. I didn't know him at first. He looked like another corpse, but one with a face. I asked:

"Where's his head?"

"They took it. They took it," Parsons was saying over and over. "Good God! He said they would, and they did."

I went over to Parsons, and O'Rourke joined us. He shook hands with me and I asked him about the wife and the girls. He beamed when he told me his second daughter was going to be married in the spring.

"No kidding," I said. "You'll be a grandfather soon." And I poked him in the ribs. He poked me and laughed.

"I hope so. The old girl won't like it, but me— I will. About the head, Race. Mr. Parsons here says someone phoned him the other day and said— What did he say, Mr. Parsons? This fellow Sarah is marrying has his own business. What about the head, Mr. Parsons? Of course we're listening."

Parsons stammered again.

"It was yesterday, Sergeant. It was over the phone. A voice said, 'Mr. Parsons, if you have any further business with Joe Mack, attend to it now. I want Mack's head.'"

"Is that all?" asked O'Rourke.

"That was all. He hung up."

Nelson horned in with:

"Did he say 'Mr. Parsons?' Come on, yes or no?"

"Yes—no—perhaps not. I don't remember."

"Huh," said Nelson and turned to the medical examiner, Dr. Steer, who had just come in.

Dr. Steer said: "Detruncated, eh?"

"Decapitated," said Nelson.

"They cut his head off," nodded O'Rourke, which is all a lot of ways of saying the same thing. And then to Parsons: "Now how was it you happened to come here?" And when Parsons said he had already explained twice: "There, there. Tell us again for Mr. Williams. Anyway, you might as well get used to it. You'll be telling it a lot."

"Someone telephoned a message to my house, apparently from Mr. Mack. He said that Mr. Williams had reconsidered his proposition and asked me to come over at once. He said—"

"So that's why you sent for me." I looked at O'Rourke. "Well, Joe Mack lied. I'd starve before I'd work for him."

Nelson said to Parsons:

"So you walked in and found the body. Anyone let you in? Was the door open?"

"I told you"—Parsons ran a hand across his forehead; the perspiration stood out in big drops—"the party on the phone who purported to be Mr. Mack left word that he had let his servant off for the evening; that I was to walk in, and that he'd be in the library. I saw the body. After I got over the shock I telephoned you."

"A client of yours, Williams, and he's slaughtered." Nelson was sarcastic. "I know, I know. He's no client of yours now. But he thought he was."

Then Dr. Steer said:

"Well, boys will be boys. Come, come, Inspector, at your time of life. Where's the head?"

Nelson never went in for comedy. He glared at the doctor.

"How long has he been dead? What killed him?"

"What killed him?" Dr. Steer was in a jolly mood. "I can't tell for sure, but I'd say he lost his head." And then when Nelson just stared at him: "I can only make a guess, but I'd say he's been dead about twelve hours."

"Twelve hours! He couldn't be," Nelson snapped.

"No?" The doctor drew his tiny figure erect. "You'll get your official report of the autopsy finding in the morning." He wrote rapidly and handed the slip to Nelson. "Permission to remove the body," he said stiffly as he started toward the door. Then he turned. "At least twelve hours," he said again. "Good-night."

"He's a smart man," O'Rourke nodded. "What time did you get the telephone message to come and see Mack?"

"This evening," said the lawyer in a hushed voice, "when I came home from the office."

"Why," asked Nelson, "do you think the murderer took the head, Mr. Parsons?"

"Because he said he wanted it, I suppose." And seeing Nelson looking steadily, almost accusingly at him, he stammered, "I don't know. How should I know?"

"He took the head," said Nelson as if he had second sight, "because of the size of the trunk. The body wouldn't have fitted in and the top closed with the head on the body. Look!" He walked to the trunk, grabbed the cover, demonstrating this point. "Get the idea? The murderer carried the head away in a suitcase and he intended to come back for the trunk later. But something prevented him from returning."

"And he left that card here just in case he didn't come back," I said sarcastically.

Mack's manservant came in then and he rather complicated things. He said Mack had let him go away on Friday to visit his mother in Albany. He was expected back Monday night, and he was there. He said, too, that Mack had intended to go deep sea fishing down at Key West. When Nelson stupidly asked him if he knew of any enemies Joe Mack might have had, he brought a grin with his serious crack.

"He was a liberal and kind man to work for," he said. Then he added thoughtfully: "Though I heard talk around that he was unpopular in certain quarters."

O'Rourke shrugged his shoulders and said:

"I daresay he's popular where he's gone now."

Which, by the way, was the general opinion of the newspaper boys, though they didn't express it in their sheets exactly that way.

AND THAT WAS how things stood about the murder up at the old Mack house in the Fifties. That the police knew a lot more than I did and that they suspected that I knew a lot more than I told them was certain. But events afterward were so surprising, even startling, that I don't blame O'Rourke for wondering about my position in the whole matter.

Things broke early the next morning when I was asked to visit the president of the First Avenue National Bank at twelve o'clock. I was pleased, of course. Large banking institutions are generally not up my alley. They hire the big, recognized detective agencies.

H. Townsend Maule took me into his private office. He shook hands, gave me the smile that I knew went only with heavy deposits, and then the joy was wiped off my face. Sitting there with his brief-case on the flat, shiny desk and a bunch of papers beside it was Charles Phillip Parsons, nose glasses, smooth hair, immaculate attire and all in order. He was just a little nervous with his hands and his papers. A little severe when he addressed me, too.

"You'll be most agreeably surprised, Mr. Williams," he said, "and perhaps a little conscience-stricken by the tragic series of events. You might have been instrumental in keeping Joseph P. Mack alive."

"Now, now," said the president of the bank, "no mortal man can prevent an act of fate."

I said bluntly enough:

"I wasn't interested in keeping Joe Mack alive. I'm not weeping tears over his death. He had it coming to him."

Charles Phillip Parsons shook his head, but the president of the bank nodded his approval. Somehow, somewhere, I was the man to please.

I sat down then and Mr. Maule took a chair behind the desk, removed one pair of glasses, placed them carefully in a case, produced another case, and taking a pair of glasses from them, placed them carefully on his nose. Then he lifted up some papers, held them in his hands, and said:

"Mr. Parsons has explained to me that this whole procedure is unknown to you.

He wishes to enlighten you and begs that you do not interrupt him until he is finished."

I said:

"Let him talk."

And Parsons did. He said a mouthful and no mistake.

"To begin with, gentlemen, this is the strangest matter that has ever been brought to my attention. I must go back some years to the Pierot family, an old and established name. My father had charge of the Pierot affairs before me. The older people died leaving one son, Francis Huston Pierot. He married an orphan and had one child. On his wife's death I am grieved to say that he became a dipsomaniac"—and looking at me as if I were a dummy—"a heavy drinker, Mr. Williams. It was a disease with him rather than a vice. He dissipated his inheritance and invested a great part of it in a business with Joseph P. Mack. That money was lost entirely and though Francis Pierot accused Mack of fraud, there was nothing that he could do about it.

"I lost touch with him over a good many years. Then he died. He had been drinking and was found shot to death. No one was ever brought to trial for that crime. Now for the strange part. Sometime ago Mr. Joseph P. Mack came to my office. He told me that he was creating a trust fund for the daughter of Francis Pierot. That, without detail, is the sum and substance of the whole matter."

He waited so long, and they both looked at me so hard that I felt I should say something. The best I could get off was:

"So what?"

"So the man was human after all." Parsons snapped at me for the first time. "The voice of conscience pricked him. He was righting a great wrong just as he told you he wished to do the other night when you would not heed him. He was under no legal obligation to do this, understand. It was simply that he must have felt it was a moral obligation. You misjudged the man."

"I didn't misjudge Joe Mack," I said. "He was born rotten; he died rotten. There was a joker in it some place, and his death surprised him. But surely, Mr. Parsons, you didn't bring me down here to lecture me on my proper feeling toward my fellow man. Where do I fit?"

"You," said the banker, leaning forward and putting on a smile that put all his other smiles to shame, "are the trustee of this fund." And if that wasn't enough to throw me, he went on, "To serve without bond and pass final judgment on all matters of expenditures. We spent an hour with the surrogate this morning."

"Is that so?" I was trying to absorb the shock. "And what about our friend, Mr. Parsons, here? Where does he fit in the picture?"

"He," Mr. Maule beamed, "is the young lady's guardian." He extended a hand to me then. "Congratulations, Mr. Williams."

But I didn't take the hand. I said:

"Nix. I'm out. I don't want any part of anything Joe Mack had a hand in. There, don't stare at me. That's flat. I won't serve."

"But"—if I had taken a mop and rubbed it down his face I couldn't have wiped that smile away quicker—"you don't know the amount or the terms of the trust."

"And I don't care." And after a couple of seconds: "How much is it, a couple of thousand dollars?"

"Its," said the president, and his voice lowered as one who speaks of the sacred, "exact value is nine hundred and thirty-two thousand dollars."

Sure, I was stunned. So would you be. Something warned me to stay out of it. Something told me there was a catch in it. But to have the handling of all that money, more money than— I said: "Get thee behind me, Satan," to myself, but out loud I asked: "What are the terms?"

"Ah, the terms." Mr. Maule coughed behind his hand. "Not complicated, no. Rather simple." He came to his feet then. "Mr. Parsons will explain things to you. I hope, Mr. Williams, that you will find it convenient to use the vast facilities of our bank, its many departments, its proven financial experts in the administration of this fund. Don't hesitate to call upon me." He took my hand and worked it up and down a bit. "No obligation—a favor—an honor, I assure you."

He went out then. Parsons took his place behind the desk and lifted up the papers. He said as he looked them over:

"The trust is so that if Margaret Pierot, the beneficiary of the trust, dies before her twenty-first birthday, the principal sum or the trust together with whatever accumulated interest may still be available, reverts back to the maker of the trust, Joseph P. Mack."

"But, hell," I gasped, "he's dead."

"I know." Parsons nodded. "The money returns to his estate. It will be administered as his will directs. That was very clearly laid down when he drew up the trust in my presence."

"I see. Not that it matters much, but who gets the money now if this daughter of his dead partner should die?"

"I don't know." Parsons shook his head. "I have not yet had a copy of the will. That was drawn up by his own attorneys, Welk & Welk. Does it matter? I was the former attorney for the Pierots. Mr. Mack would not make up the agreement of trust unless I agreed to act as guardian for the young lady. And, of course, unless I was familiar with the trust I would not agree. I am pleased to say that Judge Randolph looked very happily upon and, indeed, was quite enthusiastic that Mrs. Parsons and myself should act as guardians of the young lady."

"Well," I said, "it's a peculiar arrangement. He intended to set up that trust even if he lived."

"But, my dear Mr. Williams, the trust was already set up. The money was turned over to the bank. They have been buying gilt-edged securities with it for sometime past. Now may I ask your decision?"

"I don't want any part of it," I told him.

"I see." And for a single moment I thought he was pleased. "That, then, is final?"

"That—" I started, and stopped. Then I asked him, though I thought I had an answer to the question: "Why do you suppose he wanted me in it?"

"I haven't the slightest idea, Mr. Williams."

"I have." I leaned forward. "It was a bribe. He was in fear of his life. He was naming me trustee of this money to try to convince me he was a different man, and in return I was to protect his life. Yes, he was hoping that I would shoot to death the men he feared most."

"But why you above anyone else?"

"Because," I said, "I was the only man he was sure would stand between him and death."

A little conceited that? Well, maybe. But, after all, I was quoting Joe Mack's opinion, not my own. And I was right, wasn't I? I hadn't taken the job, and he had been killed. But he should have known that I wouldn't protect his life.

Parsons' eyes widened.

"Well," he said, "the surrogate was a little surprised upon finding your name as trustee. However, if—"

"He was, eh?" I stopped him there. "And the girl— What does she say?"

"She doesn't know, Mr. Williams. I—"

"I think I'll see the young woman," I said. "Where is she?"

"She'll be at my home for dinner. If you think it necessary under the—"

"I do think it necessary," I told him flatly. "I'll be at your place for dinner, too."

And I was at his place for dinner. I met his wife. I waited in their big living-room for the coming of Margaret Pierot. But she didn't come. Mrs. Parsons said:

"She seemed anything but bashful. I can't understand it. She came downstairs, looked into the room, and then went up again. I'll go up and bring her down."

But she didn't bring her down. She came back, looking puzzled. She shook her head saying: "She wants to meet you alone in the upstairs sitting room." She bit her lip, looking a little annoyed. "I think we'll humor her."

We did, and I followed a servant up the stairs and walked into the small upstairs living-room. I was surprised at the size of Margaret Pierot. Parsons hadn't spoken of her as a child. I had an idea that she would be about nineteen or twenty. But she wasn't. She was just a kid in her teens. She was back by the lamp near the window, leaning over the couch as if she were looking for something that had dropped behind it. She didn't look over her shoulder when she spoke. Her voice was husky, grating. She said:

"Close the door. I want to talk to you alone."

Funny? Sure, I thought it was funny. But I closed the door. And then the girl turned and ran across the room. The next moment two arms were around my neck, wet eyes were against my face, and she was crying and laughing all at once.

"Oh, Feller, Feller," she sobbed over and over. "My father's dream—my dream— it's all come true. And there's a prince in the story, and the prince is you, Feller."

CHAPTER 3

YOU GUESSED IT, all right, it was the kid, Peggy. And was I a dummy not to guess it? I was not. I was living the whole life where too often there is no beginning and no end, just a middle, while you knew from all I told you about the kid that she had to come back into my life again.

That's the difference. I'm telling things on the level to you; life doesn't always treat you on the level, though.

Yes, it was the kid. There she was straightening out my tie.

"We're going to be rich," she said over and over again. Then we got down to earth, and I asked her if Aunt Clarice were still with her.

"Yeah." Her face fell a little, then brightened again. "But we're rich now, Feller, you and I. We'll tie a can to her."

"Peggy," I said, "is that nice?"

But we didn't "tie a can" to Clarice. Later I found out that the trust suggested, "That for loyal and faithful service to Margaret Pierot, it is suggested that Clarice Clark be retained as companion with the salary of twenty-five hundred dollars a year, her board and room, and traveling expenses." "Suggested," understand, not "required." But under the circumstances I did not think it was ethical or even advisable to "tie a can" to Clarice.

I had considerable to think about that night before going to bed. I had been wrong, of course, as to why Joe Mack had named me as trustee. The thing was well planned, yet somehow I don't think the plan entered his head until he found out that I had already met Peggy in Florida. Besides which, not being much at deducing things, I put it straight to Clarice before I left the Parsons home that night. She admitted taking my picture and sending it to Joe Mack in New York. And she told me quite frankly that he had telephoned her and told her who I was and to encourage my friendship with the kid Peggy. But I was waiting for a visit from Clarice that night. I had asked her to call and see me as soon as Peggy was in bed. And since I controlled the purse strings, you can have two guesses as to who controlled Clarice.

Clarice came. Her face was still hard and cold.

"Sit down, Clarice," I said. "Now let's start right. How did you first meet Joe Mack, and what do you know about him?"

"Frankly, I don't know much about him. He hired me to watch over Peggy, take care of her and travel with her. He seldom came to see her. That's really all I know."

"Clarice"—I gave it to her straight; I thought she was the kind of woman who could take it—"I'm very much interested in Peggy. Everything I do will be for her good. There are no strings on me in that trust fund. I could drop you like a hot potato and will if I find out you have lied to me. So tell me all of it."

She didn't burst out crying or become hysterical. She didn't complain of environment or say she had had a hard life. She just nodded her head and spilled it.

"I had met Joe Mack once or twice. I used to run around with Frankie Evans. I wasn't twenty then. I… I toted a gun for him. He was my man, and I stuck to him. When he was dead I talked and saved myself a rap. But I stuck to him while he lived. He did some work for Joe Mack, I think. Anyway, Joe Mack came to me. I told him I wanted to run straight. I meant it. He hired me to take care of that kid; to watch over her and protect her."

"From what? And when did he hire you?"

"I don't know from what. Twice someone tried to snatch Peggy. We moved on. The police were not to be notified. Peggy was living with a poor but decent enough family on the East Side before I took her. They weren't crooks. I guess they were good enough to her. That's all I know."

That was the simple story of Clarice. And though I looked her up and O'Rourke looked her up, I didn't find out different then.

Now the handling of a trust fund is as much or as little work as you want to make it. The lawyer does this, and the bank does that, and the accountants do another thing, and everyone collects a piece of change out of it. Of course, there were papers to sign, but it was finally all settled, and Peggy and I led a high life. I had a private phone installed in her own room at Parsons' so that she could "call me up day or night," which was a mistake as she did just that. She talked of a trip to South America, and even if we didn't take it, we got every advantage but the sunburn from the multitude of circulars.

It was great times for us and then, *pop!* just like that, a car pulled alongside the one she was driving in with a chauffeur and just about tore Peggy's car apart with a machine gun. The chauffeur was killed. The car hit a pole and turned over, and— miracle of miracles—Peggy crawled out through the broken window with a cut lip, scratch of which I couldn't even find when I went to see her.

Peggy had dough. The Parsons were some fish in the city, and Chief Inspector Gilihanty who visited the house in person was inclined to view the whole thing as an unfortunate coincidence and point out that Larry Darvin, fresh out of Sing Sing after a three-year rap, was entering a drug store directly across from Peggy's car. There was some sense to his suggestion, for Larry Darvin had sent three pals to the chair and only escaped the hot seat himself because he had turned State's evidence.

But one thing about it I didn't like. Clarice was not in the car with Peggy at the time, and her orders were to go every place with Peggy when I wasn't on the job. Clarice had an out, to be sure, and a good one. Peggy had insisted that she ride alone, and she was on her way to my office when the shooting took place.

That night O'Rourke called on me. He wasn't his easy-going self. He was sort of strained. He even watered his whiskey, and he never mentioned his daughters. I said:

"Anything new on Joe Mack's death? How about the time? Was the medical examiner right?" And when he just nodded: "Of course you haven't caught the murderer. Your police system of looking for someone with a motive must be tough in this case. You could drag a net down Broadway any night and catch at least a couple of hundred with motive enough to murder him. Did his manservant have an alibi? Did you ever locate Joe's head?"

"His manservant," said O'Rourke sullenly, "didn't kill anyone. And we didn't find his head."

"Well," I asked, "why not tell me all about it?"

"Why don't you tell me?"

I shrugged.

"I told you all I know, O'Rourke. That's gospel. Why should I hold out on you?"

"I don't know why." O'Rourke got interested then and so far forgot himself as to reach for the bottle and down a drink without watering it. "But, Joe Mack, the one man in the whole city whose entire life shows not one act of decency toward his fellow man, let alone kindness, suddenly impoverishing himself to the extent of setting up a trust fund of close to a million dollars for a kid of a former sucker he took over. Then hiring you, whom he has every reason to detest—" And when I shook my head: "Well, then, without even telling you, he makes you trustee of that fund. You expect me to believe that?"

I grinned.

"God's truth, sarge. I have to admit I pinch myself even yet to see if I'm awake. It's a surprise to me, too. I can't believe, don't believe even now that there was a touch of conscience or remorse or kindness in Joe Mack's whole rotten system."

"Then why pull this one—and you above all people? Understand, Joe Mack used all his money for that fund and then died. Who killed him? Who knew about the trust fund? Who would profit by it?"

I laughed at that.

"Peggy or I, eh? Well, I got an alibi. And I daresay I can fix one up for the kid."

"And the woman Clarice. She got a job for life." He hesitated then. "She hasn't got a nice past, Race, though there's nothing against her lately."

"I know."

"You do?" He opened his eyes. "Well, she has no grip on the trust. Then there is

Parsons. Business isn't so good with him. I'm not saying he's broke. I don't know. He may be lousy with money. He'll draw down a bit of change in fees, anyway. He's Peggy's only living relative, you know. Sort of a distant cousin."

"I didn't know that," I admitted. "So that's why he went to see Mack. Blood is thicker than his reputation." Then I gave O'Rourke advice. "If I was looking for Mack's killers, I'd go first to his two partners, the jailbirds, Carlson and Sneider."

"That's because you're a big gun-toting dick with no head. Mack was worth more to them alive. At least to Sneider he was. Mack's lawyer found a lot of canceled checks payable to Sneider. He'd been blackmailing Mack. You can't blackmail a dead man."

"Did you say Mack died poor? That he impoverished himself when he made over this trust fund to the girl?" And shaking my head: "He wanted to hire me as a bodyguard. He must have suspected death."

"Yeah." O'Rourke looked steadily at me. "Have you seen his will?"

"No." I had forgotten about that, or as a matter of fact had not been interested in it and never had asked Parsons about it. But now since that shooting I was interested again because the beneficiaries of that will would receive the principal of the trust if Peggy would die before she became twenty-one.

"Well"—O'Rourke leaned back—"you should have looked into that. Mack left everything he had to be equally divided between his two former associates, Carl Carlson and Adolph Sneider, and the

sum was just about eighty-four dollars and fifty-five cents." He came to his feet then and walked to the window. "I just came from Mack's lawyer. The shooting took place this afternoon, an attempt on Peggy's life, and only this morning the lawyer notified both Carlson and Sneider of their windfall and how if Peggy were dead they might inherit the trust."

"Hell!" I came to my feet. "The rats! They knew about the trust. They killed Mack, and then decided to kill the kid. So the police missed that one. Well, I'm not going to." I was grabbing up my hat when O'Rourke stopped me.

"No, Race, I saw them both, and they are both alive."

"What of that?"

"Nothing except that you'd better take a look at the peculiar clause in Mack's last will and testament. It even puzzled his lawyer, but it's simple enough and clear enough and I understand binding enough. Here, I had a typed copy made of it." He handed me a slip of paper, and I read it.

It was all dolled up in legal words and though odd, was clear enough when you stripped it of the "whereases" and the "therefores." I'll just put down the meaning of it and what it had to do with the trust fund. In the first place, if Peggy lived to be twenty-one she had the power to will the trust fund as she pleased, as the principal sum became hers then. Which the president of the bank had assured me was the usual thing in such trusts.

So the only thing the will had to do with was what became of that trust if Peggy died before she was twenty-one.

Then that trust fund reverted to Joe Mack if he were alive. If he were dead, the entire principal of the fund was disposed of under the following terms of Mack's will:

1. If both Carlson and Sneider were dead the entire fund went to Peggy's nearest living relative. (Which it seems was Charles Phillip Parsons.)

2. If both Carlson and Sneider were alive the entire fund also went to Peggy's nearest living relative. (Again Parsons.)

3. But if either Sneider or Carlson were dead, then the entire fund went to the one of the pair living. Yes, one of them had to be dead for either of them to get that dough.

Oh, there was an explanation by Mack in his will. He said he knew Carlson and Sneider were devoted friends, and if both were alive they could take care of each other and would have no need for the money. It didn't sound like a good explanation, but that was the explanation he gave. I more than half suspected that there was another and real reason that wouldn't look so good in writing. I looked up at O'Rourke and said:

"It looks like Mack hated them both and hoped that one would kill the other so as to get the money." And suddenly: "So that's what you meant when you said they couldn't have shot at Peggy because both of them were alive."

"Something like that," said O'Rourke. "If they both are alive and the kid dies, Parsons collects. If they both are dead and the kid dies, Parsons collects. But if one of them is dead and the other living, then the living one collects. It's a will to kill."

"And they haven't killed each other yet?"

"Not yet." O'Rourke grinned.

"They're still in the city? I haven't heard much about them. Are they doing all right?"

"They're still in the city. I saw them both right after the shooting. It is pretty well understood that Sneider lived by shaking down Joe Mack. Carl Carlson is going straight. He's got religion. Don't grin, Race, I think he's a little gone in the head, stir batty. But for the last three years he's been preaching down in the mission. He's a sick man mentally and physically. I haven't been fooled by crooks for a long time, and from what I've seen and what I've heard around, Carlson has turned almost fanatic, but Sneider would still slit his own mother's throat for a dollar." He shook his head. "Sneider's known to be partial to a knife rather than a gun."

I went back to my thought, said: "It looks like Mack set one man to kill the other by that clause in his will."

"But why? They couldn't profit until he was dead. Understand, Race, if Peggy died and Mack were still alive, the money would go back to Mack. What good would having them kill each other do when he was dead?"

"I don't know. I guess Mack's soul was just rotten. He expected it to live on and enjoy his bit of vengeance."

"For a guy who came into a soft snap because of Mack, you seem pretty ungrateful. Maybe Mack's soul is hoping that you'll kill both of them."

"Maybe it is," I said listlessly, and then jumped to my feet. "Come on, O'Rourke, beat it. I've got to make a call on a couple of lads."

"Who and why?" He joined me at the door.

"Carlson and Sneider," I told him grimly. "Mack's soul has a damned good idea. I'm going to tell both those boys about it. That's right, sarge, I'm going to let them know that the next shot they take at that kid will be their last. I'm going to let them know that if they go after that kid I'm going after them and that I'll be on the kill."

"That," O'Rourke pointed out, "will only put them on the kill for you first."

I grinned as I closed the door.

"That would certainly simplify things."

ADOLPH SNEIDER WASN'T hard to find. He worked in a cheap gambling joint. He was a bloated-faced, pop-eyed, big-eared hood. He opened up when I was trying to feel him out.

"I don't know what your purpose is here, Williams." He stood with his hands on his hips, his legs far apart. "But I'm warning you. If you came here looking for trouble, you'll get all the trouble you want when you want it. Is that straight talk?"

"That," I said, "is straight talk. So we'll let it go that way, Adolph. I do want trouble. I came here looking for it. Now let me have it."

Adolph changed his tune. He let his face crack up. The scowl went. He came down to earth. He wanted no part of me when I meant business.

"What's come over you, Race? What's your beef? You used to take a kidding with the best of them. Getting touchy? The cops were here about Joe Mack. They thought I was shaking him down when he was really paying me back some of the money he owed me. I'm in the clear on his knock-over. The cops were satisfied."

"Hell," I said, "I'm satisfied about Mack, too. I don't care if you croaked him or not."

"You shouldn't after the nice spot it put you in. Well, what's the beef?" And his eyes widening: "Not that bit of gun-play today? Better look elsewhere for that, Race. If that kid had been killed someone else would have got the dough. Read Mack's will and figure out if I'd shoot myself out of all that jack."

"You understood Mack's will then?"

He laughed.

"After that lawyer impressed it on me. Sure, Mack thought he'd set us against each other. Now why did you come to see me?"

"Only this, Sneider." I laid a finger on his chest. "If that girl dies so that you profit by it, I'm going to kill you. Remember with all that money at stake, you could get a lone wolf to pull the job and alibi yourself. It's like this. I'm not a cop and I don't need evidence. I'm not the law, so I don't need twelve men to prove you guilty to me. I'm just telling you now that if the child dies and you profit, you die."

"Just how and just where?" His sneer was not too good.

"Any time, any place," I told him. "I'll shoot you to death the first minute I see you, even if that happens to be when you testify before the grand jury."

With that, I turned on my heel and went out the door. Across the street was a drug store. I went in and buzzed my apartment and got Jerry on the phone.

"Know Adolph Sneider?" I asked.

"Sure, boss, by both sight and smell."

"Good. Get down here to this gambling joint he works at. When he comes out, tail him. Stick close to him and let me know every place he goes. And, Jerry, this is important. Every chance you get, phone me and report what he's doing. I'll be home shortly and stick around for your calls. But call at two o'clock under any circumstances for further instructions."

Finding Carl Carlson was a little more trouble, though not much. I got his address by ringing up a mission, and later found him in a cheap tenement over on First Avenue. He let me in and seemed glad enough to see me. His eyes were sunken balls of fire.

"Come in, Race Williams," he said. "Come in and sit down. In your way you are doing your best to eliminate crime, but what are you doing for the souls of men?"

"Getting ready," I said "to send a couple of souls crashing the gates of hell." He didn't look like a phony, but I couldn't be sure.

"In your way then"—he set those eyes hard on me—"you serve a God of wrath and perhaps, too, protect the innocent from being contaminated by the devil's work. If you can't save the soul of a man, then destroy that man. I have thought on that. Well, you've come with a threat to me. I rang up my former associate in sin, and I know of your threat. His soul is beyond saving, but have you the right to destroy the body that harbors it? Don't threaten me. I'm not afraid to die and surely you can't look at me and suspect that I would harm that innocent lamb."

"Not for nearly a million?" I was puzzled. He sure seemed crazy as hell.

"Not for all the gold of the world nor its false temples nor for the adoration of its women of sin." He laughed then, pointed to a chair, and I sat down. Certainly he couldn't be putting on an act. It was too real. But he was saying:

"Why should I destroy the good I accomplished? Yes, Race Williams, you are looking at the man who forced Joe Mack to give to the daughter of his dead partner all his worldly possessions." He stood before me then with his hand raised in the air. "I offered my own life, my own soul to my Maker as well as his soul. There was Mack and Sneider and myself, and each one of us knew enough about the other to send the other to the electric chair. Sneider blackmailed Mack for small sums, for Sneider knew that he could not expose Mack without exposing himself and Mack knew that, too. But I— Well, I finally saw the light. I spent close to two years in discovering just how much wealth Mack possessed. Then I told him, showed him my evidence, the sworn statements of others, everything that would convict him before man, I told him that the day he signed over all—not part of his worldly possessions but all of them—to that child of a robbed and murdered father, then and then only would I destroy the evidence I had."

I sat erect in the chair. There was truth in what he said. A real explanation of why Joe Mack had created that trust fund. He had had to create it.

"It's a wonder he didn't kill you."

"Kill me? But I would have left behind all the evidence that would destroy him."

"And now?"

"I kept my word to Mack, kept it to him dead as well as alive. I destroyed all the evidence against him and sealed my tongue in silence. A wrong has been made right."

I got up to go then. But at the door I said:

"You knew that an attempt was made on that child's life. Who do you think did it? Parsons?"

"The lawyer?" He seemed surprised. "No, it was Adolph Sneider, or course, or someone he hired."

"But"—I gave it to him brutally—"you understand the will of Mack's. With you alive, Sneider would have shot himself out of a fortune if he had been successful."

"I know. And I guess he knows now. But his brain was always warped and his mind slow to understand. I have pleaded with him. On my knees I—" So he was going on, and I walked out of the room. I believed that Carlson had put the finger on Joe Mack all right and forced him into setting up that trust fund for Peggy. Sure, after looking at Carlson I could easily believe that he would give up his own life—not because of vengeance against Joe Mack, but because of justice. And what's more, Joe Mack had believed it, too.

And what's more I had other ideas after I got home. I thought I knew who killed Joe Mack. I thought I had the explanation of the missing head. There would have to be a purpose behind the taking of the head of Joe Mack unless a madman took it. So I sat and smoked and thought the thing over. A couple of hours went by.

Then O'Rourke walked in on me.

"Race, Nelson is about to make an arrest in the Joe Mack affair. You were interested in the shooting and the child's escape. Well, we've placed a lad who was seen in the vicinity of the Mack house early Monday morning."

"Is that enough to cause an arrest? Did he want Mack's head?"

"No"—O'Rourke was emphatic—"he said he didn't want his head but his soul."

"Carl Carlson then."

"That's right, Race, Carlson. Who else but a madman would cut off Mack's head, cart it away, and leave a card behind?"

"That," I said, "will be nice for Sneider. If Carlson is electrocuted, Sneider is in direct line to profit by Peggy's death, and what's more, he can't be blamed for killing Carlson that way. Yes, nice for Sneider, but hard on the kid."

"No," O'Rourke told me, "a lease on life for Peggy. For if Carlson is found guilty of murder, he'll never go to the chair. He's as crazy as a loon. Then she's safe—that is, if you eliminate Parsons from any interest in that money."

"Well, I don't know," I told him. "I think Peggy's safe. It wouldn't be hard to prove a motive if she were killed."

O'Rourke shook his head.

"Lads don't think about that with a million dollars at stake. Guys have been willing to face the chair for less. And you can get a lot of lads to do dirty work for you for a lot of money."

"Not killing a child." I shook my head.

"Well, an alibi for you while you do it. By the way, Race, did you see your two birds and make your threat?"

"I sure did," I said as I got up to go with O'Rourke.

Nelson was already at the dirty tenement house when we arrived. We met him coming down the stairs. He looked sourer than usual.

"Well, did you make your arrest?" I asked.

"No." He shook his head.

"Why not?"

"He's too dead," he said and went out into the street.

And he was right. O'Rourke and I went up the stairs. Someone had made quick work of Carlson; had just walked into the room and stuck a knife in his heart. The body was still warm.

O'Rourke looked down at the body and said, a little sadly for him and I must admit with some feeling:

"Well, he knows now if he saved his soul. Surely, anyone who made Joe Mack come across for that child as he did deserves some consideration at the pearly gates, and I think he'll get it."

Which let me know that Carlson already had talked to O'Rourke and O'Rourke had not told me about it. But we both took off our hats.

"It's a long time since Adolph Sneider had a real piece of change," O'Rourke said. "Funny what a pile of money will do. Within twelve hours after Sneider learns that Carl Carlson stands between him and real dough, Carlson dies."

"He must be as mad as Carlson to try anything like that," I answered. "Certainly he wouldn't dare kill the girl and expect to get away with it when the motive's so well defined."

"No?" O'Rourke stroked his chin. "You can't convict lads on motive alone. A million dollars would buy plenty of proof that he had nothing to do with the killing of the child. And—"

I cut in with: "I think I'll go up to Parsons' and see Peggy."

"O.K." O'Rourke nodded. "Nelson will have the net out for Sneider. We'll see where he was. It's my bet that his character witnesses will even surprise the cops."

It was after one o'clock when I pushed Parsons aside and stepped into his big front hall. His eyes blinked with sleep.

"Is Peggy all right?" I demanded. "Where is she?"

"Peggy? Why, what's the matter, Mr. Williams? Of course, she's all right. She's asleep in her bed where she belongs. Come in, man, and have a drink."

I followed him to the library, but I didn't want a drink. I snapped:

"Why didn't you tell me about that will, who would get the money if Peggy died? Don't tell me you don't know about it."

"Yes, of course I know. I looked it up as a matter of form. But you didn't ask me about it. Good heavens, man, why should I tell you? What's wrong?"

"Didn't it ever strike you that the one who would inherit that money might commit murder to get it? Didn't that strike you?"

"Why, no." He seemed genuinely surprised. "I have handled a lot of estates and there is always some heir when other people die. It's natural. But murder— Heavens, man, there were complications enough to the final distribution of that trust if Peggy should die. But Peggy's only a child. Her health is perfect. There is no reason why—"

Well, perhaps not from his standpoint. Even in his bathrobe and slippers, with his hair uncombed, he still had his dignity and seemed surprised at my questions, nothing more. I said abruptly:

"Carl Carlson is dead. He was murdered less than an hour ago."

"Carl Carlson?" He seemed perplexed. And then suddenly: "One of the beneficiaries of the trust under the will and—" His eyes widened; the sleep left them. "That makes the other man—what was his name?—Sneider, the possible— Good God, you don't think— You do think then—"

"Yes," I broke in, "I do think just that. And after the attempt on Peggy's life today and—"

"But the police explained that. Some gang vengeance, wasn't it? And—"

"I think," I told him, "I'll go up and see Peggy."

"And wake the child up?"

"Look at her anyway." I went to the stairs and he followed me. "After this I'll sleep in the house here, or better still we'll let her go away for a bit, take a trip."

"You don't really believe that someone would make an attempt on her life here in my home, in my very residence?"

"What's immune about your home?" We were up the stairs now, turning down the long hall to the large room and bath in the rear that Peggy occupied. I found her door, opened it softly, stood and listened. There was no noise, not even a sound of breathing at first. Then there was a sound of breathing, but it came from within me. Something was turning over inside me. I wasn't my calm, steady self when I groped for the light-switch, finally found it. There was a click. The room was flooded with light.

The bed, the open closet door, then the entire room popped into view, and it was empty. I dropped to my knees and looked under the bed. Then I crossed to the bathroom, jerked open the door. It was true. It had to be true. Peggy was gone!

CHAPTER 4

I turned to Parsons.

"She's gone," I said. "She's not here." And then for a moment my composure left me and I stepped into the hall and hollered, "Peggy!" so that it rang through the house.

There was confusion, of course. A search. All the servants were up. Mrs. Parsons was rushing about. The house from cellar to attic and even the rear court behind was thoroughly gone over, but the kid was gone. There was no sign of a struggle in her bedroom. It was then for the first time that I realized that Clarice was missing. She had gone to the movies, Mrs. Parsons finally told me, and it appeared that she had not returned.

So there you were, Mrs. Parsons had seen Peggy to bed at nine-thirty. It was now half past one; four hours had gone by. But how did anyone get into that house and carry off such an active child? A maid checking up on her clothes proved beyond a doubt that the clothes Peggy wore that evening were also missing. But that didn't prove she had dressed and left the house. Anyone who carried her out might have bundled up the clothes and taken them along.

But Clarice. The whole thing looked fishy. Who would profit by her disappearance? No one that I could think of. And then another thought, a terrible thought. I looked at the white face of Parsons, the shaking legs, his frantic walking up and down. But while we were waiting for the police whom Parsons had called, I got him alone in the library.

"Parsons," I said, "why didn't you tell me you were related to the Pierots?"

"So you know that. Well, it hardly matters, does it, now?"

"It matters a lot—maybe." He drew back as I advanced on him.

"Why—well, I was not proud of the connection, I suppose. Pierot, Peggy's father, was not an estimable character. But can't you see that's why I went to see Joseph P. Mack? After all, blood is thicker than water. That's why I was willing to be guardian, to open my home to her, a child without proper bringing up. I felt it my duty." And then in what might have been real feeling: "In the short while she has been with us, Mrs. Parsons and I have grown to love her. We'll be glad to recognize the relationship. We feel it may establish her more firmly in the social position she's entitled to."

The cops came then. O'Rourke and Nelson. Nelson started in to ride me.

"Hired to protect the man who created the fund, and now he's gone. Hired, paid big money to protect the girl and—well, she's gone. What the hell was that phone doing in her room? There isn't a phone in every room in the house, is there?"

"No," I said, "I had that put in so she could reach me any minute of the day or night and—" It came to me then. "That's it. She walked out herself, thought that she got a message from me and—" I stopped. "No, she would be too bright to be fooled that way."

"Hell," said O'Rourke, "she wouldn't expect you to call her up and ask her to leave."

"What about Sneider?" I asked Nelson. "Did you locate him?"

"No," said Nelson. "He's a fool. He's hiding out, and what's more he was at that tenement; at least we think he was. A couple of people have turned up who saw someone who looked like him. But he'd kill the child, not just snatch her."

"I don't think he snatched her," O'Rourke put in. "Even for all that money, he'd hardly go straight to Carlson and kill him and then come up here and grab off the girl and— It don't tie up right." And suddenly as he looked from Parsons to me: "Listen, Race, did you tell anyone you'd kill these two birds if they harmed the child? Anyone like Mr. Parsons, for instance?"

"No"—Parsons beat me to it on the answer—"he didn't tell me anything like that."

I had to agree on that. And we all had to agree that if Peggy wanted to leave the house, filled with servants or not, it would have been a simple matter for her to go downstairs, open the front or back door, and walk right out into the night. To be carried out presented more problems.

Someone would have had to break into the house first. And there was nothing to show that an entrance had been forced.

"No bolt or chain on the front door, nor even on the kitchen door," said O'Rourke. "If Clarice didn't have a key she could easily have had one made and slipped it to someone else."

A long and useless talk then about the trust and the terms of Mack's will and whether Clarice was familiar with it or not. But the consensus of opinion was that she wasn't. Certainly none of us had told her and Peggy did not know.

"I am inclined to think," said a young detective who had a studious appearance and who was a protégé of Nelson's and thus was permitted to think, "that the inheritance itself has nothing to do with this abduction. I don't know this Clarice woman's record, but she might be in a common ordinary snatch and a ransom note will be received in the morning."

"Too coincidental with Carlson's murder," said O'Rourke.

As for me, I don't believe in coincidence. They didn't want me to leave, but I did. Jerry was still on the job. At two o'clock he'd try to report no matter where he was.

I spent a miserable fifteen minutes waiting for my phone to ring. Finally, it did. It was Jerry.

"Well," I gasped, "did you put Sneider to bed? Did the police nail him?"

"No, he's still up," Jerry yawned. "He's having coffee in an all-night beanery over on First Avenue, I just—"

I cut in there and got the address.

"Hold him, Jerry. Hold him if you have to shoot him as he leaves the place. I'll be right down."

I drove my own car in a mad dash downtown. I pulled up in the dark a bit up from the lighted all-night restaurant. Jerry came over.

"He's still there," Jerry told me. "Hell, boss, you look white as a couple of ghosts." Then he told me of his trailing of Sneider. Sneider had left the gambling club and walked leisurely across town and straight to the tenement where Carlson was murdered. He hadn't been there but a few minutes when he came out, seemingly pleased with himself and putting something in his pocket. That was just about the time that Carlson had been knifed. Either a few minutes before or a few minutes after. Take your choice. And if your choice was my choice at that moment, you would have been wrong.

Then Sneider went to a newsreel theatre and stayed a long time. Finally, he had come to the restaurant, and Jerry had telephoned me. It was the first chance he had had to get me on the phone. And just after Jerry had come out of the telephone booth in the same restaurant a boy had walked in and given Sneider a note.

"It was in a sealed envelope," said Jerry. "I saw Sneider tear it open and read it. He must have read it several times, then he looked up at the clock. Then he ordered more coffee and— Here he comes now, boss."

"Good. Get behind the wheel, Jerry. If he goes the other way, follow me along in the car. If he comes this way, all right. We're going to pick him up."

"He's heeled, boss. Under the left arm. I know by the way he straightened himself a couple of times."

"I know anyway," I said and fell back in a doorway.

There were no breaks. Adolph Sneider came out of the restaurant, stood there for a moment free and easy, and then pitched his toothpick onto the sidewalk. Certainly he didn't look like a lad who had come fresh from a murder. Oh, not that Sneider wouldn't go to murder and no doubt had, but he never struck me as a lad who would stand around picking his teeth afterward. But he turned and started up the street, and I started after him.

It was dark and it was lonely, and Sneider no more than lifted his head until I had stuck my gun in his back and said:

"Race Williams talking, Sneider. There's the car. It's a ride. Get in and have a chance for life; hesitate and take the dose here on the sidewalk."

Adolph Sneider had been around. He didn't hesitate. He walked straight to the car and got in. Where there's life there's hope. He was a very much surprised and shocked man. And what's more he had a right to be. He knew me and knew that I didn't talk just to hear my own voice.

The door closed; the car moved away from the curb. I had taken Sneider's gun, tossed it onto the floor, and had him by the throat.

"I warned you, rat," I told him. "Talk! Where's the kid? Before I blow you apart!"

He talked. He was scared. He spluttered. But his talk did me no good. It was just a claim that he knew nothing about Peggy. I didn't have the time and the patience to go to work on him and force the words I wanted to hear out. But I said:

"For a quick word on where the girl is—if she's still alive—I'll let you get a start on the cops. Don't look so stupid. They know. Not only did my boy follow you to Carl Carlson's, but the cops have two other people who saw you leave the tenement after you murdered Carlson."

"Carlson… dead… murdered!" Sneider gasped.

And I gasped, too. The thing was too real to be play acting. He just fell to pieces. He didn't want any chance to escape. He didn't know anything about the kid. He got a telephone call to go and visit his old friend Carlson. He was afraid that Carlson's mind was going. Carlson was always after him to reform. He was afraid that Carlson was going to make a full confession of all his past misdeeds and involve him.

But Carlson had assured him he wasn't, after he had assured Carlson that he had no intention of killing him.

"Good God, Williams," he said with some semblance of truth, "am I a fool? That will was left by Mack in vengeance. He hoped I'd kill Carlson and roast for it."

I couldn't get any more out of him and he fought like hell when I went after the note. I finally had to crown him with my gun and get it out of his pocket. Did it mean anything to me? I didn't know. I read it over there under the light of the car.

Dear Mr. Sneider:

As I told you I'd help you against this man Mack, I will. He harmed me enough. Now I have found out about a lot of money. Come to Mack's house at five A.M. And come alone. I'll want half the money, and I'll want your protection from them that want it. It is hidden in the house. But don't come before five A.M. They'll still be there. Be sure to come alone and don't let anyone know you're coming. The back door will be open, so come right in. I will leave a note what we have done if you try to harm me or do me out of my share. It is a lot of money. Obey instructions or all is lost.

Manuel.

Then I found another note that said:

Mr. Sneider:

I am leaving this note at Carl Carlson's for you. You are to keep out of seeing anyone from now until two o'clock when you are to go to Eddie's restaurant (and here the address of the restaurant I found him in) and wait there for another note from me. I am sorry to be so mysterious. But someone will be watching to see that you don't meet anyone.

Manuel.

That was clear enough, and it was also clear why Jerry could follow Sneider so easily. Sneider expected that someone would be following him and didn't want to do anything to interfere with the arrangements. Manuel, of course, was Joe Mack's old servant.

What did it mean? Did it mean what is said and just involved money and had nothing to do with Peggy at all? "Don't come until five o'clock." I looked at my watch. It was twenty minutes past three. I turned to Jerry and told him to drive me up to within a block of the Mack house.

Thoughts on the way. Sure, I had thoughts. Hopes, anyway. And my hopes were that the kid would be at that house and still be alive. How did I figure that? Well, like this. And I know it sounds silly and makes a victim out of Adolph Sneider instead of the villain of the piece. My idea was that the Mack house—now closed up—was to be used at a death trap for Adolph Sneider. The time was set for some reason at exactly five o'clock. He was to walk in there and be shot to death. Then later—and I gulped over the thought— Peggy was to be killed. Why later? Well, because the time of death would have to be established according to law. If Peggy should die before Sneider, then Sneider would inherit the money, but if Sneider should die first and Peggy be found dead later, then Sneider would not inherit it.

Who would inherit it? And that was the part hard to stomach, Charles Phillip Parsons would inherit the money. There were no two ways about that. It was a horrible thought, and it was a hopeful thought. Because if it were true and Parsons was actually back of the fiendish plot, it meant that the kid was still alive and would be alive until Sneider was dead.

How would Parsons work it? I don't know the answer to that. Was Clarice in it with him? She must have been. Surely it wasn't conceivable that Parsons had made arrangements with such scum of the underworld as would murder a child for him and for his money. It also seemed inconceivable to me that Clarice could work it alone. But why not? There was really nothing to do but shoot Sneider to death as he entered the house and then—yes, then kill Peggy.

But these were simply wild thoughts and speculations. The answer to the problem lay, I hoped, inside that old house.

I told Jerry to take Sneider back to our apartment, tie him up, and watch over him with a gun. For all I knew the notes and everything else might be a fake of some kind, and since Sneider was the logical one to kill Carlson, I'd have him for the police.

WITH THAT I left the car and walked around the block.

It was a dark, cold morning, and I didn't meet a soul there on the side street. I know directions all right, and it didn't take me long to slip down the alley of the house directly behind Joe Mack's, climb over the fence at the corner, and, crouching low in the deeper shadows, make my way close against the back of the Mack house unseen. I hoped unseen—at least no one shot at me. How to get in was a problem. Oh, yes, I remembered the instructions in the letter about the back door being open. But if my idea was correct it called for one or more bullets in the body of the man who came in that back door. And that I hoped was where my idea went astray.

Breaking into a house may seem a simple enough matter. And it is when everyone is asleep and you've got a kit of burglar tools handy and have practiced your profession. A cellar window in those old houses is easy to unhook, but if the door from the cellar to the rest of the house was locked I'd be out of luck.

There was a covered shed by the back of the house and far enough away from the rear door. It was a sort of added attraction for keeping logs for the fireplace. Anyway, that's the conclusion I drew when I saw some kindling wood beside it. It was a jump and a climb, and I figured it gave onto the kitchen window. I chanced it. With my gun in my hand and lying flat on the dirty, worn, shingled roof, I pushed my way up to the window.

A bit tricky that, lying and listening and hugging close under the window. Not a sound from behind that window, not a light; just a dead stillness. I braced myself, then steadied my body and pushed it against the glass. I had a feeling that Peggy was in that house, and come what may, I was going in.

I didn't want to do anything to endanger her life if—my body pressed closer against the glass—my idea were right and she was still alive. If someone were behind that window, that someone would watch me try to enter and shoot at the best opportunity. Well, there wasn't going to be any best opportunity, if I could help it. If someone were in that room, I was going to hurl myself through the glass and take part in the shooting right at the first shot. If no one were there, then I'd chance a slow and quiet entry.

How would I accomplish that? Simple. I did it then. I held my gun in my right hand, my flash in my left, and the flash was pressed hard against the glass. My body swung far to one side then, I pressed the button and glued my eye to the glass. Desperately, I listened for the sound that didn't come. Desperately, I peered into the darkness cut by the glare of my flash. A shot, a movement of any kind and I'd go crashing in that window.

Just stillness and a bit of a bad break. It was a long, narrow room, quite evidently the butler's pantry that so many of those old houses sport. And the bad break. The sink was directly below the window. I saw the white of it plainly.

It was too late now to choose another window. This room was unoccupied. I was in the back of the house. So far my presence was unsuspected. The bad break was simply the noise that the glass would make falling into the sink. For the window was locked. I could see that the catch was in place. I raised the nose of my gun, reversed it so that the sight crashed the glass first. There was a crack, a tinkle as the glass hit the sink. Then silence.

I didn't wait to see if the sound had been heard inside that house. Heard or not, I was going in. My fingers slipped through the broken glass, caught the catch, and slipped it back. Then the window was up and I had one foot in the sink. Both feet. I was on the floor of the butler's pantry and had snapped on my flash. A swinging door to the left and one to the right. And not a sound in the house.

I hit the wrong door first. It led to the kitchen. I tried the other one. It was my meat. Old, heavy dining-room furniture snapped up in the flash of the torch. Of course, I wanted to go by the front of the house. I might be heard mounting the back stairs. Experience has taught me that nearly all criminals commit deeds of violence on the upper floors in a rear room. That's not just guess-work. It's the safest part of a house, free from observation from the street or the possibility of a cry being heard.

The single flash of light was enough. I felt out the furniture as I crossed the dining-room and passed through wide open doors to the front room beyond. There would be a hall then and across the hall the library where I had met Joe Mack that night he offered me money to be his bodyguard. But in that hall would be the stairs leading above.

A bad thought then—that, after all, I was on a wild goose chase. The notes to Sneider had been fakes. But I didn't believe that. Then a good thought. I was not only on time, I was ahead of time. Whoever was to come to the house had not come yet. I had better find a place to hide out then. To deal with Manuel would have been a simple matter. But now I might have to deal with others; the ones Manuel had written about in his notes.

Hopes then. Hopes that Manuel was just an opportunist; that he with some others had kidnaped Peggy and that they were holding her to shake down Sneider. The point of that? Simple but sickening. If Sneider kicked in they'd see that the girl was found dead. If he didn't—

I turned into the hall and heard the voices. I drew up short. Someone was talking in the library. I felt my way toward it, stretched out my hand, remembered the thick curtains that were there, parted them slightly, and looked through. A single dull lamp glowed. A man and a woman were standing by the tightly-drawn shade of the front window. It was too dark to see more than the whiteness of their faces. The man was evidently finishing his conversation. He was saying:

"And that's the whole story, Clarice.

Rather clever, isn't it? I pick you up in South America later and we live on the money in grand style!"

His voice was low and soft with a familiar ring in it, yet I couldn't place it. Then Clarice spoke.

"You fiend!" She breathed hard. "And I thought of living the rest of my life with you."

The man's hand gripped her shoulder. I could see the whiteness of his fingers.

"You'll get used to it, my dear." He held Clarice as she tried to pull away. "You're to take the knife and kill her with it. Sneider is known as handy with a knife. He'll be along on time. I'll telephone Race Williams when to come, and they should meet here. The knife!"

"No, no!" She was struggling now, and her voice was strained so that she hardly got the words out. "Where is Peggy? I'm going to tell. I'm going to scream that you murdered Carlson, that you intend to kill the child."

The man laughed. He spoke again, and still I could not place that voice.

"She's dying slowly now," he told her. "You will put her out of her misery, Clarice. Don't you see? Don't you understand? My own protection, my only safety in you and with you, is that you do this for me. You could never talk then. I love you, Clarice, but you do this or you must die, too."

"Die? But I want to die." And suddenly crying out: "No, no, not that child! Where is she? This Williams will know. He will kill you."

The man's laugh was not pleasant.

"All right, Clarice. You want it that way. Sneider can be blamed for you, too." He swung the woman around, and I saw his hand go up. I raised my gun, moved the curtains slightly, and oozed through them. I was about to speak when his hand came down to his side. He said almost hurriedly, and I thought there was panic in his voice:

"I am going to tell you where the child is. Listen!"

I listened, too. That was what I wanted to know. That was what had kept me quiet. Things suddenly happened fast. The man grabbed the woman. She cried out. I knew the truth. The man had seen me there by the curtains. He had spoken to distract my attention and to hold my gun-fire and to give him a chance for the move he now made.

I found the light button and pressed it. The picture was clear enough. The man was now masked. The woman was in front of him. He knew me and knew that I would know him if I saw his face. His voice, too, was cracked and quite plainly disguised when he spoke.

"Drop your gun, Williams. You'll have to shoot the woman to get me."

I held my gun straight on the woman. The man crouched low behind her. His arm was around her throat. Her wide, terror-stricken eyes stared at me, not blinking in the sudden glare. The man said still in that disguised voice:

"Drop your gun and I'll tell you where the child is. You'll have to shoot the woman."

"That," I said coldly, "will be just too bad for Clarice. Drop your own gun, mister, or I'll plug you right through her."

His gun wavered there by the side of the woman.

"You couldn't do it. You—"

And his gun blasted and heat that was cold shot across my left arm. I saw the white of his ear then to the right of the woman. Clearly it stood out beyond the black of the mask. I closed my finger once. Red showed on the white, and he did what I thought he'd do. His head jarred quickly to the other side of the woman. For a moment eyes glared through slits in the mask and Clarice's arm was the only thing that stood between that man and death and—yes, I thought of that when I fired—between Peggy and death.

Clarice screamed and fell to the floor. But the man in the mask didn't scream. And he didn't fall to the floor right away either. He jumped erect and fired again. Plaster fell somewhere high behind me. I jerked up my gun. It was then that I saw the tiny hole in the center of his mask, a red that seeped through the black. So I guess I was wrong unless the dead at times do queer things. But my personal opinion is that the lad didn't jump erect. I must have shot him into the air.

Anyway, he hit the floor now and I was across to him, tearing the mask from his face. I wanted him to speak. I wanted him to tell me where Peggy was. I wanted him— But he was dead and he was—

It knocked me. It would have knocked you, too. I came up from my knees and staggered back. I was saying:

"You… you—" The thing seemed so impossible.

Clarice pulled herself to her knees. "Peggy—Peggy!" she cried. "He couldn't have taken her from the house. The back room—to the right upstairs."

Poor Clarice. How badly she was hurt I didn't know. I won't say I didn't care, for the truth is that I didn't think about her enough to care. I was out in the hall, jabbing light buttons as I ran. Up the stairs, a light in the hall. The bedroom at the right, down the hall. The door was locked. The wood was strong. They say that the doors in those old houses can't be broken inside of ten minutes by a strong man alone. I don't know about that. Once, twice I hit that door. It shattered like papier-mâché, and I tumbled into the room. The push button—the light—Peggy. My heart sank. She wasn't there. The room was empty.

Clarice had been wrong then. Maybe it was the room on the other side of the hall. I turned toward the door and stopped. A door there behind me, a closet door. I hurried to it, jerked at it. It was locked. But the key was there. I turned it and opened the door. Lengths of newspaper fell to the floor. Nothing there. Then I looked down, and I drew back. Peggy was there all right. Her hands and feet were bound. There was a gag in her mouth. Her eyes were— The air was stale, and I knew. The paper had been stuffed in the jamb so as to prevent any air from entering the closet at all. I leaned down and swept her up in my arms. Was she dead?

I remember tearing the gag from her mouth, carrying her downstairs, calling loudly for water. Clarice was there now. We had Peggy in the kitchen. No sign of life; no breathing. But her eyes weren't—well, weren't as they had been and her mouth—

Five minutes, ten minutes, Clarice and I worked over her. My hands were red. So was Clarice's dress. Yet Peggy had no wound. It wasn't until Peggy began to gasp and light—not that horrible glare—come back into her eyes that I realized the truth. The blood was from Clarice where I had shot her and from my arm. Fair is fair. I doubt very much if Peggy would be alive today if it weren't for Clarice.

At last it happened. Peggy's eyes were wide, and she knew me. Twice she tried to raise her arms and finally she did and they were both around my neck. They came, the tears and the sobs, but they were pleasant to hear.

"Oh, Feller, Feller!" She clung tightly to me. "It was the ogre again, and it was terrible."

A noise outside then and pounding at the door and the breaking of glass. I jerked out my gun and, leaving Peggy with Clarice, dashed out into the hall. O'Rourke was there, and Nelson and Jerry behind him.

"I couldn't help it, boss. They were waiting for you, and they piped the hood Sneider and he told them about the notes and… and here they are!"

"I hope the little girl's all right, Race," O'Rourke said. "Maybe we cops should have taken you more into our confidence. But you seemed to be holding out on us, too. We have reason to believe that there was something pretty phony about the death of—" He broke off then as we all went into the library, and Nelson went over and looked down at the body.

O'Rourke said: "Listen, Race, we… we don't think that Joe Mack is dead at all."

"You don't?" I said. "Well, you're wrong."

It was then that O'Rourke looked down at the body. He said:

"Good God, it's Joe Mack!"

"Yes," I said. "He's got his head this time, but he's dead enough to bury."

CHAPTER 5

We got the whole story from Clarice later in the hospital, Nelson, O'Rourke, and myself. She said:

"I suppose I thought I loved Joe Mack or I never could have seen anything good in him. He was always afraid that Carlson, whom he thought half crazy, would disclose some terrible thing in their pasts and which I know now would have sent him to the electric chair. As for Sneider, he was slowly draining Mack of his vast wealth by blackmail. Carlson had but one obsession, and that was that Mack must right his wrong to Peggy, Francis Pierot's child. So Joe made up that trust fund, turning the money over to the child. I didn't know about the will. I just thought that Joe had some way of controlling the money again if he turned up alive. It was planned that I should bring the child to his house for him. Then I was to go to South America and he was to meet me there later. But it was then that I learned the truth, that he intended to kill Peggy. Indeed, he wanted me to kill Peggy so that I would be guilty of murder and he would be safe from my ever talking."

She began to cry then, something I hadn't thought Clarice capable of.

"What manner of woman am I that he could believe such a thing of me, that I would kill Peggy, that I would see her harmed?"

"And the notes and Manuel? And the body?" Nelson was anxious to know.

"Yes," she nodded, "that was clever. Joe told me the whole story while he waited for Sneider. I didn't know then, and I don't know now if he intended to kill Sneider himself or if he intended to telephone Race Williams and have him arrive at the house just as Sneider did and find the child dead and naturally presume that Sneider had killed her. And so—yes, I think he expected you, Mr. Williams, to kill Sneider and so rid him of all his enemies. At any rate, it would be assumed that Sneider had killed Peggy. Manuel had been with Mack a long time, and Mack trusted him. He had Manuel pretend to be friendly to Sneider and tell him that Mack really had a lot of money hidden away. Then when the time came, as it did come, Sneider would walk into Mack's trap.

"Oh, Mack was proud of his scheme. He stood in the street outside the tenement where Carlson lived and as soon as Sneider came out he went in and stabbed Carlson to death because Sneider was known to use a knife."

"But how," questioned O'Rourke, "was Mack going to prove an alibi, and how did he get the headless body into the house? And why did he get Race Williams into it?"

"Was it because Williams is known as a killer and he hoped that he would kill one of these men for him?" That, of course, came from Nelson.

Clarice took a sip of water and answered the questions.

"I believe he hoped that Mr. Williams might do just that. But bringing Williams into it was quite by accident. Mr. Williams met Peggy in Florida, became fond of her, and she of him. And—well, it showed honesty of purpose to have such a man as Race Williams to protect the child. Besides, he hated Race Williams for some reason and wanted the blame of the child's death to rest on him."

"But mainly," insisted Nelson as he glared at me, "it was because he hoped Race Williams would kill this Sneider for him."

Clarice didn't answer, and I couldn't be blamed for any opinion the now-dead Joe Mack might have about my failings or abilities, according to how you look at it. But Clarice was answering the other questions.

"I don't know just what alibi Joe Mack would have had but he seemed satisfied that it was a good one. He never thought he would be suspected of murder. He was sure these influential people who would alibi him on a fishing trip down at Key West wouldn't suspect why they were doing it. And I think the headless body was the work of Manuel. I'm not sure, but I think it was a man about Mack's size and build who was dying and whom Manuel had befriended and kept in a house in the country until he died."

"That's about right," Nelson agreed. "But we'll never get the truth from Manuel. He read the papers today and hung himself. The medical examiner said if the head had not been cut off he would have thought the death a natural one and did anyway, though we laughed at him down at Headquarters."

"Sure," said O'Rourke. "And the head was cut off and hidden away because Mack's dentist could have positively said it wasn't Mack no matter how badly the face was disfigured. So I suppose the call to Parsons and the card in the trunk, 'I want your head,' was to make us not too suspicious of the missing head. It would look like the act of a madman. It wasn't a bad scheme at that. Mack, no doubt, would just show up from his fishing trip, be surprised at the body being found in his house, and get control of the trust fund because it reverted to him if he were alive and the child dead."

"Yes," Nelson nodded. "It sounds complicated now. But it would really have been simple. A madman like Carlson would be blamed for killing the wrong man or simply be blamed for trying to intimidate Mack by putting a headless body in his library. And, of course, Sneider would be blamed for Carlson's murder and the child's murder. Vengeance and greed, freedom from blackmail and even freedom from death in the electric chair, a death Carlson had threatened, was to be Mack's reward for lack of virtue. How well Mack's alibi would have stood up at the trial I don't know. But, hell, he probably wouldn't have been suspected and there wouldn't have been any trial. He would just say that he had been threatened by Carlson and, believing Carlson mad, he had slipped away on a fishing trip without telling anyone."

I asked Clarice then:

"How about the attempt to kidnap Peggy in Florida that night?"

"That, I believe," said Clarice, "was to arouse your interest in Peggy, Mr. Williams, and was a fake put up by Mack. Also it was to make you believe later that there were attempts being made to harm Peggy by Sneider because Sneider suspected that Mack was fond of the child and intended to set up the trust fund for her. Yes, Mack even made me believe he liked the child and that she needed protection. That's why he insisted I carry a gun. To think that I nearly brought Peggy to her death!"

"The other shooting?" O'Rourke wanted to know. "The attempt on Peggy's life in the car the other afternoon. Did Mack explain that, Clarice, did he have anything to do with it?"

Clarice looked blank and shook her head. Also she looked very worn and tired. Nelson coughed and said:

"I think I can explain that, though Sneider won't admit it. I talked with the lawyer who advised Sneider about Mack's will, and I don't think Sneider understood that either he or Carlson had to be dead to inherit before that shooting. At least, Sneider called on the lawyer right afterward and the lawyer said Sneider seemed surprised when he explained it again. So that's why Sneider knew when you called on him, Williams."

I nodded at that. Carlson had more than hinted that Sneider was dumb that way. O'Rourke said:

"Mack had his vengeance, anyway. At least partly. Carlson might have been crazy, but he wasn't any fool. He left enough information behind him to roast

Sneider half a dozen times. The district attorney got it in the mail this morning. No doubt Carlson left it with some friend to mail if he should be murdered. So I guess that's about that."

And that was about that. Only a month later I stood by the balcony rail outside the suite in the smart South American hotel Clarice and Peggy had taken. My room was on the same floor, but down the hall. We had had a nice trip and Peggy was still fascinated by it all. I was holding her close to me and we were looking out over the moonlit hotel garden below. Suddenly Clarice called out sharply:

"Nearly twelve o'clock, Peggy. Long after your bedtime."

"Hell—I mean good gracious"—Peggy smiled up at me—"why did we have to bring that pain along?"

"Peggy," I said, "she's a right guy. Be on the level."

Peggy was. She turned and ran straight to Clarice and lifted her face to be kissed. She was careful, too, not to lean against Clarice's arm which had just come out of the sling.

"You're a white woman, Clarice," she said. And to me: "Don't forget your promise, Feller, to tell me a story when I'm in bed."

"I'm afraid I'm not good at fairy stories, kid." I shook my head.

"Fairy stories!" she sniffed. "I don't want them. I want something exciting and thrilling, a good murder."

She threw her arms around me, then, with a laugh, was gone. And that was all the effect the tragedy had on her. It's great to be that young.

Unremem- bered Murder

CHAPTER 1

I CHECKED INTO the hotel, hesitated a moment over the register, and finally wrote my name—Race Williams. I was taking off my coat when the phone rang. Too early for my client whose urgent request had brought me to Norton, but not too early for the shadow who had played the little lamb to my Mary from the railroad station to the hotel. I juggled the phone and said, "Hello."

The voice with the smile said:

"A gentleman to see you, Mr. Williams. He says that his business brooks of no delay."

"Did he say 'brooks?' " I grinned.

The voice wasn't tossed for a yard loss. It repeated:

"He said exactly that, 'brooks of no delay.' "

"Well," I said, "give me five minutes to wash, then send him up."

I went into the bathroom, did myself a cleaning, carefully rearranged my shoulder holster, balanced my gun properly, and putting on my jacket, came out as the knock sounded on the door.

The man was big—some six-feet-two

of him—with broad shoulders and a long, stern face. He was over thirty but not much over it, though his back-room eyes aged him. He looked like an ex-drinker that was not long ex. He stepped by me and came into the room, closed the door and faced me.

"You were expecting a friend," he said. "I am a friend, a very good friend to you for the moment." His eyes grew rather hard and his nose sort of set while his lips tightened like an actor putting over a piece of dialogue. "I simply wish to tell you that the last train leaves Norton at ten o'clock tonight, the last train *ever* for you. You'd better take it."

"Like that." I led him along. "That means I must live here the rest of my life or it means that I die here." I snapped in with the added attraction at almost the same time he started to say the words.

It jarred him a little, but it didn't throw him.

"Mr. Williams," he said, very slowly, "stupid men and reckless men more often than courageous men laugh at the inevitable. It is possible that you do not appreciate the real peril you face, the tragedy that you are permitting yourself to be engulfed in. I have gone out of my way to save a human life, your life."

I looked at him with a new interest. I won't go so far as to say he was sincere. He was too theatrical for that.

"It's damned white of you to show an interest in the welfare of a stranger. Believe me, sir, you're a humanitarian, that's what you are. You, no doubt, open cans of sardines for starving cats and all that sort of thing!"

"You sound like a man whistling in the dark," he cracked. "Stay in town and I cannot save you, the police cannot save you."

"But," I told him, "I might save myself."

"No." He shook his head. "Believe me, the threat does not come from me as an individual. I am simply a messenger of fate, of an inescapable fate."

"Now that's really pretty. If I believed you, if I let myself—"

He cut in, "If you believed me you'd leave town at once."

"No!" My words rapped in hard now for the first time. "If I believed you I'd shoot you dead here in this room on that Persian rug"—and being a stickler for truth I added—"or near-Persian rug."

He straightened, if he could straighten any more. Then he spun on his heels and walked toward the door. I wasn't in a kidding mood as he reached the door. And then suddenly I was; at least, in a grim sort of humor. I called to him sharply as I walked to the window.

"One moment," I said, and when he stopped at the door, "You've had your say. Now I'll have mine. The next time I see your face I'll blow you apart. And don't take the train to New York. I live there."

For a split second the color left his face, his eyes flickered, and the determined mouth seemed to drop slightly at the ends. But he didn't speak. He turned and walked back to the door, and this time when he opened it and went out into the hall, I thought that he was not quite so erect, that his broad shoulders sagged slightly.

CARROLL JOHN DALY

I went down to lunch, got myself the Norton *Daily Reporter,* propped it up, and looked over the news. It was all about the murder of Judge Anderson and the coming trial of the young man held as the judge's slayer.

There was no doubt that young Fletcher Martin had been standing on the lonely road beside the judge's dead body. Graves Hudson, a theatre manager for a chain of show houses, had been driving over from the county seat to Norton when he saw young Martin beside the body. There were five shots from a heavy-caliber revolver in the judge's chest. The police had been unable to trace the gun to Martin, but, then, they had been unable to trace the gun at all. It might have been true, as young Martin said, that he had an appointment to meet the judge out on that lonely road and that he had come upon the body and was standing stunned beside it. He said he would have notified the authorities if the theatre manager had not come along.

Why was I so interested in that bit of local news? Because that was the reason I was in Norton. I was there to see that someone who would give evidence in the defense of young Fletcher Martin was there to give such evidence. I was there to see that a witness was not intimidated, coerced or—a little gulp on that one— too dead to climb on the witness stand and give the evidence that would acquit Fletcher Martin. What that evidence was I didn't know. I had received from a firm of lawyers a check to come to Norton. The check was good and I came.

I got myself a taxi and went to see a

good lawyer; at least, a lawyer who had been good enough to send me a check. Not that I didn't think the firm was class and respectable. That was the trouble. They were too respectable. Redstone, Redstone, Johnson & Redstone sported the entire sixth floor of the biggest office building in town.

I got a bit of a shock when I was alone with Bartholomew Redstone. Sr., with his nose glasses, black ribbon and round face. So this was the lawyer for the defense, all of him. I could see Fletcher Martin sizzling in the chair.

"Mr. Williams"—he beamed at me over the glasses—"your reputation has reached even to Norton. I am afraid, though, that if you expect excitement and adventure you will be disappointed. Experience teaches us that groundless fears are just as great as though they were real. Now your client, Miss Charlotte Thorn, will not strike you as a young woman who would be easily intimidated or one who would have imaginary fears. But she has gone through a great deal, a great deal, indeed. I am sure that you will give her the attention she feels that she needs just as if you were sure that she actually did need it."

"Your letter was short, Mr. Redstone, and I thought rather cautious. You must remember that I had never heard of Miss Charlotte Thorn."

"But she has heard of you." He went into a beam. "Your interest is rather a peculiar one. Miss Thorn is secretly engaged to young Fletcher Martin who is now in the county jail awaiting trial for the murder of Judge Anderson.

I handled all her father's business and now hers. I know young Martin, too, of course, and am, indeed, happy to defend him, though… though—" He pulled at his chin there. "But your interest is in Miss Thorn. Miss Thorn has advised the district attorney that she has been in communication with someone who actually saw the murderer, the foul murderer of Judge Anderson. She has been threatened and has received police protection. She no longer desires such protection and so retains you."

"You have talked with this witness? Where is he?"

"It is not a he; it is a she," he said, and his mouth tightened and he came as near to a frown as that fat face would permit. "No, I have not seen this witness. I do not believe that Miss Thorn knows her whereabouts at the present time. Your only interest, Mr. Williams, is in protecting Miss Thorn, as she entertains some fear that the district attorney will bend every effort to prevent her witness from appearing and herself from giving evidence on the stand as having talked with the witness."

"And you don't take any stock in that?"

"None whatever." He didn't hesitate. "I have known Laurence Gibson, the district attorney, for a great many years. He is incapable of such a thought. He is the coming governor of this state. Your job, then, is to watch over Miss Thorn. Take good care of her. She is not only a valued client but the child of a dear departed friend."

I left him then to go to the Thorn house and see my client.

CHARLOTTE THORN DIDN'T look like a young woman who would be panicked into imagining things. She sat on the end of her chair, a straight, erect little figure and put two steady blue eyes on me. She was paying money for my services and she wanted to see what she was getting. She began:

"I'm Charlotte Thorn, Mr. Williams. My mother died when I was a baby; my father while I was in high school. An old aunt took care of me according to the accepted version of things. Actually, I took care of her. I have managed my own life since I was sixteen." She smiled then, and I liked the smile. "I hope that with your help it will not be necessary for me to manage my own life much longer."

"I don't," I told her, "understand what you mean."

"It is a shy young girl's way of telling you that I intend to marry a man accused of murder," she said, about as shyly as a girl reporter. "Now, Mr. Williams, don't try and give me fatherly advice about not marrying Fletch. I don't mind that coming from Mr. Redstone. He wouldn't be running true to character if it didn't."

"So long as you pay me for my services, Miss Thorn, I am not interested in whom you marry."

Her eyes widened, her lips parted, she leaned over and shook my hand.

"You and I," she said, "are going to get along." Then she tossed it at me.

"Judge Anderson was shot to death a little over a month ago. It was on a lonely road. You know the details. Well, a young married woman driving along that road saw the murderer plainly. She saw him dragging the judge's body from the judge's blue sedan. She didn't know that it was a murder then. When she read the papers later she did. Her headlights shone directly on the face of the guilty man. She would recognize him again and she knows the man was not Fletcher Martin. I have seen and talked with her and shown her pictures of Fletcher."

"Did you recognize the murderer?" I asked.

"No." And then rushing into it as if she wanted to get this part over with, "You see, fortunately, she was a girl who was at college when I was, quite a bit older, missing a year here and there while she worked. But she had done me a service and she needed money and was coming to see me."

"To get money when she saw the murderer?" I gasped.

"Yes. Why? What's wrong with that? You're as suspicious about things as the district attorney himself. How else would she reach my house but along that particular road? I hadn't seen her since her marriage. She called me up that afternoon. Her husband was in trouble, a question of money. She drove over to see me that night and saw the murderer. It was not Fletch." A long pause, and then, "You don't like that story?"

"It's not a question of my liking it or not liking it," I told her. "It will be up to twelve men. Where is this young lady now?"

"She's... she's disappeared."

That was a tough one to swallow, but I've taken a lot of tough ones in my time and swallowed them, too.

"What's her name?" I asked.

"That," she said, and she looked straight at me, and though her eyes were still steady her lips quivered a bit, "I can't tell you. I gave my word of honor to her that I wouldn't mention her name, ever."

"So-o!" was the best I could do.

"Any more questions?" she asked.

"It isn't for me to ask questions." I shrugged my shoulders. "You're managing things."

"Well, what do you think of our case?"

"Terrible," I said, and let it go at that. "Now, what am I to do? What am I engaged for?"

She looked at me a long time before she answered. Then she said:

"You are to watch over me. I am the important witness in this case. My life has been threatened over the telephone. I have been shot at twice in my car."

My eyes widened. "Were you alone when these attempts were made on your life?"

"Of course!" she snapped. "You don't think anyone would risk trying to kill anyone as well-known in town as I am before a witness?"

"Did you complain to the police?"

"I notified the police. And the district attorney has been to see me. I told him about this woman who had seen the murderer, that my life was in danger, that I was the witness for the defense who would save Fletch Martin if my other witness was missing."

"Miss Thorn"—I was very patient—"I'm afraid I'm rather dull. I don't see how any testimony you can give would save Fletcher Martin without the personal appearance of the important witness to the murderer's carrying the body from the car."

"Why," she said, "I can go on the stand and swear to this woman's having come to me and having told her story of what she saw. I can swear that she positively stated to me, after examining carefully a dozen pictures of Fletcher, that he was not the man. You don't think that will have influence?"

I didn't, but I only said:

"What did the district attorney have to say?"

"Well"—she brushed back the hair from her face—"he wanted me to make an affidavit so that he could interview the woman, but I had given my word not to give out her name. At the trial to protect Fletch I will have to give her name, I suppose. You see my predicament?"

"Better than you think," I said to myself. To her I nodded gravely. I was not her lawyer. I was hired simply to protect her. She was money; she was position in town. I daresay, both would protect her from being arrested for perjury if she went on the stand with such a line. But somewhere, some place, there was truth in her story. She had buried it in the trimmings. And where did I find some truth?

About three o'clock we had a couple of callers. There was a dark, gaunt man who took Charlotte Thorn's hand with difficulty and was introduced as Laurence Gibson, the district attorney. With him was a bright-eyed, quick, tiny mustached lad of thirty odd, the assistant D.A. His name was Mark Condon.

The district attorney repeated my name with a certain familiarity. The assistant district attorney said:

"Williams—Race Williams. So, you did get a detective from New York then, Miss Thorn." It was a statement, not a question.

"Now," said Charlotte, facing the district attorney and lifting her head after smiling at Condon, "you've come to browbeat me, I suppose, and persecute Fletch, whose family and my family have been friends for years. Well, go on. Elevate yourself to governor. I'm a defenseless woman."

"Oh, I wouldn't say that, Miss Thorn." The young assistant smiled at her. "You have Mr. Williams here with you. No one is defenseless with him present."

She smiled back and the district attorney spoke.

"Charlotte—" he began.

"Miss Thorn," she snapped.

"Miss Thorn, then," he said, a little stiffly. "I have something I wish to say to you." He looked over at me, like a hint to leave.

"You might need a lawyer present, Miss Thorn, if you are to answer questions or make a statement."

"There will be no questions that need an immediate answer." Gibson was getting stiffer. "Nor any statement that I wish. It is perhaps as well for Mr. Williams to remain. He may be able to advise you, Charlotte, if anyone can advise you about anything." He looked then at Mark Condon, his assistant. "It is very easy for Mr. Condon to be in sympathy with you, as he is not acting officially in this matter and will be on his vacation and out of town when the case comes to trial. For myself, it is a most unpleasant duty to hurt a little girl I have watched grow into a charming woman and whose grandfather served on the board that admitted me to the bar and whose father I claimed as one of my most valued friends and—"

"Go on," the girl cut in. "Say what you have to say. You're not on a platform."

The D.A. reddened right up to the tips of his collar, which was some reddening. But he had a piece to speak and he spoke it.

"Charlotte, I understand it is your intention to go on the stand and tell a… a most remarkable story. I don't want you to do that."

"No?" Her lips curled. "You want to be governor. But I'm going on the stand, and I'm not afraid of your threats to arrest me for perjury. And what's more, I'm going around town and let people know that—"

He held up his hand and she stopped.

"My dear child"—his voice was very low—"it is not a question of what you think of me now, but of what I am think-ing of you. There is nothing you could say on the witness stand that would make me cite you for perjury. But I have a sworn duty to the state, to the citizens who have elected me. I will feel it my duty, my most painful duty, if you go on the stand, to discredit your testimony as a witness. I will have to drag up for the public and the press your love for Fletcher Martin and your secret engagement."

She stared at him. Finally, she said, and her voice shook not with anger but more with surprise, I think:

"You don't think I'd sacrifice the chance, the least possibility for Fletch's life because of the newspapers."

"No, child." His voice was rather husky. "Get good advice. This man here"—he pointed at me. "Your friend Bartholomew Redstone, anyone disinterested. Don't go on the stand with a story that will harm more than help young Martin and disgrace the name your grandfather and father bore so proudly." He turned and walked out of the room.

Mark Condon stayed behind long enough to say, "Whatever else you might think about the old boy, he certainly meant that one."

Then they were both gone. After the door had closed, she frankly asked for my advice, so I gave it to her.

"If you told the D.A. the story you told me and this witness didn't appear and you went on the stand, I think you'd hurt Fletcher Martin's case more than you'd help it. Don't forget that you're engaged to the man. You talk of a witness. She's disappeared. You gave her money and she testifies not to the identity of the murderer whom she doesn't know but simply to the fact that Fletcher Martin was not the murderer. Now if you can find the woman and she can point the finger at the actual murderer, then you've got something. Now tell me who this woman is and let me look for her."

"No." She shook her head. "I gave my word that I would not divulge her name. Not because I thought it the right thing to do, but because after she telephoned me that if I told her story now she would repudiate it and not appear as a witness for Fletch. She was afraid. She had been threatened."

"Like that." I nodded. "Well, you turn her over to me and I'll protect her."

"I can't. I can't." Her steadiness left her and for the moment her story rang with truth. "She's disappeared, disappeared of her own free will. She telephoned that if I disclosed her name she would not turn up for the trial. She seemed terrified. She saw the murderer's face plainly in the glare of her headlights. At the time she thought it was someone taking a drunken man from a car, and she drove on quickly. I begged her to help Fletch. I even told her that—well, if they threatened her that they had also threatened me. She said, and she meant it, 'If they harm you, Charlotte, I'll talk. I'll come back under any circumstances.'"

There was no use to push her further on that subject. So that was the way it stood when the butler came in and announced dinner.

That evening we spent together. A strange girl. She refused to discuss the case until just before she went to bed and had cautioned me that now that the police were dismissed she counted on my protection in the night. She said then:

"I'm afraid of frightening my witness out of the state, perhaps out of the country altogether, or I'd forget my word. But I believe she'll come back." And very slowly, "I think I can manage that."

CHAPTER 2

THE NEXT DAY I called up the D.A. to get permission to see Fletcher Martin. He was very affable.

"Certainly, Mr. Williams, certainly," he said. "I feel most deeply in this matter and will be glad to afford you any courtesy, any information. Really, if you could find this boy innocent, why— But there, why not talk to Mark Condon? He's young, has his career before him, and will hold my position in the near future, I hope. See Mark. He knows the town and he may be able to assist you."

Now you've got to admit that that was the damnedest gall in trying to find out what I was doing, or downright naïve, or, damn it, exactly what it sounded like, an honesty of purpose. I thanked him and said I would be down and around town and finally I arranged to have Mark Condon meet me in the Norton Hotel.

At the hotel bar I collected general information. And what I found out was amazing any way you looked at it. The D.A. certainly did Mark Condon a favor by letting him stay out of it. Judge Anderson was the straightest man Norton ever had. He never ran for an office, but if he backed a man it was tantamount to his election. And he had been backing Laurence Gibson, the D.A., for governor and Mark Condon for D.A. Now Laurence Gibson had to convict the murderer of Judge Anderson. The citizens cried out for vengeance. At the same time, Fletcher Martin was well liked and the name of Thorn was big stuff in the county, a million dollars' worth of big stuff. And Charlotte Thorn could start a whispering campaign that might turn into a shout by election time.

Mark Condon found me at the bar. We talked for a while and I tried to feel him out. Finally, he smiled, showing those even white teeth, and said:

"Look here, Williams, there is nothing regarding the Fletcher Martin case that I can tell you that I won't tell you. The chief would take a plea of guilty and recommend leniency."

"What D.A. wouldn't?"

"But," said Mark Condon, "this is an open-and-shut case, and without extenuating circumstances. Judge Anderson was our most beloved citizen. There wasn't a dishonest or a corrupt thought in his head. Fletcher Martin attempted several times to see Judge Anderson, but the judge refused to see him. Martin followed him, blocked off his car on the lonely road and shot him to death. At least, that's the logical story to believe."

"And what is Fletcher Martin's story?"

"That he had an appointment to meet the judge, that the judge's secretary telephoned him that the judge would see him. Now listen to this. He says that the secretary told him Judge Anderson would meet him on this lonely bit of road at night and talk with him. Absurd on the face of it. The judge's secretary and everyone connected with the judge denies making any such appointment."

"A trap?" I suggested. "A trap to hang the crime on young Martin."

"Not," he said, "a very elaborate or deeply laid trap. The boy hasn't an enemy that I know about."

"And the motive?"

"Simple enough. Exaggerated to you and to me, perhaps, but a big thing in the boy's mind. He thought the judge was suppressing information that would clear his dead father's name of embezzlement."

"I see. Does the boy admit this?"

"He admits having a suspicion that Judge Anderson was withholding information. There are enough witnesses to the fact that he had been suspicious for several weeks. He talked about it enough. The judge told him it was absurd and refused to see him again."

"His father was in jail?"

"No, never that. His mother at the time was very ill, a great temptation. His father was a trusted bank official. He misappropriated funds. His friends made up the amount and the matter was hushed up; that is, legally hushed up. Naturally, it was known through the city and the county. His own son was the last to hear of it. The father had left town. It hit him hard. He died within a year. Fletcher Martin did not believe the undercurrent of gossip. I admire him for that, but it was true enough. Judge Anderson was quite instrumental in saving his father from prison. I am afraid all the past will have to be dragged out into the open now. Not a nice story, and certainly not one to arouse the sympathy of a jury."

"No." I could see that. Then I asked, "What about this missing witness of Miss Thorn's?"

"Ah, yes." Mark Condon nodded his head. "Let me assure you that the district attorney is as anxious to find that witness as Miss Thorn is. At present perhaps the sympathy of the county is with Fletcher Martin. But you see, the public doesn't know the real story of Judge Anderson's help to Martin's father and the price he paid for such help. A trial will bring it all out. A popular verdict, guilty, then. You can see now the unhappy situation it will be for Miss Thorn if she goes on the stand."

"I see," I said. "But then, from a political vantage, a trial and a guilty verdict would be helpful to the district attorney since, as you say, it would be a popular verdict."

"Undoubtedly."

"And the witness, Miss Thorn's missing witness?"

"If she appears and her testimony cannot be shaken and she can identify another as the real criminal, the chief's case would blow up in his face. And I don't believe there's a man, not even Fletcher Martin himself, who would welcome that blow-up more than the chief."

"Well," I said, "we'll try and give him a pleasant surprise."

"Good," he said. "Our whole office is at your disposal in trying to locate the missing witness. The police of Norton, too, are at your service. I… I am not active in this case, Mr. Williams, and it would not do for me to go to the county jail with you. But I have arranged for you to see Martin. I have another reason besides political ambition for steering clear of this case, at least as a prosecutor. Fletcher Martin is, in a way, my friend. Nothing practical about him. A dreamer and an artist who might have some day become famous. A bit younger than I, but my friend."

"And you believe him guilty?"

He bit his lip, lifted his glass, but set it down again without drinking. Finally, he said:

"Every bit of legal training I have, every bit of logic, every bit of evidence points to his guilt. But… but he is my friend, Mr. Williams, and every bit of instinct and decency which I possess tells me that he is not, could not be guilty of such a fiendish crime."

I saw our lawyer, Bartholomew Redstone, again and asked him point-blank if he knew the story about Martin's father's embezzlement. He did. There was no doubt that he had stolen the money. No doubt that the influence and cash, too, of Judge Anderson had kept him out of jail.

Things certainly looked bad for Martin. Redstone's only foundation for his belief in the innocence of Fletcher Martin was the hottest one yet. He couldn't believe that Charlotte Thorn could love a man guilty of murder! So I left him, hired a car, and drove over to the county seat to see young Martin.

Fletcher Martin was the sort of lad for Charlotte Thorn. He sure needed management. He had a childlike belief that he'd be free as soon as it dawned on the authorities that he couldn't have done such a thing even if they had found the gun in his hand, which was damned near the truth, for Martin had picked up the gun from beside the body.

"I thought it was suicide, Mr. Williams," he told me. "The judge lying there like that, right where we were to meet."

"Did you think it was strange the judge's secretary phoned you and made a date to meet the dignified judge on a roadside?"

"Why?" was his answer to that one. And I guess that was the answer he was going to make in court. And he wasn't worried.

There you were. Everything pointed directly to the guilt of the accused and everyone, including the D.A.—if everyone could be believed—wishing he were innocent if someone could be found to take his place in the electric chair.

There was a matinee that afternoon, so having time, I decided to go down to the Criterion Theatre and have a few words with Graves Hudson, the theatre man who had seen Martin the night of the murder. There was a possibility that he might have seen someone else on the lonely road that night.

Graves Hudson turned out to be a big, jovial man. He had been over to a neighboring town to check up on one of his chain of theatres the night of the murder. He came out and met me in the lobby.

"Sorry, Mr. Williams, people in the office," he explained. "I'd like to help you; yes, I'd like very much to help you. A fine young fellow Martin, a great young lady, Miss Thorn. Has civic pride. An expense, this theatre; an artistic addition to the city. Miss Thorn supports it whole-heartedly. But this unpleasant affair. Yes, I was questioned by the police. I didn't see anything. I may or may not have noticed the judge's car by the roadside. As to the time, well, Mr. Martin may have been right. I don't recall the time."

And so he went on, a cagey individual who wasn't going to admit or deny anything. A girl called him from the office then.

He said to me:

"Pardon me a minute. Take a seat in the back of the theatre. A rather pleasant little comedy. Edgar, a seat for the gentleman."

He was gone, and I stepped into the darkened house and sat down in the back. People were talking on the stage. It was a costume piece. A girl was storming up and down, accusing a big sprawling lad in jumpers of betraying his own people. She called him "Sir George Drake."

I got to thinking about Fletcher Martin's chances and the witness that Miss Thorn hoped would appear. And a voice said:

"I never fool, mademoiselle. Take heed that I do not expose you to the mob that they may tear your lying tongue from your mouth and—"

The voice was familiar. For a second or two I didn't realize that it came from the stage. Then I looked over the footlights. The man by the fire had risen. His legs were spread far apart, his sword swung by his side, and his face— The voice came again. I knew. Sir George Drake and the man who visited me and threatened me in my hotel room at the very moment of my arrival were one and the same man.

I didn't get much chance to absorb that bit of a shock when the manager was back. I followed him into the lobby.

"Who's the heavy?" I asked him.

"Like him? That's Sydney Sawyer. Was coming up the ladder and it turned his head. Got to drinking and flopped and now—well, if his debts don't get the better of him he'll push his way up. He's got the stuff."

"That's right. I was speaking to a theatrical man in the hotel. He mentioned his name."

"Really?" he said. "It wasn't a tall, thin man from Maxie Blue's office in Chicago, was it?" And when I half nodded, "Damned if I didn't think that's who he was Tuesday night and the big slat gave me a blank look. Well, I've got Sawyer under contract. I'm not denying he's good, but I've given him a chance. There were few who would touch him."

A little more baloney which had to do with the magnanimity of managers and the ingratitude of actors and I was on my way. Things were warming up. So Sydney Sawyer had gone down the road. And what sort of pack had he run with? Well, I wanted to ask him a question, and I had an idea that he was going to answer it. I wanted to know who was behind the threat to me and where he fitted into the picture.

I called up New York and got hold of a racketeer I had never crossed and told him what I wanted in Norton.

"I don't know, Race," he said. "The D.A. is straight out that way and—"

"Hell!" I cut in. "What do you think I am? It's not a real ride, just a fake one."

So I got what I wanted. A man called simply "Harry" who had a scar and would go "up to murder" if the fee was right. He was in a garage less than three blocks away.

Then I popped into a so-called tavern, hopped into a booth, and although the show wasn't over yet, called the Criterion Theatre. I left the pay phone number and word for Mr. Sydney Sawyer, alias Sir George Drake, to call as soon as possible.

Then I sat over a drink and waited. He called back in about twenty minutes.

"I'm from Maxie Blue's office in Chicago, Mr. Sawyer," I told him. "I'm doing a bit of looking around and would like to talk to you this evening. I'm leaving the city at eight o'clock and am having my chauffeur call for you at ten minutes after seven at the stage door of the theatre."

"But I'm not at the theatre at that time," he objected, rather high-handedly, but I caught the excitement in his voice. "Can't I come to your hotel? Mr. Hudson said he heard you were in town and—"

"I'm not supposed to be in town," I snapped back. "Rather... er, confidential. I let my chauffeur go and can't locate him again now. I told him to be at the theatre at seven-ten to pick you up. Of course, if it's inconvenient—"

"No, no, not at all." He came down to earth on that line. "It's dark, you know. The stage door, you say? What make of car, so I can find him?"

"He'll find you," I told him, "at the stage door. Please don't mention my call to anyone. So disappointing if we can't come to terms."

"Terms?" He ate that one up. "But I'm sure... er, I believe we can reach an understanding."

"Good. I'm quite convinced of it myself. At seven-ten then. My chauffeur will drive you directly to my hotel."

Would he suspect? Not a chance. Maxie Blue was a big theatrical name and Sydney Sawyer was—well, he was an actor.

As if he had set his clock by Western Union, Harry pulled up in the big black sedan right on the second of seven. I climbed in the back and he lowered the window between us. He was a good listener, was Harry, and not an objector.

"Just drive along quiet streets, dark streets, after you get your man and pick me up," I said. "I'm going to try and convince a lad he should talk. He may object loudly. I don't want people to hear him object."

"The River Road," said Harry. "No traffic to amount to anything at this hour and what there is will be rolling along. Will he get rough?"

"Not too rough for me, Harry," I assured him. Then I gave him his final instructions, had him drive me to the first street that turned into the River Road, and getting out, fell back into the shadows. Harry drove away. My right hand crept under my left armpit. I smiled to myself. Sydney Sawyer was a good actor. Well, I was a bad actor.

I didn't have long to wait. Sydney Sawyer was not too anxious to keep the representative of the great Maxie Blue cooling his heels. The car swung to the curb. I opened the door, stepped inside, slammed the door behind me, and flopped into the seat as the big sedan jumped forward and turned into the River Road.

It jerked me slightly against the man in the seat beside me. Also it pounded my gun harder than I intended against his ribs. It made my words sound better, I guess. I said, simply:

"We meet again, Sydney Sawyer, and this time I threaten."

"What… what do you mean?"

"I mean," I said, "it's a one-way ride, and your body in the river at the end of it."

"Is this a joke?" he started, stopped, and then, "Good God!" he gasped. "Is that a gun?"

"A loaded one," I told him. "But it won't be loaded long."

"Why I… who… why… you're that detective fellow. Williams, isn't it? Race Williams."

"Williams is right." I twisted my mouth up pretty hard and shot the words at him. "You threatened my life. I looked you up, found that you were a man who meant what you said, so I'm shooting first, tonight, now."

Maybe I overdid it. I wanted him to talk. And he couldn't at first. At length he did say:

"Williams—Race Williams. I've heard about you since—what you really were—after I went to your hotel. Don't… don't! For God's sake, don't! I meant no harm. I needed the money. I thought it was a joke and… and—"

"A joke to kill a man? Well, perhaps it is. Laugh this one off. I'll count five and, then, out you go. One—"

I was going to lead up to it through fear; his chance of life if he talked. But he wouldn't let me. He started in to talk right away.

"She'll tell you. She'll tell you," he said, over and over, before he could get the real words out. And then, "I was simply to threaten you, to make you think there was someone else who loved her, too. I needed the money. It meant a lot to me, and I— She said it was a joke. Then afterward someone at the theatre said you were in town and who you were and I... but I had used the money. It's the truth. She'll tell you it's the truth. She said if anything went wrong she would."

"And who," I asked, "is she? I don't like lads who hide behind women's skirts."

"She?" He was surprised again. "Why, the girl, Miss Charlotte Thorn."

Surprised? Sure, I was surprised. And then I wasn't surprised any more. I understood. Charlotte Thorn, her witness, the threats to her. It was all lies, to build up a foundation of truth about the missing witness. The threat to me, to make me believe. She had tried to make a sucker out of me. Tried? Well, perhaps she had, up until now.

I dropped the gun back in my pocket and took a laugh, said:

"O.K., Sydney, I only wanted to get even with you. I thought I'd play a little joke, too."

We parted then. He wasn't angry with me; he was too relieved. And me— I wasn't relieved at all. Things looked bad for Fletcher Martin; even worse than they had, if that were possible. I wondered if he were really guilty and if Charlotte Thorn suspected it.

It was late when I reached the Thorn mansion. Charlotte Thorn looked pretty nice in her low cut dress, a little sad, and for the first time I thought very much worried. I was hard and ready to spring my surprise, but I softened up considerably when I looked at her. She was in love with a lad she would go to any lengths to save him. Her story of the witness and the threats against herself were hard even for her to put over. She wanted me to believe

her. I was big-time in my business. Her engaging me would lend color to her story, and she wanted me to back up the threat business.

She was about to retire for the night. She said:

"You saw Fletch today. What do you think? And the district attorney and his assistant, Mark Condon. Would they frame Fletch for their own political ambitions?"

"Miss Thorn," I said, "I don't think they would. And if they would, I can't see any point to it. The evidence, I fear, will be quite sufficient."

"You mean without my testimony, without my witness?"

"That's right," I smiled. "I mean without your witness."

"I was afraid, Mr. Williams, that you, too, might be threatened. You know, because you're working for me, protecting me. If you were threatened you would tell me? You wouldn't spare me?"

I grinned but said nothing. She went on:

"These men are desperate, these men who killed the judge. I was threatened while you were out. I... it's too much to ask of one man, of you. I... the police are sending up two detectives tonight. I asked them to."

"Really?" I couldn't hold it in now. "Any more actors?"

"Actors?"

"Yes, like Sydney Sawyer." And when the quick red came into her face, "I know, Miss Thorn. I think I know your reason, too. But it's a thin story. You hope to be able to go on the stand and impress in the minds of the jury that a single missing witness, withheld by fear of death, could save Fletcher Martin's life."

"So—" She came to her feet. "You knew he was an actor hired by me. And you did your best to make a fool out of me."

"I think, Miss Thorn," I corrected her, "it was the other way around. I don't particularly mind, but you can't fool the district attorney. And you can't drum up false sympathy."

"You haven't," she said, "asked for an explanation as to the reason I paid an actor to help my unbelievable story. There might be one, you know. However, I won't bore you with it. I don't suppose you told the police of the… the fake threat to you?"

"That's right, I didn't. And I won't."

"Good. Well, there was a reason." She moved toward the door now. "Your room is across the hall from mine. I have requested that detectives be stationed, one at the front door and one at the rear door. I fear for my life or my freedom tonight."

She was turning at the door, a tragic figure in her management now, playing the game up until the end, even with me.

"I'm with you all the way, Miss Thorn, even if your danger isn't real."

"But it is. It is. Please believe that it—" She came toward me, clutched suddenly at her throat, turned and left the room. It wasn't very good acting. It wasn't even necessary acting. She was paying for my service and she was getting it.

I smoked a couple of cigarettes, killed a couple of bottles of beer, and made monkeys out of some crackers and cheese the butler brought me, and then went out and saw the detectives. Whatever I thought, whatever the D.A. thought, the detectives were not taking their job as a lark. The one by the front door said to me:

"I don't know what the racket is, and I'm not asking you, Williams. My partner is at the back and I'm at the front. You're inside. Now there's an alley to the left here under Miss Thorn's window. There's a five-foot fence there. It would be a job to put a ladder up to the second story window of Miss Thorn's room. The window below here is the dining-room window. Now, you don't think anyone could bust in that window, go up the stairs, kill or kidnap the woman, and come down again without your hearing them or her?"

"Don't you worry about the inside of the house," I told him, and went in and upstairs.

I got into bed, put my gun under my pillow more from force of habit than precaution. But I didn't stay there long. I don't know why. Maybe it's routine. I was paid for a job. I got up and opened my door a bit. Then I went back to bed and went to sleep.

I am a light sleeper. It was dark when I woke up. I'm not an imaginative man, but my thought was that a key had spun in a lock. Only a thought, understand. I lay for a while listening. Then I got up, found my pocket flash, went to the door, and let the pencil of light slide along the hall outside. Darkness and silence.

I went into the hall and listened by Charlotte Thorn's door. Not a sound. Then a clock below struck three. I went down the stairs. I grinned as I turned into the dining-room, then stopped dead. The grin was blown off my face by a current of cold air. Then my flash was on the dining-room window, the window directly below Miss Thorn's room. That window was open.

A quick run up the stairs and a light tap on her door. A louder tap, and finally a bang when there was no answer. The door was locked. By the time the butler got there I had put my shoulder to that door for the third time, yes, and smashed it open. I was worried, all right. I was scared, too. Plainly, I got the unmistakable odor of chloroform.

A snap of the lights, then a quick look at the disorder in the room, with clothes scattered around the empty bed. A dash into the closet, a look under the bed and into the adjoining bath and I was downstairs yelling for the detectives.

They came; they saw; they gasped with me. But none of us conquered. The girl was gone. There were no two ways about it. Someone had entered by the dining-room window, gone up the front stairs, passed along the hall by my open door, picked the lock of the girl's room, chloroformed her, grabbed a bunch of her clothes, and carried her down the stairs, out the dining-room window, and lifted her over the five-foot fence of the alley? Impossible? I thought it was. Yet there seemed to be no other explanation.

Frantic telephone calls, then the chief of police, the commissioner, Mark Condon and later the D.A. himself arrived. And me, I was getting into my clothes and answering questions and listening to the police say over and over that she was carried off right under my nose. Sure, they were laying it all on me until Mark Condon said:

"There's no use taking that attitude. Race Williams is not known in this town. He is not official. The blame rests with us. Don't you realize that Miss Thorn asked for protection only tonight?"

The D.A. flopped into a chair.

"And to think that I didn't for one moment believe her story. But I'm glad I afforded her protection, anyway."

"Why?" I asked. It was the first chance I had had to make a crack. But I was thinking, too. I hadn't believed her story, and I thought that I saw it now. It was a wild story, but it was true. No one believed it. She had me threatened so I'd believe in her and—I gulped there—give her the proper protection.

Mark Condon said to the D.A.:

"Well, chief, you have known Miss Thorn longer and better than I. But I was always inclined to believe there was some truth in what she said. We've got to take action on this missing witness business. Miss Thorn's disappearance will be a sensation."

CHAPTER 3

CHARLOTTE THORN'S DISAPPEARANCE was a sensation, all right. The D.A. would have liked to lay the blame on me, but Mark Condon didn't see it that way. He said the next day:

"Miss Thorn seemed to feel it was coming, Williams, and she notified the police. I think if I were handling things she'd have got more attention. What do you intend to do now?"

I gulped at that one. I hadn't taken

much stock in the story of the missing witness and her danger either. And now— But there was only one answer. I was going to locate the missing witness.

The D.A. said:

"I can't understand Charlotte Thorn's abduction. There isn't any sense in it. Her testimony meant nothing in the case, and you can take that, Mr. Williams, as a personal and honest opinion, not an official and biased one. The county will bend every effort to locate Miss Thorn. I will also make every endeavor to locate this witness. You may consider the facilities of a great organization entirely at your disposal, Mr. Williams. We feel that Miss Thorn may have confided things to you. This puts a new doubt in my mind. Why should Miss Thorn be kidnaped unless she knew something?"

And so it went on. But at the end I took advantage of official help and even got a very official and open letter from the D.A. to aid me in my investigation.

I left him and went to work. I took a hired car and rode over to Wilmington, the county seat, and the first place I visited was the automobile bureau in the county building.

Things were run pretty efficiently at the Norton County Bureau of Vehicles. A four-eyed, frowsy-haired girl who looked as if she might have been hired for her ability looked intelligently up at me. So I explained my predicament without going into detail.

My idea was simple enough. The actual murderer had seen the car of the witness approach that fatal night, and the lights shone directly on him. His natural assumption was that the driver of the car had seen him. His next assumption and fear was that the driver of that car would be a witness against him. Of course, he couldn't know whether he had been recognized or not, but within the next twenty-four hours or probably twelve, he could make a pretty good guess that the driver had not recognized him or didn't know him. If the driver had, the information would have been disclosed to the police and the murderer's name would have been spread across the newspapers.

But—and a big but—there was the chance that the driver of the car would later identify him and so roast him. Under those circumstances the murderer must discover the identity of the person who saw him and either keep out of the way of that party, silence her, or intimidate her so that she would never appear as a witness against him.

First, then, the murderer must identify the driver of the witness car. So as to identify the witness and locate her. It was a hundred-to-one that after being blinded by the lights of the car the murderer couldn't identify the driver. But he would have very little difficulty in reading the numbers on the license plate of the car as it sped away. After that the murderer must find out the name from the license number and must learn it by telephoning the bureau, certainly not by appearing in person. Yet Norton County had a rule against giving such information over the phone. So I asked four eyes:

"Now suppose the mayor or the district attorney called up and asked for the name of a registered car owner from the license number. Would you give it?"

"What do you think?" She was warming up.

"And anyone else?"

"Anyone I know, maybe."

"Or anyone you thought you knew?"

"What do you mean by that?"

"Police officers, clerks in the courthouse, people like that."

She admitted she would give the license number, but told me that the D.A. never called up, that once or twice someone from his office had, but most times they sent a man around. We finally worked it down to the fact that there were offenders, lads who called up occasionally to get a name from a license number, and, of course, you guessed who those offenders were. They were cops.

We were getting somewhere. We went into a huddle. A vague hope now that she would recall the name of the party who owned the car if not the license number.

I gave her the date of the day following the murder, my best smile, and the letter from the D.A. She looked up at me in a quizzical sort of way.

"Try to think back," I pressed her. And then, "I won't say where I got the name if that is what's bothering you."

"A month ago." She put peculiar sort of eyes on me—like a distant reproach—something like you see in the eyes of a waiter when the service has been good and the tip in his opinion is not up to it. So I said:

"The cops no doubt send you candy and stuff. I'd like to buy you a box myself. You'd do me a favor, though, if you'd take ten dollars and buy a box yourself. A favor—"

"That's all right," she cut in sharply.

"I like doing people favors." She opened a drawer to her right, took out a purse, jerked the zipper and stuffed her hand in to come out with a tiny memorandum book. "The fourteenth, say?" She thumbed rapidly through the book. "Yes. A motorcycle cop, Chester Nevans. He wanted the owner of 46R651. The car was registered under the name of Cyril B. Thompkins at 746 North Avenue, Hillcrest Heights. That's about seven miles from here. Three miles north of Hillcrest. Hillcrest Heights is just a name, simply farming land."

I slipped her the ten spot, tried another smile and said:

"Lucky you jotted that down. Any special reason for it, his voice funny or something?"

"Oh, they don't call up because they're drunk," she explained simply. "Just laziness. I don't blame them."

"I didn't mean that. I meant something odd about the call, the voice of the officer—you know, you wrote it all down."

"Oh." She smiled for the first time. "I can give you the calls right back to '44. It's not my job to give out names on the phone. It takes time—and, well, there's no free lunch in life. Some cops wouldn't even send a girl a Christmas card. I like to remember them."

Then I asked her about this cop Nevans who had called. He evidently remembered when Christmas came. He worked out of the third precinct in Norton.

As easy as that you think. Well, it was and it does sound easy, but then all things do to the other fellow when you do them. However, no one else had thought of it. It was reasonable, yes. It was the logical thing to do, yes. And someone might have done it if that someone was believing in the missing witness. And then again they might not have done it. Because it is simple doesn't mean it doesn't take thought. Sure, I like to feel that I use my head once in a while. So would you, if the newspapers kept writing you up as tough, tough, and ready to kill. But don't forget you have to think before you put a bullet in a guy's head, and if you don't think of it before he does, then he puts the lead in yours.

That was all right for a start. I got into my hired bus and buzzed back to Norton. The lieutenant on the bench of the third precinct got the D.A.'s letter without my smile. Officer Nevans was on motorcycle patrol. He glanced at the clock and told me Nevans would call in in twenty minutes. I waited. He did, and got orders to meet me out on his patrol.

"You won't have any trouble in finding him," the lieutenant grinned at me. "You just follow my instructions and drive along Elm Boulevard and he'll pick you up."

So far, I was only hoping, really not hoping, to obtain information from Officer Nevans. What I wanted from him was lack of information.

Nevans picked me up so suddenly that I almost thought it was a pinch. I pulled over to the curb and gave him what was on my mind.

"What was your interest in a car on the fourteenth of last month?" And I gave him the license number.

"I'll bite." He smiled. "What was my interest?"

And that was that. Officer Nevans had not made any call to the auto bureau on the fourteenth. So the logical conclusion was that the murderer had made the call and used the cop's name. I left Nevans then, sure that there was a missing witness and that I was on the track of that witness.

I drove out to Hillcrest Heights. The car's being registered under a man's name meant nothing. His wife could very easily have been driving it. A dowdy-looking maid opened the door for me. No, Mrs. Thompkins was not in. There would be no use in waiting. She wouldn't be back shortly. She didn't know when she'd be back. Then:

"Mr. Thompkins works down in the county clerk's office. He's chief clerk in the highway department."

I drove back to the county seat. The frowsy-haired girl in the auto bureau wasn't so bright, or so dumb, according to how you looked at it. At least, she hadn't given me any information I hadn't asked for, or paid for.

I DIDN'T NEED my letter of introduction to get in to see the chief clerk. His job was a good one and could go on for years if he worked it right. He looked like a fence straddler. He was tall and slightly bent and more than slightly bald. He had a sharp face with furtive, shifty eyes, and might have been any age over thirty-five.

Alone in his private office at the end of a corridor, I came right to the point. He looked like a lad who would frighten easily. I snapped:

"Where is your wife?"

His attitude changed. Not the furtive

part of it, but the cordial part. It was odd to watch him play the indignant and wary part at the same time. But I didn't give him a chance with the surprised indignation.

"Let me tell you—" I leaned forward and put a finger hard on his chest. "I'm here to do you a favor in return for one. I want to know where your wife is."

"And what favor can you do me—" he started, but I cut in.

"I might help keep you out of jail." And when he pushed back his chair and came to his feet, "I know all about your making restitution, but the fraud still remains. Well, want to listen?"

He didn't want to, but he did. He made a dent in his chest and tucked his chin in it. Finally he spoke, and the best he could get off wasn't very good.

"I don't know what you mean," was what he said.

I told him exactly what I meant. I was on pretty sure ground now. In fact, I thought I saw the whole thing. Judge Anderson, the power behind a political party. Therefore, it was reasonable to assume that it was a political murder. A chief clerk pilfering from public moneys, some "sure thing" investments, and his easing his conscience by intending to return the money. The investment turning sour, the theft about to be discovered, and perhaps his confession to his wife, or more likely, I thought, as I looked at his weak but intelligent face, his blaming his wife for putting him in the hole by her extravagance and pleading that it was his effort to please her, her driving to her friend Charlotte Thorn pleading for money, the money being lent, and then the discovery that she had seen murder on the road.

The result was Charlotte Thorn's seemingly wild story that her friend's husband was in trouble and that that was why she had given this friend money. Not for the purpose of trying to buy a witness. Now, see the point? Others knew then, or one other knew, that the witness' husband was a crook.

"I'm pretty well informed, Mr. Thompkins," I told him. "You lifted money that belonged to the people. Your wife got money from Miss Thorn and you thought you were safe. Now, someone has put the heat on you. In plain words, you were notified that if your wife testified in this murder trial your fraud would be disclosed and you'd go to jail."

"No, no," he said. But I could see that I had hit it, all right. "It isn't true. There is no money missing."

"Not now. Not since you used Charlotte Thorn's money. Where is your wife?"

"I... I don't know," he said.

"You find out." I gave it to him straight. "If you don't find out, you'll go to jail. Listen here, wise guy. Your crime is no longer one of simple robbery. It's aiding and abetting a murderer to escape justice. I don't know but what you can be charged as accessory after the fact of murder. I wouldn't be surprised if they could roast you, too. You see, friend, I happen to know who called you up and put the finger on you, who threatened you with the disclosure of your misappropriation of funds."

"Who?" He seemed genuinely surprised.

"You don't know? Why, it was the murderer of Judge Anderson himself who called you on the phone."

"No! No!" He came out of his chair again and leaned heavily on the desk. "It couldn't be. I... I—" He ran a hand over his forehead. I could see the breaking balls of perspiration. "I don't know who it was."

I had him then. He talked. He didn't know who had telephoned him. He didn't recognize the voice at all. It was muffled and peculiar. It demanded that he keep his wife from testifying in court and said she would only be repudiated as a witness and punished for perjury and that the scandal would cost him his job. I asked:

"And nothing was said about yourself, about your books?" And when his head sank down again. "Listen." I took the snap out of my voice and put a kindly note in. "You've made your restitution. You tell me the truth, you help me, you locate your wife and I'll see that you don't get into any trouble."

"Yes, yes?" His head came up. "You can do that?"

"Without a bit of trouble," I assured him, showing him the D.A.'s letter. How I was going to do it didn't bother me then. But he finally said:

"The voice on the wire did mention that there would be no occasion to bring up anything concerning my... my books here if there was no other scandal. And really, I didn't see that Elizabeth could do any good. But it couldn't have been the... the murderer who telephoned me. He wouldn't have dared." And when I laughed that one off:

"My wife is very fond of Charlotte Thorn and very grateful to her. I was wrong. I convinced Elizabeth that her testimony would only harm the case, not help it, that Charlotte Thorn alone would testify better to the fact that there was a missing witness. I suppose I believed and made Elizabeth believe what we wanted to believe. But now... now— I talked to my wife less than an hour ago. She called me up. She has seen the papers and she'll testify when the case comes to trial. She said she'd risk anything. My reputation. Her life even, if harm came to Charlotte Thorn."

I jarred at that one. But I asked Cyril Thompkins:

"How was your wife in politics? I mean, did she know most of the politicians?"

He shook his head.

"On the contrary. I did everything to keep my wife from meeting those connected with public office."

"Well," I asked again, "where is your wife now?"

"I won't—" he started, and then corrected himself. "I'm afraid to tell you that. I'm afraid she'll be harmed. But with proper protection, she will appear later."

"No," I shook my head. "She'll appear now. At least, to me she will. I think and hope that Miss Thorn is still alive. If your wife can possibly identify this murderer and we can lay our hands on him, then we have something to work on to locate Miss Thorn." He started to shake his head, but I said, "You haven't any choice in the matter. Tell me where she is or your job and your freedom and perhaps your life will go overboard."

He busted up then. He wasn't much

of a man. He cried all over his face. And I learned a lot. He didn't believe his wife would get a chance to identify anyone. Political murders were always done by hired thugs; probably gunmen from another city had murdered the judge.

"Has there been an attempt on your wife's life?" I asked him.

"No." He shook his head on that one. "We... I... well, she left town as soon as she told me what she had seen and what she had said to Miss Thorn. But there hasn't been anyone around the house even. Nothing suspicious."

I nodded.

"So the threat to you. This is a one-man job, and I imagine a rather prominent man, a man who could meet and talk to the judge. I think he worked alone. To me the abducting of Miss Thorn was a great piece of folly. It doesn't fit in with my idea of a clever man. It smacks of panic. That was his big mistake."

I got his wife's hide-out, the address, and the name she was using. It was on a small farm just outside Elmiro, a town about six miles away. So with a caution that he was to tell no one, and since he seemed a lot more worried about himself than his wife, I assured him that his position and freedom would be safe because of my influence with the D.A., which was a lot of loose talk, but he liked it. I walked out of his office, passed through the room of clerks and into the hall of the second floor. Ignoring the elevators, I turned toward the stairs and bumped smack into Mark Condon.

"Williams," he said. "I've been trying to find you. The chief is up in the air. He wants to see you!"

TEN MINUTES LATER I was with the D.A. in his office. Mark Condon wanted to stay, I think, but the D.A. dismissed him with a wave of his hand, saying:

"You're a young man, Mark, a coming man. For your future, I think you would do well to stay out of this case entirely."

Anyway, a few minutes later I was alone with the D.A.

"Williams"—he put hard eyes on me over the huge desk—"have you had any word about Miss Thorn or received any message? Do you know anything?"

"No to all those questions," I told him.

"I think," he said, "you would have been well advised to stay at the Thorn house. This case takes on a strange significance, most strange. I have taken no one into my confidence. I have had word about Miss Thorn."

"You have? You are taking me into your confidence then?"

"I was asked to," he snapped. "I have had a mysterious telephone call. 'Get hold of Race Williams,' the voice said. 'Tell no one but Race Williams, or I won't tell you where the girl is,' the voice said."

"And he told you?"

"No. He promised to call back and talk to you."

"Did he say he knew where Miss Thorn was?"

"Not exactly. He said 'the girl.'"

"But you're sure he meant Miss Thorn?"

"Of course, I'm sure. Er... that is, who else could he mean?"

"The other woman. The witness."

"Nonsense!" he snapped. "The other woman has been missing for some time, Miss Thorn hardly more than twelve hours. I am having you here because I… he requested that you be here when the call came through."

"Ah." I didn't appreciate the confidence of the D.A. so much then. He was telling me because he had to, because he was afraid the message wouldn't be delivered unless I was there to take it. But he sure was a nervous lad. He talked about Charlotte Thorn, her childhood, his friendship for her father. A half-hour must have passed.

Then the phone rang.

The D.A. spoke into the mouth-piece. "Oh, yes, Race Williams is here now. Yes…. Oh, to me? Miss Thorn? Not Miss—" He stopped then and listened. I saw him nodding. He seemed both interested and, I thought, somewhat disappointed. He was writing something down on a bit of paper.

I heard a click over the wire, but the D.A. went on talking.

"Why, yes. I can," he said. "Call me then in five minutes in the library. The number is 24831." He put down the phone and got to his feet.

"You'll excuse me, Mr. Williams. I think the party is afraid the call may be traced. He's going to give me the address where Miss… er… where the girl is. I must take it alone."

He started from the room, stopped, and coming back tore the sheet from the pad on which he had been writing. He said:

"Please wait for me. I have the address where the missing witness is. I'll give it to you when I return."

I leaned back in the chair then, half closed my eyes. But as soon as the door closed behind the D.A., I was on my feet swinging toward the door into the hall and through it out into the corridor. I didn't blame him for trying to beat me to the woman. Naturally, it was to his interest to locate the missing witness first. I figured what he was doing. He was going to get right out to that farm if he had the address, the right address. I had heard the click and knew that he was talking to himself and for my benefit when he pulled that line about going to the library phone. But it was all right with me. I wanted to get to the missing witness first, too.

Thompkins had given me pretty good directions. I had a fair car and was in it now, burning up the highway. As I got out into the country, I wondered who could possibly have rung up the D.A. and tipped him off as to Elizabeth Thompkins' hide-out.

I didn't have much trouble locating the side road which led to the farm. I smiled pleasantly at the young girl who gave me directions. She also told me that the road ran right through to a main highway about five miles the other side of the farm. Why did I like that? Simply because I could take my witness out that way and miss the car that was coming from the county seat to fetch her. Probably it would be the D.A. himself.

I found the farm all right. It was a white house set far back from the public road. It didn't look as though much farming went on there now. There was a garden, a dirt road from the rough highway, and the house itself.

I wheeled right up to the tiny circular drive before the door, got out, and rang the bell. No answer. So Elizabeth Thompkins had decided to keep quiet. I went around and tried the back door, but no go. The men from the D.A.'s office would be coming along soon. I went up on the front porch and tried a window. It was not locked. I pushed it up and put a foot over the sill and hung there, my gun jumping into my hand. But the figure on the floor didn't move. Then it did. But it didn't speak. It couldn't speak. It was an old man and he was bound, hand and foot, and he was gagged. And then I saw the woman tied there in a chair, her eyes staring.

I tore the gag off her first. She seemed in the worse shape. Then I unbound the man. But it was the woman who talked.

"She's dead," she said. "She's dead. He'll kill her. Papa wouldn't tell where she was, but I did. I couldn't see papa murdered before my eyes."

"Who'll kill who?" I asked.

"The masked man," the woman gasped as I cut the ropes from around her body with my pocket knife. "Elizabeth Thompkins. She was afraid of something and—"

"Yes," I cut in, "Elizabeth Thompkins. Where is she?"

"The guest house in the grove over the hill. My son's an artist and before he got married we built—"

That was all I heard. I was out the back of the house and running up the short stretch of narrow dirt road that led to the top of the hill. It was only a hundred yards or so. Then trees and the little house hidden in them—yes, and a road by the house, and a car.

Was it Elizabeth Thompkins' car or was it the car of the "masked man" ready for

murder? I had my gun clutched tightly in my hand when I made the dash up that hill. Maybe the witness was dead by now. But we wouldn't need a witness if I caught the murderer, caught him right there fresh from his second crime.

It wasn't much of a run to the front door. But any second I expected a shot to come from one of the windows. No shot came; no sound came until I had almost reached the door of the tiny structure. Then a shot came all right, but no bullet plugged me.

I grabbed the knob of the door, felt the door give. The second shot came when I was inside and facing a flight of stairs, the stairs from above which the shot had come. Maybe I was too late to save Elizabeth Thompkins, but I wasn't too late to catch a murderer or catch a bullet.

I was on the stairs now, up them, turning at the landing, and almost before I realized it I had plunked into the room above. I took in the entire picture in that small bedroom.

A single person was in that room. He was a man, and his back was toward me. And he was holding his gun straight out before him. Even as I came into the room he fired it again. And I saw that he was shooting at the lock of the closet door. He was speaking, too, saying:

"You had your chance and you talked. Now talk some more. Come on, talk, or I'll shoot up and down through the door."

"I wouldn't advise it," I said, very slowly, as I covered his broad shoulders. "There's a gun pointing at your back and—" That was as far as I got.

His cue was to drop the gun and put his

hands in the air. But he didn't. He swung, firing as he turned. I suppose I should have shot the gun from his hand, and maybe I could have. But here was a man who already had committed one murder and was in the act of committing another.

He was bent slightly as he swung. We were too close together for him to miss once he got fully around. So the answer to that was a simple one and a necessary one. I held my gun as I had held it ever since I entered the room, and I closed a finger and squeezed lead. As I said, he was bent slightly, so my bullet took him in the side of the neck. It was a .45 and it really took him.

He smacked against that closet door. The gun flew from his hand, his body bounced away, wilted once, and I saw glaring eyes through slits in a torn piece of black cloth which served as a mask. He hit the floor as the door of the closet cracked open. I saw the huddled form of the woman crumpled there. Whether she was dead or not I didn't know.

I turned my attention to the man on the floor. He was moving, trying unsuccessfully to come to his knees. Finally, he toppled back and braced himself against the wall. I leaned over and jerked off the bit of black which was not yet stained with red.

CHAPTER 4

I WON'T SAY I expected to know him. He shook his head and looked up at me. He had a rather nice smile.

"So it's you, Williams," he hardly whispered. "Well, I'm going over. I had nothing against Judge Anderson, but he had against me. It wasn't so bad. Many better men than I ever hoped to be had helped themselves to campaign funds. I didn't think he would ever know. The man who donated the money died and— But the judge sent for me. The game was up. I knew it. He was a fair old man. He said I could return the money, get out of town… and no one would ever know."

"And you killed an old man when he was willing to treat you like that?"

"It wasn't greed." His voice was sort of husky now. "It wasn't vengeance or jealousy or love. I called up Fletcher Martin after I made my appointment to meet the judge, told him the judge wanted to see him. Well, it was the only way. I had one purpose, one thought—my career, ambition."

I nodded at that and asked:

"Where's the girl, Miss Thorn?"

"Ah, yes," he smiled. "Where's the girl, Miss Thorn?"

There was no more from him then. Feet beat on the stairs. A state trooper, two men in plain clothes, and the D.A. himself were in the room. The D.A. took it hard when he looked at the man on the floor. He felt his head, then staggered back like an old-time actor and cried:

"My God! No! No! Arrest Williams! He's—"

The man on the floor shook his head.

"No," he said. "I was pretty clever in seeing that Race Williams stayed in your office. I was pretty clever in not telephoning you until I was in a gas station less than a mile from this farm. That was so

I would reach here ahead of Williams and silence the witness. How did I know where the witness was? Well, I figured when I saw Williams in Thompkins' office that Thompkins had told him where his wife was." His smile was pretty weak. "I used the phone, said I was you, chief. I told him that Race Williams had told me, but I wanted him to reaffirm it. He was so excited—yes, and scared that he never questioned my identity or my voice."

The girl in the closet had come around now. She had fainted and fallen to the floor, and the bullets fired through the door had not touched her. The state trooper led her over to the heavily breathing man who was dying. The D.A. carried himself well. His voice was thick, but he did his duty.

"Mrs. Thompkins," he said, "look at this man. Do you know him? Do you recognize him?"

"I don't know him," Elizabeth Thompkins said, "but I recognize him. He is the man I saw lifting the body from the car the night of Judge Anderson's murder." And very low, "Who is he?"

"He is," said the D.A., and it took a great effort, "he is the assistant district attorney of Norton County, Mark Condon."

Mark Condon didn't talk any more; he couldn't. The doctor who was called came too late to do him any good. They put Elizabeth Thompkins to bed up at the farmhouse with the old people to look after her.

I rode back in the car with the D.A.

"I'm sorry for my subterfuge, Williams," he said. "I'm sorry, too, that that boy could go so bad. And he never said a word about

Charlotte Thorn? I could take it all, every bit of it, if I only knew now that she was safe. He might have talked before he died." And he looked at me sharply.

When I told him Mark Condon hadn't said anything to me about Charlotte either, he simply shook his head and sighed. We rode the rest of the way in silence. I don't know what he was doing, but I was thinking.

Sure, I went over the whole case in my head, backward and forward, and, yes, I guess a little sideways, too. And what's more it was all free. I hadn't been paid to think. Charlotte Thorn was doing all the thinking, yes, even to directing my thinking with that ham actor stunt. And what had she wanted me to think? That there was a witness and she was in great personal danger. And I guess I believed her until I found out about the actor stunt. Then she put on an act with me about her danger being great, and I didn't believe there was a witness nor that there was any danger. And I had been wrong.

There was a witness. We had found her. There was danger, because Charlotte Thorn had been carried off right under my nose. Then we had all hit the ceiling and started a mad chase for the witness. No time to think then, nothing but action. Time to think now and— It hit me like a thousand of bricks.

The D.A. horned in on my thoughts.

"Do you suppose the child is dead?" he said.

"Dead?" I looked up at him.

"Why not? If that... that poor, demented boy, Mark Condon, could kill one person he could kill two."

"But," I told him, "I wasn't hired to protect the witness. I wasn't even permitted to hunt for the witness. I was hired to protect Charlotte Thorn." And when he just looked at me, "Oh, I'll find her all right. Or she'll—well, she'll get in touch with me."

"How," he demanded. "How?"

"There is"—I tossed it to him like a slow ball—"a secret understanding between Charlotte Thorn and me."

"Yes." He was all eagerness. "I thought there might be. I thought that is why you should hunt for Charlotte and not for this witness." And, it suddenly dawning on him that I was not divulging the secret, "But you mustn't keep silent now. No such silly ideas of protecting the confidence of a client."

"Oh, that." I lit a cigarette. "Miss Thorn doesn't even know of the secret understanding between us, only I know it."

He opened his mouth to throw an argument against that one, and when he found he couldn't he went into oratory on the Thorn family, starting before she was born. All very cute, too.

But he dropped me off at the Thorn house, let his chin lay down on his chest like a repentant St. Bernard and went into his final number.

"You know something, suspect something." He was very sad. "And yet rather than have the police work in with you, you would endanger, maybe actually be the cause of a young girl's death. I know, Mr. Williams. Perhaps I made a sorry spectacle out there at the farmhouse. But it was not all for... er... political reasons. You are daring, rather noted for being dramatic and playing a lone hand, I thought mostly of the woman, so detained you. But I would have given you full credit"—and rather magnanimously—"as I will give you full credit now."

"For what?" I looked up at him with great surprise, then I turned and went up the stone steps of the Thorn mansion.

He called after me.

"What are you going to do now?"

"Have dinner," I told him. And I wasn't lying at that. I ate in style, all alone. A good appetite, too. I grinned a couple of times to myself, almost laughed out loud once. And then—well, twenty minutes after dinner I wasn't feeling so good, nor so cockey either. There had been no word from Charlotte Thorn, no word from the police that she was found. I was just about at the bicarbonate of soda stage when the phone rang.

I grabbed it, the phone not the bicarbonate.

The voice was husky, muffled, like tucking your mouth into a handkerchief when you want to disguise your voice.

"Race, Race," the voice said. "How fortunate it's you. They've left me here to die—gagged and bound... I—" She faltered and then, "The New Coldridge Hotel, room 654... 654... and—"

"Yes," I showed an interest.

"Come quick... come quick... they're coming back. Come alone."

The phone clicked at the other end. I took a few puffs, stubbed out my cigarette and putting on my topcoat sauntered easily from the house.

The New Coldridge Hotel was not

too big and not too busy. I passed up the elevators and found the stairs.

Room 654 was at the end of the hall around a bend, only one other room opposite it. I hesitated a moment, then moved my gun from shoulder holster to my jacket pocket. The door was not locked. I turned the knob and walked in. The girl was laid out like a wake, all set up for you to see as soon as you entered. Just the light over the bed shone down on her. She was bound and gagged, but certainly she hadn't been handled rough.

I stood looking down at her for a full minute. Then I walked over to the window and looked out. I lit a cigarette, said:

"Lovely view you have here. I thought the city was much smaller. Really, it's quite a thriving metropolis."

A grunt came from the bed. I turned around. The soft, pleading look had gone. There was smoldering anger in her eyes, she rolled them at me. I leaned down and picked up the newspaper half hidden under the bed. I read the headlines.

"Well, well," I said, walking over to the dresser and snapping on the light there. "All about the missing witness, all about—"

"Aren't you going to untie me?" she demanded.

"Oh!" I lowered the paper and looked at her. "I was wondering why you didn't talk to me before. You did over the phone, you know."

"They came back and put the gag on again," she said through her teeth. "Are you going to untie me?" And then sort of weakly, "I just forced the gag out again."

"Might be against the law." I shook my head. "The police should do that. Or the district attorney."

"All right!" she said. "Make a fool out of me. I got loose a little while ago and if you—"

"Listen, Miss Thorn," I said, "you tell too many wild stories. The police will come. They'll search for fingerprints, they'll examine your wrists and ankles. I don't know what name you are registered under but the clerk will identify you." And with a smile, "You really don't know what a fine-looking girl you are." And when she still stared at me, "Oh, I daresay, you will tell the story well, but people won't swallow it. You should have taken me into your confidence."

"With everyone thinking I was a liar!" she snapped. "You don't know the whole truth."

"No." I gave her a smoke and lighted it. "How is this for a guess? Mrs. Thompkins came to see you. Told you about her husband's trouble—and maybe discussed the drunk on the road. You lent or gave her money. Then came the murder story. You got in touch with her and found she could identify the murderer. Which was all right with her and with you, and with Fletcher Martin who should be out of jail by morning. Then she called you up, she had been threatened, was frightened, wouldn't appear. But you knew she would appear if she thought anything had happened to you. So you got up last night or early this morning, tossed chloroform around your room, sneaked downstairs, stepped out the dining-room window, climbed the fence and came to this hotel and registered. It's a wonder they didn't know you."

"It was very early morning," she said. "I wore a veil."

"All right. I should have known that no one could steal a girl from under my nose like that. But I didn't. I was sick over not believing you. I never thought of your hiding yourself out so the publicity would reach Elizabeth Thompkins and she would appear for Fletcher Martin. Now it's sort of bad, isn't it?"

"Why?" she demanded. "A girl has a perfect right to leave her own house in any manner she wishes. And there is no law against registering under an assumed name, or if there is it can't be much of a law. So what?"

"You are going to look pretty ridiculous. The papers will give it a big run. Not just in Norton papers, in Chicago, New York, headline stuff. Heiress kidnaps self while police laugh, only they didn't laugh—" And as she sobered up a bit, "It would be better to forget the kidnaping and the police of the county hunting for the men who supposedly brought you here, and then the truth coming out. Just forget it."

"Forget it? How?"

"Easy," I told her. "Amnesia. The man you love held for murder. It was too much. You went to bed last night and didn't remember another thing until I found you at this hotel tonight. How's that sound?"

"Will Laurence Gibson believe that?"

"No," I gave her the truth, "He probably won't. But I don't think he'll question it. I'll give him an idea of what might have been in your mind when you disappeared. I'll call it your subconscious mind to sort of keep things in character. He's a good guy really, and your story can't be broken. You have one answer to everything—I don't remember."

"Maybe that is best," she admitted. "There will be nothing difficult to explain then."

"Only the chloroform scattered about the room." I wasn't making it too simple for her.

She smiled. It was a nice smile, I didn't think she had it in her. And her crack was a good one then.

"About the chloroform," she said, "I'll say 'I don't remember' twice for that one."

This Corpse On Me

BLACK LIMOUSINE

WE MADE PRETTY good time but it got colder all the way down from Los Angeles. The bus was crowded even before we reached Riverside, yet the girl got on at Palm Springs. It was up to the driver if he took on passengers or not when all the seats were occupied, and with this driver it had been decidedly *not*. I had seen him shake his head at the offer of folding money at Banning. But at Palm Springs she smiled at him and he snapped down the jump seat beside him and took her along.

The girl was young and the girl was small and the girl was slim, and people would have turned to look at her in Hollywood or even back in Grand Central Station, New York.

The bus hadn't been on its way again over five minutes before the driver must have wished he had taken the cash offer at Banning. The girl still smiled at him and she did nod "yes" or shake her head "no" when he spoke to her, but it was plainly evident that she had put on the gay-lit-

110

tle-companion act just for the ride. She had other things on her mind.

Her wrist watch, at which she looked continuously, was openly one of them. The occupants of the bus were furtively another. She had nice eyes to do it with too. But they were narrowed and, yes, suspicious. But they could be big and wide and brown when they were honestly attentive, such as the time they lit for a full minute on the huge Mexican woman asleep in her seat with three dirty little dark-skinned babies somehow balancing themselves on her lap.

We hit Indio at nine o'clock on the nose. There was the place on Fargo Street that was called the 350 Club, and then we passed the Desert Theatre. The town was dead of people and alive with empty cars parked along the curb. We swung back toward Highway 99 and up between the pumps of the gas station that was the bus terminal.

Indio was a fifteen-minute rest stop and nearly all the passengers climbed off the bus. I was almost on the girl's heels as she hit the flagging. Dim lights of the restaurant ahead of me showed clearly the man who sat beside the popcorn machine, plainly the irate Mexican youth who shook the scales that wouldn't work after dropping his penny.

Then down to my left the big black limousine. It caught my eye all right. You don't see many limousines today, even in the city. And this one had its curtains drawn on the side, I could see, and at the front between the driver and the tonneau of the car.

THE LIMOUSINE ATTRACTED the girl's attention too. It was backing slowly, farther into the shadows; as if it had been there for someone to see and then retired into the deeper darkness.

A big man emerged from the back of the restaurant and sauntered in studied indifference across the space between the station and the limousine which had now come to a stop—just a great block of almost invisible blackness. The chauffeur, or a least the man in the front seat of the limousine, got out and, walking a little way from the car, turned his back to it and lit a cigarette. He remained so with his back to the big car.

The girl moved furtively. No longer the fluffy bit of naïve youth of the bus. More like some jungle animal, quick and graceful, yet leaving the impression that she was wandering about. But I had more than an idea she was going to jump that big black hunk. I moved too—leisurely—but toward the same limousine. And still the chauffeur kept his back to the girl and the car and stared hard at the back of a dilapidated building.

I was getting nearer to the car when the big man slipped nicely in between me and the girl. He wore a dirty leather jacket and had an old felt hat on the back of his head. He barred my way and spoke.

"Can't go down that way, buddy. Forbidden ground."

"Forbidden by whom?"

"Oh, by me," he snapped, and then being a man of little patience said, "Come on—before I toss you back."

"And who are you?" I edged closer to him.

A huge paw came out and gripped my shoulder.

"I'm just—me." He laughed, cursed suddenly when I stood my ground, then let his free hand shoot back and up with the evident intention of putting the heel of that hand hard against my chin.

I'm a fair-minded man. You don't have to knock me around to wise me up. You don't even have to strike me. The intention of physical violence is enough. He was so busy with his own little act that he wasn't watching my hands. At least he wasn't watching the right one, or if he was he didn't know what to do about it.

I brought it up from my knee and popped it on the end of his chin and he went down like a thousand of brick. He didn't make so much noise, though, but laid just as still. The girl was opening the limousine door about to get in—starting to draw back, too, I thought—then she suddenly disappeared into the car as if an unseen hand had grabbed her and pulled her in. And through the black curtain I thought I saw a light. Anyway I did see the chauffeur turn and, running back to the limousine, jump in behind the wheel. That was my cue.

I didn't feel any special elation about knocking that hunk of beef silly. He was strictly small time on my circuit. Rough stuff is simply business with me.

I was thinking of the business then. The limousine was coming out of the dark and swinging around toward Highway 99, which left me on the far side of the driver and within ten or fifteen yards of the car. That is, I was ten or fifteen yards away when it started to make the swing.

By the time it completed that swing and was in almost total blackness I was beside it, had grabbed the knob of the rear door and jerked the door open.

I had been right about seeing a light through the black curtains, for a tiny bulb shone dully. No sound came from within that car because of the roar of the motor—the unnecessary roar of the motor as if the driver were racing it to drown out any sounds.

A man and a woman were struggling. The man had the girl pinned down on the floor. The door slammed closed behind me and I took in the little bit of melodrama. The man was holding the girl by the throat all right. I could see the whiteness of her face, the blueness of her lips, the wideness of her eyes. I saw the two slender hands that tore at the man's wrists, and then only one as her right hand dropped back beyond my vision. And all the time the motor raced and roared.

For an instant the man's right hand left the girl's throat. Where he got the knife or how he could produce it so fast I don't know. It looked as if the blade jumped suddenly alive in his hand. He fairly hissed words at her now.

"You nearly bit my finger off, you little rat!" he said, and there was pain as well as fury in his voice. "If you have the will or not, I'll kill you anyway."

The knife moved and I reached for his neck and his right wrist at the same time. I gripped them and held them, but didn't jerk him back. I didn't get a chance. There were one, two, three shots in quick succession and he jerked himself back.

I lifted him off the girl and pushed him up against the door. The girl was lying there, her hair mussed. The little doodad that served as a hat was crushed and more off her head than on it. I hardly recognized her. She seemed much older, for one thing. For another her lips were slightly twisted at one corner, and her eyes—those childish brown eyes—were thin slits with the hardness of marble shining through them.

Or was it more glassy? And was what I saw horror or abject terror? She came to her knees with a quick staggering movement to slip onto the seat beside me. But she wasn't looking at me. She was looking down at the man by the door—the crumpled dead figure.

I took the gun out of her hand, a snubnosed automatic. Then I looked down. The man was a well-set, broad-shouldered lad. His back was against the door, his head sunk forward on his chest, his fedora over his face, almost down to his chin. His topcoat was hunched on his shoulders, his jacket had flopped open and on his white shirt a hunk of crimson stood out.

Blood? But blood didn't stand out that way. I pulled in my breath. A thought went through my head that would have gone through the head of every detective in the city of New York, seeing what I was seeing, even seeing it out there in the middle of the desert three thousand miles from Broadway.

The great hunk of red that wasn't blood was as big as a half-dollar but it wasn't as flat. It stood out like—like a stone, a crimson stone. A ruby—a fine and perfect ruby.

I let the girl slip down upon the car seat. Then I leaned over and lifted the man's right hand, pushed back his sleeve, saw the white cuff and the splash of red as big as a quarter this time. A cuff link. I ran a thumb along its smoothness, along the big red smoothness on his chest. No kidding now. It was a ruby—or a good imitation of one. A mighty good imitation.

I couldn't believe it. Yet I had to believe it, or at least I had to find out. Call it fantastic. Call it impossible. But I bent down and, putting a hand on the fedora hat, pushed it slowly back. The square jaw, the sharpness of teeth that should have been yellow—yes, and were yellow. The full thick lips. I shoved the hat all the way back.

Maybe I gasped, even though I was sure before then. This man at one time had been one of the biggest racketeers New York had ever produced. For a while he had gone downhill until he had nothing left but that exclusive little apartment hotel called the Terrace. Lately he was getting some money some place, strutting again on the Avenue.

Many had died gunning for him. And now a slip of a girl out in the lonely desert had squeezed a small slender finger on a large caliber gun and blasted him right out from behind his prize ruby. Yep. If you know your way around you guessed it.

The stiff was "Ruby" Klegg.

CHAPTER 2

A BODY ON THE ROAD

IF KLEGG HAD any other first name I never knew it. He signed his checks that way. It was said he'd had his name legally changed to Ruby. You could spot him a mile with those stones; especially when he went in for evening clothes.

I looked at the girl. She was cuddled there in a little heap, her hand stretched over the seat close to the door. She hadn't fainted. Her eyes were on me, but they were not narrow slits now. They were growing wider and wider.

The driver quite evidently had not heard the shots, since they had come when the motor had been racing and backfiring. The car moved along easily through the night now. I sat back and looked down at Ruby Klegg and thought and wondered where he fitted into the picture. The picture—the reason I was there in the desert with Ruby Klegg who had died somewhere south of Indio. And the picture flashed back.

Things had been dull for me. Then a millionaire of fifty-odd, Bertram C. Howe, had died at his desert home. He had left a will made three years previously leaving everything to his wife, with the exception of twenty-five thousand dollars to his brother, a five-thousand dollar bequest to a small college—Colebury College—and lesser amounts to old servants and employees.

The hitch was that just before he died his nurse had seen him draw up a new will entirely in his own handwriting, and two old servants on his desert estate had witnessed his signature. My job was to find the missing will, not a dead body. I was employed most confidentially by a most dignified law firm which represented the interests of Colebury College.

Somehow they had the idea that the money had been left to them. And somehow the dignified lawyer had the idea that the nurse might know something, and he wanted me to get that knowledge from her. The suspicion all around was that the widow had copped the new will.

Why me in such a job? Why pay the price that I charged? Well, the senior partner of the law firm put it to me this way:

"I understand, Mr. Williams, that this nurse has certain information. If she could produce—er—discover this missing will and it greatly benefited the institution we represent that institution would consider it a great service. If the will cannot be found, that this nurse, Miss Burton, has knowledge of, and if she is willing to go on the stand to swear under oath to a knowledge that shows an intent upon the part of the deceased to make the college his chief beneficiary—then of course we could pay you handsomely. You understand such testimony would not and could not be paid for, as our firm could have no hand in anything that even suggested bribery. But an honest woman—you know."

"You want me to bribe her personally?" I had horned in then.

"No!" He had jerked erect in his chair. "I want you to induce her to tell the truth. It might prove difficult if other interests attempted to induce her to lie. Of course, under auspicious circumstances, we would expect to pay you a satisfactory fee for any extra—er—er—difficulties you encountered."

So had spoken Edward August Castle of the firm of Castle, Bradrick and Castle, but he had never even hinted that one of those difficulties might be the dead body of a former notorious racketeer.

And where could Ruby Klegg fit into the picture? Surely, he didn't expect to inherit any money out of it. Yet he had wanted the will. Why?

I thought maybe I knew why. There was only one person—well, perhaps two—who would just as soon that missing will didn't show up. One was the widow, of course, and the other was the brother who inherited twenty-five thousand dollars. But the brother was Addison Howe, the former noted painter, and he would hardly want or need.... Then it struck me. Former noted painter. Sure. Today he could be broke.

All these thoughts flashed back through my head in seconds—less maybe. I looked down at the dead man again. I looked at the girl crouched beside me on the seat. She was stirring now. Fixing her hair. Watching me out of eyes that still were widening, eyes that were very bright. And I saw that her lips were not thin red lines but parted and generous, and that her teeth gleamed white. What was more, she seemed to be slowly growing younger while I watched her. The wrinkles, which must have been simply frown lines, were going quickly out of her forehead.

She was not in an enviable position. If she knew where the will was, now was the time for her to tell me. If the dead Bertram C. Howe had confided in her about the new will and she held the clue to the intent, now was the time to get that information from her.

SHE SPOKE FIRST and her voice did not tremble. There was a slight foreign accent to it that I won't try to put over, but it was not hard to understand and it sounded nice the way she used it.

"He's dead," she said. "Was it wrong to kill him—for that—for what he was going to do—to me?"

"Legally or morally?" I didn't browbeat her or didn't coddle her. I wanted to see where we stood first. "Where did you get the gun?"

"It came into my hand," she said, and I guess when I stared like that she understood. She hurried on. "From under his coat it slipped, and then—well, there were black spots before my eyes. I don't remember. Did you shoot him, or did I?"

"Lady"—I grinned at her—"is that a nice way to treat a friend? Don't you know?"

"Spots—they came before my eyes," she said. "I don't remember. Later perhaps I'll remember, one way or the other."

"You or me, eh?"

"Yes, I will try and remember. You jumped into the car. And then I thought you came to help me."

"You know why I came. It was to be arranged that you meet me at the bus terminal. Instead you crawled into this—this hearse." And then the big-hearted act, for after all it isn't any too pleasant for a young woman to be held for shooting strange men. "I'll help you, for that will, for—for... Well, helpful testimony about that will."

"The missing will again," she said. "Everyone wants that will. An unknown cousin from Tennessee, a little fresh-water college in some place in the East... Oh, did I do anything wrong?"

Anything wrong? I shot forward and made a lunge at Ruby Klegg. The girl had leaned against the door and it sprang suddenly open, though I'd have sworn she must have given the handle a twist first.

I might have had him, too, if she hadn't grabbed my arm.

"No—no, let him go. We do not want him. See—he does not want us either."

She was right. Ruby Klegg took a sudden back flip and tumbled out on the road. I saw his body twist, turn over in the soft sand and fold itself neatly in the deep shadow of a telegraph pole. Then we were out of sight—and I slammed the door.

Almost at once the car slowed down. It didn't stop suddenly. The driver seemed to hunt for a special spot. If so, he found it. We bounced gently off the road. The black hulk swerved slightly and the tires settled and the car stopped.

I leaned up and unscrewed the light bulb.

"I'll do the talking," I said to the girl.

"The driver's coming around for a look-see."

I couldn't see her face, but I felt her stiffen beside me.

The door opened, our driver stood there.

"What's wrong?" he demanded. There was a rough command in his words but it didn't register in his voice. There was a quiver to it.

"Why, what should be wrong?" I asked, and held my revolver on the blackness.

"Oh, you're there." He seemed relieved. "And the other one—the woman. I want to see her. I have a flash."

"You let that flash loose in here and I'll shoot it into your carcass," I told him.

"I wouldn't shine it on you," he said, "and if it's that way you want it she can hide her face. I didn't look at you when you got into the car, did I? And I didn't look at her either. I—I wasn't paid to go—to murder."

"What makes you think someone was murdered?"

"I thought I heard a shot a bit back." His voice wasn't any better now. "Now—well, like a body tumbled from the car, and the door closing and—and I thought maybe she tried to jump out."

I sat back feeling better. So the driver had not seen the man who got in his car, nor the girl either.

"You didn't hear any shot," I told him. "And you didn't hear any falling body. The door blew open, if that's what you mean. At least it was on the latch and I opened it and closed it tight. The girl is here. You know what you were paid for?"

"Yes." He gulped. "I was paid to let the girl jump in the car and for—for you to convince her she should take a ride with you." And when I didn't answer right away his voice shook slightly. "I identified you, sir, through the other half of the bill you left on the seat—thank you—but I want to see that other passenger. I know she got in, like I know you got in—sort of by back glancing." And as if quick explanation of his peeking, "Just the figures of a man and a woman, nothing more." A dumb sort of frightened guy he was.

I LAUGHED. I couldn't help it.

"Hide your head, Mabel," I said

simply. "The driver wants to be assured of your presence. He was paid too much and misunderstands our little rendezvous." And I added quickly, "I'll use my flash."

The girl ducked low, holding her arm over her face when I shot the pencil of light on her.

"That's enough," said our chauffeur. "I can tell by the way you talk, mister, that you don't belong in this part of the country. Neither do I. I'm from the city, back Riverside way. I'll be driving you on to your appointment. Can't waste too much time. I—er—borrowed this car like I was told to. I got to ditch it before the chauffeur finds it out."

I thought of the dead body back on the road, of the explanation I'd have to make to the police. The coincidence of my riding in the same car with Ruby Klegg and maybe the girl saying she didn't do it.

"Okay, buddy," I told him. "You hitch-hike back to Indio. The young lady and I will drive on alone. Now."

"No—no." His voice shook. "I can't. He wasn't small time like us, boss. He was big city stuff. Said he'd stick a knife in my chest if I didn't show up."

He was reaching for the door as if to close it when I turned up my collar, pulled down my hat and stepped out of the car. I wasn't going in for an argument. Even if there wasn't a lot of traffic we were on a main highway. Besides, I didn't like that "small time" business.

"Okay," I told him. "Take your choice. A knife in your chest when this big-timer catches up with you, or a bullet in your chest right now." He staggered slightly back, so I took advantage of his fright

and swung him around. "Start walking," I said. "On the other side of the road so I can see you better. And don't look back. Just keep going."

He did and I watched him.

Why did I want him on the other side of the road? Well, a car wouldn't see that body. A hiker wouldn't either for that matter, unless it was a hiker who had a body on his mind. But he kept going. His head erect, his shoulders straight, like a soldier's on parade—the end of the parade maybe, for his knees weren't too steady.

Five minutes later I got behind the wheel, had the girl climb in beside me. I was glad to see so little traffic on Highway 99. Then swung the car around and headed south again.

"What now?" the girl said.

"Well, it's like this," I told her. "There's a body lying down the road that we've got to pick up and move inland some place. It would take a lot of explaining."

"You're—doing this for me?"

"For you and me," I told her flat. "I'm out to find a missing will, and I think you're my lead to it. I don't want you out of circulation right now. It would confuse the situation if you and I were occupying different cells trying to explain that corpse. Besides," I added truthfully enough, "I'm not sure what sort of story you'd tell."

"If I shot him or not?" she said. "I guess I don't know what I'd say myself. I don't know how my memory would be at the time. I—well, there those—"

"Sure." I nodded. "I know. Those spots before your eyes. How do you feel about him now?"

CHAPTER 3

HANDS ACROSS A GRAVE

THE GIRL LOOKED at me a long time. I could see the whiteness of her face, feel the steadiness of her eyes. She laughed nicely, pushed close to me, and took my arm through hers. I could feel hair brush against my cheek.

"If we are not going to try and explain the body what does it matter?" she said. "You are being very kind to me, I think."

"You don't have to be kind to me."

I shoved her off a bit, then pulled up in the darkness. I felt a little jump in my throat. Did I see that body lying there by the pole plainly because I knew there was a body there—or was it that plain?—or didn't it just look like a shadow on the road. And shouldn't I let it lie there for someone to find?

But lying there, found there? I couldn't chance it. Ruby Klegg in Indio. Race Williams in Indio.

But I don't have to talk myself into things. I backed the car up quickly off the road and alongside that pole, and the shadow that curled half around it.

"I—I'll help you," the girl said, as I opened the door and slipped from behind the wheel to the roadside.

"No," I told her. "It's a quick job."

It was. A minute later I slammed the rear door closed, brushed off my hands, for the dust was thick, and found the girl behind the wheel.

"The keys," she said. "You took them. I drive. I know this country."

"Yes, I took them," I admitted. But I didn't add that I took them for the very reason that I was afraid she knew the country too well and would be driving over it while I was lifting up the body. But I handed her the keys and let her drive. I'd rather watch her alone than both her and the road. Three minutes flat after we had stopped we were off again.

You think that fast? It was. Ruby Klegg was heavy, too. But it wasn't the first body I had handled in a hurry.

"Now—off the main highway?" the girl asked. "And you'll want a shovel." When I didn't answer, she said, "Well, you didn't just pick him up to carry around. You can't leave him in the open fields—the police—the coyotes. Surely we bury him. Far off here no one will ever know." And almost sweetly, "Then you and I will not have to remember what happened in the car, and all my life I will love you very much. Though there was not much harm in it."

After I recovered, I said with some sarcasm:

"You got a shovel in your handbag?"

"But no," she answered quite seriously, and then, "You joke. Yet I know where there is a shovel, and I know where there is big date garden, and so the ground is not too hard on top if it is done before dawn, and underneath. It is for a strong man like you nothing. Then the days and the months and years pass and we forget. Is it not so?"

We were moving along the road now, had turned right where the sign read Sandy Corners. She drove well, too. I was thinking it over. And I guess I was about to say, "It is so," but instead I said:

"Step on it."

I caught the lights in the rear view mirror before I heard the siren screech. Then the police car turned too, skidding around the corner, straightening out and on our tail.

"It's a big boat," I told her. "Give it what you can. A dark lane, a quick stop, and we'll run for it. If you know this country no one will find us."

"The American Gestapo," she laughed. "I will handle them." The car crept along.

"And the body in the back?" I said frantically, as the police car pumped up on us. "Step on it!"

"No—no, they can't know." Was she telling me or was she trying to convince herself? "They can't know, and if—if… Duck down in the seat. Like I am alone."

It was in my mind, even in my hand, to push a gun against her side and order her to let the car loose. But I didn't know if it would work. In fact, I had an idea it wouldn't work. Anyway, the police car had screamed alongside, was pushing us off the road.

I ducked down on the floor of the car. I was wondering what her "if" meant. And I had an unpleasant feeling that "if" meant that if they found the body she would lay no claim to it.

"What are you doing on this road?" I heard the voice of the cop say. Or words to that effect.

And I heard the girl laugh and say:

"But Officer, what other road would I be on?"

There was talk in between, then the officer said:

"Well, you've brought excitement to the valley anyway, and, and I don't mind saying we all wish you luck with—with—" A pause. "I shouldn't be talking like this at a time like this."

THEN THE POLICE car sped away and I climbed back up on the seat.

"It was very funny," the girl said. "I could have laughed. The officer said if he wasn't alone in the car he'd have climbed in the back and seen me safely home."

"In the back?" I gasped.

"Yes," she said. "Such respect for my years and my position in life."

She knew the country all right. The car turned into a narrow side road, ran along it for half a mile, shot down a dusty lane that would hold one car, stopped. She pointed at a little shed and hopped out of the car. I waited, but I had my gun in my hand. Pretty soon she was back out again with a shovel. One shovel.

She handed it to me, climbed in behind the wheel and without a light on the car began backing and straightening out again. Then we were off, going slowly and smoothly along two well-defined ruts in a date garden.

These were good-sized date palms, for I could see the ladders against the trees. She was talking.

"Tractors have been through here, of course. We follow the wheels, make no new tracks. So we swing here, down this way. And straight away. So this is a good spot. We bury him here."

Eerie? I guess it was if you want to look at it that way. But I hauled the body out of the car and carried it over my shoulder, walking along the tractor treads. I had given it thought and made up my mind. The body had been tossed around too much to tell a straight story to the police. And I—well, we had let ourselves in for it once we lifted the body back in the car, and once when we let the cop stop us and go on his way.

"About here?" she asked and answered her own question. "Good. It is not too cold now. The ground will be soft until around five or six o'clock in the morning. Here is the shovel."

Just as simple as that. Just as indifferent as that when she should have been lying in a dead faint with me giving her smelling salts. Even remembering that she was a trained nurse didn't seem to make any difference. She was more like an undertaker.

Through the palms the stars shone down, but they gave little light. I guess they were too far up. I never saw so many stars.

I dug. The ground was soft. It was almost like a child digging in the beach at Coney Island. And all the time the girl sat on the ladder that leaned against a tree and picked herself dates and spat the pits into her hand.

"No evidence," she kept explaining.

After I had carried the body over and dropped it in and filled up the hole she came and took the shovel and patted down the dirt. She stirred it up here and there with ridges so it would look like the rest of the ground.

"It is right," she said at length. "Pickers they come and no footstep of ours remains. The wind it move the dirt about… Here, I picked some dates for

you. But first, we shake hands over the grave. Is it not so?"

It takes a lot to throw me. I think I was thrown then. But I took the hand she stretched to me across the grave. I couldn't help it. I guess she gripped mine.

"Now," she said, "we are partners. I have killed the man and you have buried him."

"No spots before your eyes then?"

"No," she said. "He is dead and buried, and let that be the end of it. It is better to forget. I always forget the unpleasant things, and remember the good things. There are so few that one must cherish the thoughts."

"What's your name?" I asked impulsively, as I took the dates from her. "I mean, your first name, Miss Burton?"

"Miss Burton, no less. My name is Ziggie. You—" She paused. "I think you may call me Ziggie."

"Ziggie?" I said. "I never heard that name. What does it come from?"

"Oh, a little French, a little Polish, perhaps some Czecho-Slovakian, and maybe—then the United States mixes it up and it comes out Ziggie."

"You are from Europe—Poland maybe?"

"Maybe. But that is the unpleasant thing I forget. Look. I will take you home with me and you will question me, because that is your business. Perhaps also it is your business to try and hurt me?"

"If you tell the truth, nothing can hurt you," I lied easily, as we got into the car and she drove it.

"Bah! That from you. And we bury a dead corpse together. They accuse me, though not yet legally of stealing that will. Do they believe the truth?"

"I just want to know what you know about it. You nursed him and… What's the matter?"

BLAMED IF I didn't think she was crying. Even to this day I don't know if she was or not. There was, though, a catch in her voice when she asked:

"Whom do you represent?"

I gave it a thought then I told her.

"The college."

"No!" She jarred straight up behind the wheel and stared at me. If it wasn't that ruts held the car we'd have been off into the date trees. "How stupid."

Suddenly the car swung, dashed into the dim light from curtained windows and we were in a gravel driveway. We came to a stop. Before us a bungalow was nestled, if you like it flowery, among the date palms.

The girl hopped out and so did I. She almost ran toward the door. I stopped dead. Sure, I knew it was a gun stuck into my back, and a voice spoke—not a voice of the desert, by any means, but the voice of a distant city.

"Not so fast, buddy," the voice said, and when the girl, almost at the door, swung around, "Sorry lady. He's a stranger to me, and he isn't going in with you until I get the word."

"That's all right, Ziggie," I said. "I'll be with you in a couple of minutes. Go in if there isn't any personal danger to you. I'll join you in a couple of minutes, like I said."

The girl hesitated, stood there.

I turned. There was enough light for the man with the gun to get a look at me. His eyes widened, his gun wavered from side to side slightly—and I did it. I knocked his gun hand to one side with my left hand and brought my right hand in and out from under my own armpit and cracked him under the chin with it. He just had time to utter a single name. It was a nice name. I sort of liked the sound of it, and the fear in his voice.

"Race Williams," he said simply.

He fell to his knees and, toppling off the little porch, rolled out into the patio.

I knew him, and I didn't know him. That is, I knew he was a private detective with not too good a reputation back in New York. But his name escaped me, if I ever had heard it.

The girl stood wide-eyed.

"Like that." She nodded emphatically. "He calls out your name and faints. He was afraid. I saw it in his face."

He had a right to be afraid. When lads stick guns in my back I assume they intend to use them and do my best to use mine first. But then I remembered that dick as a keyhole listener, a dumb-waiter juggler, and a window-peeper.

"Miss Burton," I said, and she smiled at me pleasantly, "I take it from what this guard said that Mr. Addison Howe has visitors inside who are not to be trusted. People will try to bribe you to get information about that will. People will even—well, someone tried to kill you this afternoon. Now I can walk in with you and put the dampers on the show. Or I can listen in some place, and give you any help you may need when you need it."

"Yes, yes." She seemed to be thinking. "It will be that lawyer and the phony philanthropist who is interested in the cousin. There. The French windows—thick drapes. I will unlock the window, push it open. It is in an alcove with a piano. Close the window quickly when you get inside. The cold air may tell your story. See—the windows there, around the corner of the house."

CHAPTER 4

VISITING RACKETEER

ZIGGIE WENT IN the door and I slipped around the corner of the house. The French windows were there. I waited, listening, not watching. The curtains were thick, and hardly any light came through.

I didn't hear her spring the lock on those French windows. I waited, tried them, and the windows gave. I heard the murmur of voices.

The curtains were thick, as I said, and the baby grand stood a bit into the room. I slid inside and closed the window. People were talking. One voice was high and squeaked.

"Mrs. Howe," it said, "of the present moment everything is in the manner of a civil action, an attempt to trace a missing will. Miss Burton here nursed your husband through his last illness. You are the only one who could have taken that will. Miss Burton may point the accusing finger at you. I warn you, Mrs. Howe, my patience is exhausted. I would proceed with criminal prosecution."

I had edged along the curtain and could see into the room. The bald-headed bird with the squeak looked the part of a small-town lawyer who had taken to drink and was letting his laundry suffer to buy more liquor. He was at a table with a pad before him. To his right was a woman of about thirty-five. She looked cold, efficient, determined, and mostly interested in herself. This woman I took to be Mrs. Bertram Howe, the widow, though she was not in black.

I moved around and saw Ziggie. She was leaning on the far end of the piano. A man beyond sat with his feet crossed, and a cigar in his hand and that was all I could see. The back of a large comfortable chair hid the upper part of him.

But the other occupant of the room I could see plainly. He wore a blue dressing gown with white stripes—a dressing gown, mind you. Under no circumstances, no matter how down to earth you are, could you take it for a bathrobe. His face was young, but his hair was snow-white and his eyes were the brightest blue I had ever seen. There wasn't a wrinkle on his forehead. His carriage, his apparent ease and indifference, were perfect.

The man of the cigar and the legs spoke. He addressed the white-haired man.

"Mr. Howe," he said, "your name and your reputation are nation-wide. Mrs. Bertram Howe is your sister-in-law. Why not advise her to tell us all she knows? Why let this reach the public and the press and the courts. My friend, Miss Claudia Ramson, the cousin from Idaho, would not make any complaint. Indeed, she might make a settlement. But advise your sister-in-law to produce the missing will."

The white head turned slowly, the blue eyes glimmered. The man opened his mouth and spoke softly.

"But my dear sir," he said, "I have no right to this bungalow I occupy now. To be sure, my brother let me use it during his life, but I am here now on the sufferance of Mrs. Howe. I regret that she is not interested in my advice."

The feet moved. The cigar and the hand disappeared and the man I hadn't seen stood up. And I got shock Number Two. The man was "Smiley" Henderson. And if Ruby Klegg was a has-been along the Avenue, Smiley Henderson was a comer.

Two New York racketeers on the desert on one winter's night is hardly a coincidence.

"I think," Smiley said, "I will advise Mrs. Howe myself."

He didn't go over and stand in front of the woman on the bench. He walked straight over toward the piano and stood in front of Ziggie. And what's more he said to her:

"Mrs. Bertram Howe, I am going to stay here tonight. All night if you do not speak." He stretched out a hand and took her wrist. "You can't get the police very well because we might convince them that they want you more than you want them. Now I want to know where you put that will."

"I think," Addison Howe said, as he came to his feet, "that you may be hurting Mrs. Howe's wrist."

"Of course not!" Henderson smiled over at Addison Howe. "If there is anything Mrs. Howe doesn't like about my actions she can telephone the police."

Yep, all this conversation was going on while I stood there in a daze. If I had been surprised before I had sure been tossed plenty by this time. Ziggie was Mrs. Howe! I didn't believe it at first. I could hardly believe it now. Yet Smiley Henderson thought she was. Addison Howe, her brother-in-law, thought she was.

"Get out of my house," she said suddenly.

"There is a phone," Smiley said, almost gently. "Why not call the police?"

"Let go of my wrist!"

"There's a phone. Why not—" And Smiley stopped talking.

ZIGGIE'S FREE HAND came up and smacked him across the face. She was small, yet she struck hard. Yes, and she struck viciously. It rocked the six-feet-two of Smiley Henderson. It rocked him inside too. His face went purple, all but for the white finger marks that stood out plainly on his cheek. For a moment I thought that he was going to strike her. But he didn't.

"Mrs. Howe," he said. "I want to talk to you alone, in a quiet spot. There—don't be foolish. You'll be glad you listened. Come."

He put a hand on her shoulder and I could tell by the expression on her face that his fingers bit deeply. So I stepped from behind the curtain, and was between them before Smiley even realized it. I hit his arm up so hard that it bent him backward and put him into a half-kneeling position like those living statues you see in the circus. He just stayed in the pose too, staring at me.

"You heard what the lady said, Smiley," I said. "Get out—all of you."

"The police—" He started to mouth the words. "I—Williams—Race Williams, this is a surprise."

Smiley wasn't any cheap hood. He didn't exactly turn pale. For a moment I guess he whitened around the gills, but his color came back at once.

"Imagine you hollering for the cops," I said. "Why, if I started them off on your record they'd be months following it up before they had a chance even to question Mrs. Howe."

Smiley Henderson was standing up straight now. But he favored his right arm a bit. He was strong. He kept himself in good physical shape, but jamming his arm stiff up like that wasn't in his exercises and he felt it. But he held his temper.

Smiley was a dangerous man. I knew that. But Smiley was a smart man, too. And if it came to shooting it out with me Smiley would much prefer to do the shooting into my back.

"You represent the Howe interests?" he said. "Why, that's incredible."

"He represents the college," Ziggie jammed in.

"The college." Smiley jerked his head up higher. "The college. Why, that—that's funny." And he burst out laughing, real laughter, too. No doubt about that.

"Smiley," I said, "I'm representing myself now. Come on—get out, all of you. I don't like guys who manhandle women."

"I gave her a chance," Smiley said. "I was doing what I did for her own good.

She's got that will. Because no one else could have it. I won't wait long for action. I'm at the Date Palms Hotel in Indio, Race. Get in and see me, and talk to Miss Burton. It'll do you good."

I hesitated a moment, then said:

"I have business here first. Sit around and I'll come and see you. A half hour—an hour." And when he moved toward the door, "There's a playmate of yours lying outside in the patio."

"Of course." Smiley nodded without rancor. "That's what I like about you, Race. You're so forthright." He spoke a last word to Ziggie. "You listen to Mr. Williams, Mrs. Howe. You couldn't be in better hands. Good-night."

He was the last to leave, closing the door gently behind him.

The white-haired man with the kind face and the bright dressing gown turned to the girl.

"You didn't tell me, Ziggie. Sit down, Mr. Williams. Really your fame"—his slight smile took the sting out of it—"or your notoriety for giving clients protection is well-known."

"You and Mrs. Howe, then, are good friends?"

"Why, she's my sister-in-law." Addison Howe raised his eyebrows: "She wouldn't lend me a cent if that's what you mean, and she told you how broke I am. But we are in agreement that the present will presents few difficulties. You see, it leaves me twenty-five thousand dollars which I can use, and Mrs.—Ziggie here—a fortune which I am sure she will learn how to use, or at least how to spend."

"Then," I asked, "neither one of you

would be anxious to have the lost will found?"

"The alleged lost will," Addison Howe corrected me. "Ziggie could hardly profit by such a document, and I... Well, it is bandied around among the ever multiplying legal talent that my brother was not entirely satisfied that I wasn't simply a wastrel."

"You mean your brother rang up his lawyer about changing the will, and directed them to cut you off with a dollar."

"Yes." He smiled. "That is indisputable, I believe."

"But they never drew up that will—his lawyers?"

"Oh, yes they did, but my brother never signed it. As a matter of fact, he called them back and told them to tear it up. But I presume you are familiar with that."

I was. I knew all the details.

"But," I said, "right after that your brother made a will himself. Was he still displeased with you, and did he make it after having a row with his wife?"

"You didn't know my brother, Mr. Williams. He never permitted such a thing as a row. The servants heard loud and insistent talk on my brother's part while his wife, Ziggie, was in the room with him. Miss Burton, the nurse, makes them loud and bitter sounds. But Miss Burton has not put that in an affidavit yet. She is an opportunist, Mr. Williams. I don't know if you go in for bribery, but there is a thought."

"But she saw your brother draw up a will."

"She says she watched him write it."

"Then you deny that he made another will?"

"Why, no. He told the servants it was a will. Malcom, who had been with him years, was one of the witnesses. One could hardly doubt Malcom's word."

"And what do you think became of the will?"

"Oh—" Addison Howe shrugged, and the gesture was artistic more than theatrical. "He no doubt destroyed it, as he had his lawyers destroy the other one."

"Addison." Ziggie came over and sat on the arm of his chair and ran long slender fingers through his hair. "Mr. Williams represents the college."

"I know," Addison Howe said simply. "He amused us greatly tonight, and besides, he is entitled to any information he wants. Let's make it easy for him. Isn't that your idea about the will, Ziggie?"

"I am not interested," Ziggie said. "My husband adored me. One will or another he would have taken care of me."

"There." Addison looked up at me. "You see now both parties who would find a new will perhaps inconvenient."

"And," I said, "who realize the seriousness of concealing or destroying a will."

"Quite." Addison nodded. "I wouldn't think of such a thing. I am afraid it is a most difficult problem." He turned to the girl. "Tell me, Ziggie—it has been such an exciting and charming evening—where did you meet up with Mr. Williams?"

She shrugged.

"At the bus station. Miss Burton was to meet me there. I wanted to talk to her. She was to be waiting in my car. But she wasn't and Mack was missing from behind the wheel and—well, Mr. Williams had been kind to me on the bus—recognized me, of course. He wanted to talk to the nurse also, and to you, so I drove him out here."

"He recognized you twice, didn't he?" Addison grinned. "Mack, my dear, was drunk again. He telephoned that the car had been stolen and that he had been lured—yes, I believe his word was lured—into one of the card rooms in Indio. Imagine, Mr. Williams. Open and legal card rooms in Indio. Like an old-time Western thriller, isn't it?"

"Who is this cousin that Henderson and his lawyer represent?" I asked. "What's to that?"

"I wouldn't know." Addison frowned. "The lawyer seemed a rugged individual, or perhaps just an individual. I don't recall the cousin, but then one wouldn't. They don't say it, understand, they don't even hint it, but I gather that my brother might have written her that he was leaving her money. Else why their interest. Certainly the man you called Smiley seems hardly the type who would go around righting wrongs and spending money without compensation." After a pause, he suggested, "Ziggie, why not—to put it very bluntly—hire Mr. Williams to watch over you?"

"I am already engaged in the case," I said swiftly. "And why would Mrs. Howe need protection?"

"Well"—Addison Howe sat up straighter and became more serious—"maybe I'm seeing too many pictures or reading too much mystery, but this outfit tonight seemed rather as if they might go to extreme measures to extract

information if they really thought Ziggie was hiding the will. Certainly everything seems to center around her. You'd be in on the ground floor, so to speak. She could pay you handsomely. Couldn't you, Ziggie?"

I ignored him. "May I borrow your car, Mrs. Howe?" I said to Ziggie. "I want to drive in and talk with the troupe who were out here. I'll return the car, send it back in the morning."

"But you'll stay here?" She came over, put both her hands on my shoulders, and looked up at me. "You find out things. You ask questions. In the night maybe you search the house and the grounds. And I get the protection free of charge. For if you are here and I need you, then you have to protect. Is it not so?"

"I'll see," I told her. "I'll come back anyway."

"You'll be back in a couple of hours—maybe less. Take the convertible. I show you."

CHAPTER 5

WHY SHOULD SHE DIE?

HOWE CAME TO his feet protesting. "No—no," he said quickly. "I have the key to the car. And I give better directions. Besides, Ziggie, you would be apt to ride in with him, and that he would not want." He glanced at me. "A child of Nature, isn't she?"

Addison talked on as, holding the flash in his hand, he led me to the garage, the door of which was open.

CARROLL JOHN DALY

"We lock nothing in the desert," he explained and chuckled. "No one does. It is so safe. Nothing but Ziggie's life is in danger. I think you should watch over her."

"She is fond of you—you are fond of her," I said.

"Of course." He rattled on. "I was surprised at my brother's marriage, but I said nothing to him. Somehow one never said anything to Bertram. He was that way. In my silent way I scoffed and sneered at the marriage. She hates me for it. If she had five million dollars and I was starving she would not help me. Odd people here tonight... Take care of yourself."

Just before I drove away, he said:

"Rather fun, isn't it, the envy and greed and hopes of men, the vicissitudes of life. I could make a few thousand dollars in a morning, not so far back, but the touch, you know, the divine spark—it burnt out suddenly. Just like that. I couldn't make a nickel with my brush now. Though I did paint the chairs in the kitchen. Good luck—not a nickel from her, not a nickel from painting. Well—well... Fun, isn't it? Rather."

I was gone then. Following the direction he had given me. The car was a honey, a long, low-hung job with all the trimmings.

I had time to think going into town. It was clear now how Ziggie had fixed it with the cop. Naturally she had been driving her own car, and since she lived on the desert part of the year and was big money she was known.

As for me, I had been told I would meet the nurse, Miss Burton, in Indio. She might be late. She might even get on the same bus I was on, but I was not to try and identify her. There might be people who wouldn't want me to meet the nurse. Or she might have changed her mind and wouldn't bother meeting me. The change of mind, I understood, meant she might have been bought over.

So Ziggie was the widow of the multi-millionaire, Bertram C. Howe. I had heard something about the widow, but only in a general manner. Bertram Howe had married her abroad a few years back either before we entered the war or in the early part of it.

That she was much younger than he was, I knew, but I hadn't thought she would be that much younger. The lawyer for the college had said she was old enough to want the money, and young enough perhaps not to deserve to get it.

"Rather fun," Addison Howe had said. And hanged if he hadn't seemed to mean it. A great painter a few years back—less than that even—his work always in demand, his price—well, he had practically named his own figure.

That Ziggie Howe needed protection there seemed little doubt. Witness Ruby Klegg, the careful, sure Ruby Klegg down on the desert. Ruby had come a long way down the ladder, yet I think he had scraped up enough money to hang on to the Terrace Hotel.

And Smiley Henderson. Where did he fit in? The only answer I could get to that was that by chance he had heard that Bertram Howe was leaving his money to his distant cousin. So Smiley had got hold of the cousin, and no doubt there was an agreement that she would give him half or maybe even more of the money.

Where could Smiley have heard that? Through the nurse most likely. He must have been pretty sure. Look at the broken-down lawyer he had hired. For despite what the brother and wife thought about the unknown cousin, a dying man might in sudden anger as a vicious gesture of his hate and disapproval leave all his money to this unknown cousin. Or to the college, for that matter. Perhaps the college thought so, too.

I asked myself, was Ziggie capable of hiding or destroying a will? I didn't have to think over the answer. She certainly was.

Was the nurse capable of hiding the will?

Well, she'd had the chance. And if she could make a nice piece of change out of finding it, I guess she would. She wouldn't destroy it. I don't think any woman would destroy it, not even Ziggie. Women generally keep things like that well-hidden, of course, but with an unexplained, perhaps subconscious feeling that it is an ace in the hole if things go wrong.

THEN I WAS in Indio. There was plenty of space for me to park the car. I swung up the steps and entered the almost deserted lobby of the Royal Date Palm Hotel. Not a bad little place. I say almost deserted, for Smiley came out of a seat and met me before I was half-way across the lobby.

"Glad you made it, Williams." He lifted my hand, shook it, then put it back at my side where he found it. "We know all about each other to begin with. You take an innocent job of hunting a lost will and come across me. Then you try to connect this up with pinballs and horse-racing or some big city racket. You see danger to Mrs. Howe. But I want exactly what you want and nothing more. I want that missing mill. This is no place to talk, though. Come up to my room." When I hesitated, he laughed. "Good glory, Race, you're not afraid?"

"I wouldn't be afraid of you any place, Smiley," I told him, and followed him up the stairs, down a corridor and, of all places, into the bridal suite.

"Look it over, fellow." He clapped me on the back. "I may have to bring the little cousin on here. Want to treat her right. Sit down. You think maybe I wanted to get tough with Mrs. Howe. Well, I did. But not any tougher than the police will get, and I won't put her in jail for five years at the end of it. Sure, I'd have scared the devil out of her to get that will." He grinned. "And so would you. If there was enough dough in it for you."

"How much dough is there in it for you?" I asked.

"Plenty." He threw back his head and laughed. "I'm not posing as a philanthropist, Race. This little cousin lady has signed up a good tight agreement with me. It wasn't drawn up by that Riverside lawyer I picked up either. He simply makes things look legal. We find the will. It's in my client's favor, so she gets the money. No legal tangle there."

"You feel pretty sure she gets the money. Why? And why do you want to talk to me?"

"I only play sure things," he said. "How do I know? That's my business." He frowned then. "It's like this, Race. I don't know what arrangement you have with that college. But they can't afford to pay you much if they don't collect. Now you come down here—and show up nice and friendly with Mrs. Howe. The college hasn't much dough. I'm not blaming you, boy. Mrs. Howe will have plenty if the missing will is never found. You might arrange that it is never found. You might even find a witness who saw Howe tear it up, who even heard him say he was making a new will giving Mrs. Howe everything. Then my client or anyone else can't show intent upon the part of the dead Bertram Howe when the will isn't found."

"You think I'd commit perjury?"

"With over a million involved? Don't kid me, boy."

"So you think I might switch clients and fix the nurse?"

"I've got a statement from the nurse," he said emphatically. "But she's a smart woman. I can pay only if the will is found. Mrs. Howe can pay if the will isn't found. I don't think the nurse has the will. I do think that Mrs. Howe has it. Still has it. She was the only one who could get it."

"Couldn't Howe have got out of bed and hid it away himself?"

"Sure he could. He was up and around until the night he died. Heart trouble, you know. But his lawyers were out at the estate after he died. They nearly tore the house apart looking for that new will. It's a big house, about four hundred yards from the bungalow the brother uses. The brother was in New York when Howe popped off, so that leaves Addison out. Nothing was burnt in the fireplace, no torn document found in the trash. Nothing to show that Howe tore up the will, everything to show that he kept it. And that she took it."

"And I can see the nurse now?"

"Too bad. Smiley shook his head. "She took the car and went off to see some relatives in Banning, or Beaumont, or some place."

I grinned. "So the only reason you wanted me to come to Indio was to tell me that you suspected me of switching from the college to Mrs. Howe. And you've hidden the nurse so I won't buy her over. Even knowing me you're a bit afraid, or pretending to be, that Mrs. Howe will buy me over if she hasn't done so already. Now what else?"

"Well"—he rubbed at his chin—"I know you won't work for me. But if you're straight, Race, you might pretend to help Mrs. Howe, discover the missing will, and—" He ducked his hand in his pocket and pulled out a roll of bills, dragged a grand note from inside and tossed it on the couch. "That," he said, "is my honesty of purpose. A donation to the common cause of you finding the will and turning it over to the proper people—the lawyers for the estate of the dead Bertram C. Howe."

"Even if it won't favor this cousin?"

"No matter who it favors."

"You must be pretty sure, Smiley."

"I'm certain," he said. "Take it. You'll owe me nothing. Maybe I'll owe you a lot." And when I let the thousand lay there, he said, "Get that will, Race. If it shoots the works or most of the works to this cousin, I'll slip you ten grand."

I SHOOK MY head. Funny that, because I'm not high-minded as a rule. And I certainly did intend to turn that will over to the proper people if I found it.

"Keep it, Smiley," I said stiffly, for I was tempted. "I take one client at a time."

I started to leave him and stopped. "Smiley—" I said. I was just going to tell him, warn him not to shove Ziggie around. But I didn't. It would more than ever convince him that I was going over to her side.

"What?" He waited, and I simply shook my head. "Okay, Race. You're a funny guy with a funny racket. But show up with that will, and I'll slip you a little gift that—" He paused and laughed. "Well, that will put a new wing on the college if you're so noble-minded."

That was all. I left him then. I went downstairs. Certainly it would seem that Smiley Henderson was sincere enough about wanting that lost will. If he killed Ziggie that wouldn't get it for him.

Why did I think he might want to kill Ziggie? Why, because Ruby Klegg had wanted to kill Ziggie and naturally I had connected Ruby and Smiley up together. Certainly it would be far too much of a coincidence to have the two of them mixed up in the same case, with different interests. Yet—

And suddenly it struck me. There was only one will in existence today that was worth a hoot. That was the will in which Ziggie—Mrs. Howe—inherited the entire estate. But if she was dead, who would inherit?

I went straight to the phone booth and called up the lawyer in New York who had hired me.

"Yes, of course I read the will," he said. "No, no. I'm positive that there was nothing in it for the college if Mrs. Howe died."

But he didn't know if the cousin would get it, or who would get it. He didn't even know if Mrs. Howe had the power to will the money or if it was in trust until she died or reached a certain age. Of course he had a copy of the will but it was at his office.

"What?" he said. "Get it this time of night? Impossible!"

"You've got to get it!" I laid it hard on the line. "A human life may depend on it."

I knew that "human" part was corny, but he was half-asleep and it sounded melodramatic and it did have an effect on him. He arranged to get in touch with one of his clerks in New York. He lived in White Plains himself. And if I would call back he would let me know.

I told him I would call him in an hour or so, and hung up just as he was getting wider awake and asking how the interest of the college was developing.

CHAPTER 6

FROM DESERT DARKNESS

SURE I HAD a lot of things to think about on the way back to the Howe ranch. But I didn't think about them. I like things to develop and then do my thinking and my action right on the spot when they turn up.

I recalled Addison Howe's paintings. None of this arty stuff. His simple desert scenes. What color! He must have made a fortune. In all the national magazines—double page spreads too and often paid for by some big advertiser. They said he could name his own figure.

And now—well, he had burned himself out. That was the verdict I had heard. But he had been tops in his profession. When I hear of an artist and remember his work he has to be good. I don't go in for art.

I swung off Jackson Avenue, did the correct turn, and was coming down the narrow but paved road that the Howe estate faced. Then I made a mistake. I turned in too soon. I knew as soon as I hit the softness of the road that I was not on the gravel of the Howe entrance. But I saw the lights of the bungalow ahead and to my right and got an idea.

I switched off the car lights and came to a stop. I was back pretty early. Maybe if I nosed around a bit I'd learn something, perhaps run across that dick Smiley Henderson had along with him.

The stars were still bright. There were thousands of them. But they cast no light, at least no light down on the ground. It was all upstairs. However, the little road was not hard to follow and I went easily along it toward the bungalow. I did see a little better. One's eyes do get accustomed to the darkness, even the desert darkness.

I paused as I neared the bungalow, to get my bearings. I guess I must have been smack in the center of the desert. Mountains all around me and all about the same distance apart excepting those far distant toward Indio. Some of them looked phony. Especially a small one that looked like a piece of scenery. Then those mountains, like a chain, getting higher and higher—distant black things.

Enough of the view. I remembered the French windows and wondered if Ziggie had thought to lock them again. If not, it might be interesting to know what she and Addison Howe talked about, if anything.

It was pitch black there against the bungalow. Little light showed through the thick drapes by the windows. I pressed close, gave a gentle push. The window swung in. A voice reached me, low, inarticulate. I stepped inside and, taking Ziggie's former warning about the cold air, pushed the window closed. It slipped back without a sound.

I edged closer down the room, by the piano.

"Addison, your brother is dead," Ziggie was saying, hardly breathing the words. "I need you so much. I love you so much. He would want you to have me. I am so alone."

"Ziggie, Ziggie," Addison told her, "if it were anyone but you who talked like that—"

"Yes, yes." She ran in on him. "People would say we marry so soon. Look at me, Addison. I served your brother faithfully. I was in a way a creature of his whims. I did make him happy, Addison. You know that. You loved him so, like a brother loves a brother, only in the books."

"Yes," he said.

I looked through the curtains and saw his face. His lips were not smiling now but were tight, and his blue eyes were slightly blurred. Ziggie was standing in front of him, both her hands on his shoulders and her eyes were big and wondrous. Why didn't he just grab her?

"Yes," Addison said again. "You made him happy, Ziggie. Very happy. It was a strange romance for a man like my brother. You saved his life in Paris, and—"

"No, no, that is not so. He saved my life and I belonged to him. He took me and he married me and brought me to America right after my mother died. Look, I am still young. Scarcely twenty-five yet. And I am so alone in this land where your brother's friends did not want me. I am very rich—you are very poor." And suddenly putting those arms around his neck and lifting herself up on her toes until her face was close to him, she said, "Look, Addison, we get married or I will not give you one cent!"

I THOUGHT HE was going to crush her in his arms. He had more will power than I would have had, or would have wanted to have had for that matter. He pushed her away, threw back his head and laughed.

"Ziggie," he said, "you live in such a different world."

She laughed too, shrugged her shoulders.

"It is the way of America," she said. "Money, money, money. But you tell me you are an artist, that you live also in a different world. So we live in that world together. We forget other people, we see alike."

"No." He smiled now. "I do not see spots before my eyes."

"Oh," she said. "Those spots they are of convenience. I will not see them if you do not want it so. You make me as you want me. I have seen life and death that you have never seen, that you can not understand. I was very young in years, but very old in living. I see dead in the streets, dead in the trees, dead hanging from the windows. I see piles of dead. Once I walk in our cellar and there are six bodies there, but not seven. I laugh and shout with joy because the seventh would have been my mother."

She was running on almost furiously now.

"Is it strange then that I am different from other women? The German officer he kiss me and hold me and I scratch at his eyes, and he say it is me or this knife and takes me in his arms. His lips are warm and sickening against my face. Ah, Addison you do not like that. You pale so slightly. But me, I choose the knife but I choose it for him not myself. I stick it in him—once, twice, three times. He dies and I—"

Slender shoulders went up and down with almost indifference.

"I was very, very young and America is not yet at war, and your brother come and he raise the devil because he has much money, and no one is sure and he swears I was with him. I say I belong to him. And so I did."

"As simple as that." Addison spoke half-aloud. "He never told me that. I knew it was bad, Ziggie, but not how bad. You never told me either."

"We forget all that, your brother tell me. So I put it out of my mind, but sometimes at night it is there, and Ziggie does not laugh." She turned suddenly then and left him.

I moved, too, opening the window and passing into the night. What had I learned? I had learned that Ziggie had killed before, but I might have suspected that from the easy way she had shrugged off the killing of Ruby Klegg. And I had learned, too, that there must be thousands of girls—maybe tens of thousands— just like Ziggie, who didn't shrug it off, couldn't shrug it off. And I learned that Ziggie could not only dish it out but that she could take it, had taken it.

Five minutes later I had swung the convertible through the Howe entrance, and came noisily down the driveway. I jumped out of the car and banged along the little porch of the bungalow.

Addison Howe opened the door and let me in.

"You must be half-frozen," he said. "It's down to thirty-eight. It will hit freezing before morning. Dawn is the coldest part of our day. Go over by the fire." He pulled up an easy-chair, sat down in another, lit a pipe, and crossed his legs.

"We are having quite a time, Mr. Williams," he said. "But don't think I resent the interference. Or should I say the interest of these outside parties in my brother's money. It is inconceivable that he would not take care of his wife, Ziggie. He adored her. And as for myself"—he smiled—"I knew he would think of me. I believe he left me this little house, too. I'll be here most of the time now."

"Painting?" I asked.

He looked at me for a moment. Not shrewdly, just as if he weighed the question.

"I'll daub at it," he said then. "I don't care to talk about—my painting. You may understand. Now, Mr. Williams, Malcom is here, and his wife Augusta. They witnessed this will which so many think is lost. Do you wish to question them?"

I shook my head. "I rather imagine that has been gone into. I am paid simply to locate the will. There is no doubt that it was drawn. What do you think became of it, Mr. Howe?"

"I think my brother tore it up. A whim of some kind, and even if he didn't, Ziggie and I wouldn't have to worry."

"Suppose it did turn up?" I asked him. "And suppose he did leave you out of it. Would you contest it? Unsound mind? Undue influence?"

"Nonsense!" He laughed. "I never knew a sounder mind. I never knew a man less likely to be influenced by anyone or anything. I would not contest anything my brother wished. And I am sure Ziggie feels the same."

PERHAPS, I THOUGHT, but I was not sure.

"But your brother and his wife had a row, you know," I reminded.

"I don't know," Addison said firmly. "My brother did not row. He did not permit of argument. He may have been giving Ziggie some advice. He might even have been admonishing her rather loudly."

"But," I objected, "he did intend to

cut you out of his will when he called his lawyers that day."

"He must have had some reason which he may have felt was for my own good." When I sat up and stared at him, for that was a lulu, he went on, "He thought I could paint again if I had to. He may have meant it as an incentive. Poverty, you know. Perhaps he wished to frighten me." Again that kindly smile. "Yet I have always contended that an artist can do better work on caviar and champagne than on beer and pretzels. Then, of course, in fear that he might die suddenly he never signed that will."

He got up abruptly.

"We are going to offer you the living-room here for the night," he said. "It will be warm, and that couch makes a comfortable bed." I guess he noticed my look of surprise. "We have only the two bedrooms and the small room off the kitchen which Malcom and his wife share. My brother's big house is far back. We've closed it up since he died." He crossed to the window. "A lovely place," he went on, pulling back the shades as if he could really see out. "Nearly a hundred acres in dates. Over fifty in spinach, another fifty in carrots. We lost the beans in the early frost. The rest is rough desert land, except for the pool and lawns. He liked to have it that way."

"I may have to use the telephone later," I said. "Long distance."

"It is there on the desk." He waved a hand toward it. "Ziggie, I believe, has retired. She had a trying day I understand. I do not know how you and Ziggie met." And when I said nothing, "Ziggie

is not like other women. The passing of a loved one to her has been more of an everyday happening than a tragedy never to be forgotten. She is not callous, Mr. Williams, though my brother's lawyers think that. They do not understand that in Poland she walked among the dead for days and nights. There were weeks, perhaps months, when the dead were closer companions to her than the living."

"Why are you telling me this?"

"Because I think she may need protection. I don't know from what. But I am sensitive to impending dangers or disasters. I felt it when my brother passed away, though I was in New York. She was devoted to my brother. She thought I disappointed and hurt my brother when I ceased to produce works worthy of my former skill. It is not Ziggie's fault that she feels about me as she does."

I waited but he didn't continue.

"How does she feel about you?" I asked.

"She does not like me, Mr. Williams. I won't say that she hates me, but detest might be the word. Good-night."

Then he too was gone down the little hall.

What did I think of that? Well, what do you think of it? After the act I had just witnessed it stunned me at first. Then I thought that love is close to hate, they say, and what about a woman being scorned? But Ziggie didn't strike me as a woman who would be scorned so quickly, if she wanted something. If she wanted Addison, she would go after him and take a couple of scornings without batting an eye.

There was no bed made up for me. Just the wide couch, a dozen or more pillows that I could toss off on the floor. The fire was still going strong. I looked at my watch.

Not quite twelve o'clock. A lot had happened in three hours.

How long would it take the lawyer back in White Plains to telephone, get his clerk down to the office and then have him read the will to him? All I wanted to know was who inherited if Ziggie died, and if she had the right to will what she got. And that lawyer—you'd think I had got him out of bed at the crack of dawn.

Then I remembered the difference in time. It would be three o'clock in New York. I would wait another half hour and then give him a buzz. Surely an hour and a half would do the trick. You see, I was trying to fit Ruby Klegg into the picture.

I PUT OUT the lights, not knowing if someone could see in from outside and maybe take a pot shot at me. Why? I don't know why. But people had taken pot shots at me before. Surely they would do it again if they thought I had anything to do with depriving them of a few million bucks.

Why not? I'd probably take a pot shot at someone myself.

I half-dozed.

My hand was under a pillow, the gun close to my hand.

It was about a quarter to one when I snapped on the light again and called White Plains. I got my lawyer almost at once.

He had started to read the whole will when I stopped him.

"Just tell me can Ziggie—er—I mean Howe's widow dispose of by will the money her husband left her?"

"Of course not," he said at once. "It's in trust. Mr. Bertram Howe's attorneys, Blake and Blake, a very reputable concern, are trustees."

"Okay," I cut in. "And if Mrs. Howe dies who gets the money?"

"Addison Howe, of course."

I almost dropped the telephone.

CHAPTER 7

CARBON MONOXIDE

ADDISON HOWE INHERITED if Ziggie died. So that was why he didn't think the idea of marriage so hot. Sure he might marry her and chisel some of the dough out of her.

Or he might not marry her and have nothing. Or if she were dead have it all in cash. Cash on the line. Her death would give him a great fortune.

"Take it easy, Race," I said to myself. "Addison Howe is the last person in the world who would kill. And if he did kill her and got the money he would be the first suspect."

I went over to the fire and sat down and started to think it out.

After all, maybe I could fit Ruby Klegg into the picture. Maybe the trouble was that I had never believed in coincidence and it would have been quite a coincidence to find Smiley Henderson and

Ruby Klegg both down in the little town of Indio and each there unknown to the other and for a different purpose.

Smiley Henderson was there to collect most of the money that would come to the cousin if the new will should be found. Ruby Klegg had been there—well he could have been there to kill Ziggie Howe so that Addison Howe would get the money if the present and only will was the legal one.

But Addison Howe would need an alibi. It was a sure thing he would have had one if Ruby Klegg had rubbed out little Ziggie in that big black sedan. Witness the people sitting around his house. A nurse, a racketeer, a New York detective, a bum lawyer and two servants.

Well I'm not a guy to let grass grow under my feet, or carpet either for that matter, so I went straight down the hall looking for Addison Howe's room.

I tapped at the door.

"Come in," he said almost at once.

I opened the door, let my flash slip into the room and got a good break as the panel of light lit on Addison Howe. He was reaching over to turn on the little lamp beside his bed, and he was also slipping something under the pillow.

"Really, Mr. Williams," he said. "Not anything wrong?"

"Not at all."

I went over and sat down on the edge of the bed and looked at his keen sparkling blue eyes, his touseled hair so white, his young face almost boyish.

"Mr. Howe," I said, "you asked me about giving Mrs. Howe protection. Do you still think she needs it? Do you still want me to give it to her? Or would you rather say after something had happened that you tried to get her protection. That I wouldn't take the job."

"Good heavens!" His eyes opened wide. "What good would that do if she were dead?"

"Why do you think she needs protection?"

"Well—" He licked at his lips. "There are those who think she has a later will and they might do anything to obtain it."

"No other reason?"

"What else but money?"

"All right," I told him. "I'll protect Ziggie. And if anything happens to her I'll get the men if it's my last living act."

"Nothing must happen to her," he told me. "You see, that's why she is staying here. That's why I don't want her out of my sight. Nothing can happen to her while she's here with me, near me."

"You mean that gun under your pillow?"

He reddened slightly, then laughed. It was a nice laugh too.

"I guess I'm not very clever, am I, Mr. Williams? Still, I wouldn't have to know much about a gun to stick it against a man's back and fire. But I want the gun to keep anyone from dragging Ziggie away from this house. From me. I can't explain it, Mr. Williams, but I know that nothing will happen to her while she is with me, if people know she is with me. Sounds stupid, doesn't it?"

It did, and it didn't. It sounded to me as if he were trying to keep himself from getting the opportunity of killing her. That he knew he would be blamed for it. Or a strange quirk of mind. A man perhaps trying to prevent himself from committing murder.

"I am rather confused," Addison Howe was saying. "My little world of indifference has been slowly toppling around me. Perhaps I have lived wrong. It is time maybe that I pushed life."

He sat up then, tossed back the bed clothes and stuck his foot out, reached over and lifted a robe from the little chair. Standing up he slowly put it on. He was a fine, handsome man—no mistake about that.

"It is over an hour since I looked into her room," he said. "I want to be sure she is there."

"What would make her leave? Why would she leave?"

"Why does the wind blow?" Then he got down to earth. "Ziggie is unpredictable."

WE WALKED LEISURELY down the few steps to the end of the hall and he carefully opened the door at the right. A cold breeze hit us, and my flash covered the room. The bed was there. It had been slept in, at least mussed up. But the window was wide open. Ziggie was gone. I saw the phone by the side of the bed.

"Outside phone?" I asked.

"Yes," Addison gasped. "You don't think someone telephoned her and lured her out?"

"What do you think?" I demanded harshly.

My thoughts were back on the same line again. Ruby Klegg was a killer—for three million dollars. Smiley Henderson was a killer, for a good deal less. Could the girl have been lured to her death? Addison Howe inherited the money, had me for his alibi. I turned on him sharply but never spoke the words. I swung around, grabbed an old man who had just come in. Addison explained he was the servant Malcom.

"I called after her, Mr. Addison," Malcom was saying, his voice shaking. "I called but she went off in the big car. I watched like you said, but she got away."

I guess I nearly knocked Malcom over in my hurry to get out. They followed me. The convertible was still there. I grinned, or at least set my lips grimly, still had the ignition key in my pocket.

I saw the gun in Addison's hand as he came out the door. I didn't figure what he thought of doing with it. I only figured what he might do with it. I was mad, good and mad. I smacked his wrist with the nose of my gun, knocking his to the ground. Then I rushed to the convertible.

"Don't leave this house, Addison Howe!" I hollered back over my shoulder. "I know—" I cut that line short and was in the car.

Out the gate and turning north toward Indio. Where else could she have gone? Who would have telephoned her? Why? Something about the missing will. Then she didn't have it. Or did she have it and did someone put the bee on her and make her believe he knew she had it, and would make a financial deal with her to produce it?

Who? Smiley Henderson? Or the nurse, Miss Burton?

Maybe the nurse had the will and was willing to sell it. Well, that would be just a question of money. But Smiley would kill to get what he wanted. I had been a fool to sit there with Addison.

So I rolled north, turned right, then left, and was on the straightaway into Indio.

I got a break. I was simply watching the road ahead for a speeding car. I wasn't looking to left or right, but there was a slight curve to the road, not one you would notice, but my headlights for an instant shot off the road. I saw it, and put the brakes on slowly.

A black object had loomed up off the road. It was the big Lincoln in which we had carried Ruby Klegg's body.

I didn't know if she had run off the road there by accident or with a flat, but I hoped she had. Mostly, I thought this was the rendezvous.

I didn't like the sand at the side of the road. I didn't want to get stuck. I drove a bit farther, saw a side road, at least a place where a car could turn. I swung into it, clicked off the lights, pulled on the brake and hopped out of the car.

Cold and silent, and then it wasn't silent any more. From somewhere, far distant, came the cry of coyotes. Then not too far distant, more cries.

I went straight back toward the big black limousine. Not in the center of the road but stumbling along in the soft sand at the side. I could see a little better now in the endless vastness. To the east through a grove of date palms I thought I caught a glimpse of a rising moon.

Was the girl still in the car? Had she run off the road on purpose? Was that the date garden to my right, the one in which we buried Ruby Klegg? Had anyone telephoned her, after all? Had she come out of her own accord, come out to—I gulped—dig up the body of Ruby Klegg?

But why? To get the will, perhaps. The will Ruby might have carried in his pocket. But she knew he didn't have it. She had heard as I heard Ruby Klegg's demand for that will when he threatened her with the knife.

No, Ruby didn't have any will in his pocket because—

I stopped dead on the road, listening and thinking. Listening for the sound of a shovel in soft dirt maybe. And thinking that Ruby Klegg might have had the will in his pocket but hadn't known it. He couldn't have known it because the will was put in his pocket after he was dead. Put there because the one who had it was afraid I would get it. I hadn't searched Ziggie, but she couldn't be sure I wouldn't. And she couldn't—wouldn't—have that will found on her. So in fear and panic she had—

I STOPPED THAT line of thought. Fear was hardly a part of Ziggie's make-up, and panic with her was out of the question. No, if she had put that will in Ruby's pocket she had done it deliberately and carefully.

Yet how easy it would have been to do it. Open the car door and let the body roll out on the road. Hoping perhaps that she would reach that body before anyone else would, maybe even planning in that shrewd, clever mind of hers the burying of the dead man and later, like this now, digging up the body.

Or maybe she had kept that will on her. Maybe she had waited to be sure I wouldn't search Ruby, and had slipped that will in his pocket just before I buried him.

I didn't find the car right away. I couldn't see it. Then I heard it. At least I heard some car. A low, purring rhythm as if the engine idled. I pulled out my gun, crouched low, and moved toward that sound, finally pushing my way through a clump of tamarac trees and almost bumping into the big car.

Edging along the side I reached the driver's seat. Was the girl behind the wheel, getting ready to back out? No shadowy figure was there. My gun half-raised, I chanced a single ribbon of light from my flash. The front of the car was empty.

I walked carefully around the car in the dark. I tripped, caught at the rear tire. It was flat. I flashed on my light—a second was enough. The next moment I held the flash lit, swung back to the car, tore open the rear door.

What I had seen on the back of that car was a hose attached to the exhaust, and that hose was wound up and through the rear window of the car which was a little open at the top. Even as I swung open that door I saw the newspaper that had been shoved in the top of the window, hard around the hose, keeping out the cold desert air.

Ziggie was there. She lay on the floor. There was a bruise across her forehead. She was gagged, and bound. Instantly, I had her out of that car and lying on the hard powdered earth. She didn't move. I tore the gag from her mouth. I knew she was alive—not conscious, but alive. And conscious or unconscious Ziggie fought to live. She had gone through too much in life to die now, I guess. She drew in air, drew at it until she choked on it.

There were thick pads about her wrists under the rope that bound them, and the same about her ankles. A nice little attention on the murderer's part, I thought. No scars to mar her beautiful young body, except the single bruise on her forehead.

Ziggie spoke.

"Race—Race Williams." I hadn't spoken, and I don't think the flash had shone upon my face. "I prayed—" A funny little laugh then. "Yes, I prayed you'd come. I knew you'd come. You're different, you know. Other people don't give a care about Ziggie."

"Tell me," I said, "exactly how it happened."

"A woman telephoned, said she was the nurse, Burton. She wanted to talk to me about the will." Ziggie hesitated, drew in her breath, then said, "She said she had information. She hinted would I buy it, and I hinted I might."

"She told you to come here?"

"Yes," she said. "I'm a bit dazed. The bump, you know. He hit me on the head, said he would tie me up so he wouldn't leave any marks on my wrists or ankles. Then he would come back and remove the ropes when I was dead. He said the bump on my head would look as if it hit the wheel when I went off the road. Yes, he would remove the hose and close the window. I went off the road. Things are clearer now."

Something jabbed hard against my back as I knelt upon the ground:

"The little lady has had a rough time, Mr. Race Williams," a cold voice said. "Let me tell you about it. Stand up. Drop the gun!"

CHAPTER 8

DEAD SHOT WILLIAMS

QUITE WELL I know my way around. I knew what I faced. I knew I would be dead in a second. No one would be fool enough to let me live longer with a gun in my hand. So I dropped the gun, half-tossed it a dozen feet from me, to my right.

I was trapped. Trapped like any novice. For I knew that voice. And I knew, too, that I had to die and that the girl had to die. The jig was up for the man with the gun if either one of us lived.

Fool! Sure, I was a fool. The carefully bound hands and feet all should have told me the man would be back, that he wouldn't go far away.

All this went through my mind in an instant, and in that instant that I started to stand up and take lead in the back. Stand up and die. Die without even raising a finger to save myself and the girl. Okay, maybe I would die. Maybe I wouldn't. This man with the gun knew the law of the gun, the law of the night. He knew that when a gun is stuck into your back you obey that gun.

I was only half up when I dived. I dived to the right, my hand reaching for my gun, my body twisting in the air even as I grabbed it. He fired once and missed me, because my body was twisting. He fired again and missed me, because he wasn't satisfied in pounding lead into my body. He knew his business and knew that a bullet in my body might not kill me, and that if I turned and fired I wouldn't miss.

He was shooting for my head and shooting to kill when I turned over and raised my gun. He had the drop on me. There was death before I could squeeze lead. I saw it in his face, saw it in his eyes, in the bright gleam there—the deadly eyes of a killer just before he kills.

We didn't fire together, for I was bringing my hand up and twisting my head when he shot. There was something cold and hard across my throat like a piece of ice, then it was warm, and he didn't fire again.

I closed my finger once. That was all. I saw the tiny hole in the center of his forehead, saw it turn from purple to red and widen slightly. Then he dropped to his knees and fell forward on his face.

I was coming to my feet before I realized the truth. How in that dead blackness I had seen his face, his eyes, the tiny ever-widening hole in his forehead. It was because there was a light on his face and now I saw it plainly. The moon smack through the palms, the moon that my moving body had manipulated into the bit of gun-play. Or maybe I was wrong, and it was simply the moon's own idea.

The girl was on her knees, clutching at my arm now, trying to come to her feet despite the ankles which were still bound. I pulled out my knife, cut her loose. She staggered erect, hung on to me.

"Is he dead?" she asked.

"They don't come any deader," I told her.

I picked up my light, flashed it down on Henderson, cut it off almost at once, not wanting her to see. So it was a shock at first when she said:

"Do we bury him too?"

Then I remembered her past and her present also, as I thought of Ruby Klegg. But I felt of my throat, found that the side of it was wet and slippery. I shook my head at her.

"No, Ziggie," I said. "This corpse is on me. They know he's in Indio. They know I'm in Indio. Someone may have heard the shot."

"No one would hear it out here, or pay any attention to it if they did."

"It doesn't matter, Ziggie."

I pulled my fingers from my throat. They showed red in the moonlight. But then I could hardly expect a guy like Smiley to miss entirely.

"His lawyer will look for him," I said. "His detective will look for him. The police will look for me, but I have a scratch to show self-defense."

I took her arm then, for I had a shock coming for her. But she had snatched the flash from my hand and was looking at my neck, daubing at the wound with a handkerchief.

"It isn't anything," I told her. "I was hired to protect you."

"And you did." Her voice was low. Then she said, "Why do you think this man Henderson wanted to kill me?"

"You don't know?" I asked.

"You do?"

"I think I do, Ziggie. Who gets the money if you die? Who? Do you know?"

"Not him." There was a forced sort of laugh in her voice.

"No," I said. "But the man who hired him to kill you would get the money. Don't you know who inherits, if you die?"

"Why, Addison, of course. What could this man… Why, you think—but you don't even think it!"

"Yes," I said. "Addison Howe gets the money if you die."

I WASN'T PREPARED for the way she would take it. I didn't expect her to faint. But I thought it would crack up the almost easy indifference with which she faced death herself and saw others die. And as I said, I wasn't prepared for the way she did take it.

She laughed. Then she hoisted the flash up into my face. And suddenly she was gone. Just like that she had disappeared in the night.

I started after her. I thought of my car, started that way, and stopped. She couldn't know where the car was. But she could return to the body of Smiley Henderson and remove anything he might have in his clothing. A ghastly job even for a man. I didn't like it myself. Still that didn't mean that Ziggie couldn't do it.

Suppose there was another will, and this one left Addison Howe out of it and Ziggie had it? Suppose Smiley Henderson had got it from her? I know I didn't make sense, but I certainly was going to take a look for that will.

I went through Smiley's pockets. Not a thing. No will. No letters. No document of any kind. Well, I'd get the car, go back to the house, give Ziggie the protection she still needed. I would telephone the police about this corpse. My end of it seemed legal enough, perhaps even noble if you have an open mind.

I stood up. A motor roared, a car ground into gear and I let out with all speed toward the road. The moon helped again. I saw the road plainly.

I made it, too, and was running toward Indio when Ziggie backed out the convertible and turned toward the Howe ranch. It was a simple matter to swing open the door and jump in beside her.

"Ziggie," I said, "you had an extra key to the ignition."

"I have an extra key to all the cars," she said, as we moved along slowly. "I forget so often. I'm sorry I left you like that. But you see I love Addison. I love him beyond life, beyond death—my death or another's. I would kill anyone who would harm him."

"Well," I said, "that may be very true, but it doesn't alter the picture. Take it easy now. Stop the car."

"Why?"

"The big Lincoln, for instance. The shovel we used. It wouldn't still be in the car, would it?"

"But yes," she said. "Will I go and get it?"

"It is a heavy shovel." I smiled. "We'll carry it together."

When we returned to the car, I said:

"Ziggie, I want you to drive me to where we buried Ruby Klegg."

"Who?" And suddenly, "Oh, was that the name?"

"I simply want to be sure it's a good job," I lied easily. "The police may start looking around when I tell them about one body. I just want a look."

"Okay."

She nodded and she put a nice bit of accent on the okay.

She showed no suspicion, no interest any more than a shrug of her shoulders as if she thought I was the nervous type. But she sure knew her way about that desert.

I'd have spent hours, maybe days finding the place in the daytime but she drove me right to the spot in and out among the date palms again.

I made sure it was the right spot. I took both ignition keys, got the shovel out of the car, and started to dig.

"Now, Ziggie," I said, "I want to talk to you like a Dutch uncle while I do this little job."

That was that. I can't say I expected it. I can't say I didn't. But she was out of the car and was gone. I let out one holler after her.

"As you value your life, Ziggie, don't go back to Addison Howe!"

Alone in the ever-brightening desert moonlight I dug. Before, I had been worried I hadn't buried Ruby deep enough; now I was worried that I had buried him too deep.

But the soil was easy-going, and pretty soon, if you'll excuse that expression, I struck pay-dirt.

I won't go into the gruesome details. I didn't like the job any more than you would have; maybe not so much.

I found an envelope. A long manila

CARROLL JOHN DALY

envelope. It was sealed. It was bound around with twine. I opened it. It wasn't the will.

It was something else, something that made me whistle as, crouched down there in that open grave, I read it beneath my small flash.

I made a neat job of putting the dirt back, patted it down, and went toward the car. I felt pretty good. I felt pretty cockey, though why I felt that way I didn't know. In the car I read the document again.

It was short and to the point and written by hand in ink. It read simply:

So that no one else will ever be blamed for it, I herewith state that on the night of March 11, 1945, I, Addison Howe, shot and killed Morris Snead.

Addison Howe

How HAD RUBY Klegg come to have that confession, or rather more simply that statement by Addison Howe, that he had killed a man?

I put the envelope into my pocket. It gave me a comfortable feeling that Addison Howe had killed a man, and that I had something that would make him talk.

Then it gave me an uncomfortable feeling that since Addison Howe had killed before he would kill again—if not a man, a woman.

Had I figured things out? Were they more confused? The answer was yes to both questions. I knew how Ruby Klegg was mixed up with Addison Howe. Somewhere between them was the killing of a man named Morris Snead, and

Ruby Klegg had wanted to be sure he never would be blamed for it.

I thought, too, I knew why Ruby was willing to kill Ziggie for Addison. That little document was worth a lot of money to Ruby Klegg if Addison was rich. It wasn't worth a hoot if Addison didn't get hold of his brother's money.

I stepped on the gas, tried to follow in the ruts as Ziggie had, but took a beating over the mounds most of the time. Then I saw the lights of the bungalow.

I wanted to get back to that house before Addison took a powder.

The door was not locked, and I walked in. The man and the girl broke. I don't know what kind of a clinch it was. But the girl was breathing heavily, which might have been from running back to the bungalow, or from Addison grabbing her by the throat. Or—or—well, from Addison not grabbing her by the throat.

ADDISON HOWE TURNED and looked at me. There was a misty something deep in those blue eyes. He smiled when I said:

"Mr. Howe, I'll have to talk to you alone, after I call the police."

His face never changed when I went to the phone, but Ziggie's did. There was nothing phony about her unless it was "spots before my eyes." Her emotions showed too plainly. She reached the phone before me, jammed the instrument aside.

"You're not going to tell the police that silly thing you told me about Addison!"

"We'll see," I fenced, as I lifted the French phone.

"Leave us alone, Ziggie," Addison

Howe said, and to my surprise she left the room without a word.

I dropped the phone.

"The police will pick up the body of Smiley Henderson," I said to Addison Howe, "then come here to talk to me, Mrs. Howe, and you."

HOWE WALKED OVER and leisurely put a log on the fire, motioned me to a chair, and lit his pipe.

"I take it, Mr. Williams, I am in for a few unpleasant moments. Is it true that Ruby Klegg is dead?" And when I just stared at him, he added, "Ziggie lost her head and then told me everything."

I took a grin.

"I believe she told you everything," I said. "But losing her head, I doubt that."

"I doubt that too. I hate to stoop to subterfuge, selfish subterfuge." He looked at me keenly. "Your attitude toward me tonight before we found Ziggie missing was decidedly suspicious, but uncertain. Now I feel that you are no longer uncertain, have entire command of the situation and peculiarly, too, I do not feel that you are suspicious."

"I am certain that you killed a man called Morris Snead. The police would like to know that."

"Like to know? Then you wish something from me. Am I to understand that for that something you'll pay with silence?"

"I'm not a policeman," I told him. "I'm not hired to look for the slayer of Morris Snead. If the killing was justified, my ethics do not even make it necessary for me to mention it. Tell me about it."

"Ruby Klegg and Smiley Henderson are both dead?"

"Yes."

"May I see the document?"

CHAPTER 9

FINISHED BUSINESS

WITHOUT ANOTHER WORD I took the manila envelope from my pocket and handed it over to Howe. He gazed toward the fire, looked at me, smiled, read the document, then handed it back to me.

"You are not a foolish man or a trusting man, Mr. Williams," he said. "But a man very sure of himself. Now what do you want?"

"First, about this killing of Snead. In detail as to time and place."

"Simple, Mr. Williams. The date you have there—the time about one o'clock in the morning. The place, the Terrace Hotel Apartments, New York City. I kept a suite there for years."

"Klegg's hotel?"

"Yes. I was being blackmailed by Morris Snead. He was a clerk there. I bought some letters back one at a time, until the important one. Then he just showed it to me, took the money and laughed in my face—and kept the letter. One night—I guess it was his laugh, for there must have been some reason. I had a gun and I shot him dead. I took the letter and burned it, just before Ruby Klegg and this Smiley man walked in."

"And then?"

"I had been a guest of the hotel a great

many years. Ruby and his friend Henderson removed the body. I believe, from the evening papers, it was found later in Prospect Park in Brooklyn. Owning the hotel, it was not too difficult for Klegg. In case of trouble for Mr. Klegg or my untimely death, I signed that little paper for him."

"And he in return blackmailed you."

"To the tune of something over one hundred thousand dollars."

"You had that much money?"

"No. My brother helped me out. He knew nothing of the blackmailing." He paused, then said, "So Klegg carried the document with him once too often."

"He always brought it with him when he demanded money from you?"

"Yes, he was quite a psychologist, Mr. Williams. It always made me go to my brother, until my brother would give no longer, and I had nothing more to give."

"So that is why your brother called his lawyers to draw a new will leaving you out of it. Did he know about the blackmail?"

"He thought me a fool, or maybe guessed at the blackmail. I don't know. He quite evidently thought better of it later, and drew the new will."

"Then there is another will." I came to my feet, tapped the folded confession of the killing of Snead. "The police will be here soon," I said. "I want that will—now."

"What makes you think I have the will?"

"I don't think you have, but I think you can get it from Ziggie. I have figured things out pretty fair, Mr. Howe. There wasn't any cousin. That was simply an invention to put Smiley on the scene, to show honesty of purpose. He and Klegg intended to kill Ziggie so you would inherit the money, then they could get it from you with this confession of your killing Morris Snead."

"Oh"—he stretched out his legs—"there is a cousin. But my brother had never even met her. Henderson did locate her, did give her to believe she might get some money, and did have her sign over a share if he got it for her."

"And"—I was thinking—"you and Ziggie pretended not to like each other. That's why you couldn't marry her—because they'd make you chisel the money out of her for them, or kill her anyway." I stopped and then said, puzzled, "But suppose this new will was found and Ziggie was dead, and it went to the college. The college seemed pretty sure about the money."

"The college." He shook his head. "That was another red herring that Klegg and Henderson drew across the path. They had someone anonymously telephone the dean of that college—a grasping, greedy man—and inform him that the will of Bertram Howe left everything to the college. That the nurse could tell things." He shrugged. "It put an honest and interested institution into the search for the will." He smiled now. "It was rather fun, wasn't it? They were shrewd, clever men. I watched their plot develop with considerable interest, until I feared for Ziggie's life. But as you once said, Mr. Williams, you were retained simply to recover the missing will. I—I'll give you the will for that document."

"And bankrupt yourself and Ziggie?"

"I didn't say that." His blue eyes sparkled. "I have some paintings hidden away, and my touch is as sure as ever. But I wouldn't paint just so these blackmailers could have the money from my work. Yes, I'll give you the will in a minute—for that paper."

I GRINNED AT such assurance of promptness.

"Make it thirty seconds and the confession is yours," I said facetiously as I held out the confession to him.

He put his right hand suddenly into the pocket of his dressing gown. When he pulled it out again it held a long white envelope.

"My brother's missing will," he said, and laid it in my hand.

Sure I was stunned. So would you be. I opened the envelope and drew out the will, saw the date, the signature, the names of the three witnesses. He was tossing his confession of killing Morris Snead into the fire when I started to read the will.

I looked up, said suddenly:

"I don't believe you ever killed that man Morris Snead."

"And he didn't." Ziggie came from behind the same curtains by the piano. "It was I who was being blackmailed. Addison didn't know then. I asked Addison to let me use his rooms at the Terrace Hotel. I met this Morris Snead there, gave him ten thousand dollars in cash. He refused me the letter. I saw spots before—"

She stopped and actually broke into a slight ripple of laughter.

"Well, I shot him dead anyway and took the letter. After that it is as Addison says. Klegg and Henderson came, but Addison hid me in the bathroom and they thought he shot Snead. So Addison gave up all the money he had. Gave up all he could borrow from his brother."

"For you?" I cut in.

"No." She shook her head. "For his brother. So his brother would never know. But I didn't know he was paying out money. Addison simply told me that friends helped him hide the body."

"Why didn't you tell her about the money you were paying out?" I asked Addison.

But it was Ziggie who answered.

"Addison was afraid I would tell his brother the truth," she said. "And I did tell him the truth. I told him—yes, I told him I killed Snead. I told him when he rang up his lawyers to make another will cutting Addison out of it because he suspected Addison was being blackmailed for something—spending such great sums of money."

"Did you tell your husband why you killed this man? About your being blackmailed?"

"N-no." She hesitated. "I let him think the blackmail started after I killed him. I said this Snead lured me to his apartment posing as a Federal Agent, that he acted as a German officer did once, and—and—and—" She jerked her head up straight. "Yes, I told him that I saw black spots before my eyes."

I looked at the will again. With the exception of a few small bequests, one to the college, which would just about pay my fee, everything was left to Addison Howe "to take care of my widow as he sees fit, and with the hope that he may find it in his heart to watch over and cherish her as I have cherished her."

"Ziggie," I said, "did your husband think that his brother paid out this blackmail purposely, or that he gave the money to you to pay it?"

"I told him," she said, "that Addison gave all the money, both his own and what his brother gave him, to me to pay it. That Addison knew nothing of the killing. And I led Bertram to believe that the last cent had been paid. That was when he ordered his lawyers to tear up that unsigned will. Then he drew a new one himself."

"I see," I said.

I thought I did see. Bertram Howe didn't want to trust Ziggie with his vast fortune, and he thought his brother would see that she kept free of future trouble, so she would not have the money to squander.

"Where did you get this will?" I asked Addison.

Addison smiled.

"My brother sent it to me the day he died. I guess he felt the attack coming on. He simply put it in an envelope, addressed it and gave it to Malcom to mail. He let Malcom think it was a letter, but swore Malcom to silence about it." He paused, watched Ziggie as I gave her the will and let her read it. Then he said, "Bertram sent me a letter with the will, elaborating upon the peculiar wording of the will, about watching over and cherishing Ziggie."

"He meant for us to get—" Ziggie started and stopped.

Addison went on speaking.

"You see, of course, Mr. Williams, the incredible, yet slightly humorous position I was in. Both Klegg and Henderson knew what was in the will. The nurse, Miss Burton, had told Henderson—no doubt for a handsome price. But neither Henderson nor Klegg nor the nurse knew that I had the will. They were sure Ziggie had it, and later must have determined that Ziggie had destroyed it.

"What was I to do? If I produced the will they would take everything away from me, and so from Ziggie too. I hadn't thought of them killing Ziggie, because I was the only one who would have a motive, and I would hardly give them any money to keep quiet about my killing one man who was a blackguard and a thief while being tried for killing a young and charming widow.

"But last night when they were all here but Klegg, when Henderson seemed to be building up such an elaborate alibi for me, I was afraid. A short while ago Ziggie told me that Klegg was dead, had died while brutally attempting to murder her, and that Henderson, much the shrewder of the two, had made an elaborate attempt to kill her and make it appear suicide. You see the predicament I was in before that. Yet I dared not produce that will."

"Without paying Henderson and Klegg everything or going to jail for murder?" I said.

"No. No." He was very thoughtful. "There was no danger of my going to jail for murder. I knew Ziggie too well for that. If the showdown came she would tell the truth just as she told you the truth now. That was my real predicament."

"And," I said, "what was the blackmail in the beginning? What did Snead have on Ziggie?"

Addison Howe sat up rather straight.

"Really, Mr. Williams, I don't know. Ziggie didn't tell me and quite frankly, I never thought to ask her."

It jarred me all right. Not the words in themselves, but the fact that I believed him.

"Okay, Mr. Howe," I said simply. "Give me the key to the main house."

"What for?" He was surprised.

"Why, the police will be here. I'll want to earn my fee from the college, give the police the missing will I found hidden away in Bertram Howe's library, if he has a library. Surely you don't expect to confuse the police with such a complicated story as yours, especially since you have gone to such lengths to conceal it."

Addison Howe remained seated before the fire, and it was Ziggie who got the key and took me up to the main house. It was early morning now, but the moon was a crescent-shaped bit of brilliance.

"The letter Bertram wrote Addison," she said. "I guess it was that he would like Addison to marry me." She paused and when I said nothing, she murmured, "I would like that too."

"So would Addison." I gave her encouragement.

"Yes," she said. "I love him so much. I tried to tell him when I used to go to New York and pose for him in his studio at the Terrace Hotel. I couldn't tell him. I tried to hint at it in letters I wrote. I wanted him to know. I thought maybe if he loved me, we should tell Bertram."

"Why do you tell me this?"

"Oh, unfinished business is so unsatisfactory. Maybe I want advice from you. Maybe I want you to say 'Go ahead, Ziggie, find happiness at last.' I admired Bertram. I was devoted to him. But I didn't know what love was until—well, Addison."

"Yes?" I waited.

"I was living a lie with Bertram. Addison seemed so dense when I hinted around things, so I wrote Addison a letter, a long letter. I said so clearly in it 'I love you—I love you. Tell me what to do. Shall I tell Bertram?' "

"So!" I whistled. "That was the letter then, that you killed Snead to get. What did Addison think of it?"

"He never saw it," she told me. "Morris Snead was the night clerk. He saw more in my eyes when I visited Addison than Addison or Bertram ever saw there. He stole the letter from the mail. He told me about it and I paid what I could, and then I killed him."

There was a long pause.

"So there it is," she said. "Am I worthy? Should I—can I marry Addison?"

"No spots before your eyes?" I grinned.

"No." There was no laughter in her voice.

"Sure, kid," I said. "Marry him, make him happy."

She threw her arms around me then and kissed me. At that I thought maybe I had given Addison more of a break than I gave Ziggie.

I'll Feel Better When You're Dead

CHAPTER 1

ROUGH ON RATS

IT WAS A joint. It was a cheap dive with a shabby door about fifteen feet down from the entrance to the saloon. It said "Crescent Hotel," and under that "Entrance" with the "r" missing. You walked up one flight, and the hotel itself was above the bar. It was the Crescent Bar, I suppose, but it didn't say anything over the door. And the windows were blacked out with dirt and curtains. Even being modern you couldn't call it a tavern let alone a cocktail bar. It was simply a dive.

The minute I looked at it I thought Riley had given me a bad steer. This was no place to hide out a young girl of wealth and what passes for education in our best girls' school. The first time one of the customers got a look at her or she opened her mouth and hollered through the papier-mâché walls, the police would swarm down on the dump.

What difference did it make if her old man was in no position to put up a holler. The young girl was, and would as soon as she got the chance. And too many people, no matter how shady or shabby or how fearful of the police, have their pet hates and would drop a nickel in a slot and phone the cops to make trouble for someone. At least, people who lived in the Crescent Hotel would.

The barroom was dark and dirty. There were no booths, but a back room with tables in it and a dull light that made the dismal bar seem bright in comparison. The bartender wasn't too clean himself. He wore what might pass for a white coat on a particularly dark night, with a little fog thrown in to sustain the illusion. He was not a sociable guy and he took my order for a bottle of beer as a personal outrage. I wouldn't drink anything in that place that wasn't hermetically sealed and opened in front of me.

I TOOK THE bottle of beer he slid along the unpolished mahogany with my own handkerchief, though I'm anything but particular, and called the bartender's attention to the fact that he was a dime short on the change. Then started in to talk to him a little.

I talked about women. I talked about girls. I talked about one particular girl who might be a stranger to the Crescent Hotel, and when he stiffened up from his former indifference, I took another bottle of beer, counted the change carefully from a five spot and told him to keep the four seventy-five.

He looked nasty about that but he pocketed the dough.

He waited on another customer then—a flashy bit of clothes, a hood's idea of a perfect gent. Then he came back to me.

"What sort of a girl would it be?" he asked. "One you like?"

"One," I grinned, "who might like me."

"Do girls like you?" He tossed a sneer up under my slouch hat.

"Do bartenders?" I asked, and slid a hundred-dollar-bill over the bar. And as his stubby yellow fingers grasped it greedily I told him, "It's not for keeps—unless I locate this girl."

"And how," he raised beery eyes to mine, "do you think you could get that century back from me."

"I could try." I smiled pleasantly.

"For your sake," he leaned on the bar now, "I hope you won't want to."

"Good." I nodded. "Now about this girl."

"What did she look like?"

"No, no." I wagged a finger at him. "I paid the money. I ask the questions and get the answers." But he was walking away from me again to the lad who fancied himself as tough up at the end of the bar. After a while the bartender came back, leaned on the bar and looked at me—or as much of my face as he could see.

"You look slightly familiar," he said.

I smiled and tried, "That is almost an insult. Do I look like a guy who'd drink in a dirty dump like this—for pleasure I mean?"

That jarred him a bit. Maybe it should. I had paid a hundred bucks and been mighty pleasant—now I wasn't. I wanted to jar him, and I wanted to confuse him, and I turned my head away from him long enough to let him nod up toward the end of the bar.

You see I wasn't sure. It seemed like a

bum set up. No place, as I said, to take a high class girl and hide her out. Yet Riley had told me she was there. I had burrowed into the subway and taken myself downtown under the shadow of the bridge. Riley wasn't one to give me a bum steer.

Besides which, if I could put Judson Masters' daughter back in his house without letting the police or the newspapers in on the stunt, why there would be ten grand in it for me, according to Riley. So far there wasn't a cent. I had even laid out one hundred and four dollars and seventy-five cents. The beer I didn't count. It wasn't too bad. Things were slow and it is quite possible that I would have had a couple of bottles some place anyway.

The bartender twisted up his face, shot it forward, put a hand over the bar as if to grab my tie, but didn't. He said instead, picking up the conversation where I left off, "It's not too clean. That's because I often got to wipe up the place with guys like you." And with a laugh, "Do you know what I'm going to do with that hundred?"

"Get a clean apron?" I asked, and then before he could bust a blood vessel, "Fellow," I said, "You tip me off about this dame and I walk out with her—and I'll match that century note for you like that."

He smacked his lips hard together and looked toward the door. I followed his look this time. The broad-shouldered guy was standing by the door half looking at its worn grimy surface, half looking back at me.

I was getting what I wanted to get— and getting it before any phone calls could be made and big-time talent brought into play. Maybe I was even getting a little more than I wanted. If the girl was there they would never let me leave that bar until she was removed—maybe not even then. Guys who played these sort of games play them rough.

THE LAD AT the door gave me the tip off. He started to move slowly down the filthy floor toward me. Other feet moved too. A shadow was coming from the back room, another just behind it. A fourth man had opened and shut a door I couldn't see, and was walking from some place across from the bar toward me.

I knew their kind. Small time gangsters and rats. I was alone. The guy at the bar should have been enough, especially if the bartender was playing ball with him. Not these mugs. They run in packs like wolves. Their boss knew his stuff when he worked them together. One of them alone wouldn't have the nerve to take the proverbial candy from a baby unless he had a pal to hold a gun at the baby's chest.

The truth is that I wanted action and it looked like I was going to get it. The feel of the revolver in my right hand coat pocket was good. I fisted the butt, and slipped my finger inside the trigger guard.

I let them come and waited. As the four converged I turned.

"Hello, boys. What will you have?" I said to them. And to the bartender: "Okay, dirty apron, give the lads anything they want not to exceed twenty-five cents."

"You might," and this lad who came toward me was a little slicker than the others, "give us a girl who's worth two Cs to discover. Come on, smart guy." The man had a scar on his face. He took me by the shoulder and swung me around to face the semicircle of four. I nearly cracked him then, but I didn't. I wasn't in this to start a barroom brawl. I was out to find a girl, worth exactly ten thousand dollars in cash to me. When things broke I wanted them to break hard and sudden and deadly.

So this was the leader. Or was he? I fancied the smaller one who stood back a bit in the shadows. He was stocky with a wise face, and was older, and had been long in the business. My friend who had been at the end of the bar and another member of the party were a bit on the young side and went in for making tough faces and keeping them that way. You know, like at a children's party.

The one that swung me, I'd say, was an up and coming boy. He was doing the talking now, though the stocky guy seemed to be directing the show. So this lad with the scar said to the bartender:

"A bottle of gin, Fred." And taking the bottle the bartender handed over to him he smashed it across the bar leaving the neck of the broken bottle in his hand.

"Now, friend." He looked at me. "Who sent you? I'll count five—then I'll scrape this bit of glass down your face. Come on. Talk."

I said, "Aren't you moving a little fast. I mightn't like that."

The stocky lad said:

"Scratch him up, Pinkus. He'll talk afterwards." And pulling out a gun he stepped up close to my right side which was near the bar and nodding at me he spat. "Move and I'll plug you. Okay, Pinkus, let him have it."

And Pinkus shot up his right hand with the jagged glass and started it swiftly down toward my face. I had no choice. I closed my finger in my right hand jacket pocket and squeezed out some lead. Pinkus was pretty close to me when I fired. I use a forty-five caliber revolver— and naturally it tore a hole in his chest you could have hidden the gin bottle. It picked him up and tossed him back, and laid him out as cold and neat as if he had paid spot cash to a high-priced under-taker.

Surprised? Of course they were surprised. Three heads turned and watched Pinkus do his act. I turned too, but not to watch Pinkus. I had him placed all right. I swung and grabbed the wrist of the stocky leader with my left hand, lifted my right one out of my pocket and brought the gun down hard on his head. I hit him with the nose, not the butt. I knew the butt is the polite way of doing it, but if you ever had a slug run up your sleeve from that bit of horse play you'd use the nose too. What's more, I pressed the trigger as I crashed the runt. I thought it might carry a little more drama to it if the others thought I had killed him too.

I turned to cover the other two before they could jump me. There they stood. No guns in their hands. No threatening looks on their faces, nothing but stunned horror. If I waited for them to recover from their surprise I'd be there all night. From the pans on the two of them you'd think surprise had set in permanently.

There wasn't much trouble after that. The two boys lined up for me and stuck their hands in the air and the bartender came around to join them when I stopped him; pushed my gun against his fat stomach and said:

"Well, do I take it off your dead body?"

I never got a hundred dollar bill back so fast before. Then I talked to them nice and kindly about leading me to the girl, since I knew she was there or they wouldn't have put on the heavy villain act.

"But—but—" One of the boys with the surprised pans stammered. "But suppose there isn't any girl. I don't know of any."

"Don't be a sap, Harry," the bartender jammed in then. "You see what he done. I don't know the racket, but I know there was a dame brought in here. Take him to her, or I'll take him." And being made of sterner stuff than the two kid punks, "Do I get those two 'Cs,' mister?"

The crack was so good and so much in line that I took a laugh. What's more, if the amount had been a couple of bucks or even a five I might have given it to him. But as it was all he got was the laugh. Maybe he could cash in on it when he was old and living with his memories, if he ever did get old.

He did me a good turn at that. The other two were simply youths with distorted ideas. Kids that had grown up with vicious associates and made to think decency was found only in the dictionary, and that only suckers worked. Even though it might be a good thing for the community, I never liked to plug kids.

So we paraded across that floor, the bartender in advance, the two young punks right behind him and me bringing up the rear. The bartender opened a door across the room, and we started into the dimness beyond. I said simply:

"All set, boys. Lead me to the girl. The first false move is the last move of any kind."

We all went up three steps, turned into the hall of the hotel which had a little more light, and then up the stairs. They creaked and they groaned but we moved right along, passed what might have been an office behind a partly closed door at the top of the flight, straight down another dim hall; a right turn, a shorter hall, and halted before a door numbered 112.

The bartender tapped. There were guttural inarticulate sounds from inside and the bartender said:

"None of your lip, Gertie. Open up." And when foul words came through the door the bartender said in a tired sort of voice, "Pinkus is dead and Granger's dead. Sure. I'm supposed not to know, but open up."

More argument from within, and I said:

"Boys. Boys. Things are going too slow."

The leader of the two young hoods spoke up fast and his words were obscene but effective. The door opened and we paraded in. The woman who stood by the door was a big rawboned creature and if the way you live is written on your face you could have taken a microscope and checked up on her life by hours and minutes—maybe seconds even if you had the patience. The woman was talking, and I said:

"You boys line up against the wall and reach—and stay that way. Now where's the girl?"

THE WOMAN LOOKED at me belligerently.

She put her hands on her hips and opened her thick lipped mouth, but it was the bartender who spoke.

"He shot Pinkus and Granger dead—just like that. Better produce."

The woman turned on me, but I sized her up and she never quite got going. I knew her type and how to talk to her. I knew she was used to men who gave her a bat on the head if they were big enough to do it and get away with it. So I flipped out a gun, knocked her chin up none too gently, stared into her hard colorless eyes.

"If we have to look further we'll leave you here dead on the floor," I said. "Give, sister."

She gave, caved in. Not like the men had. Not through fear of death but through long association with men. She simply changed her character.

She bent slightly and rubbed her hands together and started to sniffle and mutter.

"Why yes, sir. She's quite all right, poor dear. I was taking charge of her so no harm would come to her. But she got crying like, and noisy, and I put her in the closet there for fear she'd attract those who would have harmed her."

She turned the key in the closet almost at her elbow and pulled open the door and a little bundle rolled out. I saw only the tip of small feet in tiny black pumps.

I leaned down and pulled off the cloak that covered her. It was a nice bit of blue with a fur collar. She was trussed up all right. Her hands and feet were bound and a rope was tied from her neck to her feet to keep her in that bent position. I wondered if her back was broken. But it couldn't be. She must have been leaning against the door to roll out like that.

The woman shrunk away from me. I guess I looked that bad.

"I tried to untie the knots but my hands aren't steady," she whimpered. "I did it for her own good. I—I—"

"Okay, dirty apron." I tossed the nose of my gun toward the bartender. "Get those ropes off her. Got a knife?"

He had and he did. If his hands shook I didn't notice them. He seemed startled when he first saw the way the girl was tied and I doubted if he was in on the show. Me—I was wondering how I'd get her out of there. I didn't want to drag in the cops and lose my ten grand. And the girl would hardly be able to walk if she had been tied up like a bundle of dirty wash very long. Well, clean wash, now that I saw her better.

The ropes were off, and the girl was up—straight up on her feet. She tore loose the dirty rag that was wound tightly across her mouth. I saw her chest sink and heard the air whistle into her lungs. Her clothes and her hair were rumpled, and she gave herself a couple of twists and her head a few shakes. And suddenly she looked like a movie heroine after she has been dragged through horror after horror and the camera takes a close up.

Her face was fine—the side of it that I could see now—and sharply defined with the jet black straight hair neatly in place as if she had combed it for hours. She was small and wiry and supple, and every movement was as natural as a highly trained dancer's. The muscles of her legs stood out like a dancer's too.

She looked all those faces over before she turned to me. Then she put those black eyes on me, steady and piercing and bright, terribly bright.

"Someone killed?" she asked very slowly and then, "But why would anyone take a chance of being shot dead a hundred times a day for me when—when—"

Suddenly she stepped forward and lifted my hat and looked straight at me. "Race Williams," she said. "Yes. I can believe the killing part now. Race Williams. I didn't think you even knew I was alive."

"I know it now." I smiled down at her. "Suppose you put that wrap around you and we get going." I hope my voice sounded pleasant and enthusiastic, which is a lot to hope, for I got a good look at the girl now and saw that ten thousand bucks fluttering out that door down the stairs and right back into the pocket of Judson Masters. That's right. You've guessed it. This was not the daughter of the wealthy Masters, the racketeer of prohibition days now turned gentleman and business man. The girl was Sally Evers— night-club entertainer, contortionist and "Dancer Extraordinary" up at Johnny Rainer's Night Club. The contortionist part explained why she hadn't been busted in two or at least had charley horse for a couple of weeks.

I HAD SEEN her often enough— admired her too, but not enough to go around killing guys free of charge just to see her dance again. She was a nice

eye-full and I did think she was the most graceful thing in an eccentric sort of way on Broadway. But a call to the cops would have been my contribution to her rescue. I'm not an endowed institution. But I said to the girl:

"Put that coat around you and we'll get going." Then, noticing the little swelling that was turning blue above her left eye I asked, "Who gave you that?"

"Him." She pointed at the tallest of the gangsters. Harry was his handle.

I walked over to the tall lad who wasn't so tough-looking now. In fact, he looked a bit scared. I held my gun low in my hand and spoke to him soft and gently about the respect youth needs for women today. It was a nice lecture for the color came back into his face and his lip went back into its perpetual sneer that had disappeared for a while when the surprise took over his ugly puss. Then I let him have it. I jerked up the gun and reversing it quickly tore the front sight once, twice, down his face in a crisscross movement. He squealed like a stuck pig, dropped to his knees and began to beg for his life.

But that was the whole show; nothing more except to tap him good right on the head and let him fold up on the floor. It would mark him of course and a gun sight does hurt a bit but what would you have.

I turned to his friend, and believe me that warrior's legs were shaking in his pants. I didn't talk to him so gently. I near scared him to death before I tossed up my gun and knocked him cold. A cruel streak in me, you think. Well, it's a matter of opinion. To my mind, guys like that have to have a moral lesson. They forget too easy. They have to have something to remember.

There was a thud beside me. I turned sharply, pulled up my gun, and got a real laugh. The tough, dirty-aproned, unshaven bartender was lying flat on his back. He had fainted dead away.

"Come on, kid." I took Sally's coat and tossing it over her shoulders walked toward the door. No one watched us but the woman.

Sally Evers was not the bold, belligerent, angry little animal that she had been a few minutes before. I took her arm on the stairs and I knew that her legs were rubbery, and though she smiled when she looked up at me the color had gone out of her face. Even in the darkness she was a real beauty—and I mean real. I don't think there was a touch of make-up on her, and her straight hair was combed and set by a simple jerk of her head.

CHAPTER 2

FOR LOVE—OR MONEY

DRIZZLING RAIN HAD begun to fall so I got a cab down the block. The driver lived in the neighborhood, and had gone home to eat. I gave him the address of the O'Shauncy girls over in the Village and pushing Sally in settled back. I made the first break.

"I suppose Johnny Rainer will be glad to get you back," I said. "It doesn't seem like something you want to go to the police about."

"No. No," she said. "That wouldn't help. You couldn't stick it on the right person."

"You know who the right person is then."

"Yes, I—" she started and stopped and tried to peer into my face in the dull flashes from the street lights as the cab shot along deserted streets. She said, "You don't know? No one hired you?" A little hopeful, that last, I thought.

"No," I told her. "I don't know. And— no one hired me."

"Like that. Just like that. You knew I was there and you came—and there was nothing in it for you." She hesitated a long time and then, "You—you're not— well—I mean—you're not in love with me?"

"I know what you mean, Sally," I told her. "And I'm not in love with you." And when she just looked at me, I made it easier for her and said, "And I don't want anything from you, either."

"Gosh." She suddenly burst out with it. "I'm an awful heel to have such thoughts. But then, I never knew a man who didn't want something—not since—as long as I can remember. Or maybe I'm just suspicious."

"Or run with the wrong pack," I told her. "There are lots of swell guys, Sally. Better guys than I ever hope to be."

"Oh—no," she cut in quickly. "I used to see you come to the door and slip inside and I'd pretend you came to watch me. I used to think that if ever I was in a jam why maybe you'd—and then tonight. You didn't come there by accident, did you?"

"No—I came there on purpose."

"Gosh." I could feel those eyes sparkle, catch a faint flash in a passing light. "Gosh, Mr. Williams—it's hardly believable. Why would a big shot like you go out of his way to save a little punk like me?"

I'm no better than the next guy. She was pretty, and she had talent. With any backing she would get places. Men went to see her all right. I even stepped in to look at her as she had said. I guess I felt a bit cockey. Anyway, I blurted it out—easy like—and smart—and maybe indifferently.

"It wasn't much to do for you." And when she asked me how I knew where she was, I carried the lie on without exactly lying by saying, "Someone told me where to go."

So we sat in the O'Shauncy girls' little Tea Room in the Village. And although they had been closed since the dinner hour, they opened up and trotted out a pretty good meal. The O'Shauncy girls being old girls as gentle as lambs if they liked you, as hard as nails if they didn't. At the time they liked me.

I got an earful then from Sally. And I didn't feel so cockey or so flattered. It looked like I had walked into something that should have paid me a lot of dough if you can measure personal danger in dollars and cents. She didn't crab, she only told me facts. They paid her seventy-five dollars a week up at Johnny Rainer's Club. Others who came in got several times that salary and didn't draw like Sally did. She called them "the regular profession." She had come up from the streets of New York, danced around since she was ten, and the final fling was her getting a movie offer—a good contract—and through a good agent, Ben Tyler. It was then that

they clamped down on her. The night-club had a contract and they wouldn't let her break it, though she hadn't even signed it the last time it was presented to her.

"I don't get it," I told her. "Why not simply walk out?"

"No." She shook her head. "I'm of the night like they are. I don't think it's my success, my loss to the club, the money I'll be making. I'm part of a system, a criminal system, those outside the law. He's afraid I'll talk. Though I don't know what about."

"And this 'he,' I suppose, has something on you. Something you would be ashamed of. Something that would send you to prison."

"No." She seemed to be thinking. "I guess there are a lot of things that I would be ashamed of. And I guess maybe a few crimes here and there as I moved up out of the tenements. But nothing that even a second rate lawyer couldn't get me sprung for."

"Then what?"

"Then—like tonight. I tossed everything to the wind. I said I was breaking clean. I was old enough. I was going to take that movie contract. Two hours later I was snatched on my way to my apartment."

I LIT A butt and blew toward the ceiling. I'd give the girl a break.

"I know what you mean by the system," I told her. "But Johnny Rainer is talking through his hat. He can hire a few thugs like those tonight. But Johnny doesn't really cut much ice." And when she would have come in, and started to in a little frightened voice, I told her, "I'll have a talk with Johnny. Then you can simply go on your way."

"Race—Mr. Williams." She leaned over and took my hand. "It's you—who should be on your way. I'm mighty selfish. I know Johnny Rainer would mean nothing to you, nor any other man but one—" and as I stuck out my chest—"Johnny doesn't own the night-club. He operates it for another—for—for George Latham— *the* George Latham."

I did sit a little straighter but my chest wasn't out so far. I knew Latham owned the building, but I didn't think he had any interest in the club except to keep an office there. And certainly none in the welfare of obscure little Sally Evers. Maybe I showed it on my face. For she said:

"It's George Latham who holds my contract—holds me, Race. Race—I'm sorry I brought you into this. Go—forget me—and maybe he'll forget you—and I'll—I'll do what he asks and take my chances."

Take her chances. I sat there and looked at her. Of course I knew George Latham. Everyone in New York knew George Latham—and I guess no one knew any good about him—maybe not any bad about him lately—or anything about him. He was big stuff along the Avenue. So big—that, with a gulp, I thought even I had let him alone. Not that the occasion to cross him had ever arisen. There had been offers once or twice but the price hadn't been big enough for the job or that's what I'd told myself. Horse-faced George was a mysterious shadowy figure who was always mentioned in any big and questionable, and often pretty rotten deals, but never any more than a mention. No one could lay a finger on him. That is no one could now. Every time some famous name in crime or sometimes out of crime for that matter was picked up dead and no motive seemed to be in order a little wave of current went along the Avenue— that the stiff had known George Latham when, when it would have been better for him if he hadn't.

To be frank I had turned down cases that would have bucked Latham. And I had always told myself that the cause wasn't worthy enough or there wasn't enough money in it. Now—well, there was nothing in this for me. I hardly knew the girl, and certainly there was no dough in it, nothing but headaches. I never posed as a philanthropist. I'm no amateur detective. I'm a highly paid one. The girl said suddenly, "You've been swell, Race. Of course you must have thought it was Johnny Rainer. No man in his right senses would cross Latham. I can go away— take another name—start over—dancing other places."

"You're too good," I told her. "Your picture would be in the papers. No. You can't do that."

"No—I can't—can I?"

She was looking straight at me. "Besides there is you. Maybe I'd be dead now if it wasn't for you. I'll go and see George. I'll explain you never thought he was in it, that—well—you just stumbled into the Crescent Hotel looking for something else." And how right she had hit that. "I have no right to think of myself now."

She leaned across the table and clutched my wrist. "I must think of you; the first guy who ever did anything for me—and wanted nothing in return." She started to her feet. "You wouldn't have a chance, Race. He'd wipe a lone wolf like you out like that. I'll go now, before he learns we were together even this long. I'll promise him anything—if he'll leave you alone."

I SAT THERE and took it. I watched her pick up her purse, slip from the table, go half-way across the room, turn and wave sort of sadly, sort of bravely at me. That was all of that. I got up and dragged her back by the arm. I was talking a blue streak.

Whatever put it into her head that George Latham had my number. Was she crazy with terror that she thought anyone pushed Race Williams around. Where had she been that she didn't know that Race Williams didn't take guff from anyone. What? Yes, I'm stuck on myself all right. It's been said enough and I never denied it. I suppose I have blown my own horn a little at times. But mostly I don't have to blow it. There were enough people blowing it for me.

I guess I blew the top right off it. Sure, I always thought pretty good of myself, but when I got through talking then, I was surprised at what a guy I really was. I was puffed like a pouter pigeon. She was impressed too.

She said, "You see—I would be old enough—and I'd go on my own way—and told Latham that."

"How old?" I asked.

"Twenty-one."

She looked older, I mean inside—back of her eyes. I asked her when she'd be twenty-one.

"Tomorrow," she said, and I looked up at the clock. It was five minutes after twelve. She followed my eyes toward the clock.

"Today? Now?" I asked.

"Yes," she said, "today—now—twenty-one. I didn't realize."

So I called over Grace O'Shauncy and whispered in her ear, and she said she'd see what she could do. Then I left the kid and went out and used the telephone.

Johnny Rainer answered the phone and said:

"I don't care, Race, if you are the King of England. You can't talk to him now, and you can't see George Latham later. And—"

"I got Sally Evers with me," I cut in—and cut him out too. There was a queer silence at the other end of the wire, no click of a hang up, yet no sound, not even of heavy breathing. Then the breath came in a gasp like Johnny had held it a long time.

I said, "Sure, I know, Johnny. I suppose George said you needn't expect to see Sally around any more. Well, he was wrong, or you misunderstood the implication. I'll be there with her at two o'clock—and her agent."

"Here with her—you—with her— What have you got to do with Sally Evers, Race? She hasn't got a nickel."

"I'll lend her a nickel," I told him airily. "I'm liberal that way. No more talk, Johnny. If you know what's good for you round up George. And if you know what's good for him—have him there. I'll be wanting that phony contract of Sally's."

I hung up on his gasp. He hadn't been talked to that way about George Latham and I guess he couldn't believe it now. Maybe I couldn't either for that matter. But I was into the thing—into the thing the moment I dragged Sally Evers out of the Crescent Hotel.

I went back to the table as Grace O'Shauncy came in with the birthday cake, and twenty-one candles on it. It wasn't a fresh cake, but it wasn't exactly a stale one either. A sort of an in between, but tops for such short notice.

"Forget George," I told the kid. "We'll be seeing him later. We'll pick up your phony contract. Have your agent there and—"

"But my agent will be afraid to—"

"Forget it," I said again. "I'll manage things from now on. Come on. Blow out your candles like I'll blow out George if he—if he wants it that way."

And there you are. No amount of money could talk me into something I didn't want to be mixed up in. No woman could flatter me into it. And a slip of kid exactly twenty-one with a thought for my life and a feeling that I wasn't a match for horse-faced George Latham had made me talk myself into it. Talk myself into being as hard as George, as dangerous as George.

She blew out the candles and I blew out my chest. I was right, of course. None of them had ever come too tough for me. Anyway, I might as well die now as forty years from now with cramps in my stom-ach. Certainly George and I would cross sometime, and why not when I was in the right and in the mood. And I sure was in the mood tonight. Sally Evers had created a mood that portended evil for—I gulped—for George Latham of course.

WHEN I GOT Ben Tyler, Sally's agent, on the phone he was a little tough to handle. He hinted around the name George Latham but didn't come right out and say that George had rubbed out his offer to Sally. He admitted, too, that Superior Pictures were very anxious to have the girl and that Kent Mason of Superior was on from the Coast and around town some place right then.

He finished with, "I haven't any doubt that they'd make Sally Evers, nor any doubt she'd make the picture they have in mind a box office whirlwind. I've crossed a lot of people, Race, and so have you, but I never heard of you crossing Latham. I have had my hint and I quit playing with fire and dynamite and T.N.T."

"Try mixing them all together. It's fun." Then I laughed good-naturedly. "You misunderstood, Ben. There's been a change of heart. I'm seeing George tonight and he's all for the little girl going to Hollywood and doing it right. You be up at Johnny Rainer's Five Star Night Club—ready to make it a four star club. And get Mason if you can."

"The very fact that you are in it, Race, makes me more skeptical. I think it can wait and—"

"Okay," I told him. "If you think it can wait—then wait. But she'll be sign-ing Hollywood before breakfast. If you are not there I'll know you don't want part of the little gold mine." That was when I clicked the receiver down—but hard.

It was then I decided. If I was going to cross George Latham I'd cross him in grand style. I'd swing into the Five Star with the gorgeous Sally Evers draped over my arm. Draped—I looked at her now. She wasn't dressed for the party I wanted. I told her so.

"Well—" she said. "I wasn't exactly dressed for a party tonight. I was sticking my nose in where it didn't belong. And though George couldn't be sure, he thought I was getting to know too much. I don't think he suspects how little I do know about him. The idea that he would really harm me came so suddenly.

"I met him quite by accident coming out of a house up in the seventies and he looked sort of surprised and—well, he wanted to know what I was doing there—and when I admired the house he took me right by the arm and led me down the street. I remember the number and—you're not listening, are you, Race?"

No—I wasn't listening. I wanted to do things right. I wanted to swagger and toss my weight about a bit. I wanted to swing into the night-club with Sally on my arm, dressed up in her best. So I asked how long it would take her to make her apartment and get herself decked out.

She nodded and smiled but I didn't care for the humor in her voice when she said:

"Yes, Race. If I'm going to die I might as well look my best. I have a dress—just the thing for—for—"

"Nothing is going to happen to you," I told her, and meant it. I was a little annoyed. After all, I had a reputation in the city. It wasn't like George Latham's reputation, built on mysterious rumors, low whispers, sudden and unexplained deaths. I had pushed over some pretty big lads, a few of the biggest, and anyone could have a look at the corpse and know my bullet was in his carcass just as if the slug had my name on it.

Anyway, I was skating on thin ice, I'd cut figures on it. But I decided not to let Sally go for her clothes herself. A little talk, and I discovered that Sally had a friend who lived in a small apartment three floors down from hers and they exchanged keys in case one wanted something in a hurry and couldn't make it home. I had Sally call her up and arrange for her to go into Sally's apartment and pick up that certain dress for this occasion and what equipment went with it.

She was a good kid was Sally, and after asking only once why she couldn't go and get the things herself and dress in her own rooms she made the call.

"I'm fussy," was my only explanation. "I'll call for the things and bring them to you at a hotel, and you can dress there. I don't want anyone to know where you are until I sweep you into the Five Star Club."

"But, someone might follow you to the hotel I'm in."

I grinned at her and said, "Only in a hearse, Sally."

Then I called a taxi, and we went outside to wait—which proved to have been a good idea a few minutes later. I simply thought we were pressed for time and we could wander down to the corner and watch for the taxi. And that was why I saw the car, the heavily curtained black car that swung into the block, turned at the next corner and began to cruise up and down the street. It was going the other way when the taxi came but turned back again almost as soon as we got into the cab.

CERTAINLY IT LOOKED like a death car. How did I know? I've seen enough of them. And today crime was sweeping the city at a pace that was going to make prohibition times look like simple juvenile delinquency.

If George had sent that car it was fast work and, what's more, he would have had to trace that phone call. Or we were shadowed from the Crescent Hotel. I believed he could trace the call all right. He had that much influence. But I didn't believe he had done it at one-fifteen in the morning. That sort of influence didn't stay up all night.

I said to our driver, "Swing around— and head west." As we made the turn I saw that the other car was turning too, making a nice job of it considering its length. And I had to make up my mind then whether to run for it or face it out. I thought of Sally but I thought of our chances too, so I decided to face it out. If I gave orders to speed up the death car would be down on us like a P-38. If we went along leisurely—well—they'd try for a surprise attack. Maybe even push us to the curb and throw some fancy talk first. I like fancy talk. It's been the death of some famous gunmen.

As the long black job came silently and swiftly down on us I asked our driver casually:

"Small rear window—unbreakable glass?"

"Naw." He didn't turn around but tossed it over his shoulder. "Used to be, but it busted. I put in that hunk of glass myself. The crack is my job too."

"Nice job." I nodded, and kneeling on the seat I smacked the nose of my gun through the glass, cleaned out a nice hole. Guns shoot through glass of course and often do good work for I've done it myself. But I never put obstacles in my way if I have time to avoid them.

The car was pulling right up on us. I said, "Easy does it, Sally—" and squeezed out lead twice. It was then for the first time I saw the machine gun and the brown fedora on the man's head.

I didn't hear the tires go out. But I did hear the machine gun and I did see the car swerve, hesitate a second, then smack itself up on the sidewalk and against one of those iron railings before an old house.

Our own cab jumped a bit. The driver said, "What's that?" But he was a long time in the city, and stepped on the gas instead of the brake.

I told him, "I think some fellow fired at a car—gang war. Don't want to stop, do you?"

He didn't, and we didn't. I shook the cab about four blocks from the Carter Hotel, a nice little respectable family affair where I occasionally park my clients. I was hesitating between giving the driver a twenty or even a century note when he said:

"No reason to report that, mister—that shooting—if it was shooting. It doesn't do a guy like me any good. In my business it's wise to keep your nose clean."

I put the large folding money back in my pocket. Gave him a buck and told him to keep the change. I assured him that since I was a stranger in the city for simply a day or two I wouldn't care to be mixed up in police procedure. I watched him drive away after that, then took Sally down to the Carter and booked her—nice expression that, eh—under the unflattering moniker of Amelia D. Amerstave.

As for Sally, she just grasped my hand and said she'd wait—for me to be careful. She only showed her woman's curiosity in one sentence.

"Did—did you kill anyone?"

"I'm afraid not, Sally," I told her with regret. "Still there is a chance."

CHAPTER 3

HORSE-FACED GEORGE

AFTER I LEFT the hotel I took the subway uptown, walked a block south, turned two east and hit Sally's apartment house. I gave myself plenty of room, too, though I didn't anticipate any more trouble. I won't go as far as say I didn't expect trouble, for I always expect it and am always ready for it. I never like to be surprised. In my business surprised men are dead men.

So I met Sally's friend, a nice little number who wanted to chat a bit and wanted to know if Sally was doing a "special."

"You can't wear much and do her dances," was the way she put it.

"No," I said, "you can't." And "Yes, I said, this is a special."

It was late and it was dark, and there were few people on the street. But that's the way of New York. It's hard to hit a time or hit a street without someone coming along to spoil your show—especially if your show is murder.

After I had left Sally's friend, and was walking away from her apartment, I saw another girl in the doorway, heard her too, muttering to herself as she tried to fit her key in her lock. And I was surprised, but not in the way you'd think. I had come around the corner and there was no one ahead of me. I had walked part way down the block. No one came from the other direction, and yet the girl was having trouble getting the key in the lock. She turned as I neared and stepped out of the little entrance way and said:

"I can't turn it. I hurt my wrist I wonder if you'd—"

"Walk in and do it for you?" I turned sharply and almost ran through that doorway. "Of course I will."

The girl shouted.

"He's got a gun in his hand."

That meant the lad's death. I had only intended to knock him silly. But the girl's warning brought action. He was up from his crouching position like a flash, the knife high in his hand and coming down fast. Very fast. There was nothing to do but let him have it. I don't know how bad he took it. But there was inches, not feet, between us when the yellow-blue flame spat out at him and slugs cracked him back—far back into the vestibule. I think I heard the knife hit the floor. Anyway, something clattered, and I stepped out onto the sidewalk again. High heels beat along a side alley. And I walked down the street feeling pretty good about things.

Of course I knew there would be a man in that hallway. It was old stuff. Why didn't I walk on, you think. Well, it would be better and healthier to settle things right then than have the guy peek out and take pot shots at me from the rear. No. I wasn't looking for trouble. But I wasn't going out of my way to avoid it.

Yes, I was feeling pretty cockey. No coincidence now. George was out to get me, and I was giving a pretty good account of myself, which would stand in my favor when we had our showdown— less than an hour from then. Why if that was the best Georgie could do I—I—

I heard it and swung and saw the pointing rifle from behind the ash can—think I detected the slightest ping—or swish or whatever you call it and my gun was out and—that was all. I took it high up on the shoulder—more over on the arm. It spun me slightly. The guy was gone, and blood was running down my sleeve.

I DIDN'T LIKE it. What's more I didn't feel I had had to take the dose of lead. I saw how Georgie had foxed me. The stupid doorway trick wouldn't fool a rookie cop— and my strutting away with ease and confidence and too much indifference. Then the gun with the silencer. A twenty-two, no doubt. So the lad was a crack shot. And— the ping before the swish had saved me. Anyway, I had turned and the bullet had caught me in the left arm. So the ping was the touch of steel against the tin of the garbage can—or maybe the ping was in my subconscious mind.

Yes. George had foxed me, pulling that fast clever one after the slow stupid one. I set my lips grimly. I remembered a conversation I once had with Georgie— about his set-up and his gunmen and I guess he remembered it too.

As I made my way to the corner I thought that was the last attack. So it was odd to find that I held a gun in my hand, and once I almost took a pot shot at a drunk sitting against some stone steps.

I took a taxi because I couldn't be sure how bad the hit was. Not inside—but outside, and if blood seeped through. In the taxi I found where the bullet had gone in and gone out. No hole in the jacket to notice. The lead had skipped through by the seam and skipped out leaving a hole almost too tiny to find.

I thought of a doctor. I knew I should go see a doctor. But time wouldn't permit. I was going to land at the Five Star Club smack on the minute of two—and I needed all the time I'd have.

I sent the suitcase up to Sally's room when I reached the hotel. I got a look at myself in the mirror, and didn't like what I found. Sort of white. No, I didn't go to the men's room and take my coat off and patch myself up. I had a feeling if I did I wouldn't finish out the trip on time.

I sat there in the lobby and waited for Sally, thankful that there was no blood showing. I sat and waited. My thoughts were black—and I was mad. I tried to pull myself together. In my business it is as bad to let yourself get mad as it is in prize-fighting. But I was mad.

Sally came and I forgot my arm. I got to my feet and stared at her. I guess I smacked my lips too. No, I wasn't thinking of Sally then or even myself, except in the general way of the impression she'd make swinging into the Five Star Club. I almost wished I was wearing a tuck—almost.

"What's the matter, Race?" She ran over to me. "You look white as a ghost. Anything happened?"

"Only you, Sally," I told her. "Only you. You're like the ghost of all the beautiful and best dressed women in New York rolled into one. All the charm of—"

"Race—" she said. "That—doesn't sound like you."

"No, it doesn't." I shut up. Blood was trickling down my arm.

WE SWUNG INTO the club—the girl on my right arm, and a bullet-hole in my left arm. Johnny Rainer was there, and when I tapped him he turned in that imperious way of his—and his jaw sagged. Maybe I was white from loss of blood. Maybe Johnny Rainer was pink-cheeked from vintage wine. But he turned white, a good deal whiter than I was. He started to speak.

"Race—Race Williams. I thought you wouldn't—" He stopped talking and stopped thinking, and I smiled at him.

"You mean you were told not to expect me after all. Is that it?" And when he looked at me I said, "It might save your family an expensive funeral if you didn't know any more than that."

"I—I didn't expect you. I thought—I was told—"

"Johnny," I said, as the headwaiter came over. "Don't make me smear you all over the floor. I got some respect for high priced rugs." And to the headwaiter, "Take Miss Sally Evers over to Mr. Ben Tyler's table."

"Yes, yes; he's expecting her." The headwaiter looked at Sally then, and let himself go for once. "I must say, Miss Sally," he said, and there was real respect in his voice or he wouldn't be still on his feet, "I must say, Miss Sally, that I never saw you look more charming—more radiant—and that is a rare compliment indeed."

It was and she was. People watched our entrance all right. If the big shot Mason was with Ben, he'd have his pen in his hand before she reached the table. I'll say this for the headwaiter. He wasn't in any racket. He had come out of a swank hotel, and he took Sally across that room as if he was negotiating an international treaty and making way for a queen.

I turned to Johnny Rainer. It was just two o'clock on the dot. I said, "Take me up to George."

When he started something about announcing me I shook my head and gave him exactly what was on my chest. "No, Johnny," I told him. "You made the date. He'll be in his office. You've got push buttons all over the dive. Half of them have been pressed already."

When he still looked doubtful and some of that B picture assurance had come back into his boiled shirt and nicely padded shoulders, I added. "You don't know what happened tonight, Johnny, for if you did you'd know I was only kidding about not messing up expensive rugs."

Johnny's mouth opened and closed again. He turned and walked back toward the bar and when I crowded him he said simply, "This way, Race. I gave the boss your message. He's waiting."

We went past the bar along the brightly-lighted hallway and suddenly into the semi-darkness, turned through a door, large packing case both sides of us. We were walking under a bright light with darkness on either side of us. It wasn't a nice spot for the fellow in the light. I jogged Johnny up unpleasantly I hoped. I told him so.

"Not nice for the lad in the light, Johnny," I said, "nor the one with him."

"What's the matter with you, Race?" He stopped suddenly and looked straight at me. "What in heck is the matter. I never saw you so jumpy before. Never heard of you jumpy before. Why in thunder do you and Georgie have to cross? If you're afraid, why do you go and see him now?"

"If he's afraid—why does he see me?"

"He's afraid of nothing, Race. You must know that. You must know—"

"That he kills what he fears," I said. "That's my cue, Johnny. I'm not afraid of Georgie Latham."

"No—of course not." Johnny stopped before a small elevator. The elevator took us slowly up and stopped. The door opened and soft thick rugs appeared. A few paces down was a heavy door. We had hardly reached that door when it opened and a young, efficient, not to say handsome girl, trotted out and said with a smile:

"Mr. Williams, isn't it? You are to go right in. Mr. Latham can give you fifteen minutes. All right, Mr. Rainer. Mr. Latham says for you to go down and take care of things. He won't need you." As she stood aside from the door she told me, "Go right in, Mr. Williams. I'm going home."

I stepped inside the big room. It was an office and library combined. There were handsomely bound books, soft leather upholstered chairs, a small desk over by some mahogany filing cabinets, and a big flat-topped desk with a glass on it. The door closed behind me and I faced that big desk. Behind that desk was horse-faced Georgie Latham.

He might be thirty. He might be forty-five. Like a horse, you couldn't tell his age by seeing him, and unlike a horse you couldn't tell his age by looking in his mouth. At least I couldn't. He smiled. His chin went down, his loose jowls straightened out and his eyelids blinked. His eyes were just about as soft-looking as cement coated with ice. His hands were big and his fingers were thick but they were long and reputed to be quick on a trigger, for Georgie was not above personally pumping a bit of lead into a friend's chest. Not that it was sentiment upon Georgie's part. But if a man was big enough to be classed around as Georgie's friend, he was big enough to die by Georgie's own hand. He didn't want to blame anyone for messing up an important job. Georgie faced his responsibilities.

"Sit down, Race. Sit down, boy." He put a cigar into his face, but did not light it. "The inevitable moment. Well, I never ducked it but you did."

I took the chair he indicated smack in front of the desk, sat down and said, "I never ducked it either."

"Oh, come now." His chin fell down and the jowls disappeared. "There was the Morse affair and the Blandon mix up."

"Not enough money." I shook my head.

"And the Warren case—what of that then?" The cigar moved slowly across his mouth and granite behind the ice watched me closely.

"Too crooked," I told him.

"Ah, well." He leaned back in his chair and the lock of hair that curved down onto his forehead receded a bit. "Then we must assume that your interest now involves money and is honest." And when I said nothing, "I mean your visit to me."

"I'm afraid," I said slowly, "my visit doesn't involve either one—now."

"So you've changed." He picked up a pencil and tapped lightly on the blotter of the desk. "Now let me see, Race. Sally Evers is a cute number, but I didn't think you were the kind of a man to cross me for that. So I dismissed the idea. As for the money in her—understand I didn't say in me—but in her—well, I dismissed that idea too. She has talent, yes, but her Hollywood contract wouldn't bring too much, and the future in pictures is uncertain. So I dismissed that. I felt my animosity wouldn't be worth it to you."

I looked at him a little blankly. I could feel the blood going out of my face, but I could see him clearly enough and I was steady enough. I said simply, "So you dismissed that—and then what?"

"Well—" he said, "I have a lot of dough. A lot of people have tried to take it from me. No one has ever succeeded—for long—and lived. You recall what I told you the last time we met. It was over at the Ritz, wasn't it, some years back. Warren had approached you, and I came over and sat down and talked to you. Remember?"

"Yes," I nodded very solemnly because I felt very solemn. "I remember that. You told me that you had only to lift the phone to have a hundred men at a hundred spots I frequented and unless I was a better shot than you thought I was I would be dead before I reached the second spot."

"And now."

"Now," I said. "You know I can reach the second spot. You made two mistakes, Georgie. I never blackmail anyone, and besides I don't believe Sally Evers knew enough of your past to really harm you. If she did you'd have killed her right off the bat. If you thought she had it sunk away in writing, you'd have tortured the truth out of her and found it and destroyed it. You know I am known for one thing— I've built that up in the underworld, along Broadway. I never break my word. And I give you my word now that Sally Evers told me nothing."

"Ah." He raised his eyes. "Why do you think—she was where she was?"

"I don't know," I told him. "I can't even guess."

THE JAW DROPPED down and came up again. It was like running a towel rapidly back and forth through the wringer.

"So that's how it is." He pulled his great hands up and let the fingers touch very slowly one at a time. The thumbs touched last. I remember that. "Well, Race, we might straighten things out then. We might—arrange to let the girl go into pictures. I know you have admired her. Often dropped in to watch her perform. Yes. Yes. I think we might reach an agreement. You assure me that you'll not capitalize on any of her knowledge—nothing special, was there?"

"No," I said, "nothing special." I was feeling rather tired. I could feel the warm blood trickling down my arm.

"Well then, boy, don't be so somber. You have the reputation of being so light-hearted about everything—even when facing death. I've always admired you for that. Shoot with a laugh—take lead with a laugh. Perhaps tomorrow we can arrange things. Indeed I'm sure we can settle the girl's problem."

"No." I kept my eyes on him. Mostly on his hands. "The girl no longer has a problem. She no longer has to fear you. I guess maybe I—well, I no longer have to fear you."

He was looking at me funny now—maybe I was acting funny. But he said:

"Then you did fear me?"

"I don't know." I gave him the truth. "I've fought men. I've fought gangs. I've done stretches in the hospitals. But I've always won out. I'm alive—here to prove that. I'm tired tonight. Awfully tired. I remember what you said, Georgie. A hundred men on a hundred spots, and I believe you." I took a breath then and told him flat. "It's too much for me."

"Of course it is." He was still looking at me oddly and his jaw didn't drop down. "It's too much for anyone man. Any ten

men for that matter. So—you want to withdraw—you want—"

"Georgie," I interrupted very slowly. "You didn't ask me what your second mistake was."

"No, no, Race. What was that?" I thought he was getting cockey.

I got up out of the chair then with a slight effort and leaning over put my left hand down on the clean white blotter on the shining spotless desk. It didn't take but half a minute—maybe not that long, but he didn't see it at first. Then he followed the direction of my gaze, and saw the blood dripping down my hand on the whiteness of the blotter.

"That, Georgie," I said, "is the second mistake and it's going to cost you your life. You work fast, Georgie. As soon as you discovered I was going to take something from you, you acted. You picked up that phone and put a hundred guys on a hundred spots. Well, the first guy missed. His bullet went right past my head. And the second guy, Georgie. He lies dead up in a side street. The third guy must have used a silencer. I heard the whirr and I felt the pain, but I didn't get him."

He was staring up at me now, and staring too at the gun that had dropped into my right hand and was centering right about the middle of the horse's mouth. "To me, Georgie—all those guys were one guy, and that one guy was you. And three attempts at my life is all any one man is entitled to have. That's right, Georgie. I'm going to kill you—now."

CHAPTER 4

HOT FOR HOLLYWOOD

HE DIDN'T LAUGH. He didn't speak right away. He gulped once. His face was set and pasty. Georgie had been around. Georgie looked me straight in the eyes. And Georgie knew the truth. I was going to kill him all right. Finally he spoke. His voice was in his chest, and the best he could get out was:

"That—that will be murder."

"All right, Georgie." I shrugged my right shoulder. "If you can get any satisfaction out of that it's okay with me. Murder it is then." I stiffened the gun up. Things were getting a bit foggy.

"No—no." I'm not sure but I think there was panic in his voice. I know though that there was fear. "It don't have to be that way, Race. I'll do what you ask, Race—tonight. Now. Ben Tyler is downstairs. Mason from the pictures, too. Come on. We'll go down and settle it. We—man, why—why—"

"One of us has to die, Georgie." My voice sounded a long way off. "I'm not afraid to die. But I'm not going to be wiped out so a rotten rat like you can live."

"You're mad—man." He started to rise from his seat, saw something in my eyes or my gun that moved toward him—anyway, he sat down again. "You're delirious, Race. Let me get a doctor. I swear I had nothing to do with the shot that—"

"No, Georgie," I told him. "One shot might be coincidental—hardly two, and certainly not three." And with a sigh, "Anyway, Georgie, I'll feel better when you're dead."

The sweat broke out on his forehead, then. He knew I wasn't bluffing, and I knew I wasn't bluffing. I was very tired. Very tired of looking at the horse face and very anxious to shoot it right out of the picture when he started to talk.

He wasn't in a panic. He was talking to save his life. But he wasn't smooth any more. He slipped back into the gutter where he came from. I got what he was saying. It didn't register emotionally. It was simply words, and I thought what a rotten little punk Georgie really was at heart. It was about Sally. That she wasn't downstairs anymore. He had had her grabbed the minute I got in the elevator. A fake message from me. A description of the torture she'd go through. And the death she'd meet if anything happened to him. I remember saying clearly:

"That's tough on the kid, Georgie—but no skin off my nose."

I was going to kill him. And suddenly I looked down and saw the girl. Saw Sally Evers' face as plain as anything right there on the shiny desk. She was smiling up at me and—and—and I guess that cleared my head all right, for the face disappeared, and I was sweating and sort of shaky all over. I was back to normal.

I didn't collapse—either mentally or physically. I suddenly knew I wasn't going to kill him, but Georgie didn't know that. I said:

"Lift the phone and get the girl here."

"And then you—"

"Lift the phone and get the girl here."

He did lift the phone and did give quick orders into it. Then he talked, got up, watching me apprehensively. He opened a little cabinet and took a drink of brandy, offered me one. I took it. Things were better. I looked down at the desk. No girl's face this time.

SALLY EVERS CAME. She was frightened, but she was unhurt. She had gone to speak to me in the back on the phone and had been grabbed and kept in a room, but nothing had happened to her. She assured Georgie that she would never mention anything she knew about him—and all she knew he had told her. Peculiarly, Georgie listened to her very intensively.

Then I cut in: "He isn't going to harm you. You have nothing to fear."

Georgie went into his act. He didn't deny nor he didn't admit that he had Sally grabbed up and shoved away in the Crescent Hotel. He said he didn't understand her great desire to go on to be famous, that the pictures were a rough and dangerous road. She was too young. He said he was going downstairs with us right then—with a glance at me—and he'd see Ben Tyler and everything would be fine. Then he patted her on the head in a friendly way and told me I was a fine friend and she should be glad to do anything for me. Yes—I'd say Georgie had been scared and wasn't over it yet. It wasn't until then that I put the gun in my pocket—or realized that I was holding it in my right hand and was still balancing the empty brandy glass there too.

I took another brandy, but not too big. Then I stuck a handkerchief up my sleeve. I guessed things weren't so bad with me now.

Johnny Rainer's eyes bulged when he saw the way the show had turned out. So did Ben Tyler's, but for a different reason. For Georgie who seldom made even an appearance in the main room of the club walked among the tables, and stopped the show.

I flopped into a chair at the table with Ben Tyler and Mason.

Georgie did it in grand style. He took Sally up under the lights—made her take a bow. Told everyone how she had come along. How they themselves had come night after night to see her dance, and as was inevitable, the pictures wanted her. He said they all knew Johnny Rainer would never stand in the way of the success of one of his finds, "good old unselfish Johnny, though it is money right out of his pocket." And then he made the final crack that may not have knocked the others but did knock me.

"And I can say without fear of contradiction that despite her great talents our little Sally Evers owes the opportunity that is being given to her tonight to Broadway's roughest play-boy. You've seen his picture in the papers. You've read about him. The man who is frowned on by police and criminals alike, yet has done more to suppress crime than any other single man in the city of New York— The roughest, toughest, hardest-hitting, straightest-shooting private dick that ever pounded the pavements of Broadway— my friend, Race Williams. Take a bow, Race."

I was stunned. So would you be. An hour ago he was gunning for me. Twenty minutes ago I was planning to kill him. But he was right. She owed it to me all right. None knew that better than he did. Maybe I'm not over modest. I took the bow. I work for a living, and it was good advertising—no two ways about that.

I said, "You all know Sally Evers. You've seen her dance. Her feet kicked the sense inside my head and I told Georgie how I felt about it. Yes, exactly what I thought about it. And Georgie, a man who knows when to listen and when to talk, has done both tonight." I raised my glass then. "To Sally Evers. When she comes back to Broadway in her own show, let's all go and tear the theatre apart."

I went over big. Why not? Few people had ever heard Georgie give anyone a boost before.

Georgie took Sally from table to table, and I took another brandy. Yet I knew it wasn't doing me any good. The blood was coming again and the handkerchief up my sleeve was soaked.

Georgie shook hands with Ben Tyler and Mason and leaning over whispered to me.

"Better see a doctor, Race. I have one of my own who could fix up gunshot wounds without talking, but I daresay you have your own man."

"Yes," I said.

"Yes." His jaw dropped down and he looked like a real pleasant horse—a horse maybe you'd bet on. "You won't be long on your feet, Race. And don't worry about the girl—or the hundred spots. I've washed this thing up unless you lied to me. And when I wash a thing up I wash it up completely. Good show, wasn't it?"

"Good," I admitted. It wasn't too easy to talk. "There will only be one shot next time, Georgie. Just one."

"Okay." He still smiled pleasantly. "If the occasion arises again, Race, it will be a good shot. I know. I'll fire it myself. You can take my word for that. Good-night."

Ben leaned over to me and whispered. "First time I ever heard of your being drunk, Race, let alone seeing you drunk."

I tried to look him straight in the eyes. My head wobbled, but I said:

"Okay—it's the first time I've seen you sober." Then I felt the throb of pain. I came to—I got to my feet, whispered to Ben. "Not a word to Sally. Say I've been called away."

I made the door, got a cab and gave the address of Doc Stoddard. A good man Doc Stoddard. Never gave any trouble and had a certain ring that got him out of bed day or night. This time it was somewhere between day and night.

I gave his bell the two long and three short rings and was surprised how quick he opened the door.

"Hello, Doc," I said, and fell flat on my face. Yes, that was how close I had played it.

I came to after a bit. It was like waking up after a big night—all the meanness of a hangover. There was a light in the room. I could feel it—and someone present, I thought. I wanted to think, so I didn't bother to open my eyes.

I went over the past twelve hours—or was it more. Anyway, I went over the past from the time Riley first told me how I could pick up ten grand until I landed on my face in Doc Stoddard's doorway.

From an altruistic point of view it wasn't a bad recapitulation. From a business one it was terrible. Or was it? I had received a bit of advertisement, and I had let Georgie Latham know exactly how I felt about him.

The whole set-up was so phony. Sally Evers picked up like that—snatched by cheap hoods. There could be but one reason. She had to be snatched in a hurry—so fast, in fact, that Georgie must have used the first lad he could get his hands on—or see even. And— And— Suddenly the whole thing came to me. I knew what Sally knew and what George knew she knew. But George didn't know if she knew it or not—and certainly didn't know if I knew she knew it. Yes, and when she was telling me I was dumb. I hadn't listened. But I'd listen to her now.

Sounds confused, doesn't it. But it wasn't anymore. It was clear. Crystal clear. Georgie Latham was tops in the city. Fifteen years ago he was a raw kid, coming along, feeling his way, ingratiating himself with the big shots of that day. The big shot then was Jud Masters, of course—now known as Judson Masters. And it was Judson Masters' daughter who was missing and whom Riley had told me about. Riley, who was never wrong. Riley, who made his living slipping out such information to interested parties outside the law. Riley who—and drat his soul, he hadn't told me who had snatched the daughter and why and—I cooled down a bit. Riley was a careful man. Riley in a way was a timid man. The answer could be that Riley didn't know who snatched Masters' daughter.

I opened my eyes then and looked straight at Doc Stoddard. He smiled.

"You can't fool the old Doc, Race," he said. "You've been awake for some time—thinking and planning and not wanting to be disturbed. Planning no doubt to go out and put a little lead in a lad who put a little lead in you." He wagged a finger at me. "No killing. Not for a while yet."

I didn't grin. I said abruptly:

"What day is—or night is it, for that matter?"

"It is eight-thirty Friday night." He consulted the watch on his wrist. "You dumped yourself on my doorstep so to speak at exactly three-ten this morning. Not a long time, is it." And then giving me the old wheeze. "If you had been shot in the head instead of the arm no damage would have been done."

"I remember," I said, ignoring the wisecrack. "I was alone."

"Maybe." Doc Stoddard smiled. "But there was a girl on your tail. She was not the usual type of hysterical woman. She got in and saw you."

"How?"

"Oh, she didn't break the chain off the door, or knock me around, or point a gun at me if that's what you're thinking. She knew you were here, said she'd bust in every window unless she could see you, that she was part of your act. That you had saved her life." And twisting up his lips, he added, "And that she wouldn't have you butchered by some old quack. I didn't like the word old, Race."

"And then?"

"I convinced her that you wouldn't have come here if you didn't want quiet, both for yourself and the authorities. And she helped me dress the wound, offered a pint of blood, stood by without batting an eye until you were safely tucked away in bed. Then she promptly folded up on the floor. Just like a woman."

"Where is she now?" I asked.

"Oh, she left. Said to tell you she'd be back for breakfast. She never showed up though. Just like a woman again."

I started to nod at that—stopped—and sat bolt upright in bed. Then I started to climb out. Things were a bit woozy, but I came to my feet, wavering. The Doc just stood and looked at me.

"I didn't think you could do it," he said. "Now walk toward me. I'll catch you if you fall."

I STOOD THERE. The blood was coming back into my head—or maybe it was going away. I didn't know which. It felt like a mixture of both.

I said, "I've got to go out, Doc. I've got to go."

He walked across the room and pulled a curtain aside.

"There are your clothes," he said. "I could lend you a jacket and shirt. Yours were a mess, and I didn't like to send them out to be cleaned. The police being curious like they are. And my forgetting to report a gunshot wound."

He went right on without raising his voice. "Your guns are there in the drawer of the bureau. They'll both need reloading. I'm not curious. But the afternoon papers report unsavory characters being found shot dead hither and yon in our fair city. You seem to get around."

"You don't think I can get dressed and go out."

"My dear boy." Those fish eyes settled on me. "My dear boy, I have seen too many people do too many things to hazard an opinion on the determination of the human spirit."

I sat down on the bed.

"That girl's life depends on my getting around tonight. Couldn't you give me something to jazz me up?"

He sat down on the bed beside me.

"I could float you out of here—yes." He took his hands and held his left knee in them. "I could give you a shot that would move you in five minutes. But if you'll give yourself a couple of hours—well you can run around a bit—and no morphine in you." He shook his head at me. "I never saw any of this courage they rave about come out of a needle—nor out of the neck of a bottle."

I started to argue that one when he interrupted.

"Do you know where you want to go?"

"Yes." And then as I stopped to think, "I've got to see someone to tell me."

"If it's an enemy you have to beat the information out of you can't do it. If it's a friend have him here."

"I don't know which he is—and—and—"

Doc raised a finger and going to the curtained alcove leaned in and took out a telephone. Dragging a long wire behind him he handed it over to me.

"Unlisted number—" he said. "Couldn't be tapped." Doc Stoddard walked out of the room and closed the door.

I buzzed Jerry, my assistant at my apartment, and got the word that I wanted.

"Riley's been burning up the wires," he said. "He's got to see you. He's that excited." Then he gave me a telephone number, said, "That'll be a Mrs. Brown. She'll give you the number of a Mrs. Flannigan, and she'll get you Riley."

"Okay, Jerry," I said. "You do the buzzing. And bring Riley here to Doc Stoddard's. Over the fence and through the alley. Don't be seen. And bring him if you have to drag him here."

"I'll promise him a buck," said Jerry. "He thinks of nothing but money." And when I let him know it was no laughing matter, "All right—I'll put a ring through his nose."

Then I told him what clothes and ammunition I needed.

I was fully dressed when Riley came. If the man had a first name I never heard it. He was a dapper little old guy—though hardly as old as he pretended to be. He wore black shoes with gray spats, blue serge suit, the nose glasses with a ribbon. Even though the place was warm, he kept the white muffler around his neck. He had a cane hooked over his arm, and a very pale gray fedora in his hand. I could see the handkerchief in his breast pocket, the tiny bud in his lapel and guess that the slight bulge in his jacket pocket could be suddenly turned into a pair of yellow gloves.

"So." He put those little gray ferret eyes on me. Eyes that could twinkle at times, but didn't then. "I read the papers and spotted the holocaust down at the Crescent Hotel. Don't tell me that a South American revolution started in that joint."

His eyes widened. "I see you favor your left arm. Well, what became of the girl?"

CHAPTER 5

WILLIE, THE WEAPON

I POINTED TO a chair, sat down in one myself when Riley parked on the end of his. I gave him the whole story. That is, without mentioning Sally's name, simply that I pulled the wrong woman out of the hat.

"Like that." He stood up, and made a bow to me. "My apologies to you, Mr. Williams—and I suppose there wasn't a cent in it for you." There was an odd sort of courtesy about Riley, but none of the stage Irishman and none of the brogue so popular on the radio. "Put two and two together and get four," he went on. "I've read it a thousand times, done it a thousand times, and now I put two and two together and get zero. And so did you."

"Do you?" I asked, "know how it happened?"

"Of course," he said. "We always know how things happen after they happen, or we can make a good guess at it. I got a tip the Masters girl had been taken into the Crescent Hotel. I don't believe in coincidence anymore than you do. But—that's what it was. Business will be booming for you and I, Mr. Williams."

"We'll be spreading more happiness, I suppose," I said sarcastically.

"We will—and it is not something to point the finger of scorn at. We get paid for it, but so do the doctors when an epidemic hits the city. It's unfortunate for the citizens who have loved ones taken ill—but fortunate for them, too, that they have the doctors to call to make them well. Mental ills, my boy, can be far more devastating than ills of the body. And we—you and I are doctors of the mind, surgeons of the soul."

I didn't want to hear all that again. So I cut in with:

"Have you any idea who snatched the Masters girl?"

"I know there was a snatch. And I imagine someone who knew Masters when—and has something on him that would keep him from talking. Not much of a mob from the newspaper account of those in the Crescent and—"

"Would it surprise you if it was Georgie Latham who grabbed the Masters girl?"

"No—it couldn't be—couldn't—" And Riley came up out of his chair. The ruddiness went out of his cheeks. His cane slipped from his wrist to the floor. He grabbed a table for support as he stared at me. And then when I nodded the words oozed out of his mouth—sort of dribbled out.

"God help us then, Williams. I never suspected."

His head bobbed up and down as he sought the chair and sank into it.

"The only man who would know the whole truth about Masters. A word from Georgie, and Masters would fry." A cough. "Die—I mean of course."

Riley was not his usual cockey genteel self. I said, "Don't tell me you didn't know it—didn't know it was Georgie who snatched Gloria Masters."

"No—no—" he said. "I don't believe it—not even now. He couldn't. Masters was very close to Georgie in the big days. Georgie was pretty young. Masters got out, and Georgie took over. Then Georgie began killing off those in the know, but Masters was too smart. He had it in writing. Had affidavits that would send Georgie to the chair—himself also. Masters is sick, too. If anything happens to Masters the D.A. gets it all. Georgie wouldn't dare and—"

"Don't give me that," I cut in on him. "It's my hunch that Georgie got the Masters girl, all right. Now does the ten grand still go?" And when he just stared at me. "It's your racket, Riley. Am I to bring her to you?"

"No. No." He drew back from me as if I had the plague. "I got a bad steer, Race—somewhere along the line. If you had trouble—if you had work for nothing—think of other times."

And when I put the glassy look on him. "I was wrong. I should pay you for your trouble."

"That isn't it." I grinned. "I simply want to know if I'm dealing you out or in."

"You mean would I want a nickel of it. No, no, Race. I don't want any part of it. It's all yours—just keep my skirts clean. I didn't know. I want no part of it. I don't think the one who gave me the tip off had any idea Georgie had a hand in it."

"And who was that?"

"Mr. Williams." Riley shoved the ribboned glasses far back on his nose. "Mr. Williams, I never divulge information given me by my clients. May I wish you luck and—good evening."

"One minute, Riley."

I GOT BETWEEN him and the door and was surprised how well I did it. Doc Stoddard's medicine was beginning to work. "You didn't ask me how I was going to find out where this Masters girl is."

"No." Riley eyed me a moment. "I don't know how."

And when I pulled a gun slowly out of my pocket he straightened instead of cowering. "I don't know, Race—if you are any judge of people you should know that. I crossed Georgie Latham once, four years back. It was an accident. He believed that. But he said if it happened once more—two accidents—I'd never cross him or any living man again. I don't know—Race. I don't know. Reason should tell you Georgie don't need money bad enough to make a snatch. And not from Masters. Masters hasn't long to live. Georgie hasn't long to fear him. Yes—he's that sick."

"Riley." I looked at him steadily. "It's Sally Evers I want, not the Masters girl. She's been grabbed again, I think. What do you know about her?"

He started to talk, paused, wet his lips and finally said:

"I know she must be the girl who came to you by coincidence. It's all through the city the speech Georgie made about you and her. But I didn't until this moment connect her up with the kidnaping. I thought—maybe—why did Georgie want to snatch her? It sounds silly."

"Does it?" I asked him. "Maybe it was because she knew where the Masters girl was hidden."

Riley looked at me. "He'd have her killed if she knew that," he said.

"But—" I watched Riley carefully—"Georgie wasn't sure she knew." And when Riley stared at me. "It's like this,

Riley. Sally Evers saw Georgie coming out of a house in the seventies. She didn't even reach home before she was grabbed. Now she couldn't suspect why Georgie was in that house, but Georgie was afraid she had. And what would the great Georgie fear her knowing? One thing only. That Gloria Masters was in that house." Then I told him what Sally had told me, and what I had guessed, about the house in the seventies.

"But you simply guess that she's been grabbed up again."

"Well—" I went across the room and picked up the phone. It was early yet, and I was lucky enough to catch Ben Tyler at his apartment. He talked before I could.

"Thank gosh it's you, Race. I've been trying to get you all over town. First she's tied up with a night-club, and now your message that she's got to be with her sick mother upstate. I didn't know Sally Evers had a mother."

I didn't know it, either. But I said simply, my heart pounding a bit, "How did my message reach you?"

"Telegram, of course. Don't you remember? Haven't you sobered up yet? What will Mason think? And how long is indefinitely? What do you mean?"

"Oh, she'll be with you shortly. I called up to ease your mind, Ben—"

I hung up, but Ben kept on talking. How long I don't know. Then I reached for the phone again to ask Ben to keep quiet about my calling him—and decided against that. But I was pretty sure now where Sally Evers was. In the house in the seventies. And I wasn't listening when she talked about that house at the O'Shauncy girls' restaurant. She wasn't interested in it, either. But Georgie was. Yes, I was sure now that Georgie was.

It was then that Jerry walked into the room. In a great many ways he was still the kid I had picked up years back and saved from the penitentiary. His hat was on the side of his head. A butt hung from his mouth. His hat came off and the cigarette came out when I put the disapproving eye on him. But I knew he had important news to impart.

"Spill it, Jerry," I said, and when he jerked a thumb toward Riley. "Spill it anyway."

"Well—" Jerry stiffened up a bit. "We got company. They rode around the block for a bit. Then the car parked down the block. A lad is watching this house. I did myself a walk and spotted him." And when my eyebrows went up. "I think they decided not to hide out on you, but the gun who's casing this joint is class, Willie Sims."

RILEY TOOK IT kind of bad. I didn't think he'd be in such a hurry to leave now. He muttered, "Georgie's classic killer—" and then with a gulp—"but also known as the guy who can bring them in alive when Georgie wants to hear someone sing."

I knew Willie as a gun, yes. But the last part about bringing them in alive I didn't know. But it struck a chord with me. Would Georgie like to hear me talk? Maybe. Or did George have his pride. His promise that that next time he'd be his own killer. I paced the room and gave things considerable thought. Sally was prominent in that thought, the Masters

girl, too. That is, to the extent that she represented ten grand.

I pushed Jerry into a corner and buzzed him, too. He argued and he cursed and kept saying, "No, Boss, no," but I went right on talking. I went into detail. I said, "I've done it before and I'll do it again and—"

"But not like that, Boss," he still objected. "You'll be dead sure."

"Jerry," I finished with him now. "You drive that car smack around to the front door." And when he left grumbling I turned to Riley. "Georgia wants to see me and I want to see him, and Willie Sims must know it's that way. If he doesn't I'll tell him."

Half an hour later I walked out of that house, turned left and a minute later smashed right into Willie Sims, gun and all.

The driver stopped the car before a house in the seventies and I got out with Willie Sims. He was shaking pretty hard as he walked beside me up the stone steps—rapped on a door and whispered when it opened:

"Not afraid, are you, Willie?" I said, "after such slick work. Such a slick capture—regular bring 'em back alive stuff."

"No." He mumbled it, but he was scared, good and scared. I don't blame him, for he had been close to death.

The man who let us in didn't bother us as Willie linked his arm in mine, and pressing his big cannon against my side led me along a dimly lit hall and finally down a wider one and at last up a broad flight of stairs. We turned toward the back of the house, and Willie tapped at a large door. I mean larger than an ordinary room door. It was as if there had been folding doors there—taken down and one wide door put up.

We passed into the room together. The man at the door shut it behind us and stayed out in the hall. I took in the picture.

It was a spacious library, done up in style with big comfortable chairs, softly shaded table lamps and little bronze ones with dull bulbs in them along the wall. There was another door across the room, and what I thought was a fake Spanish balcony. There were iron bars about a foot apart and black, and, I thought, some thin material hiding the balcony. The material didn't go with the massive solidness of the room.

I SAW THE desk, a smaller stretch of mahogany than at the office, and the man behind it. It was horse-faced George—a rather skittish-looking horse this time. He smiled and nodded to me.

"It was nice of you to come—Race," he said. Then, nodding to Willie Sims. "So good of you to bring him, Willie." And leaning forward, "You look shaky, Willie—a little pale—surely there was no trouble."

"No—" said Willie, turning paler. I half faced Georgie and half faced Willie. "I—I had to knock a gun out of his hand to bring him in," Willie explained.

"Really?" Georgie frowned. "I didn't know it was in you, Willie. I thought he'd want to come." And smiling at me. "And I didn't know it was in you, Race." And back to Willie. "I know I suggested

bringing him in alive, Willie, but I didn't want you to play it that close." He leaned forward and smiled. "You may go, Willie. See that the latch is on when you close the door. I won't want to be disturbed."

And as Willie reached the door. "If the bell rings twice, you'll find the door open—kindly dispose of anything—er—anything that may be cluttering up the floor here. Far into the country—Willie—side by side."

Georgie waited until Willie had departed and the door closed before he said to me, "I get sentimental at times, Williams, and I really think it appeals to the boys." He motioned to me to take a seat, motioning by the way of the point of a gun he lifted up from the desk, he went on, "So all the time you were after the Masters girl. You lied to me."

"No," I said. "I didn't lie to you, Georgie. Is Sally dead?"

"Really—" Georgie smiled at me. "You anticipate things. Sort of clairvoyant, aren't you? No, Race, she isn't dead." And his voice rising slightly, "You made a fool out of me last night at the club. But I don't think any of them guessed it. I played it so they wouldn't guess it." He smacked his lips. His voice was hard and cold. "But I knew it—and—"

"Georgie," I said. "Before you go too far, or talk too much, let me tell you a few things. In the first place the Masters racket is going to back-fire on you. Do you suppose a smart man like that hasn't left a record with someone that will get you for murder over and over—first if anything happens to him, and secondly if anything should happen to his daughter?"

And when he would have talked. "I know, you were afraid Masters had gone soft and intended to atone for his sins by exposing you, and therefore himself. The thought of his daughter kept him from it. But it has preyed on his conscience and you must have known that when he came to die that he'd leave a record behind—daughter or no daughter."

"Exactly." Georgie nodded. "Jack Masters was a smart man. He taught me my business. I respected him. When he suddenly ran straight, I feared him. But he can't expose me without exposing himself. And he worships that girl of his. I've let him know that she will be all right, as long as he keeps his mouth shut and hasn't any record to spring."

"You slipped up, Georgie," I told him. "Masters hasn't got long to live. You didn't know that?"

I thought that would throw Georgie, but it didn't. He smiled and said simply:

"That was what hastened things. I went to see Masters, Race. We had quite a talk. He hasn't got long to live, poor chap. And do you know he made a new will leaving me half of his estate for old times' sake and his daughter half of it. Touching, isn't it."

I took a laugh.

"He'll change that will."

"No." Georgie shook his head. "Why should he? There is a clause that if his daughter is at the lawyer's office, sound and well, a week after his death the will is valid. If she isn't, then the entire estate is left to his daughter when she 'returns from abroad.' If she doesn't return, it all goes to some charity. Of course, there are

minor benefits and I believe a few thousand dollars to a cousin in the south."

"But the daughter, Georgie. She won't forget. She'll—"

"Tut, tut, Race. Gloria Masters has never seen my face—and will not until she is released. Why, I might even rescue her." And with a frown. "There was a strict understanding that Masters would make no attempt to locate her." And then off-handedly, "I had her beaten up a bit this morning. I have the photograph to send to him, since he hired you."

"But he didn't hire me."

"In a way," Georgie looked directly at me, "I believe you. But someone set you on the track. That's what I want to know from you. I'll show you the picture." He half turned from the desk and when I moved forward he said, "I can use a gun very quickly, Race. I know you are unarmed, even to a toothpick. Willie is always so thorough. Yet I know how melodramatic you are, and you wish to die fighting like a man. And I know that I seem careless but with reason."

He put a hand under his desk and I heard the soft rustle of moving curtains and turned my head.

The thin curtains before the balcony had parted. There was a small platform there and room enough on it for a stool and a man. I saw both. The man sat staring straight at me, and he was not too good to look at—not too bad either, if it wasn't for the thing over his knee. Yes, it was a sub-machine gun and it had a bead drawn right on me.

"So don't precipitate things, Race," Georgie advised. "He's an expert marksman, but if we tangled together you see he could hardly fail to hit me if he shot at you. Therefore his instructions are quite strict. I wouldn't move too much in the chair, if I were you. There—" when I straightened up, "be comfortable. You mustn't take me too literally. Perhaps I should say don't move too far out of the chair—or out of it at all."

"I made a mistake last night then?"

"A grievous one, Race, and one that cannot be remedied. I sincerely hope. But you coined a phrase worthy of the immortal bard. I think I will borrow it tonight. 'I will feel better when you're dead.' "

"Nice set-up," I told him. And when the curtains didn't go back I figured though the lad with the Tommy gun could see through them he could see better without them.

Georgie Latham took two pictures from his desk and handed them to me. The first was a beautiful blonde girl. Head erect, chin up, but a bit of fear in the clear eyes. Then I looked at the second picture he handed me. "Before and after." He said grinning. I had to grip my chair.

THERE WERE WELTS across the bare legs and arms, and one of her eyes was puffed. I didn't look at it any more.

"Nothing that can't be repaired," Georgie said. "Remember the will said she must be sound and well. Tut—tut, Race. And this girl a stranger to you. But there— I won't send it to her father if you convince me he didn't hire you."

"No one hired me, Georgie," I said. "You're pretty rotten all the way through and you only crawled out of the gutter to creep along the curb and drop back in again. But the truth is that I came across Sally when I wasn't looking for her and then—"

"Sally talked." He stopped me there. "I believed you last night, and believed her too. I felt around things and she gave the street and number of this house—and yes, Race, she gave them to you. Don't stare at me. You were getting ready to come here unescorted.

"Now," he said, getting to his feet and looking over the desk at me, "you want to talk. You want to make a deal. But Sally talked. No, she didn't know what information she had. But she saw me going out of this house. She admitted she noticed the number. And she admitted she told you that number."

"But it was just conversation. I didn't even remember any number. Can't you see, Georgie. I'm giving you a last chance to make good on your word. On—"

"I made good," he snapped in on me. "I told Willie Sims to bring you here alive. I said—there would be no more hundred spots—just one spot when you needed killing—and I'd attend to it personally. Now you no doubt want to make a deal. Turn you loose and turn Salty Evers loose and neither of you will ever mention the Masters girl.

"Well there is something else I want to know. Who tipped you off to the Masters snatch to begin with? And don't tell me it was Jud Masters. His attitude would decide how his daughter was treated. He doesn't expect ever to see her again—and with a shock like this he mightn't live a week."

"Well—" I shrugged. "I don't know anything about it. Even if I did there is no way you could make me talk."

"Is that so? I almost fell for that last night. But now, I'm bringing Sally in here. Believe me, Race, I'll cut her to ribbons to make you talk."

"Fine." I crossed my legs. "You've known her longer than I have. If you can do it, I can take it."

"Like that." He looked at me steadily, then he crossed the room, unlocked and tapped on the other door. It opened and Georgie said, "The little one."

For a minute I saw the man. Then the girl came into the room. It was Salty all right. She walked hesitantly. Her head was down. Slowly she lifted it and saw me. I could see her stiffen and then start to shake all over.

"It's not true, Race," she said. "Not true. I told him if I ever gave you the number you had forgotten it. That you weren't listening. It was an accident you found me, downtown."

"All right, kid," I told her. "Don't worry. Georgie's just a big bluff. And—" I took a chance and moved slightly from the chair. Of course the guy in the alcove wouldn't shoot yet. For one thing I was too far from Georgie and Georgie held a gun. For another thing my death would kill all Georgie's plans.

Georgie turned to the man in the alcove with the machine gun trained on me. Georgie started to speak and the man's eyes swung for a split second—maybe a full second—toward Georgie. I don't know. But it was enough. The machine gun was still pointing at me; his finger

had begun to tighten on the trigger; his eyes were fixed back on mine when I fired.

CHAPTER 6

WITH HIS EYES WIDE OPEN

THAT'S RIGHT. I fired. I just crossed my right hand over and under my left armpit and out again. The result was amazing, at least to Georgie. What the lad with machine gun thought I don't know. Three bullets bounced into his face so fast that I don't think he even kept track of them. The dead man, for he was a dead man even before he hit the little railing, was heavy, and I guess the bronze of the balcony was fake for he and the machine gun clattered and thudded to the floor—if you must have your sound effects.

Then ducking low I pulled my gun up for Georgie—and stopped. I thought I'd get him before he closed his finger on the trigger. I knew I'd get him before he ever got a real effective shot in. But not Georgie.

The gun that was hanging in his hand fell to the floor even as I crouched there. Though his lips had trouble, the words came out just the same.

"It'll be murder, Race, and I call on this girl Salty to witness that."

"Horse radish," I said disgustedly. I straightened and drew a bead on him. "Are we going through that crying act again?" Then I dropped my gun slightly and took a laugh. I couldn't help it. He had staggered back against the wall, his knees sagging slightly, his arm half resting on a rather large gaudily-framed painting of the Blue Grotto.

"All right, Georgie," I told him. "But I have an idea that I'll feel better before the night is over. You seem surprised." And when he only looked at me. "No. Willie Sims didn't frame you. Willie was a smart boy. Willie pulled the Frank Buck with me. You told him to bring me back alive and Willie did. Yes, Willie fell hard—and I took a chance."

"What happened?" Georgie asked as I frisked him.

"Well," I said, "I figured you wanted me alive. For your own pride, for one thing, but mostly to know where you stood. For if I should die you'd never know who was onto the Gloria Masters steal. A nice thing it would be, wouldn't it, if someone buzzed your ear every week or so and shook you down for a couple of grand. But you weren't sure what I knew, if anything. You couldn't be. And I didn't know. But I did figure it out before Willie Sims stuck his rod in my side.

"Willie was smooth; Willie was polite; and Willie told me that you wanted to see me. He said nothing bad would come of it if I came along nice; and he went through me with a fine tooth comb. He got me in the back of his car with another smart guy you had driving; and what do you think happened?"

"You got the gun from him."

"No." I shook my head. "Not from Willie. I know how fast he is. He had a flat tire. I think Jerry must have dropped a nail in it. Willie didn't have time to change it, and I pretended great interest in seeing you and suggested a taxi. But a taxi could be trailed, and Willie wouldn't hear of it. Then someone thought of my car right up in front of Doc Stoddards. Jerry, my boy, had brought it there.

"So we started for here—and I don't know if Willie suggested it or I suggested it, but anyway it would be easier for Willie if I held my hands in the air—and safer. I did; and my right hand touched the roof of my car. And Georgie, what do you think I found there?"

"The fool!" Georgie said. "I told him—to—to kill you if there was the least—the faintest chance—or—or—"

"Well—" I think I told my story good for I was enjoying it—"of all things, I found a gun up there—right in the roof of my car. And when I stuck it down Willie's neck, I think he was more surprised than I was."

"The idiot! The double crosser!"

"Not a double crosser." I shook my head. "Willie thinks more of you and your life than anything—but his own life. And Willie listened to reason. Whispered reason right there in the traffic. And somehow all my hardware came back to me, and the bullets fell out of Willie's gun. Even your driver didn't know of our little deal. So when we marched in here, Willie's arm in mine and Willie's gun against my side—and my right hand in my pocket—well, Willie was in great and immediate danger."

"The fool." Georgie cursed now for the first time and I think I saw what was coming. "There's a phone there on the desk. He could have rung it."

"No." I shook my head. "Willie is very

fond of you, Georgie. Very fond of you. I told him if a phone rang in this room, even for the most innocent reason—that before the bell ceased ringing you would be dead. Willie believed me, and I think Willie was right."

I WATCHED HIM carefully as I went to the door Sally had come out of and unlocking it pulled it open a bit and whispered: "The big one this time."

And I was right. She was a big blonde, not in the derogatory sense of the words, but rather complimentary—if you like them tall and muscular and clear eyed. Well, one eye was clear. She was bewildered and after I closed the door and locked it I said:

"Gloria Masters?" And when she nodded and looked about confused. "It's all right now. I've come to take you home. Isn't that right, Georgie?"

Georgie gulped and said it was. The picture on the wall shook as his unsteady hand wavered on it.

And no one can say Georgie didn't have his chance then. I gave it to him. As a matter of fact I gave Georgie two chances, and he took the wrong one from his point of view.

I said simply, "I think it would be a nice gesture, Georgie, if you lifted the phone there and told all the boys to clear out of the house. The phone there, Georgie." I turned my head for a split second and nodded toward the phone. Sally screamed. But I think it was slightly before the scream that I turned my head back.

It was too late then for Georgie to change his mind and he knew it. But I knew something else. I knew that Georgie wasn't as old as I had thought he was or if he was, he was much quicker than I thought he was. For in that second that I nodded my head away Georgie's hand had swept behind the picture, flashed out again and, the gun it held was spitting lead.

George didn't count on accuracy, at least to begin with. I guess he thought the spitting lead would surprise and confuse me. It didn't. It only made my purpose the more definite. By the time Georgie had found the range—as a matter of fact a split second before Georgie had found the range—I had fired twice.

You didn't have to have sharp eyes to see where those two bullets had gone. Georgie grasped at his chest with his left hand and jerked twice. The gun in his right hand wavered with his jumping body, but his eyes were still clear, and there was a determination in his set mouth as he steadied—aimed—and I shot him some place in the center of that horse-face of his.

I walked over and I looked down at Georgie. I guess I said it aloud—certainly I thought it. "Well. Georgie, I feel better that you're dead."

It was then that the big blonde began to do tricks and sob and Sally had her hands full. And me, I walked over to the dead man under the little balcony and lifted up the machine gun. I looked it over pretty well, nodded, tucked it under my arm, went to the phone and picked it up. It was a house phone and a low voice said, "We heard the racket—but did nothing like you told us. Is everything all right?"

I whispered too. I said, "Everything is fine. Put Willie on the wire." And when Willie came I said, "Race, Willie. You haven't talked—have you?"

"No. No—I haven't—I was—I kept my word."

What he meant to say was that he was afraid to tell the others what had happened, but I didn't argue with him.

I said, "Listen, Willie—you're a nice lad and I'm going to give you a break. Georgie is deader than a salted codfish. I burnt him down a couple of minutes ago. Now you have five minutes to clear the crowd out of the house. Then turn up all the lights—every light in the house. Be at the wheel of a car outside—yes, the front. I'm leaving with a couple of ladies, in style. Got that?"

"Yes—yeah," he said.

"Okay. I'll be walking down with the machine gun that used to belong to the guy in the balcony. One unpleasant gesture and I open up and the cops come in and things break wide open. Follow my orders—and the cops are out. Can do— exactly as instructed?"

"Yes—yes," he said. His voice was tight with fear.

I WENT OVER to the blonde girl, balanced the machine gun against my knees, took both her hands in one of mine and lifted up her chin. This was my case. She might as well know where we stood, and what I had done.

"Gloria," I said, "this was a kidnaping like you read about in the papers, but never quite believe because it doesn't happen to you. Well it did. Your father obeyed instructions and didn't notify the police. He—" I was going to say he hired me but instead tried, "I'm a private detective and get ten thousand dollars for this job—taking care of you and bringing you home. Maybe he'll never want the police to know. So you keep quiet."

When she nodded I turned to Sally. Good old Sally. She was shaking a little on her pins, but straightened when I spoke to her.

"Sally," I said, "You'll have to keep that chin up." And when she nodded. "I'll find something to pass for a veil for Miss Masters. She'll need a doctor, and Stoddard will call it an auto accident or anything else for a few hundred bucks."

There was a muffler of Georgie's, a classy white silk affair. I put it around Gloria Masters' head and made a veil so good she could hardly see where she was going. Then they followed me out the door. The machine gun was swinging easily in my hands. The first shadow—and I'd blast the whole lower floor.

Our retreat from that house was an orderly affair. Willie Sims stood by the door of a sporty sedan like a first class footman. His eyes went this way and that like a scared rabbit's when he saw the gun. But I guess he wasn't afraid so much that I'd shoot him as he was that someone would see the gun.

The street was deserted. The girls piled in. I smiled at Willie.

"No one but you, Willie, need know the truth—if you are careful. If you aren't— well, the boys wouldn't like the way George took the dose. Drive on. You have my car left at my address—or I'll come after it."

He gulped and nodded.

Unfortunately Masters was at his city apartment which was a swanky affair, and we had to make our entrance rather dramatic. I tossed the machine gun in the back of the car and saw Willie drive off. Then had to put off the door man with, "Miss Masters had an accident."

We got too much attention all the way through the thing. From the hall men— that's right, there were more than one— to the elevator men, and then Masters' butler. But there was one lad who earned his onions. He was an owlish-looking man with a bald head and glasses who turned out to be Mr. Masters' secretary. Maybe he didn't know anything, but he certainly suspected everything.

He said he had better send for the doctor. Mr. Masters was not expected to live for the next twenty-four hours. His daughter's sudden return might be the shock that killed him—or again the one that pulled him through. But he might die at any moment. The doctor lived only two floors below.

"Okay," I said to him. "It's like this. Telephone Doctor Stoddard to come at once and look over Miss Masters." I gave him the number. "He'll say she was in an automobile accident. Get a lawyer— anyone in the building. Mr. Masters will want to change his will at once. My name's Williams—Race Williams. Private investigator. I got his daughter out of this—"

I paused and looked him straight in the eyes. "What we may all choose to call an auto wreck. Do you understand that?"

"I will try to understand it to the best of my ability."

"And—" I still held his eye—"make out a check payable to me for ten thousand dollars. I'll want it signed before I leave. But get Stoddard here and we'll fix the girl up before her father sees her. Also this lawyer—any lawyer."

"Was—was she treated badly—in the accident I mean?" The secretary turned suddenly human and suddenly wise.

"Bad enough. Don't think that what I'm telling you to do is silly."

"I've been with Mr. Masters eighteen years," he said. "I'm not altogether a fool. This check of course is assurance of your silence."

"My silence," I told him stiffly, "is assured without pay. The check is a darn small fee for what he got and what I nearly got. But it was my agreed upon price."

Doc Stoddard's work was good, especially when the nurse conveniently couldn't find Mr. Masters' glasses. Seeing his daughter proved a tonic rather than a shock, and the glasses turned up in time for him to sign the check. Sally I took home with me, for I was going to see she made the plane to the coast. And it was Sally who told the story of the shooting to the delighted Jerry.

"Behind a picture, eh?" Jerry was enthusiastic. "That was clever." He paused and then, "But Mr. Williams has done that before. Gee, Mr. Williams, you must have been sick not to see it when he played around the picture like that— especially when you've pulled the same stunt and—and—" Jerry stopped again and his eyes got big. "Why you knew and—and—"

"That's enough, Jerry," I slammed in. "I had never been in the room before. I couldn't possibly know he had a gun behind that picture."

"That's right," said Jerry, in that innocent voice of his. "You couldn't know—you could only—only guess."

Maybe that was the truth. Maybe it wasn't. But Georgie was deader than dog meat.

CARROLL JOHN DALY

Not My Corpse

DEATH COMES TWICE

THERE MAY BE likable crooks and there may even be likable killers, but Jake O'Hara was not one of them. He curried favor with everyone who needed currying. He was rubbing his hands when he came into my office. "Well, what do you want?" I demanded.

"I don't know, Race," he said. "That's a fact." He opened his wallet and placed two century notes on my desk. "I'll pay that to find out."

"I don't like anything about you, Jake," I told him. "Beat it."

"But," he insisted, "you're a private eye, aren't you? I got trouble. We've never crossed."

I shrugged. "You don't cross anyone in the open. You do your shooting from behind garbage cans and the corners of buildings." And when his eyes widened, "I understand you even peddle the stuff."

Jake didn't get mad. "I never sold a dime's worth of the stuff."

"Okay, Jake. I hear you can't make a

dame unless you feed her stuff. It all adds up the same. I don't like you."

"We can't like everyone." Jake stood there and agreed with me. "Remember the dirty little man in the dirty little room."

"Harvey Rath?" I was startled. "I never believed that myth, Jake—and he's been dead, anyhow out of circulation, for a long time."

"He ain't out now." O'Hara laid a card on the desk before me. On it was printed:

THERE'S A DIRTY LITTLE MAN IN A
DIRTY LITTLE ROOM

"Would you like to get a card like that?" Jake asked me.

"I wouldn't mind," I told him.

BUT I WAS curious. I noticed that there was a nervous twitching to his fingers and that his usually ruddy face was pale.

"Go back a couple of years, Race." He wet his lips. "Guys were being shook down, bumped for no reason at all. Tough Tony walked into Eddie Smart's place. Eddie was behind the bar. Him and Tony were friends, see. Tony pulled out a gun and shot him through the head. 'That,' said Tony, 'is straight from a dirty little guy in a dirty little room.' Tony was hopped up all right. What more he might have said we don't know. Milligan was in the bar and he pulled out a rod and blew Tony apart."

"Jake," I said, shoving the two Cs back into his hand, "I'll give you some free advice. I think someone is trying to scare you to death." I opened the door. "On your way, Jake."

"It isn't me so much as my girl," Jake whimpered, as I let him out of the office.

Five minutes later Jerry, my boy, came in.

"Boss," he said, "wasn't that Jake O'Hara who left you a little while ago?"

"Yes," I said. "So what?"

"So I know something about him you don't know. He's lying dead in the gutter. Two doors down the street. Someone stopped a car, beckoned him over and spat lead in his face."

"Where do you get your information?"

"Clarice—on the newsstand downstairs. She buzzed me. I know it was O'Hara. I put the glasses on him out the window."

They were moving the body and the crowd too when I put my six-ply glasses on the street below. I guessed Jake O'Hara wasn't worrying so much now. I shrugged—and gulped. What of the girl?

"Has Jake got a girl?" I hollered to Jerry. "And do you know where she lives?"

"A dame called Sissy Pierson," he said. "She slipped down from the upper crust too. Does a number in one of the night spots. I'll get her address for you."

Jerry was efficient that way. In five minutes he had her address, on Ninety-second Street.

"If she's got a phone," he said, "it's a secret."

I went out and took a taxi to Ninety-second Street to a small walk-up apartment.

Sissy Pierson's card in the mail-box read "4D." I pressed the bell and held my hand on the door waiting for the latch to click. There was no click. Perhaps she wasn't in. Perhaps she was in danger and Jake had told her not to answer the bell.

I pressed a buzzer of a ground floor apartment and got service. I was in the door fast and on the stairs before 2A could get a look out at me. Though you can always apologize. On the fourth floor I found 4D and it didn't take too keen an eye to see that the door latch wasn't caught. Someone could do that going out quietly; someone could do it going in quietly. A lad could shove that door open and walk into a lot of trouble. A burst of gun-fire, or a tap on the head from someone hiding behind a door. I gave the bell a ring, heard it plainly back in the apartment. No response.

I thought I'd go in and wait for Sissy Pierson. I was there to do her a favor. Most normal people don't like getting themselves killed that's quite certain.

The hall was fairly dark so I swung my gun into my right hand, crouched low, hoping if it was gun-fire they'd shoot high or I'd shoot first, and started to push the door, to put the squeeze on anyone hiding behind it.

Nothing stirred. I got the door back as far as it would go. I looked down a long straight hall and into a living-room with curtains drawn back from the windows. I had plenty of light now.

I STEPPED IN, closed the door and with my gun still in my hand walked slowly down the hall. A kitchen loomed up to my right and I took a look-see—empty—so I went to the living-room. The furniture was comfortable, expensive, too, and in surprisingly good taste.

Living-room empty. No dining-room. The door to the room down the side hall was closed. I raised my gun slightly and pushed this door open.

I didn't even have to enter the room. I was looking straight at the bed and the girl that was huddled on it—a dead girl. Despite the rope that bound her feet to the foot of the bed and her hands to the head of it, she was curled up, half-turned on her side.

Her lips were torn and the skin on either side of that mouth was raw with little bits of whitish linen still clinging to it. Strips of adhesive tape lay on the floor, evidently tossed there as they had been stripped from the lips they sealed.

She was fully dressed but her feet were bare—and blistered and burnt, and many burnt matches and cigarette butts were in the deep ash tray.

Someone had tied that girl on the bed and before killing her had tortured her for information. If he got it or not I didn't know.

There are times for lads in my business to get from under. This was not one of the times. I lifted the phone by the bed, dialed Headquarters, and got Sergeant O'Rourke.

"I've walked in on a body, O'Rourke," I said. "It's murder." I gave him the address and the apartment number. "I'll give you the set-up and don't bring Inspector Nelson with you."

"He's Homicide, Race," O'Rourke said easily. "He's got to come along."

Which was true enough.

I took a quick look-see in the bathroom, then sat down in the living-room and took a smoke. I guessed the dame was Sissy Pierson all right. Her picture was around the place enough, in all sorts of poses—mostly costume stuff or lack of costume stuff.

How had she died? I thought offhand she'd been choked to death from the marks on her throat. How long had she been dead? Not long—her body was still warm. I didn't question further. She was not my corpse. She belonged to the Police Department.

I went into the kitchen and looked for a bottle of whiskey. I've seen a lot of mean killings. I can take them, but that don't mean you ever get exactly used to them. She hadn't been a bad-looking kid. I took a stiff drink.

She couldn't have been a day over twenty-three. I took another hooker, went back in the living-room and sat down to wait. I was thinking she wouldn't mind about the whiskey.

Pretty soon they came—O'Rourke, the same friendly cop as ever, his gray hair beginning to whiten, and Inspector Nelson. O'Rourke was only a sergeant in rank, but he was close to Commissioner Porter. He could have been an inspector a long time ago but as he said, and meant it, a copper learns more when he keeps close to his men.

Inspector Nelson acted with his usual belligerency, as if he had just found me after I'd murdered the woman. He disliked all private dicks, and me in particular. But I wouldn't be shoved around like a lot of the other cops and he knew it.

CHAPTER 2

DAUGHTER OF WEALTH— AND RESPECTABILITY

DR. SPEAR, THE assistant medical examiner, came on the heels of the boys who were setting up cameras and going over the place.

Dr. Spear was not the public's idea of a big city medical examiner. He never complained that he was pulled away from his dinner, never made flippant remarks about the corpse, never kidded with the police or permitted levity from them. It was a hard, cold and serious business with him.

I was wrong about the choking to death. She had been stabbed. Right through the heart. No knife was found. The time of death he set within the hour. That made Nelson look at me sharply.

"I suppose, Williams," he said, loud enough for the cops in the living-room to hear, "you can account for your time?"

"Sure," I said, just as loud. "I was out looking for the Malone brothers."

Which held Nelson. The Malone brothers had disappeared a couple of years ago not five minutes before Nelson dropped down on them. And Nelson had had the anonymous tip and the evidence that would convict them of murder for more than four hours. But he had checked up before even trying to make an arrest. The story still went over big—if you wanted to get under that thick skin of Nelson's.

The girl might have been killed in anger at not getting the information the murderer wanted. But it was Dr. Spear's opinion that the torture had gone on for some time.

One thing more. A card had been thrust down the girl's blouse. I didn't need to see it to know what was printed on it.

"Come around to my office and I'll match that card for you," I said to O'Rourke.

He showed the card to me then. Of course it read:

A DIRTY LITTLE MAN IN A
DIRTY LITTLE ROOM

O'Rourke came around and I told him all about O'Hara's visit.

" 'A dirty little man in a dirty little room,' " he thought aloud. "Remember Harvey Rath? He was a fence for over forty years. He lived back of his pawn-shop—yes, in a dirty little room, and he was a little man, not overly clean. There were hints that he started to cash in on some of his knowledge. Tough Tony blurted it out before he died. But we never found out anything. Rath disappeared—we never found his body… O'Hara say anything else to you?"

"Not a word."

"And you never saw the girl before?"

"Not until I saw her on the bed dead. No skin off your nose, O'Rourke—another cheap gangster and his dame."

O'Rourke looked at me steadily. "She had a scrap book in her apartment, Race. She was Daniel Pierson's daughter. The stock broker. Plenty of money and society, though he was rather pushed out of it a few years back when he was divorced. A mess. His daughter blew up and got a job singing in a Chicago night-club. Made pretty good money, at first. Then she met O'Hara. Doc Spear said she needled herself."

I nodded. "O'Hara would get his girl that way. I told him so. I guess he deserved the dose…."

Only Foster of the *Journal* put me into the morning papers—a line about O'Hara taking the dose "almost immediately after leaving the office of a private detective." Evidently the advertising department wouldn't let him put my name in.

The wages of sin and hints at the sins of the parents and so on were played up good. O'Hara and the dope were pushed down as if the divorce had everything to do with it.

There were pictures of the girl when a child, and at an exclusive girls' school, and the information that last summer she had done a song and dance act at the invitation of the Junior League up in Maine for a new hospital opening on Moose-head Lake.

O'ROURKE TROTTED IN to my office several times to see if I had heard anything and it was surprising the things he knew about that girl—alive—and how little he knew about her dead.

"A couple of guys were making a play for her," he told me about a week after the murder, "and in spite of the dope O'Hara was having a tough time keeping her in line. If O'Hara hadn't come to you, Race, I'd think he threatened the wrong man in a jealous rage, and got himself knocked over."

"And the card—the dirty little man?"

"Just a red herring of O'Hara's."

"So the guy gets rid of O'Hara because he wants the girl, then tortures and kills her because she won't tell him what she saw in O'Hara. How does Nelson cater to that idea?"

"Nelson," said O'Rourke, "has it all sewed up. He liked the idea of the lover killing O'Hara, and explains it that the girl has a new boy friend. O'Hara tortures the girl to find out his name. She won't talk, so O'Hara kills her. The boy friend walks in on the body, goes after O'Hara and pops him off. The time element makes it possible."

"And I suppose I was to help alibi O'Hara."

"Could be." O'Rourke shrugged. "Anyway, a lot of guys liked her and O'Hara wasn't one to scare a man much."

"No." I shook my head. "O'Hara was scared himself."

Jerry came in then.

"I've plugged it in here." He nodded toward the phone then at O'Rourke, who took it and listened.

"Sure," he said. "I know where it is. Loft building. Body, huh? Why? She was—" O'Rourke straightened. This was not simply another body to him. He said, "Like that, eh?" dropped the phone back in the cradle and walked toward the door.

"It's a dead girl," he said slowly. "Tortured, too—burnt matches and butts."

"And a card?" I asked.

"Yes—and a card." His lips set tightly. "And if you ask me what was on it, I'll bash all your teeth down your throat. Want to come along?"

I went. And I didn't need to ask him what was on the card.

I knew.

The loft building was in the Bronx. We made time in a police car.

Nelson was already there. The Homicide boys had set up their cameras, the place was being dusted for fingerprints and Dr. Spear was finishing up his job. I got a look at the girl lying on a dilapidated couch, an old chair beside her, a tin box full of butts and matches, and the torn lips and scarred face where the adhesive tape had been torn off repeatedly as the girl evidently had been given a chance to talk.

And that was all I did see. Nelson wanted no part of me and O'Rourke didn't try to buck him.

Nelson was within his rights, so I went out into the hall and talked to the reporters.

The girl was identified two hours later at the city morgue and the papers had a field day. She was not simply the child of wealth and respectability and society. There was no personal blot on her character and certainly no family scandal back of her.

She was Elsa Ames, daughter of Otis Ames, the real estate man, and Mrs. Ames, the former Constance Barrow of the Barrow Chemical Works and the Barrow fortune. Those two names, Ames and Barrow, meant plenty of dough, and the Barrow name took care of the society, back a few generations.

The card made the papers this time. The speculations were most anything you wished to name.

What's more, the Ames girl had

disappeared in broad daylight. She had been shopping in a well-known Fifth Avenue shop and had walked out onto the Avenue—or at least walked toward the door. The store wanted her all the way out, but O'Rourke told me the girl had last been seen walking toward the Fifth Avenue entrance by a saleslady who knew her.

That was at half-past eleven in the morning. She was not seen again until four in the afternoon. Then she was dead.

Some kids playing in the condemned building had found her.

The underworld of New York— the dives and the gambling houses came in for a bad time. Even night-clubs were investigated.

I went around personally and couldn't find anything. In one of the big uptown clubs Bill Cruthers who owned the place came over and sat down at my table.

"It's a rotten racket, Race," he said. "Look at this club. Of course we have shady customers." He waved a hand. "They're all missing tonight. It's the same in the big hotels. Lads who can't stand being questioned. They've run. Not a bit of harm in—well, ninety percent of them."

"What do you think, Bill?" I said. "You've been around a long time."

"Off the record?" He grinned at me and I nodded. "Understand, Race, it's only my opinion—not anything I've heard. But the bad boys of the city are scared. There is a sort of code in the underworld of self preservation. They keep their quarrels and their wars among themselves. They don't murder respected citizens any more than they kill cops, if they can avoid it. It's bad for business—from the pickpocket in the subway to the lad at the roulette wheel. Look what it does to the night life—a respectable place like this, too, almost deserted."

"Why don't you chuck it up? There's nothing to hold you—nothing shady."

He put that nice smile on me. "Perhaps the dough I brought along in the beginning and put into different spots wasn't made by the sweat of my brow. But how many big business men wouldn't say the same thing if they told the truth? I don't let myself get pushed around and I don't push too much myself. But I'm not a sucker."

"And your idea?"

"Well—" He rubbed his clean-shaven chin. "I don't take too much stock in that card business. I never knew Harvey Rath, but I think he did use the threat of disclosing things to get a few enemies bumped off. Then someone got to him. I think, Race, the cops have a tough job. I think someone is trying to cover something."

"How?"

"Well," he said, "it's hard to connect up the two murders. I don't think O'Hara counts too much. He was only in the way. The girls had met, I suppose, and that would make it appear like a link to the police. But I think a certain guy wants to do in a certain girl and that these are preliminaries."

"So it will look like the work of a maniac?"

"Sure." He grinned. "Maybe I read too

many detective stories—but maybe the killer did too."

"But the torture business," I said.

"Why not?" He shrugged. "It's got to look macabre."

"But a man couldn't work it alone," I said. "Remember the death car, and O'Hara."

"Don't spoil a good story, Race." He got up from the table. "Here's news for you. I've sold out my interest in the night spots to some A Number One lads—Harry Long, Spencer Clarke, Malcolm Drew. They're forming a syndicate and pulling in bank money from outside. But I'll stick around a bit, see this through. The cops are running roughshod through the night. It would be something, Race, if you broke this case. If I hear anything—it's yours for a little bit of quiet when I blossom out as a gentleman, maybe a financier."

He gripped my hand again and was gone.

I liked Bill Cruthers. Never saw anything bad about him, though I heard plenty—but then I heard the same things about myself. Still I knew he'd be a mean man to cross. He was like me.

He wouldn't be shoved around.

CHAPTER 3

THE NEXT VICTIM

THE NEXT DAY Mr. Otis Ames made several statements. One of them was that his daughter had never been in a nightclub in her life.

The best one was that it was quite possible that his daughter had met Sissy Pierson, since they were both up at Moosehead Lake in Maine on the occasion of the opening of the hospital.

The police were raising the roof through the underworld and men were talking who had never talked before. The general feeling was that Harvey Rath was alive and had returned. He had passed the word along that certain people must be killed and that these killings not only included the two girls but Jake O'Hara as well, and anyone else whose death could not be satisfactorily explained. When two gunmen were fished out from under a wrecked car alongside the reservoir by Kensico Dam above White Plains the word traveled fast that these were the birds who had picked up the Ames girl and spirited her to Harvey Rath up in the warehouse in the Bronx.

O'Rourke was too busy to have any talks with me.

Then things broke wide open. A girl named Dorothy Sears Briggs, of the Austin Briggs clan, not yet twenty-one, received a message during a late dinner at a smart night spot. There were eight in her party. Every one of the eight, including her escort, the idiotic but extremely wealthy Mortimer Chase, saw her read the note carefully before excusing herself. Two of the party were sure she carried the note from the room with her.

That was the end of Dorothy Sears Briggs. At one-twenty the following morning they found her body behind some bushes in Central Park. There were no burnt matches, but her bare feet showed signs of the use of fire. Her face

CARROLL JOHN DALY

and lips were torn like those of the other two girls, though the tape was missing. Fingers that had gripped her smooth white throat finished the job.

O'Rourke came to see me again. Even his voice was tired.

"I want to check my thinking with yours, Race," he said. "You can lie in bed and do your thinking."

"Well," I told him, "I think each of these girls knew something. Maybe the first victim told them."

"Yes, yes. We figured on that, but it doesn't jell. The Pierson girl, yes. She might have been afraid to talk, for in a way she was one of the mob. But the others—why should they keep a secret, one so terrible to the murderer that he would kill horribly to prevent it being known? And O'Hara—and the two thugs who were picked up, and—"

"Wait a minute, O'Rourke," I stopped him. "Did these last two girls know each other—and did they know Sissy Pierson?"

"They knew each other socially. Dorothy Sears Briggs was a nice kid, and so was Elsa Ames, but she wasn't as far up the ladder. They met at social affairs, but weren't chummy if that's what you mean."

"Well," I said, "someone knows something and won't or can't talk."

I asked him what the Department was doing.

"Plenty," O'Rourke told me. "Since the Briggs girl was found dead Nelson has got the names of nearly every young girl in the social set, or trying to get in. He's got the name of everyone who knew Dorothy Briggs personally, and a few who knew Sissy Pierson. He's interviewed most of them."

"And the results?" I wanted to know.

"Irate papas and friends of irate papas, and lawyers of irate papas have been calling the commissioner. But Nelson's not backing down."

"What did he find out?"

"That the daughters of the rich have their secrets as well as the daughters of the poor—and that some of their so-called friends are about as willing to talk about it. But the killer's hot. Some day he'll make someone talk—say exactly what he wants to hear."

"I'm lucky to be out of it," I told him.

"But you're not out of it." He looked straight at me. "No citizen is out of it—no decent citizen. The alert is on for eight million people in New York. Someone is sure to talk. Something is sure to break any minute. No, Race, you're not out of it."

I shrugged that off....

THE SHOCK CAME exactly one week after the death of Dorothy Sears Briggs. And it jarred me like an explosion.

I got a phone call to meet a man named Riley. He was a familiar figure to be seen strolling along Broadway. A dapper old guy, though not as old as he'd like you to think. He had come up from the gutter, but wasn't going back into it—not alive. He had been a pickpocket, a common stick-up and a con man, but all that was years ago. Riley had slipped from one thing to another so fast that the cops never had been able to put the finger on him. Then suddenly he went in for high class literature and poetry, and could misquote most any authority you named.

But he did get around. And he did

know what was going on. And now he was the go-between for so many things, and stepped on so few toes doing it, and never shook anyone down or made any enemies, that he was taken for granted around the underworld when anything diplomatic had to be pulled off. So he had his nose in everything.

I got his secret call—everything about Riley was secret. He wanted me to have dinner with him in a delicatessen restaurant in Brooklyn. I wondered who thought I was after his hide and wanted Riley to sound me out on what Riley always called "a meeting of the minds."

This cheap but large restaurant was doing a big business. But they had booths for two and poor lighting in the back. It was in one of these booths that I found Riley.

"I know how fastidious you are, Race," he said, as I sat down, "so I ate my dinner before you came. We haven't got more than a moment to give to each other, but it's a moment of some importance."

There was a note of excitement in his voice—strange to Riley—and a trembling to his hand and a furtiveness in the way he looked around. It was all the more strange because Riley always had the direct look, an honest, steady handclasp and a voice of assurance.

"Important to me or you?" I grinned at him.

"To me," he said. "There is ten thousand cash in it." Riley never said "grand" any more. "For you, as much as you can make the traffic bear above that. Maybe a small fortune." He leaned across the table, "And maybe death."

Riley always could be melodramatic. Then he went into swearing me to secrecy, insisting on my solemn oath that I would not divulge the source of my information.

I gave him all the assurance he needed. "Since the thing is big and it will take time," I said, "get talking. What have you got worth ten thousand dollars?"

He coughed, and prepared to give me his usual spiel about how he served mankind, then suddenly thought better of it, and said in a hoarse, unnatural voice:

"I've got the name of the next victim of the dirty little man in the dirty little room."

"What!"

The dishes rattled on the table. If Riley had wanted to throw me he certainly had. He hushed me to silence.

"That's it," he said, his voice hardly a whisper. "The name of the next—shall I say intended victim?"

"What do you mean, intended?" I said.

"You might gather a large fortune preventing it."

"And who will pay you this ten thousand? You don't think I have it."

"I think you could get it," he told me. "Her father should pay. He's worth enough."

I wanted to tell him he was crazy. But Riley was not crazy. And when Riley gave, or rather sold, information it was good information. You got all you paid for.

"Look," he was saying. "I only want your word that the ten thousand is mine. Then I'll give you the name of the girl. Then you'll send me the ten thousand. I'll be out of the city until the vicious fiend is dead, the girl is dead, or you are dead. Don't you see, Race, the chance I'm taking—for a measly ten thousand?"

"I'm to go to the girl's father and ask him for ten thousand dollars to tell him his daughter is the next victim. Why, he'll know it as soon as I peep the request for money." I thought a moment. "I see. You give the name. I'm to collect the money. He'd run to the phone and the police would be in. Give me the name, Riley. Maybe I can work something. Certainly you'll be entitled to a reward after—"

"No. Listen, Race. If I was as young as you, as quick with a gun as you, as willing to die as you are—and as much of a fool as you are—I'd work into it myself. This guy's millions. I'm risking my life."

I SHOOK MY head, and felt my jaw harden.

"Riley," I said slowly, "you're risking your life more right now by not telling me. When I think of the way those girls died—and that another is to die horribly if you don't speak—why, I'd choke the truth out of you for a lead nickel." I looked around the crowded restaurant. "If the place wasn't so crowded I'd start now."

"It does you credit." Riley was more himself now. "I thought of that when I picked this crowded haven of hungry mortals. No, Race. I must have the money—and I have a plan."

"In the meantime a girl dies."

"I think not."

"Riley." I was recovering now. "You can't know. If the money was obtained and then—the girl—well, we'd want her to live, of course."

"Of course. And for once I'll break my rule and tell you how I know. Tiny Prague—you know him?" I nodded. "Bad he was back in the days when guns worked more. He did his stretch and I guess he was lucky he didn't sit down on a chair for murder. He's been straight since. Has charge of the bar at the Golden Eagle. I think Cruthers gave him his chance. Big handsome fellow, Tiny Prague.

"Well, I was at the Golden Eagle and Tiny took a phone call in the booth. I happened to be in the next one and heard him curse—a frightened, but a determined curse—and heard him swear if he fried he wouldn't do it. Then he mentioned a girl's name, and there was horror in his voice. 'I'll go to the police,' he said. 'I'll go to Bill Cruthers!' Then I heard the girl's name again, and when he came out of the booth he was white. Perspiration was running down his face. He didn't drink, but he did then, and put on his hat and coat and went out."

"Anything else?"

"Yes. He muttered over the phone like he was repeating what he heard—'A dirty little man in a dirty little room.'"

I looked carefully at Riley. "Well, Bill Cruthers is straight. If he goes to Bill—" And I was thinking of Bill's promise to deal me in if he heard anything.

"He won't go to Cruthers." Riley was saying. "Tiny's dead, Race. Stabbed in his own apartment—through the back. And no card, Race." He paused. "That's significant, isn't it?"

"Could be." But I couldn't think of anything significant about it.

"So," said Riley, "ten thousand is dirt

cheap. Listen how you can work it. Of course you don't go to the girl's father. You go see—"

And Riley talked....

I had done some work for the Second National Bank. In a way I knew the president. He had bowed stiffly when the others had shaken my hand at that board meeting. But he hadn't liked my method and my ethics, though he congratulated me begrudgingly on behalf of the stockholders and the depositors.

"I'll be satisfied with what he says, Race," Riley went on. "If you don't get the money—" he shrugged—"I've done my duty. But I expect you to get the money."

"I don't like it, Riley," I told him, "but I'll play it your way. If it doesn't pan out, and you don't give me the girl's name, or go to the police with it, I'll get the information out of you."

Riley smiled as we both stood up.

"You'll mail me the money, Race—in cash—or you won't find me."

CHAPTER 4

BODY BLOW

Now to walk in at night and call on J. Fletcher Logan, President of the Second National Bank, for a private conference—as Riley wanted me to do—was something. I had to pull a few fast ones to do it.

I decided to work through Frank Rainer, play-boy with plenty to play with. Not that he'd have any influence with J. Fletcher Logan, but his eccentric aunt would. She was both society and money,

and even J. Fletcher Logan would respect her wishes.

It took me a couple of precious hours to work it. Enough to say that "a gentleman would call on J. Fletcher Logan on a matter of the gravest importance." The gentleman was me. But Rainer insisted on it that way, since anything less wouldn't impress his aunt.

At that I guess it wasn't the first secret visit J. Fletcher ever had. His secretary met me in the alley of his Fifth Avenue home, at the door. He was a bald-headed, horse-faced individual with eyes like a ferret, and he knew me at once.

"Mr. Logan will see you briefly in his upstairs study," he said. "The hour is late. You will understand that."

I said I would and followed him along a dim narrow hall to a small elevator. It shot up like a snail.

J. Fletcher Logan was as formidable-looking as his name and position in the financial and social world indicated he would be. He was in a dark purple dressing gown. His white hair was neatly combed and parted in the middle with mathematical precision.

He was standing behind a desk, tall and rather on the thin side, and with a slight stoop. There were two pairs of glasses on his desk, the nose type and spectacles. His eyes were blue—not fishlike, not bright and pleasant—just a steady sort of pale blue.

"Mr. Williams—with a message of the gravest importance," he said simply.

I looked at the secretary who closed the door and stood by it, and he got the point and said:

"My secretary, Mr. Norman Hilton, has been with me twenty years. You may proceed."

I proceeded. His dark eyebrows went up when I broke into the society murder cases, but although I didn't like the man, I'll admit he heard me through, even to details. His face expressed nothing when I came to the ten-thousand-dollar part. I finished with the final crack that I believed in my informant, that he had never misled me, and that he wanted to know if Mr. J. Fletcher Logan would advise the father of this girl to pay the money. Even before I knew the father's name.

"A close personal friend of yours, who accepts your advice always," I finished, just as Riley had put it.

J. Fletcher Logan spoke then.

"Mr. Williams, this girl's father, whom your informant has in mind, is quite evidently a personal friend of mine or one who is in a position or in the habit of seeking my advice and reasonably certain of acting on that advice. Would I advise him then to place in the hands of this doubtful character the sum of ten thousand dollars for information of a most tragic and horrifying nature, affecting the welfare of his home, actually, as you believe, the life or death of his daughter? Now suppose that this informant, being as you frankly state of an unsavory character, made the same offer to a dozen different men at the same time through different intermediaries."

"Mr. Logan," I interrupted, "I have stated the case to the best of my ability. I want a yes or a no."

"Really. Then—"

"If I may suggest," the secretary cut in, "we have had dealings with Mr. Williams before, Mr. Logan. Perhaps we might—compromise on a small amount in advance and later—"

"With a girl's life in the balance and every moment precious?" I said. "If the price was low enough I'd pay it myself. I wouldn't be here."

"How low?" Mr. Logan's voice was soft now.

"I can raise five thousand," I told him. "I found that out tonight. And it's from people you wouldn't even meet."

"Very well, Mr. Williams," Mr. Logan said. "The bank will lend you the other five. I'll go on your note myself."

He bowed stiffly, and was about to dismiss me when I saw a phone across the room and asked to use it. When he nodded I lifted the phone and dialed my number. I heard Riley answer as Logan was rebuking his secretary in a soft voice for bringing me so neatly into making my offer.

"All right," I said to Riley. "The money goes to you at the opening of the bank tomorrow. Never mind congratulating me. I don't want congratulations. The girl's name! What?" I guess my voice went up. "And her father is—her—?"

I dropped the phone in its cradle, turned and faced J. Fletcher Logan.

"You look a little stunned." For the first time he actually smiled. "I hope you found your investment—satisfactory."

I couldn't speak. I simply looked at him. When I did speak, my voice sounded far off. "Not satisfactory at all, Mr. Logan— not at all."

"Well, I won't question you. You have your ethics, or so you told me once. Our little talk will be confidential and the bank will take care of you in the morning. I am not to know the girl's name, of course."

"But you are to know it." I guess a hundred ways to break it to him were dashing through my muddled brain. Then I tossed it out. "The girl's your daughter." And when his face remained the same, "Your daughter Martha. Martha Logan."

People have taken blows before too heavy for the mind to accept at once, and I thought that was what had happened to Logan. I guess the secretary did too, for he came over and took his arms.

"It's true, Mr. Logan," he said. "Somehow I knew the moment Mr. Williams spoke, yet he couldn't have guessed it."

No, I hadn't guessed it. Maybe I should have. Later I knew I shouldn't have. Not J. Fletcher Logan's daughter. Not Riley actually sending me to the father.

I'll say this for J. Fletcher Logan. He could take it—plenty. He opened his mouth to speak, but no words came. But he didn't let his mouth hang open. He closed it firmly and leaned on the desk, not gripping it for support exactly, at least not giving me that impression. Logan had faced crises before, though not like this, and he was gathering his mental strength to face this one.

His secretary suggested a brandy, and that he sit down. Logan waved him aside.

"No, Norman," he said. "I like to take things standing—a little brandy perhaps in a moment." Then looking at me, "I recall your doing some work for us at the bank. I did not approve your methods, yet I did not question your integrity. Now—is it possible that your information is erroneous?"

"Anything is possible," I told him, "but I'd say the odds were twenty to one that my information is correct."

"There is nothing from my point of view to substantiate this—this horror. I am thinking."

Logan waited a full minute, took the brandy Norman offered him.

"Nothing strange about Martha's actions lately," he murmured. "Not even little things. She is an especially level-headed girl, Williams. The police must be notified at once."

"I wonder, sir." Norman was in it now. "The police are capable, honest, and without doubt anxious to protect you and yours, and prevent what would be tantamount to a national disaster. But you know yourself, Mr. Logan, that things leak out."

"Leak out!" Logan's voice raised. This strong man of finance was using all that strength now to fight hysteria. "What does it matter? A cordon of police day and night! I'll call the commissioner."

I broke in hurriedly.

"Where," I asked, "is Miss Logan now?"

"Ah!" He swung then. "Norman, she's in bed, isn't she? Or did I see her at dinner? Mr. Williams, you think—"

"I don't think," I told him. "Who knows where she is? The thing to do is to find her at once." And as he moved toward the phone, I said, "I don't know if your phone is tapped or not, but a call to the police might bring immediate and disastrous action. I want to find her."

"Her maid—Walters," Norman said, and pressed a button. "But I think Miss Martha is out of town."

Walters came. She was not a frivolous young French maid, but rather stout, motherly, and dependable-looking.

Martha Logan had gone up Westchester way to a party, she said. But she was not staying the night. "Her work at the hospital, you know." Her train would arrive at eleven twenty-seven. Thomas, the chauffeur, was to meet her at the Roosevelt Hotel. Yes, the maid thought she was returning alone.

I got a good description of how Martha Logan was dressed before the maid left us.

CHAPTER 5

A GUN ROARS

I GUESS THE same thought entered the minds of all three of us at the same time. That thought was that there was a long underground tunnel, the passage from the station to the Roosevelt Hotel.

I walked over to the desk and lifted a small picture from it.

"Miss Logan?" I asked, and when both men nodded I shoved it into my pocket, grabbed up my hat and went to the door.

"Better let me out as quietly and quickly as possible," I said to Norman. "The house might be watched."

"Yes—yes." Logan was still beside the telephone. "Norman will see you down. Williams, don't hesitate to protect Martha in any way necessary."

"In the way perhaps that you objected to when I worked for the bank last year," I couldn't help but throw it at him.

He faced me squarely.

"I was a narrow-minded man then. Perhaps I am a narrow-minded man now." His lips set grimly. "Strike without mercy. Kill, if it is necessary. My name, my money, and my lawyers will stand behind you."

"I don't think it will come to that yet, Mr. Logan," I said. "I've got plenty of time to reach the station. Wait until I contact your daughter before using that phone."

As I left the room, J. Fletcher Logan called after me:

"Are you armed?"

I grinned and swung a gun into my hand from a shoulder holster so fast that Norman jumped. I stepped into the elevator with him and crawled down three floors. If I had had an acetylene torch I'd have burned the cable and dropped the car.

Norman said, as he let me out the back:

"Think nothing of that ten thousand, Mr. Williams. I'll have a check ready for you as soon as you return...."

That long tunnel that runs from the Grand Central Station to the Roosevelt Hotel is hardly ever full of people at eleven-thirty at night. As a matter of fact, I've seen it deserted sometimes at seven P.M.

A good place for a murder, but not too hot for a kidnaping. The girl would scream if conscious, and if unconscious would have to be carried out. That would be my meat. At least this three-time murderer of young girls had to get his prey alone where he could torture information out of them.

I was thinking it over as I got out of the taxi and walked into the Grand Central Station, coming down the ramp from Forty-second Street. I still had seven minutes before the train came in. I'd had a good look at the girl's picture and I had liked what I had seen. A little on the ritzy side maybe, but good.

She held her head as if she was somebody, and I guess she was, at that. Her features were sharply defined, but not too sharply cut. There was a delicate fineness to her face, like that in those old-time paintings, with a little firmness tossed in. A hands-off sort of look.

She was a blonde and her eyes were blue. Best of all, I had a full description of what she was wearing.

I got up to the gate where the train came in but not too close. I couldn't spot anyone in the theatre crowd returning up Westchester way who looked too out of place.

Thomas had already left with her car, but my idea was to introduce myself to Martha Logan, preferably after she left the tunnel and came up in the Roosevelt Hotel. I'd take her home in a taxi in case this was the payoff and an accident had been arranged for the Logan car.

The station was pretty crowded. People hustling for trains, the after-theatre crowd, and there was quite a mob around the gate where she would arrive.

The train came in. The gates opened and people poured through. The train must have come from well upstate because it was pretty crowded and a lot of people were coming through and a lot more were meeting them—and I saw the girl.

IF YOU DIDN'T know there was great wealth and family behind her you'd fall for her right away. She walked like a thoroughbred. It was only knowing about the dough that gave you the idea she might be snooty.

Blonde hair peeped out from a little hat. The weather was still cold but she carried her coat over her arm. A plain coat, a plain tailor-made suit—but I expect it cost heavy dough. It fitted her perfectly, or she fitted it perfectly. Fine straight body, fine quick walk, nice blue eyes.

I turned in after her when she was in the thickest part of the crowd.

I was closing in to get on her heels when I saw the man. Short, stocky, well-dressed, nothing loud. I didn't know him, but he didn't give me a pleasant impression. He walked through the crowd, got close to the girl, and I saw his hand come out of his overcoat pocket. There was a gun in it.

A place like that seemed no place to intimidate a girl and make her walk quietly to the nearest exit and disappear into the night. Certainly the gun was jammed close to her. Certainly other people saw. One woman saw it, for she cried out—and my right hand swung up under my left armpit. A man alongside of me was jarred back with my sudden movement. Maybe I could have shot the gun out of that fellow's hand under ordinary circumstances. But heads were bobbing in and out between me and the girl.

There was the man's body. There was the man's face. There was the man's gun—and I read death in that face. Death for the girl. In that hard, cold, evil face of a killer. For an instant his face was clear, his eyes were clear, his gun clear and raised close to the girl's head. All clear—and I squeezed lead once.

The roar of the gun. A woman alongside of me looking at me and folding up and fainting. The screams of another. The—yes, the gunman going down amid the small, jammed-up crowd.

I moved fast then. I knew the man was dead. You don't lay a .45 into a man's head at twenty-five or thirty feet and not get results. Hysteria took the crowd as I reached Martha Logan. Women were screaming. Men were shoving and yelling, and that inevitable man in every crowd who can handle things was shouting orders to stand back and give the man air, and "Where the devil did that shot come from anyway?" As many people were trying to break into that circle that held death as were trying to get out.

"This way, Miss Logan." I had her by the arm and steered her along quickly. "I'm from your father," I told her, weaving in and out. "Keep your head now. Remember the notoriety if you get into the papers. Take it easy—this way."

I steered her toward the restaurant, twisted right, joined those who were going up the ramp and avoided those who were coming down asking what had happened.

It wasn't hard to get away. The gunman had figured that. People who were close to that shooting were fighting to get away from it. Those who weren't close were running toward the excitement.

The ride to the Logan house in the taxi was something. A lot of class was sitting alongside me needing protection—a few million dollars' worth of class. Also she was asking questions and I was avoiding them and telling her to ask her father. I handed her one of my cards which she made out in flashing lights.

"Race Williams, isn't it?" she said. "Yes, Race Williams, the detective."

I liked the way she put "the detective."

But I wasn't talking.

When we reached the house I hustled her in, and the place was already overrun by the law. O'Rourke was there, and Commissioner Porter himself. Logan, telling Norman to give me a check, was tossing his arms around his daughter. She wanted an explanation. Logan telling her there had been trouble at the bank and hustling her off to her rooms. But before she went she tossed a parting shot that hit the bull's-eye.

"The bank?" she said. "But Father, if it has anything to do with—with these awful murders, I want that man there." She pointed at me, smiled. "Yes. I mean Race Williams. I like him."

SHE WAS GONE up the stairs then and they were all questioning me. Had I told her? Why had I told her. To my surprise I got the drift of what Logan was saying—that he was dismissing me, handing me a check.

"Norman considers it my duty," he said. "Ten thousand dollars for the man who furnished you with such information." He bowed slightly toward the commissioner. "Of course, Williams, I realized after you had left the impossibility of my daughter actually being involved in such a sordid—" He choked that off. "I'm inclined to agree with the commissioner that you yourself were taken in and had nothing to do with the—extortion."

I looked at the check. It was for ten grand all right. I looked at the commissioner and at O'Rourke. They knew nothing about the shooting at the station. Then I turned to Logan, but I didn't throw in his face his suggestion that I kill if necessary, that his lawyer and his money would stand back of me.

"The ten thousand, Mr. Logan, is simply expense money," I said. "There is a small fee for escorting your daughter home from the station. I get twenty-five dollars an hour or for any part of an hour."

"Very well," Logan said, but the commissioner's eyebrows went up and O'Rourke grinned. "Norman, make Mr.—this man—out another check for twenty-five dollars."

"One moment." I was calm, but I was good and mad. "There is a small extra charge for additional service. I don't know what the other agencies charge, but I always demand three dollars and seventy-five cents extra when I kill a man in protecting the life of my client's daughters. If you think it too high, why mail me what you think it's worth." I turned then and started toward the door—just in time to bump into Inspector Nelson.

"So," said Nelson, grabbing me by the shoulder, "you shot him—just like that."

"Just like that," I repeated. "So what?"

Ten minutes later we were all in the upstairs study. All but the girl. Intended victim Number Four—Miss Martha Logan.

CHAPTER 6

RACE HAS A THEORY

THE COMMISSIONER WAS heavy and quiet and composed. Nelson was pacing the room and talking. O'Rourke was standing beside the door, and J. Fletcher Logan was sitting uncomfortably in the big chair by the flat desk, Norman beside him as if ready to take notes, but without his usual secretary's pencil and notebook.

"If this is a pinch, say so," I said, "and I'll get my lawyer. Not yours." I looked at J. Fletcher Logan who had made no remark.

"Come, come." Commissioner Porter was pouring the oil around. He was a good commissioner and he was a good politician too. "Let us have it all, Williams. Tell us what happened at the station."

So I told it. The killer's face, the gun in his hand, death in his eyes.

"It was a split second or death for Miss Logan," I said. "A wound would only have jarred him and he'd have fired. So I shot to kill—and he died."

"Like that." Nelson stopped walking and glared at me. "You know these girls have never been killed on sight. They've been kidnaped or lured away, and tortured before they died. Don't say you didn't think of that. You claim you think of everything."

"Sure," I said, "I thought of it. I thought, too, that maybe the murderer could have changed the pattern. All right, Nelson." I glared back at him now. "If you were there, you'd wait and see what his plans were—is that it?"

"I'm asking the questions." Nelson pulled the iron jaw on me.

"You're not asking this one, Nelson. I'm asking it." I turned to J. Fletcher Logan. "What would you expect from the police? A wait-and-see game? I had an instant decision to make."

"Why—er—" J. Fletcher sort of stiffened. "Under the circumstances—"

"You'd prefer the newspapers to carry a story about how quick-acting Inspector Nelson wounds murderer five seconds *after* brutal slaying? How would it read to you—the girl's father?"

"Come—come," said the commissioner. "The inspector is merely questioning whether your action was necessary. Let us presume it was necessary. I think perhaps the least publicity given to the whole affair in the station, the better for all concerned. We must assume that this was a hired assassin, who misunderstood his orders. It's about your information, Williams—we'd like to know about that?"

I told them all except Riley's name.

"Well, well," said the commissioner, "I think Williams has perhaps performed a commendable action. What do you say, O'Rourke?"

"I know Williams," said O'Rourke. "He

calls them as he sees them. No man can do better than that, Commissioner."

I'll give all of them credit for respecting my position and not trying to get Riley's name out of me. Nelson, no doubt, because the commissioner hamstrung him a bit.

"You feel certain you got all the information available from your—informer, Williams?" the commissioner asked.

"I'd have wrung his neck for what I got, if he hadn't made that impossible. And I'd have paid him myself. Ask Mr. Logan about that."

"Yes, yes," said the commissioner. "I am quite aware of the dramatic denouement in naming his daughter. Now, Williams, you are to understand that in a case of this importance your protection alone would hardly be satisfactory. Miss Logan must have complete protection. I would request your silence. Leave this entirely in our hands. And be so kind as to give us your opinion on the matter."

"For free?" I asked.

"For the benefit of the citizens of New York," he said slowly. "I know you too well to offer you money from the public funds."

"Nicely put."

THE COMMISSIONER WAS a smooth lad.

He didn't like my methods. But he was honest in that dislike. He never had hounded me. Cautioned me at times, yes. Maybe threatened me once or twice. But he was no hard-driving, bull-headed Nelson.

He knew there would be nothing in it for him and a lot out for him if he started driving me for killing a man in saving the life of Martha Logan. Logan—like it or not—would have to stand behind me, or the newspapers would make him. I had a story and it was a beaut.

"Well," I said, and this was my big moment, for I'd had this in my mind ever since the last girl was killed, "all of these victims held a secret—a secret of a crime—and each one who knew that secret must die."

"And the torture?" The commissioner was interested.

"The murderer knew the name of one girl who held the secret in the beginning, but he knew that there were others. He tortured Sissy Pierson to get the names of the others and got only one name. Let us say Sissy Pierson knew only one name—Elsa Ames. So he tortured Elsa Ames to get the other names, and she knew but one name. He got that name and tortured the third victim, Dorothy Sears Briggs, to get the other names—and got only one name. Martha Logan."

"Would girls like that keep a secret that was so important?" said Nelson. "You're out of your mind. We had that idea but it wouldn't fit in after the second death and certainly not after the third girl died. Now there's Martha Logan. None of these girls showed any fright, or the least apprehension even, at any time before they were killed."

"These girls didn't know what the secret they held was," I said. "Martha Logan doesn't know it now. Can't you see? All of them were at the scene of some crime. All of them saw the murderer's face. Not one of them even knew a crime was committed."

"Then why trouble to kill them?"

"Because," I said, "all of them saw the murderer. That must be the only solution. They saw the murderer, no doubt fresh from his crime, but they didn't know he was a murderer because they didn't know a crime had been committed."

"Then why would the murderer kill them?"

"Because the murderer knows that sooner or later they *will* know a crime was committed, and remember him. Now, my suggestion for solving the case, if you're interested—"

"Yes," said the commissioner, "we would be interested in that."

"Well," I said, "make a list of every unsolved murder committed in New York within the last year, or out of New York at any time Martha Logan was out of the city. Try to place her at the scene of any of those crimes. Martha Logan has seen this murderer smack at the scene of his crime but she doesn't know it, because she never heard of the crime. Good-night, gentlemen."

I turned and walked out of the room. And out of the house. Cops were all over the place....

The next night I went down to the Bright Spot, a small new night-club that was coming along. The talent was not expensive but it was good. Boys and girls got a chance to show their stuff there and make names. They had a fine talent scout combing the city. It was like a proving ground for some of the big clubs.

I wasn't there to be entertained. I wanted to see what I could pick up. Big shots dropped in there; not so big shots

CARROLL JOHN DALY

too—lads who would be barred when café society discovered it.

I guess I wasn't the only one who hoped to get some information. Lieutenant Hogan from the Broadway Squad was sitting at a table looking for all the world like an old-time matinee idol. A plain clothes man named Cohen was with him, dolled up for the sporting mob.

JOEY PALENO, THE wise-eyed, olive-skinned, smooth manager came over and flopped into a chair beside me.

"Business not so good," I said.

"Bad," he said. "I've been asked a dozen times already if the regulars were all here last night, and when they left, or if they acted nervous—and I don't know who are regulars and who aren't any more. They all got up and left last night at about the same time, except a few."

"A telephone call tipped them off that something was wrong?"

"Just nothing, Race." Paleno spread his hands. "You know how those things are. Everyone knows something at once. I was out at the bar and Fingers Levine is drinking alone. Suddenly he puts his half-drunk glass down and walks straight out of the place. It was a double whiskey sour at that. Talk about mental telepathy. Duke University should do its experimenting here. It's uncanny. I've seen it hundreds of times. They were all out by midnight when the cops were on the prowl."

He got up as Lieutenant Hogan went by and beckoned to him.

"See?" Paleno tossed out those expressive arms again. "Now it'll be what time some of the drunks got playing musical chairs."

I watched the show. The girl who was on had talent. "Feather" Falon they billed her. And I appreciated the club a little more. Her old man had been shot to death in a gang war when she was a kid. Feather was tough. Feather was afraid of nothing.

Feather looked like a million dollars. Maybe two million, for that was the first time it struck me that Feather looked like Martha Logan. Or was it simply that the Logan girl was on my brain? No. She looked like her all right. Not that they were twins. Just a likeness in height, color of hair, fair skin.

I saw Bill Cruthers. I gave him the hand as he passed and he came over and sat down at the table beside me.

"They'll have me down to Headquarters, Race, for associating with you," he said. "It'll be my first trip, too."

"What are you doing down here?" I asked him.

"Getting around. The Bright Spot is part of the syndicate, but it won't be known until we branch out and welcome the big money. I'm trying to smooth the rough spots. The cops are at it again."

"So Joe told me. Another big—crime?"

Bill Cruthers had a nice smile. "Don't be coy, Race," he said. "A shot was fired and everyone who should know knows. The cops go into a panic and start raiding again." He leaned forward. "How deep are you in it?"

I ignored that.

"What are you doing down here?" I asked him again. "You've got bigger business."

"Well," he said, and he was serious, "it

isn't known and I wouldn't like a guy who started guessing. When this panic clears up I'm going to marry Feather Falon and take her out of this business."

"Feather Falon?" I was surprised.

"She's the cutest, straightest little shooter that ever trod the Avenue. Anyway, I'm for her if she likes it or not. She'll take a chance on anything for money and she's ambitious, so I guess I'm set. I'll take her to South America—abroad if things are right—to the West Coast, and I won't be back until they've forgotten—if then. Then maybe I'll star her on Broadway. The truth is—"

"Yes?" I waited.

"I'm in love with her, Race."

Then he went on to talk about his age. Thirty-eight not being so old. That he'd make it up to her in many ways. He'd run straight for years. Her old man had been no good, but the kid was straight. Loyal.

"Bill," I told him, "you don't have to cry all over your face to me. It will be a real break for her. She's getting a swell guy." I shook his hand. "I wish you luck and I'll send you a wedding present."

He hesitated a moment before he spoke.

"You might do something for me now," he said. "I don't want to mix my name up with hers or I'd do it myself. Inspector Nelson is buzzing her back stage. Every once in a while they drag her in because of her old man. But the girl's straight as a die—I know that. I thought maybe you'd slip back and break it up. I've got to toddle. Nelson would forget anything to jump on you. Give him the Malone brothers gag."

I didn't like it, but I did wander back stage. I'd had no idea that Bill Cruthers was gone on Feather Falon, but it explained how she got her chance at the club.

I didn't cross Nelson and I didn't see Feather Falon. I found out enough to know that she had gone off with Nelson, but if he had dragged her down for questioning I couldn't tell. The watchman back stage said he didn't know.

"Cops are like that," he said, adding that Feather had a temper but she hadn't been using it. "Believe me, son," he said, "she ain't tongue-tied, either. He must have offered a few bucks. That kid will do anything for money."

So I left without any information except the item of Bill Cruthers' heart throb that any gossip columnist would give his right eye to have.

CHAPTER 7

A DIFFERENT PATTERN

A late edition of the paper had not a word about Martha Logan, nor had I been mentioned yet in the Grand Central Station shooting. The commissioner was soft-pedaling things until he got the breaks.

I wondered. Three girls had never got the breaks. Martha Logan—I rather liked the kid. At least she'd had a break the other girls didn't have. The police knew that her number was up.

Did that give her safety? It should, for a while. Surely they'd toss enough police around her. She would have an escort every place she went, if they let her go any place. No. It looked as if she would have to stay in her own house until she—or the killer—died.

The next day I liked her better. I went down to the *Times* and went through some old papers with the help of a doll who knew the society angle. Martha Logan had done her stuff. She held a record for war bond sales and not to the millionaire set either. She had gone out and done her part at public gatherings. Sold them on her personality, too, without benefit of identification.

She had been a nurses' aid. None of this stuff of running around in a pretty uniform and meeting important visitors to the hospital. She had done more than straighten flowers and hand over vases to be filled with water by someone else. She had worked. Seven o'clock in the morning stuff—six days a week, and sometimes seven.

What's more, she hadn't simply waved the flag and folded it up when the war folded. She had kept right on at the hospital. More work and less pictures in the papers than any girl in the city was the way the superintendent of the hospital put it. She said the boys needed her as much now as then.

More—because the glamour had gone out of it when the drums stopped beating, and no glamour, no girls. They had quit by the hundreds. If she had done two girls' work during the war she had been doing five girls' work since.

Sure, I felt a little proud. I had given her a chance to carry on, and now the police were watching her, so she couldn't carry on until the thing was settled....

O'Rourke came in to see me the next day before I had breakfast. He still looked worried, but he looked as though he'd had more sleep. He had some typewritten data in his hand.

"Here," he said, "is a list of every murder for the past two years in the city of New York, and out of it on the dates we can fix the Logan girl as out of it. She has never been near most of the places at any time. The Central Park killing—well, she rides in the park once in a while but never at the right time to have been near when killing was pulled off. Besides, she's never had the other three girls riding with her. She's sure of that."

"Has she ever been with them? I mean all at once."

"She doubts it," said O'Rourke. "Sissy Pierson, she remembers meeting—but don't know where. She identified her from the picture. Both the other girls she knows. The first one to die after Sissy—Elsa Ames—she didn't know too well, but had met her around. The third one she knew better. That was Dorothy Sears Briggs. But only met her at parties."

"Have you ever placed the four together?"

"Yes," said O'Rourke. "At the Plaza in April of Forty-four, and Madison Square Garden in December of Forty-five. Uptown at the Armory on New Year's Eve of the same year. A lawn fête on the old Untermeyer Estate up in Yonkers last May. There may have been other affairs, but we can't be sure. Like the docking of a troop ship in Forty-four. Sissy Pierson is hard to place always. Then last Labor Day up in Maine on Moosehead Lake." And when I looked up at him, he said, "There were one hundred and thirty-seven guests that came from New York. At the other affairs, all but the Plaza, there were over a hundred, at the Garden nearly two hundred—and no one was killed at the Plaza, or the other places."

"She's not keeping anything back?"

"No," said O'Rourke. "It's a wonder she remembers as much as she does. All she did was entertain, sell bonds, and work at the hospitals. Half the time she didn't know where she was going, even when the time came. Says she met a lot of people a lot of places. I was out early this morning talking to all the girls she knew well. Boy, are they a suspicious lot! I didn't mention her name in particular. I let them think I was asking her questions, too. They remember a lot of the blamedest things, and make up a lot of the blamedest things. For my money, I'd bury the Logan girl in the Tombs until we clear up this thing."

"You showed her pictures, I suppose."

O'Rourke chuckled, and shrugged.

"Practically moved the Rogues' Gallery up into her sitting room." He shook his head then. "She recognized one guy for us. Said she didn't know where she had seen him, but remembered his face. Nelson hit the ceiling and had every cop in the city after him—picked him up in twenty-seven minutes. He has a record, yes, but the fact was he served the Logan girl at a luncheon in a midtown hotel two years ago. She's got a memory all right. Nelson wanted to pin something on the bird, but as soon as he spoke of that luncheon the girl recalled him. Said he served the soup cold."

"Did he?"

"Well he—" O'Rourke stopped. "What the devil are you talking about? You're not serious? Cold soup."

"No," I said, "I'm not serious about that. Why tell me all this?"

"Old friends, Race. The police have their place and you have yours. There are a lot of things you can do we can't do."

I asked O'Rourke about Harvey Rath.

"We showed her pictures of him, but she said she had never seen him. Of course she couldn't be sure from the pictures. I knew Rath well."

"Tell me about him—his character." And when O'Rourke's eyebrows went up, "We all have character, O'Rourke, good or bad."

"His," said O'Rourke, "was just bad. He fenced things in a small way for years. Then he went in for bigger stuff. We never could lay the finger on him after he hit the high priced stuff. Suddenly he got real smart. We were sure some big stuff went through him, but we couldn't prove a thing."

"Used blackmail, put the finger on big shot crooks too," I said, and when O'Rourke nodded, "That's dangerous stuff."

"There was talk he had a little book and that it would go to the cops if he was ever knocked over. I guess it was only talk. He disappeared sudden. Two, three years now. He's dead, of course."

"Why of course? No body."

"It is easier to hide a dead body than a

live one. Racketeers, politicians, far bigger lads than Harvey Rath have died and their bodies have never been found. I come in to pump you, and you start pumping me dry. I'll have to be on my way, Race. I'm worrying about the chances this killer will take."

"He can't get through a real police block, O'Rourke," I told him seriously. "But it is a desperate situation for the killer. I think Miss Logan is the last of his victims. So this time it has only to be a quick and a sudden death, and no doubt soon. Look at how the other deaths followed one upon the other."

"But we didn't know then," said O'Rourke. "We know now. We've taken every precaution possible without letting the press in on it. The girl has seen pictures of everyone worth seeing." O'Rourke grinned. "She's recognized a few big shot racketeers, a couple spotted for black market stuff, but nothing to remember about them. Just one." His smile was a tired one. "A pickpocket at the Plaza two years back. He was acting odd. We'll get some small stuff back through it. What a memory!"

"That's what the murderer is thinking, O'Rourke. That's what he fears. Four girls saw something that will stand out in their minds when it is forced back into conscious memory through something startling, no doubt. Something that is going to happen soon. Take care of the little lady, O'Rourke. She's got lots on the ball."

"Don't you worry," O'Rourke said with great confidence, but he was still worrying his head off when he left me....

FOUR DAYS LATER, what happened knocked the opening of "Aida" with the newly discovered young opera star right onto Page Five. A woman looking out a window saw it. She didn't report it right away. She didn't have any phone and was afraid to go out to telephone.

Early in the morning, along about three, she saw a car come down the side street past a brownstone front that had been turned into a rooming house. She saw the door open, and something pushed into the street. Saw it roll over and lay in the gutter.

She hadn't been able to sleep and was sitting at the window. She sat there for quite a long time staring, fascinated. Then she woke up the girl across the hall in the back. It was almost a full hour though before the landlady called the police. Yep, the body laid there undiscovered right in the city of New York.

The man had been shot dead only a few hours before they found him. He hadn't been identified when Jerry brought me the early editions of the afternoon papers. But there had been a neatly typed card pinned on his chest—not the same terrifying note that had startled millions and struck terror to those who had daughters. It was not the same simple message that had sent the underworld into a panic. It read a little bit differently. It said:

THIS IS FOR YOU
YOU DIRTY LITTLE MAN IN A
DIRTY LITTLE GUTTER

O'Rourke fairly breezed in to see me. His eyes were bright, the wrinkles gone out of his forehead.

"You were right, Race." He patted me on the back, chuckled. "It was Harvey Rath. I knew him well. Been hiding out all right. What Martha Logan knew about him will never be known now."

"Did she see the body?"

"Her old man hit the ceiling at the very idea. And to tell you the truth, Race, I was timid about taking her down to the morgue." In a matter of fact voice he added: "But he wasn't mussed up any. A bullet-hole in his heart. We had some mighty good pictures made and sent up for her to look at. She said she had never seen him."

"That wonderful memory!" I took a silent laugh. "So Rath had all his trouble for nothing. Got anything on his killing?"

"No." O'Rourke looked at me steadily. "This Norman lad, the Logan secretary. He hasn't been in touch with you, has he?"

"Not a peep. What's on your chest?" I inquired.

"The pattern. The bullet-hole in Rath's chest. Sort of different. Not true to form. Like the Grand Central Station."

I came to my feet.

"You think I killed him!" Then I laughed. "The pattern is all right, O'Rourke, for remember, this is a different pattern. This is someone that Rath put the finger on to do some killing for him—out of the book maybe. And this guy—well, he was big or he was mad or he knew where the book was, and he plugged Rath." I nodded. "I'll admit that card on the body was a classic, and worthy of me. Was it Nelson's idea?"

"Well"—O'Rourke scratched his head—"don't blame Nelson too much. I

was wondering—the commissioner was wondering. What's so strange or insulting about it. It's like you, isn't it? Nelson thought maybe Logan had his secretary send you around some dough, too, for the job."

"I'm flattered, not insulted," I told O'Rourke. "And if you never find the lad who dished it out to Harvey Rath, you can give me the credit."

O'Rourke put cow-like eyes on me and went out chuckling. He was in a rare good humor.

CHAPTER 8

SITTING DUCK

OF COURSE I thought that was the end of it. The papers thought so too. The boys of the press surmised and conjectured and went all out according to their imaginations. They made a lot out of Nelson's ambiguous statements. But never once was the name of Martha Logan brought into the story.

The following day I saw her picture in the society column. She was among those who would attend the opera "Aida."

My first thought was that the police were finally convinced all danger was past for Martha. Then I saw the point, or thought I did. Dislike Nelson or not dislike him, he was a good cop and a careful one—at least with a name like J. Fletcher Logan. He'd have cops watching that girl at the opera. At that it seemed like he was setting her out to see if there would be any attempt on her life. Well,

I'd probably never see Martha Logan again, unless I went to the opera to get a peek at her. And that I wouldn't do for any woman.

Logan had sent me a check for twenty-five hundred, so I had made a few bucks out of it.

That night I went to Johnny Swan's Grill to eat. It was surprising the food he could dig up right out of his vest pocket if you had the money to pay for it. It was surprising, too, the people you could dig up there, and this night was no exception. As I passed through the grill an important voice spoke up.

"Mr. Williams, sir," it said, "the tables are crowded. I dislike dining alone. Be my guest, please."

A dapper little man was on his feet, half-bowing from the waist. I tried to keep the surprise out of my voice, but I knew, or thought I knew then, that Martha Logan's peril was a thing of the past. Riley was back in the city.

"Sit down, sir." He waited for me to fall into the chair across from him. "You've missed me, I see. Well, I went up to northern Michigan for a bit of shooting. Or was it fishing, or was it even Michigan?" He smiled pleasantly as he beckoned a waiter. "A little business transaction called me back. A deal that came through quite handsomely." He lowered his voice. "No doubt you read about it in the papers." And, with a stiff little bow, "Let me thank you for your promptness in our little deal."

When the waiter had brought my steak and gone Riley started in again.

"It's like this, Race." He lit up an expensive cigar. "I like to look after my friends.

There's a man now, an upright, wealthy, and distinguished gentleman who could use your services. Worked hard, you know, and played a bit too hard. A doctor has kept his body in good shape, but even a psychiatrist can't help his mental condition. You and I can—at a handsome figure."

I looked at him. "And I'm to buy back the letters. I don't like blackmail."

His sharp eyes appraised me. "If I didn't expect to live to a ripe old age I'd manage you, Race," he said. "Say twenty percent and I'd be a millionaire in a couple of years. I don't object to your swaggering in and out of places daring guys to take a shot at you, but I'd see that you got big money for each swagger—plenty of swag! I'll bet you didn't drag down what I got in our little deal."

"I didn't," I told him. "And I wouldn't have wanted to drag down what you would have got that night if we'd been alone… What's the trouble at the bar?"

Riley was out of his seat at once. If there was anything he could cash in on he wanted to have that nose of his in it first. While others were digesting what had happened, Riley would be at a phone to see what was in it for him. When I reached the door I saw him disappearing out the side entrance.

Small knots of men were talking. Other little knots were breaking up and leaving the place. Then I heard an excited guy blubbering what the commotion was all about.

"I saw it, I tell you! The car came down the street right behind the big Caddy. They poured tons of lead into it. The

Caddy hit a pole but didn't turn over. And of all things, a police car shot after that black Packard and dumped it over at the next corner. But she was dead. Her face shot away almost. Conley of the *News* was there. Got pictures."

THINGS WERE SORT of swimming. I don't think I heard someone asking questions, but I heard the little guy answer them.

"Sure, it was the financier's daughter, Martha Logan. There were cops in her car with her, going to the opera, too."

For the first time in my life my stomach went back on me. I went into the men's room and was violently sick. I must have thought a lot of that girl. And what I thought of Nelson! A sitting duck—a trial balloon to see if things were all right! Harvey Rath. All a plant to get the girl out in the open. A dead man planted to kill a live girl!

Those thoughts came later. At the time, only the words going through my head. Martha Logan's face shot half away. Conley of the *News* had pictures. Cops in the car. Following the car. The killers turned over. Martha Logan.

I had the boy bring me three whiskey sours before I got one to stay down. I gave him a five-dollar bill and told him to keep the change, then smacked him such a wallop with my open hand that he sat down on the floor. Why did I smack him? He'd started to tell me the story of the shooting, because he thought I'd been out of the café so long I hadn't heard. I slapped him down and went out onto the sidewalk.

An extra was on the street, by now. I got a copy, walked into a strange dump and read it. Not a thing new. It seemed like everyone had been killed until you read the big print over again. And there was nothing but big print. Only one thing seemed to be certain—that was that Martha Logan was dead. Cops had been riding in the car with her, and another police car following along behind. But you couldn't tell from the newspaper story whether the police car was there by accident or design.

I knew that it had been planted. And Martha had hardly left her house before the gun-fire had broken loose. Two machine guns had peppered the Logan's big Cadillac.

If the *News* had pictures, they would be in a later edition, so I didn't buy it. Martha Logan's picture covered what part of the front page was free from black print. The black print read:

FINANCIER'S DAUGHTER DIES IN CAR
AS POLICE BATTLE THUGS

So that was the end. I'd go out and get gloriously drunk.

That wasn't my usual line. Too many people want my hide, and if I was caught staggering, or caught reaching slowly for a gun, it would be my last drunk.

Anyway the stuff went down bad, so I spent my time walking up and down side streets. I didn't want to hear any more details. I simply walked. Not thinking; only walking.

Finally I shrugged and headed for home. After all, it wasn't as though I'd had a client shot from under me. She was a girl I had seen only one night. Ten to one I'd never have seen her again anyway. I'd go home, sleep it off. If I could sleep.

I have a nice apartment. Nice guys work there. It wasn't yet twelve o'clock. The doorman was still on the job. He was just about to go off duty. He looked at me, shook his head.

"Bad business," he said.

I nodded and walked back to the automatic elevators and took myself upstairs. I shoved my key in the lock, pushed the door and got no results. So Jerry had heard, hadn't gone home yet, and was guessing how things would be. Jerry was like a dog. He knew if things weren't right, if they weren't going to be right.

I gave the buzzer a couple of shorts and one long, and got action. Not that I heard his feet. The walls and the door are too thick for that. I like my joint built well. I like quiet for myself, and I like quiet for the other tenants if I intend to be noisy.

The bolt clicked off, the door opened the length of the chain.

"Okay, Boss," Jerry said. "Okay."

I remembered my instructions in case I ever walked up to my door with a gun in my back.

"Hunkery dorey," I told him. Sounds silly—but you don't live like I do.

"I know," I told him when he let me in. "You've been reading the papers."

He grinned. "I've been listening to the radio and I'm—"

"I don't want to hear anything about it," I cut in, and walked past him into the living-room.

He was saying something about a visitor when I turned, half-facing him, half-facing the bedroom door that was slowly opening.

When it opened wide I was knocked into a tailspin. If you had put a hand grenade into my mitt and told me it was an apple and asked me to take a bite and I did, I couldn't have been more surprised.

Standing in that doorway was Martha Logan, or a reasonable facsimile thereof. And me? I stood there with my mouth open.

"Boy," Jerry was saying, "like a play, isn't it?"

The girl ran over and took both my hands. She was real all right and her hands were little and soft; and all that stuff on the radio about smooth, soft hands that had sounded like hooey was suddenly true.

"I—I thought—" I said, and let it go at that.

"I know," she said. "You thought I was dead. But didn't you hear? It was on the radio after—after what happened."

"Sure," Jerry chimed in. "I tried to tell you, Boss. There was another girl in that car. But it isn't explained yet how she got there. Miss Logan here come in and wanted to wait for you and I seen the society page you folded to—"

"That's enough, Jerry," I told him. "Beat it into the kitchen. Close the door and don't try to listen."

Jerry went and I turned to the girl.

"You shouldn't have come here. Don't you know your danger?"

"That isn't like the Race Williams I've been hearing about—from Norman of course. They don't know I'm here, Race. No one can know. If they wanted to kill me, they think I'm dead. I slipped out. Even the servants watched the other girl go. I climbed out the window. How terrible! How horrible! I don't care what she was paid, I didn't want her to die for me! I came to engage you—to have you take me off some place." She stepped back and looked at me. Her smile was something. "Why, Race Williams," she said. "I believe you are really glad to see me!"

I put my hands on her shoulders and shook her up a bit. Like she was a kid. I was glad and relieved and even my stomach felt better.

"I was never more glad to see anyone in my life," I told her, and meant it. "But still you shouldn't have come."

"I had to. I couldn't be cooped up there any longer. They hired this girl, Race— maybe a not too nice girl, for her face was hard—but she didn't want to die. They wanted to take her out before that man Rath was found but I wouldn't let them. Then when it seemed all over, they did take her tonight and she was killed. I feel to blame."

"You needn't," I said. "How much did they tell you? The police, I mean."

"They tried to tell me very little, but I guessed the truth. I had to look at pictures—nothing but pictures. They wanted to know if I kept a diary, but I didn't have one. I had a date book and they went back over everything." And when I would have questioned her she said quickly, "Don't, Race—don't. I've thought and thought and thought. I've never seen a murder committed, never

been near any place where a murder was committed. It's all a horrible mistake!"

CHAPTER 9

THE REGULAR ROUTINE

JUST AS IF I believed Martha Logan, I nodded, but I knew it wasn't any mistake. I went down the hall and put the chain on the door. I tried all the windows, but Jerry had locked them.

"You can't stay here," I said to the girl, "and on the level I'm afraid to take you out alone."

"But I won't go back. I can't stand it! If I get up in the night there's a rap on the door and a policeman wants to know 'Are you all right, miss?' "

"Look." I was thinking it over. "I don't like running away. You are too well-known. The safest place for you is home with the cops."

"Race—" She came close to me. "My place is in the hospital, but if that may endanger the patients I won't go. I saw the truth of that when that understanding Sergeant O'Rourke spoke to me."

The phone rang. I picked it up. I didn't recognize the voice at first, then I knew it was Bill Cruthers.

"You wanted information, Race," he said, and his voice was hard, determined. "I'll give it to you tonight. I want to come around and see you now."

"How much do you know?" I said.

"Enough to give you a chance to burn this fiend down. And you are the one to do it. Can I get into your apartment without being seen by anyone—anyone, understand? I'm less than a block away."

I hesitated, then gave him the dope. "The rear door. Jerry, my boy, will have it open." And when he objected strenuously to Jerry seeing him, I told him, "It's pitch dark. Jerry will stand there with his back to you and you can slip right into the elevator."

I told him how to reach that door.

Then he began to holler about Jerry. Being seen might mean his life. Girls had been tortured and had talked, and so would Jerry. I saw his point of view and explained how Jerry simply stood downstairs by the automatic elevator that the superintendent dropped into the basement for my private use. Jerry stood by the door so clients wouldn't make a mistake—his back to my visitors.

"No worry, Bill," I told him. "I've worked it a long time. A hundred guys have come in that way. Big shots in the rackets. Little punks. Millionaire playboys. A couple of society women even, to say nothing of a well-known broker. They didn't want to be seen by anyone but me either. They never were."

After a pause he said, "Your word, Race, that this Jerry won't see my face or body?"

"My word," I told him, and that word meant something in the underworld. "Just run the car up to the seventh floor. I'll be watching for you."

"Ten minutes," he said. "Exactly."

I was puzzled. Why would Bill Cruthers risk his life to give me a break?

"This may be the big moment," I told Martha Logan. "A lad is coming up to empty his chest." And then, offhand, "This girl who took your place in the car—what did she look like?"

"Oh, about my build and size. And my carriage and features, that inspector said. Feather Falon they called her… What's the matter, Race?"

"Nothing," I said, after I rocked back on my toes again.

I knew now why Nelson had been in the Bright Spot the other night. This case was a series of jolts. I knew now why Bill Cruthers was coming over to spill it all. Feather Falon! The girl he was going to marry. The girl he was going to star. The girl he was going to build up and—

Had Bill Cruthers known the truth of these murders for some time? He must have had something to go on. But he wouldn't have talked before. After all, he was of the night. Those of the night who talked, died. Now, Bill Cruthers would even chance that. He must have thought a lot of the Falon girl.

I DRAGGED JERRY out of the kitchen and gave him his instructions.

"Usual thing," he said. "No peeking even a little bit?"

"Not even a little bit, Jerry." I was deadly serious. Bill Cruthers was a swell guy, but anyone knew he wasn't a lad to fool with. "We play this always on the level."

After Jerry had gone, I said: "Listen, Martha. I want you to go in that bedroom. I'll lock the door and you stay there until I tell you to come out. A visitor—maybe a break on the case."

She went without a word. There was no fire-escape on that window. I was seven floors up, so she was in no danger from intruders. Then I went to the front door, held it open slightly and dropped my gun into my right hand.

Bill came quickly, his coat collar turned up, his fedora pulled well down over his face. He was breathing heavily when I let him in, closed the door, put on the chain.

I was seeing a new Bill Cruthers—nothing calm and suave about him now.

"You know why I came," he said, and preceded me into the living-room.

"Yes," I said. "Feather. Feather Falon. You didn't know she took the job?"

"I never suspected. That devil Nelson!"

He flopped into a chair, got up almost at once, walked to the kitchen, the bathroom, down the hall, tried the closet door, looked inside. All slowly and deliberately. Then he went to the bedroom door, tried the knob, turned and looked at me.

"Your word of honor, Race, that there is no one in the apartment."

I hesitated. He swung on me almost viciously.

"Okay, Bill," I told him. "I have the key. It's a—well, it's a woman."

"I see." He seemed relieved. "All right, Race. I'm not going to waste time. Pick up that telephone book. I'm giving you the name, the telephone number—and the truth."

I started to turn to the phone book, my back half to Cruthers.

Something was wrong. Something was missing from the picture. I swung back, and my gun was in my hand. It didn't seem to make sense. But my hand was steady and my eyes were straight and my finger was on the trigger.

I couldn't have shot him to death like that. So he had time to aim and fire and put me out smack through the head, if he had waited a second longer.

He must have seen my right hand jerk up under my left armpit as I swung. And he was afraid to wait. He fired as he stood and it took me high in the chest, spun me around a fraction of a second faster than I would have made it.

No, I didn't have the same chance Bill Cruthers had. The cards were dealt and he held all the aces. I saw his body as I staggered back and I pumped lead into it. He had lifted his gun for my head. But my head wasn't there. It wasn't there because his shot in my chest had knocked me down and taken my head out of the picture. His bullet cracked against the wall and I heard the picture crash and I remembered in a dull sort of way that it had cost me seven dollars and fifty cents—and wasn't worth it.

I didn't understand it all when the shooting ended. I simply knew that I was on my feet again and that Cruthers wasn't. He was on his knees and holding his stomach and bent over like the dying gladiator, only not looking so noble about it.

My vision wasn't too good but it was clearing now, and I heard a woman screaming. Not an hysterical girl pounding on the door. A woman had her head out a window some place and was shouting into the night.

Cruthers wasn't taking it too well. But who would, full of lead? I leaned down and took his gun from his hand. He rolled slightly and turned his agonized face up at me. Then he went all the way over and stretched himself out on the floor. It was almost too theatrical to be real—but it was real, terribly real. He was unconscious now and his face wasn't agonized. It looked sort of drawn, but his eyes were closed and he was white.

No SOUND FROM the bedroom. I leaned down and gave Cruthers a quick search. No other gun. But there was a knife. It might have been the knife that—

I jerked erect, felt the sharp pain up by my shoulder. I got my hand in my pocket and went to the bedroom door. My stomach was bad again. But not from the shot. Things were too quiet behind the door. I hoped she hadn't fainted, but she didn't seem the fainting kind. Could she have jumped from the window? But she wouldn't be the jumping kind either.

I swung open the door, and she stood by the open window holding her throat.

"It's you—you—" she said. "Then I shouldn't have screamed, but I thought that—"

"Stay here." I told her. "I've got to use the phone."

Then I was buzzing 'round trying to locate O'Rourke, and did get his friend, Detective Kahn. I got my message through too.

By that time people were pounding at the door. I started toward it. Martha stopped me. Her voice was sort of uncertain, then it wasn't. She was looking straight down at Bill Cruthers. He opened his eyes.

"I know that man," she said. "I saw him. Why we flashed the searchlight from the

boat right on his face. He was kneeling on the dock, or just getting up from it, or something. I remember asking him what he was doing on the dock. It was Dorothy Briggs' boat."

"I was right," Cruthers groaned. "I knew one of them would remember, and it *would* be the last one." Then he passed out again.

When I swung open the apartment door a tenant who had wanted in jumped back ten feet, and several others crowding behind him made for the stairs. Funny how people will demand entrance, then wish they hadn't.

The cops came all right—lots of them. I came around and hollered about Jerry. They wouldn't let me out, but they found him in the elevator and brought him in.

"What a skull the kid must have," the doctor said in admiration. "The wallop he took with a gun, I think, should have cracked it like an egg shell. But he'll be all right."

Jerry opened his eyes, winked once at me.

"The regular routine," he said. "You killed the guy, I hope."

"He killed him all right," said the doctor. "Sort of on the installment plan, but he won't last another twelve hours."

CHAPTER 10

END OF A LOVE LIFE

LEAD I HAD taken had gone in high up in my chest and far over to the left side, and didn't give me much trouble. I was at the hospital when Bill Cruthers made his antemortem statement. He was willing to talk, insisted only that I should be there.

Cruthers said it started in Pittsburgh when he was little more than a kid. A few drinks, kidding around at a dance hall with a girl because some tough guy didn't like it, a street fight later, his grabbing the gun from the thug's hand. Cruthers killed him.

"I'd have got a few years at the most," he said, "but I was young and I was scared, and Harvey Rath took care of me. That was when he first put the hooks into me.

"And here's something no one knew. Harvey Rath had a daughter who lived in Pittsburgh. He kept her out of the picture entirely. She was a devil, all right. Don't ask me how I knew about her—I married her. And I had to visit her once a month, too.

"Why? Well, Rath said to me some ten years back when I was beginning to make the night-clubs pay—his clubs, 'I've treated you like a son, Bill, and now I'm going to make you really my son. I'm going to give you my daughter.' He put those rat-like eyes on me then. 'I could turn you in for murder, but you're smart—my child loves you. Shall we say the wedding will take place on Saturday?'

"There wasn't a decent thing about that she-devil except that she thought I was heaven's gift to this earth. She was the only thing in the world Rath cared about, the only person he really trusted. There was money in those night spots and none but his daughter and I knew he had a hand in it. I ran everything and he took the money. No matter how much he made

he lived in the same dirty little room alone back of the pawnshop, and some place was that yellow folder in which he kept everything about me, everything about others. Most people thought it was a book, but it was a folder. He had fenced more stuff than any man in the city. Then when the night-club business wasn't too good he began to shake down the boys themselves. When he fenced things he knew if murder went with it."

Cruthers did a bit of coughing, but refused a drink of water. He seemed anxious to spill it all.

"So Rath started to run roughshod over the boys. Then he went too far. He got the Malone brothers to knock over a rival fence in the Bronx with the promise of big money, but paid them nothing—simply threatened them with what he knew about them. He had affidavits and all. Both the Malone boys were hard, but it worked once. Rath tried it a second time and there are still a couple of bullet-holes in his bed to show how much they disliked it.

"He sent the information about them to the police, even planned to have them at a certain spot so the cops could pick them up—all anonymous. But the Malones sensed the trap, got from under and disappeared. After that Rath was nearly killed twice. He had no threats to hold over their heads now. They were fugitives from the electric chair and Rath believed—and he was right—that their one mission in life was to get him. That's why he disappeared—hiding until they were caught by the police or he could have them traced. I was to help him." With a grimace that was meant for a smile, he added, "I didn't.

"That was over two years ago. Rath hid out in Pittsburgh. Then he didn't like the way I treated his daughter. Treat her? It was a wonder I didn't crush her skull long ago. Then I met Feather. After that there was one girl only for me, Feather Falon."

"Then you didn't plant her on the cops—on Nelson?" I came in quick with that one.

"No!" he almost shouted the words. "They killed her! On my orders and with the money I paid them, and with the threat I pretended came from Harvey Rath. I arranged it all on the phone, but I thought it was the Logan—girl."

CRUTHERS SEEMED TO have difficulty in breathing. The doctor shook his head at Nelson.

"We're not interested in your love life, Cruthers," Nelson said brutally. "Why did you kill those three girls?"

"My wife stole that hidden yellow folder from her father and gave it to me," Cruthers went on slowly. "It helped me to get men to bring those girls to me—they thought they were doing it for Harvey Rath. They never saw me. Those girls had seen me up in Maine on a dock at Moosehead Lake. They were coming from some hospital dance, but I thought they had all reached the dock and gone when a big boat had disembarked dozens of them twenty-five minutes earlier. Four girls came in the speed boat later. I couldn't see their faces, but they could see me. Their spotlight lit right on my face."

"What were you doing?" O'Rourke asked.

"Sinking my wife. I drove her up to Maine, strangled her in the car and sank her by the dock. No one knew Rath had a daughter. No one knew I had a wife. I don't know how Williams finally suspected. I was pretty clever."

"Very smart," I cut in. "But what made you kill the girls? What made you think they'd know you again, and would suspect you of anything?"

Cruthers gave an odd little gurgling laugh that brought the doctor half erect. Cruthers said:

"I haven't any conscience and I never believed in this subconscious mind business. But it exists. One killing—a gun battle years back, a short stretch would have been all I got—and it all came from that. Sissy Pierson was the first. O'Hara introduced her to me one night, and she tried to remember where she had met me. I knew where and knew she would too, later. I got a couple of guys to knock over O'Hara in case she had told him anything.

"I went to see Sissy. She swore up and down she knew only one of the girls on the dock that night—and as soon as I mentioned the dock she knew where she had seen me. I taped her mouth to stop her screaming and put her through the works for more information. I had to kill her.

"The second girl—not too difficult. I got a couple of boys to snatch her and bring her to that loft. They never saw me. And she remembered the name of only one other in the boat! I got that other later with a simple telephone call. The last name came up. Logan's daughter.

"You know the rest. Somehow Logan was tipped off, and Williams killed the guy who had the girl in Grand Central Station. I was almost free—and the police all around the house, and time running short."

"What do you mean short?" I asked.

"The ice would be breaking up in Moosehead lake. They'd find the body. It would be spread all over the papers. The police were questioning society girls, and the Logan girl might see me and remember. She wouldn't, if there was no body. That's that subconscious mind you read about."

"But why would they find the body?" I asked. "You weighted it down, must have picked a deep spot."

"Deep—yes, good and deep, and plenty of weight. But don't you read the papers about Maine? The place belonged to the father of the Ames girl. He sold it for a quarry, no less, that wanted deep water. They were going to dredge when the ice broke up. They'd find the body."

"How did you know that Martha Logan was at my place?" Me again.

"I saw her leave her house. I thought she was a maid. She slipped out a window. I could have killed her then—easy. But I thought she was dead in the car. When I learned different I guessed where she would go, but I made sure she was at your apartment by asking for your word that no one was there. I wouldn't have tried to kill you, if you hadn't admitted a woman was there.

"I had intended to toss Rath's body into the picture after the Logan girl was dead, so all the blame could rest on him. But

with half the cops in the city guarding Martha Logan I had to act. I hoped to convince them that the show was over by dumping Rath into the street. But the cops were still timid and hired Feather Falon to ride the death car. Feather—well, she gave me my chance to see you, Williams. It would seem natural that I'd talk."

BILL CRUTHERS STOPPED then and his pain was apparent, his face contorted. It was to me he spoke now, or rather gasped.

"I planned it all, Race—carefully. I don't know how I could have slipped up. I didn't even take a chance that Jerry didn't take a look at visitors. I cracked him because I wanted to be sure he didn't get a look at me. How could you have suspected—and turned shooting like that? How—did you know it was—me?"

Nelson looked at me then. O'Rourke too. I heard Logan breathing heavily from where he stood back against the closed door. I almost blurted it out. But I didn't.

The doctor looked up at me, shrugged white coated shoulders which said quite plainly, "It won't be long now."

Cruthers half lifted a hand. There was a plea in the gesture, in his eyes, in his voice.

"I've known you a long time, Race. We—you always liked me. I'm going out. I want to know. I got to know. It will help me go—easier."

"Hurry, sir," the doc said, and when I didn't speak, "He went through torment last night. Five shots in his stomach. If you can ease things, do it in the name of humanity."

I guess I laughed, but I didn't feel like

laughing. I was thinking of the girls who had died, and how they had died—not the attempt to kill me. I was thinking, too, of the load of lead he had dumped into the machine, and which was meant for Martha Logan.

"Ease things." I shot the words at them. "Let the dirty rat go out with the lead in his insides." And when Cruthers made an agonized twist, I growled, "So you don't like it now. All right—take this with you. You were a fool. I knew. It all fitted. It couldn't be anyone but you. You rotten—"

He cried out once, and died. Logan took off his hat. O'Rourke hesitated, put up his hand, dropped it, raised it again and lifting his hat off, held it at his side. Nelson and I stood looking down. Nelson maybe because he didn't know any better. Me—well, I had had a lot of respect for Cruthers living, because I hadn't known any better. But I knew better now, and I didn't have any respect for him dead. My hat stayed on.

The doctor tossed a sheet over Cruthers' head. We turned and left the room. Nelson wanted to know all I knew. Logan wanted to pay. He did, and plenty, I took the check, and I told Nelson that if he was half a cop he would have known the answers long ago. With a wink at O'Rourke I invited him up to my place for a drink.

"It was mighty clever work, Race," said O'Rourke, over his whiskey, the third by the way. "The newspapers will get the whole story. I understand Miss Logan is making a hero out of you, so any hush-hush is off the books. Listen, Race, I

always knew you had a head, but I never thought you'd bother to use it. Cruthers made a mistake some place and you caught on. We boys either didn't recognize it or didn't have your chance to see it."

"Yes," I said, "he made a mistake. And my solution and how and when I solved the crime is strictly off the record—and for your ear alone."

"Not for the papers?"

"Not unless I can think up a better story than the truth. I'm still a man of action, O'Rourke."

"Yes, I know." O'Rourke nodded. "You turned your back and gave him a chance to use his gun, and he blame near killed you. What was his first mistake?"

"He made only one," I told O'Rourke. "Otherwise he could have walked in here, shot me through the back of the head and killed me, then shot the girl dead, walked upstairs, straddled a few low walls from roof to roof and have been as free as the air."

"Yes, I know that. Come on."

"Well," I said, "it was Jerry. You heard Cruthers say that he didn't quite swallow that stuff of Jerry not seeing visitors. He should have believed it, because it's true. Jerry does leave the rear door open and lean against the elevator my secret visitors are to enter. It's hard enough to get people to trust me without asking them to trust him. Cruthers thought Jerry might watch, give me some signal. So he flattened him. And that, O'Rourke, was my signal."

"How?" O'Rourke stiffened.

I LAUGHED a little at his puzzlement. "We have a routine," I said. "When the client is in the elevator, Jerry goes out and sees that our meal ticket wasn't shadowed. If things are right, he gives me a buzz. It's a protection I furnish my clients. If Jerry doesn't telephone me, I know that things are all wrong. Well, he didn't buzz. Cruthers had made his one mistake."

"And yet you turned your back and went for the phone book."

"Sure." I grinned. "I never suspected Cruthers. It never entered my head until he put it there. He said for me to take a look at the telephone book. That was to get my back to him. I wasn't suspicious. I was facing him with my hands at my side. He had every chance to draw and kill me. But he was too careful, had planned things too well. Also he was a bit afraid of that shooting hand of mine. I turned to the book, saw the phone, missed Jerry's ring—and it was that subconscious stuff that Cruthers was talking about. If Cruthers had waited a breath of time he could have shot me through the head. I wasn't shooting as I swung, but he thought the swing meant death to him." I poured O'Rourke another drink, and said, "And it did."

O'Rourke downed the drink.

"Sometimes," I told him, "one hunk of lead is worth all the thought in the world. You never saw a fighter think himself out of one of Joe Louis' fights. Cruthers had a sight better head than I have, but I'll be using what I got a lot longer."

"I'll be hanged," said O'Rourke.

Then the phone rang.

"I'll be hanged," said O'Rourke again, when I put the phone down and told him I'd have to give him the air, for I was having lunch with society. Martha Logan herself.

"I'm paying for the lunch, too," I told O'Rourke, "but she says she's needed so badly at the hospital she can only give me forty-five minutes. Blamed if I don't like that girl!"

Race Williams' Double Date

THE LADY AND THE HOOD

I SUPPOSED IT was stock or bonds, but someone had left them at my office with a fifty-dollar bill if I delivered them to the clerk of the Astoria Hotel downtown. The Astoria had a nice bar and served you draft beer that would float you up and down, it was that smooth.

From where I sat I could look down into the dining-room and see the row of tables below street level along the windows. It was pretty well crowded, but not enough for the scene that was going on.

I have seen lads who get mad enough to play bumpsy with the back of another lad's chair when they think he is hogging all the room, but now I was seeing it being played rather viciously. So much so that the waiter had to move the last customer from the corner table entirely. The man who had been banging his chair against the other's was now satisfied. He leaned back comfortably and smiled at his companion—who looked as though she shouldn't have been found dead with the guy.

I knew the man. He was Jake Haggerty, a common gangster in anybody's language—except that he worked for Ward Anderson: slick racketeer, night-club owner and trying to mix with society.

The more I looked at the empty chair behind Haggerty, the more I wanted to go sit in it. He had been shooting off his big mouth about me lately, and it is not good for my business to have gangsters telling tall yarns as to why I leave them alone.

The more I thought of the idea the better I liked it. I walked into the dining-room from the far end, and before a captain got hold of me, was almost at the corner table directly behind Haggerty.

The captain tried to steer me away, but finally pulled out the distant chair so that I would not be within bumping distance of Haggerty. I wiped off his satisfied smile by taking the chair with its back to Haggerty.

The captain was apprehensive and whispered: "The gentleman behind you, sir—a little gay perhaps. He may annoy you…."

"Hell," I said with a sort of twang in my voice, "I'll sit here no matter who doesn't like it. Free country, isn't it?"

Nothing happened until I got my soup. I was leaning over for the first sip when I got a push that nearly buried my face right in the plate. That was not quite so funny as I expected. But if Haggerty wanted to play bumpsy then I could play bumpsy. That's what I'd come there for.

I moved my table well forward—then

I shot back my chair against Haggerty like a bus hitting a truck. I heard him grunt. Dishes rattled and a glass fell to the floor. I held my breath. When I heard his chair squeak, I slid forward hard and fast against my own table four or five feet away.

The crash told me that Haggerty had put all he had into this bump—missed me and crashed to the floor. A few old ladies gasped and several people burst out laughing.

I started buttering a roll just as if I didn't know anything had happened.

Then Haggerty's hand fell on my shoulder. His face was twisted in rage as he swung me around and jerked me to my feet. I let him have it. I doubt if anyone in the room saw the blow. Certainly not Haggerty until it caught him on his chin and straightened him up.

Another man would have gone down. Some would have stayed down. But Haggerty stayed on his feet, although his eyes were glassy and his legs were rubber. I could have knocked him down and kept him down then with a smack across the mouth.

But I didn't. I watched Haggerty do his dance of the rubber legs and get ready for a comeback. Then his eyes began to clear and see—yes, see plainly. His words choked in his throat.

"Williams—Race Williams! I thought you were a—a stranger."

"Oh come, come Haggerty," I said. "We don't play games with strangers." Then in a lower voice: "Maybe you'd like to pull a gun and have some real fun…. Beat it, punk."

Haggerty turned and left without even a look at the girl.

A waiter lifted up the chair, set it by the table. The girl looked up at me at an angle. Her eyes weren't wide and they weren't wondering. I grinned.

She said: "Very pretty, sir. Good clean fun. But what about me? Darkness coming on—and the dinner to be paid for."

I sat down and looked at the girl.

"Tell me about yourself," she said slowly. "Did you come up from unspeakable poverty? Did you build yourself up alone, flouting law and order—laughing at mere man?"

"Maybe," I told her. "At least I've got a better line than Haggerty. He was surprised, I presume. And you?"

She smiled. "Haggerty looked surprised. Stunned, too, or he wouldn't have left me. As for me—I don't know. I saw you come along the back of the room close to the wall and take the seat at that table."

"And you didn't tell him?"

"I didn't think he would be interested." She paused. "If you slapped Mr. Haggerty around for pleasure, then I think you might pay for my meal."

I liked the girl. That is I liked to look at her. It was such a strange sort of face, the eyes slightly narrowed. She had a strange smile which I have no description for. I thought there was a trembling to the lips, and though it looked like derision I had an idea it wasn't. Her lips were much too red, and her eyes were shaded, her eyebrows overdrawn.

"And if," I said, "I slapped him around by accident?"

SHE SHOOK HER head. "That might have been true if you had originally been at that table. Jake was doing his chair bumping without the slightest idea who he was bumping." She let her eyes open a bit. "It was the first time I ever laughed out loud at him. There was terror in his face—a surprised sort of terror like a man who expects to pick up a bit of clothes line and finds it is a high voltage wire."

I was about to crack wise, but she stopped me. "Don't—please. Take me very seriously. It may be worth real money to you."

And damned if she didn't place her elbows on the table, put her chin on her delicate hands and stare directly at me. After a bit she said:

"So you're Race Williams, the private detective. Okay, Mr. Williams, I think you'll do. Played right—and it will be played right—I can get my hands on two hundred grand within the month. Honest money, every penny of it. How would you like to have a share of it?"

I'm not often thrown, but she sure tossed me a bit. For a moment, I was sure I had the secret of her eyes. She was hopped up to the gills.

She came slowly to her feet, picked up her purse and gloves. Her eyes were narrow slits. Now she was not beautiful—she was not even pretty. Or perhaps she was….

She laughed, and there was something mighty cold about it—nice but cold. "So you don't want to share that money with me. Well, perhaps you are right. You couldn't spend it if you were dead. Good evening." She turned, then swung back. "Thanks for the show. I was amused."

She was gone and I was left holding the fort—that is, holding the table. I watched her walk down the room. She was rather tall and most of it was legs. Nice legs that had a long stride to them.

I tossed a ten-dollar bill on the table and went after her. But I was no further than the door when I looked out one of the windows and saw her long legs climbing into a taxi.

The waiter approached me with the manager. The manager said, "Ten dollars, sir? The bill was eighteen-fifty."

"What bill?"

"Mr. Haggerty and—er—the young lady."

"What have I got to do with Haggerty?" I asked him. "The ten bucks was a tip to the waiter. I liked his face."

I turned up my collar and went out into the rain….

It was pretty late, so I decided to go home, fix up a bit and wander around a few of the spots. Maybe Haggerty wanted to make something out of the smack he had. I always like the boys to have their chance early before someone talks them into a lot of courage. Also, I was wondering if I would see the girl again.

Thinking a little of Haggerty and more of Ward Anderson, his boss, I buzzed my boy Jerry at my apartment. He was slow to answer the phone. Though his voice was about right, there was a little bit of—oh, bitterness in it.

"It's all right, Jerry," I told him. "I'll be coming home right away. By the way, we've wound up our case with Mrs. Moffet—did you make the train reservations for her?" And when he gulped that

he had, I asked casually, "For what time tomorrow afternoon?"

He said it was half past two. I let it go at that and hung up.

I MADE SURE that no one was sitting on my tail and jumped a taxi. I got out half a block away from my apartment.

I went in the side door and grabbed off one of the automatic elevators in the rear. It is one of those apartments where you pay high for the service at the front door and more for the lack of service at the side door. It gives me real privacy, and no copper can find out from the help when someone visited me or left.

The car took me to the seventh floor. I let myself out and went whistling toward my door.

My gun was in my hand when I swung the door open and stepped into the small foyer. I could look straight down the length of the hall into the living-room, and see the heavy curtains by the window and the wide double doors, now open.

All this took only a couple of seconds. Then I pulled the other gun from under my armpit and, with a gun in each hand, went down the hall at my usual even pace. "Jerry," I called. "Did Milligan call up about the suitcase stolen out of his car?"

I went on talking, watching the curtains ahead. They were flat against the window and did not move. So I took a peek at the cracks between the double doors and the wall. With a final "Hi, Jerry," and a sigh of contentment about being home again, I stuck a gun through the large crack in each door and I fired two shots.

The results were immediate and pleasant. To my right a man screamed out in pain and thudded to the floor. To my left a man staggered out into the room as though doing a dance. His left hand was held against his chest, his right hand waved a gun. If it weren't for the blood, you might have thought it was a Russian ballet.

I looked at the other man on the floor. He was holding his leg and his gun was beside him. I picked it up and kept my eye on the dancer. I recognized him, of course. It was Jake Haggerty.

"Drop the rod," I told him. But he had already fallen full length on his face and the gun had shot across the floor—just to the edge of the couch where I could now see legs kicking.

That would be Jerry. But I looked around the room, at the closed doors that led to the kitchen, the bedrooms, my den.

Somewhere in the apartment another figure lurked. Not too dangerous—for Jerry had said half past two, which meant two tough birds and one that didn't count too much.

Stupid things, gunmen, to think they could hide in my apartment and plug me. Of course I had called Jerry first. He had tipped me off easily with that time business.

The wounded boy by the door was scared stiff. And he had reason to be. Guys couldn't go around trying to blast me out of the picture and get away with it. He wasn't over twenty, a juvenile delinquent of the war years developed into a full-fledged gunman, or so he thought.

"You're going to kill me," he kept crying over and over.

"You knew that when you came, kid." I patted him gently on the shoulder. "Don't you worry—you're no more than a child. I'll blow you out easy—a single shot in the mouth."

I got Haggerty's artillery, then watching both doors, I backed over to Jerry and tore the rag out of his mouth. It took him a full five seconds to get his breath. Then he let out some of the foulest language I ever heard.

"Jerry," I said, "I pulled you out of the gutter some years back. You talk like that again and I'll toss you back. Now, where is the half?"

"The frail," he said. "She's in the kitchen. She didn't come with me. They forced in on her heels.... Get these damned ropes offa me, will you?"

"Got to get a knife," I told him. I walked into the kitchen, slamming open the door. A lad can be just as dead from lead squeezed by the dainty fingers of a woman as he can be by a man.

The kitchen was deserted. One glance told me that. It was one of these kitchens you don't have to hunt around in.

THE WINDOW WAS open. I looked out—and I gasped for breath. She was walking along the ledge. She had her back close against the cement of the building and was moving very slowly.

What to do? Go after her? Sure, very noble. But I lay no claim to being noble. Besides, if I went after her she might jump. This way, she would try to pass my bedroom window and make the fire-escape.

Of course I could call softly to her to

come back, that all was forgiven. But I didn't. I had a plan. It might break her heart, but it wouldn't break her head.

I went back into the living-room. Things hadn't changed much, except that Haggerty had reached a chair and was trying to pull himself up. I cut Jerry free and rubbed his hands and legs until I had him on his feet. Then I walked him into the little hall and got the truth out of him.

"The girl came to the door," he told me. "She was a pippin and she squeezed by in a hurry like a lot of them do." He killed my raising eyebrows there. "And then I was rushed from behind her. I had my gun drawn and—"

"Never mind that. They rushed you. What about the girl? She was part of the racket for them to get in, eh?"

"I didn't think so, boss. She whispered something about not letting anyone in. And then she lit out for the kitchen."

"Did they search the whole apartment?"

"Over and over, boss, until you telephoned. They told me to talk natural." He grinned.

I said quickly: "Watch over this team, Jerry. I have business back in my room. And if someone pounds hell out of the door, tip me off and I'll be telephoning the police."

I went down the hall to my bedroom. I wasn't in any special hurry. Not a great distance for her to travel, of course—but under the circumstances almost a marathon. Sure I was worried; that was natural. No one likes a girl to fall from the 7th story window of his apartment.

I didn't switch on the light but felt my way across the room and took a tiny flash from a desk drawer. I used it carefully. I got the curtains drawn well back from the window—and then silently opened the French window. I left one window closed for the girl to pass, the other open to bar her progress. I wanted her to fall, all right—but I wanted her to fall in, not out.

I was tempted to look out but I was afraid. I tried listening, but couldn't even hear a squeak of moving feet. Nothing but the distant toots of cars.

She came, faster than I expected. I saw her slim legs. They moved like a wooden soldier's, side-stepping. I didn't see the whiteness of her hands; she had them both buried hard against her sides.

I stood close to the open window and waited for her to fall in. Then she was there. I almost laughed as she started leaning backward into the room, and stepped forward to catch her.

I didn't catch her. There was the sharp intake of breath. Her falling body straightened—went too far forward—and started to pitch into the outer darkness.

CHAPTER 2

MY FAVORITE CLIENT

I SHOULD HAVE grabbed her when she first appeared by the window. I leaped forward and caught her just back of the knees. I braced my feet, bent backward and tried to hold her.

I'm as strong as the next guy, but believe it or not, I went forward with the girl and damn near went over. We seesawed back and forth for what seemed ten years, and neither one of us said a word. One thing was certain—she didn't want to die.

I gave it to her straight as I felt my arms begin to tear apart in the sockets. "Toss yourself backwards when we come in," I gulped.

We teetered back—and she gave a quick spasmatic twist of her body.

Here we go! I thought, and then I laughed. We were on the floor.

I quit laughing as I took a cute little toy gun from the handbag she'd dropped. The cute little toy was a .25 automatic. I came to my feet and half held her in my arm.

She clung to me and cried softly, which wasn't too bad. She was very limp and wobbly. I laid her down on the bed and snapped on the lamp.

And there she was—the little lady of the affair with Haggerty.

That is, she was a spitting image of her, figure, features and—but I didn't know. There was something softer about her face, about her lips, and certainly her eyes were wide open. And she wasn't wearing any lipstick or other make-up.

"Where am I?" She sat up and ran a hand across her forehead. She didn't act as if she ever saw me before. "I—the bath-room, please?"

That was hardly what Emily Post would suggest for teen-age etiquette for a girl who'd just been snatched from death. But I like people who are not trite, so I showed her to the bathroom—and went back to the living-room.

I didn't mention the girl. I looked things over. Haggerty had pulled himself up and was half leaning on the couch.

Jerry said, "Look at the blood—the rug's ruined. Tough guy," he turned to the kid who sat across the room, "has been crying that you're going to kill him. Haggerty told him you wouldn't."

"Haggerty told him that?" I took a look at Haggerty. He didn't look too bad. His eyes were glassy, but he knew what was going on. "Haggerty," I said, "wouldn't bet with the kid on that."

The phone rang then and Jerry answered it. He turned to me.

"Ward Anderson," he said.

I lifted the phone, spoke easily.

"How are you, Ward? Haven't been around to your place for a long time. Can I do anything for you?"

"Yes," Ward said. "You can come around here right away. I've got a case for you—real money in it."

"I don't work for mugs."

"*What?*" I think Ward was genuinely surprised.

"I don't work for mugs," I told him again. "Mugs that send punks out to knock me off."

"You—you mean Haggerty?"

"No one else," I said. "Want to listen to his last breath?"

"Is Haggerty in your apartment?"

"With a slug in his chest," I told him.

Muttered stuff came over the phone. When he paused, I said:

"There's a kid with Haggerty—I don't know him. Killer something, probably. He's right out of a horse opera. Maybe I should have the cops take him away."

"Suit yourself." Ward had his breath back now. "I didn't send Haggerty and a punk after you. What do you think

I am?" When I told him, he gave in suddenly. "Okay. Deliver them both here to me at the club—side entrance—and I'll give you a grand for each of them."

"They're not in very good condition."

"I don't care what condition they're in."

"And the girl?" I tossed it in casually.

"What girl?" He said it as if it had no significance, and then suddenly it had. He gasped. "I'll be right over!" The phone went dead.

I said: "Don't mention any girl to him, Jerry. I didn't see any. You didn't see any. And the two mugs didn't see any. Ward Anderson would slaughter them if he thought they even saw the shadow of a girl. He's coming over."

When I went down the hall and saw the bathroom door open, I hurried to my room. Maybe the girl was on the loose again.

She was sitting in front of my mirror fixing up her hair. And I could really see the difference. Not that she wasn't the same girl of the window sill and the *affaire* Haggerty—but it was as if she had recovered from, well, a long illness or— Damn it, I couldn't put a name on it.

She turned, stood up, and faced me.

"You're Race Williams, aren't you?" she asked.

I said that was true and then asked her point-blank why she was on my window ledge. She knitted her brows and said nothing.

Then I asked bluntly: "What brought you here—to help two men to trap me to my death?"

HER EYES OPENED even wider. They were deep and green, and sort of blue, too. And she really did look surprised.

She didn't deny it. She said simply, "It can't be true. It—it doesn't make sense."

She came closer to me, and I saw how small and dainty she was and how she looked right up into my eyes. She said, "I don't think you'll lie to me. Did I—did I bring two men here to—to kill you?" And when I didn't answer right away she put both her hands up to my shoulders and shook me slightly. "I wouldn't like to believe that. Did I?"

I shrugged off her hands. "I don't know if you did or not, but it sure looked like it. Why did you come, then?"

"To see you. That is, I was coming. I had a note to come—" A pause. "I did come—" She shuddered suddenly. "There were shots—and then I was falling and you were holding me." She bit her mouth. "I guess I better talk to you—when I'm more composed."

"Your name?" I knew an act was going on, but I had come in late and the curtain had gone up. She was the girl of the restaurant and yet she wasn't. She certainly didn't act the same, and she wasn't wearing any make-up now. But unless identical twins were in the picture, ten could get you fifty it was the same girl.

"Must I tell you that? My name?"

"I have no way of making you," I said, nodding toward her bag. "Unless of course there are some cards or letters in the bag you carry."

She looked startled.

"Alyce Joyce Reed," she said. When I reached out for the bag, she tried to pull it away. The struggle was not much of a

CARROLL JOHN DALY

one—and I don't mean because she didn't try. But I opened the bag and emptied the contents on my bed.

There was the usual junk a woman carries. Mirror. Comb. Lipstick. A handkerchief with initials *A.J.R.* No cigarette case. No vanity. A wad of dough and two letters.

She stood there and watched me read the letters. One was from a girl friend inviting her to spend a couple of weeks at her Booth Bay home in Maine. The second envelope had no postmark and was simply addressed *Alyce.* I opened it and read aloud:

"Go see Race Williams. Pay him to watch over me. My life is in danger and your life is my life. Go see him."

It was signed *Martha.*

I shook something else out of the envelope. It was a check for twenty-five hundred dollars and was made payable—yes, to me. And it was signed *Alyce Joyce Reed.*

"Who is Martha?" I asked.

"Martha." She thought a moment. "They call her Martha Dale. You'll find her at the Crescent Club. "

"Ward Anderson's place." I straightened a bit. "Do you know him?"

"Yes," she said. "I am engaged to be married to him. It's not public yet."

"Good Lord." I took a good look at her now. "You know who he is—what he is? Does he know you are retaining me—for Martha?" She really had me going.

She surprised me with her first laugh, and it was a nice one. Her lips and teeth came into the picture and she looked good. In fact she looked good all over.

"Yes," she said, "I know who he is and what he is." She paused. "And you might as well know now that—that my uncle is William Evans. Yes, the politician." She bit her lips. "He has taken care of me and I love him. I'd do anything for him."

I tossed back lightly, "Ward Anderson thinks you are here and is coming over. Do you want to see him?"

She seemed to pull back.

"All right, you don't have to. He can't search the place, you know." When she seemed about to say Ward Anderson could do anything, I told her, "I think I can convince him I haven't seen you if you leave now. By the fire-escape with Jerry—that's my boy. But you'll have to hurry."

"And you'll watch over Martha?"

"Yes."

She turned toward the hall. "It's Martha's money, too, you know. She won't like it if you don't understand. And when Martha gets sore she raises hell with me."

"Everything back in your bag?" I asked.

"Yes. Yes, thank you." She was closing the bag.

"All but this." I took the small gun and tossed it over on the bed. "Now tell me that belongs to Martha."

"Yes—it must," she said. "She must have slipped it in my bag."

"Martha," I said, "is quite a girl."

I went and got Jerry and gave him his instructions. When Jerry was gone with the girl, I listened to Haggerty tell me about how he was dying.

The kid was sullen now. He was pretty sure I wasn't going to kill him. The phone rang and Anderson was downstairs, doing everything gentle and aboveboard. He said he had two men with him.

I said, "All right. Park the rough stuff downstairs and come up alone. I mean alone, Ward. I'm deep into it now and one or two more wouldn't bother me."

"All right." He didn't argue—just hung up.

Ward Anderson was a chesty guy, not too little or too large—just a chesty guy who didn't talk too much around things. He was alone. He preceded me down the hall and looked at his two stooges. He noted the punk's leg and sniffed. Then he went and bent over Haggerty.

He straightened up, looked down at Haggerty and said, "Get up."

Haggerty floundered and got to one knee and fell back again.

Ward Anderson turned to me. "Let me bring up the boys and help them out—no one need know."

"No."

"Okay." Ward Anderson used snap judgment. "I'll stand them up against the wall in the hall, and let the boys take them from there. Good boys. You know them—Charlie and Eddie."

I knew them and nodded.

Ward said, "Give me a hand."

"Not me." I sat down on the window seat.

"You want the cops here?" he said. When I said that was all right with me—which it wasn't—he turned to the punk and said, "Get up—get up on your feet." And the punk did. At least he stood on one foot.

"Now you, Haggerty," he said, "you would come here to knock Williams off! Get up, damn you! Get up!"

Haggerty thought he couldn't, but he did, just the same. Ward Anderson literally kicked him to his feet. Then Anderson led Haggerty down the hall and to the door, the young punk hopping on one foot after them. He came back and lifted the house phone and spoke into it.

"Put Mr. Charles Emons on the phone, please." Which was the first time I ever heard Charlie's last name. "Oh, Charlie, They're here in front of the door. Suite 720. Drunk, I suppose. Get them out the back. You and Eddie take them over, understand? Take Haggerty over—now!"

"Now, Race." Ward Anderson turned to me as if he had come for a little chat. "Tell me what happened. And what's this about a girl?" The easy indifference was not so good about the girl.

"Well," I told Ward, "I walked in and they had guns in their hands and my boy was tied up—and I shot the pair of them. They had some story that they followed a girl in—but they could have lied." Then with a shrug, "Or the girl could have jumped out a window."

"Nothing to be funny about," Ward Anderson scowled.

"Maybe not," I told him. "You and I haven't crossed yet—but if this is the way it's going to be, it's all right with me."

Ward changed his tune. "Come now, Race—how did you get that way?"

"Well," I told him, "Haggerty and I had a little cross talk downtown. There was a girl with him and—"

"That's it!" Ward Anderson cut in quickly. "He's on his own, see? There was this girl. He liked her—you know how Haggerty is to talk himself up. Well, you knocked him around. It doesn't do a lad good to get knocked around in front of his girl, so he pulled at his vest. You won't have to worry about Haggerty any more—I'll promise you that."

"Haggerty wouldn't worry me."

"Well," Ward got up and walked toward the door, "Come down to the club sometime. Look it over—put it on the cuff." He started toward the long hall to the door and swung suddenly back. "Oh, Race." He was familiar and friendly. "I got a little business to throw your way."

"I don't want your business."

He laughed pleasantly and pulled out a wad of bills. "There's five grand here, Race—just for *not* taking a case."

"Sold." I put the money in my pocket. "I'll think up a case not to take."

"A *certain* case." The humor had gone out of his eyes.

"Not Haggerty's girl friend?" I prodded him.

He stared at me then for a long time. "Haggerty hasn't any girl friend. You see—by now there isn't any Haggerty to have any girl friend."

"As fast as that."

"Your bullet in his chest. I'd accept that five grand if I were you, Williams."

I tossed the money back to him just as Jerry came in the front door. I called Jerry over. I took the gun that had plugged Haggerty and the boy and handed it to Jerry.

"Take that up to—well, our little friend. If he can't fix it up so that bullets that came out of it before will never come out of it again—okay. If not, let him melt it

down and make a bracelet for Mr. Anderson here."

I turned to the night-club man. "Sit down a few minutes, Ward. I'd like to talk things over with you."

Ward Anderson had been around. I didn't even need the simple gesture of exposing my left armpit and the holster there. He sat down leisurely, took a cigarette, lit it and said easily, "Sure, Race."

I was pleasant, too. "This girl's name is Martha Dale. You know her?"

"Yes," he said, very, very evenly. "I know her."

"Is there any reason why you object to my giving her protection?"

He laughed out loud.

"We'd get along, boy. Really get along…. No, I can see no objection to you giving her protection. I'll give it to her myself, any time you wish."

"Then it is not you she fears."

"Now, now." His finger was playful. "You can ask her about all that easy enough."

"If she gets to see me again."

He frowned then, and he looked at me for a full minute.

"If I could keep her from seeing you again—if I could lift her by the throat and squeeze every bit of evil out of her—I'd do it."

"You'd strangle her?"

"I'd give my right arm to strangle her!" he said viciously. "Yet I'd shoot you to death, Race, if I thought you were going to harm her—any harm, do you understand?"

"Guys don't harm their clients," I told him.

"Don't they?" He was still looking at me. "You stick to that idea and we'll be friends. I might toss you a few grand myself."

The phone rang. It was Jerry. All things were arranged. The gun would never tie me to Haggerty's corpse.

"Was that the all-clear signal?" Ward asked. When I nodded, he got up and straightened his tie. "Maybe I'll see you at the club," he said. "That is where your client will probably be."

CHAPTER 3

TWO-TIME QUEEN

I MET HER at the Crescent Club, all right. She was sitting at a table off in the corner where great drapes hid her from view of most of the people. I didn't see her until the waiter came to me and said she wanted to talk to me.

The girl smiled up at me. "I'm Martha, you know."

I sat down and said, "No, you're Alyce Joyce Reed and putting on an act."

"I'm not putting on an act—and I'm not Alyce. How could I be that damned little society prude? Look," she said, "did you ever hear of dual personality?"

"I know lots of guys with it. They treat all the boys to dinner. Smile all over the place and go home and beat the children—and the wife, too, if she isn't too big."

"That," said Martha, "is a double life. Have you ever heard of Dr. Raymond Halton?"

"The psychiatrist?" I asked. "He must be a hundred years old."

"He's very famous. Also, have you heard of Dr. Johnston—another psychiatrist? Rather young, though he's the coming man in the profession."

"Doctors are not much in my line. Generally when I finish up a case we use the medical examiner."

She leaned over and let her two hands rest on my left one. "I talked about a lot of money this afternoon, Race, and you didn't believe it. But it's there. We've got to get our hands on it. Suppose we did—I'm not bad to look at. We'd split it—get married and travel around the world."

"What," I said, "made you think that I'd marry for money?"

"Haggerty gave me trouble—was about to give me real trouble—and you killed him. They picked him out of the East River less than half an hour ago."

"How distressing."

"Hmmm." She took her hand away.

"Martha," I told her. "I'm just a regular guy trying to make a living. I don't go much for this hocus-pocus business. If anyone is holding out money you're legally entitled to, I'll get you the best lawyer in this city—and ten to one you get your dough. All your dough, outside of his fee."

"And your charge?"

"Nothing. I've been paid. But for the life of me, I don't see why you play these two parts. I like you much better this way. Personally, if there weren't that mean streak in you and your eyes opened a little wider and you took off some of the paint—I'd say you were a better-looking girl than Alyce Joyce.... Now, if you'll give me that gun in your bag and ask to go places where you won't be known, I'll take you."

"Why?" she demanded. "To find out things—to cause me to make slips?"

"No." I shook my head. "I won't try to trip you. But I want to see this Dr. Johnston and ask him what's what."

She looked at me for a long time, then said, "Yes, I think maybe you better see him. Yes—see him tonight. Tell him that I know he's planning to murder me."

"Tell him that?"

"Yes," she said. "He'll admit it if you corner him."

She excused herself and was gone....

Inspector Nelson nailed me before I even got to the bar. He went into a long recital about the trouble I had with Jake Haggerty down at the restaurant and that I was right to slap him around. And suddenly he shot it at me.

"So we dragged Haggerty out of the East River. He had a slug in his chest. Your slug."

"No." I shook my head. "My slug and his chest—but they are not mixed up together."

Nelson understood. He grinned. "He went gunning for you. You killed him in self-defense. He's better off dead. Just tell the truth, and you won't have much trouble." He paused a moment. "Just the way you disposed of the body. That's not like you, Race."

"No," I agreed, "it isn't."

"It isn't much of a crime—leaving the body."

I leaned over. "You still want my license, don't you?"

"So you have an alibi? Who?"

"Well—" I pulled at my chin. "It might be the mayor."

"And it might be a racketeer—the owner of this club, Ward Anderson."

"It might be that," I said. "Or maybe he saw me toss the body into the river."

"You'd have a lad like Ward Anderson give you an alibi?"

"Nelson," I said, "I don't know quite what you are talking about. I don't know what time I need an alibi for. But if Ward Anderson—or even a guy like you—can give me one that will stick, I'll take it."

A waiter was bringing us a drink. Nelson barked at him, "I don't drink free. And I wouldn't drink here at any price. Come on, Williams. Now, waiter, the shortest way to Ward Anderson's private office."

Nelson disliked me all right, and I guess I wasn't exactly stuck on him. He was a rough, tough cop of the old school. We got to Ward's office the shortest way. I guess Ward had warning ahead—but he didn't try to cross Nelson up.

HE WAS STANDING at his desk when Nelson pushed himself in. He wasn't in a friendly mood.

"Don't like it, eh?" Nelson said.

"No," Ward Anderson said very slowly, "I don't like it. And I'm not going to take it much longer."

Nelson wasn't feeling friendly, either. "I want to know something about Haggerty."

I went over to the bookcase and looked

over the books. I was surprised at Ward's reading habits. I didn't listen to Nelson shooting off.

The phone rang and I heard Ward say after a moment, "It's for you, Inspector."

Nelson lifted the phone, barked his name into it. After a few moments, he jammed the phone down. He walked straight to the door—turned and looked at me.

"There was water in his lungs, Williams. Haggerty died of drowning." Then he walked out, slamming the door behind him.

Ward Anderson looked at me.

"I'll get him broke one of these days. I gave you an alibi, Race."

"And yourself one." I nodded. "Nelson is anything but a dumb cop."

Ward Anderson was thoughtful. "You think he had something on his mind about my alibi?"

"Sure." I nodded. "My bullet and your water."

Ward Anderson shrugged his shoulders.

"It's your body," he said in great seriousness. "He must have got away from the boys. Been delirious from the shot—and tumbled into the river."

I nodded. I was looking at a book called "The Dissociation of a Personality." Anderson grabbed it from me.

We eyed each other for a few minutes; then the little door behind him opened and the girl came in. It was Martha, all right—if you went by the make-up. And you did because there wasn't anything else to go by.

She smiled at me and looked at Ward Anderson a long time before she spoke. Then she said:

"I'm short of money, Ward. Can you give me that couple of hundred I asked you to keep for me?"

He handed it out to her, peeling it off a large roll of bills without hesitation. His eyes never left the girl.

She said: "I think Race better go up and see Dr. Johnston tonight. Damn it, Ward, don't look so despondent. We like you a lot. Joyce and I are going to marry you. Joyce, poor fool, because she loves you, and I—" She laughed then. "You see that I have the money—and you won't wake up some morning with a knife in your back."

Ward Anderson was sort of pale as the girl and I left his room. His body swung slowly and his fixed gaze followed us.

"You see," Martha said when we reached the stairs, "this is hard on Ward. He loves Joyce and he hates me. He'd kill me in a minute—but he'd have to kill Joyce, too. At first—well, he nearly strangled me. It gave him quite a shock later when he saw the marks on Joyce's throat. I never told her, though...."

Dr. Edward H. Johnston was a rather young man to have the degrees he had. I asked to see every diploma, and he showed them to me without hesitation. He was a tall thin man, slightly stooped and very pleasant, but his eyes were certainly direct and penetrating.

"You needn't apologize, Mr. Williams, for asking for my credentials. If more patients would do the same thing, they'd soon put the quacks out of business. We'll

CARROLL JOHN DALY

sit here in the library. There now, begin your questions."

"Well—" I started right in—"what is a dual personality? A sort of Dr. Jekyll and Mr. Hyde affair?"

"Not at all." He laughed. "That was a fancy of Stevenson's—an impossible chemical and physical metamorphosis as science understands it today. With Miss Reed, the change is entirely in the personality, Joyce is tempered in her dress, gentle in her manner. Martha, on the other hand, goes in for startling creations, daubs herself with lipstick and blackens her eyebrows. Their thoughts and motives are different. They—"

"Have there been any other such cases?"

"Yes, although they are not numerous. However, in that book you mentioned, there is a case of a young lady with four separate personalities. The girl herself was a very religious but sickly young lady."

"Is this case on record?"

"My dear man, it's medical history. One of the personalities was a child of nine; she would go on long hikes. Another personality was a rather unpleasant character who used to frequent disreputable drinking places and abandon the girl there to resume her own personality."

THIS WAS ALL pretty much over my head. I said, "You are being paid for attending this case?"

He nodded. "My regular fee. As a matter of fact, I would be glad to spend twenty-four hours a day on it for nothing if that were possible. Some of these cases make medical history, you know. But Miss Reed and her uncle and some owner of a night-club she is engaged to wish to avoid all publicity."

"Martha," I said abruptly, "said you wished to murder her."

He leaned back and laughed.

"Quite right," he said. "Psychological murder. I would like to shove her back into the subconscious mind where she came from. I have also consulted with Dr. Raymond Halton. It is his considered opinion that my treatment is correct—and that it is quite safe for Miss Alyce Joyce Reed to travel around as she pleases."

"Miss Reed wasn't always like this, was she?"

"No," he said, "she wasn't. It came on her suddenly, almost immediately before her engagement to this Ward Anderson."

"You draw conclusions from that?"

"Yes, we do—although this, Mr. Williams, is in the strictest confidence. I have told Miss Reed's uncle but not Miss Reed. But I think this personality Martha is a defense mechanism set up to prevent her marriage."

"She doesn't want to marry Anderson, is that it? You think the marriage may be under pressure?"

"I thought of that." He shook his head dubiously. "But she has given me no reason to accept such a theory. It is my belief that she loves the man consciously— but something inside of her revolts at marrying such a man. And that something suddenly developed as Martha. Not a pleasant defense, perhaps—but certainly an effective one. Ward Anderson, I believe, more than hesitates about marrying under the circumstances."

"He's afraid of Martha," I admitted. "I saw it in his eyes. He believes in this thoroughly?"

"He should." Dr. Johnston smiled. "He's questioned every authority of note in the country on the subject. A very interesting character, Martha. Don't you think so, Mr. Williams?"

"You talk as if she were a real person—a real and separate person."

"And so she is, to all purposes." He looked straight at me. "I have to keep Martha in line by threatening her at times with confinement in an institution."

"Does Anderson know all this?" I asked.

"Of course." Dr. Johnston nodded. "I told him everything. He is engaged to her. It was my duty to tell him." He added with a tired smile, "I imagine you could talk to him. I don't doubt that by now he is almost as well informed on dual and multiple personalities as I am. Good-day, Mr. Williams."

Now you've got to admit that was a tough jolt to swallow. Sure, I had heard of cases of amnesia when lads got hit on the head. I knew other lads who got tired of living home and took a powder, and when they got picked up pulled the blank act. But this was pretty hard to believe.

I slept on it that night. Most of all it was Ward Anderson who bothered me. As far as the human mind could be, he was out on a limb. Yet he had checked up around and found out it was gospel. For a guy like Ward Anderson to believe such stuff was—was— I went to sleep.

The next day I got around and was amazed. I hired a research specialist I knew, and he went down to the library and got the dope. There were several such cases on record. I don't recall one being exactly like Joyce Reed but some were worse.

I even went and saw the old doctor who had taught Dr. Johnston what he knew. Dr. Raymond Halton wasn't seeing as well as he used to, and he was crowding eighty. I started to toss questions at him.

"My dear man," he said. "You are attempting to seek knowledge that your life and habits—and may I say from some of your questions—your intellect has not been prepared to receive. Science has always sought that which is behind the curtain of the mind. These are questions which man has studied for centuries, and you request me to solve them in five minutes."

"Okay, doctor." I didn't crack wise. I wanted information. "Just the simple question then. Is this girl's condition— two separate people—possible?"

He hesitated a long time. Then said slowly, "One person, two separate personalities—that I presume to your limited vision is two separate people in one body. The answer is yes. Good afternoon."

CHAPTER 4

SAY "UNCLE," UNCLE

I LEFT THE doctor's old Madison Avenue house. It was raining, and the few people plodding along that street were ducking under umbrellas. That was all the atmosphere there was—nothing exciting or terrifying or leading up to sudden and violent death. I half slipped on a deep depression in one of the stone steps—and a guy poked a gun out from the next alley.

I ducked and he fired. He fired once more as I crawled to the sidewalk. My gun exploded twice as I half ran, half crawled into that alley.

My third shot was carefully aimed and carefully placed, even if I had but part of a second to do it in. I had nothing more to shoot at than a leg, a leg disappearing over the fence in the rear of a stone yard, but a buck would get you ten that the bullet hit the whiteness of flesh above the short dark sock.

I came to my feet, not too steadily, and I put my hands up to my neck. It was wet and warm, and when I looked at my fingers they were red.

I didn't try to run. I don't leave scenes of shooting—at least not like this one. People were gathering around. A cop was on the job—and an ambulance was making a hell of a clatter.

Some said the lad who fired was masked. Others that he had a handkerchief over his face. He wore everything from a funereal black coat to a pea-green raincoat. I wouldn't go to the hospital, but I let the interne get a little practice bandaging up my neck.

A cop that knew me showed up. Someone discovered that I had fired a few shots myself. But there was nothing to that.

I had learned something. This was no ordinary warning to lay off. This lad had popped up and shot to kill. There aren't many guys who are interested in doing that to me—and those that were are dead.

What would you figure? In the Alyce Joyce Reed—Martha personality disassociation case, there was only one man that I knew was a killer.

I was surprised at how easy I got up to see Ward Anderson. He was sitting behind his desk. His humor was not good.

"Look, Williams," he said. "I wanted to see you. I've decided that Martha doesn't need any more protection from you—and she's not going to get it. That's final." If he had nicked me in the neck an hour before, he didn't take much notice of it. He was sitting down and so I couldn't examine his leg.

"And," I asked him, "how are you going to stop me?"

"First," he said, "I'll try and appeal to your sense of justice. I am going to marry this young lady. I'm going to be her husband."

"Why don't you want me to protect her?"

"Because," he leaned forward, "I have made a decision. I have read the books and I have listened to the men of medicine. It's in the books—and it's gospel. There will be no fuss about it. A simple wedding with her uncle there—and maybe Doc Johnston. Then I'm her husband and you are out."

"You're marrying Alyce Joyce Reed," I told him. "She paid me to protect Martha."

"I'm marrying both of them. If a woman had four feet or three eyes or two hearts, I'd be marrying just one woman. Now if I marry a woman who simply believes she is someone else at certain times, I'm still marrying one woman."

"You sound like a lawyer."

"Sure," he nodded, "I'm quoting. Benny Zisson gave me those facts. I got an author to ask him. This thing isn't coming out in the papers."

"Well," I looked at him, "I've got a couple of thousand dollars to ride on yet."

"You can keep the money." He graciously tossed away the girl's money. "You see, we're going on a honeymoon— just the two of us. And no one will know where we are."

"You mean the three of you, don't you?" The thing would seem ridiculous if it weren't so terribly tragic. I changed the subject suddenly. "I got shot in the side of the neck this afternoon."

"You did?" He wasn't very interested.

"I came to ask you if you did it—and to tell you that if you did, there isn't going to be any wedding. You'll be too dead."

"Give me the time of the shooting and I'll fix an alibi up for myself."

"Never mind, Ward," I said. "I want you to take off your shoes and stockings. Silly, isn't it?" I added, at his blank look. "But I've got a gun and I'll use it if you don't."

He hesitated a moment, sat down in a big chair and lifted up one of his feet. Then he stopped.

"You're nuts, Williams," he told me. "There's a man by the door you came in with a gun in his hand. It would be inconvenient to kill you here—but I've been inconvenienced before."

"I know." I moved my pocket up slightly. "But I'm covering you."

"Not much good if he plugged you."

"Not much good for you either, Ward." I let the gun slip into view now. "We'd both be too dead to attend the wedding."

"Don't shoot, you fool!" Anderson called over my shoulder. "Well, what sort of a deal do you want to make?"

"Take off your shoes and socks," I told him. "I'm looking for a hunk of lead I lost before—or the foot it went through."

He didn't spar for time. He jerked off his oxford and the sock—and then it happened.

The girl's voice: "Drop the rifle, Shorty. Tell him to, Ward. I'm not half as bad as you paint me—yet."

A buzzer went off somewhere in the room. The man at the door spoke.

"The police, boss—and only Nelson would come through like that."

We moved after that. The girl led me by the arm, through the door in the rear, along a narrow hallway to narrow stairs. We raced down them and made the alley.

Her frail form trembled on my arm. In the dimness the make-up didn't seem so heavy. The dress was conservative—the dress of Joyce Reed. But the face was the face of Martha.

She held my arm tightly. I hailed a taxi.

"Some little restaurant," I said as we climbed in.

"No, no," she said. "Home. Oh, Race—" She flung her arms about me. "He's going to marry me. He's going to marry me although I've warned that he'll always have me, never Alyce Joyce.

"He told me so today. Told me that he's going to commit a psychological murder of his own. He's giving me twenty-four hours to go back where I came from. He said he'd bought a whip—and he'd beat me back where I belonged. He said if the doctors could do it with psychiatry, he could do it with a whip. He'd beat me back!"

And damned if she wasn't clinging to me, crying. This terror of the night—this mad little devil who took over another woman's body and mind.

"Maybe," I said slowly, "it would do you good. Maybe it would be the best thing for you."

Something shut me up. Martha was sitting up. She was looking at the mirror, and she was sobbing.

"Again!" she cried. She grabbed at the door, but I caught her arm.

"Mr. Williams," she said desperately. "Race Williams, I'm not—I'm not Martha. I'm Joyce Reed." She shook me by both shoulders. "I tell you I'm Joyce Reed! You see that—you know that. What happened? How did I get here?"

Well, it was like a guy being half drunk—or all drunk for that matter. "Well," I tried again, "you *were* Martha...."

"Of course—I'm used to that now. She didn't use to leave me this suddenly. It would be only in the morning when I'd wake up. Have—I done anything? Were you with Martha—every minute of the time?"

I wasn't and I didn't see how I could be. I watched Alyce Joyce fix her hair and wipe off the make-up. And I got to wondering about other things. Something, maybe, that no one had thought of. It burst into words.

"Suppose," I said, "Martha didn't wear any make-up and opened her eyes wide—how would anybody know who you were? Why, you might be Martha now."

"You know better than that." She wiped tears away. "This make-up business is part of us, I guess. I don't know. But I can't stand the horrid stuff—and I suppose she must have it."

The taxi stopped at the Park Avenue apartment. "You're not coming in," she said, when I followed her.

"Yes," I said. "I am. I want to talk to your uncle."

"Oh," she said slowly. "Do—do you think that is wise?"

"Wise or not I'm going to talk to him. Does he approve of your marriage?"

"Uncle William," she said, "would approve of anything that would make me happy."

And that was as hammy as any melodrama. You know where the girl says to save the mortgage, "Father, I love him," and everyone in the audience knows it's a lie. But here was Joyce Reed's uncle, reputed to be one of the cleverest politicians in the city, playing the heavy sucker in the drama. Hard to believe that. But the rest was harder to believe still.

She didn't want me to come in. And she didn't think her uncle was home and she thought he was awfully busy with something, and—

We went up in the elevator. Still objecting, she opened the door of William Evans' apartment. There he was. Heavy of jowl, moist of eye, and taking her in his arms and saying how worried he had been about her.

If it was an act, it was a good one. I was wondering if I hadn't seen a lot of good performances since I met Alyce.

WHEN HE SUDDENLY looked up and saw me, it was a masterpiece. One could almost see his brain working smack through his forehead, trying to place me. His eyes were cold and unfriendly, and then suddenly they weren't. He put his hand out.

"Mr. Williams—our well-known investigator. This is indeed a pleasure."

I said, "Mr. Evans, I want to talk to you."

"I told him you were busy, Uncle."

"I see." He looked down at the girl. "And the nature of our talk, Mr. Williams?"

"Your niece here."

"I see. In the interest of my niece… Run upstairs, dear."

He pushed her away and led me into a little library. He closed the door behind him and locked it.

"This check my niece made out—they called me from the bank. It was for you. You are working for her then?"

"Yes," I said. "At least at present. You might say I was working for Martha."

"Martha." He took off his glasses, twirled them around a few times, and finally said, "I have never met Martha."

This was sort of a foul blow, but I staggered back quickly.

"But you believe in Martha? You understand the whole situation fully?"

"Fully?" He hung on that word a bit. "I don't think anyone understands it fully. But I am sure I understand it quite as well as you do—and this Anderson. And better than Dr. Johnston thinks I do."

"Johnston and his colleagues," I went a little high hat, "have been toying with the idea that it might have something to do with you. Something Anderson has on you—something that makes you agree to this marriage." I stopped and waited for his indignant reply.

I didn't get it.

"Go on, Mr. Williams," he said. "Let me have it all. Proof—evidence—guesswork." He smiled a little. "Come on, throw the book at me. You haven't the reputation of being timid."

Here was no indignant uncle—no hurt politician.

Well, if he wanted it that way, I would give it to him. "Anderson might be in love with your niece. Or he might wish to have your political influence behind him."

"He might even be paying me money." Evans smiled. "No, no, Williams, don't leave that out of all your calculations about me.

"Let me try to take this up reasonably. I am pretty well known—and fairly well respected, which is rare in politics. I call some of our best citizens by their first names. I also know the underworld from which Ward Anderson has sprung. I doubt that any underworld character would be so foolhardy as to try to blackmail me."

"That," I told him, "is a matter of opinion. Isn't it possible there is something in your life you'd give a great deal—a great deal indeed—to keep secret?"

"We all have our soiled linen. Few of us enjoy having it washed in public. But if you mean by a great deal that I would sacrifice my niece's happiness—the answer is no!"

"What would you do if the issue were forced?"

He smiled. "I'd hire you, of course, to eliminate the holder of my great secret." While I tried to swallow that one, he went on: "I sometimes wonder if Dr. Johnston or his colleagues have reached the wrong conclusion. You know my niece was not always brought up in ease and comfort."

"Really?" I was surprised.

"Her mother, a very charming woman, was my sister. She married—well, it sounds a little melodramatic—a scoundrel in a carnival show. Alyce Joyce was born in a tent. When she got old enough, she rode bareback, I believe, while shooting glass globes tossed into the air. My sister loved him and the child did, too. He was the only man who ever blackmailed me—and it was not really blackmail. Occasionally he would write me that my sister was ill and needed money—or the child needed this and that. I always sent it, of course.

"And then," he went on, "my sister was killed." His lips set tightly. "He left Alyce Joyce with me and sailed to fill an engagement in England. It was war then—and he went down with the ship. Alyce Joyce was sixteen."

Evans straightening slightly. "I have never said one harsh word to her about her father. She has to me. Indeed, Mr. Williams, the story is all rather hush-hush stuff. A man in my position avoids such publicity. I might say that I would be glad to pay you ten thousand dollars if you brought to a satisfactory conclusion this unholy mess."

"And just what is the satisfactory conclusion?"

"I'm sure I don't know," he told me, shaking his head. "If she wants Ward Anderson, I suppose she must have him. I know, I know—he's a disreputable scoundrel. But if she wants him, she can have him."

"Do you think she does?"

"I'm sure I don't know. She seemed until lately a sensible girl. I know men. I know women. I know life. But no man knows love."

I put my last question.

"You have not thought then of sending her some place—not exactly an institution but—"

"I have not," he said emphatically. "Neither an institution or anyplace else. She may not be a very fine woman in the eyes of others, but she is all I've got and I'll stick to her."

I didn't see the girl on the way out. I inquired of one of the servants, but she was lying down.

CHAPTER 5

I.O.U. A MURDER

I WENT OVER every sentence, every word—yes, and every thought that might be behind what Evans had just said. Had he been sincere? Just one thing—he said he had never met Martha. Why? And then I shrugged. I'd met Martha.

I went toward the elevator and saw the leg of a man draw back on the stairs. I got into the automatic lift, but instead of going down, I went up one flight.

No one was in the hallway. I took off my shoes and tucked them in my overcoat pockets and crept silently down the stairs.

I peeked around the corner and there he was—still looking out toward the elevator. Hymie Rath. Not one of Ward Anderson's boys. Hymie Rath was in business for himself. He was the last of those really high-class professional murderers who worked alone.

I soft-footed down the stone steps, hesitated as the man moved and reached for his gun. Then I let him have it—with my gun barrel against his forehead.

Hymie Rath's eyes rolled like an old-time comedian's; his legs grew rubbery. I caught him easily and sat him down on the stairs. I grabbed the gun from his loosening fingers and found another under his right arm—and a knife in his belt.

An elevator door opened. Footsteps beat it straight for the Evans' apartment. I took a careful look-see and there was Ward Anderson swinging a cane. He heard my stockinged feet and muttered:

"Back, Hymie. Back—"

I cracked him. A little more finesse to this. It was in the approved fashion—just behind the right ear. Perhaps this blow was a little more vicious, for Hymie was only earning his living while Ward Anderson was paying him to earn it.

I eased him down gently. I didn't bother about his artillery. I simply lifted his trouser leg—the left foot—and pulled down his sock. I got up then, walked over to Hymie and put one of my cards in his hand. Then as I saw Ward Anderson beginning to twist a little, I pressed the button for the automatic lift.

I went down and outside onto Park Avenue. I had given Hymie Rath a big clue—my card in his hand. But I had given Ward Anderson a little clue which should have been big enough. I had left his pants leg turned up and his sock turned down. Also, I hadn't bothered to put the bandage on again.

I went whistling down the street.

It was late in the afternoon when Hymie Rath called me on the phone.

"I found your card, Race. I was wondering—what's it mean?"

"It means what you think it means, Hymie. On sight."

He coughed, cleared his throat. "As a matter of fact," he tried, "I was only bodyguarding someone."

"No, Hymie," I told him. "That's not your business."

"Suppose," he tried again, "suppose I told you I had no idea it was to be you?"

"Hymie," I said. "You and I go the same places in the city a lot. I'm sure to meet up with you—and my business will be your business… on sight."

"You mean that, Race?"

"Yes."

"No kidding?"

"No kidding."

"Okay. I'll be visiting my folks upstate for a bit." He gave me a phone number. "You can find me there with my Aunt Grace. I'll come back in a week, eh?"

"You'll come back," I told him, "when

I'm sure you no longer have a financial interest in me."

Funny conversation. Hymie, the killer, believed that I would shoot him on sight. Was it bluff? Hymie was one of the wisest boys along the Avenue—and he believed it.

Things were coming to a head. Ward Anderson was getting cockey. He had enough people of his own to do his killings for him—but not too long ago he had taken a pot shot at me himself.

I didn't like it. If the underworld thought a guy could have two chances at me, I'd have been dead years ago. A couple of blazing guns are all right when you are surprised into an attack. But when you know a guy intends to kill you—has tried it once—law or no law, it's self-defense to get that guy before he gets you.

I took a shower and was getting ready to go out when Jerry nailed me.

"Both of them girls—I mean—well, there is one of them in the library to see you now."

"Which one?" I asked.

"The best one—the one who paints up and looks nice and don't put on airs."

I walked in and there was Martha.

"Race," she said. "Do you want any more money?"

"What for?"

"To protect me. You might get killed."

"No." I shook my head. "You haven't used up the twenty-five hundred bucks yet. There's been only one attempt on my life so far, plus one killer hired. I don't charge extra for that."

SHE LEANED WAY across and took my hand. I looked at her and I thought that if it wasn't for the paint, she'd be a better-looking dame than the real one. And then I saw the paint wasn't so much. It was just that the hair was different. She looked nice—and for the first time she looked natural. I said without thinking:

"How do you know that you aren't the real girl and the other one the fake?"

She sat back suddenly and stared at me.

I said, "Well, if you wouldn't twist your lips and let your cigarette hang down, if you'd talk somewhere between the tough style and the high-hat way you put on when Alyce Joyce takes over, I'm damned if you wouldn't be not too bad a bit of goods."

She sort of stiffened, and for a moment I thought maybe she really was half-way between. But she said, "Where did you get such a ridiculous idea?"

I said, "I got it out of the books the doctors told me about—those cases had four different personalities." She looked sort of disturbed and I laughed. "You strike me as a girl who might like to do it in a big way."

"Wouldn't you find just one extra personality a little terrifying—if it happened to you?" she asked.

"Yes," I admitted, thinking it over. It would be tough if I turned soft at times, and guys got to gunning for me hoping I'd be in the sissy mood. "But it would be sporting," I added. "They couldn't tell when I'd turn back to Race Williams and pull a couple of guns and lay them out."

Then I got serious and asked her what she came to see me about.

"Ward's going to marry us. Alyce Joyce

or me—whoever it happens to be. He says he'll beat hell out of me if I ever appear."

"Nuts." I was in it again. "He'd only be hurting Alice Joyce."

"What good would that do me? Alyce Joyce is at a stage where she will go through anything to be rid of me. That's where Haggerty came in…. I think she loves Ward. I think she'll marry him. I think she has to. It couldn't be me because I know everything I ever did and Anderson fears me. It couldn't be Alyce Joyce—" with a tinge of bitterness—"because she is too sweet. And too weak."

"Then?"

"Then it is my uncle. Alyce Joyce loves him. And I guess I love him—because I've never let him see me."

"You think the shock would be too much for him?"

"For Uncle William?" She laughed. "No, but it might be for me." She came to her feet. "I've stayed too long." She opened her bag and took a bit of paper from it.

"Here's the address of the hide-out Ward will take Alyce Joyce to. If you don't hear from me by ten tonight, you'll know the worst has happened—that he's married her, just to scare me into oblivion. I'll call you every night by ten o'clock. If I don't—come for me at that address. Enter through the basement window." She pointed to a spot on the little drawing she had made. "Then do as you please—for me."

"How?" I asked, "do I know you won't be at that window and shoot my head off?"

"You don't," she said. "That was why I asked if you wanted more money. But I really have only a minute. I must go."

"Listen," I told her. "You killed a lot of time here for someone who had only a minute—and a single message. Why?"

"Because—" she looked straight at me—"I want you to like me… maybe more than like me." And with that she came quickly forward, put both arms around my neck and kissed me on the mouth. Then she was gone.

I licked my lips. Her mouth had been real enough. I ran my hand across my mouth. The lipstick had been real, too. I jerked myself together and went out into the hall. But she was already out the door.

Yes. The kiss had been real enough. In fact it was a honey….

Along around dinner time, I put through two calls to Ward Anderson. Neither stirred him up, so I went down to his classy dive. On my second drink, Ward Anderson came in. He didn't make any bones about it. He sat down and said simply:

"You could hardly kill a man here and get away with it."

I said, "It could be done. You'd be surprised how quick I could start a fight, force out a gun, and blow holes in you."

He didn't laugh any more. "Are you on the kill, Race?"

When I said I was, he spoke his piece like Hymie. "No kidding?"

"No kidding."

"You wouldn't believe I'd hired Hymie only as a bodyguard?"

"Hymie," I told him, "has his pride. Besides, from the way you frame that question you haven't spoken to Hymie lately."

He paled slightly and looked around the bar. But he wasn't yellow—not Ward. He said:

"You knocked him over—already?"

"I came here to discuss you, not Hymie."

"Well—" he said. "I'll settle on your terms. How can I convince you it won't happen again?"

I gave it to him just as I gave it to Hymie. "The city isn't big enough for both of us any more, Ward. And I'm not getting out."

"So that's how it is." He came to his feet.

"Okay," he said. "You pushed me into it, Race. I'm not leaving either." He turned around and left the bar—his back to me.

That was a new one on me. I sure had to admire Ward Anderson's guts.

I got up and left the bar too. He had a hundred men to draw from, and I—I shrugged my shoulders as I passed out into the street.

It would be self-defense, of course. Ward Anderson would pull a gun as soon as he saw me again. I don't bluff with guys like Ward—and Anderson didn't bluff either.

Within a few days, maybe within a few hours, our kill-or-be-killed pact would be known through the city. Then the cops would hear of it. What would they do? What *could* they do? No crime had been committed. They would sit down and wait for a body and then arrest—me, I hoped.

If I happened to have a bullet or two in me, that would help. If Ward died with a gun in his hand and a couple empty shells

that had gone off into the night—that would be better still for me. Sure, he had the advantage there. I would give him a chance to draw, but he wouldn't give me one. But I didn't think I needed to be given one. Maybe it's my conceit—but I'm still alive and a lot of other lads who had the first draw are dead.

That night by ten o'clock, Martha hadn't called me. I used the phone. I even put a couple of buzzers on Ward Anderson from a private agency. And how those guys can charge!

I put down the phone, adjusted my shoulder holsters under each armpit, and jerking on a dark gray fedora, went out again into the night. I moved fast. I didn't want any cop on my tail—what with information going around the way it was. It looked like the showdown.

I had Jerry take my car out of the garage and park it down from Alf's Drug Store for me. Seven minutes later I looked at my watch. It was ten minutes after twelve, and I was on my way uptown in the car.

I swung over and passed the zoo and shot over to the Bronx. That was when I began to think a bit—although I was still going ahead no matter what conclusions I reached. I was paid to protect the girl and this was it. Ward didn't like Martha and he was going to beat her back to where she belonged. Where she belonged! I took a gulp at that one, but who was I to pooh-pooh the great of the scientific world?

Then I got mixed up in the scientific world myself. Wouldn't it be possible for Ward to get it out of Martha and have a few guys at the cellar windows I was supposed to hop through?

I decided it was very possible. The chances were even that I'd be nailed or fired on by the time I got within ten yards of the house.

Though dark, there was moon enough to see the place. It was an old, three-story affair with a slanting roof. I bent low and ran toward it.

When I came to a tree, I stood up and kept close in its shadow. I looked the house over. The window was there all right, and occasionally there was a light on it from the fading moon. Maybe I was wrong, but the cellar window seemed to be swinging a bit free.

I slipped around the house, approaching it from the other side. Then I saw the ladder. It ran straight up the side of the house to the roof—and close to a window.

The next moment I was climbing up it. Not the instructions I had, certainly. But what was to prevent Martha from suddenly turning into a child and slipping out a pail of water for me to drop into? Or even taking on another personality as a gun moll?

I climbed up the ladder, found the distance to the window was a little greater than I thought. I made the stretch over. The ladder held steady. I got one foot on the sill. The window was wide open and it wasn't screened.

I caught the frame and stepped over onto the sill. Not a bad way to come on a guy who had tried to kill you. I stood spread-eagled in the window and laughed silently.

The laugh died as a gun was thrust in my stomach. A rope or a belt jerked under my knees, and I fell sprawling into the room.

Then they knocked me silly. Maybe I was kicked a few times on the head, maybe a couple of times in the stomach to knock the wind out of me. But nothing serious.

I came around fast enough. My arms were tied behind my back. Both my guns gone, and I was being marched out into a hall and down a flight of stairs.

I must have been a pretty sight half bent from the kicks in the stomach. There was blood running down my face, too. I could feel it and taste it. And my hat was pushed down on my head. Nothing jaunty about my appearance. Though when I saw the light from the room to the left on the second story, I tossed a bit of a swagger into my walk.

Ward Anderson was alone. He was balanced against a high-backed desk that must have been brought in so he could lean against it. He had a half smile on his face, and he was all dolled up in full evening dress.

"Smart fellow, Race." He took the cigar out of his mouth. Then I saw that two guns lay on the desk and that they were my guns.

"You can't get away with this one, Ward," I told him. "It's already along the Avenue that the city isn't big enough for both of us. The cops will know."

"Yes, I know." He nodded easily. "The boys from Gregory Ford's Agency were inquiring around. But they only know you are on the kill for me. I saw that it was put that way."

He looked over at the clock on the desk. The time was close to one. "Alyce

Joyce," he said easily, "is resting. I gave her a sleeping pill."

He dismissed the two hoods from the room with a wave of his hand. "Close the door but stand by.

"Now, Race." He opened the desk and took out another gun. "I'm not a guy to drag things out. You've been in a lot of people's hair. They've always been afraid of you because they said you had a charmed life. I always knew better. You've had a hell of a lot of nerve and a magic trigger finger. That's all."

"How did you know I would come here?"

"I put the hose to Martha. She squealed like a stuck pig. But she told me before— before she turned back to— Do you believe that, Williams?"

I gave him a hoarse laugh, hoping for some break.

"You'll find out Martha's not so easy to handle," I said, "when you wake up some morning with a knife in your back."

"I've thought of that. I'll see to it that knives won't be too easy to get." He grinned. "So the smart Race Williams had suspicions about our dual Martha. I thought you would. That's why I set the ladder to make things easy for you."

He stopped as a slight scratching came from a closet door to his left.

"Remember Hymie Rath?" he asked.

"Killer-rat," I told him. "He got out of town this afternoon."

"He wanted to, but he didn't. He's in the closet now, Race. Nice and convenient for the kill between you two."

He kept his eyes and his gun on me as he went to the closet and unlocked the door. Hymie Rath crept out. He wasn't too sure of himself, and he blinked in the sudden light.

Then he saw me and started to cringe back. He stopped and straightened, and his killer eyes widened. His tongue came out and he licked at his lips.

"It's Williams. Race Williams. And you've got him trussed up like a steer ready to be slaughtered."

"That's right." Ward Anderson nodded at him. "But you see—now I can do the job myself, and it will cost me nothing."

"No, Ward," Hymie protested. "Let me kill the dirty rat. I'll do it for nothing— my way."

"Listen," Ward said slowly, "I'm not in a hurry. I want Williams to take it slowly. I want you to put a shot through his left shoulder—close to his side."

We both gasped. Ward Anderson didn't go in for vengeance, he killed simply for convenience. But Anderson said:

"Maybe I want him to talk a bit, Hymie. You're mighty sharp with a gun."

And Hymie was, particularly when my hands were tied behind my back. He simply tossed up his right arm. Yellow flame belched. There was a stab under my left armpit as cold as an icicle. That was the only way I knew I was hit. Just the coldness and the quick flow of warm water that I knew was blood.

"Nice, eh?" Hymie turned to Ward Anderson. "Now what?"

"Now—" Anderson raised one of my guns from the desk—"now it's over, Hymie. Like this." He raised his right hand slowly, took careful aim while Hymie grinned.

Then Hymie didn't grin any more. He knew.

The gun swung suddenly in Ward Anderson's hand, and he shot Hymie almost straight between the eyes.

CHAPTER 6

GUN MOLL GAL

THE ROOM REVERBERATED with that shot. The bullet went through Hymie's head as if it were paper. It picked him right up off the floor and tossed him against the wall. Even then he didn't fall right away. He stood there looking at us with sightless, glass-like eyes before he slid slowly to the floor. Then he fell forward on his chest as if he slept.

"You see," Ward Anderson smiled at me, "Hymie and you were gunning for each other. He was killed with your gun—but he shot you before he died." He crossed, still watching me, and leaned down to take Hymie's gun from him.

I thought of making a dive for him. It wasn't my style and wouldn't help my rep to be shot like—

We both paused and listened. The noise was a simple creak. Then suddenly the door opened, slammed closed again, and a lock clicked into place.

Both of us stared at the girl—her face touched heavily with make-up. Her eyes were ablaze and her red lips pale even through the thick red. There could be no doubt that it was Martha.

"Good evening, Martha," Ward Anderson said quietly. "There has been a fight here. And Mr. Williams is leaving us."

It was death then, I thought—but it was not death for me. Martha's hand came from behind her back, and the thing it held was black and small.

She seemed to fire it without aiming. It went off like a tiny machine gun—and every one of the shots bounced straight into Ward Anderson's right side. He went down slowly, dancing slightly to each bullet, looking surprised.

I hollered at the girl, "The door! Bolt it!"

She ran to the door, and I heard the bolt shoot home. I stepped forward and kicked my gun from Ward Anderson's hand. He looked up at me with soft inquiring eyes. There was no hate in them. They were the surprised eyes of a child.

I looked over at the girl. She was going through the desk. She found a penknife and walked over to me and hacked at the cord around my wrists.

"No, Martha!" I cried out. Ward's hand was stretching out to Hymie Rath's gun.

I tore myself free. Fingers stiff, body really hurting, I bent forward swiftly and grabbed up my gun.

It was as if Martha saw the gun in Anderson's hand and not the gun in mine, for she suddenly tossed both arms about my neck and cried:

"No, no, Ward! Not Race!" She clung to me.

The danger to the girl didn't stop him. He fired once, and hot lead ran across my right cheek.

I had nothing else to do. It was my life and the girl's life....

I squeezed lead once. I hit him just about where he hit Hymie—in the center of the forehead. He caught his heels against Hymie's dead feet and crashed upon the floor like a trap door with a heavy spring.

"Is he dead?" the girl whispered against my chest. "Oh, Race—I killed him. I—I killed him for you."

"No," I told her. "I killed him."

Then she saw the blood on my arm. She took my coat off, snatched a handkerchief from my pocket.

"Is it bad?" she asked. "If I had come sooner—"

"Not too bad," I told her. "Is there a phone here?"

"A phone? Here? What would you want a phone for?"

"The police," I said, "and Dr. Johnston."

"The police?" she gasped. "But they—that's what we want to avoid." She looked at the two bodies. "We can slip out."

"Lady," I said to her, "I have spent a great deal of my life explaining to clients not to leave the scene of a crime. What's the matter? What is it you can't take?"

She came close to me and looked straight up at me. I'm telling you Martha was better to look at than her other self. Even with the smear of red lipstick and a bit of powder; and half-closed eyes that were opening. She said slowly:

"I can't take remembering that I told him you were coming because of a few slaps. I thought Race—Race, hold me in your arms."

I did. It wasn't so bad. It wasn't so good either, what with a couple of stiffs lying on the floor, my arm aching like the blazes, trying to watch the windows—hell! I was hanging on to her more like a drunk to a street lamp than Race Williams in a big love scene.

Besides, I was beginning to think. She had saved my life all right, but I couldn't quite see the lady-like action of walking into the room and emptying her gun in Ward's side. Still she was a very nice bundle, and her lips were suddenly warm. I pulled her closer. She dropped back off her toes and said:

"Race—could you just let me go and—and sort of fix things up yourself?"

I shook her off. I walked over to the desk and picked up the phone. I said to Martha:

"Doc Johnston's number, kid. I know—I made a mess, but we're in it together." After she gave me the number and I had dialed it, I said, "If you can pull a third personality out of yourself—better make it the governor.... Oh, hello, Doc Johnston. Williams speaking." I gave him the direction how to get there. "It's a mess," I said. "A couple of stiffs—and our playfellow Martha."

"But I—from what you say I don't think I want to be there."

"Okay," I told him. "Lots of guys don't like to sit in the chair either, but they sit down just the same. Make it here fast."

I jammed down the receiver and turned to the girl.

"Race," she said, "deal me out of this and I'll give you fifty-thousand dollars. I—"

She must have seen the expression

on my face. Then she did it. She put her hands over her face and fainted.

She seemed comfortable enough. I took a look at the little gun she had put on the desk, saw that it was empty, then went quickly through the pockets of the two stiffs. Neither of them carried anything incriminating except that Hymie had a blackjack, a pair of brass knuckles and a knife that when it folded out looked like *something*.

The girl still sat where she had slid down against the desk. I went to the door, carrying enough hardware for any emergency, and looked out. A great silence. The others had left at the shooting. If things had gone right, I would be dead. If things had not gone as planned and they burst open the door to see how things were—then they would be dead. And they were wise guys of the night who didn't want to die.

I heard the car pull up. Going down through the dimly lighted hall, I opened the front door. It was Dr. Johnston. He looked in bad shape.

"Dead. People killed. Who killed them? Who?" He got his hand on my shoulder and shook me—more like an hysterical woman than a learned psychiatrist.

I didn't say anything. I led him up the stairs. We were almost at the door when she flew out at us, put her arms around the doctor's neck.

"Oh Doctor! Ward—he gave me something to drink. And I woke up here—like this."

Yes, the girl was Alyce Joyce now. Not rough. Little lipstick, eyes wide open, mascara gone. The niece of a well-known politician, William Evans.

"Okay," I said. "Let us hear anything you have to say, Doc. And you Miss Reed." I looked at my watch again. "Just a minute or two. You can't stall the cops." Then I gave Johnston the whole story.

I don't know what he wanted to say when I finished, but I cut in on it anyway. "No time, Doc. I got to get the cops. She can't walk out on the show because—well, there are five or six small bullet-holes in Ward Anderson."

"But that's awful!" Her voice came rich and musical. "I was not myself—"

"You'd be locked up as a dangerous criminal anyway. They can't keep one half of you in jail and one half of you out. Okay, Doc. What do you know about such instances? I mean the law. Where do you stand—and how far will you back the girl up?"

"We're engaged to be married." The girl went over to the doctor and clung to his arm. He pulled back like he never saw her before.

She turned to me frantically. "Martha will never appear again—I know it! I can feel that her personality is dead. And after all, she saved your life and—"

I hesitated a moment. "Yes, she saved it all right. But, damn it, I killed Ward Anderson for her—for Martha!"

"No, no." Dr. Johnston jerked himself away. "It wasn't Martha. It was she—Alyce Joyce."

When I stared at him, he cried, "Don't you see? Don't you understand? There never has been a Martha! Just the one girl. She was acting a part—a part that needed no disguise and very little acting. She simply acted herself. Williams, don't you see? Don't you understand? I taught her how to do it. Told what to say to old Dr. Halton, the famous psychiatrist. Half-deaf, half-blind—Lord! I—I thought I loved her."

"Thought?" The girl turned on him now. "You did love me! What you *thought* was that I loved you!"

I picked up the phone while the incriminations were still flying back and forth. Johnston was through with her, all right. He kept saying so. But she wasn't through with him.

When I put down the phone, I saw that they were whispering quietly together.

I said simply and in a sort of daze, "I knew all along there was something fishy about this dual personality."

But I knew even as I said the words that I was lying. I had believed it right up to that moment—what with the books, the learned men, Ward Anderson consulting every authority. Well, the answer was simple. It *could* be—but it *wasn't*.

I didn't have much time to think about it because the girl was talking—or a mixture between Martha and herself was. She was talking about money. She was pointing out how we could all profit by being careful, and how her Uncle William would clear the decks if we made it look on the up and up.

The girl was right, she made sense. After all, it wasn't a bad set-up with the girl there to give testimony. Two hoods were wiped out. The papers would give me a good play for that. I even had a wound of my own. The girl shooting to save me—her fear and terror and my calling her doctor—it could be explained.

"Okay," I told her. "I don't know what he had on you but he deserved to die."

I BUZZED HER uncle. A little political influence couldn't be bad. He listened, asked one or two questions, then said he'd be right over, as if his niece were mixed up in a murder a day.

The police arrived, including Inspector Nelson. The assistant medical examiner was there, too. He said in his jovial manner:

"I'd recognize your work any place, Williams. Clean as a whistle right through the head. But the stitching up the side with a small gun? Tut, tut. You'll be going in for embroidery next."

"Would he have died of those side wounds?" I asked.

"Tut, tut," said Steel. "That is like shooting a man off the top of the Empire State building and asking if the fall would have killed him. He's dead—and the bullet in his forehead did the trick. And if you were to take another shot at him now, he wouldn't be any deader."

Just then William Evans was shown into the room by a cop. David Edward Goamer, the big-shot lawyer, was walking softly behind him.

My story was a good one. The truth— at least most of the truth. William Evans, the big politician, had hired me to protect his niece, Alyce Joyce Reed, who was being seen too much with Ward Anderson and even talking of marriage. Miss Reed had disappeared on me. I was searching the city for her. Then I got a call where she was. I thought the call was from some stoolie that I knew and would collect from me later—and came rushing out to this house.

I climbed the ladder. They could see the busted plane of glass there. I rushed down the stairs and met Hymie in the room. I shot him after he winged me. Then the gang was on me. Ward Anderson had them tie my hands behind my back. Then he chased them—told me he was going to kill me. He had fired one shot when the girl came into the room, screamed and fired. Then she cut me loose and Anderson grabbed a gun, smeared lead across my face, and I put a slug in him.

The girl did her part. She sobbed hysterically, "It was to save my life! I was clinging to him—clinging to Mr. Williams. I didn't think Ward would shoot me—but—but he would have. I saw it in his eyes!"

"Just a minute," Inspector Nelson cut. Not even William Evans could frown Nelson down when he thought he was doing his duty. He had a question to ask. It was a nasty question.

"Miss Reed—just why were you in this house here with the notorious Mr. Ward Anderson?"

She said, "I think he was afraid. He wanted to keep hidden until we could get out of the city."

"But that doesn't answer my question," said Nelson. "Why were you here alone with a notorious gangster?"

"Oh—" she opened her big eyes wide— "Ward and I were married this afternoon. Very quietly, in Greenwich, Connecticut."

That bombshell about broke up the party. It hit me a little below the belt. She said it so quietly and easily and simply—

as if it were the most natural thing in the world for us to expect. Which it wasn't—not by a barrelful it wasn't.

WE LEFT AFTER that. Everyone seemed to fade away in different directions.

I had my wound fixed up by my doctor and went home.

I saw my friend Sergeant O'Rourke the next morning but not the reporters. O'Rourke had some of the early editions of the morning papers. It didn't look too bad.

One of them read:

TRAPPED, BEATEN AND TIED WITH THICK ROPES, RACE WILLIAMS BREAKS FREE AND SHOOTS NOTORIOUS MURDERERS.

I didn't care much for the second one, though:

BRIDE OF A FEW HOURS SEES KILLER AND HUSBAND SHOT DOWN BY NOTORIOUS DETECTIVE.

Yes, that could have been better. Another headline put it much more nicely:

TWO OF THE CITY'S WORST HOODLUMS SLAIN IN TERRIFIC GUN BATTLE BY THE FAMOUS RACE WILLIAMS.

I liked that one and read a bit more of the article, which had me lying at death's door and a "grateful young widow who had been forced into wedlock crying on the hospital stairway."

"It doesn't mention," said Sergeant O'Rourke, "That you got up, served me liquor, then laughed yourself to sleep. Don't get livid, Race. Nothing will come of it. So far Nelson has heard that the girl could turn herself into five or six women at once—and I think a snake or two. And a fortune teller claims to have predicted Anderson's death to the minute.

"Nelson's thinking," said O'Rourke, "what I'm thinking. You said you'd kill them and you did. And I don't care."

I HATED LIKE hell staying in the house for a couple of days but I did want to make it look like a real gun battle.

Then who walks in on me but William Evans himself—the big shot in person.

I chased Jerry, folded up the note I had just received and looked up at Evans.

"Here is a check for ten-thousand dollars." When I started to refuse, he said, "No, no. You remember me? I'm the man who never saw Martha. I don't read those kind of books and if I did I wouldn't believe them. But it's the nice way you handled things—your taking all the blame."

Evans grinned there and tossed me the evening paper he was carrying. "That ten grand you earned—consider it a fee for not worrying too much why things happened as they did. I offered you that much for bringing things to a satisfactory conclusion."

He picked up his hat and cane. "Incidentally, Williams, here's some plain advice from an old guy. There isn't any Martha—so don't bother going out with her."

He turned and left the room.

I looked down at his check. Then I picked the note I had so hastily thrust in my pocket. Was Evans a mind reader? The note was simple enough.

Hi, Race!

You and I will dine out tonight. Meet me at the Astoria at seven-thirty. I'll be the best-dressed and best-looking woman there. Two personalities mixed into one—for you.

Martha.

Of course I wouldn't go. I was indignant. But I called Jerry and told him to get out the soup and fish.

Then I opened the paper to see if I was still on the front page. I wasn't. But the front page rocked me just the same. I read:

SLAIN RACKETEER'S WIDOW TO INHERIT OVER HALF A MILLION.

Ward Anderson's will, made a few hours before his death, left everything to his widow....

Did Ward Anderson have something on the girl that forced the marriage—even a threat to kill her? Did Ward Anderson have something on her uncle, despite William Evans' simple and assured denial that he could ever be blackmailed?

Was it all coincidence that I met Martha and she talked about two-hundred grand? Did she misjudge the amount and mean half a million? Did she plan the marriage and his death like that? It all seemed too clever? Still, Martha was a clever girl.

I sort of liked Martha. But I like the

truth, too—and I hoped I'd find it out at the Astoria that night.

"You look swell." Jerry came over and straightened my tie.

The phone rang. I hesitated at the door, then strode back into the room and answered it myself. It was Inspector Nelson. His lips smacked with pleasure, so I knew that something very unpleasant was coming up. He said:

"So you think you are having dinner with Miss Alyce Joyce Reed at the Astoria, do you?"

"Why not?"

"Because," Nelson spoke very slowly, "even you don't dine with the dead, Race.... It just happened. That psychiatrist Johnston went nuts and pumped five shots into her body—then swallowed the last slug himself. What do you think?"

I wasn't thinking. I dropped the phone.

I got up and walked toward the kitchen to open a can of beans. Then I changed my mind. Come to think of it, I had never had dinner at the Astoria.

The Wrong Corpse

"I AM NOT JANNY CORT"

IT LOOKED LIKE a swanky joint. A small stone balcony with French windows three feet behind the stone railing. It was real class.

I pressed the bell and got service from two directions: a man peeked through a side window and a butler opened the door. There was a chain attached to it. No use putting my foot in, unless I wanted to play a game of hollering back and forth for a few hours—which I didn't.

"Sorry, sir," the butler said, "Mr. Carlander is with his solicitor and is seeing no one. Absolutely no one!"

"Good!" I nodded pleasantly. "He'd only be in the way. I'm here to see Miss Cort—Miss Janny Cort."

"Sorry, sir." He turned on the record again. "Miss Cort is indisposed and not seeing anyone."

I gave my fedora a jerk down then, stuck my face close to the crack but not close enough to get my nose caught, and told him flat.

"I didn't say I *wanted* to see her," I said.

259

"I am here at her request and I am *going* to see her. There is a difference between want and going to."

"Close the door, Edwards." A masculine voice came from behind the butler. "Tell him to go away."

"Better let the chain off. I'm coming in anyway." I meant it.

A quick order and the door slammed shut.

I don't play jokes. I wasn't playing one then. I turned, hopped the little rail onto the balcony, faced the French windows. Raising my right foot, I shot it hard against the center wood of the windows.

It was a good kick. The windows flew open like saloon swinging doors and smacked back against the wall. A half dozen or so little panes of glass clattered into the room.

I stepped inside. It wasn't a big room. I suppose it was what you might call a small reception room. Anyway, I was getting my reception. Two men stood in the curtained doorway that led to the hall. Both looked money. Both were dressed money. And despite their rich appearance, both were darned well good and surprised. Both mouths hung open. The smaller man began to use his mouth first.

"The police—" he half cried out and rushed toward the white, cradled phone on a side table.

"If you are calling the cops, it suits me," I said.

"Just a moment, Carlander," the taller man, thin and bent forward slightly at the shoulders, said. "We—ah—have ample protection here, I believe—if this man is a crank. And—ah!" This "Ah" as a heavy-set, youngish and strong-looking lad slipped into the room. "Just take care of this man, Mr. Cummings—er—and no disturbance before the police get here—understand?"

"Yes, sir." Cummings walked rapidly toward me, and nearly lost his life by putting his hand in his jacket pocket. But what he pulled out was a pair of handcuffs, and he said, "Stick them out!" He approached me carelessly and stopped as if to talk. He followed up his clever ruse by jumping forward suddenly, grabbing my left arm and slightly raising his knee.

I stepped about a foot back. His knee missed me. And I hit him a blow behind the ear that knocked him half-way across the room and brought him up sitting in a flower pot.

I knew his sort, all right—a licensed private detective.

As the private dick started to climb to his feet and reach toward his hip-pocket, I said:

"Look, guy! You pull that gun on me and you'll wind up in the morgue!"

I pushed my hat back, and I liked the respect he paid to my face. His gun went slowly back into his pocket. He had never met me before, but somehow he knew. It just slipped out of him.

"Williams—" he said. "Race Williams!"

"That's right." I nodded at the lawyer and his friend Carlander. "Now, gentlemen—if you wish to call the cops, go ahead."

"Just who are you—and why are you here?" Carlander wanted to know that.

"The name," I said, "is Williams—as

our good friend told you. I'm here on behalf of my client, Miss Cort. I'm going to see her."

"I don't know, Mr. Carmical—" Carlander tried this on the shyster "solicitor." "Must I be subject to such breaking and entering—isn't that what they call it?"

"That is what they call it," the lawyer, Carmical, admitted, but he put beady eyes on me. "Perhaps the young man is excited, presumes Miss Janny Cort is his client—"

"Boys," I told them, "I'm not excited yet. You've got two minutes to put that bloodhound Edwards on Miss Cort's trail, or I'm going through the house."

"I think"—the lawyer put his hand on the phone—"that we had better have the police in. He *did* break and enter your house, Carlander."

"Not *his* house," I cut in then. And when they both looked at me, I said, "I looked up the deed. This is the house of the estate of Miss Janny Cort. Look! I'll give you a break. Maybe we could quibble over the title to the property, but I certainly have a memorandum from Miss Cort telling me to call here today, at this hour, and to see her over any objections or obstructions. You gentlemen are the objections." I glanced at the busted glass and doors, and being an honest man, added, "The window was the obstruction. All very legal, eh, what?"

"Really!" Carmical seemed surprised. "Really, Mr. Williams, you should have told us this at the door. Might I see this—er—odd request from Miss Cort? You needn't be afraid I'll keep it."

I took a laugh at that. Fished out the paper and let him see it. Lawyer Carmical and Carlander both had a look at the note. They read it carefully, and I thought of the girl who had sent it to me and the five hundred dollars.

Carlander spoke then. He took off the spectacles he had used to read the note and put on unrimmed nose glasses and became the gentleman of the world.

"Edwards," he called, "ask Miss Cort to step down for a few minutes, please." And then to me: "I am afraid we owe you apologies, Mr. Williams—but we had one detective here today to protect Miss Cort. She is—well, I would not like to say erratic. Perhaps an impulsive young woman would be better. But she seems to fear something." He jerked a thumb at the detective. "Since this gentleman has identified you, I presume we must commend Miss Cort's good judgment, but not her discretion."

"You needn't worry about the discretion. You gentlemen did all the hollering." But I was still wondering why I had to break into the house if things were on the up and up.

And sure, I knew "Slippery Joe" Carmical, but never had any dealings with him. I tried like a book detective. "You, Mr. Carlander, might I ask your position here?"

The little man laughed.

"Really," he said. "I am trustee of the estate. Miss Cort's guardian, in a way. And her dead father's devoted friend."

"And this gentleman?"

"I don't see—" the lawyer started, and then: "I'm Joseph Carmical."

"Oh!" I put up an eyebrow at that. "Carmical."

"Yes."

"Hardly the lawyer for the estate."

"Not the lawyer for the estate, no." And, bristling, "But why the 'hardly?' "

"Obvious," I told him with my best smile. Then, turning to Carlander, "What do you mean, 'Miss Cort's guardian in a way?' "

He didn't have too bad a smile as he said, "I mean she's over twenty-one. Twenty-four, to be exact. And a girl that age is in the habit of having her own way quite a lot."

"And entitled to it." I nodded.

Joe Camrical was in again. "Might I ask, Mr. Williams, if you have—er—do you know anything detrimental to my legal practice, or my name?"

"Want to catch me in a libel suit?" I grinned, and when he seemed appeased, "I don't know anything good of it, either."

Which was true enough. Shyster was the name for him. High-class shyster, if you make a distinction.

The girl came in. Her face was like fine-cut ivory, her eyes and hair black.

She had something bright and yellow holding her hair severely back. And to top it off she had on a long, white dress—maybe what the ads call a hostess gown.

She came right over and held out her hand to me.

"You are Mr. Williams, aren't you?" And when I nodded, for the hand was soft with long, slim fingers, she said, "I asked you to come." And turning to Carlander, "Not against your wishes, Uncle dear—but against what I knew would be your judgment."

She tossed him a smile with eyes that opened so wide you could see yourself televised in them.

"Will you come to the den, Mr. Williams? Alone, please."

So this was the Janny of a couple of newspaper unpleasantries. Rich and willful, with a snootful too often now and then.

Maybe I had seen her before, but I didn't think so.

No one made a yap as I followed the girl out through the hall. Edwards, the butler, was there.

His eyes shifted to right and left, then his frozen face cracked up and he smiled. It was something like the end of the ice age.

We went into the little den, the girl locked the door, got us seated in comfortable chairs, with me close to a small bookcase, and said:

"Race Williams. Now what do I get for my five hundred dollars?"

I liked her smile and I liked her eyes, but I like also to know where I stand. So I opened my little book, took out a pencil and started to itemize.

"For the chances of being shot at the front door—twenty dollars," I said. "For kicking in the window and discussing the cops with your guardian and lawyer—a hundred bucks. For coming in here—"

"You forgot. Edwards tells me you knocked down that rough detective."

"To be sure." I smiled. "That's another fifty cents. Now, Miss Cort, the rest of your money entitles you to walk out of here with me, and go where you please.

With smiles and bows from your guardian and his lawyer—or stepping over their chests. Well—how does that I sound?"

"It sounds very gruesome!" Her laugh was real. "There is no finer man than Uncle Carlander. No finer." She was out of her chair while she was talking. "Now, I'll tell you what I want from you, Mr. Williams. I have clothes in the closet here. I want to change. I want to leave by that window, hop the fence behind in the alley and go my own way, I want you to sit here for ten minutes. Give me a chance to go." She looked at me a moment. "You are not overbright, but you are honest and you are strong. And I understand you are, at times, ruthless."

"What do you mean?" And I certainly meant exactly that.

"That—*I am not Janny Cort*. We both have brown hair and brown eyes. And she does affect this Grecian get-up when meeting people she wants to impress with her intellect—or absence of it. Now, wait a moment. Janny Cort doesn't look very much like me. It is just a matter of our coloring, and a few other features. She's shorter, perhaps not so slim."

CHAPTER 2

MURDER DRAWS A FULL HOUSE FAST

It took me a few moments getting back my breath.

"So what?" I said. "I let you get out of the house. What good does that do the real Janny Cort and me?"

"Oh!" She shrugged her shoulders. "I'll tell you where she is—or where she will be at a certain time. There is real money in her, Mr. Williams, real money. She has made me promise that I'll see that you find her?"

"What's the set-up?" I asked her.

"I don't know that. But she's afraid—really afraid. She said to tell you the pay would be generous."

"But the set-up here—it must have been planted sometime."

"Yes. I have been here a week, as Mr. Carlander's secretary. But I saw no one but Edwards and the new servants. The others were dismissed and replaced within the week."

"All this for me?"

"No, I don't think it was for you. I think you were a complete surprise. As for me, I was to impersonate Janny Cort to anyone they permitted me to see. So naturally it must have been for people who did not know the real Janny Cort. Few in the city knew her. Contrary to gossip, she didn't go out often. Lately she has not been out at all. Now she's fled—and she wants to see you."

"And what's in it for you?"

"I was paid. Quite frankly, Mr. Williams, I came up the hard way. I don't want to go back. In a way, I'm an actress."

"And where did Carlander discover you?"

"Mr. Carmical," she corrected me. "I don't care to discuss it. The more I think of it, the more it alarms me." She lifted a pencil now and wrote rapidly and for some little time. "There." She handed me the paper. "Janny Cort will be on that train tonight. Drawing-room. It's all written down."

She turned and hurried over to a closet. It wasn't very deep. I could see flashing white flesh—long slender legs. Sure, I watched. I might see a hand with a gun in it. Silly thought, that. But guys in my job have died because of sillier thoughts.

She looked nice when she came out in her blue suit, ready for the street. She looked more real, too.

"Okay," she said, and nodded toward the window. "Give me ten minutes and I don't care what you tell them, Let them think you believe me the real Janny Cort." And as someone tapped at the door, she looked at me, smiled, asked, "Okay?"

"Okay, kid," I told her, and walked over to the door. It was the lawyer, Joseph Carmical, calling through the panel. He appeared genuinely worried.

"We're getting along all right," I called to him. "Give us—" I hesitated and turned, and saw that the girl was gone— "Oh, say ten minutes."

Ten minutes wasn't so bad. I didn't know how I'd like Janny Cort, but I liked her impersonator well enough. And the two birds outside—I could see Joseph Carmical mixed up with anything shady. As far Carlander, I didn't know. He looked character. They might have good reason for not wanting the police in. Then again they might be afraid to have them in. Any way you look at it, I was sitting pretty.

Again a pound at the door, this time louder. I looked at my watch. There were two minutes to go. I walked over to the door, started to open my yap when a voice shouted:

"Unlock that door, Williams, or I'll break it in!"

I UNLOCKED THE door. I know the voice of authority when I hear it. I know the voice of Inspector Nelson—"Iron Man" Nelson—when I hear it, too. I didn't like Nelson. But dislike and respect are two different things. He was no dumb cop. The City of New York does not breed dumb cops.

I swung open the door and faced the irate Nelson. There was just one thing he wanted from me—my license.

"Well," Nelson bellowed. He paused, stood staring as Carlander stepped into the room. But it was Joe Carmical who did the running around looking for the girl. It was he who demanded of me.

"Where's the girl—Janny?"

"Oh," I waved a hand, "out there in the alleyway."

"What did she go out there for?" Nelson demanded.

"Smoke a cigar." I shrugged. "She said her uncle didn't like the smell of cigars, so she always smoked them in the alley."

There were questions after that, plenty of them. But nothing I couldn't shrug off. I let Nelson take the girl's note. He read it over and over, maybe upside down and sideways.

"She owns the house," I said. "She is of legal age and owns herself. As for me, I'm only acting under the Bill of Rights. This Miss Cort sent me a retainer, requested I come here even if I had to break in. I came and I broke in. No cops then. Why now?"

"Maybe," said Nelson, "because Mr. Carlander suspected you were letting her out."

I took a loud laugh on that one.

Both Carlander and Joe Carmical had disappeared now. We could hear them calling in the alley farther back. Nelson leaned over close to me, whispered:

"As a matter of fact, she just stepped out in the alley, didn't intend to come back. Right?"

I grinned and shrugged. "Looks like it," And as Nelson glared, I said quite seriously, "As a matter of fact, she didn't have any cigar with her."

He didn't grin. He didn't blast out. He walked back to the door as the two men returned, and was saying to Carlander in a not too pleasant voice.

"Sure, sure! I appreciate that the commissioner mentioned my name to you once at a dinner. I appreciate that you know the commissioner—or at least ate with him. But I'm Homicide. We're busy people. When I'm called I expect a body, a dead body—not a live, wisecracking second-rate private cop!"

I grinned as I walked past them to the door. "If you want a body, Inspector, why not search the house?"

"Yes, yes!" Carlander chimed in suddenly. "She couldn't have gone. She must be some place. Search the house. Search it now. I demand it!"

"Have you any reason to believe—" Nelson was saying. But that was my cue, and I left.

Of course, I wanted the house searched. After all, I still had a client I had never seen. She could still be in the house. It was a big one. The cops could search it better than I could. How did I know if the girl lied?

EDWARDS, THE BUTLER, was just coming along the street as I went down it. He tipped his hat, half stopped. I remembered the break up of ice and walked over to him.

"Let's walk a block, Edwards," I said, and when he went along with me, I couldn't tell if he wore a frozen face or a smile—it was getting dark.

"Edwards"—I put on my high-hat detective make-up, which consists of a stern voice, a straightening of my fedora, and a slight rise in my chest—"Edwards, you're just a pawn in a game of big money. Shove Mr. Carlander in a cell and Slippery Joe will spring him. Shove *you* in a cell, then what?"

"A cell, sir? You mean prison? Really, sir!"

"Really," I told him. "You went upstairs and came down with a girl. In plain words, you were in with Carlander, and I guess the lawyer, and you passed off a phony on me. That girl was not Janny Cort."

"You astound me, sir!" He was very polite. "But it was Miss Janny Cort I brought downstairs."

"Edwards," I told him, "you don't know the trouble you can get into. How long have you been with Mr. Carlander? And how long have you known Miss Cort?" And when he hesitated, "And don't think up a good one."

"Lie, sir? That would be quite unlike me. I was with Miss Janny Cort's mother when Miss Janny was born. I was with her mother when she died. And Mr. Franklin Cort, her father, met with his tragic death hurrying back from Europe. It was the sinking of the *Conada,* sir. Mr. Carlander took over then, sir, and— Pardon me, sir, but there's a cab. I've been looking for one."

He ran out into the street. I started after him—then dropped to the sidewalk, my gun in my hand.

A heavy black-pointed object had protruded from that cab, and a machine gun sent Edwards dancing in the air before he hit the pavement. Behind that machine gun was a white face. I saw the whiteness plainly as the nose of the machine gun raised slightly, twisted back and drew a bead on me as the cab sped on.

I fired once. I don't know exactly where my bullet went, but I do know the white face disappeared from the window, the machine gun turned up in the air, popped a few shots, then also dropped back into the cab. I chased a few useless bullets down the street after it.

I reached the body of Edwards first. Nelson was a poor second. He has his usual line. Whenever he saw a body, and whenever he saw me, he connected us up together.

"Listen, Nelson," I told him, "I'm sporting two guns. I emptied all but one shot of one gun after the death cab. This Edwards lad has half a hundred slugs in him. Do you think I shot them through my teeth?"

Nelson didn't smile. Rather, he looked at me as if he were actually weighing the possibilities that maybe I did just that.

It had been a dark and empty street at dinnertime, except for the passing cars. Now it was beginning to fill up like 42nd Street and Broadway. Things get around in New York. Murder draws a full house fast.

The lawyer was out and Carlander was out and I told my story three times or more. Nelson wanted to know what the driver looked like. I didn't know. Carlander seemed dazed, while Slippery Joe Carmical kept asking if there was a woman in the taxi.

"You don't think Janny Cort played the tune on Edwards, do you?" I finally said.

His denial was lost in Nelson's wanting to know what sort of a detective I was. It seemed I could do enough shooting when it looked darned suspicious—and he blathered on.

"A century will get you a grand, Nelson," I said, "that if you find that cab in time you'll find a body in it—and that my slug is in the corpse's head."

"Sure," Nelson said. "Let me see them guns of yours."

CHAPTER 3

THINGS ARE NEVER DULL WITH RACE

THAT WAS A big moment. I knew if Nelson got his hands on my guns I wouldn't see them again for a long time. And I'm a guy who needs guns. Nelson held out his hand and waited. I compromised and gave him one gun. The nearly empty one.

"Come on, smart guy," he said, "you just said you had two guns."

"The other gun played no part in this," I said. "I got a license for it. No cop can revoke it, or take it."

"Think not?" he said. We were standing in a little circle now, the cops having pushed back the crowd, and the photographers were snapping pictures of the body. "Want to make an issue of it, Race?"

"Yes!" I set my face grim. "How do I know that the attack wasn't made on me, not that poor guy? I need a gun—always!"

"Quite right, Inspector." Slippery Joe Carmical stepped forward. "I represent Mr. Williams, you see. He is not involved in any crime. He simply was attacked upon the public street. He is not a defendant, but a plaintiff. Every judge, every newspaper man, knows how you feel about Williams, and your threats to get his license. I hope we won't have to make an issue of that. Unpleasant."

But I agreed to go with Nelson and make a statement. In the taxi following Nelson, I let Carmical know that I had a good lawyer of my own and didn't expect to play along with him—and get stuck a fee.

"Nonsense!" He seemed smoother than he had when I first broke in that window. "You needed a lawyer on the spot. I know all about you, Williams. You would not be the sort of man to be turned loose on the public streets without a gun, even for a few minutes. Miss Cort is your client. I'll collect my feel there."

"Is she your client too?" I put it to him straight.

"In a manner of speaking—yes. That is, a feeling that she would like to be, will be glad to be."

There was little doing downtown at Headquarters. Nelson had changed. My gun was taken and marked and I was given a receipt for it. I was allowed to keep my other gun. So I shook Carmical, took a taxi home and restocked my left shoulder holster.

I read over the little memorandum the girl who was not Janny Cort had given me. Simple and direct—the time the train left the Grand Central Terminal, the number of the drawing-room Janny Cort would occupy; that Janny was going to a rest home upstate, though there was nothing the matter with her; that she was not going against her will but that she was afraid of something—and above all wanted me to meet her on that train. And the little note was signed "Deb."

I looked at my watch. There was time. More even if I went uptown and got the train at 125th Street. Also I had time enough to eat a quick meal.

So I hoisted my guns, got them perfectly balanced under my jacket and left the apartment. I hadn't gone half a block when I knew that someone was playing the lamb to my little Mary. I didn't have to look back. I had seen the shadow, felt the steps, and decided to have it out. At the next corner, I turned quickly and stopped. A voice said:

"Oh, come, come, Mr. Williams! Surely I would tread the light fantastic more elegantly if I were trying to hide my presence. I was simply hoping to catch up with you, turn into the side street and talk. Okay, now?"

"Okay, Riley." I stepped out by the curb as the little old man joined me.

Riley had been a hardened criminal—but back so many years, it was long before my time. Few remember him now except as a genial, smiling, smartly-dressed little gray-haired man. I hadn't seen him in some time, except at a distance in some night spot. I knew his racket. He was the best informed man along the Avenue—by far the best informed. His information came high, was very confidential, and as far as I was concerned, never wrong.

HE SWUNG HIS cane to his other hand, clutched my arm and went along with me down the street.

"Well," he pulled at his little waxed mustache, "I saw you and I thought we might stroll along together. Things with me have been dull—but I know that things with you are *never* dull."

"Perhaps, but I thought things are never dull with you, Riley."

"No!" He sounded shocked. "Why, I spent my time this afternoon looking through files, wills—one particular will. Whenever I read of money about to come due to someone, and overhear that person's name in—er—shall I say unsavory places, I am always interested." And when I stopped and grabbed his arm for a change: "Tut, tut, Williams. I was looking up the will of Franklin Cort. He has been dead twenty-four years. I found out that his daughter Janny Cort inherited it all in trust—and on her twenty-fifth birthday gets the principal of the estate. A lot of money for a young girl."

"What else?" I asked him, but I did walk along at his suggestion.

"I was wondering who got the money if she died," he said, "and if she could dispose of it by will before she received the principal sum."

"And?" I was interested.

"Why, it's a matter of record. I had no idea you'd be so interested in my little pastime. Her cousin, Thomas Slater, gets the money. He sort of hangs out down at what was the Turkey Club. Hideous name, isn't it, for a club. But then Johnny Johnson had no idea it would make so much money, be such class, and move over on Broadway. He's changed the name to Toi-Kay now."

"Riley," I told him as we reached a cross street, "what do you know about Janny Cort—and my connection with her? And where do you fit in?" I hesitated a long time. "There's no money in it for me, or for you, either."

"What do I know about it?" He turned me around and we started back, Riley explaining blandly. "You are a fine chap and all that, Williams—but I prefer your company at present on dark side streets. Certainly, I know more about it than you do. If there is no money for you, there should be. As for me, I lost my amateur standing in helping the unfortunate when I was eleven. Today I am an honest man. A statistician and a research expert. I turn up some of the oddest things!"

"I dare say," I cut in on Riley, "that Miss Janny Cort would be willing to pay you a handsome sum if you really helped her in some slight difficulty."

"Really!" Riley stiffened. "Your willingness to use a gun and kill people with it has warped your sense of proportion. I am sure that Miss Janny Cort would not consider her intended murder as a slight difficulty."

With that I turned, ran to the corner and grabbed a taxi. I'd be sure of riding

CARROLL JOHN DALY

the rest of the way with Janny Cort. Riley was a surprising man.

I made the 125th Street Station in nice time, hesitated, then bought a ticket to Albany in case it was a longer ride than I thought. If Janny Cort was aboard that train, I'd see and speak with her. The train pulled in and I boarded it.

Then I saw the girl—the dark-eyed beauty who had *not* been Miss Janny Cort.

She didn't avoid me. As a matter of fact she seemed relieved to see me, as if she had been watching for me. I shook my head as I approached her and gave a jerk of it for her to follow me. I started toward the club car. She caught up to me in the vestibule between two cars and grabbed my arm.

"She's aboard with a man—yes, Janny Cort! I think it is the detective. I didn't get a good look at him, but they both disappeared into the drawing-room."

"What's your name? What are you doing here?"

I was pretty blunt.

"Call me Deb," she said. "I promised—and she paid me to stick until you met her," and when I still stared at her, "Deb—Deborah Layton."

She let me know exactly where the drawing-room was, and when I asked her what she was going to do, she said:

"Get off at Yonkers somehow. I shouldn't be here. Something drove me on, though I was told not to come—*warned* not to come."

"By whom?" I swung on her.

Deborah hesitated a moment, as if marshaling her thoughts.

"I don't know. A dapper little man. I was in Grand Central Station, came there directly from the Cort Carlander residence. He seemed to find me without any trouble. His voice was soft, but his hat was pulled down and he stayed close to my shoulder so I couldn't turn around. He said, 'Don't do it, my dear. Stay away from that train. Send Race Williams word where you are. You can trust him. He'll come high—and maybe I will too.'

She paused as a train screeched by, continued. "When I told him I didn't know what he was talking about, and that I didn't have any money, he laughed, whispered, 'You'll have enough. It's like hiding out; that's it. You'll pretend like in a book that you are hiding out.' And with a snap that wasn't so gentle, 'You're in danger, my child!' And then, when I would have turned on him, 'No, no! I'll have nothing to do with it but to offer advice and information. You've been seen too much now. Your life is in grave danger.' And then he left."

"Are you sure," I started, "he didn't say 'You've seen too much or know too much—' " But she was gone as a porter came along, slipping through to the car ahead. I didn't follow her. Who she was or what she was shouldn't be too hard to find out. Slippery Joe Carmical must know who she was; no doubt Carlander, too. And certainly if I bet a hundred to one that the dapper little man was Riley, I wouldn't be giving high odds.

I figured it about time now to find my client, and made for Janny Cort's drawing-room.

It was in a narrow passageway, deserted,

not too brightly lighted. I rapped, waited. No one answered my knock.

I tried the door. It opened easily, then caught. I slipped a gun into my hand, stepped through the opening quickly and closed the door behind me. I groped for the light-switch; stopped dead. I had kicked against something. I pressed my small flash. It was a leg—a man's leg—that had been blocking the door.

Trouble? I straightened back against the door. I let the flash hunt out the switch and snapped on the light. The man on the floor was twisted sideways. His profile was visible. There was a nasty gash in his head and some blood flowing down. I knew him, all right. He was the detective bird of that evening up at Carlander's, known to me simply as Mr. Cummings.

The thing that caught me was the outline of the figure on the couch—the bed hadn't been made up yet. There was no doubt that a body was under that sheet. A very still body. And down from beneath the sheet at the head of the couch was a length of wire—a couple of feet of it hanging down, as if it had been tied and knotted and this much was left over.

I crossed quickly to where the wire was, lifted the sheet. It was a girl. And she was dead. Glassy black eyes that stared up. A swollen mouth and a protruding tongue. And a wire that was wound so tightly about her throat that it disappeared into blue flesh.

She was not much to look at, now. I didn't need to go through her handbag to know who she was; yet I did. There was no doubt. It was Janny Cort, all right. And the thought went through my head that

some cousin called Thomas Slater, who was working around the Toi-Kay place for Johnny Johnson, was the lad who would get the money.

As for me— There I stood with the dead body of the girl and the unconscious body of the private detective.

CHAPTER 4

THE TOI-KAY CLUB

No DOUBT ABOUT it, I had lots to think about then. The natural impulse was to leave the drawing-room, slip outside and get off at Yonkers. If the detective came to in the meantime, it would be all right. I hate being found at the scene of two killings on the same day.

The best stunt of course would be to wait for Yonkers, or near Yonkers— anyway over the city line of New York. Then the Yonkers cops would have the case—and things would be better for me. Also the girl Deb was entitled to a break and—quick thought—the murderer might be preparing escape that very moment! I just raised my hand, braced myself for the results, and pulled the emergency cord.

The emergency cord worked like magic. The train jerked and the great wheels caught and let go again, and caught again—and I struggled to the door and opened it.

I ran into a guy with a wild look trying to decide which side of the train he'd lean against. I gripped him hard and gave it to him straight.

"Murder!" I said, leaving the death-chamber door open. "Sit here and see that no one comes in."

There was a conductor on the platform of the car. I said to him:

"Murder! That compartment there. Don't let anyone off the train until the cops come. Don't open any of the doors." And I swung the platform door open, and said, "I'll drop down and watch here. I'm a detective."

He hesitated, uncertainty in his face, then said, "All right, Officer."

I had seen the Deb girl behind him listening. She came leaping down to the ground after me.

"Ludlow Station." She pointed up to a few lights. "South Yonkers. Thanks a lot, Race Williams. I won't forget this break!" Then she disappeared in the darkness across the tracks and was gone.

Just in time, too. Doors had opened. Brakemen were walking along the track. A conductor with glasses on the edge of his nose had a couple of brakemen by the door and was taking down my statement, and wondering half aloud if I should have pulled the cord or not.

"It is for emergency," I told him, "and if an unconscious man and a horribly strangled woman isn't an emergency, I don't know what is!"

The cops came. A lieutenant of police. And my chance to button-hole him and take a few cracks at the New York Police—which he liked. And then he got wondering if the girl had died in New York City or Yonkers—and who would get the case, Westchester County or New York. He knew who I was and shook hands with me twice—and I had about got myself clear and permission to leave, when he suddenly asked:

"But if she's your client, you—well, you would want to stay here, wouldn't you? Sort of take care of the body."

"Look," I told him, "I'm a detective not a mortician!" And I gave him Carlander's name and address. "I got a telephone call that she was on this train—was hunting through the cars and found her, dead. I want to get back and see if I can lay a finger— By golly, she could have been murdered before I got on at 125th Street!"

"That," and his face fell, "would put the crime in New York City and—"

He let me go, with my final thought that I would keep in touch with him, maybe let him in on the showdown. I went all the way back to town in a taxi, got the driver's license and everything else. Nelson would want to know about this. Only a guy who wanted a dead body pretty badly wouldn't realize that the girl was killed in New York City. Why, we weren't a block hardly over the city line.

As soon as I hit 42nd Street, I called up Carlander's place. Nelson answered the phone. He bellowed at me.

"You get up here right away, Williams! What's this I hear of your finding a body on the train right after it pulled out of the Grand Central Station?"

"That," I said, "was in Yonkers. I'm all clear up there."

"What do those cops know? You get up here, if you know what's good for you! Edwards, the butler, had ten thousand dollars scattered all over him. What do you know about that?"

"Nothing—except I'd like to have got my hands on it before the cops did. Call up my apartment later, and I might arrange to see you."

"Now, now, Race." His voice was calming down a bit. "We found the taxi lad you plugged," he went on, "in the gutter over on the East Side. There was one slug through his mouth. Doc Steel found it, and ballistics turned it out as yours. Nice shooting. Where can I meet you now?"

I wouldn't give. I even got a little cockey. I said I had important information to look up, and when he asked where, I laughed.

"All right, boy." The voice soured. "I'll send out a dragnet for you. Nice success with your business."

"On the level?" I just wanted to be sure. "You'll be obstructing justice—and maybe letting the murderer get away."

"On the level," he told me. And I knew he meant it.

Nothing to do then, so I made a deal with him. I'd tell him where I was going if he'd give me forty minutes alone on my job before he tried to find me. His agreement was a grunt.

"Okay, Nelson, I'm counting on your word." Though he didn't give me any. "Forty minutes in the Toi-Kay Club."

And that was all. I hung up.

I went into the street and found out that there are no secrets in life. Everyone knew of the murder of Janny Cort. An extra was already out. There wasn't much in it.

Heiress Murdered. Lieutenant Arthur Gillmore of the Yonkers police force was in charge of the case. New York Ace Private Detective Race Williams flags train at discovery of body, etc., etc. With plenty about the Yonkers police taking care of things. It wasn't bad. Gilmore had boomed my name, hoping I might boom his.

Anyway, I went right to the Toi-Kay Club. I went into the bar, picked out a likely-looking chap who seemed to be a habitué and not too drunk, and said offhandedly:

"See Tom tonight?" And when he half looked up at me, I added, "Slater, you know."

"Oh, sure! Inside. All alone at a table."

I walked right into the dining-room and was half-way across it before a waiter captain stopped me. No rough stuff here. The Toi-Kay was all class and on the up and up downstairs.

"Mr. Slater," I said offhand, "Thomas Slater. He said he'd be here waiting for me." And with a grin, "And sober."

"He's both, sir." The captain grinned back and led me across the room where a young, not unpleasant-looking and hardly dissipated man was sitting. He was lanky, had nice brown eyes. He looked like a healthy small-town boy who was being taken by the great city.

It was so easy finding him that I wished I had given the captain of waiters a single dollar, rather than the ten bucks I did. It was too late now. I pulled out a chair and sat down across from Thomas Slater, who was looking at the floor show.

"Hello, Slater," I said, and leaned over the table and handed him the newspaper. "On your way"—this to a waiter hovering nearby.

Slater looked at the paper.

"Yes, I know," he said, in a slightly tired voice. "At least, I heard. You think it's wrong for me to sit here like this." He straightened slightly. "No, it isn't wrong. I saw her but once in my life. She chased me away from the door, said she would see the police if I bothered her again. I didn't. I wanted nothing from her. I—I shouldn't be talking to you, should I?"

He looked down at the paper. "It was rather nasty for her, wasn't it? I'm sorry, of course, just like I'd be sorry for any stranger." He looked up, reddened slightly. "I can't talk—not for the papers."

"I'm not from the papers," I told him, and went right on as a smooth gent in a tux slipped another chair up and sat down. "I'm a detective. Naturally, I'm interested. I found the body."

THE SMOOTH GENT said, "Don't talk any more, Tommy." And to me, "So you found the body—on the train. Quite a coincidence, wasn't it?"

"Not too much of a one." I looked right at him now. Pudgy-faced, pudgy body, probably thirty—looked forty. "I was sort of looking for her."

"Dead?" He leaned over.

"Dead or alive," I told him. "I was looking for her."

"And you are here. Why?"

"Why not?" I shrugged. "He's the cousin, isn't he? He's the heir, isn't he? He gets a pile of jack, doesn't he?"

"Smart guy, eh?" He even let his teeth show now. "You'd be surprised to know I got a gun covering you under the table."

I raised my eyebrows slightly, studied

him a good ten seconds. Then I said, "I don't believe you. If I did, I'd have shot you in the stomach before you finished telling me about it. Lift your hands slowly—" And when he sneered, I gave it to him straight. "Lift them—or I'll spread your insides all over the floor!"

He lifted quickly, involuntarily maybe, as if he didn't want to. They were empty.

"See, the waiters that are making a circle—gunmen all of them," he said. "There's a little door just behind Mr. Slater. Get going through it." And when I laughed: "No harm, Mr. Williams. Johnny Johnson wants to see you—and when he wants to see a guy, he sees him!"

I pushed my chair up against the wall, leaned back, stuck my hands in the armholes of my vest. For a split second maybe my guns showed. Then I grinned at Jason.

Jason spoke very low. "We never like trouble downstairs, Mr. Williams. But orders are orders. Things can move fast. I snap my fingers, those four men standing there move quickly and you are through that door—"

"All four won't move."

"No?" And with irony, "How's that?"

"Some of them will be too dead. Be your age, Jason. You've been seeing too many movies!"

"Four men—and me." He seemed really surprised. "You think you could handle us?"

"I don't know," I told him, "but I can try."

He stood up, half raised his right hand. "We'll see," he said.

"Why you four-flushing, mug-making ape in a monkey suit!" I burst out. "Don't you know you are suggesting a slaughter? I'll hit what I shoot at! Will they if—"

I stopped. There was no doubt of the intention of the man who was crossing the room to reach our table. No doubt too that he was not one to use finesse. He brushed off the head waiter, cursed as he cut into the table.

Jason turned, half put up an arm, and just touched the arm of Inspector Nelson, who was in plain clothes, and got a smack across his mouth from the back of Nelson's hand that sat him down on the floor. Nelson even ignored me. He leaned over and stuck a finger in Thomas Slater's chest.

"So—" he said. "Where have you been all evening? Come on, talk. It's murder!"

CHAPTER 5

A MAIL-BOX

SURE, I DIDN'T like Nelson! There was nothing smooth or slick about him. He's one of the old school. But like him or hate him, he was the nastiest yet the most efficient cop on the entire force.

Things quieted down then. And I got up and started to leave without, I thought, Nelson even noticing me. But he did notice me.

"Get yourself a drink at the bar," he said. "I'll want to see you later. You and them Yonkers cops."

I went into the bar and it looked like Old Home Week. Slippery Joe Carmi-

cal was there. He turned almost at the moment I came in.

"Oh, Williams, isn't it?" There was a nice shade of doubt in his voice and the assurance to everyone that if he had ever seen me at all, he hardly remembered. "Join me, will you?"

He got up and went over to a quiet booth. I flopped into a seat across from him. He ordered a drink for me, having his own still in his hand. Then he said in a low voice.

"Edwards had ten thousand dollars on him when he reached the morgue. You couldn't know that. But why didn't you tell me he mailed a letter just before he was killed?"

"Mailed a letter?" I was surprised. "I didn't see him mail a letter. I simply thought he was going for a stroll."

"No, that's not so," he said.

"Look," I said, "he ran right out to the taxi and got killed!"

Joe Carmical let his hands come apart. "I think his number was up anyway," he said. "I think someone watched that mailbox. I think someone saw him drop in the letter, then signaled the death car—and he got the works. You'd have got it with him if he had stayed on the sidewalk a couple of seconds longer.

"Maybe so," I admitted. "Again maybe neither one of us would have got it. I've handled death cars before. With Edwards—" I shrugged. "He was between me and the car."

"That doesn't matter." Joe leaned over and very quietly said, "Do you know, Williams, I'd give five thousand dollars for the letter Edwards put in that mailbox on the corner."

And then I got it. "Are you suggesting that I break into the box—the U.S. Mail?"

Carmical's laugh seemed real and pleasant. "What nonsense, Mr. Williams! I was just thinking if—if you bring me that letter I'll give you five thousand dollars for it—no questions asked."

"Well," I said, "that is a nice way to put it. No, Mr. Carmical. My ethics are peculiar, I know. Rather loose in some things to some people, and strict in others. I—" And I stopped short, then leaned across the table. "What time is the mail picked up at that box?"

"Two A.M. You have plenty of time—"

"Who," I asked, "is your client?"

"I don't know yet." He looked straight at me and I felt he was telling the truth. "I'll decide after I get the letter—one way or the other."

"Then it must involve the Cort estate," I said. "You have some doubts as to the cousin being the heir?"

"I have grave doubts! The thing involves close to, perhaps may exceed, a million dollars."

I stopped to think. Riley had some such idea, too. And then, "Carlander—what does he think?"

"Carlander," Carmical said, "doesn't think."

"This girl Deb—Deborah Layton—you hired her to impersonate Miss Cort, and maybe take the jolt." And when he started, "You know what I mean! You set her up to establish her identity as Janny Cort to strangers who might visit the home—got Miss Cort off on a train—and if there was shooting, Deb was to take the lead."

"You don't know what you are saying!"

"Don't I? They were too smart for you. They got the right girl. Now who are they? Johnny Johnson? Is that why the cousin Thomas Slater hangs around here, signs checks, runs into debt? He inherits the money—and Johnny collects and leaves him enough to go back to the little town he came from. Is that true?"

I COULD SEE Carmical's respect for me was going up, as he said, "It shows that you get around. That, Mr. Williams, is not the picture as I paint it. As you say, Johnny Johnson may have figured on killing the girl—and did. But if you get that letter—the documents Edwards mailed in that envelope—we can dump over Johnny Johnson's applecart and realize some real money. Otherwise—"

He stopped. Nelson had walked into the bar. He came straight to our little booth and sat down.

"The lawyer, too," he said at Carmical, and then, "The heir apparent has an alibi like a parade. He's been with any number of people all evening. His picture taken by flash bulb right in the dining-room, with the time marked. I say that is overdoing the alibi. Not too smart."

"But it will stand up in court, won't it?" Joe said in a soft voice.

"It's a cinch he hired someone to knock her over," Nelson growled. "She treated him like a rat. He gets the money. What more would you want?"

"*I* want?" Joe showed surprise.

"He hired someone to do it. I think I'll go up and see Johnny Johnson."

I followed Nelson out into the lobby.

"I got an idea," I told him. "You better listen."

I told Nelson a few things. His eyes widened. He listened and was interested. Then he laughed.

"Silly stuff," he said. "Everybody mails letters—we can't tamper with the mail. Forget it!"

I didn't forget it. That was like Nelson—to deal me out when I gave him a break. He went and made a telephone call.

So I went up to see Johnny Johnson. I knew Nelson watched me from the phone booth. It was not yet one o'clock. I had no trouble getting in to see Johnny. He was behind a big desk counting money, going over papers.

"Sit down, Williams," he said. Johnny Johnson tossed his pencil on the desk, sat up and faced me. You often say a guy looks like a mobster or he doesn't look like a mobster. With Johnny it was neither one. He was a little on the bald side, a little cultured in speech or uncouth, according to his mood. Now he was a mixture of the two.

"What's on your mind?" he asked.

"My mind? What's on yours—what about Jason getting tough?"

"Oh!" he laughed. "I told the boys I wanted to see you, and they just followed orders." His face turned serious. "I really want to talk to you. I don't like what's going on."

"You can't please all of the people all the time," I said.

"Cut it," he said sharply. "I never did cater to wisecracks. I'll tell you what's what! You are hired to protect a girl. And you find her body—and her cousin, Thomas Slater, gets the dough. He has plenty of alibi, so he didn't do it. I have plenty of alibi, so I didn't do it."

"But I hear too that she's a hard dame, a money grabber. Bad friends with Slater—real enemies. Anyway, she nearly got herself killed a couple of times. So, I watch this cousin. If the girl is going to be bumped, he's not going to get the blame. Nor me, because he owes me a little money."

He let out a big breath then, expanded his chest and finished with, "So that's how it is! If you want Tom Slater for murder, produce a warrant and pull him in. If you want me, get the same paper."

He was looking over my shoulder now, still talking.

"That goes for you—and the big cop in the doorway. How are you, Nelson? Glad you heard it all. The kid, Tom Slater, isn't talking any more, I'm not talking any more—but we both have the same mouth-piece, who will talk plenty!"

He looked at his wrist watch. "I haven't called him yet—because he adds a couple of grand to a bill if he gets out of bed." And when neither Nelson nor I said anything: "All I told you is hard truth. You can check it up. What the joker is to do the kid out of his money, I don't know—but it will have to be good. Now what?"

"I think you can save a couple of grand tonight," Nelson said. "Better get to see your lawyer tomorrow, though—early."

"Thanks for the tip," said Johnny Johnson. "I'll make a note of it." And darned if he didn't write it down.

Nelson and I went downstairs together and out on to the street.

"He painted the girl pretty bad," I said. "Was she like that?"

"Carlander was her guardian," Nelson said. "He got little pay for it—and from what I heard about her he earned it ten times over. She's been questioning his accounts since she was sixteen—she's twenty-four now. She had a certain allowance, and saved like a miser. But it could have been blackmail. Don't worry about that postal business. There's nothing to it. Good-night."

We went different ways, and at one-thirty we came together again. That is Nelson didn't know we came together because I was there first. I was resting easily down in the areaway not far from the mail-box, and Nelson and another man were sitting in a car across the street.

No, I didn't see him. But I'd bet it was Nelson. And I didn't think the other man was a Postal Inspector. Nelson would have waited to see if the mail was worth it.

The postman came to collect the mail at one-forty, not two A.M. as Joe Carmical had told me he would. Across the street, a man moved from the shadows. Carmical, I'd bet anything. But he didn't move far. He turned and walked rapidly away—because Inspector Nelson, in uniform, hopped from his car before the mailman's key was more than in the box. Nelson liked to be impressive, and he had a harness bull with him.

I saw the postman hesitate, look at them again, then pick out the mail, lock the box and stand his ground facing them. What they said, I didn't hear. But Nelson got a look at the mail. There wasn't much of it. He patted the postman on the back.

"Just a false alarm, boy," he said, loud enough for me to hear. "Sure, sure, nothing irregular! We'd have wasted your time and government time by going straight to the Postal authorities."

The postman was on his way. Nelson and the cop climbed back into the car, and after a bit they went away, too.

I didn't go away. I sat there, crouched in the same position, waiting for Joe Carmical to come back. Somehow I didn't believe the mail-box was empty. There had been that sudden look of the mailman as Nelson got from the car, a quick pickup of the mail and—and yes, that was what I thought—a quick putting back of mail, too. One thick envelope!

Yet I waited. There was nothing phony about that postman in any way except— he had dropped something back in that box. And he was twenty minutes ahead of time.

Against all this, Nelson had talked to the postman and— I started to my feet quick, crouched low again. A car came around the corner, stopped across the street in the darkness. A man slid from behind the wheel. He looked up and down the dark, deserted street, made straight for the mail-box. Metal scraped against metal. The whiteness of his hand disappeared in the box, came out again. He sighed with relief.

I think he was aware of something even before my hand reached over and grabbed the thick envelope. He was smart. He was fast. There was a gun in his hand and he was half facing me when I brought my gun down with a low-chopping swinging motion before I turned it. It was a hard blow. But we weren't playing games. I heard the thud of steel against bone.

No slipping easily to the sidewalk. He hit that pavement like an axed steer in the stock yards.

And me—I ran across the street. The silence inside his car was reassuring, the soft purr of the motor more so. I put the car in gear and got away from there.

CHAPTER 6

RILEY MAKES AN EXPLANATION

OBVIOUSLY, THE LETTER was no longer in the hands of the United States Government when I got it. It was addressed to Johnny Johnson, and the guy I took it from was certainly his agent, sent to get it for him.

So what? Everyone had had a crack at that letter. The bogus postman—the real one was probably tied up in some alley, or dead. Nelson had had a go for it. The shadowy form I felt sure was Slippery Joe Carmical had at least hovered around it. And me—I *had* it! One can't be all ethics.

Johnson, Thomas Slater, Carmical, even Riley, saw a lot of jack in something. I felt sure that jack was this document. I drove about ten blocks more, and left the car after giving a few preliminary wipes to the wheel and door.

I rode the subway a few blocks, then went up to my apartment. I got the envelope opened and had seen enough to pop my eyes, when Riley turned up. He came in pulling his vest down and brushing a bit of lint from his shoulders. He gave his brown, waxed mustache a little twist, said:

"It's been a night, eh, Race?"

"Yes," I said. "What's on your stomach? It better be good—and quick. I'm busy, or going to be."

"Oh, I've been resting," he said. "One gets one's clothes dirty crouching in areaways watching— Well, you are a little forthright, Race. But very definite, very definite. I'm sure I heard his skull crack!"

I got up then and walked behind him. "You may be in a spot, Riley."

"Nonsense!" He straightened his five feet four. "I'm here to do you a good turn. Heavens, man, I have a clear conscience! I walked a block and took a taxi right here and waited outside until you went up. I had no occasion to run around town first. I see you have been examining the evidence. Daring, but not too clever, to do it right here."

"Well, what about it?"

"You don't quite understand it. I imagine it's documentary proof of the birth and identity of Janny Cort." I nodded, for that was just what it was. "I imagine it is complete proof—absolute to perfection. Such proof, after twenty-four years, would— Ah, you see the light!"

"You mean, the girl who was killed was not Janny Cort?" I said. "That she passed for Janny Cort since her infancy?"

"Exactly," Riley said. "Shall we go over the evidence together? Why, my dear man, I struck up an acquaintance with Edwards, the good and faithful butler, after I had heard of the attention this cousin, Thomas Slater, was getting. We had many a little drink together. I even let out that my business was searching lost heirs—claims. And do you know what he asked me?"

"No," I said. I was all ears.

"Well, he wanted to know if two babies got mixed up and years later it was discovered, would the statute of limitations save the mixer."

"Okay," I said to him, "you're a smart guy, Riley. The babies were switched. The dead girl was not the heiress. Edwards knew it, had the proof—and the wrong girl was killed. Right?"

"A fair guess," said Riley. "But I'd make a better one. There was no mistake in the switching. Edwards did it. Kept a nice record. Blackmailed the false Janny Cort, and finally decided to double-cross her before she got hold of the money. You see, once when the folks were away, Edwards had me as guest for a night—a single night. He was not too sound a sleeper. But fair enough. I found the phony Janny Cort's diary. Edwards was blackmailing her plenty."

"Who is the girl?" I put in. "The real Janny Cort?"

"The birth certificate is there, isn't it?" Riley seemed astonished. "My, how I searched the house for that stuff! And do you know, Edwards suspected me—so much so, that I dropped out of a window. We parted poor friends, I'm afraid."

He leaned forward suddenly. "Look, Race. I could make a good guess who the real Janny Cort is. Johnson would be astonished with that evidence. Don't you see, he killed the wrong girl." And after a long pause, "But he can correct that error by killing the right one!"

JUST THEN THE phone rang. The voice asked, "Can anyone else hear me?" I carried the phone over by the curtained window where Riley could certainly not overhear.

It was Joe Carmical.

"Listen, Williams," he was very friendly. "Events have taken a sudden and perhaps alarming turn. I am here in a young lady's apartment. She is in great fear, and she'll need your services. And she better have them now. Can you come at once?"

"Okay." I took out a pencil and on the back of an envelope I jotted down the address he gave me.

"Fourth floor—that's the top floor, he added. "The door downstairs will be open."

I forked the receiver and turned from the phone. Riley had only got my end of the conversation, but it was quite enough for him. He pointed at the stuff beside the Manila envelope.

"Not someone to get you out—so he can get in and find it?"

"I thought of that." And I added sarcastically, "Maybe you'd like to keep it for me?"

"Not me," he said quite seriously. "I'll be on my way." And lifting up his hat and stick and walking to the door. "I'd guess the change was made like this: The mother was dying, the father lost at sea. Edwards simply changed the babies— kept the record to cash in on later. Not too difficult. It happens by accident often enough. We are getting near some real dough, Race. Don't get yourself killed."

And just before he went, he said, "I'd lay you a fiver that someone was not far from the mail-box and recognized you—or the lad you hit."

"And didn't come out, or take a shot?" I laughed.

"Now really—" He grinned. "I've got the courage of a lion, Race, but if I had recognized you, I certainly would not have come out. One man shot to death; another crashed to the pavement like a clothing-store dummy. And the little affair at the Toi-Kay." He wagged a finger at me. "You know, my boy, you get around. Will me the documents if you get killed."

"Where," I asked him, "will I find you if I want you?"

His laugh was quite genuine. "I'll find you," he said, and was gone.

I took another quick glance through the contents of that envelope. There was a letter addressed to Johnson. If there was humor in it or not, you can make your guess. It read:

Esteemed Sir:

Ten thousand dollars was a paltry sum for the help I had given you. The threat of my death if I asked for more was contemptible and ridiculous. But I promised you some information that would amaze and astonish you.

I was alarmed to learn that you would go to murder. That is unnecessary now. You may make a deal with the real heiress. As for me—I will be out of the country by the time you receive this.

Your most respected servant,

E.

So Johnson knew some information was coming. He never had any idea what it would be, though. But he wanted it, and he didn't want Edwards blackmailing him from a distance later—so he planned to have the car there and Edwards murdered once the information was mailed.

And that information was complete. Edwards had done a remarkable job in keeping track of the real Janny Cort over the years. There was no doubt that the dead girl on the train was not Janny Cort.

There were even pictures of the real Janny Cort from childhood up, and a remarkably good picture of her taken—well, I stared at it now—taken within the last few months, certainly. And the real Janny Cort was the girl I knew as Deb—Deborah Layton. There could be no mistake about that.

Did Deborah Layton know that she was actually Janny Cort and heiress to a fortune? I didn't think so.

I gathered all the evidence together, put it into an envelope, sealed it carefully. I would simply slip it in the mail-box, stamped and addressed to myself.

Five minutes later I dropped it in a mail-box on my way across town. No one saw me—for no one shot at me.

I HAD NO trouble in finding the house where Carmical was. This was a real old-time brownstone front—not fixed up much, but I guess with the housing shortage the boys and girls with property didn't bother with those little things.

I was turning the second flight when I saw the shadow. My flash tossed a finger of light and a figure came erect. There was a startled surprised look. It was Joe Carmical. I gave him the word in a whisper.

"Good heavens!" he said. "I was waiting

here to caution you to silence and didn't even hear you on those old stairs."

"That," I said, "is because I don't pussy-foot. What gives?"

He was excited and nervous. He took me by the arm and started to push me upward.

"You lead." I dropped back. "You know the place."

"I was never here before in my life," he said, but he led the way just the same. I crowded him pretty close, stumbled against him once or twice in the semi-darkness, half held on to him for support. After that, I did all right. Also I knew for a fact that he wasn't carrying a gun.

We were at the door. It was wide open. A lamp was lit. The room was class. The furniture was comfortable, easy-chairs, a lounge. This was the place. Joe Carmical stepped inside. So did I. My hands sunk deep into my pockets, gripping the guns there.

"Deb," Joe called, not too loud. Then swinging back, he closed the door, said something about more light. Two things happened at once.

Joe's arms went around me, pinning both my hands to my sides. From the doorway on the right stepped Jason—the lad who thought he wanted to play rough at the Toi-Kay. He didn't say a word. He just leveled his gun on me, let his thick lips part and his mouth split open from ear to ear in a deadly grin.

His hand was on the trigger of his gun. His gun was aimed smack on my fore-head. There was hatred and death in his eyes. I closed the trigger finger of my right hand once, shot through my coat pocket. And his gun wavered. Twice, and it slipped from his fingers and fell to the floor. He clutched at his stomach, slumped to the floor. No, it wasn't fancy shooting. But my hand was held that way by Joe Carmical's grip.

I heard Joe holler, "Oh, this can't be!" Then I felt the gun in my back. There was ice in the soft voice of Johnny John-son.

"Okay, Williams," he said, "drop the rod!... A nice mess you made of it, Joe!"

I've been around. I pulled out, dropped the gun. Johnny Johnson went through me expertly, lifted the other one. Joe Carmical was crying out, "You killed him, Race! I grabbed your arms so you wouldn't—and now you killed him!"

"All right, Johnny," I said. "What now?" And getting my eyes shifted slightly, I put them on Carmical. "As for you, Joe—you're the only man alive today that's trapped me for a killing."

"No, no, I didn't, Race!" Joe squealed. "He said he was only going to disarm you."

"Brace up, Joe," Johnson said to the lawyer. "This lad Williams will never bother you. Take a seat over there, Race. All right, Joe. Get a bedspread and toss it over the body, if you're going to be sick. And tell Lefty to come in. This Williams is as slippery as a bag full of shucked clams!"

Joe came back with a sheet, tossed it over Jason. And I looked at "Lefty" Caron. He just nodded, held a .45 automatic in hand and sat down beside me. He never moved, he never talked.

CHAPTER 7

RACE WILLIAMS
HAS ETHICS

Joe Carmical kept telling me they only wanted to talk to me; that Johnny Johnson meant no harm.

"Shut up!" Johnson raised his hand. "Look at the body, Joe—and shut up! Whatever happens, you are in on the show." He lifted a small chair, put the back of it close to me and sat down cross-legged, leaning over the back looking at me.

"Race," he said, "it's like this. There was a small-town boy called Thomas Slater. He came up to the city with a few dollars; had a cousin who was a mighty rich doll: Janny Cort. I didn't know then that she was one of the meanest dolls in New York. Now this Thomas Slater was a nice boy except he drank too much. The bright lights got him. And he gambled too much. He was into me for quite a pile. Then he went to see this cousin. She wouldn't even let him in the kitchen entrance. Tough on me, wasn't it?"

He smiled pleasantly, said, "No, things weren't that bad, though I beefed a bit. Looked into the thing—and what do you think I found out? Janny Cort was a phony! Edwards, the butler, told me. I paid him ten grand for that." He spread his hands far apart. "Someone knew he had the dough on him, so someone smoked him out. Anyway," he went on, "Edwards mailed me the proof last night. Never mind the burlesque around the mail-box."

His lips sort of curled. "You got the proof that this dead girl was an impostor. I'll give you fifty grand cash now for the evidence—and you can walk out of here a free man. Don't you see, I never killed that girl on the train. Why should I? I already knew that she was a phony—from Edwards."

I thought of the letter, and I shook my head. "Edwards never told you."

"How would I know—how could I possibly know then?" he asked.

"Joe Carmical," I said. "He knew. He told you, when I wouldn't swipe the letter for him. So you sent for it—and got it. You killed the girl because you didn't know. It was Edwards' little joke."

"All right!" He fairly shot the words at me. "I—" He paused as the phone rang; answered it, listened, jammed it back on its cradle. "So the envelope wasn't in your apartment—the boys just searched it." And watching me shrewdly, "The old stunt, eh? Mailed it to yourself? Well, I'll put enough men on to pick it up at your office or apartment. Why not make a deal?"

And almost before I could shake my head no, he said, "Okay. So I killed the girl. I'm in it deep. But I'll have the dough if I—"

Then he searched me. He got very little, but he was so thorough he got his fingers cut on a safety-razor blade I had hidden in the lining of the cuff of my trousers. It comes in handy with cords and ropes and such at times. He cursed a bit and said, "And you won't play?"

"No play," I said.

"Rather be dead?"

"I'm still working for Janny Cort—the *real* Janny Cort."

"And the man you killed—Jason," said Joe Carmical, "he'll have to be explained."

I shrugged my shoulders. "It won't be the first corpse I've had to explain."

"Okay!" Johnny Johnson snapped. "Keep your eye on him, Caron....Joe, you stay here."

I took one look at the locked drawer of the table where both my guns now reposed. I heard Lefty Caron whisper in my ear to take it easy, felt his gun back up his soft voice with the hard truth. Then I was ordered to follow Johnson.

We turned into a lighted bedroom. Certainly a man's bedroom. And this was the first I knew that we were not in Deb's apartment. But she was there stretched out on the bed. Rope held her arms above her head, twisted around the bed post. Her feet were tied, too—one to each post. She was stretched quite a bit, and she was lying very still.

Her eyes were open and they lighted up for a second and her lips parted—then the smile, the look of hope that had come, was gone. She took in the entire picture. I noticed that her feet were bare and there were burns on them.

MY MUSCLES STIFFENED. Lefty noticed it.

"Easy, Race," he whispered behind me. "You nearly had it then."

"Don't let him burn me again, Race!" the girl cried out, though she must have known I was useless. "I tell you again—my name's Deb! Yes, it is really Deborah Layton. Not any other name."

"Funny girl," said Johnny Johnson. "I'm not one to go in for hurting women, Race. But I had to be sure she didn't know it all.... Now listen, Deborah Layton. Williams here has an idea that he has information which would make you a very rich woman. For that information, you can go free and happy. He won't give it. It isn't true—but if it was, wouldn't you rather live?"

"Yes, yes," she cried out. "Mr. Williams—Race—" You could see her arms tied to the bed quiver as if she thought she was raising them to me. "Anything—I want nothing! Get me out of here!"

They'd kill her anyway. They'd have to. It was tough.

"Listen, Johnny," I said, "we might make a deal. Afterwards, so much money. It isn't as if—"

"No," he said. "I'm through. I wouldn't trust any of you. The devil with the information! Who's to know—"

He swung a knife from his pocket, snapped it open. It was quite a size.

"The information," I said quickly, as he leaned over Deb and pushed back her chin, "would tie up the estate for a long time. If—"

"No." He cursed now. "They'll find the body—" He looked at the knife. He was like a boy apologizing. "A gun makes too much noise."

The knife went up. No chance to save my life—a possible one to save the girl if I stuck that knife in Johnson's heart before Lefty smoked me out. Enough noise to startle the tenants, maybe scare what nerve Joe Carmical had out of him.

So that was the way it was to be. Go out after all this time with a bullet in my back. Oh, well. I dove forward.

The shot came. I was on my way and felt no pain. The knife was coming down. I hit Johnny hard and it missed. And Johnny Johnson and I were on the floor across from the bed.

A man—a tall, thin man—was standing in the doorway of the bedroom. His hands were over his face. He seemed to be sobbing. And then there was a gun in Johnny Johnson's hand and I wrenched it from him as if he had been a child, but I didn't know then that the knife was sticking in his side, where he'd fallen on it. I got to my feet, swung from the sobbing man toward Lefty Caron, and he wasn't there. And then he was.

He was sitting on the floor, with his back against the wall and the gun was in his hand—and I raised the gun I'd taken from Johnson and sprang toward him and stopped. Lefty Caron was dead.

Johnson spoke. "Okay, Williams. In your back where it belongs. Don't turn."

This time I did turn, crouching as I swung. And it was my first break. Johnny Johnson fired twice, I think—at least it sounded like two shots. I heard the plaster fall behind me and a picture crash to the floor.

Johnny jerked his head back as I fired. I had been so sure it would be right in the center of his forehead, but it wasn't. I guess even the best of us can go through a little too much. And I must have when I dove for that knife and was sure of death, for I shot him in the neck. It was a mess.

I turned to the sobbing man and saw a gun at his feet. My gun. I jerked his hands away from his face. The reek of liquor nearly knocked me over.

"I killed a man, I killed a man," he said over and over. Maybe his shot killed Lefty Caron. "I couldn't help it. When I saw you there, and the knife and the man with the gun, and the girl, and you, risking your life for her—"

He went to the bed then, and knelt down beside her. "Janny, Janny!" He pulled at her arm, not seeming to know it was tied. "I knew the other one couldn't be—I'm your cousin, Tom Slater!"

The girl had fainted. I cut her loose, carried her from the room, placed her on the couch.

Joe Carmical was shouting at me, "What happened? I called the police. The cousin, Tom Slater—I told him who the girl really was and he opened the drawer and took your gun. This is his apartment. Johnson owned the house and fixed up the top floor for him. The rest is vacant."

The cousin wobbled out then, white, staggering. He sank slowly to his knees, then collapsed. I thought he'd been shot, but he had simply passed out.

"What a—" I started, and then said, "He did his part in the end." I took the bottle of whiskey from Joe and poured Slater a drink. Got him to his feet, sat him in a chair.

I took a drink myself and threw myself into a chair and lighted a butt. I was sort of washed up.

Joe Carmical pulled himself together and started in to talk. He even had on his glasses with the long ribbon.

He explained to the girl who she was. Said he knew for some time, from a little informant who would have to be paid. He was still talking and I wasn't listening, except to notice he brought me into it a lot. I had an idea he was playing both ends against the middle.

He had gone to Johnny Johnson when he thought Johnson would get the evidence anyway, and tried to make a deal. I was pretty sure he hadn't thought anything was to happen to the girl or to me. I saw now where he really thought that lad could stick a gun on me and get away with it—for Johnny Johnson had wanted to talk to me and he wouldn't want me knocked over that soon. Maybe it was just Jason's idea for the way I had treated him, and Johnny didn't care particularly whether I got killed right away or later.

Slippery Joe had most of the dope in his head that was in the envelope, but he would have difficulty in proving it without the affidavits of this and that person, some now dead. Yes, Edwards had been an efficient man. I guess if the phony Janny had played ball, it would have been all right with him. He had waited twenty-four years to cash in—a careful, patient man, Edwards.

But why go into all that. The girl looked tired, looked pleadingly at me. I went over and shoved Slippery Joe aside, said to the girl:

"You are the real Janny Cort. You get all the money. The proof is safe. So you don't have to be bored.... Come on, Joe. Go down and meet the cops. Who did you call?"

"Nelson," he said. "Inspector Nelson.

He was handling things, you know. I thought it would look better—and I didn't know if you were alive. I said you had the evidence—that was mailed." And when I half raised a hand, "Now, look here, Williams. I know more than anyone about this case. You'd be wise to let me represent the girl and—er—you can name my fee. All unpleasant things can be left out of it."

THE GIRL WAS glancing toward the sheet over the body when I sat down and took her hand.

"Don't worry, kid," I told her. "I'll see that you don't get stuck."

She clutched my hand. "It's been pretty awful! You saved my life and—" She looked over at the staring cousin. "He's not bad—good when the time came. I'll want to see that he's taken care of. And oh, Mr. Race"—she had her arms around me and was crying on my shoulder—"how was I so fortunate as to have you interested in me!"

"You," I said, "were my client—the real Janny Cort. I don't work for phonys."

A gruff voice spoke behind me. "This must be the money girl. And Race Williams in on the show already—and another dead man."

Carmical talked up at once. "Mr. Williams killed him in defense of this heiress' life, my life—and his life."

I turned and looked at Nelson. "It would have been a feather in your cap, Inspector, if you had found that envelope when the fake postman put it back into the box."

"I know!" Nelson glared. "We found

the real postman, sapped, gagged and bound, between two houses. Yeah, and a guy on the sidewalk by the mail-box—well-known crook. Said he was walking along when he was hit by—"

"Really," I cut in quickly. "Well, someone sent me the envelope." And when Nelson was about to explode and talk about getting my license now, I said, "I'm rather a naïve lad, Nelson. The real credit for this case—giving an heiress back her inheritance—should go to you." And then I went close to him and whispered, "I mailed that evidence to you. You'll get it later this morning."

The anger went out of Nelson's face. He actually smiled.

"Well, Williams," he said gruffly and a little patronizingly, "the police like to work with outsiders who are doing their duty. Is this the heiress?" He went and shook hands with the girl, and with a wave of his hand to me, "Take her home. Carlander should be more pleased with her than the other. I'll talk to you later."

As Carmical started to follow us, Nelson grabbed the lawyer by the arm and actually winked at me. "I'll need you, Joe—for the facts," he said.

I took the girl downstairs and located a taxi. No, I didn't like Nelson. I didn't even like him now, with the girl snuggled close to me. It will just show you how far I will go for a client. And how far Nelson would go for a big break like this.

Sure, I had mailed the envelope to Nelson. That's my ethics!

Half a Corpse

THE MUNSON PEARLS

No one saw me go in. I was positive of that. It wasn't too hard to get in and out of that apartment house without being seen. If it wasn't exactly built for that purpose, a good many of its tenants rented there because of that very convenience.

The automatic elevator lifted me to the eighth floor. I walked down the hall and around the L to what was called, on the door, Suite D.

I didn't ring the bell and my knock was not too loud but the occupant opened the door almost at once and I slipped in, closing the door.

"Hello, tall and virile if not handsome," the girl said and followed me down to the living-room, a flashy but comfortable set-up at the end of a long narrow hall. She was surprised to see me but she didn't show it except for the half-quizzical, not startled look in her eyes.

She wasn't a bad eye-full and had cut down a bit on her weight since I last saw her. A luscious blonde if you like them that way. A little on the fat side, if you didn't. She had purple lounging pajamas on under the light drape she was wearing.

She wasn't a woman easy to throw and in a way I was there to throw her. She said simply:

"Park your hat and coat around and sit down. Can I buy you a drink?"

I took off my coat, tossed it over a chair, and threw my hat on top of it. I was willing to give the impression that it might be a little while before I left.

I said, "Thanks, Doris. Anything you mix will suit me. Not surprised to see me, eh?"

"If you mean was I expecting you, Race, no." She stood there, a cigarette between red lips and a match waiting to flare up. Then she burned up the end of the smoke, took a long inhale and waited. After a bit she tried:

"It's almost midnight. Not too late for a social call, not too late for a business one. I'm not throwing you out anyway, if that's what you mean." She walked to the sideboard in the alcove and poured me out a drink of rye, pushed a glass forward for herself, changed her mind and handed me my drink. "You take rye?"

"Right," I said. "Good guess."

"No." She shook her head. "I don't guess, Race. I know what people like, people who I figure are worth knowing."

"Flattered." I tossed off the drink. "Not having one?"

"No. I don't know how clear your head is after a half dozen or so, but I know about mine. Tell me what's on your chest and I'll figure if six won't matter."

"Half business, half pleasure. Half to your advantage and half to mine."

"Tell me," she said coldly without sitting down, "the half to my advantage—my pleasure."

"Well." I put the empty glass down on the arm of the chair. "Were you waiting for Jimmy Ferris when you let me in?"

"Why?" She never took those blue eyes off me, china blue with the hard coldness of china now. "Did he send you to see me?"

"No one sends me any place." And before she could frame the question, "Nor did he ask me or pay me to come. I'm on my own, Doris. If you could tell me anything about the Munson pearls, I'd do you a favor in return, give you information."

"What," she said, "made you think I'd know anything about the Munson pearls?"

And that was Doris Wheeler for you. There was nothing of surprise in her voice at my question. Nothing to give me the slightest hint that she didn't know all about the Munson pearls.

How did I know she didn't know anything about the Munson pearls? Simple, that. I didn't know anything about them myself. In fact, I had just made up both the name and the pearls. I went right on. I wanted to confuse the reason for my visit.

"It's like this, Doris," I told her with an air of great ease. "You used to be soft on Harry Hamilton and he had a liking for such baubles."

"Harry." She laughed. "A rich man's son. Yes, I liked Harry. You know what he thought of me. It's nearly four years since he copped that string from his aunt and put them around my neck. He was just a kid who wanted to dress up a woman. His first and last and—" She stopped.

"And only woman."

"Perhaps." She smiled. "His old man came around and threatened me with arrest and what not. Finally I sold him back the pearls plus twenty percent for loss of Harry."

"Plus Ferris, though Harry's old man didn't know you had had Ferris in mind for some time."

"You're uncanny," she told me. "What made you think of Harry Hamilton and what is the lay?"

"No lay." I shook my head and with a smile, "And no full value for the pearls back. Harry Hamilton got them and he forks over—there might be a little something in it for you. But then you would hardly need money. Ferris never was tight-fisted."

"A girl," she said slowly, "can always use money. As for Harry Hamilton—a girl and boy affair. I haven't seen Harry in four years." She was very emphatic. "I'm a one-man woman. I'll stick to Ferris. He don't ever need to worry about that. He won't lose me. Tell him that. He won't ever lose me. Is that clear?"

"Clear enough," I told her. "Did you ever think maybe he might want to lose you?"

"No." She looked straight at me and the china blue came through slits. "He may think he wants to lose me, Race—but he really doesn't."

I got up now and went over and put both my hands on her shoulders. "Doris," I said, "I'll tell you what's on my mind. The Ferris romance is a washout. You're through."

"Thanks." She looked straight at me. "Is that all?"

"You know the truth, don't you, Doris? You've heard the gossip. He's owner of a swanky club now. He entertains café society. He is café society. His past is forgotten. He's tossing you over for— He's thinking of getting married, Doris."

"I heard that too." She still stared at me. "What else?"

"You might," I said, "make trouble. You've known Ferris for a long time. You know what happens to people who make trouble for him."

"He fights back," she said. "Okay, Race, I know that."

"You don't know all of it." I framed the words carefully—not exactly a lie. "Doris, he couldn't stand you buzzing in his ear. In the girl's family ear. She's money; respectable. She's a kid. He'll hop off and marry her. If you can give me any dope on Ferris, I'll see you don't lose him to this girl."

"I see." She hesitated a long time. "No, I won't double-cross Ferris. I don't work that way. And I won't lose him either."

"Doris," I told her. "Give it a thought. He'd wring your neck if you stand in his way."

Not even her long lashes flickered. But back through the slits there was the smallest break in the china, maybe not doubt— let us say, speculation. She walked by me and out of the room. She was back in less than a minute. China was wide now. She held a bottle up in her hand for me to look at. The plain mark *'Poison'* and also *'Carbolic Acid'* stood out.

"Good lord," I said. "You wouldn't—not kill yourself."

For the first time her face cracked up and she laughed. It was a real laugh, a pleasant laugh. She said:

"This doll, Diana Van Court. Not a blemish on her baby face. You know, Race, I was born in a small town outside of Albany. Had a boy who promised to marry me. I was only eighteen and we kept our love a secret. He tossed me over for another girl." And letting me have it with a bit of venom, "No one suspected me, of course—I was just a kid and he never talked. But someone threw acid in her face. She was a mess. Beautiful she had been, too. She killed herself a year later. Ferris doesn't know that story. Tell it to him."

"I'm not from Ferris," I said after I got my breath back. I'm not easily startled; seldom shocked. But I was shocked now. It never entered my head to tell her she wouldn't dare. I knew she wasn't bluffing. Somehow, with a little shudder; I knew that she'd toss it in the girl's face as quickly as she'd snap her fingers.

I had wanted to make a deal with her. If she would give me information about Ferris that would be worth a prison term for him, I'd threaten him with it and make him lay off the Van Court girl. I told her that now. She said:

"I wouldn't double-cross Ferris. I'll always stick to him."

"And the acid throwing. Is that sticking to him?"

"Oh," she said. "That will be protect-ing him from himself. No, Race, there is nothing in it for you—through me."

Nice going that. But I never pretended to understand women. I didn't press her. I simply said, as I looked around the room:

"Okay, Doris. I gave you a friendly tip about the neck wringing."

"I have nothing against you." She followed me to the door and just before I opened it: "About Harry Hamilton and the pearls?"

"What about them?"

"Oh nothing. You get around, Race. You hear things. I was wondering. Is Harry—is he in some sort of a jam where he might need money?" And when I looked at her and started to turn the door knob, "I won't tell anyone, Race."

I said nothing.

"Tell me." She gripped my sleeve. "I—I—got to know."

She bit her lip then and caught herself up. It was the first bit of expression or feel-ing that she had shown. As far as I knew, she had not even looked at Harry Hamil-ton in—well since she went with Ferris. But I was through now. The shock had turned to disgust and, yes, a little fear and she still had the bottle of acid in her hand.

I went out and closed the door. I slipped out of the apartment as carefully as I went in. No one had seen me come or go.

Nice girl, Doris, eh what?

THAT WAS THAT. I had found out one thing. Diana Van Court was in actual danger. I hadn't figured out how to take care of that. If Doris had been a man I might have stuck a finger against her chest and said simply, "The day you lay a finger on that kid, I'll push a gun against your stomach and blow you apart."

That wasn't the point. I was under wraps. I was paid by Diana Van Court's father to protect her and break up the marriage—the possible marriage of his daughter to Jimmy Ferris.

It wasn't the free-and-easy job it seemed. I couldn't threaten anyone. Diana must not know I was hired. It was a good stipulation at that, for if she knew the truth, she would probably up and marry Jimmy Ferris right away.

I could see her father's point of view, but I had a point of view too. I went over Jimmy Ferris' past. It was not a good past. It was, in fact, a very bad past. He had killed men. You could get that from most any city dick in on the know. But knowledge was not evidence. Now he was a big-time night-club operator.

It was late but I found my car parked around the corner and went up and visited Hatton Force, the young attorney. He met me in the hall of his apartment in a classy bathrobe that he liked to call his dressing gown. He was rubbing one hand through his uncombed hair and the knuckles of the other in his sleepy eyes.

He wasn't a bad-looking lad, hardly more than thirty. Inheritance stuck out all over him—breeding and money. He was the junior partner of Lennard, Hayward and Force—no doubt putting plenty of money into the firm. He said:

"My man has gone to bed. It is better this way, I suppose. Now, what could bring you to me at this hour of the morning. Almost one, isn't it?"

"Well," I gave it to him straight. "Doris Wheeler, the woman Ferris tossed over for Diana Van Court, is getting ready to throw a bottle of acid in Diana's face. I just left her. Should her father know that?"

It threw him all right. He didn't pull any more 'my man' stuff.

"What have you done to prevent it?" he said at length. "The agreement is that her father never appears in this at all. You have had a retainer and the assurance of five thousand dollars when this affair is broken up—permanently. You haven't spoken to Mr. Van Court, of course?"

"I've never seen him in my life," I told Hatton Force. "And I don't like my job. I'm to protect the girl, prevent her marriage to Ferris. At the same time she mustn't know it. Ferris mustn't know it."

"I think," he said, "you are exaggerating. The single stipulation is that no one should know the part I played in it, or her father played in it. I expected you would eliminate this—Ferris entirely."

"Any way at all," I murmured. "You know what those words imply."

"They are rather final," he smiled.

"You mean shoot him to death?"

"Are you serious?" His eyes opened so wide that I thought they'd roll out of their sockets. "If I thought for one moment you were serious, I'd throw you out that door," and with the slightest smile as I stiffened, "or try to throw you out the door. If you could push this Ferris back into the arms of the woman—Doris, what's her name—that would be final."

The speech could have been a phony. If it was, he did it well.

We talked a bit after that, but didn't get

any place. I admitted I had no trouble in meeting Diana, even dancing with her.

"I—we foresaw that." Hatton Force took some of the credit. "You see, Mr. Williams, Diana always admired you. She spoke of you often. Read all there was to read about you, at different times in your career. That is the reason I chose you for this mission. Of course," he hastened on, piling it up with a bit of lather, "Your fearlessness, integrity and—"

"And I knew your check would be good," I cut in there. "All right, Mr. Force. We understand each other. I thought her father might want to talk to her, take her away on some long trip."

"No, no. Her father has a rule never to interfere with what she does. He—" and as he saw me watching him closely— "That is, in this instance the situation was drastic and called for drastic measures. I'm sure I can count on you, Mr. Williams."

"You have nothing to lose if I don't pull it off—or have you, Mr. Force? You're not in love with Diana yourself?"

"Good lord," he gasped and reddened. "I'm in a way of being her relative—er—first cousin, so to speak." And when I waited for more: "The Van Courts and Forces do not believe in marriage between cousins, first cousins."

"Fine." I smiled at him for he seemed to be embarrassed. "I'll do the best I can—up to killing him, eh?"

"Yes, yes." He gripped my hand. "Look at that man, that terrible man Ferris—and that fine girl—look at Diana."

"Right. I'll go and look at her now."

I left him. This time I landed on Park Avenue.

CHAPTER 2

MORE THREATS

I WENT AROUND to The Silver Swallow owned by Jimmy Ferris. He was a smart lad, was Ferris. He had not stuck to his old friends. No flat-nosed, cauliflower-eared, through-the-side-of-the-mouth talkers had been carried along with him on his wagon to success. He didn't want those who knew too much of his past. His staff was high class. Smooth talkers, smooth dressers. Their rough part was on the inside buried deep.

The first lad I spotted, sitting alone in a high-backed booth in the bar, was Harry Hamilton. They said he could make you burst out crying just to look at him. He was still supposed to be carrying the torch for Doris Wheeler.

He had a clear field there now, so far as Jimmy Ferris was concerned. But the old man—now dead—hadn't forgotten that his son had chased Doris, liked to gamble, hadn't been above swiping a string of pearls, even if they did belong to his aunt, and also was known as a rum-hound.

One thing would keep Doris from being interested in Harry Hamilton. He inherited his father's money. Sure, it was a fortune. But—there was a catch to it. Harry Hamilton still lived in the same big house. The expense and upkeep of it was paid by the trustees of the estate. Food and all was supplied, but no liquor. And get this—the papers had made something of it at the time—he was permitted an allowance of twenty-five dollars a week. Out of this he attended to his own amusement, pleasures, liquor, clothes.

When he arrived at the age of fifty, he would receive the principal of the estate; all of it to do what he pleased with it. Since Harry was now less than thirty, it was doubtful if he would live that long and pretty sure that Doris wouldn't wait that long. But he might know something about Ferris, so I sat down and gave him the merry line.

"Cheer up, Harry," I told him. "It looks like Ferris is thinking of getting married; but I suppose after she tossed you over the way she did, you wouldn't be interested in Doris Wheeler."

"Interested, Mr. Williams?" Harry was always very formal. "I've lived for no reason but Doris. My father was a stern and an unjust man. I wished to make that girl my wife. I mean to now. I thought my aunt would be glad to give her the pearls. My father held it over her head when he broke us up."

"We all sort of thought you'd take it out on Ferris for stealing her away from you." For a moment I thought there was a flash in those alcoholic eyes. "But Doris—" I shook my head. "She would hardly be one to wait over twenty years for money."

"She'd wait a lifetime with me," he said. "I kept my bargain. I have not seen her. Perhaps the trustees would let me rent the mansion. Doris and I could live quietly up in the Main woods. The income from the rent and my paltry allowance—" He straightened. "I have in mind a bit of land with lumber on it that belongs to my estate. I could fell those trees. We could raise a family and by the time the children were ready to go to college…"

"About Ferris, you must hate his guts." I cut in on his whiskey dream.

"Ferris." He shook his head. "To know Doris is to love her. She smiled on him. No man with blood in his veins could have resisted. Now," and with a slobbery grin, "she is ready to cast her smile some place else. Perhaps she is casting that smile backwards to me."

I got up to go. There would be something doing there. "Ferris may think he left her because he wished to leave her, but that is only the greatness of her heart. She saw what it did to me. I never can look at another woman. She spared him. That, Mr. Williams, is Doris. A woman with a heart of gold."

Hard as gold I thought when I left him. Harry had been going on like that for the past four years.

A waiter tapped me on the shoulder. Miss Diana Van Court wanted to see me. I wanted to see her too. She was alone at a table in the distant corner of the dining-room. I went over and sat down beside her.

"Dance?" I asked her.

"No, Race." She shook her head. "You've been rushing me lately. Being at places I'm at. Jimmy doesn't like it."

"Jealous?"

"No." She laughed. "But I want to know why?"

"Have you looked at yourself in a mirror lately? After all, you are not engaged to Jimmy, at least formally. Don't you like it?"

She hesitated, and then: "Yes." And then, "You're not afraid of Jimmy?"

"No," I told her. "I'm not afraid of Jimmy. Is he afraid of me?"

"Not in the way you think." She seemed puzzled. I looked her over while she put together the words she was going to use. Very young, yes, but plenty of poise, plenty of assurance, slim with perfect features—maybe too perfect—and plenty of red hair. Finally she got it out.

"Why did you take me up after Jimmy began—began paying attention to me?"

I laughed at that one. It was a good opening and I took it.

"You always seemed a little too high-class. Not just money; not just position; not just your august father. I felt I might be sort of pulling you down." She looked at me and reddened slightly. I took a big grin. "If you took up with a mug like Jimmy Ferris, I wouldn't be dragging you down any." She saw what I meant.

It got her all right. And it should too, for I'm a lad who thinks pretty well of himself and doesn't care who knows it. But five thousand dollars was a lot of money—and besides, I hated to see a nice kid like that hitched up with Jimmy Ferris.

"You sort of felt I was—in the gutter—with you now?"

Maybe I flushed up too. I didn't expect she'd be that direct. But I tried to talk my way out of it.

"Hardly that." I hoped my laugh sounded better to her than to me. "Let us say you were an angel come to earth." I couldn't help adding, "Down into the dirt with Ferris—and me."

"That's not the point," she switched quickly. "Ferris thinks you came on the scene for another reason. He thinks my father hired you to break us up. If that was so he said he'd—he'd—"

"He'd kill me." I filled it in for her. "What did you say?"

"I talked him out of it, I hope. I know my father never hired you." My eyebrows went up at such clairvoyance, and such false clairvoyance. "I know my father. I know he would not in any way interfere with my life. When there is a question in his mind, he says simply, 'Diana, you are a Van Court. I know you will do the right thing.'"

"Has he ever been shocked?"

"No."

"Is he going to be?" I said it lightly, hoping it would go home. A waiter came then. Mr. Jimmy Ferris wished to speak to me up in his private office.

"It is all right to go." The girl leaned over and took me by the arm. "I have made him promise that he won't do anything." I smiled. "I never met a man like Jimmy before. Do you know he—he'd die for me."

"Good." I got up. "You make him keep that promise about not doing anything to me, or he may do just that."

"Do what?"

"Die for you."

JIMMY FERRIS HAD had his office done over. No bar, no rare wines or hundred-year-old brandy. At least, none showing. Books had taken their place. The furniture was comfortable but more subdued.

Jimmy sat behind the desk with his dark hair standing out on a background of leather-bound books. His shirt was clean and he didn't wear his tux like a waiter. But his eyes were still hard and black, and his straight nose still had the little bump in it where someone had sapped him in his younger days. Big and broad and not an ounce of fat on him.

"Sit down, Race," he said, and added before I was in the comfortable leather chair: "So you like my girl?" I simply smiled. "For a time, you know, I thought her father had hired you to bust us up. I wouldn't have liked that." Leaning back, he put those cold black eyes on me. "We never crossed, Race, you and me. That's why we both are still alive. You know when I wanted anything, I wasn't above— anything to get what I wanted. I want to marry Diana more than anything. She's far too good for me."

"Sure," I agreed. "No one will argue that point."

It didn't throw him. "Everything I've gone after has been far above me. I got it just the same. Now I've got a little job for you."

"Yes?"

He counted out five century notes and flung them on the desk. "That is for dropping around and telling Doris Wheeler that if she so much as makes a threat about Miss Van Court, I'll wring her neck for her."

I had just told Doris that very thing. But I already had one client who was paying me to work against Ferris. I couldn't very well work for him. Ferris went right on talking.

"Now," he said, "we can multiply that if you can convince Doris that it will be worth her while to hand me back that diamond necklace I gave her." He hesitated. "It has a clasp on it. Inside the clasp, so small you need a magnifying glass to read it, it says *'to the only girl in the world— Jimmy.'* I want to give it to Diana."

"Getting tight," I said. "You didn't buy her off then."

"Buy her off?" He was sore. "That dame has close to—well, over a hundred thousand dollars' worth of cash and bonds, negotiable bonds, to say nothing of jewelry. Sort of keeping it for me." He smiled and shrugged. "A lad in my position needs stuff sunk away in case of trouble. At least I did. I was willing to let her have twenty-five grand, keep most of the jewelry and all the furs and the beach place. Hell, Race. That woman turned everything I ever gave her into cash— and never spent a nickel of it."

"And you haven't been rough about it?"

"Rough about it?" He came to his feet now. "I nearly knocked all her teeth down her throat. But the safe I gave her was empty. Her bank account is less than a grand. The safe deposit box we shared had a couple of half-smoked butts in it. I don't care much about the money—except I could use some big cash right now. I hate to think of a dame putting it over on me."

I could have laughed in his face. All he ever thought about all his life was money. And now a dame put it over on him. I shoved back the five hundred, shook my head and when he looked ready to bite the desk I said:

"I don't high-pressure dames, Jimmy. Besides, what makes you think Diana's father didn't hire me to break up your marriage, that he wouldn't interfere with his daughter?"

"So she told you." He stuck a cigarette in his face. "She said she would. Family tradition." He smiled. "Anyway if it was true, I'd kill you the first chance I got. You could count on that."

He went on again to my going over and seeing Doris Wheeler. He had some idea that she intended to harm Diana Van Court all right but he never put it exactly. And he did want the necklace—and finally he came out with something about letters.

"Blackmail?" I was a little surprised.

"No, no, nothing like that. Of course not. But they could make me look ridiculous to Diana. Okay. Race, I'd have a go at it myself except that I'm honestly afraid of what I might do. Won't you go see her?"

"No," I told him. "And I am not interested in what you might do." He started pulling out bills of larger denominations, "No, Ferris. Is your engagement announced? Do you want me to lay off your girl and pass the word around?"

"No, no." He came right in with it. "She's a popular girl; she enjoys that popularity. I'm not afraid of losing her. I—I—but no, Doris wouldn't dare harm her with me—alive. I'm giving Harry Hamilton a job here at a hundred or so a week. But I don't know." With a touch of pride, he bemoaned, "Doris can't see anyone but me. I don't know why."

"Money," I said. "Glamour, power, big-time stuff. Nothing else."

I left him. So far I had five hundred bucks out of Hatton Force. Ferris seemed bothered about the money Doris Wheeler had. Still, a hundred thousand dollars one way or the other shouldn't mean much to Jimmy Ferris. Maybe, like other lads who had a lot of money, he wanted more. Too,

a man who had done everyone else, hates to be done himself. And by a dame like Doris Wheeler, at that.

I called it a night.

CHAPTER 3

CUPID'S KILLING

SOMETHING DID BREAK when I was shaving the next morning. I opened the door and Inspector Nelson brushed by me and went down the living-room like he owned the place. Behind him was Sergeant O'Rourke, the whitest man on the force. It was a lot of Homicide even if you took it simply by numbers. If you took it by weight, it was still a lot.

Inspector Nelson turned, in the living-room. "Okay, Williams." He took out a notebook and a pencil and held them ready. "You left the Silver Swallow at exactly one-forty-eight this morning. Then where did you go?"

"I left the Silver Swallow at exactly one-forty-one. Then I went home to bed."

"One-forty-one. How do you know the exact time?"

"I looked at my watch, wondering if I'd go to the park and feed the squirrels and—"

"That," Nelson cut in, "will be enough of that. It isn't far to your apartment here. Say ten minutes. Twelve if you stopped to pat a stray cat." That last was considered heavy sarcasm. "Who saw you come in?"

"I don't know." I shook my head and when he frowned, "I imagine most of the tenants stay up to keep tabs on me."

"Okay, okay." Nelson closed up the book and his manner changed. It was free and easy and pleasant. "Sort of routine, Race, old boy. We'll be checking up on dozens of people who even knew her by sight. You didn't happen to call on Doris Wheeler last night or early this morning?"

It wasn't Nelson's way of putting things. He should have shoved his face forward and growled, "What were you doing at Doris Wheeler's apartment last night?" I stalled a bit.

"Is it important?" I tried.

"Oh, not too important." Nelson looked over toward the window, then he turned back. "She was strangled to death early this morning. Well?"

"I was there," I told him without hesitation. "Got there a little before twelve and left a little after."

"Don't know the exact moment." He twisted his face up close to mine.

"I left," I said, "at twelve twenty-two."

"Don't mind telling me what you were there about? Or will we go downtown?"

"I went there in the interest of a client—confidential." Before he could twist his lips up in a sneer, I added, "Mr. Richard Hilton Van Court, President of the Agriculture Trust Company."

"And his interest?"

"Information about Jimmy Ferris that might make his daughter lose interest in him. There is more than a rumor around that she might marry him."

"I read the papers," Nelson said. "What did you learn?"

"Nothing. Doris still liked the lad Ferris and had hopes."

"Like that." Nelson thought that I would lie. He had been trying to get my license for a long time. To O'Rourke, he said, "Like always, we'll be settling up Williams' problems for him. That will be all for the present Williams. It's funny when we find a body, you've always been around."

"Always?" And then, "Can I ask you a question, Nelson. Who told you I called on Doris Wheeler?"

"Sure," Nelson turned toward the door. "It's a free country. You can ask all the questions you want. You can even call spirits from the vastly deep, but will they come?"

With that he went roaring down the hall. Nelson didn't have any sense of humor but the trouble was, he thought he had....

I was sorry I had to divulge my client's name but it was a big enough name for Nelson not to blab it to the newspapers. I finished shaving, swallowed a glass of grapefruit juice, went downstairs, did the grapefruit juice again but this time I added a couple of fried eggs and ham to it and washed it down with coffee.

I was still convinced that no one had seen me go in and out of that apartment last night. But Nelson knew I was there. No one knew—except Hatton Force. But surely the cops had not gotten it out of Hatton Force. Certainly his name couldn't come into it, not this fast.

The case looked open and shut. Jimmy Ferris had told me he would twist Doris' neck for her—and he had.

Things moved fast in Homicide. Willis, a plainclothes dick, was waiting for me when I went into my office. He was a tall, lanky lad whose conversation was mostly "huh" and "uh huh." Nelson wanted to see me downtown. I didn't argue. I went downtown.

There were a desk and half-a-dozen uncomfortable chairs and a spittoon and bare floor to impress you how hard cops work and how little comfort they have. There was also Nelson. He was writing at a desk. He didn't raise his head but said:

"Sit down, Race." After a moment he added, "How long have you known Mr. Van Court?"

"I never met him personally," I said easily.

"Didn't he engage you to protect his daughter from Jimmy Ferris?" Nelson snapped into life. "Isn't that what you told me an hour ago?"

"Yes, through a lawyer."

"What lawyer?"

"Hatton Force, of Lennard, Hayward and Force."

"Damn it! Why didn't you tell me that at first? Willis, show Mr. Van Court in."

NELSON CAME TO his feet as Mr. Richard Hilton Van Court stood in the doorway. He was exactly what you would expect from the name and the position. I suppose he had the stuff inside but outside he looked just that—a stuffed shirt. Now he was annoyed. He made his little speech as he looked at me.

"I don't recall seeing this man before, though his face is familiar. I believe my daughter kept—er—had some pictures of him."

"Do you know Hatton Force?" Nelson was no respecter of persons. He jammed the question right in.

"Yes, yes, of course. I knew his father. A friend of the family. Lennard, Hayward and Force are my solicitors. For the bank too. A reputable firm, highly reputable, a fine man Mr. Force. Young, a promising career."

"This man here. Race Williams says Hatton Force hired him to break up the romance between one James Ferris and your daughter." Van Court simply stared at him. "Do you believe that?"

Mr. Van Court put cold blue eyes on the inspector. "I do not believe nor disbelieve it until all the facts have been placed before me. What does Mr. Force say?"

"I don't know." The inspector frowned at Van Court but he wasted the effort. "Do you condone such an act, approve of it, if it is true?"

"Well…" Van Court stroked his chin. "If it isn't true, an ethical discussion would be quite useless. If it is, I must have facts. I have not been led by emotions in a great many years."

I tried one of my own. "Is Mr. Hatton Force related to you?"

"No, he is no relation."

"Perhaps he would like to be?" I tried.

"Ah, perhaps he would. I'm a busy man, Inspector. For matters that concern Hatton Force, I would suggest that you discuss them with Mr. Force."

"Yes, yes." Nelson was thrown for once. "Thank you, Mr. Van Court. I'll let you know what develops to your interest."

"My interests." Van Court permitted himself the semblance of a smile. "I am afraid you will find that Mr. Hatton Force was protecting his own interest rather than mine. Good-day."

Nelson had Hatton Force on the phone as soon as Van Court left. I guess he didn't feel he could go two of them in one day. Force must have admitted that he had engaged me and he must have talked around it a bit, too, for when Nelson hung up, he wiped the perspiration from his forehead and said:

"Okay, Williams, run along. And after this, know who you are working for."

Willis grinned, opened the door and said, "Uh huh" to my "Good afternoon."

I did go up to see Hatton Force. He received me cordially enough.

"I'm sorry, Mr. Williams," he said, "that it caused you so much inconvenience. Certainly I did lead you to believe that you were acting in behalf of Mr. Van Court. Since you have met Mr. Van Court, you must see that you are acting in his interests. I'm in love with the girl and wish to protect her from her own folly."

"And to marry you."

"That is my hope. A slim hope, perhaps, but surely she can do no worse than marry Ferris."

"You'd do anything for her."

"Yes, I think I would."

"Die to protect her?"

"That," he smiled, "always seemed a bit melodramatic to me."

"How about killing for her?"

"Really, Mr. Williams, that is rather worse."

If he had any idea what I was driving at, certainly he didn't show it. But he was shrewd enough to see I was annoyed and clever enough to help clear away that annoyance.

"I hope," he said, "that our understanding will continue and—er—don't you think I should advance you another, say five hundred dollars?"

I thought he should and he did. Then I asked him if I disturbed his sleep last night, or if I worried him about Diana with the threat Doris Wheeler had made. "Maybe like me, you got dressed and took a bit of walk to get some air."

"No." He came in with it rather sharply. "I went to bed and to sleep."

Somehow I thought that he wasn't telling the truth, but I smiled pleasantly at him, said:

"You don't need to worry. That woman won't harm Diana. You read about it in the early edition of the paper."

"What—what exactly?" We had both looked toward the newspaper on his desk.

"The murder of Doris Wheeler?" When his face went a sort of pasty white, I said, "That was the girl who threatened Diana with the acid."

"Oh, yes," he said. "For a moment I didn't connect the names."

I folded up the check he had given me. "Better keep up on the names. Now that your interest in Diana is established, it would be the natural thing for you to do. Not that I care—but the police will."

"The police! But surely the police won't have any interest in me?"

"They might," I told him. "You'd be surprised how they get around." With that I left him....

"It seems like a dumb act for Ferris," O'Rourke later told me, "But you know Nelson. He is pretty sure he can make it stick. And he's been after Jimmy Ferris for years. I'm not so sure."

"Why?" It was all right by me.

"For one thing, Ferris hasn't any alibi for the time of the killing—two and three in the morning. In the old days when we suspected Ferris, he had plenty of alibis. Of course if a lad should lose his head—you know. Nelson will be asking you about that acid tossing the dead woman threatened to do." My eyebrows lifted. "Hatton Force hasn't withheld anything from the police. You told him, and the assumption is you told Ferris."

"But I didn't tell Ferris anything."

"No?" O'Rourke lifted his eyebrows. "But Nelson let Ferris assume you did. And Ferris knows you were hired to bust up his marriage. Ferris took it calmly, too calmly. I thought I'd warn you. I don't want him for your murder." He grinned.

"I'll watch out. What else?"

"Well," O'Rourke said, "Doris Wheeler had all her possessions in cash and jewelry and negotiable bonds, yet her bank account only ran a little over two hundred dollars. Ferris was trying to get hold of the bonds and a necklace anyway. Her little wall safe was empty. We can't trace a nickel that belongs to her. Her lawyer said she told him she had it in a safe place."

"Lawyer?"

"MacPherson. Not too well known but nothing against him. He drew up her will. She left everything to her mother upstate. Funny, eh? One doesn't think of a dame like that having a mother. Never gave her so much as a dime when she was alive. Got anyone else in view for the killing?"

"Have you?"

"There could be Hatton Force," O'Ro-urke said. "But it's a little far-fetched. Saves Diana Van Court from the acid threat and fixes up Ferris. But the missing money and bonds doesn't fit him. Anyhow how would Force know about it? It might have been a killing for cash.

"Or—there's a lad upstate. Edward Toussey. He tossed her over for another dame. And do you know, Race, it looks like she used acid on that girl. Of course, that's six years back, a long time. But Edward Toussey never married after that. And he was in New York on business at the time of the murder. His alibi? He was in bed and asleep."

"Anyone else?"

"Well, Harry Hamilton, an old flame. He's taking it bad. And—"

"And?"

"And you." O'Rourke grinned. "Now, now, Race. But you did go to see her and if we know you, you did threaten her—to protect your client's interest, Miss Van Court, of course. A struggle and things happened. At least Nelson likes to have you in mind."

"I didn't threaten her," I told O'Ro-urke with a grin. "Now tell me something. How did Nelson find out I was there at Doris Wheeler's apartment?" O'Rourke didn't answer right away. "He found it out fast and it was before he saw Hatton Force, wasn't it?"

"Yes." O'Rourke hesitated. "Someone telephoned the dead woman's apartment while we were there. Just a muffled voice, probably speaking through a handkerchief. It said, 'Ask Williams, he was there this morning, early'—then hung up. Why did you want to know?"

"Why?" I looked at him. "Because—" and then I stopped.

"Anyone might have done it who saw you go in or go out," O'Rourke said. "An honest tenant who didn't want to get mixed up in a murder investigation. Nelson is trying to trace the caller." O'Rourke got up then. "Since you might be interested in seeing Ferris put away, Nelson thinks you might have something to add. Serve law and order."

"And myself, eh?" I took a grin as I let O'Rourke out.

Then I sat down and did some thinking.

No one knew I was there but one person besides Doris—Hatton Force. Maybe two persons. The murderer would know I had been there. How? Because Doris Wheeler knew the murderer well enough to let him into her apartment at two or three in the morning, and she might have told him that I had been there. That would be the only way he could find out.

Sure, it looked bad for Jimmy Ferris. Despite the warning I had given Doris, I knew she would see Jimmy Ferris any time day or night. Was it the simple case of Jimmy Ferris saying he would wring her neck—and doing so? But after all, it hadn't anything to do with me.

Or had it? If Jimmy Ferris said he'd wring her neck—he had also said that if I was hired to break up his marriage he would kill me.

CHAPTER 4

A SHOOTING MATTER

I WENT DOWNTOWN to the Lawyers Building to see Hatton Force again. In the downstairs lobby, I met Harry Hamilton. He was surprised to see me, and I thought a little alarmed.

"What are you following me for Mr. Williams?" he demanded. "You've hounded me ever since that—that string of pearls business and—and—"

"Easy does it, Harry," I told him. "I've hardly seen you a dozen times, since then."

"Well," he was blearly eyed and had been drinking, "every time there are any pearls missing, you—you— What do you want to see me about anyway?"

"I don't want to see you." Since he did look a mess and I felt pretty sorry for him, I said, "What pearls did you get hold of, Harry?"

"Pearls—pearls. I—I—"

I had to explain to him it was a joke. But Harry was not in a joking mood. I guess he did take the death of Doris pretty bad. I took him up to the corner and bought him a drink. He needed it. He always needed a drink.

I got him to talk about Doris then. But it wasn't much good to me. It was all in the past. To hear him go on, you'd think an angel had been taken back to heaven on wings of gold.

"I've been to see my lawyers," he said before I left him. "A little money, just a few hundred, even less for flowers, Mr. Williams. You—you knew her."

It served me right. He touched me for

twenty-five bucks. But I kissed it good-bye and went back into the office building and rode up to the seventeenth floor and went into the stuffily correct and conservatively sumptuous offices of Lennard, Hayward and Force.

Hatton Force was glad to see me. Indeed he nailed me in the outer office, dragged me down the hall and into his suite of rooms.

"You've got to act, Mr. Williams." He went right into his act. "Diana was here. She knows. She called me a contemptible cad. She's going to run off and marry this Ferris person. Says he needs her now. Practically accuses me—us—of framing Ferris—is framing the word?"

"That's the word," I told him. "Is she marrying him to get even with you?"

"No, no. Loyalty and that sort of talk. Standing by him. Showing the public— and— And I've had a call from this Ferris person."

"A threat?"

"I don't know. He said to—er—keep my nose clean. I'm not afraid of him. I'd like to meet him man to man."

"Well," I grinned at him, "you'd need a blackjack, a knife, brass knuckles and a gun or two to meet him on even terms. Don't worry too much. The cops are closing in on him. Do you know Harry Hamilton?"

"Hamilton?" He seemed to think a moment. "Why, I think I have met him, yes."

"Think? Was he in to see you a few minutes ago?" Force looked blank: "I met him downstairs. I thought he said he was in here."

"He could—" And then it seemed to dawn on him. "Of course, that peculiar will. Mr. Lennard handles the Hamilton estate. Harry Hamilton. Good heavens! This Wheeler woman. That was the woman was it?"

"It was," I told him.

Then I saw Mr. Lennard. Mr. Lennard was older and stuffier, but with a little pushing from Hatton Force I got what information I wanted—whether the death of Doris Wheeler would make any difference in Harry Hamilton's wait for the money.

"I'm afraid not," Lennard told me. "The will was a severe shock to a young man who used to have everything. I thought the terms of the will were unnecessarily severe, Mr. Williams, in view of the fact that he did not see this woman any more.

"But the Surrogate pointed out that since no woman was mentioned in the will, we had no right to assume that one was responsible for the drawing of it. We had as much right to assume that his general conduct of living was as much responsible. No, Mr. Williams, this unfortunate woman's tragic end will make no difference in Harry Hamilton's er—status quo."

I went out with the words of Hatton Force buzzing in my ears that I must do something to stop the marriage. What, he didn't suggest.

WHEN I GOT back to my office I had a surprise. I wasn't sure if it was pleasant or not. Diana Van Court was waiting to see me. I hadn't more than closed my door when she put it straight to me.

"Did you frame Jimmy Ferris?"

"What do you think?"

She looked at me a long time, nervously. "Race," she came close to me and put a hand up on my shoulder, "I don't want to believe it. I didn't want to believe a lot of things. So your only interest in me was—money?"

"In the beginning," I said. "Then it was nice to try and prevent a girl like you from marrying—" I took a fast warning from her look—"out of her line."

The eyes she put on me were meant to be alluring. Her other hand was on my shoulder now. "Race," she started softly—dropped her hands and turned her head away. Then she said: "All right, I'll give you a chance to convince me. But not here. Jimmy might come. I'll take you to a little place for tea."

"Fine." I got my hat off the rack again. "It might as well be now as any other time."

"What do you mean by that?"

"To try and convince you. Will you pick the place or will I?"

She would pick it. It was a little place on a side street. You went down a few steps. We arrived in a taxi and not in her flashy car. There were a couple of other people having tea. There was a curtain in the back. A dumpy little man smiled at her, said:

"Quiet, no music, this way, miss."

Four booths were behind that curtain. The light on the table was soft. I slid into a booth. She sat down opposite me. I began to talk. I talked about her; her father; her name. I said:

"Maybe Hatton Force is stuffy on the outside, but he doesn't know you'll marry

him. He's out to keep you from being a little idiot. He made me a business offer. He didn't go around with a lovesick cow-like look. Yes, I'm talking about you. Glamor—a lad who came up stabbing his friends in the back and shooting his enemies the same way. A lad who has learned to change his outside shirt every day but whose undershirt—"

"What do you mean, whose undershirt," she came in with.

"Well," I said. "A man who goes through life getting even his girl friend to set traps so—" her eyes went wide—"like Doris Wheeler. Don't you suppose she ever set a trap to kill a man? Maybe he'd tell her something different but…"

She suddenly looked at her wrist watch; jarred to her feet.

"I've got to telephone my father," she said, "about my marriage. I'll be right back. I don't believe anything you said and I don't—" and suddenly— "Yes, I'll give you a chance to say more. Wait!"

She swung from the seat out between the curtains and I heard her feet beat across the room beyond. I got a peek too. The two couples had gone. The room was empty. Diana and I were the only ones in the tea room. In another minute I felt sure I would be the only one, the only customer there.

I was right. The slick dark-haired figure oozed into the seat across from me. There was a napkin covering his hand. Hard eyes watched me. A mean, grating voice said:

"Okay, Williams. There's a gun under this napkin. Put both your hands on the table. I said I'd kill you." The napkin fell from the automatic in his hand.

Both my hands were on my own knees. I didn't lift them. I looked straight at him, asked:

"Are you on the kill, Jimmy?"

"Yes," he said, and his thin lips were grim. "There is no other way. I'm on the kill now."

Tough that. I believed him. I closed the index finger of my right hand twice, and put two slugs some place in his stomach.

I pitched to one side as I fired. At that he got me, burned me along the left arm with one shot and buried the other one some place in the ceiling. Lead in the stomach is rather unpleasant and not conducive to good shooting. I finally came to my feet and listened. I was alone with the dead man.

Ferris was slumped over the table. His hand clutched the still warm gun. I felt relieved. Ferris was a guy who, if he intended to kill you, would go through with it. That was settled.

Sure, I knew the set-up from the beginning. I had that gun in my hand ten seconds after I sat down. The girl had not been a very good actress. She had trapped me for Ferris. But did she know he intended to kill me?

No one came into the room. No one stirred beyond the curtains. There was no cry of alarm in the streets, nor the screech of a police siren. There wasn't meant to be. There was meant to be death there all right. It was simply the wrong corpse.

It was okay with me. I looked toward the phone on the wall behind me. I had noticed it the moment I came into the room. Maybe she thought I hadn't. I could leave the body there and walk out. But why? It was self-defense.

I swung from the phone. My gun jumped into my hand. The words came again.

"Williams, Race—you're not dead?"

It sent chills up and down my spine. It was the corpse talking. I went over, lifted up Ferris' head. His eyes rolled. He was alive, all right.

"Water," he gasped. After I gave it to him: "Am I going to die?"

"I shot you," I told him. "You or me, Ferris. I'm no doctor but you should be dead now."

"What are you going to do?"

"Call the cops."

"No—no," he gasped. "They want me for murder. I didn't do it. I was there, yes. I had a key. I walked in. Doris was dead like that. I—you framed me. The letters—Nelson found them in my room. You framed me."

"Nix," I told him. "I don't frame people, Ferris."

"You just—wanted to prevent the marriage—for what was in it?"

"That's right."

"You, you know I didn't kill Doris. The cops will stick it on me. Those letters. It's open and shut." He mumbled a bit after that and I didn't get it but I went to the phone and called O'Rourke. Luck was with me.

"Jimmy Ferris?" O'Rourke was pleased. "Sure, Nelson wants him dead or alive."

"How about half dead?" I asked, and then, "Okay, O'Rourke, I got him for you. Send an ambulance and a doctor."

"You know, Race," Ferris was talking

when I got back to the table. "You're a smart dick. Five grand to put me in the chair. I'll make it ten to keep me out, if I'm going to live. You know who killed her?"

"No." I shook my head. "Besides I got one client. Can't work against that client."

"Well…" Ferris tried to grin at me. "Make a deal with you then. Won't marry the girl if you clear me. Fair enough." He mumbled on, "What you got against Harry Hamilton? Poor Harry. I gave him a rotten deal. So did Doris. Never resented it. Got to do something for him. Don't want to die without doing something for Harry. He says he never even heard of those pearls. But I know you and I know Harry. Is it an insurance company?"

I thought he was out of his head. I said:

"What are you talking about?"

"Look, I'll square it with cash. Insurance company should like that. Even Munson should like that."

I hadn't been paying much attention. I swung back now and bent down close to him.

"What Munson?" The name was only vaguely familiar.

"The Munson pearls. That's the name Harry used. But if you don't know—can't find the murderer of Doris, why, come on Race—clear me." He jarred up then as a siren screamed in the street. "Hell, there are other girls. There is only one Jimmy Ferris. Come on, I'll toss her over like a rotten tomato if—if you clear me."

"I can clear you," I told Ferris. "Yes, I know who killed Doris Wheeler. Your word about the girl, not to see her again."

"Never." He had trouble in getting the word out. People were pounding at the door. "Never, I swear it."

He pitched forward again as glass crashed. I tossed back the curtain to let in Nelson and O'Rourke.

Nelson saw me and came forward. He saw Ferris and stopped. Then he went over to the table and lifted up Ferris' head. He swung on me, asked:

"What happened?"

I looked at Ferris. There was intelligence in his eyes. I said: "I guess he thought I was framing him. He fired." I pointed to the hole in my left sleeve, "and I fired. Ask the doc."

The little man with the bag was Doctor Steel, the assistant medical examiner. He said:

"No corpse—that's what a man gets for hanging around gassing with cops. What's the matter with his own doctor? Here, help me lay him out on the floor there. My, my, Williams, no lead in his head."

Ferris shrieked once and was quiet. Nelson wanted to know if Ferris would live.

"Now, now," Doctor Steel said. "You're always wanting to know how and when a corpse died. I've been so used to dead men that I'm not much good on live ones." But Nelson wanted a guess. "Damn it man, I don't know. The holes look clean."

I took O'Rourke out in the front room. He was sort of stern and hard. I fixed that up by asking about his daughter. Then I told O'Rourke, "Ferris isn't your man. He's been framed but nice. Listen." O'Rourke's eyes widened. He made clucking sounds and kept shaking his head while I talked.

"No one will believe it," he said finally. "Least of all Nelson. Yes, Race, we do have to take Nelson along."

One thing about Nelson. When he went into a thing, he went into it the whole way.

"Like that." He looked at me after the ambulance had driven away. "Well, it's like this, O'Rourke. I'd rather have Ferris anyway. So would Race. This way there's nothing in it for any of us."

"Only seeing a murderer punished," I said sarcastically.

We got into the big house in the seventies without trouble. Nelson had his warrant and his men searched it well. In less than an hour he had turned up the missing cash and securities.

"How did you solve it, Race?" There was admiration in O'Rourke's voice.

"Yeah." Nelson had to keep the sarcasm. "Don't tell me you have been using your head."

"What do you care?" I lit a cigarette as the three of us stood looking out the window. "Here comes the killer home now. Pull your stuff, Nelson."

Nelson did. As soon as the man walked in the door, Nelson said in that official voice of his, "Harry Hamilton, I arrest you for the murder of Doris Wheeler."

Before Harry Hamilton could recover, I came in with:

"It will be easier for you, Harry, if you say what you did with those pearls."

"Pearls," Harry gasped at me. "I never saw the Munson pearls. I never even heard of Munson."

"Of course you didn't," I told him. "Only I knew about them—and Doris Wheeler. She told you before you killed her."

HARRY HAMILTON MADE a full confession. He said it came to him suddenly. The one really fooled was cynical Doris Wheeler—who had never trusted anyone in her life. Here was a man who she kicked around, trampled on, got disinherited—and yet he went mooning around about his everlasting love for her. She believed it as did everyone else. She handed bonds, jewels and cash to Harry to keep for her. She felt certain he wouldn't touch a penny of it. He was her slave. He was the only one she could trust.

But Harry was used to money. His father cut him off. He got to thinking what he could do with it. If he had loved Doris, he also feared her—and Ferris. He knew the letters that Doris gave him, she could use to blackmail Ferris.

He planned to kill her and frame Ferris. He planned it for over a year. By now he hated both of them. He knew how he'd do it but he didn't know when. It was even nice for him to think about.

Then I went to see Doris Wheeler. I made up the story of the Munson pearls and Harry Hamilton having an interest in them. It frightened her. Harry wanting money—and having hers.

"Sure, O'Rourke," I told the sergeant. "I remember now how it worried Doris. She got to thinking about it after I left, wondered if Harry would swipe her stuff. She telephoned for him—and he came. Maybe she wanted the stuff back, but she didn't fear him. Anyway, as Harry said, he strangled her."

"And she told him of your accusation about the Munson pearls."

"Right," I said. "I made up the name at the spur of the moment and forgot it. Harry already had Doris' valuables and the letters hidden in his house. And Ferris was giving him a job to take Doris off his hands. It was easy to plant a few of the letters in Ferris' office, or his home, for that matter—as Harry confessed."

"Yeah." O'Rourke threw down his last slug of liquor and got up. "Do you know, Race, he's still denying he had anything to do with the Munson pearls—but they had a lot to do with him. I hear Ferris leaves the hospital tomorrow as good as ever—or as bad. Diana nursed him...."

She must have been waiting down the hall from my apartment for she rang the bell almost the moment I heard the elevator go down.

"It's the little idiot," she said when I opened the door. "I want to come and talk to you. Jimmy Ferris told me you'd say he swore not to see me again, because you cleared him of murder. He told me I wasn't to believe you."

"Yes." I looked at her.

"I'd believe you. So tell me." She was starry-eyed.

"I have nothing to tell you, Diana," I said very seriously. "I've quit the case. I'm not going to ruin your life."

"What?" She was surprised. "You think preventing my marriage to Jimmy Ferris would ruin my life?"

"Maybe. There are worse guys than Jimmy Ferris hanging around. Oh, I can't think of any off-hand, but you're the kind of girl who would go out and find one."

She came close to me, stretched up both her hands and put them on my shoulders. Suddenly she pulled my head down and kissed me.

It was really surprising. For a moment I understood Jimmy Ferris. Then she stood back looking at me, while I colored.

"I've found one," she said. "But I don't think he's worse than Jimmy Ferris. I think he's the grandest person in the world.

"If my life must be ruined, then I want him to ruin it. Race, I've been with Jimmy constantly. I don't want any part of him. He would have—have murdered you."

It tossed me. I looked at her in a new light. She was pretty. She was class. She was rich. The name Van Court had stood for something for many generations. Even her worst enemy wouldn't say she wasn't a nice armful. I put an arm out toward her, when she suddenly turned and tossed an official-looking manila envelope on the desk.

"Yes," she said. "I found one. Hatton and I were married this afternoon. I'm glad you shot Ferris and he didn't shoot you.

"Thanks—from an ex-idiot."

She was gone and I was absently tearing open the envelope on the desk. It was a check from Hatton Force. I sat down and lit a butt.

Well, now what about Jimmy Ferris? Would we have to go through that shooting all over again?

Race Williams Cooks a Goose

CHAPTER 1

PHOTO-FINISH LIZZIE

THE WOMAN WAS dead. Someone had put a wire around her neck and twisted it tight. She lay there by the couch, her eyes protruding and her lips swollen. One leg was twisted under her and the mend in a well-worn stocking showed plainly. Her clothes were awry and her gray hair pulled down over her forehead.

Nothing sensational for the papers. A murder. Yet, somehow to me the most bitter I had ever seen, for the woman had been my client. There was the name on the door of the apartment, as drab as the three rooms she occupied. Simply— Lizzie Dell.

I looked the place over before calling the police. It didn't look as if the killer wanted anything he could carry away with him. Rather something he could leave behind with the dead woman. Silence.

There was one touch of the personal on the bureau in her bedroom. A worn photograph. Third grade, Public School 0023, 1931. A bunch of kids and the teacher at the desk before them. A woman who might have been Lizzie Dell, or a million other women for that matter. The years had not been kind to the dead woman. I put the picture in my pocket, went into the main hall and down the three flights of stairs to the phone, and called the police.

Sergeant O'Rourke from Homicide arrived a few minutes after the squad car. After that, the experts from the department.

"Client eh?" O'Rourke shook his head and ordered another cup of coffee in the little lunch room down the street. "Didn't look like she could afford your rates. Not holding out, Race?"

"Nothing to hold out," I told him bitterly. "She came to me with a wild story, O'Rourke, and a check I haven't cashed—because I didn't think it would be good. She walked into my office three days ago. Laid a check for a hundred bucks on the desk. Flattered me to the skies about my being afraid of nothing.

"She wanted to be my client so she could tell someone she was my client. She said she wanted to keep this someone in line by threatening to tell me something unless he 'relinquished his evil desire' to do something. I warned her of her danger. She shook her head and said this person never would find her. But he did."

"How did you happen to come to her place tonight?" O'Rourke wanted to know.

I shrugged. "My boy, little Jerry, was in the outer office that afternoon. I gave him the buzz and he tailed her. Tonight I was in the neighborhood and dropped in. A hunch."

"Huh." O'Rourke shook his gray head. "This is Wednesday. She came to see you on Monday. The M.E., Doc Steel says she's been dead for—" he paused and his lips moved as he counted to himself—"she got it sometime Monday night." With a harsh sort of chuckle, "This guy, whoever he was, didn't scare much when she threatened him with you."

"Don't rub it in. I did everything to get his name from her. But I thought she had a screw loose." I took out my wallet and showed the check to him. "I bet it was good."

"Maybe," O'Rourke agreed. "But it won't be much good to you now she's dead."

"Nor to the lad who killed her. I'm going to get him, O'Rourke. She knew something and had to die."

"It isn't that easy," O'Rourke said. "She knew something—yet wasn't the type to share any great secret. My guess is she saw something by accident, an innocent bystander. She wasn't sure what to do and waited too long. We'll go back over crimes of murder committed in the last couple of weeks and see if she could fit in."

"No," I said. "It was something definite. No accident. She was very earnest, very sure of something."

"You thought she had hallucinations."

"The wire around her neck," I told him, "is no hallucination."

"She was a rabbit." O'Rourke shrugged his shoulders. "Too frightened to talk, and too frightened not to talk. The morgue gets them before they can make up their minds." He put a hand on my shoulder. "Don't take it so hard, boy. We'll put a name on her and give you her history by noon tomorrow...."

They didn't put a name on her—except the same one, Lizzie Dell. No one identified her. They tried tracing her back and the trail went cold. Just Lizzie Dell. One of thousands of lonely, unknown women who sewed a little here, scrubbed a little there, and somehow stayed alive in a great heartless city. Unwanted and unknown. I never felt so bad about anything in my life.

However, those cops didn't have the one clue I had. The picture. I didn't have much trouble in tracing back Lizzie Dell. She had been Elizabeth Delton—third grade teacher in public school 0023, until she simply faded out of the picture about eleven or twelve years back.

All who remembered Elizabeth Delton had good words for her. A real guide to youth. No one could put a finger on exactly what she had accomplished— simply that she was always helping someone.

I gave O'Rourke the dope on the identification without mentioning the picture, and he gave me a bit of news.

"The Old Man," he said, "has offered to give the woman decent burial."

By the Old Man, O'Rourke meant J. Farrell O'Neil. The man behind about everything on the East Side. Lately he had been getting his name mixed up with rackets which he had never been a part of for at least thirty years. The Old Man hadn't risen to notoriety in the city and then become the power behind things. He had started out behind things and never fully emerged into the open.

He was the last of the old-time political influences. If he copped a few hundred thousand dollars on a city building contract, he gave away about as much to the poor of the city, or added a wing to some hospital. If it was whispered that he had broken more than one man who had questioned his rule, it was openly shouted that he had saved thousands of others. If you got in to see the Old Man with a hard-luck story—it was a hard-luck story no longer. There wasn't a widow or an orphan in his district who ever needed a pair of shoes or went to bed hungry.

O'Rourke explained, "It used to be nothing for the Old Man to do something like that, Race—but lately it's been different with him."

"I know." I had always liked the Old Man. "They say he's been preying on the small business man lately. I hear he's been slowly going to pieces."

"No, no." O'Rourke was thoughtful. "It's been five years now since he took in that cheap killer, Eddie Marco. Sort of wanted to use him to handle the rough element. Now Eddie seems to have control. Some say he's got the Old Man by the ear. Others say the Old Man went hard, and is using Eddie as an excuse. Whatever it is, Eddie Marco is a power today, a real menace."

"Sure." I had heard, but never had anything to do with Eddie Marco. "If you see the Old Man now, it's clear things through Eddie. Eddie's supposed to be engaged to the Old Man's daughter."

"I've heard that." O'Rourke nodded indifferently. "That's not the point. The point is that the Old Man's daughter, Yola O'Neil, walked into the morgue and took a look at Lizzie Dell."

"Identified her?"

"No, simply took a look at her. Then the Old Man came across with the burial offer. You might try and connect the Old Man up with Elizabeth Delton." Which meant that as a private investigator, it might be better for me than for O'Rourke to step on the Old Man's toes.

That afternoon I made a call on Yola O'Neil....

The Old Man's house had stood for years in a poor section. Then enterprising real estate men discovered it. There was a good view of the river, so they built apartments taller and taller so the tenants could see farther and farther out over the river. But the Old Man hung on to his house. It was remodeled if not entirely rebuilt, and though a bit incongruous among the towering apartments of wealth, not exactly an eyesore.

Yola O'Neil was no eyesore either. She didn't need her Old Man's money, or his influence, to make her stand out. She was fairly tall and not too slim, and her hair was blonde. Her eyes were green, green and blue. I couldn't figure out the changing colors. Just as I thought I had—she went the wrong color on my figuring, and that sort of distracted me from the woman herself.

Beauty and brains. No doubt about that.

She knew who I was and took me into the library, and of all things didn't ask me to have a drink. I was watching her eyes change and came to it rather abruptly.

I asked, "Did you know Elizabeth Delton? The woman was murdered under the name of Lizzie Dell."

She smiled pleasantly and let the blue go to green, and asked me to sit down. Then she said:

"I know you are a detective, Mr. Williams. A very good one too. I presume you are investigating her murder. Tell me about it."

All right. I told her brutally enough to make her squirm a little and chase the smile off her face. She cleared her throat before she spoke.

"I guess I asked for it," she said, very seriously. "No—I didn't know her."

"You went to the morgue the other day, and recognized her."

"I went to the morgue to see if I would recognize her. You see, a woman giving the name of Lizzie Dell had called me on the phone. But I didn't know her."

"What did she call you about?"

"That, Mr. Williams, was not very clear."

"What exactly did she say?"

"She said she wanted to hear the sound of my voice. Wanted to know if I was happy. Things like that. Very odd. I had an idea she might have known me when I was little. But I'm sure I never saw her before."

"And what did you tell your father?"

"Not what I am telling you." She looked toward the open door. "I didn't want to disturb him. I asked him if he ever knew or heard of Lizzie Dell. I didn't tell him that I had been to the morgue."

"Did you suggest he take care of the burial?"

"I think I did. Anyway, father used to do such things."

"Used to?" She let that ride. "But doesn't now, you mean?"

"I don't exactly mean anything."

I took a shot in the dark, saying, "Did this woman say anything about your intended marriage?"

"What marriage?" She flashed that one and the eyes were definitely green.

"To Eddie Marco?"

"There has been no announcement. How could she possibly have known anything about my intentions in such a matter, when no one knows?"

"She could have known as I know," I said. "She could have read some of the columns."

"Oh, that." Yola seemed relieved. "Yes. She wanted to know if I was happy in my coming marriage."

"Not mentioning Eddie Marco by name?"

"Not mentioning Eddie Marco by name, no."

"Did you tell Eddie Marco about this woman—this telephone call?"

"Perhaps," Yola said. "You'd rather ask Eddie about that?" There was a challenge in her voice.

"If you prefer."

"You wouldn't hesitate to ask him?"

"No."

"You wouldn't be afraid?"

"No. Why?" I said.

"I mean you wouldn't be afraid of Eddie—under any circumstances?"

Now that was an odd way to put it. I gave her a straight answer. "No. I wouldn't be afraid of Eddie Marco under any circumstances. Why?"

"Most people are."

I tried the photograph on her then.

"That," I said, "is the murdered Lizzie Dell. You'd hardly recognize her though, for she aged considerably. Are you looking at the woman? Do you know her?"

"No, no," she said. But there was a tremor in her voice and her face was very white.

"You do know her."

"No—no," she said again. "I don't. I swear I don't. I never saw her in my life."

Her fingers seemed to stick to the photograph as I took it away from her. Funny too, I believed her. Believed her, yet couldn't account for her shock. For certainly the photograph had given her a shock, and I had an idea she was looking at the pupils rather than the teacher.

"Well," I said, getting to my feet. "I've got a job to do. I'm going back downtown and talk to Eddie Marco."

"Don't go yet." She got up and put a hand on my arm. "I don't want you to talk to Eddie—yet. Sit down a minute. I want to think."

I sat down. Her eyes watched me. They were capable of a direct, unblinking look. After a while she said:

"Mine has been a very strange life, Race Williams. I don't remember my mother. My father has been everything to me—and to a great many people. And sometimes the things he has done have not seemed entirely right. But where he may have done wrong things, he has never done a contemptible thing. I would do anything for him."

I waited a bit and when nothing else came, I said:

"That's a nice feeling for a daughter to have about her father. I've heard plenty good of him too. Although not so much lately."

"That's Eddie," she said at once. "Eddie has had a strange life too. No one to help him. There have been some terrible stories around about Eddie but they're only stories. Aren't they?"

"If you mean there has never been any evidence that would stand up in a court of law—that's true."

"Do you—" she leaned forward—"believe that he has killed people—shot people down in cold blood?"

"Sure," I said easily. "I believe that all right."

"Can you prove it?"

"No," I said, "I can't."

"Can you— Is Eddie connected in any way with the death of this woman?"

"Not that I know of." I told her the truth. "Listen, Miss O'Neil, I didn't come here to discuss Eddie Marco with you. Just Lizzie Dell. I'm going to find the person who killed her."

"You mean—a sort of conceit with you?"

"I mean—" I stopped. Maybe she was right. "I hope not entirely that," I told her. "But I guess it's partly true. Now have you any reason to believe that Eddie had anything to do with it?"

"No, no." She couldn't get the words out fast enough. "I haven't. Believe me, I haven't." And then both her hands were on my shoulders and she was very close to me. "Race, Race," she said over and over. "Wait. Don't go see Eddie yet. Give me time to think. The telephone calls I've had regarding Eddie since—since that columnist first hinted I was engaged to

him. They can't be true. Why do they call me on the phone and say such terrible things about Eddie?"

"Because you have helped people." Which was true enough.

"Wait." She was almost clinging to me now. Yet you couldn't put it down as romance—nor entirely fear. You couldn't put it down as anything. "Don't talk to Eddie yet."

"Why should I wait?" I was unwinding myself uneasily from foreign entanglements.

"Because—if I can find out anything, no matter what it is, I'll tell you."

CHAPTER 2

HELP YOURSELF TO TROUBLE

Feet upon stairs. Heavy slow feet on hard wood. Feet that slowly crossed the outside hall and came toward us. The Old Man walked into the room. If he had lost his grip, he didn't show it.

He was dressed for the street, and he was a very impressive sight. Not simply tall and heavy, he was huge. Heavy of jowl with a few hanging chins and, of all things, a stiff-winged collar. Gold nose-glasses too. His face was pleasant, but a little too big for his features. His hair was snow white and his eyes bright china blue. But his mouth was too small, and his nose was too small; and his eyes were set too close together. Age—sixty to seventy.

The Old Man showed no surprise at seeing me. He walked slowly across the room, slipping off a spotless yellow glove and tucking his cane up under his arm. Then he extended his hand to me.

"Race Williams," he said. "We are honored, I am sure." There was no sarcasm in his voice and his blue eyes twinkled. That was the Old Man. He could make the most extraordinary statements sound real, even sincere.

"We haven't," he went on after shaking my hand, "come under that private eye of yours?" His chuckle was friendly and pleasant. "Run along, my dear," he said to his daughter. "Race, no doubt, has a word or two he wishes with me." After the girl had left, he said, "Well, Mr. Williams. Lizzie Dell of the morgue, no doubt."

"Did you know her?" I asked.

"Know her? Of course, I knew her—as I know *all* people in the great city. Are you interested in her life or her death?"

"Her death," I told him.

"I have always told myself that if I ever needed the services of a private investigator, it would be you. In what way can I help you? What other information can I give you?"

"You haven't told me what you know about her."

"Know about her?" He seemed undecided then. I knew the Old Man and how he talked around things. Now he talked on, saying nothing definite, and I reached the conclusion that he wanted to find out things from me, that he suspected something.

I asked him direct questions. I never got a direct answer.

"What can one do for the dead?" he said once, in answer to my question why he paid for her burial. "I thought perhaps she would like it. A resting place of her own. I have often done the same before, for our unknown dead."

"But you didn't know her to speak to."

"Perhaps." He wouldn't even come one way or the other on that. "I meet and talk to everyone. If this Lizzie Dell was part of the city, then I knew her." He seemed to be thinking. "But it does you credit, Race Williams, and belies the stories that you think only of money. You have someone in mind for this murder?"

"No," I said. "I haven't. What made you think that?"

"You're coming here to see, perhaps, if you would step on my toes."

"I don't care whose toes I step on," I told him a bit sharply.

"Good. Good." He really seemed pleased. "The police perhaps spoil me. But this is murder. Ask me anything you wish. You couldn't be thinking of my young friend, Eddie Marco?"

"I could," I said.

"What," he said, "do you think of Eddie Marco?"

"No doubt the greatest scoundrel unhung."

"A strong man, Eddie." The Old Man nodded. "Capable of making enemies."

"Capable of removing them too."

He put those sharp blue eyes on me. "Ambitious, too. He is going places. I am afraid at times he is selfish. Doesn't think of people." He took my arm and led me to the door. "Call on me again, Race. Any time, for anything. And good luck."

I was out the door and it was closed. Was the Old Man slipping? I had seen him before when he could make snap decisions. A likable old scoundrel. Eddie a deadly menace to the city. What a duo to team together.

Well, they had learned what I thought of Eddie Marco. Eddie and I had never crossed. But more than once Eddie had let it be known that I had turned down a job offer because it meant tackling him. I couldn't pin that on Eddie. But it hurt my pride.

Anyway, I got one thing out of Yola O'Neil. The classroom photograph had jarred her.

THERE ARE TIMES when I use more than my brawn and my trigger finger, and do more than talk through the side of my mouth. I went to work on the kids in that photograph. I was interested only in the boys—fourteen of them.

The picture had been taken by a professional photographer. It had been sold to the members of the class at ten cents a copy. But the photographer was no longer in business. The lack of school records was also appalling.

Finally I got two of the boys identified. One was a young doctor in Brooklyn. He remembered the names of some of the kids. One of them built me up a bit.

"Little Eddie Marcolina," he said, and he let me look at the dark-eyed boy through his long-handled, powerful, magnifying glass. "Cute kid. But crooked as a ram's horn. He'd swipe your lunch for no reason at all. Never hungry. Miss—what was her name now?"

I told him.

"Yes—Delton, that was it. She'd buy him lunch and take him home with her.

He sure played her for a sucker. She believed nothing but good of him. She was killed, eh? No, I wouldn't have known her from the newspaper picture."

He moved the glass on. "Nellie Braumwich. On the end in the third row. I used to carry her books and—this one, Mr. Williams—I'll get the name in a minute."

I wasn't interested any more. I couldn't get to O'Rourke fast enough. I wanted to be sure it wasn't the closeness of the two names that made me see the likeness of the boy under the glass to the man....

It didn't take O'Rourke over ten minutes to dig out the truth for me. "Sure." He came back with some records. "He must have dropped the 'lina' part a good many years back. If he ever had it legally changed. It would be the first thing he ever did that was legal. All very interesting, Race—but what does this tie Eddie up with?"

"Have you," I asked him, "tried to tie Eddie up with the murder of Lizzie Dell, formerly Elizabeth Delton?"

"No, no." He looked at me. "Why should we?"

"You'd like to, wouldn't you?"

"I'd like to tie him up with anything that will put him away." O'Rourke was emphatic. "It seems far-fetched."

"He was in her class at school. Third grade."

"She taught school for twenty years." O'Rourke shook his head. "Thousands must have been in her class at one time or another." With a grin, he added, "Lots of kids want to kill the teacher. Some even plan it out as a pleasant relaxation—but none of them ever do it."

"Can you link them up together?"

O'Rourke shook his head. "An old-maid school teacher who went downhill, and a killer who went up. Where would they come together, Race, and how could we link them?"

"You could go back over Eddie's record."

"That won't be hard. It's long enough I guess the cops have questioned him for every crime on the calendar. But we never put the finger on him. Now—" O'Rourke shrugged—"he's hit the big time and getting bigger. I'll give you a buzz if anything turns up. But don't hope. Eddie killed women, I guess—but not her kind."

I went to see another lad who lived in the Bronx and had attended that third grade class of Elizabeth Delton's with Eddie Marco. I had hopes that someone would have followed his classmates a bit and connect up Eddie and the teacher for me. But this man had less to give than the doctor.

He remembered the dark-haired boy with the dark eyes most unpleasantly, but couldn't remember his name. He remembered losing a pen and a pencil, and a watch.

"Bad kid." He shook his head. "Pulled a penknife on me down in the basement. I was bigger than he was and nearly bashed his head in." The Bronxite said more about the teacher liking Eddie. Then he wanted to buy the picture—went as high as offering five dollars for it. "I wasn't a bad-looking kid," he said by way of explanation. Looking at him now, I couldn't blame him for wanting something to recall such an idea.

When I got back, my office boy, little Jerry pointed toward my door marked private and pulled at his nose, so I knew it was the law. I went in, and O'Rourke said:

"You called the turn all right, Race. It goes back to 1937. I wasn't in Homicide or I would have remembered. It was the first time Eddie Marco was dragged in on a major charge." He consulted his notebook.

"George Wyton was knifed and robbed, and bled to death in an alley. A number of men were pulled in for questioning. Eddie, only a kid then, was one of them. It was no dice. He had an alibi, maybe his first fixed one. Guess who gave it to him?"

"Lizzie Dell," I said.

"Right. She was still a teacher then, had a good reputation. We really had nothing on Eddie Marco, and didn't take him seriously after she said he was with her in her apartment. Eddie was sprung, of course. But he could have knifed George Wyton."

"Then the murder was never solved?"

O'Rourke admitted, "No, it was never solved. But it simply links up a former pupil visiting his old teacher, who gave her time and her savings to helping kids. That is no reason he should kill her. More reason he shouldn't."

"Don't be a sap, O'Rourke," I said.

"What's on your mind, Race? Why did he kill her?"

"Because of that alibi," I told O'Rourke. "Suppose she was ready to repudiate it? There is no statute of limitations in murder."

"Why would she repudiate the alibi? And if she was going to, why wait this long? Why give it to him in the first place if it wasn't true?"

"Because," I said, "she was crazy about that kid. She couldn't see any wrong in him. She didn't believe him guilty. Just a poor kid who was hounded by the police. If she couldn't believe he'd swipe a pen or a lad's lunch, she wouldn't believe he'd knife a man. So she gave him the alibi, believing his story of police persecution."

"And why the sudden change?"

"Sudden?" I laughed. "That was eleven years ago. She began to doubt. Or she found out about something that Eddie was going to do that she didn't want him to do. That is what she came to see me about. She got in touch with Eddie. Maybe she hadn't seen him in years. But she told him if he does this or that—whatever it was—then she'll repudiate that alibi. There's the reason for his killing her."

"Sure," agreed O'Rourke. "If?"

"If what?"

"If Eddie killed her."

"But she talked to me and told me that—"

"Yeah, I know. You told me. She wanted to make someone do something, or not do something. She didn't mention Eddie Marco by name. With eight million people in the city of New York, and millions outside of it, you pick out Eddie. All right. All right. He was in her class. How many others were in it?" Leaning forward suddenly, O'Rourke said, "What are you holding out on me? Don't tell me all this is headwork."

So I told him about the picture. I didn't tell him I picked it up from the dead woman's bureau. I said she dropped it from her bag in my office.

He didn't believe me, but he didn't argue the point while he looked at the photo.

"It's good work anyway, Race," he said. "She didn't also drop a repudiation of that alibi, did she? I'm not saying you haven't got a good story. But I could spend hours pointing out to you the holes a defense counsel would plug in your case. Why, the D.A. wouldn't touch it with a second-story man—let alone a big shot like Eddie Marco."

"Well," I said. "I know Eddie killed her. And you know Eddie killed her."

"Yes." O'Rourke nodded his head quite seriously. "I'll agree to that. Then you'll agree, too, that there are other killers walking the streets today. I know they killed and who they killed—but I can't do anything about it."

"So you want Eddie to be another. I bring you stuff like this, and you do nothing about it."

"Why don't you do something yourself?" O'Rourke asked.

"What?"

"Spring what you told me on Eddie. If he pulls a gun on you and kills you, we'll know you were right and we'll fry him for killing you. If you must serve the state, that would be a glorious finish."

"And if I should kill him?"

"Then it will be self-defense—I hope." O'Rourke grinned. Then he walked out of the office.

He left me with an idea. I would spring it on Eddie Marco and see what he did. O'Rourke was right. I'd never make a good department dick. I didn't have the patience.

CHAPTER 3

THE MOVING CURTAIN

THAT NIGHT CAME the first of my mysterious telephone calls about Lizzie Dell. Where you might like to ignore anonymous calls, in my business you can't. Nine-tenths of them are phony or misleading—but the one-tenth pays off.

"Lizzie Dell," the voice said, and you couldn't tell if it was a man, woman, or a child; so I gathered it was someone talking through a handkerchief. "Lizzie Dell left some writing with me. Keep after Eddie Marco. The time will come when I will put proof in your hands that he murdered Lizzie Dell because of George Wyton."

"I see," I said easily. "Lizzie Dell a friend of yours?"

"Oh, yes. She went to see you. I know all about that. Frighten Eddie into the open. There is writing. I'll make him believe in the writing. But he may try and kill you. Be careful."

The phone clicked. The connection was broken. I went to bed. I'd see Eddie tomorrow all right. I didn't need any voice to egg me on. Still, it was the first time in my life I had butterflies in my stomach....

A few years back, Eddie was a rat running in the gutters of the East Side. Maybe Eddie had had a hard life. But if he made life hard for others, he could always claim that he made death easy for them. Eddie was lucky. He had actually shot himself into power. Everyone who knew his way around, knew that. No one had ever put the finger on him.

How he ever got so close to the Old Man, no one seemed to know. Eddie had a way about him. He was smooth and slick, and the rough edges had been polished down. Eddie was ambitious. If his best friend stood in his way, then that best friend had to go.

And there was Eddie Marco greeting me now, in his high class offices labeled:

INVESTMENTS INCORPORATED

"You know, Race—" he was shaking my hand—"I've admired you since I was a kid. Fighting it alone; the halfway house between the cops and big business." Eddie always called crime big business. "Come on back, boy, and see my private room. Something special for the elite." I followed him down long halls from the new building into an old one.

He finally let me into a room that might have been a nightmarish idea of how a cross between a big-game hunter, a college librarian, and a guy on the verge of the D.T.s would have his room fixed up.

A moose head, a lion head, and a rhinoceros head crowded over the large fireplace. On the floor, not yet set up, were some pretty odd-looking mounted fish. On the other side of the room were books. Rare editions. Fine bindings. Eddie called them off to me with prices.

At the back of the room, behind a large desk, were tapestries. To top it all off, the carpet upon the floor was thick enough to tickle your ankles. Even then, there were

a couple of animal skin rugs tossed over the carpet.

Eddie explained the stuff.

"I'm fitting myself in," he said in all seriousness. "Creating a background. I'm to be married, Race, and I don't mind telling you, it's Yola O'Neil. She went to some swanky schools and knows the right people. We'll buy a place up Westchester way, join the clubs and what not. A big-game hunter gives a lad a bit of standing among the sporting men."

"And the carpets hanging from the walls?" I asked him.

"Carpets," he frowned. "They are rare oriental pieces. They better be or a smart dealer will wake up some morning with a belly full of lead. Turkey or Persia; or some such place. World traveler. Explorer. Big-game hunter. Books for culture. What are you grinning at?

"Look at Yola. Her old man's a big-time grafter. It didn't set well on the stomach of the high and mighty. So she was a politician's daughter at the first school she went to. Then the Old Man got smart and gave the school a new wing for the girls' gym, and he became a statesman. But look here!"

He walked over in front of the big expensive desk. *"The pièce de résistance."* He smacked his lips when he pulled that one, and eyed me carefully. He liked the sound of it for he repeated, "Yeah—the *pièce de résistance.* Something anyone can sink his teeth in. Look at that."

I looked at the heavy revolver encased in a plush-lined niche built right in the front of the desk. He lifted the gun out and handed it to me.

"Dummy bullets," he explained it's deadly appearance. "That's real, Race. Got it from Chicago. Danny Logan's gun. It's supposed to hold the record for deaths. Killed thirty-seven people with it, Danny did. Men, women, and children and five cops."

I bounced the gun in my hand. It might have been one of my own. Just the sort of a gun I fancied. It was scratched a bit on the nose, and black along the barrel. A nice, heavy, revolver.

"What are you going to tell the elite about this rod?" I asked him.

"The truth, maybe," he nodded. "If I can doctor it up a bit. The story behind it will come in handy if anyone needs a bit of—a bit of a scare. That's right, Race. The D.A. gave it to me in appreciation. The cops took credit for the killing of Danny Logan but it was me who gunned him out."

I didn't laugh. I remembered Danny Logan, of course. There had always been some doubt as to how he took the dose. What Eddie Marco said might very easily be true.

"All the cops in the country looking for him." Eddie put the gun carefully back in its exposed velvet case. You could see it was his prize possession. "But they couldn't put the finger on Danny."

"And they asked you to get him?"

"No," he scoffed. "I don't do the cops' work. I had a little deal. Danny horned in on it. I went looking for him. We met one night in the Loop. I was coming out of the Greek's place. Logan knew it was him or me. He had the draw, and he had the drop—so I jerked out my gun and tore him apart. Just like that. They hushed it up. I got the slaps on the back, his gun as a souvenir, and they took the credit. That's the truth how Danny died. Guys never cross me but once. Now, Race, what did you want to see me about?"

I TOOK A grin out of that. You've got to admit it was a nice build-up to that final question. I guess I was supposed to shake at the knees and cry that I was collecting for indigent detectives. Instead I said:

"I'm trying to wrap you up for the wire murder of Lizzie Dell."

That could have been his cue to go for his gun. Maybe that would have been the simplest solution all around. I think ten years ago he would have gone for it. Maybe five—maybe even a year or two. Certainly his fingers twitched, and his black eyes grew blacker and a little narrower. But he only laughed. His voice, when he spoke, was steady.

"You know, Race," he said. "You and I have never crossed. When I was younger, you were my hero, but I often thought of pulling a gun on you just to see how fast you were. I wasn't sure then. But now—"

"Now?" I asked.

"Now it would be murder," he said. "You wouldn't get your hand out of your armpit before you were dead. Who is this Lizzie Dell?"

I told him, showing him the picture.

"I was a nice kid." He glanced down at the photography. "I got a picture taken about that time, gave it to Yola. Miss Delton, eh? Sure, I remember her now. She liked me. Fussy old maid. Poor old Pussy—we always called her Pussy."

"She saved your life," I said and watched him. "The stabbing of George Wyton!"

"Wyton." He half-thought aloud. "Was that his name? I was with her when the old guy croaked off." He laughed. "She thought I'd grow up to be president. I didn't do so bad."

"Not sorry she's dead? She gave you an alibi!"

"Don't be dramatic." He was watching me carefully. "If it wasn't Pussy, it would be another. You're not—not trying to shake me down?"

"No, no," I told him. "She was my client, Eddie. I let her down. I'm going to make it up to her now. I'm going to pin her murder on you!"

He didn't speak for a long time. It was as if he was trying to figure things out.

"Someone hire you to dump me over?" His eyes were shrewd, searching.

"Only Lizzie Dell," I told him. "She was going to deny that alibi, and—" as if I had something—"maybe she did, in writing."

"Baloney." He shook his head from side to side. "She's dead. There would be nothing in it for you there. You say this dame gave me a phony alibi? That's years ago. Suppose it was true. How would that connect me up with Wyton?"

I looked serious and said: "Maybe I got more to go on?"

"Like what?" When I didn't say anything, "You know, Race, I can't make you out. You got nothing. You come and lay a four flush down on the table." He looked at me long and steadily. "I'll think it over and let you know how I'm taking it."

"Better." I nodded at him. "Did it ever strike you, Eddie, that Elizabeth Delton, Lizzie Dell, Pussy—was a dame who liked to keep things in writing."

"She did?" he said. "Well, what have you got in writing? I might pay for some writing. Is that what you mean?"

"Writing that would fry you?"

"Do you know, Race," he said in a clear even voice, "no one in years has talked to me as you are talking now. And no man alive ever talked to me like you have. What do you want?" He leaned forward then. "A belly full of lead?"

"You have a gun," I told him. "I know you killed Lizzie Dell. I just want you to know you're going to die for it, Eddie."

He looked as if he was going to reach and draw. He didn't. I don't think he was afraid. I don't think Eddie Marco feared anything at any time. He said:

"All right, boy. You're out to get me. You want me to know it. Is that it?"

"That's it," I said to him. "There's a shorter way out of this room, isn't there?"

There was, and he showed it to me. A private door back of one tapestry. I went right down the stairs and out on the side street.

ONE O'CLOCK THAT morning, Yola O'Neil called me on the phone. Her voice was hoarse and low, and seemed to have panic in it. Would I come and see her at once? I would, and I did.

She saw me in a little room that gave onto a large room, and was closed off by thick curtains. She looked nervous, had been crying. She didn't ask me to sit down. Indeed, she stood before me all the time as she talked, her back to the curtains. She did not give a very good performance. Somehow I got the impression that she did not want to give a good performance.

"Lizzie Dell." She would hardly let me get a word in sideways. "Have you any idea that he—that Eddie killed her?" I said:

"This is where I came in before, Yola." I looked at my watch. "It's late, unless there is something you really want to tell me."

"What could I tell you?" I half moved to one side, and she was between me and the curtains again. "Have you anything in writing? From Elizabeth Dell, I mean."

"I might have." I didn't whisper. I was watching the curtains over her shoulder. There was no movement to them. Yet, I had the idea we were not alone. Someone was listening, and that someone had a gun in his hand and—

The whole idea came from Yola O'Neil's actions. It was as if she expected a gun to blast and lead come from behind those curtains, and for that lead to bury itself in me. I gave her credit for one thing. She didn't want it to happen… at least, not yet.

She didn't like it when I started to play her game. I let her put herself between me and the curtains all right. But I kept backing her closer and closer to them.

Suddenly I shoved the girl aside. Jerking out my gun with my right hand, I pulled the curtains aside with my left hand. Very dramatic. I looked into a darkened dining-room, half crouched, gun up, finger tight against a trigger—and I saw the body and straightened.

There on the floor, on his back, lay

Eddie Marco. His right hand was crossed over and up under his left armpit. He was breathing heavily.

I thought he had been shot. That would be the natural thought if one saw Eddie Marco stretched out on his back, and his hand reaching for a gun. But instead, someone had tapped this boy on the back of the head, underneath the right ear. It was a nice clean blow and had felled him like a steer in a stock yard.

Yola O'Neil, behind me, said:

"Eddie said he simply wanted to listen. He had me ask you here. But I was afraid he might harm you. Still—"

"Still you beaned him." I turned and looked at the girl. "Then you don't love him. Do you, Yola?"

"No," she said. "No, I don't love him." She was twisting a handkerchief around in her fingers.

"You were afraid he was going to kill me. So you struck him down."

"No, no." She sure was mixed up. "I didn't think he would; not with me here." Her blue-green eyes looked startled.

"You were afraid he would regain consciousness and take a shot at me. Why did you bring me in here, after you struck him down?"

"After I struck him down—" she repeated my words as if in a daze—"I don't know. He said to bring you here, to ask you certain questions. He wanted to hear the answers. I was afraid for you."

"Sure," I said. "You're a good kid, Yola. Why do you run with that rat?"

"Because I have to. He always wins out. Always. I—I— We mustn't talk here. What will he say when he comes around? He will, won't he? He's not—not going to die?"

"No," I said. With a sudden idea that I rather liked, I asked, "Did he see you hit him?"

"See me hit him? No, no, he didn't. What will he believe?"

"This." I looked down at the unconscious man and led Yola out of the room before I told her. "You tell him you let me in. I came around through the hall behind him, and knocked him cold. The first thing you knew he was out like a light. I was mad and left." She looked at me.

I added, "Then he won't think you did it."

"Oh, no. He won't think I did it." Suddenly brightening up, for she was acting like one doped, she now said, "Thank you, Mr. Williams. Thank you, Race." Both her hands were around my neck now. "You—they told me you were hard and cruel. Why do you do this for me?"

She was close, and she was a nice armful. She had conked the boy friend, Eddie, for me, and I felt pretty good.

I told her when I saw Eddie I'd admit, in fact, I would glory in, having knocked him for a loop. Whatever story she told him would be my story. I wouldn't go into it in detail for Eddie until I heard from her.

"Thank you," she said. "I suppose it's all a waste of time. Eddie has his star. It guides him. For good or evil, it guides him. He can't be beaten. Even father couldn't arrange that—could he?"

"I don't suppose the Old Man wants to," I said.

"No—no." She shook her head. "I don't suppose he does."

I left then. I laughed more than once as I drove home. I was laughing when I went in to little Jerry's bedroom to wake him up for an early snack. Jerry was always ready to eat, and he could put food together real tasty.

Only Jerry was not home. That was funny.

CHAPTER 4

HARDWARE ON THE HOUSE

JERRY MISSING PUZZLED me and bothered me, but not too much—until the next day when I was having lunch in a good old chop house. The chair moved across the table from me in the crowded restaurant, and Eddie Marco slid into the seat and faced me.

"Hello, Race." He grinned over at me. "Still feeling sentimental about that old doll—what was her name, Lizzie Dell?"

"Lizzie Dell is right." I was pleased I had Eddie's goat. "Surprised to find I have a bit of sentiment?"

"Sure, sure," Eddie said. He dismissed the waiter, saying he had eaten. "I like it in you, Race. That pre-shrunk boy of yours, Jerry—attached to him aren't you?"

I wasn't so pleased then. I was jarred. Eddie saw it all right and showed his teeth.

"Smart boy, little Jerry," Eddie went on. "You couldn't fool him. Except he has a bit of sentiment, too. I often heard how

you worked out codes together, and put the finger on guys who meant to put it on you. Nothing clever about me, Race. Just an excited voice on the phone saying you'd been shot, was in the hospital—and for Jerry to come at once. You were dying.

"All training went then. Jerry dashed out of the apartment, grabbed the first taxi—the first one—understand? A lad with a gun in it. As easy at that."

"You—you didn't kill him?"

"No. I'm sentimental too. You know, Race, you made your mistake last night when you knocked me out. Should have put a bullet in my head. Guess you thought of it. But—" his hands spread apart—"your sentiment again. Didn't like to do it in front of the girl, Yola, eh?"

I said: "If anything happens to Jerry, I'll kill you, Eddie."

"We wouldn't like that—would we, Race?" Eddie was master of the situation now. "I wouldn't want to be dead, and you wouldn't want to kill me. So we'll make a little deal. Listen. You'll come to my office, say at eleven o'clock tonight. You'll bring all this written stuff you've got. And I'll turn over Jerry to you!" He came to his feet then. "The door on the side street, Race."

He started to turn. I whispered sharply: "Eddie."

He stopped dead. I said, "Sit down Eddie. I've got a gun on you—under the table. One step and I'll plug you."

He looked at me a long time over his shoulder. Then he shook his head.

"No one has ever called your bluff, Race. If it wasn't for Jerry, I wouldn't call it now." With a shrug, he added, "but if it wasn't for Jerry, you could shoot and would shoot. Okay—boy—shoot!"

He turned and, with his back to me, strode toward the door. He was right. I knew that the minute he disappeared around the bend near the door to 34th Street. I did have a gun on him under the table. And my finger was pretty tight on the trigger. But it must have been a bluff because I didn't squeeze lead, and he didn't die. Or was I thinking then of the living Jerry and not the dead Lizzie Dell?

Mechanically I finished my chop. The best chops, the best cooking in the city— tasting like leather.

Eddie knew I would come to him that night, but he hadn't mentioned anything about my not coming armed. Why? Because he was willing to face me alone with a gun? No, because Eddie thought I wouldn't plan to come without a gun. At the last minute he'd arrange it so I couldn't see him with a gun—figuring I wouldn't turn back.

He was right. Once on my way, I'd go and see him without a gun if it meant Jerry's life. I hadn't much doubt it did mean Jerry's life....

The next few hours I spent trying to find Eddie Marco in his usual haunts. If I could get him alone, I'd have taken him apart to find out where Jerry was. But I couldn't find him.

I went to my apartment and tried to think it out. I had no writing to bring to Eddie. What good would it do to go unarmed to Eddie, with no chance of making a deal? Then came the flash.

I left my apartment. I wasn't toting two guns now; I was toting three. The odd one sunk deep in my coat pocket. I had scratched it up a bit on the nose, and blackened up the silver of the barrel where it would show. To be sure I wasn't followed, I worked a couple of taxis, crossed in a few subway stations. Then I called Yola O'Neil on the phone. It was twenty minutes of five in the afternoon.

"Yola," I put it to her. "You said you'd do anything for me. Does that go now?"

"Yes," she said over the wire. "Anything up to murder." Up to murder. I didn't like the stipulation she made there.

I asked her could she get in to Eddie's private office. She could; she had a key and often met him there. I breathed easier. Then I wanted to know if she could meet me some place, and be sure she was not followed. She was expecting Eddie to telephone; so I decided to see her at her home. Her father was busy in his office at the back of the house. If Eddie was going to telephone her, he didn't expect to be there.

SHE SAW ME in the library, but this time the doors were closed and the curtains drawn over the window. I told her about Jerry and what I wanted her to do. She listened with her hands folded in her lap. She took the gun I gave her from my coat pocket.

Like a child reciting a lesson, she said:

"You want me to go to his den. You want me to take the gun that is in the case cut into the front of his desk. You want me to put this loaded gun of yours in its place. You want to kill him?"

"I want to save Jerry," I said. "In a way, it may save you too from him. Why are you marrying him, Yola? You don't love him." I tried to keep the doubt out of my voice when I said that.

"No." She shook her head. "This may be fate working things out for me. Still, if you kill him, it will be like—like I killed him."

"It isn't a question of killing him." I objected. "It's a question of saving Jerry."

"You won't kill him."

"Not unless—Yola." I went over and lifted her from the couch and put my arms around her. "You can do it, can't you? And you will do it, won't you?"

"Yes, yes." She hardly breathed the words. "I can do it—and I will do it—if I can."

"But you said you could—"

"I can take myself unseen to his office, put the gun there, and take away the other one. What I mean is—unless something beyond me holds me back, tells me it is wrong." Suddenly raising those now blue eyes to mine, Yola declared, "Yes, Race. I believe that he has killed and killed. I believe that if anything happens to you tonight, my life is no longer worth living. Yes, yes I'll do it—if I can efface the picture that I am murdering a living human being."

"But you'll do it."

"If the moral courage does not fail me."

"If you want to see me alive again, you'll do it?"

I kissed her then, and I think she liked it. Anyway I did. I kissed her once more and left her with the statement that my life was in her hands. She clung to me too and cried softly, and let her hands run up the back of my head and through my hair....

I didn't return to my apartment. I stayed along the city streets. At eleven o'clock I'd show up at that door on the side street—and I'd have two guns with me.

There was a man lounging against the building when I arrived on the deserted street at exactly eleven. His hands were conspicuously empty. He made sure I noticed that as he swung over to me. I knew him. Cockey Elman, a rough-and-ready lad close to Eddie Marco.

"Hello, Race," he said. "I got a mean job. Don't be sore, fellow. I understand you want to visit someone upstairs. I've got to frisk you first."

I laughed, saying, "You don't think I'd go up there unarmed?"

"I don't think, period." Elman grinned at me. "I'm not to make a point of it. The lad you want to see won't be there unless I take your hardware. Suit yourself. It's no skin off my nose."

"No guts? He's afraid to see me?" I had expected this, but I didn't want to agree too easy.

"Maybe," he said. "I don't know from nothing. I'm to tell you that if you want to see a certain party again alive—I frisk you. Suit yourself."

I let him frisk me. A real courageous act, you think. Just how brave, I didn't know at the time. For I didn't know then that for the last two hours Yola O'Neil was trying frantically to get me on the phone to tell me she couldn't—wouldn't go through with planting the gun.

I let Elman go over me and take the two guns. Also, he hesitated over my penknife, and finally kept it.

With an ease I did not feel, I said: "You'll return those to me tomorrow?"

I was clean now, so he spoke right up.

"I'll see that they are buried with you, Race." He thought that was pretty funny and almost split a gut laughing. Then he pointed toward the door. "Go on up," he said, "and good luck."

I didn't pussy-foot up those stairs. I climbed them quickly and easily in the dim light from an overhanging electric bulb. I was showing a confidence I didn't feel. The door to that weird room was open. I saw Eddie under the light as soon as I turned on the landing at the top. He was sitting behind the desk. Both his hands were on the flat surface, one clutching a .45 automatic. He said:

"Come in, Race. You're on time. Close the door after you."

I went in quickly, slamming the door behind me. I crossed right to the chair before the desk and sat down in it quickly. I was facing the gun. Was it mine? I thought it was. I didn't feel so bad.

THEN I LOOKED over by the fireplace and my eyes widened. Little Jerry was there. He was tied in a big, high-backed wooden chair. He wasn't gagged. The kid had found it tough. But he said:

"You shouldn't have come, boss. I could take all this rat could offer."

Eddie Marco said:

"You're a sap, Race. Those telephone calls didn't fool me. Though how you got to my private wire, I don't know. It was kid stuff. That voice saying, 'You have written proof.' But if you had, you'd have sprung it!"

So he had been having telephone calls too.

"Well," I put it to Eddie. "If you didn't believe it, why this elaborate trap, this snatching of Jerry? You went to a lot of trouble for something that wasn't true."

"Did I? You did get the wind up me. But it wasn't Lizzie Dell. It was Yola O'Neil. I could make her believe most anything until you came along." His voice grew hard and cold now. "You crossed me, Race. No guy ever crossed me and lived."

"You think if you kill me, Yola will marry you, that she really could love you."

"She'll serve me," he said brutally, "and she'd marry me. I'm the coming lad, Race. As soon as I marry the Old Man's daughter, I'll wipe out the Old Man. He hates my guts."

"Yeah." I edged my chair closer to the desk and to the gun. I watched Eddie's right hand. "Why does the Old Man stand for you?"

"Because I'm the only living soul who's got anything on him." He held up some papers on the desk. "He killed once, someone else nearly took the dose for it. The Old Man had sentiment like you have. He wrote a confession of that killing in case this other—friend was in danger of taking the rap for it. I got that confession." He waved to the paper with his left hand. "The Old Man had to kill. But that confession would break him."

"That's why the Old Man had a rat like you running things, and why Yola is marrying you."

"One of the reasons she's marrying me, maybe. I'm going to clean things up, boy."

"Why kill the Old Man? Why kill me?"

"The Old Man," he said, "is just that— an old man. He's shrewd, he's smart. He has always been able to arrange things. I don't want him to arrange anything for me."

I came forward on the chair, said, "If you don't believe I have anything, why take this chance on killing me?"

"It's no chance," he said. "There are a dozen gunmen, maybe fifty gunmen who'd like to kill you. The police may think of even more. But the point is, Race—you know I killed Lizzie Dell."

"So you did kill her?"

"Did you doubt it?"

"Never for a moment. But if I can't prove it—why kill me?"

He leaned forward then. His gun raised, and I bent slightly.

"Because you know," he told me. "It's your life, or mine, Race. Maybe you don't know it yourself, but you were going to kill me. I know killers. I saw it in your eyes the other day. You may deny it. But it's a matter of time, as the thing would grow on you. You think you only kill in self-defense; but I know better. It was my life or yours."

I was about to deny it. I had never shot anyone down in cold blood. Yet, at lunch time, how close it had been. But it wasn't true.

Eddie Marco raised his right hand. His eyes were black slits. He said simply:

"This is it."

I dove at the front of the desk and the gun that was there. I guess I tossed myself sideways as I shot out of that chair and away from Eddie Marco's vision.

His gun roared. The kid, Jerry, cried out. A stab that was warm seemed to take a chunk out of my shoulders and burn cold across my neck. I missed my grab for the gun. I had reached it all right, but his shot and the jar of it made my fingers bang against it. Then I was flat on my back on the floor.

Something pounded down on my chest. I put up my hand. It was the gun I had knocked loose from the niche in the desk. My hand gripped it, and I could tell from the feel of it that it was my gun. I could tell from the weight that it was loaded. Then Eddie Marco leaned far over the desk and pointed his automatic down at me.

There was a surprised look on his face at first, when he spotted the gun I held. Then he grinned as he saw the empty cavity where his gun with the dummy bullets had been. He said:

"Playing games, Race?" His fingers started to tighten on the trigger.

I raised my right hand; closed my finger once, and blasted lead right into the center of Eddie's smiling boyish face.

The shock blew Eddie right back from his leaning position over the desk. I heard his body hit the desk as it crashed forward again.

I climbed slowly to my feet, gripped the desk and straightened. I couldn't help laughing. Never had I seen such an expression as I saw on little Jerry's face. It was like a rainbow after a storm.

The door was slowly opening. I thought it was Elman come to dispose of my body. But it was the Old Man.

"Ah, Race." The Old Man came slowly into the room and closed the door behind him. He lifted his cane and pointed it at

Eddie Marco there on the floor. "Dead?" he asked.

"Quite," I said. "Do you want to make something out of it?"

"Hardly." He shook his head. "You did that." He walked over to the desk and reached for the phone. Then I saw the paper. His confession. I scooped it up. His sharp little blue eyes watched me. He lifted the phone. "I'm calling the police," he said.

"We'll need them," I agreed. "There was a killing some years back. You wrote it up, I understand."

After a bit he got O'Rourke. Then he put down the phone, turned to me, said: "Why not burn that confession, Race? I had to kill that man years ago just as you had to kill this one tonight. I'm an old man now. Oh, yes, Eddie Marco killed Elizabeth Delton. She came to see me. I have a statement from her that the alibi she gave Eddie was false. At last she had found out the truth about 'her boy' Eddie. I told her to get in touch with you."

He put his hand in his pocket and laid an envelope on the desk. "Elizabeth Delton's statement for the police," he explained. "Not enough to convict Eddie but Eddie doesn't need convicting now."

"You told Lizzie Dell to get in touch with me?"

"Yes," he said. "And I made those telephone calls to both you and Eddie." I went to work untying Jerry and rubbing at his hands and legs, while the Old Man went on. "Yes, I have been arranging for Eddie's end for some time. Yola was planning to marry him because of me. She didn't think I knew. I couldn't have that.

Besides, if Eddie took over, it would be bad for the people." He added, with a wonderful smile, "That confession of my little dereliction so many years back— you'll destroy that."

"I think, Mr. O'Neil," I said slowly, "I've acted outside the law enough for one night."

"Nonsense." He still smiled. "You'll destroy it. Eddie snatched your faithful assistant, the boy there. You came. He shot you. I see that." He was looking high up on my arm where the blood was drying. "You drew and killed him. I think I might even say that I had grown suspicious of Eddie and hired you. At least, I will commend you to the police and press. You'd be dead without me."

"You saved my life?"

The phone rang. It was Yola.

"He's dead, Yola. I had to kill him."

"I'm glad I had nothing to do with it. I've been so worried. I tried to get you for hours. But you know now I couldn't put the gun there. I just couldn't."

"You— Are you saying you didn't put the gun there—here?"

"Of course, I didn't. It wasn't there, was it?"

"No. No," I said. I hung up.

"The gun. You—" I looked at the Old Man—"you put it there."

"Yes. Yola doesn't know. You mustn't trust women, Race. I saved you before."

"The fire tongs, you know. I came up behind Eddie in my stocking feet when he was behind the curtains. He thought it was you. You thought it was Yola. But Yola must have known. Dear child, she never spoke of it even to me."

"But the gun—" I was watching him put back the genuine gun now—"how did you know?"

"Listening." He smiled at me. "I have an intercommunication system hidden in my library. I listened to all you and Yola had to say and—"

"All of it?"

"Yes." His smile now was like a setting sun. "No matter. If you wish to turn that document over to the police, all right. I was nearly resigned to it...."

O'Rourke was pleased when he saw the dead Eddie. He thought I was lucky the Old Man took it so well. I still had the confession in my pocket when I sat down to have a drink and a bite to eat with Yola and the Old Man up at his house. I was thinking what Eddie said about my being a killer. I was wondering if the Old Man had arranged that too, planted that idea in Eddie's head. But I was wondering mostly if it was true. Eddie's bullet hadn't bothered me—much.

The Old Man never said a word about that confession even when he saw me to the door on leaving. It was then I handed it to him, on sudden impulse I guess.

He smiled and thanked me, saying:

"You could go far, Race, with me to arrange things for you. Have you ever thought of it?"

"No, I haven't," I said, and meant it. "And I'm not going to think about it either. Good-night."

The $100,000 Corpse

CHAPTER 1

MURDER ON 34TH STREET

THERE WAS SOMETHING very likable about Johnny Sharp. He was a gunman and a killer, but I liked him. He had come up through the East Side and made himself felt in the rackets. Johnny could not be shoved around.

He dressed expensively and flashily. He swaggered when he walked, but Sergeant O'Rourke said I did too when I wanted to throw my weight around with the tough boys. I've killed too. Though you might say I kill within the law. But within the law, or outside the law, it's all about the same for the lad who takes the dose. He's just as dead—legal or illegal.

Anyway, Johnny Sharp showed white even teeth as he slid into the booth opposite me in Chauncey's Chop House on 34th Street.

"I'm still above ground. Race," he told me after he had ordered his fried chicken. Fried chicken in Chauncey's, that was known in and out of the city for its steaks and chops. But, then, Johnny never did appreciate good food.

"So I see," I told him. "But you are not so old—yet."

"Twenty-nine," he said. "You warned me to take it easy, that I was going up too fast. And I said I was shooting my way to the top. You got wrong ideas on that. The more a lad is willing to shoot it out, the less he has to shoot it out. I don't know how many slugs I've had dug out of me. I have real news for you, Race. I'm leaving town."

"Business? Pleasure? How long?"

"For good," he said. "Johnny Sharp, tough guy and public enemy, is through. I'm going west today. Change my name—be a rancher or a farmer."

"Sounds stuffy," I said. "Someone got the finger on you?"

"No more," he told me, and with a grin, "I'm in love, Race. I'm quitting the rackets. I'm quitting the city for good. I'm going away, get settled and send for the girl. Then we'll be married. Raise a family and all that rot like in books."

"Fine," I said, "if you can get from under. What do the boys say?"

"Big Butch didn't like it." The grin went and he was very serious. So was I. For that was the first time I suspected that Johnny had gunned out Big Butch Barlow up in the Bronx on Monday night.

"And who is the night club lady?"

HE IGNORED MY question for the moment, said, "Sneaky guy—Butch. He was afraid of me. Took me out to treat me. One final fling." His broad shoulders shrugged. "It didn't work. I'm in the clear on that." And, suddenly, "It isn't any flossy. No night-club fluff. This is a kid from the East Side. I baby sat for her when I was twelve. No one knows about her and me—even she don't know yet!"

"Wish you luck, Johnny." I shook my head. "It's a tough game to walk out of. Got a stake?"

"Yeah—a hundred grand. All in cash. I thought that was fair enough. I held it out on collections. But Himmie Zimmerman knows that. After all, I built the uptown business. The numbers alone paid half a million last year. You see, I hadn't saved, and the idea struck me like that."

"I hope you make it," I told him.

"I'll make it," he said grimly. "I didn't sneak out. I didn't run out. No powder for Johnny Sharp. I told the boys. Those that don't like it have had a chance to squawk. Butch was one of them."

"They are bad playmates, Johnny. You'd have done better to simply drop from under. Run out."

"No," he said. "I'm like you, Race. You never ran from any guy. You're a straight shooter."

"I'm not part of the rackets, Johnny."

"You play a more dangerous game. Between the cops and robbers. With no friends. Listen, Race." He leaned forward now and whispered the words. "The girl's Angelina Ferra. Her father had a push cart down on Delaney Street. She's a real lady. You don't need birth or money for that. Nothing is going to happen to me. But getting set with a farm in the West has its dangers. You can't tell what might happen. I want to know if you'll look out for her."

"Me?" I straightened up. "No kidding, Johnny. You can't pass your girl off on another guy like that."

"Dough," he said. "Money. See that she gets it."

"They'd cut her heart out for it—your pals."

"Nix, nix." He was very confident. "They don't know. No one knows. I've only seen her a couple of times in years. This is all in my head—not hers. It just come to me like a flash. I got it figured out like a movie. I get settled. Then I arrange a good job for Angelina. She comes out. We meet. I make my play. She remembers."

"She's not in love with you?"

He shook his head. "She was when she was twelve. She said then she'd grow up and marry me. Last time I saw her I knew she would. You know how you feel things. Just like I feel now. Nothing can happen to me."

"You mean you're willing the money to me—for her? Why—"

"You talk like I was a sap," he cut in. "Don't tell me, Race. I know how to fix things. You a detective. Last one they'd suspect I'd confide in. She a little sales girl in the slums. Last dame I'd be even seen with." He looked down at the expensive watch on his wrist. "In half an hour I'll be pulling out of New York. No place where the wise money ever goes. I'm riding my star, Race." He came to his feet. "I never felt more sure of myself than I do right now."

He didn't shake hands. He simply grabbed his coat and slipped into it. Jerked his fedora down on his head, gave a quick feel under his left arm, then he was gone, swaggering between the tables to the door. I could see him plainly as he walked out on 34th Street.

Yes, I could see him plainly. I even saw the car, but I didn't know it yet. I heard the shots as everyone else in the place heard the shots. I made the street quicker than most of the patrons. Maybe the dark sedan weaving down the street was the death car. Maybe it was any one of a half dozen other cars.

Sure—34th Street a little after one o'clock in the afternoon. The street was crowded. A hundred people must have seen the shooting. Thousands could see Johnny now. I saw him all right. He was stretched out there on the sidewalk. The bullets of a Tommy gun had ripped him apart. His right hand was under his left armpit and his gun was half drawn.

Johnny wasn't the only one dead. There was a man lying in the gutter. An innocent bystander. He didn't count. He was in the way and had to go. There was a young girl, too. She wasn't dead. She was moving there in pain on the sidewalk. It didn't matter. Johnny had to die. And what had he just said? He never felt more sure.

The cops were thick now. I moved off. I couldn't do Johnny any good. I couldn't do myself any good. The cops always wonder when I'm around right after a killing— and most times they have a right to. This time they didn't have any right, and I wasn't going to give them any reason for wondering.

CHAPTER 2

RETRIBUTION

So THAT WAS the end of Johnny Sharp and his romance, and his settling down on a farm and going straight. Maybe, after all, racketeers have hearts. A little sloppy, eh? The heart of a gangster!

Two days later the package came. It was large and it was heavy and it was shipped by express and, of all things, insured for ten dollars. Maybe I had forgotten. Maybe I wasn't thinking about it. Anyway, I was surprised—and so would you be. That's right. It was full of folding money. All denominations. New and old bills, large and small. There were some mighty pretty pictures on that green background.

There was a hundred grand, all right. And the note was like Johnny. It read simply:

You were right and I was wrong, or you wouldn't be handling this dough. I don't want vengeance—just retribution. See that Angelina has the money. If you think it best she doesn't know it came from me—okay? Otherwise— well, I'm a conceited guy. It would flatter my bones to know she knew I was a success—and hadn't forgotten. Angelina Ferra—Pearlman's Department Store, Delancey Street. Sales Girl.

Johnny.

A success. That was a laugh. I looked at my watch. There was time yet. I shoved it all in a suitcase and made the bank. I didn't deposit it. Not that it could ever be traced, but I'm not in the habit of making deposits of a hundred grand. I got myself a new safe deposit box, of good size, and shoved the money away.

I'd look up this Angelina Ferra. And I'd decide then if I'd give her the lump sum, or make a trust fund out of it. Or have it paid to her by installments, through a lawyer of course. Any thought of returning the money to its rightful owners was out of the question. It might have come from a thousand and one different places. Maybe more. It was a lot of jack.

In a way it was fun. The heart of a gangster. Like a movie. A killer and a criminal and a crook—and a poor girl on the lower East Side that Johnny Sharp had secretly, and evidently subconsciously, loved all his life. And at his death—the payoff.

Delancey Street hasn't changed so much over the years. It was a Saturday night. The street was crowded. The sign over the door read simply, PEARL-MAN'S. It was called a department store and did have a second story and a basement.

Business was terrific. A mass of humanity struggled through the place. I pushed through the mob and, with a little help from other sales girls, found Angelina Ferra. Slim and delicate, and tired-looking—but pretty with great black eyes. Tiny too.

I told her I had to see her. That my business was extremely confidential, and she mustn't mention to anyone that it was about money she might receive.

She was smart, too. She put those dark eyes on me.

"It would cost me my job if I left now," and she wrote down her address for me, said, "Go see my father. I'll be home in an hour." And when I put in the confidential part, "Tell father everything. I keep nothing from my father."

I went to see her old man. They could use Johnny's money all right. It was three dingy rooms and a kitchen on a side street. The place was clean, but the odors from the rest of the house and the dampness seeped in.

HER FATHER WAS old and had rheumatism. He took me in to what he called the sitting room. And I guess it was.

"Tell me something about yourself—about Angelina," I said.

"Lawyer?" he looked at me as he tried to arrange his bad leg. "You say something of interest to my girl. Money. No, no, she is not thinking of getting married. She thinks only of me, of feeding me, and housing me. Perhaps when I am dead. You have not stated your business clearly, Mr. Williams."

I told him there might be some money coming to Angelina. What would she do with it? What would he suggest?

"Suggest?" He looked at me with tired eyes. "I'm an old man now. No longer can I push the cart. For years and years I pushed. I save money. Much money for a store of my own. Then the money was taken from me."

"Stolen?"

"Taken. He wanted it and he took it. No, no. I did not go to the police. Understand, sir, I am not against the police. They serve their purpose. But they are not for my kind. I go to the police—and this man, he kill me. Maybe Angelina, too. I could have bought a store then. Yes—even Pearlman's—I had enough saved."

"Today it would cost more?"

"Today," he said, "Pearlman's is a great bargain. But Pearlman is an old man and the relatives, they do not agree. He would sell out for a song."

"A few thousand dollars?" I thought of the dump.

"You joke?" He looked at me. "It is worth—perhaps a hundred and ten thousand dollars. But for seventy, it can be bought. Lease and good will and stock. Angelina. She knows the clothing business. She could help me run it. Now she wastes money to study painting. An artist. Bah! There is no money in it. Her painting, it is not a help for me."

"What became of the money you had saved? What happened to the man who took it? Has he money today?"

"Today?" Old Ferra straightened in the worn rocker. "He has nothing. He is dead. As he lived, so did he die. He was shot to death."

"Johnny Sharp?" The words jarred out of me.

"You know him?" He came to his feet, wavered slightly. And when I explained that I had read it in the papers, he was somewhat mollified. But it took a bit of time to get the story out of him.

He had been kind to Johnny Sharp as a boy. Johnny's aunt had a great deal of trouble with him. But old Ferra thought there was good in Johnny. Little Angelina had worshipped him.

"I never let her know. Good fortune had it that she was staying with a friend that night. Johnny came here. He knew where the money was hidden. He had to have it. I begged and screamed, but he knocked me down and took it, and told me that he would give it back to me. He had to have it. I did not let her know—not Angelina—not anyone. That is all."

"That is all?" I asked.

"All, but that he held me by the throat and said that he would kill me. Then, too, I half believed him he would give it back. But no. Already he had killed a man. Since then he has killed men. One hears. I never saw him again."

"But Angelina has seen him?"

"No."

"Does she speak about him often? Was she in love with him?"

"But she hardly knew him. As a child, she adored him. Yes, yes." He bobbed his head. "He had his ways. But he was no good."

I CAUTIONED HIM then about telling no one of Angelina's good fortune. That things were not yet arranged. I put off all his questions about who left the money to Angelina, as he rattled off names of relatives who were long since dead, and others he had not heard of since he left Europe forty-seven years before. But he was the one who hit on the idea I left with him. That some wealthy person that Angelina had been kind to, had left her the money.

I did see Angelina. I did have a long talk with her—alone. I did see some of her paintings. And where I don't know much about art, it made me favor the dry goods business. She did know that business—and did want her father to have a store. In fact, she thought of nothing but her father. And she wasn't suspicious of me.

"Why, you are Race Williams," she said, and I liked the way she put it. "I have known of you all my life. There was a boy once. He read me all about you. How you hunted criminals. You were his hero, yet he became a—a—I guess he always was a criminal."

"You were in love with this boy?"

She smiled rather sadly. "When I was a child, I used to think I would marry him when I grew up. I wouldn't have, of course. He stole all my father's savings."

"Johnny Sharp?"

"You know him—knew him?"

"Your father told me. He doesn't know you knew about the money."

"No, father doesn't know. It is better that way, I think."

"Now this Johnny Sharp is dead?"

"He's been dead to me a very long time."

"You didn't go on—loving him?"

"No. It didn't matter. I guess there were two Johnny Sharps. The one I knew died a long time ago. The other one, I never knew. Now they are both dead."

"You never saw him again?"

"Yes—at least I think so. At least twice by the store—and once here across the street. But maybe I was imagining things. He couldn't have thought we had any more money."

I got her promise to say nothing. Assured her that her days of being poor were over. Said I wasn't at liberty to divulge where the money came from— that I wasn't sure myself. Which was true enough. I cautioned her again to silence.

I turned for a last look at her in the doorway downstairs as I went into the night. She was a picture framed there in the dim light of the dirty, electric bulb. A picture that Johnny had seen waiting in the doorway of some distant farm house. The only hitch was that—that she wouldn't have been there.

Likable guy Johnny. The heart of a gangster, eh? The copy books are right. Gangsters don't have any hearts. I didn't feel so bad about Johnny getting the dose, now. Retribution? And I thought Johnny had misused the word. But—retribution was right.

CHAPTER 3

COUGH UP—OR COFFIN

PICKING UP MY car, I drove leisurely uptown. I parked a little way down from the door of my apartment house, stepped from the car, then drew back hard against it. My gun jumped from under my armpit into my jacket pocket. My hand gripped it tightly and my finger caressed the trigger.

Standing by my apartment door was the rugged, broad figure of Himmie Zimmerman. The numbers man, the shake-down artist. A leader in the system that played upon the public and fixed the right people. Parked, one on each side of him, were two men. Two men, who like myself, kept their hands sunk in coat pockets.

Himmie Zimmerman spotted me almost at once, and moved slowly across the sidewalk toward me. The two men detached themselves from the building and joined him; crowding close on either

side of him. It was a rough-looking trio. Slowly they paced toward me.

Like a movie scene you think. You wouldn't if it was you pressed with your back against the car and you knew Zimmerman's rep, and saw the two figures with him and heard the tramp of their feet. Slow, even, moving feet. It was done for effect, all right. And it got the effect. What's more, it pretty nearly got Himmie a breadbasket full of lead.

"Hello, Race!" Himmie said in that slow even voice of his. "What's the idea of leaning against the car? Afraid the old boat will collapse on you? Not nervous, are you boy?"

"No," I said. "Anything to be nervous about?"

"I wouldn't think so," he said. "I'm here to put some money in your hands."

"That's nice." I could see that Himmie's hands swung free and empty at his sides, but I had to watch the hands of the other two. It was not a nice job.

He waited perhaps thirty seconds after that. In fact I think he counted them off. Then he said.

"Okay, Race. You and I are going to have a little talk. Turn, walk across the street and step into my car. I'll point it out to you."

"I'm not walking, Himmie," I told him.

"Nervous, eh? A little scared. That isn't like you. Race. Maybe I didn't make things quite clear. I'll count five and then—"

"Himmie!" My wrist stiffened. My finger tightened. "I'll do the counting. I'm counting to three, and then if those hoods of yours don't pull their hands out of their pockets empty—I'll plug you."

"No kidding, Race," he said quite seriously.

"No kidding," I told him.

"Okay, boys." Himmie's laugh was pleasant. "Pull you hands out empty. We had our little joke."

The hands came out empty. Had I bluffed Himmie successfully? No—for I wasn't bluffing. I'd have shot him all right. I know Himmie. It would have been his life, or mine. More likely both of us. And where that wouldn't do me any good, it wouldn't do Himmie any good either.

"Well," Himmie said, "it's nice to meet up with a guy so you know where you stand. Can I come up to your diggings and have a little talk with you?"

"Minus the gorillas," I told him.

"Sure, Race. Sure, boy," he said easily. "I wasn't thinking of you, Race, when I brought the boys along. Okay, boys. You wait for me here. You know them, Race?"

"I know Jordan," I said, nodding at the one on the right. He raised his head then and I saw his face.

"The other boy is Fitzgerald," Himmie said. "Meet Mr. Williams, Fitz," and when that fedora-clad head jerked up and down, "A new boy, Race. Hopes to take Butch's place some day. Poor old Butch." And walking toward the apartment door, "Say—you don't mind? I have a rod."

"That's all right, Himmie," I told him, and loud enough for the others to hear as we turned in the doorway. "It's all right if you want to try and use it, too, Himmie."

"All right for you or for me?" Himmie's laugh rang out loud in the deserted lobby.

WE WENT UP in the automatic elevator and into my apartment. Himmie tossed his coat over on the couch and dropped into an easy-chair. He was a broad, squat man in his middle thirties. He tried to make his face jovial, but only succeeded in showing his teeth and opening his eyes too wide.

"Would you have shot downstairs?" he asked.

"Yes," I said. "Don't worry that you were bluffed."

"You must have thought it something important then, something big."

"It should be—to bring you out in person."

He was a bit flattered, for he waved a deprecating hand. "You, Race. You're big in your line, and I'm big in mine. You've been smart and never crossed the system—nor me. Now it's like this. There are a hundred good shots in my organization," and when my eyes widened, "well I might say I could lay my hands on a hundred good shots. Maybe only two or three as quick and as sure as you. Maybe I'm the only one who could drop you like a log. But a hundred men shooting from cars or behind ash cans—well—you wouldn't like that, would you?"

"It might be annoying," I admitted.

"Now, I'd have to have a good reason. A very good reason for putting the finger on you like that. You wouldn't take it as friendly, would you?"

"Why not try it out," I said, "and see what happens?"

That puzzled him. His mouth closed and set hard, and his eyes tightened. "I don't get you," he said. "Elucidate."

"Try it," I repeated, "and I'll elucidate."

"You mean you'd shoot all of them to death?" His supposedly jovial look was coming back.

"Look, Himmie," I told him. "I'm no superman. Remember, too, that your idea is not an original one—to threaten me with half the gunmen in New York. It's been done before. I'd simply figure that the man who gives the orders is the same as the man who fires the shots. So make your first gunman a good one. If he misses me, why I'll plug you the first time I see you—and I'll be looking for you."

"A good point under ordinary circumstances." Himmie bobbed his head up and down in agreement. "A couple of things wrong with it though. I wouldn't be acting as an individual, so my death, if you were lucky enough to pull it off, would not call off the hundred men. The system would still want you."

"Okay," I said, "think of that when they toss the dirt in on your face and take what satisfaction you can out of it. I'm simply telling you I'm no hood. You can't finger me. Is that all you have to tell me?"

"Now, now, Race. I'm simply stating a hypothetical case. Don't you want to know the reason for my coming?"

"I thought you told me. To put the finger on me."

"No, no. It's to put some money in your pocket." He leaned forward suddenly and his eyes got narrow and his mouth grew hard. "Johnny Sharp," he said, "was a crook and a double-crosser. He copped himself one hundred grand, and was running out on the boys. He was dumped over on Thirty-fourth in broad daylight.

He sent that hundred grand to you. I want it. I want it now."

I WHISTLED, LOOKED at the ceiling. "You don't believe that?" I said, finally.

"Can it, Race. I'm laying my cards on the table. I know. Now you're a square shooter, so you are not planning on copping the money. Johnny offered you a rake-off to—"

He paused there, so I knew he didn't know what I was to do with it.

"To do what?" I lit a cigarette and smiled at Himmie with disbelief, or what I hoped he would think was disbelief.

"Look, Race," he said. "It wasn't Johnny's money. It belongs to the system. Once the system knows who has it—think of your chances of living."

"So." I understood now. "The system doesn't know. Only you know. An idea that. You'd like the money for yourself."

"No, no." He shook his head and tried to look sad at my lack of understanding. "I'm giving you a break, Race. I'm the only one who knows about the money, and who has it. Look, boy. You don't want what don't belong to you. I know that. I know you. I'll give you five—no—ten grand, and never a complaint. Surely Johnny promised you something."

"Use your head, Himmie," I said. "Why would Johnny Sharp give me money? Can you think of one reason?"

"I can think of a half a dozen." He jammed that in on me as he came to his feet. "It came to you by express. You got it today. You took it to the bank."

That jarred me a bit. If I had been followed to the bank, why I could have been followed downtown and to Angelina's. But good sense saved me there. One hundred grand was a lot of money. I'd never have reached the bank with it, if I was followed—if Himmie knew. Johnny Sharp was shot down on Thirty-fourth Street because of a hundred grand he didn't have. What would have happened to me on a side street with the money in my possession, is not hard to guess. No, Himmie knew that I would naturally take it to a bank.

"Okay, Race." Himmie was putting on his coat now. "You'll see things my way. You better come and tell me. If I have to come and tell you, why there won't be any ten grand in it for you—just a wooden box."

He was walking toward the door when I threw myself back in the chair and burst out laughing. I was still laughing when I went to the front door and put the chain on. I came back into the living-room and finished my laugh. Get the point?

A hundred gunmen out to kill me? Nonsense. Himmie would think more of my life than I did of it myself. Why? Because the moment I died he lost the hundred thousand dollars. A hundred thousand dollars of tax free money. It sure was a lot of jack. And Himmie Zimmerman was known as a man of greed, of great greed.

At that, the laugh might have served a good purpose. It might have made Himmie doubt that I had the money after all. Though how he had found out, I couldn't figure.

I was perfectly safe until Himmie was sure he couldn't get the money from me.

Until he let the system in on the truth—and he forgot greed and the underworld cried out for vengeance.

When would that be? That would be when Himmie was sure, beyond all doubt, he couldn't put the dough deep down in his own pocket. But how had he known? I felt that he couldn't have known—that he was only guessing. Not good figuring, that. Maybe not. You figure it out then. I went to bed.

CHAPTER 4

HIMMIE WINS

Next morning, my newspaper told me in a rather alarming way that Himmie Zimmerman was not guessing. Himmie Zimmerman knew. And it told me just how he knew.

It was buried away inside the paper. A couple of paragraphs only. It was not nice reading. A Marie Canope, a long time resident of the East Side, had been tortured and beaten to death. The article gave no reason for the fiendish crime except to hint that the "aged woman must have been suspected of having hidden funds." But it was the last line that gave the show away—at least to me. It read:

The old woman, so brutally done to death, was a distant cousin or aunt of the gunman shot to death on 34th Street the other day. She took care of him as a young boy.

So Himmie Zimmerman used his head as well as his gun. He knew that Johnny

Sharp had the money. He knew that Johnny Sharp would have to go back a good many years to find anyone he could trust with it. And the old woman had told Himmie, before she died, that she had sent the money to me.

I worried a bit. Himmie would know the money was not given me to keep. Witness how he had gone straight to the last relative that Johnny Sharp had had. Look how Himmie had gone back into Johnny's past. So far, he had avoided the dames, in the racket and around the clubs, that Johnny played along with. Would he continue to go back into Johnny's past and come up with old man Ferra and his daughter Angelina? That didn't seem possible. I was building up fears that were groundless.

My apartment house was watched all right. I felt no personal danger, as my life was as important to Himmie Zimmerman as it was to myself—at least while the hundred grand was tied up I wasn't followed.

I made sure of that.

I went to my office and attended to a little business. Then I went to Frank Donigan, the lawyer—and a good one. I didn't pull names on him, as yet. I told him a hundred grand was coming to a certain young girl, and it would be used to purchase a business. I asked which was the best way to go about it.

"Hot money?" Frank had a most unpleasant direct way of stating things.

"Not hot," I told him. "A gift from the dead, but she's entitled to it."

"Spill it," he said. "Disguise it all you want, but make it about the same story."

I did.

"You say—" he looked at me—"the business will cost all of seventy thousand dollars? Restitution of some kind. That will be the thing, Racc. Maybe it can be swung for thirty thousand dollars, but I don't—"

"Robber—" I started in, but Frank stopped me.

"Easy does it, boy," he said. "There's the government tax you know. The income tax, to say nothing of an inheritance tax."

I HADN'T THOUGHT of all that. If I had, I wouldn't have needed a smart lawyer. I told him that.

"Too bad that you are set on buying this young lady a business. I knew a man once—" Frank set back and let his fingers pound together—"who found twice that much money. His partner swiped it on him thirty years before. No tax there, but it cost something to convince the government. Now, if it was simply a trust fund that we could set up through some bank, I could work it. Indeed I could. Not tax free, of course—but where there would be plenty of money in it for everyone. Not hot money you say?"

"No, it isn't. I'll be seeing you about it later."

And that was all I told him then. And I decided, too, after Himmie's visit, that I better stay away from Angelina and her father for a bit.

A hundred grand is a lot of money. Yet, there wasn't a peep out of Himmie Zimmerman all that day. I should have been relieved, but I wasn't. It wasn't natural. There wasn't a more vicious or a greedier man in the criminal life of the city.

The doorman, Gus, at my apartment

handed me a sealed envelope. I tore it and stared at the faintly perfumed blue paper, and the name Angelina Ferra printed across the top amid some flowers. Note paper that was a Christmas or birthday present—and bought at "the store," no doubt. Each of the three times I read the note, I grew more alarmed.

The note said:

Dear Mr. Williams:

I know I shouldn't have come, but father insisted on it. He hardly slept all night. He was so excited.

He wants to know if it will be all right for him to go and have a talk with Mr. Pearlman. He's afraid the business might be sold.

I telephoned your office, but didn't go there, as you said the money was all very confidential.

If I did wrong, please forgive me. But father is that way. You are turning out like the prince in a young girl's dreams.

Affectionately and gratefully yours,
Angie.

I questioned Gus Brown, the doorman. He was a big, good-natured lad who's only claim to greatness was that he was a prize fighter who had never been knocked off his feet. I went about it so as not to make him suspicious. A hundred grand was a lot of money.

"Still never been knocked off your feet, Gus?" I asked.

"You will have your little joke, Mr. Williams," he laughed. "Some day you'll have to feel that chin of mine—take a crack at it. Iron jaw, they called me. I doubt if I'd feel it if you hit me. Now what was it you wanted to know?"

I put it to him—about Angie. No, he hadn't seen anyone watching the apartment. No, no one had questioned him.

"She was a sweet, shy, delicate little thing, Mr. Williams—I watched her around the corner." And when I gave him a generous tip, "Thank you, Mr. Williams. It will come in handy. I get a couple of days off starting tomorrow."

Did she do wrong? Angie had written. How wrong? I thought of that as I rode the subway downtown.

THINGS WERE WRONG all right. I knew that as soon as I saw Angie's old man. She had returned from trying to see me. Gone to her job at the store. She left the store with a man. The same man who had visited and questioned her father.

It was unpleasant and it was tough. I was mad and scared too. She was a nice little thing, was Angie. I should have shipped the two of them out of the city at once. I thought of the store that her father wanted and of the painting that Angie wanted.

"She looked so sweet." Old Ferra nodded his head. "A new dress to call on you, Mr. Williams. It took all her savings, but it was a bargain. She went to the store. Then this man came here to see me. It was, perhaps, an hour after she got back from looking for you. He said it was about money. She didn't return from the store. I went there. She had left with this man."

"And Johnny Sharp." I almost shook the old man. "Did this man ask about him?"

"Yes, yes." He laughed nervously.

"I thought he said Johnny left her the money."

"Did you let him know you knew Sharp?"

"Yes." Ferra thought he was pretty shrewd. "I said very little. That we knew Sharp, yes. But not that he robbed me. Not that I didn't like Johnny even, not that. I thought this man was a lawyer. About the money for Angelina. You didn't send him?"

"No, I didn't send him."

It was then that it hit him. He wasn't all greed now. He gripped me by both shoulders.

"Angie. Angie. It is something terrible about her. It's that Johnny Sharp."

"Sharp is dead."

"Dead or alive, he's evil. He's visited us again with evil."

How right he was, he couldn't know. Didn't know.

I got him to pack a bag. Scribbled him a note where he was to go and saw him started off in a taxi. Then I made a telephone call to the place in Jersey where I was sending him.

A good sign that. I must have had hope of rescuing the girl. For my only idea in shipping off the old man was, well it would be stupid to find the girl, then have Himmie snatch her father and so make her fork over the dough for his life.

But it did look bad. I could make a deal with Himmie, no doubt. He had the girl and I had the money. But I knew what kind of a deal I could make with that hood. Pearlman's seventy thousand dollar store. Blooey. They'd be lucky if there was enough money left to get out the old push cart and give it a coat of fresh paint.

Himmie Zimmerman was a clever lad. No mistake about that. I sat in my apartment until close to eleven o'clock and wondered what was happening to the girl. That was what Himmie wanted me to do. Then he wanted me to come and see him. That was the last thing I would do, or rather the last thing I should do.

Going to the police or the system would knock Himmie right out of the cash. And, no doubt, cost the girl her life.

Going to Himmie would cost the girl the money. Sitting tight would bring—what?

Himmie won out. At eleven-fifteen I had done enough thinking about the girl. I went downtown and saw Himmie.

CHAPTER 5

RECORD OF A SCREAM

Himmie Zimmerman had what he called offices up over Andy's Tavern, just off Broadway. What's more, he kept me waiting close to half an hour. He was sitting behind a big desk when I came in. He spoke to the silent, rough-looking Jordon, who showed me up to his office.

"Leave us alone, Jordon. Wait outside the door. You know how nervous Race is. He might be afraid to be alone with me. Okay, close the door."

When we were alone, I said, "What makes you think I'll pay money for the girl? Would you?"

"No, I wouldn't," he said abruptly, and grinned at me. "But, then, I haven't got your high ideals. I'm sort of sorry you came in, Race. I was looking forward to a bit of fun tonight." And letting that sink in, "But business is business."

"Okay." I shrugged. "What's the deal? How much?"

"One hundred thousand dollars." He leaned forward over the desk. "All of it. Every single penny of it. And for every day you wait, it goes up a thousand."

"Out of my pocket." I took a laugh at that. But not a very good laugh.

"Yes, out of your pocket. And out of the girl's hide. She's your client. You're her prince." He sneered. "Give me that spiel about your sacred duty to a client that I've heard up and down the Avenue." He leaned back in his chair. "Think of it. Johnny Sharp. Some of the swellest dames along the Avenue, and he dumps all that dough on that bit of fluff. I know he never trusted any of the crowd. That's why I put the heat on the old dame downtown and found out where the money went. Yet, if it hadn't been for you, and Angie Ferra calling on you, I never would have found her."

"You—you saw her go in. How did you know?"

"Gus, the doorman," he said, and when I stared at him, "Sure—sure. You give him a buck now and then, and a few bucks at Christmas. I slipped him a hundred dollar bill, so we steamed open the note. As easy as that. Money will do anything."

"Okay," I said. I tried to hold in from boiling over. "When you feel reasonable, give me a buzz."

"In the meantime?" he asked.

"I'll sit tight, or spring it on the boys in your racket. They don't know, do they?"

"No." He shook his head. "They don't know. They are not going to. My own little transaction. Of course, if you sing—" he shrugged his shoulders—"you'll have to fork over the dough or have those hundred gunners on your tail. I don't like you, Race. I don't like you at all. I didn't like your laugh last night." His mouth was very tight. "I'll cut her to ribbons, and every nick I take in her, will be a nick in you."

Himmie was a bad actor. None worse along the Avenue. I had never seen such pate and viciousness in a human face before. And greed. Himmie had money. How much I didn't know. I thought plenty. Yet, above everything, he wanted that hundred grand.

My right hand was half raised and across my chest—and so was his.

"Pull a gun if you want to, Race. What good would it do you? The boys would burn you down."

"At the worst," I said, "it would get me a one hundred thousand dollar funeral."

"On me," he nodded. "It might be worth it. It might be, at that. I hope you sleep well tonight. Angie won't."

"If anything happens to that girl—I'll kill you," I told him.

"She's worth a lot of money alive," he said. And when I backed to the door, "Nothing will happen to her yet. Nothing a good plastic surgeon can't fix up."

What was I trying to do? Why, salvage as much of that money for Angie as I could. He couldn't kill the girl, for he knew I wouldn't hand over the money until I knew that she was safe. And there was always the chance that something might break. I might get a lead on where the girl was. Sure, I told myself that nothing would happen to the girl. Himmie was too greedy. But it bothered me.

I didn't sleep too well that night. In fact it was a tough night.

UNQUESTIONABLY, HIMMIE HELD the cards. I was about to pay him another visit the next day. Maybe I could salvage some money for Angie.

I didn't see Gus Brown, the doorman, when I left the apartment. Big good-natured Gus—the dirty two-timer!

There across the street, watching my apartment house, was Jordon. He didn't try and hide himself or duck me. I never figured Jordon as a lad who used his head. A sort of brainless Himmie—who never used two words if one would do—and never used one if none would fill the bill. A bodyguard, an animal of the night. An easy killer that Himmie gave a few century notes to now and then to go off and get drunk. That was Jordon. A dame and liquor. Then broke and back to Himmie again. Never a drop on duty. That was his life. The only life he wanted. I bet he never had over three hundred bucks at one time.

And it hit me. It was Himmie's idea. Just as simple as that. Himmie had told me. I walked across the street and straight up to Jordon. He grinned. At least he showed his teeth. Jordon's business was being tough. He was. He never quit playing the part.

I didn't say anything. I simply grinned back at him, tossed open my coat a little, and drove my gun hard into his stomach.

"You and I are going to take a little trip together, Jordon," I said. "Want to come easy, or will I take a look at what you had for breakfast?"

Jordon was dumfounded. This was something that happened to others—not to him. This was something he did, but did not have done to him. But he knew the rule of life. The man with the gun talks—the man without, listens.

"You wouldn't blast me out. Not here, Race. You wouldn't dare."

"Reach for a gun—and find out, Jordon," I told him. "Now listen. I've got something to show you. It's not a one way trip. My word on that. Have I ever broken my word?"

He thought that over a long time. I saw his head nod up and down. He knew that I hadn't. I had built that reputation along the Avenue. Every criminal knew I kept my word. It was what made my business possible. Jordon knew it. I suppose he thought I was a sap for keeping it.

"Yeah," he said.

"Remember Doggie Joe?" And when I saw recognition dawning in those odorless eyes, "I went to bat for him. Got in bad with the cops, and he double-crossed me too. But I stuck to my word—remember?"

"Yeah, yeah, I remember all right. I never figured why."

"Business," I told him. "It's paid me off handsome. You know I work often between you guys and the cops. I arranged that Long Island snatch ransom for Porkey Stokes, the gambler. The ruby necklace for Henley, the race track booky."

I was giving him all this for a purpose. It was true, too. Everyone knew about those cases. Even the cops knew, but they couldn't prove it. But Jordon knew. He nodded vigorously in understanding.

"What's it to me?" he asked.

"You'll find out," I told him. "Come along. It will be worth your while."

He came. I put him in my car and frisked him. One rod, nothing else. I was surprised.

"No sap? No knife?"

"Nix," he said. "I got a license for that gun. Himmie knows the right people. Where we going?"

"A place you'd like to go alone."

His narrow eyes widened when we reached the bank. When we went down to the safety deposit vaults, he fairly purred. I explained him to the old man who unlocked the heavy steel door and let us in.

"Value some stuff for me," was all I said.

Jordon hesitated a moment, but he knew his way around, and signed in the big book under my signature. Not too dumb there, either. No Jones or Smith—and certainly not Jordon. Alfred G. Arden was what he put down.

Jordon was interested. He didn't speak. He watched the guard put his key alongside mine in the box and open it. He didn't say a word as I counted out ten thousand dollars. I did it slowly and deliberately.

He watched me put those bills in an envelope. Ten thousand dollars' worth of them, but he didn't see the rest of the money. I put an elastic band around that envelope, and back we went with my steel box. I shoved it into the wall and locked it up. Then Jordon and I left the bank.

I took him to a little tavern on a side street. We slipped into a darkened booth. He hesitated, then took a cup of coffee.

"Jordon," I said. "You're a good listener. I'm interested in a girl that Himmie is interested in. He wants something from me that I can't give him. If he doesn't get it, he'll harm the girl. I wouldn't like that. Himmie can't win, but I can lose. Now, you saw that ten grand go in that envelope. If someone should call me on the phone tonight before ten o'clock, and tell me where that girl is—and I should get her—and if I was alive at twelve noon tomorrow, I'd come back to this bar and give you that ten grand in cash."

I drank half my beer and waited. He didn't say anything.

"Of course," I said, "this is very hush hush. So hush that Himmie is playing it alone. I mean it as a personal business—not with the system. But you would know that."

I came to my feet then, and watched Jordon sip his coffee. There was no expression on his face. He simply nodded when I gave him his gun back and slipped it into his pocket as carelessly as if it was a pack of cigarettes.

I leaned both my hands on the table. "My word on that," I said. "My word that I will never bring up the name of the man I may think telephoned me."

Jordon still said nothing.

"Good-bye for the time being, Jordon," I said. "Ten grand for a one-minute phone call."

I walked out of the tavern and climbed into my car. I spent the rest of the time at my apartment. I didn't see the doorman who could be bought for a hundred bucks. Then I remembered his few days off.

I waited by the phone. We'd see how good Himmie was on what you could do with money. Greed again!

The call came at ten o'clock exactly. I would guess it was Jordon's voice. It said, "The package is at Three Forty-one, A, West Seventy-sixth Street. Mr. Big will be alone with it. He has to sleep. Third floor, rear room, right. Go by way of the cellar, rear window."

That was all. The phone clicked up. Was it a real break? Was Jordon simply assuring himself of the money by making it easy for me? Or had he spilled to Himmie and was he following instructions? Was I to walk into a trap? I didn't know. But I was going. Himmie would not be above torturing the girl to get the money from me. And what's more, he would get it if I didn't get Angie first.

I had doubts and thoughts. Should I go at two o'clock? Or should I improvise on Jordon's instructions? Hit the house a couple of hours earlier. Go in by a different window. Spring the trap before it was ready. Be smart. Be clever or—be myself?

Okay, I had taken this leaf from Himmie's book. I'd stick to his book. If I was a fool, I'd be a fool all the way. Not just half an idiot.

Maybe I was smart by playing it Himmie's way—Jordon's way. At one o'clock the phone rang. It was Himmie.

"Still up?" he said. "Worrying about little Angie? Want to hear a good record? Something new? Listen."

It came, Sharp and shrill, and tore at me inside. The agonized shriek of a girl in pain. Angie, of course. I wanted to display an indifference, would have if I'd had any warning. But it came so suddenly. The curse and threat of what I'd do to Himmie shot out of my mouth. Himmie laughed.

"That soul of honor, eh, Race?" he said. "That great interest in your client! You can't do anything boy, because I have the girl. And you think I can't do anything because you have the money. Six o'clock tomorrow night, with all the dough, or I'll put on a show for you that'll— Listen!"

Again the shriek of agony. This time I didn't break out. I held myself.

"Six o'clock tomorrow, Himmie, I'll see you," I said. There was no answer, but he was listening, for the phone did not click. Then the click came. I hung up. I looked at the clock. It was eight minutes after one a.m.

All right. I had the two o'clock appointment at the house on 76th Street. If it failed… I shrugged my shoulders. It was a lot of money to turn over to that slimy hood, Himmie Zimmerman.

But, then, I had heard the girl scream and you hadn't.

CHAPTER 6

WOULD IT BE MURDER?

I DIDN'T THINK there would be an outside watch at the house on 76th Street. I drove by to make sure. There wasn't. I left my car at the corner and walked back. The houses were all alike. Stone steps, iron railings, four-story affairs. Well worn old-timers, mostly in need of paint.

A few of them were still private dwellings. All had been in their day. Now most of them rented rooms. Some of them were divided into apartments.

I turned into an alley a couple houses down, and went through the yards in the back. Small yards they were, with wooden fences, one of which I had to climb. The others I simply moved, loose boards.

I found the cellar window. I used my gun. It was nice to have it in my hand. I tapped out a hunk of glass. The tinkle as it hit the floor inside was hardly audible. I put my hand through the hole I had made and unhooked the window. As easy as that. It is always easy to get into a place. Not so easy to get out—that is, get out alive.

The window was narrow and long. There was room enough and I made it. A bad minute that. For I had to slide in with my back to any flash of light—and flash of a gun. Sure I thought about a gun, and lead too. But I was gambling on greed. Jordon's greed for ten thousand dollars that there wouldn't be a man with a gun there. Himmie Zimmerman's greed for one hundred thousand dollars that if he was there with a gun—he wouldn't use it.

No crack on the head. No gun against my ribs. I breathed better. I was in the cellar, both feet flat on the floor, and I had turned around. Certainly that window had been the logical point of attack.

My pocket flash found the cellar stairs. I cat footed up them, found the door at the top, sprung the knob. It was locked. An annoyance, that. Nothing more. My skeleton key, the kind you can buy in almost any dime store, did the trick. A quick stab against the key on the other side, the thud as it hit the kitchen floor, and I had the door open and was in the kitchen. Gun ready. Waiting.

The fall of the key disturbed no one. Why should it? A little after two in the morning. If Jordon had given me a right steer—and so far it seemed he had, why should it disturb anyone? Surely Himmie would be up on the third floor keeping close to his hundred thousand dollar "package."

The house was strange to me. I had to use my flash. The furniture in the dining-room was old, substantial, even massive. There was a side door to the hall at the back of the stairs. I didn't hesitate. A lad makes as much noise, and more, creeping around as he does fast stepping it.

THE GUN IN my right hand was raised. The flash in my left cast a pencil of light as I moved quickly up the two flights of stairs to the third floor. The old boards of the stairs gave up their dead.

I made the third floor. I had to go easy on the light now. A door was open down the hall. Another door at the end to the right—the room Jordon told me held the girl.

It could be a trap yet. It could be—well, the girl didn't have to be there. Any time bullets could come out of the dark.

I slipped by the first open door and made the room at the end. I listened. Was there labored breathing? I stepped inside. A bit of a wait then until I had located that breathing. Was it the girl, or was it the man, Himmie? And let me tell you it is not easy to locate breathing in a dark room, and I've had a lot of experience.

Then it came. A sob, plainly a sob. A relief, that. Jordon had not played me false. That could hardly be Himmie. But was Himmie in the room also? I crouched low on the floor and chanced it.

"Angie," I whispered. "Quiet! Are you alone?"

And out of the darkness, her voice. "Race—Race. It is you! I knew you'd come!"

"Are you alone?"

"Yes—oh yes! He looks in every now and then and—and—"

My light found her. She was crouched on some rugs in the corner of the room. Her hands were tied. Her feet were tied. Heavy rope was wound around those legs. I was across to her. My knife was out. I made quick work of the ropes. She cried softly and clutched at me frantically.

I couldn't stop her crying. Indeed, there was no necessity. Tears and sobs would be natural enough and shouldn't disturb, or at least alarm, Himmie. If he came now, that might be best. He couldn't talk to the system if he were dead. And Himmie dead, meant me—alive!

He was coming.

The flash of light out in the hall from that open door. The dull thud of a foot hitting the floor, then another, as a man got out of bed. A gruff sound that might have been a curse. The soft but determined sound of bare feet that were set hard down.

I cautioned the girl once to silence, stepped to one side, lifted up my gun as Himmie Zimmerman entered that room. "Cut out the sniffling," he was saying. "I'll teach you."

The light flashed on. And there was Himmie Zimmerman. Of all things, in baby blue pajamas. His eyes were puffed in sleep. He had a stick in his hand that he raised when he snapped on the light. He held it so and looked at me. What's more, he looked at my gun, too.

Himmie, the killer, the gunman. He was caught flat footed. And, surprisingly, he didn't look nearly so formidable. He went through more expressions than a television comedian. It was some mugging.

"Good evening, Mr. Zimmerman!" I said. I felt pretty good. Wouldn't you? And to the girl, "Can you walk, Angie?"

HIMMIE MADE A quick recovery. It wasn't hard to tell now why he was one of the big shots in the payoff racket.

"Take it easy, Race," he said. "Don't go off half cocked. After all, you can't shoot me dead you know. Murder isn't your line. Sure, boy, you are smart. Very smart. But it is only for one night. I'll make a deal with you—fifty-fifty on that hundred grand and no trouble afterwards. My word."

I took a laugh.

But Himmie went right on talking. "Remember the hundred lads with a hundred guns I spoke about? Cop that money and they'll all be looking for you. I'll tell the boys what became of the money. They'll hunt the girl down no matter where you hide her out. As for you—well, your business is in the city. You can't hide out forever."

"We'll talk about it tomorrow, Himmie," I told him. What he said was true. And I might as well have as long as I could to fix the girl up.

"No, no." Himmie shook his head. "You're simply stalling for time. I'll use the phone as soon as you've gone. A split, boy—"

And, suddenly realizing that I wasn't going to split with him, he turned nasty—that is, in his thoughts. He didn't come out with it. A lad without a gun doesn't get nasty with a lad who is holding one.

"So you found me and the girl. How? I know. I know. Just one person—Jordon. What did you pay him? It would have to be—"

It was then that I hit him. I had edged closer to him as he talked. I got him back of the ear with my gun. He went down like a stuck pig. He had the blow coming to him because of the scream of the girl over the phone. But that isn't why I hit him. I like to tell myself that it was simply business to cover our get-away. I didn't want him getting a gun and shooting at us as we left the house—or went down the street.

But I could have tied him up. There was plenty of rope. No, I think mostly I struck him to save his life. Anyway, to save me from killing him. Everything he had said was true. They'd hunt the girl down and kill her if they could find her. They'd hunt me until they got me, or I got all of them. For I did have my business in the city, and I wouldn't run out.

I wished Himmie had come in with a gun belching lead and we had shot it out. Let us say, I simply struck him down. I don't know why. Maybe I was just mad. Maybe it was simply to keep myself from committing murder. For it is hard, at least I would have found it hard, to pump lead into an unconscious man on the floor.

Would it have been murder to save the girl's life and my life that way? Would it—

But enough of that. It's not nice thinking.

CHAPTER 7

KNOCKOUT FINISH

WE LEFT THEN. Angie could walk pretty well. She was such a slip of a thing that I could have carried her easily enough. Would have, too, except I didn't know what might turn up—and I wanted my gun arm and hand free.

I was right too. We left by the front door. It was a second before I closed it, that I heard the shot upstairs behind us. Where the bullet struck I don't know. I whistled softly. What a head Himmie must have had. Two minutes—well, three at most since I crashed him, and already he had come-to, run to his room, found a gun, and taken a pot shot at us down the stairs. But we were out of the house and away.

It was an easy drive downtown that time of morning. No traffic. I left Angie with Miss Duncan in Greenwich Village. Miss Duncan could be trusted, and in a day or two I'd get Angie out of the city.

She was a lovely little thing. Plenty of romance. She clung to me like a wet sock there in Miss Duncan's front room, and I would have liked it except I had so much on my mind.

"Father," she said. "He'll get the store after all. He'll be thrilled."

"No, Angie," I told her. "The money

has been left as an income for you—by someone who knew you, knew you painted. Now there will be enough for you to study painting and—"

"But father, he will be so disappointed."

"He'll have to take it," I told her. "There will be enough income for you to get out of that dirty dive and live in the country."

She was crying. Of all things. She liked where they were living, wanted to live and die and paint there.

I didn't tell her then that she couldn't do that. She should have known from the line Himmie had pulled. But, somehow, I don't think she got it. I left her with Miss Duncan.

In the morning, early, I saw Frank Donigan, the lawyer. He was pleased about the new arrangements. An income for Angie for life. He figured that he could do it for ten thousand dollars. All up and aboveboard and no squawk from the government. I let it go that way.

I met Jordon on time. If I expected him to be nervous and excited and scared, I was wrong. Perhaps he hadn't seen Himmie yet. I almost wished that I could have held off on the money. I felt pretty sure that in another twelve hours Jordon wouldn't be alive to collect. I thought I'd give him a little tip.

"You can't tell, Jordon," I told him. "If I were you, I'd hide out for a while, or take a powder."

He looked up at me. Poor dumb Jordon—just a silent gunman who always did what he was told—what he was paid for—and never a thought for himself. But now he made a little speech, almost an oration for Jordon.

"Himmie liked money too much," he said. "He was mean too. I'll never mention that you shot him to death last night. No more than you would mention it if I had done it."

"Better be careful," I warned him. I was anxious to see the last of Jordon. But I didn't tell him I hadn't shot Himmie to death.

"I got nothing to worry me. Just like you got nothing to worry you." Jordon pushed the envelope with the money in it back to me. "I'll call for it tonight. It wouldn't be a good time for me to be found with ten grand on me."

"Suppose you don't make it tonight—or ever." I was thinking of Himmie's suspicions.

"Then split it with the kid," he said, and when I nodded, he added quickly, "I'll be around for it. Here—" Jordon got suddenly to his feet and thrust a newspaper into my hand. "Extra. Just came out. You'll find it interesting reading."

He was gone and the bartender wanted to know what I'd have. I took a small beer, sat down and spread out the paper. It made the front page.

I guess my eyes popped. Himmie Zimmerman had been shot to death early that morning.

His body has been found in the house of a small time politician on 76th Street. A woman next door had heard the shot and notified the police. They had got in touch with the owner of the house who said he had lent it to Himmie Zimmerman while he was on an extended vacation.

Then it went on about the activities of Himmie Zimmerman. It left you with the impression that the police might suspect anyone of hundreds in the city of New York of the killing.

Poor, silent, dumb Jordon. He was a smarter man than Himmie—for he was alive, with ten thousand dollars coming to him, and Himmie was dead. It was simple enough. Jordon could be bought. But he wasn't one to pay with his life. He must have been there in that house when I found the girl. He had stepped into that room and put a bullet in Himmie's head as he lay there on the floor. That, then, was the shot I heard. It's rather nice having no scruples, like Jordon.

Jordon who had shot men for a few hundred dollars—even less. Why wouldn't he shoot Himmie for ten grand? The answer was that he did. After all, Himmie had made Jordon what he was. A professional killer. Why should friendship enter into it? It was simply business with Jordon.

Good business at that. Angie could stay down on the East Side and live and die there, and paint her pictures there and—well, you got to admit that a hundred men gunning for you is not a pleasant way to spend your time.

You think, perhaps, that I am morally responsible for Himmie Zimmerman's death. You think, perhaps, that it might even be suggested that I paid ten thousand dollars to have him killed. I don't think so. But I'm not one to argue the point. I don't know of another man in the city of New York who isn't better off dead, than Himmie Zimmerman.

Maybe I was wrong about Jordon. Maybe he wasn't so smart. Maybe all guys in his racket are dumb in the long run. He didn't come to see me that night. He wouldn't be coming any other might. It came over the air while I was waiting for his visit.

The system worked fast and violently. Maybe they didn't know for sure who gave the dose to Himmie Zimmerman. But they evidently knew who could have and who should have. I don't know. But it was simply a guess, it was a good one—and a quick one. That's right. Jordon's body was picked up alongside the golf course in Van Cortlandt Park. It was riddled with bullets.

I sighed and shrugged my shoulders. Then I took the money out of the envelope and started to count it.

Angie painted a picture of me. She sent it up to me. I was glad she had an income after seeing it. I wasn't mad. No one who saw it recognized me, though many were puzzled by the vacant look in the face. Maybe it was art. But it gave me an idea what to do with that extra ten thousand dollars. Half of it, say, for quick work on Angie's art. Half of it for my fee, and, maybe, a course for me in appreciation of art.

Is there more to tell? Just that Gus Brown, the hearty ex pug, was back on the job as doorman when I came in that night.

"Good evening, Mr. Williams," he beamed.

"Good evening, Gus," I said, and then, "Is it true that when you were in the ring you were never knocked off your feet?"

"That's true, sir." He beamed more and stuck his chin out. "They called me iron jaw. Just touch that chin, sir."

I touched it. I touched it with everything I had in my right hand. I was pleased, too. Maybe Gus had slipped since his days in the ring. Maybe for that single blow I was given superhuman strength. Anyway, Gus clicked his heels like soldiers on parade, and went down with his head in a potted plant—or what passed for a potted plant.

Gus got the point. I never did see him again.

CARROLL JOHN DALY

The Strange Case of Alta May

THE LYING GIRL

HE LOOKED MONEY. He looked class. He looked like the idle son of wealth. He swung into my office with a cane over his arm and a flower in his button hole. Big, broad-shouldered, handsome. Honest blue eyes. Nothing dissipated about him. I'd put him at close to thirty. The twenty side of it. He spoke his piece easily.

"I've read about you, Mr. Williams. Like the Canadian Mounted, you always get your man." And with that pleasant smile, "Though this time, it is a woman. The point is, what do you charge to listen—if you refuse a case?"

"Nothing," I told him. "But I listen better with a check in my hand. If I'm not interested, I'll return it. Any objection to that?"

"None whatsoever." His white even teeth showed. "But my bank might not like it. May I talk anyway?"

"Of course." Maybe I was not quite so cordial now. "You do have some means of digging up my fee, though?"

"With your aid, I believe so." And his

smile went and his lips tightened somewhat. "I could spend hours over the story with an enthusiasm and dramatic emotion that would surprise you. But I've boiled it down to cold facts. Shall I let you have it?"

"Let me have it," I said, "without the dramatics."

"My uncle," he began, "was Jarvis Harrington. He had no children of his own, but he adopted a daughter—Katherine. It was all legal and aboveboard. Aunt Clara—that was Uncle Jarvis' wife—died, and Uncle had the girl on his hands.

"She had a tough life. I guess he wanted her to be proficient at everything. So she simply messed around with music and painting and the classics—and stuff like that. She couldn't have boy friends and she couldn't have anything a young girl normally should have.

"I guess Katherine had spirit though, for in the long run she jumped the traces and married Uncle Jarvis' secretary, Tom Bronson, a man who really wanted to paint. Uncle Jarvis didn't just chuck her out and disinherit her. He hounded—yes, just like in an old melodrama—he hounded the man she had married. I guess he even accused him of stealing. Anyway, he fixed it up so Bronson couldn't get a job again. And I think he finally put it right up to Katherine. That if she didn't throw over Bronson—divorce him—why he'd press criminal charges and send him to jail."

For a moment, he paused, before continuing, "Then, according to my mother, there was one more big scene between Uncle Jarvis and his adopted daughter, Katherine. And it was the daughter, this time, who made the threat—against Uncle Jarvis! Katharine laid it on the line. If Uncle Jarvis so much as made one crack, one hint of accusation against her husband, Tom Bronson, Uncle Jarvis would never see her again. Nor her child, Alta May Bronson."

"So there was a child?" I mused. "How did the old man take the threat? And what made the adopted daughter think he'd want to see her again?"

"Yes, there was a child. What made her think he'd want to see her again? Well, I don't know. I guess Katherine thought Uncle Jarvis really cared." And after another pause. "And I guess she was right. When he died last year he left his entire estate to her, or in the event of her death, to her daughter. You see, Uncle Jarvis did threaten Katherine once more. And he never saw her or her husband or the little girl again."

"Did he hunt her up?"

"I don't know. He never said. He wasn't a man you'd ask about it. My father had died and my mother always thought I would get Uncle Jarvis' money. I ran second, so to speak—all or nothing. I got nothing. It was a lot of money. Five million dollars."

I INHALED a bit—recovered—said, "What do you mean, all or nothing?"

"Well, if the adopted daughter was still alive, it went to her—or her heirs. If not, I got it. Well, Katherine Bronson and her husband, Tom, were killed some eight years back. So when Uncle Jarvis died, their daughter Alta May, now grown, got the money."

"And this Alta May—the one who inherited the money—she's got it now? What is your beef?"

"My beef," he said slowly, "is that the girl who got the money is—is not Alta May Bronson!"

"An impostor, eh?" I shook my head. "It's hard to impersonate someone else when such a fortune is involved."

"It has been done, hasn't it?"

"Yes," I told him. "But then you don't need a detective. You need a lawyer. You can contest the will—claim fraud—I don't know what the legal terms are. It won't take a good lawyer long to find out if there is any cause for your suspicions. If he thinks there is, he'll fight it for you and take a nick out of your pile of the spoils."

He had an answer for that one. Not too good an answer, though. "I wouldn't want it dragged through the press."

"Silly," I told him. "You want what rightfully belongs to you. There is no disgrace in that."

"No, no, none whatever." He started to hunt for a cigarette, took the one I offered him and said, "If I were wrong, I'd look quite an ass, wouldn't I? Not that I haven't made quite an ass of myself on other occasions. But think of the girl." And when I refused to think of her, and waited, he leaned forward and spoke almost confidentially. "There are other complications—at least one. You see, Mr. Williams, I'm in love with the girl."

"And she?"

"Is Alta May in love with me? I don't know. I did think so. I did hope so anyway. Now, I doubt it. She won't see me any more, and I don't blame her for that."

"Tough," I told him and then truthfully, "I'm not of a romantic turn of mind, Mr.—" I looked down at his card which was inscribed, Frank Huntington Roberts—"Mr. Roberts. What are your reasons for believing she's an impostor? I can understand your reason for wanting to expose her."

"No, you can't," he told me and meant it. "I suppose I want what money belongs to me. But I want to marry the girl."

"And you think if your positions were reversed, things might be better?"

"Decidedly." He smiled, and when I didn't smile back, "Oh, I wouldn't threaten her or anything like that, Mr. Williams. I'd hope to make her love me again—in time."

"Very fine. Give me the grounds for your believing she is an impostor. Without the love interest, please."

Roberts' even, white teeth showed again. He seemed to have an unshakable good humor.

"I was away." He went right back to his rehearsed part. "When this girl who calls herself Alta May came back, took over the Yonkers house, the Southhampton place, and the lodge up in Maine—" He seemed to watch me there to see if I was impressed and, even if I didn't show it, I was. "Naturally I was disappointed that the property and the money didn't come to me. But I got curious, and since she was spending the season up in Maine, I went up there and had myself introduced to her under another name."

"Another impostor."

"Exactly." He was not ruffled, and he

didn't redden. "Now for the damning evidence. Alta May was not too familiar with the family, with her family, with my family, with the names she should have known."

"You questioned her—even though you were an impostor yourself?"

"Why not? I noticed she seemed to be avoiding the people she should meet—I mean those people her mother and father might have known. Well, there was the big scene—love scene, I mean. And of course I told her who I was and—and—"

"That ended that."

"That ended that," he agreed emphatically. He sucked in his lips and ran his tongue out over them. "Alta May was more frightened than angry at my revelation. More shocked than surprised."

"Any explanation—why she wasn't familiar with past events?"

"Yes. I'm afraid I was a little rough on her there. She said that her mother spoke little of such things. In fact, fragments only. That left her with no idea she was an heiress. She was surprised when she was—found."

"That," I told him, "would be natural of her mother, under the circumstances."

"That—" he didn't like the words nor the sound of his voice when he used them—"that would be the natural thing for her to say, too, if she were an impostor."

I agreed on that one. I went over things again with him. The difficulties of impersonating someone else. And when he tossed in more facts that only bore out what I was saying, I went on with it. It meant crooked lawyers, and he admitted that the firm in question had represented his Uncle Jarvis for years and were highly respected. It meant fooling the court. In fact, it meant it couldn't be done. And we came back where we started by my admitting to him that on occasion it had been done.

I wasn't interested. Roberts had good references. He was highly respectable. He was in a brokerage firm and quite frankly admitted he sold securities because of his connections. He was on his feet, but before I could dismiss him, he leaned over the desk and turned on his dramatics.

"I didn't yet mention the fee," he said. "Five hundred thousand dollars—one half million dollars, Mr. Williams, as soon as you put me in possession of the Harrington estate. As soon as you establish my right to the inheritance. It's a lot of money."

"But you haven't got it." I grinned at him.

"It's a lot of money," he said, "whether I have it or not."

"Sit down, Mr. Roberts," I told him. "You're dead right it's a lot of money—whether you have it or not."

CHAPTER 2

TWO DEAD MEN

WHEN HE WAS seated again, I said, "Now give me one reason why you came to me."

"Then you've taken the case?"

"Not at all," I told him. "I have simply agreed that half a million dollars is a lot of money."

"Well, I came to you because you are a man who can be relied upon and because you are a man of discretion."

"There are plenty such men." And, with a grin, "If not in the detective field, certainly among top estate lawyers. I am a man who is called upon as a last resort. A man who is hired to face danger— generally death—" And, leaning forward, "mostly murder."

"All right." Mr. Roberts rose now and started to pace the room. "I did hire a detective. If you want death. I'll give you death. If you want murder, I'll give you murder. The detective working for me was shot through the back of the head."

I was interested. "What was his name?"

"Slavin—Jimmy Slavin."

I nodded. "Slavin works out of the Gregory Ford Agency. Then you went to Gregory Ford. What happened? What did Gregory Ford tell you?"

Roberts didn't like that one. He hesitated for some time. Then he said, "I ran out of money."

"But what did Gregory Ford tell you?"

"Okay, Mr. Williams." Roberts' boyish enthusiasm was back a bit. "I didn't want to go into that. Gregory Ford told me to go home and forget it." And with an effort, "He said that Alta May Bronson was not an impostor. Is half a million a lot of money?"

"It is not as much as it was before," I told him honestly enough. "What did he say about Slavin?"

Roberts didn't like that one either, but he answered it, "He said that Slavin was killed because of something else—that's all." And when I just looked at him, "Okay,

Mr. Williams." He came to his feet. "I'm convinced there is something wrong— terribly wrong. Alta May was frightened. I know fear when I see it and hear it in a voice. Now, I'm not going around begging anyone to take this case. I offer you a flat half million—take it or leave it. I want a yes or a no."

"Like that?" I asked him.

"Just like that."

"Okay then." I picked up a letter I had been reading before he came in. "The answer is no."

I said it as if I meant it. And perhaps I did. Anyway, I might as well. He turned around and walked right out of the office. I dropped the letter back on the desk— grinned and waited. Then I stopped grinning. He didn't come back.

I knew I was right. It would have cost me time and money—for nothing. Common sense told me that you couldn't go around impersonating five million dollars. I dismissed it from my mind. It didn't make sense.

That is, I dismissed it until close to twelve o'clock that night. I bought a paper right outside of Willie Chaffey's Feed Box—and it stood my hair right up on end and set my fedora wavering.

It was spread across the front page. The ink was hardly dry. If it didn't smear my fingers, it sure felt like it. Frank Huntington Roberts, scion of a prominent social family, had been shot not much more than an hour ago while entering a taxi. It was as if you'd shot a half million in folding money right out of my inside jacket pocket.

It wasn't his name so much that made

the headlines I guess. It was the time and the place and the daring behind the shooting. He was plugged almost in front of the Mercury night spot, and a dozen people had seen the shooting—and the police would have the man who did it at any moment. He had been recognized by a man on the street.

That is newspaper work for you. They had a lot of details considering the time the shooting happened. But they didn't have how seriously Roberts was hurt, though this particular paper dramatically hinted that the shot would be fatal. And it gave the name of the hospital he had been "rushed to."

I DIDN'T GET in to see Roberts until after the police had questioned him. It appeared they were convinced that he was shot by mistake for another man. Roberts had stated that the gunman had called him by another name just before he fired.

Frank Roberts was smoking a cigarette and he grinned up at me. It was simply a flesh wound in the side.

"I'm no good to you," he said. "You want a body. But you do get around. So it isn't a cold war any more."

"It looks," I told him, "like a hot one. Anyway, the shooting has started. What's this yarn about the lad calling you by another name? True?"

"No." He grinned. "I didn't want Alta May Bronson dragged into it. I told you I intend to marry her."

"You still love her after this bit of shooting? Certainly you believe it has something to do with your sticking your nose into the thing—into the money."

He shook his head. "I won't believe she engineered the shooting. I won't believe she had any part of that. Now, Mr. Williams. Still interested in that half-million—if I have it or not?"

"Forget the half million," I told him. "I'll charge you enough if things work out all right." And while he gaped at me, I added, "Tell me about it."

He did, and there was little to it. He was stepping into the taxi when he felt the gun go smack into his side. He never could explain how he knew it was a gun. But he did know, and he suddenly thought of Jimmy Slavin. Anyway, he switched his body in a split second. That was all.

I told him to take care of himself. Then I left. Did the police really have any idea who shot him—and when they found the man—well, would the man make up the same sort of story that Roberts had? That is—that he thought Roberts was someone else?

I ducked into the subway and rode up to Kingsbridge. I'd see Sergeant O'Rourke of Homicide. He was a good friend of mine.

I got the sergeant out of bed. He gave me a drink. Told me to talk as loud as I wanted to, the missus was used to visitors at all hours. Showed me the picture of his latest grandson, which now made five. Told me about his youngest girl—who had a scholarship at Smith. Then he came down to cases.

"What's on your chest. Race—wasn't just in the neighborhood?"

I didn't exactly lie to him, but I did quibble with the truth.

"It's about the Roberts shooting," I

told him. "His family is worried. They wonder if he—well, if he made an enemy—'such a romantic adventuresome boy' was the way they put it. And they wonder if he told you the truth when he said he was mistaken for someone else."

"We wondered too." O'Rourke leaned back and laughed. "I was on my way home when it happened, and I saw the boy in the hospital. If he lied, he lied well, and at the time I was inclined to think he lied well." And then, "We work fast sometimes, Race. Eddie Moran shot him. Now he didn't mean to shoot Roberts—unless, of course, Roberts has some pretty good friends, some friends pretty handy with a gun."

"What do you mean by that?"

"Well, about twenty minutes before you arrived. Detective Cohens called me up. Eddie Moran was found shot to death. Oh, we'll look Roberts up of course—but we don't think he had that kind of friends. You see, a bartender recognized Eddie Moran when he shot Roberts—that's how we know it was Moran. Tell the family not to worry. And charge them double for not leaving things to the police."

"Thanks," I told O'Rourke. "That should kill any scandal. I won't keep you up longer."

"Don't you want to know where the body of Eddie Moran was found? Well, it was found over on Eighth Avenue. Looks something like the fur racket."

"Why?" I was just making conversation before I closed the door.

"I don't know." O'Rourke stifled another yawn. "Inspector Nelson has funny ideas in the back of that head of

his. It's just about the same place where the body of that private eye Jimmy Slavin was found. Good-night."

And I was standing on the steps in the dark as O'Rourke closed the door. It would have been coincidence enough if someone had tried to shoot Roberts in mistake for another man just after Roberts had left me. But it would certainly be stretching the long arm of coincidence far out of its socket to have the body of Eddie Moran, who had shot Roberts, found at the same place as the body of Jimmy Slavin—who had been working on the case for Roberts.

Sure, it looked as if the five million was in the bag. Impossible as it may sound, it looked as if a five million dollar fraud had been put over on the Surrogates Court of New York. I'd call on Jimmy Slavin's boss, Gregory Ford, the first thing in the morning.

CHAPTER 3

RACE INVESTIGATES

GREGORY FORD HAD the biggest agency in the city. It wasn't hard to get in to see him. Half the time he thought he might learn something from me and the other half he thought maybe I'd work for him—though my methods certainly would have given him many a sleepless night.

Gregory Ford sat behind a big desk in a big office and looked exactly what he was—the head of a private detective agency. There were the beetle brows, the steady stare, the thick cigar. Even in these times he would have put on a derby hat if he thought that was what a client expected. Gregory Ford wasn't a phony. Not by a long shot he wasn't. Years ago he figured that was what the people wanted and expected and he gave it to them. It became part of him over the years.

"Sit down. Race," he said. "Sit down, boy. A cigar, a cigarette—a drink now? No—well, what's this about Jimmy Slavin and the Bronson heiress?" He was referring to my phone call of course.

"Slavin," I said, "got killed investigating the Bronson heiress—right?"

"Now, now." The brows came down and the eyes grew steady. "I wouldn't put it that way. Jimmy Slavin was killed while he was working on that little affair, yes. But he was working on other things too. He was smart, Race, as good as there was. He wasn't on my pay roll you know—just so much per day. He was good on documents and estates." After a long pause. "I think he got himself mixed up in a fur racket and—playing both ends against the middle—got knocked over. Nice boy, nice boy. Sad, but inevitable. His wife sings around cafés."

"What has that to do with it?"

"Nothing, except she can take care of herself. I expect she had to anyway."

And when I came down to gold tacks about the Bronson set-up, Gregory said, "I took that case for young Roberts. Yes, I know. He was shot. You add two and two together and get five million instead of four. This girl who calls herself Alta May Bronson is exactly that. Alta May Bronson. There can be no mistake about it." And when I just looked at him: "Do you

think I'd toss over a case of that magnitude? Common sense should tell you it couldn't be done."

"Your full report came from Slavin, didn't it? Mightn't he have been hiding something—intending to cash in on it—and been bumped?"

"Yes, yes." Gregory nodded. "The report came from Slavin. And certainly he might have hidden something. But I checked and double checked it. There wasn't much to it. The Bronson girl's mother and father left New York in 1926. She was two years old then. They arrived in Paris, changed their names to La Verne, and two years later went to live in the south of France. Bronson went in for painting. Did fairly well at it—under the name Henri La Verne. But he kept his own name too. That is, he was in touch with things here to a certain extent. The family—still with the little girl—fled to Switzerland—"

HE REFERRED TO some notes on his desk. "Lucerne it was. That would be just about the start of the war. Her parents were killed in an automobile accident. I think that was September, the latter part of 'Forty-two. A Swiss family—Blanche—took care of the little girl. Money certainly was not mentioned to them or anticipated by the girl. Let me see. Jarvis Harrington died in—oh, last year sometime. Six weeks later, they had located the girl."

"Who?"

"The law firm of Stevens, Ronalds, Blake and Stevens. You see, Stevens, Senior, took charge of all Jarvis Harrington's business. When he died a year or two back, young Mr. Stevens—" Gregory Ford permitted himself a grin— "he must be close to fifty now—had that end of the business. Wait, Race. Young Mr. Stevens, Charles Holland Stevens, was made executor of the Harrington estate. Harold Ronalds, one of the smartest, the wealthiest and the most respected men in his profession drew up the will. He was visiting Europe last year and picked up the girl himself and brought her back."

"Did the Swiss family have any idea that Alta May was the Bronson heiress?"

"Not the slightest."

"Did she?"

"Not that she was to be an heiress, no. But that she was a Bronson, yes. You go talk to Harold Ronalds if you wish. The Bronson girl wasn't supposed to know, but little things here and there that parents will talk about gave her an idea that she was someone else. Her parents did tell her a little when she questioned them. But the money came as a surprise."

"It sure is odd." I was disappointed all right. "What a coincidence that—"

"Yes, I know. You don't believe in coincidence. But it does happen. And I can see Roberts' viewpoint. Nice boy, nice family—but a little hard up. He expects the money, doesn't get it, and can make himself believe anything."

"Did you check it all personally?"

"I don't know what you mean by all," Gregory said. "If you mean did I go to Europe, no. If you mean did I interview Harold Ronalds and young Stevens, who has complete charge of the estate, yes. I didn't bring Roberts' name into it. I spoke vaguely of a claimant in France."

"That is all you did?"

"Well—" Gregory reddened a little and then laughed. "I guess I had dreams like you, Race. When Slavin was shot, it startled me. To be perfectly frank with you, I went to see the Surrogate himself—and not only was convinced but was laughed at. There wasn't the slightest irregularity in the entire procedure—not the slightest question. You should know what a reputation Judge Blenheim has in such estate matters."

I did. And I did listen to Gregory's suggestion that I take over his Chicago office.

"We need a good rough tough man there right now, Race," he told me. "I could go to a pretty good figure—in fact, a very good figure, if you'd like to take a crack at it."

I shook my head and left. Sure I was let down. I had thought for sure I had my finger on a five million dollar swindle. I looked up Stevens, Ronalds, Blake and Stevens. That afternoon I went in to see Harold Ronalds.

I GUESS I wanted to be impressed, and I was. He was a white-haired man, crowding seventy. Pleasant, too, as he looked down at my card.

"I have heard about you, Mr. Williams." He smiled at me. "Now I am not going to ask you who this mysterious foreign client of yours is. There isn't a bit of doubt of the—er—Miss Alta May Bronson's identity. I know. No doubt you are working through a firm of lawyers. Speaking for the firm and for young Mr. Stevens, who is sole executor of the Jarvis Harrington estate, I might say that under no circumstances would we consider paying out a penny to any claimant, under any circumstances. I don't know how well you have investigated the past of Miss Bronson or her parents. But we have investigated that past most thoroughly since Mr. Ford came to see us. We find nothing, absolutely nothing that would justify any intimidation of our client into settling rather than—"

"Oh nothing like that," I came in. "I'm just to make a report."

"Certainly, certainly." And when I was about to leave, he called to a man passing in the outer office. A rather chubby little fellow with gold pince-nez on his nose and his black hair streaked with gray. "Oh, Charles—one minute please," he called.

Charles came. I shook hands with "young Mr. Stevens."

"Charles," Harold Ronalds said. "This is Mr. Williams—a well-known private investigator. It's regarding Miss Bronson again—a question, I believe, of her identity."

"Well, well." Charles Stevens seemed a lively little lad. "He'll have to work fast then. She's using quite a bit of the money. I've read about you, Mr. Williams. Like a detective of fiction. But Mr. Ronalds here will have to enlighten you. I am entirely on the financial end of things. If he brought back the wrong girl, that is his lookout. Dear me, Ronalds, you did a remarkable job of establishing her identity—and you picked a very charming young lady for the role."

"I am afraid—" Ronalds permitted himself a slight smile which he wiped off at once—"that, Mr. Williams, or at least whoever he represents, would hardly appreciate your levity, Charles. Again Mr. Williams, we are not entirely unused to such investigations, such claims."

"Miss Bronson," I said, "does not seem overanxious to associate with the relatives of her late foster-grandfather."

I knew the moment I said it that I had rubbed Harold Ronalds the wrong way.

"Really," he said, "I am not familiar with—nor would I consider it proper to discuss—Miss Bronson's social activities."

"Why would she want to have anything to do with them?" I was surprised at the way Charles Stevens' little eyes snapped. "They all treated her mother most shabbily and—"

Charles Stevens stopped. He coughed. Cleared his throat. And grinned at me. His teeth were even and white and I was positive his own.

"Of course, Harold," he said to Ronalds, "of course you are right. Miss Bronson's actions and opinions are hardly a part of our function. I have a deep admiration for the young lady, Mr. Williams." He turned to me. "Let me congratulate you, too, on your efforts in behalf of someone else. You must excuse me now."

Charles Stevens walked out of the office, leaving the door open behind him. Harold Ronalds stood looking at his back. "You know," he said, as if speaking into space, "that is the first time I ever remember Charles losing his head. Do you know, I believe young Stevens is smitten with the girl!"

CHAPTER 4

ROGUES GALLERY

THAT WAS WHEN I left. But somehow I didn't believe young Stevens had lost his head. He had seemed quite natural and quite himself—though what "himself" was, I didn't know. I, too, had an idea that young Stevens might have ideas of marrying five million dollars. It bothered me at first—then it didn't. Who wouldn't entertain such an idea? A young wife and five million in cash would not be too unpleasant a way of spending your declining years.

When I reached the street, I was wondering what the inheritance tax would be. It made me sick to think of it. Under the circumstances, I thought young Stevens was bearing up very well indeed.

So—I didn't have any specially exhilarating news to take to a young man convalescing in a hospital, dreaming of five million dollars and the girl he loved.

I'd see one more person. The widow of Jimmy Slavin. Maybe he had told her something.

It was after lunch when I reached the now deceased Jimmy Slavin's apartment. Uptown and a walk-up. Mrs. Slavin was home. She was a nice bit of goods. If she was missing Jimmy, she didn't show it too much.

She invited me in and sat down on the arm of a chair.

"I'm a mess," she told me. "But I just had something to eat. I'm working a new cocktail lounge—night spot to the patrons—and what with rehearsals in the late afternoon I don't get much time."

And when I apologized for bringing up the unpleasant subject of the late lamented Jimmy, she said, "That's all right, Mr. Williams. It's like a relief. Not that I didn't love Jimmy, but I didn't know what was going to happen next. Being a detective, he always found out too much—then wondered how he could make more money from what he had found out. He wanted to do big things for me, and almost did—always *almost*. About his shooting. Well, I don't know."

And to my next question:

"Yes, I knew about the heiress racket. He was always enthusiastic. Just before he got—got it, he said, 'Dolly, ten or twenty grand will only be small change pretty soon. I'm onto something big.'"

"Then—" This was my first break. "Then he had discovered she wasn't—this girl was an impostor?"

"Oh no." Dolly Slavin shook her head and knocked me off the ladder again. "He said she was the heiress all right, but there was big money around just the same."

"Around her—for him?" And when she looked at me. "Are you sure of that?"

"Well, I thought I was." She frowned, then brightened up. "Anyway, he wasn't disturbed too much on her being the heiress—the right one, I mean."

"Do you think that had anything to do with his death?"

"His death—his death? Oh no, no. I don't like to talk about that."

"Sentiment?"

"No." She seemed reluctant now. "I just don't want to talk any more about it, Mr.

Williams. I've kept out of the rackets—always. And I'll say this for Jimmy. He never tried to bring me into them."

"The fur racket?" And when her eyes widened and she seemed frightened, I added, "Don't you want to know who killed your husband, Mrs. Slavin? Don't you want to have him punished?"

"I want to be out of it!" she cried, standing up and facing me. "I don't want any more of it. I know who killed him—and that's enough. Ed Moran was here to see him—and—" She put both her hands on my shoulders. "Jimmy was to meet Ed Moran the night he died. But don't you see, Mr. Williams? I'm through with even the thought of that life. I knew Jimmy would go too far with his easy money."

JIMMY SLAVIN, THE man working on the Bronson case, was killed by Ed Moran, the man who had tried to kill Frank Roberts. Roberts, the man who thought he was entitled to the millions....

Complicated—and how. And I like my crimes straight.

I guess I'm a tough guy to satisfy, though. Okay—so maybe I didn't believe any more that the Bronson girl was a phony. Or maybe I didn't want to let myself believe it. I had interviewed about everyone connected with the case but the heiress herself. But—well, now I went to see Roberts. He was home in his small apartment and felt fine. The police weren't bothering him any more.

"I never felt better," he said. "And the papers aren't giving it much of a whirl—except the mistaken identity." He grinned at me then. "Too many mistakes in iden-tity in this thing, Mr. Williams. I see that the man who shot at me got himself killed by— What's the matter?"

"I haven't done much looking at the newspaper," I told him, and then I gave it to him flat. "It's a washout, fellow. The girl is the real thing. There isn't a crook mixed up in the whole deal but the dead Jimmy Slavin—and you brought him in."

"You mean you're giving up already?" And, half climbing out of bed, "You can't, Mr. Williams. You haven't seen the girl. You didn't see the look on her face that I saw when I questioned her about being unfamiliar with any of us—of Jarvis Harrington's relatives. Before she knew who I was, she asked me if I'd love her if she was a fraud and a cheat. She's playing a part, I tell you. And what's more, I'm in love with her. Go to see her. You've got evidence that she's not the real Alta May Bronson. I'm that evidence—the fear I saw in her."

"Where is she now?" I asked.

"Yonkers." He leaned forward and gave me the address. "You can't miss it."

"I have an idea that might work out," I said, "if it doesn't land me in jail for disturbing the peace."

"Look." He had that nice smile working again. "I won't see you foot all the bills. I'll pay for the taxi up to see her."

"No." I shook my head. "So far, your case has cost me forty cents. Considering that my time is of some value, let us call it a half dollar flat. Not so much," I went on sarcastically, "when you think of a half million or more."

So Roberts had seen fear in the girl's eyes. Okay then, I'd go up and have a look at her, see what I'd find. And I'd take along a little picture—a photograph to make things interesting.

I didn't know much about Ed Moran. So I went down to a newspaper office, got in to see Billy Frazier, who gave me not only a photograph of the gentleman in question but a good deal about his life.

"He don't sound like any fur racket business to me," Billy said. "Look at this picture. Isn't it a beaut?"

Yes, it was at that. Moran was dressed up in top shape. Nothing flashy, understand. You might take him for a banker.

"Gentleman Ed Moran," Billy went on. "That's what the boys called him. In a way, Race, I suppose he has been a confidence man. But he took that up after he got a jolt for forgery about fifteen years ago."

And in answer to another question, Billy told me, "It's hard to tell what a man would do. Race. As far as I know, he was never found with a gun on him. And certainly he wouldn't kill a man for hire. But, if it was personal, if his whole future depended upon it, well then I think he'd shoot."

Forgery. That word stuck in my head.

"Did he come into money lately?" I asked.

"I don't know." Billy shook his head. "And I don't think you could find out. He was used to big money at one time, Race. He'd know better than to toss it around."

Billy was pretty well informed on Gentleman Ed Moran, just as he was pretty well informed on just about everything in the newspaper morgue. But he couldn't put his finger definitely on who Moran worked with. Confidence men and forgers usually worked very closely with someone. But we boiled Moran down to three possible buddies.

Then we checked up on them. One of them was dead. Another had been in jail for the past three years—which left one. George Granger. I hadn't told Billy anything about the doubts about the Bronson heiress.

"If you have the fur racket in mind," Billy said easily, "forget George Granger, though he might be the agent for the foreign stuff. He speaks several languages, is highly educated and smooth as glass. It's a wonder how such people get into crime."

I took the picture of Gentleman Ed Moran. I also had a good look at a picture of George Granger—and a promise of a copy later if I wanted it.

"George has always been sort of in the background of things," Billy said. "He's always in and out of the country. He hasn't been in England much. He likes the Continent—South of France—Monte Carlo. These are not young fellows, Race. I'm afraid they are out of your line."

"Perhaps." I thanked him. "But I'll try and put them in my line."

CHAPTER 5

HEARD IN THE DARK

It was a nice night. Pleasant for a drive. The traffic was not too bad and the home of Alta May Bronson was in the old Park Hill section of Yonkers—not too far over the city line. It was late for a call, but it was my last stand. I'd clear things up in twenty-four hours or be through with it. I'll admit forgers and smooth guys and a lad who traveled the Continent and spoke several languages gave me quite a shot in the arm.

I liked the Yonkers place. There was a wall around it and the house was set back in the trees and it wasn't too big.

Another car ahead of me swung into the gate. Curious? I'm always curious. There were no sidewalks so I ran my car up a bit and parked off the road close to the wall of the property beyond. Then I went back on foot.

That car was new, a four thousand dollar job, and I wanted a look-see at such a classy caller. I hopped the low wall in time to see the owner of the car—one person, and I thought male—pass into the house.

I looked at my watch. It was ten minutes after nine. It was a nice night, no moon, so I wandered around a bit, circling the house. I wanted to see the girl alone.

Before a tile patio there was a light through some French windows. Not a bad place to peek through. I crouched and made sure that no one was in that patio. I was ready to slip into it when one of the French windows opened. A man stood in the light. I knew him at once of course. It was young Mr. Stevens.

"Alta May," he half called, half whispered. "The maid said you were out here."

"Yes," came her answer. A figure in black suddenly materialized in the patio and came into the light.

That was how near I had come not only to being seen, but caught. Roberts was right. She didn't need five million to make a man want to marry her. In fact, a guy might need the five million to do as well, shopping any other place. Her voice was nice.

"Mr. Stevens, I was not expecting you—or anyone."

He came forward and took her hand and held on to it. "Try to call me Charles, Alta May," he said. "I'd like that."

"All right—Charles," the girl said. "You haven't come to admonish me?" And that was the first time I noticed a trace of accent in her voice. Then I thought, why not? She'd lived abroad since she was two.

"Not admonish you, child—for in many ways you are like a child. But I would be lax in my duty to you, to myself, and to the memory of your adopted grandfather, if I didn't speak out. Now, Alta May. I know you have great wealth, but it is a tremendous lot of money you have drawn."

"Isn't there plenty of money there?"

"Well, yes. But I did have to liquidate some rather valuable bonds. And I'm thinking of the purpose for which you use it."

She came rather close to him and whispered something.

"Of course, of course," he answered. "You told me that." He seemed just a trifle impatient. "These people were good to you—the child you liked so much needed an operation. I understand that. But I'm talking about much more money than that."

"I am sorry, Charles, if I appear extravagant."

"It's not that." And suddenly he put his arms around her. "I love you, Alta May," he said. "And—and God help me—I feel that you are being blackmailed."

She pushed him away, but he went on talking. He talked about blackmail breeding more blackmail. A stop should be put to it at once. If there is something that had to be bought off, it should be bought off and finished with. That the greed of a blackmailer was "insatiable."

All of it was good and all of it was true—if she were really being blackmailed. And then I saw the thing in her eyes that Roberts had seen—fear.

"Good heavens," young Mr. Stevens said suddenly, "it's not Roberts—demanding what he considered his share of his uncle's estate?"

"No," she answered quickly. "He never would do such a thing. There has not been one penny for him, though I thought—that he might—that he should receive some of it. I was going to ask you to advise me on that."

"No." Young Mr. Stevens was emphatic. "At least, not yet. It might be misunderstood by him and his family as an admission that he was really entitled to some of it."

"And isn't he?"

"No."

She looked straight at him. "Are you absolutely sure?"

"Absolutely. Understand, Alta May, he has no legal claim. As for any other claim. Well, my father drew up Jarvis Harrington's will. Our Mr. Ronalds was present at the signing of that will, and he's fully versed in its contents and Jarvis Harrington's desire in the matter."

"Then what makes you think that Frank Roberts feels I should give him money?"

"Because he's been investigating, and I know the illusions that his uncle's will is not being properly administrated. There was a detective who talked of a foreign claimant—but Mr. Ronalds readily saw through that."

Then Young Mr. Stevens went ardent. He took the girl's hand and begged her to marry him. He waved aside the difference in age. He tossed in his graying hair—called it premature—and lied when he let it lightly slip out that there was hardly more than fifteen years between them, though the girl couldn't possibly be more than twenty-five.

Alta May looked over his shoulder and I saw her blue eyes plainly. She was giving it thought all right. No doubt about that.

"It wouldn't make any difference," she asked almost speculatively, "if I weren't an heiress?"

"Only the difference that I would have spoken sooner," he told her. "I have plenty of money. And, Alta May, I'd protect you from whatever it is you fear. No, don't deny it. I see it in your eyes now. I've seen it there before."

"Could we go away?" she asked. "Travel? Change our—my name—forget I ever inherited a fortune?"

"Why you'd change your name of course." He tried to put a jocular note in his voice. "You'd have my name. I'd protect you. You will tell me everything. It can't be so bad, Alta May. And no matter what it is, don't you see—I wouldn't care."

ALTA MAY WAS almost in his arms. Then she pulled back.

"No!" she cried out. It was torn right from inside of her. "I don't love you, Charles. But it isn't only that. You're too good, too fine. I wouldn't let you throw yourself away on me. I—" She straightened now. "I tried to get money from the bank today—and couldn't!"

"Really?" He came back to business pretty good, I thought. "But there's plenty money there for you."

"They didn't have it in my account. Don't you know? Didn't they call you?"

"Yes," he said, as if he didn't want to speak. "That's why I came tonight. One hundred thousand dollars, Alta May. You said it was for some property in Europe you wanted to buy. In Europe—as vague as that."

"And you didn't believe it?"

"No," he said, "I didn't believe it."

"You—" She put her hands to her face and her body shook, and I could see the sobs and the hysterics coming. But I was wrong. She lowered her hands, and her eyes were dry.

"It was a lie, about wanting the money for some property," she told him. "It will be the last. Get this money for me, Charles, and I'll do whatever you want me to do afterwards."

"I don't want you to do or not do anything," he said. "And the money is not mine, but yours."

"Get me the money," she said, "and I'll marry you." And when he stood staring at her, "That is what you want—that is what you told me was the dearest wish of your life."

"I'll see that the money is there," he said somewhat stiffly. "It is your money, you are entitled to it. I love you, Alta May, very deeply and very sincerely. I'll propose again at another time. Good-night."

He turned toward the window, but she ran after him and took him by the arm. I don't know what she said. I don't know what he said. It went on inside, behind the French windows—closed French windows now. But it wasn't very much for I was standing close against the side of the house by the front door a few minutes later when the four thousand dollar job purred softly into life and sped easily down toward the gate.

I took to the wall and left as I had come. No, I didn't think this was the time to see Alta May Bronson. I had seen the fear in her eyes. So had young Mr. Stevens, who didn't seem too bad a lad at that, even if he lied about his age. But there was no reason to believe that her fear was because she was not the rightful heir to the Harrington millions. Certainly young Mr. Stevens didn't entertain any such fantastic idea. And young Mr. Stevens was in a position to be pretty well informed.

The next day I played bodyguard to one hundred grand. Also I ducked seeing Frank Huntington Roberts. I talked to him on the phone. I didn't give him any information—nor any encouragement. I didn't see yet where there was anything in it for him—either the girl or the money.

But I had a plan....

CHAPTER 6

DEAD MAN'S FACE

DETERMINEDLY, I WATCHED that girl and I watched that money. It wasn't hard to follow her. I simply trailed her back to Yonkers and watched the house after she went in it. After it grew dark, I went into the grounds again.

A little after eleven o'clock she slipped out a small side door and went to her private garage.

I was in my car and swung in behind her when she left the gates. It wasn't too difficult. Oh, she skipped along a bit down Broadway, but she didn't break any laws after she turned toward the river. She took me well downtown. She wound up by a warehouse.

She turned into a narrow street and stopped. Luckily, I found a particularly dark spot, parked, and jumped out. I ducked behind a loading platform as she left her car.

She clung close to the huge building and so did I. I didn't see the door, but she did. I think she used a key. She took some time at it. I was on her heels when she disappeared into the inky blackness. And she did what I hoped she'd do—and, yes, rather expected she'd do. She left the door open a crack. Sure, that was the most natural thing in the world. She was afraid. Subconsciously she would not shut out the outside world and what she thought of as her way of escape.

I pushed in and closed the door about the same—stood listening. And I heard her breathing. Yes, we were that close

together and the place was in pitch darkness. Then it wasn't.

A tiny beam of light made a circle on the floor. The girl had switched on a small electric flash. She followed that beam of light now—and so did I.

Alta May Bronson had no thought of being followed. She was simply in a hurry to get it over with, and her breathing was hard and labored, very hard for such a slip of a girl. I had worked a gun into my right hand and a flash into my left—not the little pencil of light she had, but a torch that would show up something when I let it go.

I didn't like the stairs. They were narrow and walled in and the door we passed through worked on a spring and swung shut. Sure she might spot me any moment. But it was too late for me to think of that. Too important that I stick to her—that I stick to the money. I climbed the stairs with her, not over a dozen steps behind her quick moving heels.

The door at the top of the stairs had even better springs. I took it with my arm crossed over my chest and had my fedora knocked down over my eyes for a moment. Then we were in a loft together. She didn't go far into the loft—a few steps and stood waiting, listening, though I doubted if she could hear anything above her own breathing.

She moved on again.

This was the easiest shadowing job I ever had. I followed her light across the loft floor, dodging the huge packing cases as she avoided them. There was a door finally. The girl hesitated, then opened the door and went into a small room.

I saw the room. I saw the old desk and a couple of chairs. And I saw the shadow of a figure there.

"Come in, Miss Bronson," a man said. "Ah, you have the stuff!"

For a split second I saw the brief-case as she flashed it from under her long light coat. Then the door closed and I was on the outside.

Was that my cue to enter? If it was, it would have to be a dramatic and dangerous entrance. For a key had turned in the lock.

I COULD HAVE tossed my weight against the door and got it on the first or second pound—maybe. On the third one—sure. But a lad could spray lead up and down that door, through it and into me. I didn't want things that dramatic.

I dropped to my knees to listen. I heard only a mumble of voices.

Now what? What could I do? I had plenty on that girl already—enough to scare her into talking. That is, if I could do my scaring before someone advised her that she hadn't broken any law by going to a warehouse and paying out cash that belonged to her. She would no doubt come out the way she had gone in. And the man, too, for that matter.

I listened for a few minutes more. Then there was a familiar sound. The closing of a door—another door. Feet moved. Then a creak. That door had been opened again.

My guess—and I didn't like that guess—was that the girl had left when the door first slammed. And now the man, or whoever she had met, had left—leaving that other door open behind him.

Then my listening brought results with a vengeance. The blast of a gun.

A space of time when you might count three—and I heard the thud of a heavy body, a human body crashing down on hard bare wood. Count five this time—and then the slam of a door.

Okay, count ten again. Then I was up and hurling my shoulder against that door. I've busted in doors before. My heart was in this thrust, my weight behind it. The door splintered, tore loose from its hinges and I was hurtled into the room.

I went to one knee. My left hand hit the floor, but my right was up and my gun was in it—and I was blinking at an empty room. I mean empty of life. A desk, three chairs—a clothes rack on the wall. And—yes. A dead man on the floor.

I bent down and looked at him. I've seen dead men before. I knew what had taken place in that room just as if I had seen the man killed. Someone had stuck a gun against the back of his neck, not over an inch or two away, and blown the back of his head in. He lay flat on his face. A big man. Well dressed.

I didn't like it. I didn't like the job. One of his hands was under him as I straddled the body and lifted it slightly. But no brief-case or anything else was under him.

The back of his head was a mess all right. I put my hand down, slipped it under and onto his face—lifted it slightly and twisted his head so I could see the face.

I whistled softly. I knew the man all right. I had seen his picture that afternoon in the newspaper office. Billy Frazier had shown it to me. It was George Granger, the partner of Gentleman Ed Moran.

CHAPTER 7

A FRAUD REVEALED

CAREFULLY, I LOOKED about the floor for footprints. But it was swept clear of dust. I looked up at the single light blazing down on the gruesome sight. Certainly he had been on his feet when he was killed. Witness the way he laid on the floor. Witness, too, the crash I had heard of the falling body. It hadn't been the sound from a man toppling off a chair.

I didn't go through the man's pockets. But I patted them for anything big—like wads of money. All I found was that he was packing a rod—and of all places in his right hand jacket pocket. I didn't lift it out, but a dollar will get you ten it was a thirty-two.

A question there. Was the man unfamiliar with carting a gun? Or was it in the right hand jacket pocket so he could keep his hand on it and shoot? Your guess is as good as mine. He had been a high class confidence man. A first class forger. A lad like that might not be used to a gun. Also, a man like that, especially if he had turned to blackmail, might need a gun, where his right hand could rest on it.

A couple of minutes later I was back in my car and on my way to Yonkers. The girl had a start on me. But the girl was not too familiar with the city. She couldn't be. I shot up the express route along the river, then cut toward Broadway. I made time—and hoped that I'd know the cop who stopped me.

I passed her just above 242nd Street, not over a minute after I cut out from under the tracks of the subway where it is elevated at the end of the line.

If she was frightened, she wasn't driving in the madness of panic. I saw her white face for a moment behind the wheel. And although it might be easy to imagine things, she just looked like any other woman driving a car.

This time I was standing by the rear door of her garage when she came out of it and walked toward the house. Her step was quick and steady enough. But fear was in her all right, for it made her more alert. I tripped along behind her to the side door of the house, but I knew even before she reached it that she knew I was there. At least, she knew someone was there.

She had a handbag over her arm. She was opening it when I put my hand on her arm.

"I'll take the bag, Miss Bronson," I said, and as she spun around and faced me I clapped a hand over her mouth. I had seen the parted lips and the white teeth. She was about to scream.

"I wouldn't do that," I told her. "I'm a detective. I'd like a word or two with you inside—and I'm sure you'd like a word or two with me."

Then I dropped my hand. If she wanted to holler, I couldn't keep her quiet forever. "Yes, of course—inside," she said.

"What," I said, "were you looking for in your bag?"

"The key to the door."

"Allow me." I opened the bag, stuck my hand in, and then handed her back the bag. "Okay," I said. "Get the key out and open the door."

That's right. There was no gun in the bag. I should have known that when I hefted it. Anyway, only a good-sized rattler would have made that hole in George Granger's head.

HER HAND SHOOK as she opened the door, but she didn't say anything. I followed her inside, even took her arm. I didn't like the dead silence. I didn't like her quick breathing. It was that of a desperate woman ready to do a desperate act. Or of a terror-stricken woman just come from murder.

It was a man's room she led me into, no doubt Jarvis Harrington's den. It wasn't big enough for a library, yet it was practically surrounded with books up to the ceiling on three sides. There was a fireplace, some easy-chairs, and a flat table that served as a desk. It was the French window room that gave on to the patio.

Alta May let me close the door and switch on the light. I turned her around to face me. Still she didn't speak. I even had to help her take off her coat. "Have a cigarette," I said then.

I don't think she heard me. Or if she did, I don't think she quite understood me. I lit a cigarette for myself, put one between her lips and held a match for her. After a while she got the idea and drew in on it, and reached up and took it from her mouth.

"Sit down," I said.

She sat. Her blue eyes were wide and staring and her lips were colorless. I put my hand inside my jacket pocket and produced the picture of Gentleman Ed Moran. If it was meant to startle her, it failed.

"You knew him?" I asked. And when she looked up and nodded, I said, "Did you kill him?"

"Kill him?" She looked at the picture again. "Is he dead?"

"Yes." I nodded gravely. "And so is the other one—George Granger." And when that didn't register, I explained, "A big man—gray suit with a stripe in it. Bulging eyes. He was killed in the warehouse tonight. Shot through the back of the head. Murdered in cold blood just after you gave him the money—"

I broke off. She was on her feet, swaying. I could feel her whole body vibrating as I held her in my arms and choked down the scream. And I knew then as I looked into those eyes that she hadn't done it. The slam of the door must have been when she left—the opening when someone else came in and—killed Granger.

After a bit, the shaking died down, and she nodded her promise not to scream. I let her go. She choked, but got the words out clear enough.

"I don't believe you. I saw that man in the warehouse tonight. He's—he's— I didn't kill him. I didn't. You're the police. I knew it couldn't last. Well, I don't care any more. No, I'm not the real Alta May Bronson." She flopped back in the chair. "I didn't want the money. I don't want it now. I did it for—for that poor little crippled child, and the few thousand it took, and now—I've robbed, stolen, so much money."

AND THERE IT was. A five million

dollar swindle. And the girl confessing to it. The girl was talking. Popping it all out—all of it.

She had never heard of Jarvis Harrington. Had never heard that she might inherit money. Yes, her father had been a painter—just like the real Alta May Bronson's father was. Ed Moran and George Granger had come to her in the little Swiss mountain home, though of course she knew them under different and fancier names. They talked her into it. They said the real Alta May Bronson had died.

She went on, calm now.

"It was my fault that little Celia was like that—would never walk again. I didn't watch, and she fell. No, the Verdou family never blamed me. But I blamed myself. These men said my impersonation could never be discovered. They said the real girl had known little about Jarvis Harrington, so I wouldn't have to pretend or fake anything. They told me just a few things—things the real Alta May's mother might have told her. They had everything, as they said, fixed. And I thought of the good I could do with the money." She broke down then and cried. "Later, I thought I could run away and the rightful heirs have it."

"But you didn't run?"

"I couldn't. Always they demanded more money. To fix this—fix that. And always the threat of going to jail."

"Were the lawyers in it? Mr. Stevens?"

"Oh, no," she said. "He handled only the Harrington estate. Mr. Stevens, they said, was a simple honest man. Mr. Ronalds was given all—all forged papers.

Now what will you do with me?" Sure I questioned her while I had her going.

My head was whirling a bit. The girl made no excuse for herself.

"I suppose I took advantage of Mr. Charles Stevens," she said simply. "He—he seemed to like me. It had been my intention to give the money to Mr. Roberts, then disappear. But Mr. Stevens' father, and later Mr. Stevens, were very close to Mr. Harrington. And Mr. Stevens told me that Jarvis Harrington did not want Mr. Roberts to have his money. And then came the fear of prison, and these men threatening me with exposure and arrest, and—and now you are the police and it has happened!"

"I'm not the police," I told her. She looked at me with disbelief and then fear. "I represent Mr. Frank Roberts. We'll do nothing, say nothing, until consulting him."

She watched me go to the phone, lift and call my number. Roberts answered almost at once.

"Race Williams, eh?" he said. "Where have you been?"

"I've got news for you," I told him. "Come to the Harrington house in Yonkers at once. At once, understand." And when he started to question me, "If you haven't got money for gas, charge it. Tell them you're worth—what's left of five million."

CHAPTER 8

THE LAW ARRIVES

SLOWLY, I CRADLED the phone. I told the fake Alta May to sit down.

"Look," I said, "the lad who was robbed in this transaction is Roberts. It is up to him to decide what to do about this swindle. What the law will do, I don't know."

"I make no excuse," she said flatly. "What I did was a reprehensible thing. I knew that Mr. Roberts suspected me. The child might have lived anyway, but forever horribly crippled. Now, the child will walk again—run and play. I knew I would pay a price. I am willing to pay it."

"That," I said, "is between you and my client and the laws of the state. It has nothing to do with me. But there is another thing, Miss Bronson."

"Miss La Verne," she corrected.

"Well, Miss La Verne then. A man was killed tonight. Murdered in the loft building where you were. I found the body."

"But I had nothing to do with that."

"Maybe not the actual killing. But you were there. You delivered the money. It was in a brief-case. When I found the body, both the money and the brief-case were gone. It's murder, and I'm calling the police."

I went to get that done before Roberts turned up. I didn't want to be convinced that it would be worth my while not to call the police. Not that Roberts was such a good talker, but he had a lot of money to talk with now.

The girl said nothing. I buzzed Sergeant

O'Rourke. He didn't answer at once. He wasn't wide awake and waiting, nor did he demand where I'd been. I told him.

"Ed Moran's partner, George Granger, was knocked over tonight, O'Rourke." I gave him the location of the warehouse. "How do I know? I was there, and heard the shot, and found the body."

I gave him details of where the body was. No, I wouldn't meet him at the warehouse. I was working on the case in his interest. He'd be wise to keep my name out of it for the time being. It might involve big names—and certainly a lot of money. Then I told him where I was. Yes, I'd wait for him. No, my client wasn't near the warehouse.

I lit another cigarette and sat down. I had a lot of thinking to do. I did a lot of thinking. I looked at the girl. The fear and horror were going out of her face. I watched the change come over her.

"You—you look relieved," I said after a bit.

"Yes." She tried to smile, but it wasn't too good. "I am relieved. I'm glad it is all over with. I always knew I'd have to pay. I told myself over and over I'd gladly die if it would help that child. Why, then, should I cry and scream now against the loss of my freedom?"

That was one way of figuring it.

The doorbell rang and I went to let Roberts in. I opened the door and we were both surprised. It wasn't Roberts. It was young Mr. Stevens.

"Williams, the detective," he said. And, in sudden alarm, "What has happened?"

With that he pushed by me and headed straight for the den. I could have stopped him, but why? If anyone needed a lawyer, that girl did.

I followed him into the den. Watched him walk across the room and put an arm around the girl. He swung then and faced me, looking indignant. But I spoke first.

"Remember our little talk?" I said simply. "Well, she's not spending any more of the money. Hold tight, Mr. Stevens. Miss Bronson is not Miss Bronson anymore. She confessed to the fraud a few minutes ago."

"Yes," the girl said. "I know it must be an awful shock to you, Mr. Stevens."

THERE WAS A blank incredulous look on his face. But the lawyer came out in him then.

"Not a word, Alta May. Not another word," he cautioned her. Then, to me, "I'll talk to the young lady alone, Mr. Williams." And when I shook my head, he straightened and said, "I am her lawyer. Just how do you propose to stop me?"

"We'll—" I smiled at him—"I won't serve you with any injunction, if that's what you mean." And then, having no desire to pull the strong arm act on him, "I've been in touch with the police. I've been ordered to keep her in my presence until they arrive."

"The police?" he said. "Coming here? But what—what can she have to do with the police?"

"Well," I told him, "if you don't find much harm in her masquerading as another woman and copping off a few million dollars, how will you like murder? Sure. She was at a warehouse when a man was shot to death tonight."

"How—how do you know she was?"

"She won't deny it," I told him. "If she does—I was there too."

That got him. He hadn't seemed to mind her flim-flamming good old Stevens, Ronalds, Blake & Stevens. Or maybe he didn't believe it. Maybe he didn't believe the murder part either, but it threw him, He dropped his arms from the girl as if she was—well, a cold potato. He pushed a hand up inside his collar and pulled at it slightly, as if it were choking him.

"I—I must use the phone," he said then. "Mr. Ronalds must know about this."

He went out of the room on rubbery legs. But he was right. His law partner, Mr. Ronalds, sure should know about it.

Roberts came in then. That is, he came to the little French windows and tapped and I let him in. He stood there facing the girl. She looked straight at him.

"You were right, Mr. Roberts," she said finally. "I am not Alta May Bronson. I am Alta May La Verne. I've thrown your money away to swindlers—and cheats."

Roberts looked at the girl. "Now—now. It is not as bad as that. We'll straighten this thing out, you and I. And Race Williams here of course." He brought my name in as an afterthought. "There must have been very good reasons for what you did."

"There's more." The girl looked straight at him. "Mr. Williams is holding me for the police—for murder. Do you think there is a very good reason for that?"

And then Roberts did it. He walked right over and swung her into his arms. Not like young Mr. Stevens. He did it as if she belonged there. As if she belonged to him.

"That," he said, "I simply don't believe."

"No one," said a voice from behind us at the open French windows, "likes to believe in murder. You seem completely recovered, Mr. Roberts. The young lady— is she a relative of yours?" Roberts wasn't thrown. He turned and looked at Sergeant O'Rourke.

"This young lady," he said, "I intend to make my wife."

"Really!" O'Rourke turned to me. "Well, Race—I sent the boys down to the warehouse and came up here myself. Let me know what gives."

I was half-way through what I had to say when O'Rourke interrupted me.

"I think," he said, "we had all better go downtown and discuss this matter—"

"I think—" young Mr. Stevens put in, entering from the hall—"we had better go very lightly on this matter until proper explanations—"

"Interested in the young lady?" O'Rourke turned those sharp eyes on Stevens.

"The young lady," said Stevens stiffly and he did it well, even better than Roberts, "is to be my wife."

"Well—well." O'Rourke rubbed his hands. "So now we have intended bigamy." Then the light tone went out of his voice. "And who may you be, sir?"

"I am a member of the firm of Stevens, Ronalds, Blake & Stevens. My father is dead. I am young Mr. Stevens." And Stevens said it simply and with a certain amount of dignity.

CHAPTER 9

KILLER AT BAY

EVEN I WAS impressed. But then it was an impressive sight. Five million dollars is a lot of money. Harold Ronalds sat behind the big long table in what was known as the main library of Stevens, Ronalds, Blake & Stevens. Alongside him was Mathew J. O'Donnel, Commissioner of Police. Pacing the room in sartorial splendor was Gordon Ritter, the District Attorney. I recognized in the worn busy-looking little man the Chief Clerk of the Surrogates Court. There were a couple of other clerks with him.

Inspector Nelson had joined the party and I had gone out into the hall to talk to Sergeant O'Rourke.

"Just how did you happen to find the brief-case?" O'Rourke asked me for the fifth time.

I told him again.

"Believe it or not, O'Rourke, I was looking for it. That's why I stayed at the house. I know it isn't often I use my head—and I didn't use it in this case until after you decided to invite everyone down to Headquarters. The brief-case was hidden in the patio outside the den windows. The gun was inside of it. Not money—but negotiable bonds worth a hundred grand on the market today. The bank would have taken down the serial numbers of bills, I don't suppose there were any fingerprints on the gun."

"No." O'Rourke shook his head. "But I think it's the gun all right. Ballistics will give us that soon enough. It looks bad for the girl and young Roberts running off like that."

"Like what?" I smiled at him. "They weren't under arrest. Why, you hoped they would skip out! You boys always figure that flight is a sign of guilt. But it can be a sign of fright, too, even panic." And with a shrug. "Even a sign of love. Besides, you can pick them up when you want to."

It was O'Rourke's turn to grin now. "Even in Greenwich, Connecticut," he told me. "Now listen, Race. You found that gun and brief-case after Frank Huntington Roberts went in that window. He was your client and maybe you didn't see him put it there. He lives in about the center of the city. You had to drive to Yonkers. Roberts could have been home an hour—well, forty-five minutes anyway, before you called—and still have killed George Granger at that warehouse. He could have hired Ed Moran and George Granger to blackmail her. Then he held out on them. Ed Moran shot him. Roberts decided to kill Moran and have no witnesses—and he did."

I shook my head. "It doesn't wash," I told O'Rourke. "Too many things all wrong. Why would he blackmail the girl out of his own money—and don't give me the love angle again."

"Oh well," said O'Rourke, "maybe he didn't have proof she was a phony. They want us inside."

When we went into the main library, Harold Ronalds was on his feet talking. His dignity was unruffled. He paused politely when I came in.

"Take a chair, Mr. Williams," he said. And when I sat down, "The authorities are facing a situation of great gravity—in which I am concerned but not involved. The District Attorney, the Commissioner of Police, the good inspector here, are now thoroughly convinced that there is no room for the slightest doubt that the girl we know as Alta May Bronson is in fact beyond dispute the real Alta May Bronson, and is entitled to the Harrington estate." He raised his hand when the District Attorney started to speak. "One moment, and I will be through. There was never the slightest doubt at any time as to the girl's identity. There is none now."

The District Attorney came in then. "But Mr. Williams has made a sworn statement to the fact that the girl confessed that she was not Alta May Bronson."

"Not confessed, Gordon." Ronalds permitted his lips to part in what might have been a smile. "Let us say she made a statement to that effect. I have not the slightest idea why she made such a statement. If she made it, it was false. I presume from the whole sordid and unpleasant story, as Mr. Williams unfolded it, that Miss Bronson was blackmailed. Perhaps in fear or panic—or under pressure—she made such a statement. But the statement is false. You have ample proof, gentlemen."

"Is that true?" I looked over at Ritter, the D.A.

ALL THE MEN nodded solemnly.

"But she ran away—" Inspector Nelson said.

"Ran away?" Harold Ronalds had a nice inflection in his voice and a neat way of raising his eyebrows. "Ran away from what? Certainly not from shooting a man. Mr. Williams has explained that she hardly could have done that. And certainly, Inspector, you must be glad that you did not charge her with fraud in disposing of some of her own securities. Gentlemen, I am surprised that you would entertain the thought for one moment that such a fraud could be perpetrated upon the courts of this city."

"But Miss Bronson herself said—" and I stopped. Light was beginning to break. "Yes," I went on, thinking aloud, "she said it, and she meant it."

"She might have told you that you were the man in the moon," said Inspector Nelson turning sharply on me. "And you might have believed her."

"I might have believed she meant it at that." I pulled a grin, a weak one. But things were shaping up. Clattering around in my head, but falling into place just the same.

"Are you suggesting that Miss Bronson is not in her right mind?" Harold Ronalds came in then.

"No," I told him, "I'm not suggesting any such thing. But I was with Miss Bronson and heard her make the statement. You are all convinced that it was not a true statement. You must be right. I believed it—because Miss Bronson believed it. That's it, gentlemen. The girl herself doesn't believe she's the real Alta May Bronson."

"But why?"

"Why?" I said. "Because she was told she wasn't. Don't you see? Someone got to her before she was notified of the inheritance. These two men, Ed Moran and George Granger, came to her and told her they could fix it up so that she could pose as the Bronson heiress. Understand, she never suspected she was actually an heiress. Her mother and father took that other name. La Verne. They never mentioned the name Bronson to her—or Jarvis Harrington. Harrington had put the girl's parents out of his house—threatened to frame the husband, send him to prison. Why should they ever even mention Jarvis Harrington to their daughter? Oh, they might have if they had known they were going to die, but they didn't. And these two men told Alta May they could pass her off as the heiress."

"But how would they know? How would they find her?" The D.A. was tossing the questions now. "Yes, yes—I can see how easily they might blackmail her, if it happened as you say. I can see, too, how a young girl who never had any money could more easily believe that she was a false heiress than a real one. But my dear Williams. Two such well-known crooks could not hope to get away with that for long. Certainly the lawyers for the estate, the executor, would suspect."

He turned now and looked at Harold Ronalds, but Ronalds had turned and looked at young Mr. Stevens. In fact, they were all looking at young Mr. Stevens now. Young Mr. Stevens' tongue came out and he licked at his lips.

"Well, yes," he said. "I did suspect something, but it was her money and—and—"

"I know." Harold Ronalds nodded his head at him a bit sadly. "You were in love with the girl."

"Oh, when we find the girl and question her," the D.A. slammed in, "we'll get to the bottom of it. Things that were said, things that were done. Come, Mr. Stevens. How much did she confide in you?"

"Not a thing," young Mr. Stevens said. "Not a thing. I had hoped, indeed she led me to believe, that my affection was returned—and—"

"And you'd marry her and do the paying of the blackmailer for her," I came in fast then. "Sure, Mr. Stevens—young Mr. Stevens," I said sarcastically. "You were the only one she could trust. The only one who could see she got the money in a hurry without anyone else knowing about it. A secret that she would keep, and a secret that you would keep. And after you married her, you'd pay the whole estate into the pocket of the blackmailer—not blackmailers anymore. Just one blackmailer. Don't stand up and glare at me. You killed Ed Moran and you killed George Granger. Look at his face!" I let that one go to the District Attorney. "What other man could have engineered the whole business? No other man. Young Mr. Stevens ran that show. Harold Ronalds knows it—now."

Harold Ronalds looked steadily at Charles Stevens, and if the dignity hadn't gone, the nice inflection and the raised eyebrows were dead.

"You have always come to me for advice, Charles," he said in a low tired voice. "Why didn't you about—about the huge sums the girl wanted?"

It was there written on Charles Stevens' face. He could lead the band all right, but he couldn't turn around and face the music. Sure he denied it—violently. But I think we all were certain now.

Inspector Nelson had the single thought, "Where were you last night?" Even before Charles Stevens broke down—and he did break hard—Nelson was pushing him about what he did with the gun that killed George Granger. I came in there.

"What did he do with the gun?" I said. "He had it in the car with him—it and the bonds George Granger had received from Alta May Bronson. Stevens had no idea he would be suspected. He drove leisurely out to the Bronson place in Yonkers—straight from shooting Granger through the back of the head. He wanted to be sure the girl got home all right. The light was on, so he came to the door. He got a shock when he saw me. He got more of a shock when he discovered I knew about the murder. He left the room to telephone. I guess he did. But the police were coming. His car might be searched—the bonds and the gun found. And then he got a break. He saw Roberts go in the French window. He parked the gun and bonds outside that window."

"To plant the crime on Roberts?" the D.A. asked me.

"Yes, if they were found. If not, he could slip back and get the bonds. I think he preferred the money. But Roberts was making trouble and I'll bet young Mr. Stevens was afraid Roberts would put it straight up to the girl and she'd tell him the truth. Roberts hired the detective Jimmy Slavin, and Slavin found out something—enough to die. Whether it was Granger or Moran or Stevens who killed Slavin, I don't know, but I think it was Stevens. The other two were not killers. Witness the mess Moran made of his attempted murder of Roberts. But we should be able to pin one murder on Stevens anyway—the murder of George Granger in the warehouse."

It was the low voice of Harold Ronalds, however, that got results.

"You have sought my advice in all things, Charles," he said. "I'll give you that advice now. If you are guilty, nothing will save you. A close questioning of Miss Bronson should reveal much. A close scrutiny of your finances will reveal more. A closer scrutiny of your movements will no doubt reveal the truth. The gun may be traced to you. This young girl—your responsibility and mine—may be this very moment going to marry a man who will, by reason of her distracted condition, benefit by her fortune."

And young Mr. Stevens said, "Jarvis Harrington, at the end, wanted them to share the estate. He made a will to that effect." And after a long pause, and as if it were the worst and only crime he had committed, "I—I tore that will up."

Is there more? I suppose young Mr. Stevens (for I will always think of him as that) should have whipped out the murder weapon and shot himself dead—or taken poison. But this was life, and he didn't. Also he should have gone to the hot seat. But this was law, and he didn't, though he'd be behind bars for the rest of his days. Harold Ronalds fought the thing hard, with the best criminal lawyers in the city to back him up. He believed young Mr. Stevens insane. He couldn't believe otherwise. It didn't even enter his head that a member of that great firm which he headed could have been in his right mind and done such disgraceful things.

I guess Frank Roberts and Alta May Bronson shared the estate all right, as Jarvis Harrington had wanted them to do. They did get married. And they were in love. Anyway, the check I got was signed by both of them on a joint account.

No, it wasn't for half a million dollars. But it wasn't for doughnuts either.

Little Miss Murder

CHAPTER 1

BUSINESS WAS DULL, but I did have the remains of the Madden case. Nice remains, too.

She sat across from me now in the *101 Club*—which name meant that your chances of getting your money's worth was a hundred to one against you. She was peppy and over twenty-one, for she had moved out of her parents' place upstate and was playing the big city. A nice respectable secretarial job and all that, but hitting the night spots. "Seeing life" she called it.

Cissy Madden—I remember the day her father came in to see me. A retired produce merchant from the west living upstate he said. He was worried about Cissy; she got herself mixed up with some rather bad company in New York.

There was no trouble in my straightening that out. A little dough here and a punch in the nose there; and once a gun against a fair size stomach, and things were done. Now—he had wanted to put me on the payroll to take her around. But she wouldn't have that—and neither would I.

"Listen Race," she leaned across the table. "On the level, isn't it? You are taking me out and paying it out of your own pocket—just because—you—you like me." And when I grinned at her, "Father isn't kicking in?"

"Not a cent," I told her. "Though he was willing to. But honestly—I haven't used up anywhere near what he paid me to clear you up."

Her big eyes sort of closed and her lips twisted in a little grimace. "Anyway," she said finally. "You'd come to me anytime— anywhere—if I needed you badly," and when I waited, "even if your life was endangered."

"That's right." I lit the cigarette she put between her too, too, pretty lips. "But that would go on the expense account—" She looked hurt. "Danger is my business," I told her. "Your father understood that."

"But I didn't," she pouted across at me.

"Well—" I said, "you understand now."

She was a lot of fun; she was wide-eyed and excited and innocent and I didn't get a whole lot of that. But I won't go into it; I don't pretend to understand women. I've been fooled too many times by them. I'll simply say she struck me as real class. I could be wrong and she might turn out to murder her parents with an axe; it's been done you know. I have few illusions, but I liked the kid.

After a while she perked up again. That's another thing I liked about her. You couldn't keep her down for long. "All right," she said. "Since we are making confessions—or anyway talking right out—I'll tell you something. I'm writing a book. At least—I'm going to write a book.

So you see—I'm not just dumb—but got into that trouble with those people on purpose. That's Mr. Haydon, isn't it? I'd like to meet him."

And she did. For Harry Haydon, a big frog in a particularly big and very dirty puddle, came over to our table. He owned the *101 Club* and a few spots around town. They said he was short on money now.

I DIDN'T THINK Cissy should meet Haydon; he had an eye for cute tricks and he wouldn't have met her then except she did it herself. Harry Haydon had an eye for business, too, and didn't chase patrons around his place and never made a play on the premises. But he wanted to speak to me and Cissy did the trick.

"Oh, Mr. Haydon," she said. "You are— Mr. Haydon—*the* Harry Haydon, aren't you?"

"That's right," Haydon took the hand she held out, looked over her, and liked what he saw. She fussed over him, and his place, and the floor show; Harry would certainly know her again. It was to me he spoke then.

"I'd like a few minutes of your time, Race—up in the office—if this charming young lady can spare you." When she insisted that I go, he said, "It will interest you Race." And turning to the girl as he left, "You'd be a sensation here in the show young lady. Too bad you are not a professional or—or don't dance or sing."

That was Harry; he had laid the foundation. I guess he did it a dozen times a night. Sometimes he meant it— sometimes he didn't. Anyway, if a cutie confirmed his first quick appraisal he

CARROLL JOHN DALY

could have a better look. I'll say this for Harry; he was particular.

I left the main room in the middle of the floor show, went out through the bar and up the stairs to Haydon's office. I heard the buzzer sound almost the moment I reached the door. It opened, and the ugly-faced Joe Manze smiled at me. "Hello Race," he said, "the boss is waiting for you," and as I passed by into the room, "Race Williams—Mr. Haydon."

"Yes—yes," the deep voice came from inside. "Let him in Joe—close the door. I'll buzz you if I need you." And there behind the desk sat Harry Haydon. He got up slowly from behind the desk, as if with great effort; yet I knew, despite his bulk, he could move as quickly as a jungle animal. He even walked around the desk and shook hands with me; he was on the wrong side of forty and looked it.

"How are you, Race," he said. "You look good, boy. Sit down." And seeing me seated he went back and sat behind the desk. "I sent for you, Race, because—"

"Let us get it straight Harry," I said. "No one sends for me; you came and asked me up."

"Tush, tush," he wagged a finger at me. "A poor choice of words on my part Race. Let us say, then, I humbly sought a few moments of your time. That you were considerate enough to grant my request and—"

"Okay, Harry," I grinned, "that does it."

Harry nodded. He was taking himself very serious, lately—but fair is fair; so were lots of other people for that matter, racketeers, politicians—even the police. He sat back in his chair, then—leaned over and poured milk from a thermos-bottle into a glass and took a bite of a sandwich.

"Anything to eat—drink—smoke—" and when I shook my head he grinned, "even put an I.O.U. in the till for a few thousand. I feel friendly tonight, Race. We've been a long time around the Avenue, you and me. Understand each other; never crossed. I say to myself. 'There's Race Williams now—a bad man to cross Race.' And I keep in my own back yard. And you—say the same thing to yourself about me. We're as like as two peas in a pod."

"I hope not," I said.

"Oh—I mean we take care of ourselves," He waved a hand, and though it was a big paw and huge arm, it was a graceful movement. "If we have something unpleasant to do, we do it ourselves. Lone wolves." My eyes opened wide as I thought of his mob. "I have organization, yes—for business purposes. But I rely on myself for personal matters—just as you do. When we make a threat—we mean it."

"Have I threatened you?"

"No, no," he laughed. "Why should you?"

"Are you by any chance threatening me?"

"Hardly. I'm asking you a favor. I'd appreciate it very much if you saw no more—absolutely no more of Vickey Carr." When I looked up, surprised, and started to speak he interrupted me. "And I want your word Race—for your word is good—that you will see no more of Vickey Carr."

I gave that considerable thought. The simple thing would be to tell him the truth. But then—well, I'm built that way. I played along. "Why?" I tried.

"As a favor to me. I won't offer you money, Race, because I know your ideas on being—what you call bribed. Still if there is any loss to you, any expense, I want to pay it—double it or triple it or—"

"I guess," I cut in, "that, after all, you don't know how I feel about bribes."

"Okay Race—just lay off Vickey Carr."

There was no mistaking the hardness of his voice, the coldness of his eyes. He meant it all right. I came to my feet then; I was mad. I walked toward the door—then I turned, said, "I'll see as much of Vickey Carr as I wish."

Stupid that. Maybe. For I didn't know—didn't have the slightest idea who Vickey Carr was. I had never seen her—never heard of her.

Harry Haydon's voice followed me out into the hall. "Give it a thought Race. You might cause the death of Vickey Carr. I want to help you, and—" There was more. I didn't hear it; I was out in the hall.

Cissy wanted to know what it was all about but I didn't tell her of course. She said, "Do you really think he meant that about—about my being in his floor show?" When I told her he said that to all the lookers she pouted up a bit and chirped, "But I can dance—and I can sing. And—it would be wonderful to be up there and be—be—maybe a big star some day."

I didn't like it somehow. Ten minutes later I took her home. One thought: *Who was Vickey Carr?*

Maybe you think I should have let well enough alone—at least until this Vickey Carr showed up. I let it be known around that I wouldn't be averse to meeting one Vickey Carr, and I got a surprise. Vickey was not known in the night life of the city, and I got the impression that I was not the only one looking for her.

I didn't have any luck—but I didn't find any lead in my back either. I didn't see Cissy and I didn't find any Vickey Carr—and then one night I gave Cissy a buzz.

"Oh, Race—" she said. "I wanted to get in touch with you—" and when I waited, "you see—I've changed my job."

"Not starring at the *101 Club*," I joked.

"Not exactly starring—yet," she told me. "But I've got a job, and I open there Thursday night. Just chorus. What did you say?" and then, "No—I went and put it up to Mr. Haydon. I said I knew he was kidding and all that, but I could really dance and sing—and won't you come and see me?"

"Sure," I said and hung up; was she a dumb cluck after all?

That afternoon I had a visitor. You couldn't lay an age on her—somewhere between twenty-two and thirty-two. Back of her eyes, she had lived a hundred years. Her voice was low and husky as if she sang that way. I wouldn't especially like her, but fair is fair. There are those who would.

She sat down, opened her purse, and took out a roll of bills. Which was a good beginning. She peeled off five bills and put them on the desk. "A retainer," she said.

"But," I liked her better now, "I haven't accepted your—business, yet."

"That is right," she said. "You haven't. That money is for listening to me talk." She put a cigarette in her mouth, offered me one from a gold case. They were long and thin—with Russian ends on them. I shook my head but snapped a light for her. I said. "I can stand a lot of talk for five hundred dollars."

"There will be a lot more money in it for you, Mr. Williams." She pulled the chair up close to the desk alongside of me, crossed her legs. They were long; there was a lot of them to see; they were not bad. I felt like saying the five hundred was enough. But I didn't; I waited.

"It is a question," she went on, "of money. A lot of money. A lot to you and to me." She did a double take with her legs—got them settled the other way, then said. "It won't be hard to show proof that the money belongs to me."

She waited, so I asked. "If you can prove it—what do you want me to do?"

"I want you," she said, "to see that I stay alive while I prove it. Can you do that?"

"I can try," I said modestly but I meant *you bet I can* and my smile should have told her that.

"I'll be in danger of my life," she told me, "and so you'll be in danger of yours. And the trouble is—" she frowned, "I don't know exactly where the danger will come from."

I looked her over, then; a great light was dawning. "I think I can find out where the danger will come from," I told her. "Now—who are you? And just what is it I am to do."

"I'm Vickey Carr," she said simply. It didn't toss me; I was pleased. I said:

"Could your danger come from Harry Haydon?"

"Haydon," she looked at me surprised. "I wouldn't think so. He was my father's—my dead father's friend."

"He has charge of your money—your father left it to him."

"Oh no," she said. "It's mine. He doesn't want it; he wouldn't have it—unless, of course, I were dead."

I SAT UP straight on that one. It was such an innocent crack coming from such hard lips. "You've seen Haydon?"

"No, no," she came in quickly. "He's been looking for me," and leaning forward, "Mr. Williams—should I fear Harry Haydon?"

"I think you should," I told her, and I took the stuff she handed me out of her purse. A birth certificate—Los Angeles, California; it said she was almost twenty-four. She looked older. A picture of her when she was about five—or any other girl for that matter. You know the resemblance—two eyes, one nose, a couple of legs—skinny ones then. Better ones now.

She took the stuff back, said, "It won't be easy for you Mr. Williams. You will have to appear quite openly in my behalf. Your life, then, will be in constant danger. It was suggested, Mr. Williams, that I pay you ten thousand dollars—I thought perhaps it should be more, for it is a lot of money."

I nodded at that and said, "I understand that just about this time Mr. Haydon could use a lot of money. You are not thinking of trusting him, are you?" When she looked sort of blank, "You say it was suggested that you come to me—by a friend—a lawyer—who?"

She just looked at me. I tried, "Is that all you want to tell me?"

"What else is there to tell?"

"How much the money is. If it is in a trust fund. Who your father was. How he got the money. If it is all legal and aboveboard. Who threatens your life? Has it ever been threatened before? Is this cash hidden away? Who has it? Is there a lawyer connected with it? Has your life ever been attempted?" I paused a moment and then, "Where have you been keeping yourself over the years?"

She looked at me as if about to speak, hesitated—then came to her feet. "Tomorrow night," she bobbed her head forward emphatically. "I've rented an old furnished house here in the city. I will meet you some place tomorrow night and take you to that house. Then the lawyer will come."

"Where—what time will you meet me?"

Again the hesitation. Then she named a drug store and fixed the time as midnight exactly. It was a quiet street she picked; the drug store would be closed at that hour. I told her so. I said, "Better trust me—fully."

She looked at me as if she never trusted anyone fully, and shook her head. "The lawyer will have to tell you. I promised. I'll meet you outside the drug store. Be—be most silent—and careful."

She suddenly turned and beat it out of the office. Was I a little insulted? For a moment maybe. Then I counted the five century notes, again, and felt less insulted.

CHAPTER 2

I CAME OUT of the Chelsia Steak House the next night when the little figure slid alongside of me and whispered, "Turn the corner Race. I would pour words into your ear."

The spats. The yellow gloves, the fedora at a rakish angle—and the white carnation stood out. I couldn't see the pince-nez nor the black ribbon attached to them but I knew they were there. It was Riley—the wise man of Broadway.

He must have been crowding seventy, now—maybe into it. The mystery of the city. Born with larceny in his soul. A common thug they had said in his younger days; a swindler, a confidence man, and in jail more than he was out. Then Riley suddenly changed; he had not even faced a judge in close to forty years. He was the Walter Winchell of the night—except that he didn't broadcast what he knew. But he was paid for that information. Riley seemed to know everything.

"Walk slowly, dear boy," he said. "I've been wondering if I should go out of town for a few days, or longer. I didn't want to be seen talking to you, in case you should break this case yourself."

"What case?" I asked.

He ignored that and went on. "I knew you were looking for a certain party. Nothing clever about that; you asked enough people. And I knew another certain party wouldn't like that. And I knew that certain party was also looking for—"

"Vickey Carr," I said. "What do you know about Vickey Carr?"

"I knew her father," he said. "Not too well. He knew Harry Haydon, knew him too well. Forrester Carr—quite a name but that was his real name. Fancy, wasn't it? But then his family never expected that he'd turn out bad—and I guess in the long run Forrester never expected that he'd turn out good. But he did; at least he died leaving good money."

"Listen—Riley," I stopped him. "I'm a busy man. I'm interested in Vickey Carr, but not as interested as I was a few days ago. Still if a hundred dollars."

"Boy—boy," he laughed. "I lost interest in century notes years and years ago. You see Forrester Carr left a few hundred thousand dollars in trust for his daughter, or to Harry Haydon if she was dead. The money wouldn't be distributed for twenty years," and with great meaning, "that was twenty years ago. I want five grand in cash for my help in finding Vickey Carr and—"

"You're out of your head," I told him; "I didn't need your help. And—"

I stopped dead. I never did like talking to myself. Riley was gone; he had simply merged with the night.

I kept the appointment that night. I came in my car and parked up the street from the drug store. It was already twelve o'clock. This was the big night. I smacked my lips.

VICKEY WAS LATE. I stood with my hands deep in my jacket pocket. My right one held a gun. Why not? She said a lot on money. Haydon needed money. He was a killer.

She came, slipped out of the subway and I had her by the arm and we were around the corner and down to my parked car.

"Where to?" I asked her.

"You fairly took my breath away," she breathed heavily, and I could see that she was nervous now; she was scared.

"Not far," she told me. "In the fifties. I've rented a house there."

"The lawyer fellow—he'll be there?"

"He'll come," she said as we drove across town. "Please Mr. Williams, don't question me now. He'll tell you everything; it's going to be all right."

"Of course it is," I said. "You're shaking; has anything happened since yesterday afternoon?"

"No, no. Why do you say that?" there was a bird-like tone in the husky voice now—as if fear was turning to panic. Then, as if she tried to pull herself together, "I guess it's the reaction—near the end—the end. I've been through a lot. Let us talk about some thing else. The lawyer—he will explain all; you'll be well paid."

"Sure," I said. "I'm not afraid of that. But don't worry. Buck up; I'll take care of everything in the fear line."

"Yes—of course. Let us talk about something else," and then suddenly, "Have you got a gun?"

"Two of them," I told her. "You are as safe as if you were home in your own bed."

"I know—I know."

I looked over at her; there was no leg show now.

We drove by the house, first; it was a brownstone front like the rest of them on the block. Most of them were apartments or rooming houses. I asked her and she said this was a private dwelling. She lived alone there. It didn't seem quite sensible. But she said it wouldn't be long. "It will be all over tonight, Mr. Williams. I'll keep you with me from—from now on."

I pulled to the curb a few houses down the block and climbed out. I waited for her. I didn't help her. She gripped my arm; she had a bad case of the shakes. We started along the sidewalk. I'd be glad to get her in the house and into a chair—maybe a drink into her. She was fast going to pieces.

I steadied her—said:

"Look—pull yourself together. I want a hand free." I jerked a gun suddenly into my right hand; let her see it. It shook her up rather than quieted her down.

"Put it away—put it away," she hardly could get the words out. "It makes me think of death—death—" Maybe there was another "death" but it was too low to get.

"Okay, Vickey," I parked the gun in my jacket pocket but kept my hand on it. I tucked my left arm through hers and steadied her and we started down the sidewalk.

I said to make a conversation, "What name do you go under?"

"Adams," she said. "Elizabeth Adams. Why?"

"Never told anyone your real name—Vickey Carr?"

"No—no one—why should I?"

"Who knows it?" We were getting along better.

"This lawyer who advised me to seek you—no one else. I told no one. Here it is—the next house."

We made the worn old stone steps, reached the vestibule. There were outer and inner doors on these old residences. I held her back, took the key from her. I breathed easier; we were inside.

A dead silence. The house was dark. Pitch black. I made a light with my flash. The girl grabbed at my arm, hissed hoarsely. "Don't do that." When I doused the light she added more sensibly and more naturally, "I'll find the switch—the library to the right here."

Feet moved by me. I listened. Just her feet.

Then a light snapped on and I saw the room through slightly parted thick drapes. Library? I suppose so. Anyway there were books around and some old furniture—comfortable enough, and a fireplace.

I followed her through the parted drapes saw her look to the windows—at the curtains before them. I looked, too. The curtains were drawn tight but they didn't reach the floor; no one could hide behind them without showing feet. That, I guess, was her thought and I knew it was mine.

"Better sit down," I told her. "Or if it's handy you might get a drink. What are you listening for?"

"Nothing—nothing." She was standing there, her eyes over my shoulder. Her hand raised—listening—listening—listening. And then I got it—the feeling of danger. Peril—real and immediate, was in the air. I heard it. Not feet exactly—certainly not moving feet—but the crack of old boards despite the thick carpeting.

It was a board. As if—as if—well as

if someone—some human had shifted his balance or her balance, but certainly not their balance. One person only. One board only.

"Listen," I warned and I jerked out my gun.

Things broke inside the girl, I guess. She threw out her arms—and pitched forward, leaped forward with a frightened cry and was in my arms—had knocked aside my right hand. My gun.

I saw the arm and the hand—yes and the gun come from behind those drapes at the door. I shot first. My shot was wild; she had knocked my arm up. There were three shots; then two more of mine. I was shooting wildly now, blindly, for the girl was in my way. And I knew even as I grabbed at her that she was hit—hit bad.

I could feel her body jar with each of those three shots from the curtain, well with two of them anyway. The third one, I knew, did for her even if the first two hadn't.

I WAS HOLDING a dead girl in my arms; I was shooting. Then I wasn't. There wasn't any hand there any more; there were just the drapes waving and the boards now—dulled of squeaks and sound by the running of feet. One pair of feet.

I could do nothing for the living; I could do nothing for the dead, for that matter, except give her vengeance. I let her slip to the floor and was out in the hall.

The feet beat on stairs. Going down. Then I remembered that these old houses had a basement floor that generally contained the dining-room and kitchen and servants quarters. The killer knew

the house and I didn't, and I made my mistake, then—if it was a mistake. I don't think I could have caught up with him before he was out the back door and over the fence and into the rear stone yard behind.

I thought I played it well. My flash gave me directions. I found a rear room—the window. It was not so dark that I wouldn't spot the fleeing killer as he fled for the fence. I didn't bother with locks on the window. I knocked out a pane of glass with my gun and was ready—and waiting.

Ten, fifteen, twenty seconds—half a minute passed and I knew the truth; I had been outguessed—outsmarted. Call it what you want. The killer, of course, had doubled back through the basement and gone out the front—the areaway entrance from the floor below. And now was clean away.

I went back to the library. No sound in the old house, just a dead girl on the floor. I knelt down beside her. It was useless. I knew she was dead; I knew, too, that she had feared this.

A new experience for me. A client shot down right under my nose—literally in my arms. Her final fear—her final hope—me.

She had been in a panic from the moment I met her. And I—I looked down at her again. There was nothing soft about her face in death, nothing good about it either. That wasn't the point; I had told her that she would be just as safe as if she was tucked in to bed. And now—she was dead.

I caught myself listening for the wail of the siren, the screech of the brakes of a police car. But these old houses were well built.

Panic? No, I didn't feel any panic. Mad! I was mad, all right, and my first impulse was to dash from the house and crash into the *101 Club*. I didn't. The phone was there; it stared me in the face. I knew the danger of leaving the scene of a murder. It could mean my license. It could mean more than that. I tried to tell myself that no one knew I had met the girl—had come to the house with the girl. But who might this girl have told? The lawyer lad—who hadn't showed up? Had she told him? If she hadn't? But the murderer knew; that meant that Harry Haydon knew.

I lifted the phone and buzzed the cops, tried to get my friend Sergeant O'Rourke, but he was off duty. I knew he lived up in Kingsbridge. No luck.

I swallowed hard, got Inspector Nelson. My enemy—the lad who wanted my license. But I gave it to him straight. "Race Williams—speaking," then I gave him the address. "A girl was just shot to death in this house; the killer got away. I'm reporting the crime and getting on the job."

"No," he snapped, "you stay there; you know the law." When I started to give him an argument he popped in, "Beat it out of that house, Williams, and I'll have a general order out to pick you up; you know what that will do to you."

I lit a butt and tried to kid myself. Doctors lose patients, and people think nothing of it. Big criminal lawyers have their clients burnt, up at Sing Sing, and it isn't held against them. Cops have prison-ers escape, and key witnesses in trials are spirited away from under their noses, or blown out with machine guns—and they are heroes for risking their lives in trying to prevent it.

Then why couldn't I—couldn't I. I cursed myself and lit a butt. It was no go; I felt responsible.

The police are good; in less than two minutes the first police car pulled to the curb. I didn't talk; I waited.

Nelson came, then the boys. Cameras, fingerprint men—the assistant medical examiner. At last Nelson took me across the room.

I told him all I knew about the girl. It wasn't much. Just that she had come to my office and retained me. That I met her; that I came to the house with her; that she was nervous. That she said a lawyer would be there. Then the man with the gun and the sudden panic—and her jump toward me and knocking my gun hand up.

"What's your hurry? Who do you think gave her the dose?"

And when I simply shrugged. "It's murder, Race. It won't do to hold out on the police, and it won't do to make a private vengeance out of it. Now who do you think?"

"I won't guess on murder," I said.

He kept me longer. Went over it again—wrote it all down in a little book. "Vickey Carr," he repeated after me. "Unnamed lawyer. Money she expected to get. Feared for her life. Gave you five hundred dollars—well I can check your bank deposit on that." He looked at me a long time; he was a wise bird, was Nelson.

There was a hard, speculative look in his eyes. "Okay, beat it along. Work on the case—and keep me informed. The D.A. will want to talk to you."

I was relieved; I had expected worse. Down at Headquarters until far into the morning. It was a break I might have gotten from Sergeant O'Rourke, but not from Inspector Nelson.

I drove right to the *101 Club*. It was only a few blocks. I stalked into the bar, walked back toward the stairs. An ugly-looking lad in a tux blocked my way. Joe Manse. "Oh, it's you Race. The boss is busy. A little game. Some prominent citizens. Can't be disturbed."

I kept my eyes on him and shoved my right hand up under my coat—knocked his arm down as it moved. I shoved the gun hard against his chest. "Is that good for admission?"

"Well—" he looked at me and seemed surprised. "What's the matter Race? What's wrong? I'll buzz the boss if it's that bad—and—" he moved out of the way. He was right; I would have brought the gun down on his head in another moment.

"I'm in a nasty mood, Joe," I said. "Take me up."

He never said a word; he led the way like a man in a daze. And I followed him like—well like another man in a daze, I guess. What was I going to do when I faced Harry Haydon, I didn't know. The gun was up under my arm again, so was my hand.

We went up the stairs together. The door to Haydon's private room was open. Quite evidently, he invited inspection; he had nothing to hide.

I walked into the room. Five men were there, playing poker. Haydon's alibi. Not one of them were of the night—all business men. I guess. Two of them I recognized as clients of the club. So—Haydon had done his own killing. Ten minutes— fifteen—half hour, would have been enough for the murder; maybe less if he knew what time the girl was to bring me to the house.

Harry Haydon looked up at me. He seemed surprised, but not alarmed. "Join us, Race, he said. "Another player would do; we've been at it since eleven o'clock."

"Vickey Carr was killed tonight, Haydon," I said "Shot to death— murdered—through the back."

"No," he did it well—half jarred to his feet. And then. "You were with her?"

"Yes," I said. "I was with her when she died; I want to see you alone—now."

"No—" he said. "You can't. I— I—" He came to his feet as I walked toward him; he must have seen in my eyes what Joe Manse had seen there. The smugness left his face, a startled surprised look took its place. He called, "You're mad Race; I was here all evening. These men—they—I tell you Race—" I was right in front of him. "All right, boys—" he called out suddenly and a door in the rear opened and two men came in. I guess they had guns; I don't know. I only saw them out of the corner of my eyes.

"They won't help you any, Harry," I said. "I'm not interested in myself, now— only you—just you."

I was lifting my right hand when the relief came into his face. But he wasn't looking at me; he was looking over my shoulder. He said, and his voice was calm, "I warned you Race. I told you that if you didn't leave Vickey Carr alone something would happen to the poor girl and now—now—Inspector Nelson."

At first I thought it was the old *"look out for the baby carriage behind you"* stall. Then Nelson came into the room, said, "So you knew Vickey Carr—eh Mr. Haydon? Very interesting; you and I will have to have a talk. Beat it along—Williams."

I did. Nelson was a smart man. I knew now why he let me go—so he could tail along and see where I went. And I hadn't even looked back.

CHAPTER 3

I GOT HAYDON's story, or what Nelson wanted me to have the next day when I left the District Attorney's office.

Nelson said, "Haydon has an alibi. Fake, perhaps, but I can't break it. He says he was rung up and told that Vickey Carr would be in danger if she engaged you. He said Vickey's father was his friend, he warned you, so as to protect the girl.

"Did he say he got money—if she died?"

"Yes—quite frankly. But then he pointed out that someone inherits money very often when someone dies. He appears hazy about the amount. Talked of protecting his long dead friend's daughter. He could have killed her; I hope he did." And after a pause, "There's no man I'd rather get—for murder. We know he's killed women before."

"If you know—" I started, but he stopped me.

"Don't give me that stuff Race—knowledge is not evidence to take before twelve men. You know he shot this client of yours dead in your arms and what—what are you doing about it?"

"I'd of done plenty about it if you hadn't—" I started and stopped. *So,* I thought; *Nelson would like that. I kill Haydon and he gets both of us out of his hair.* I was going to crack wise, but I didn't; I wanted to find out more.

Nelson said, "Haydon claims not to have seen the girl in nearly twenty years. Our information is simply that she suddenly appeared out of nowhere. She rented that house a month ago under the name Elizabeth Adams. Paid six months in advance. The house agents positively identified the body at the morgue. She was not hiding her name too much—or was careless. The check she gave them was signed with her own name—Vickey Carr."

"What does the bank say?"

"Nothing. She opened her account there the day she made out the check. A thousand dollars. Nothing else has been drawn against her account."

"Did you find any lawyer?"

"Not yet, but we will. We're holding the body at the morgue. Relatives, maybe. There is no one to claim the body but Haydon; he wants to pay all the funeral expenses because of his old friendship with her father."

"I can't understand Vickey Carr's father leaving money to a hood like that—especially if his daughter was dead. Haydon's a known killer for money."

"He wasn't twenty years ago. Haydon didn't even have a record them; he was unknown in New York. Still," Nelson paused, "I don't see how he could have killed Vickey Carr. How he knew where she'd be—the exact time. And he'd have to know that. Those lads he was playing cards with wouldn't alibi him for the brutal murder of a young woman: somehow they think he didn't have the time to do it—if he wasn't with them all evening. Well—" he shrugged his shoulders. "It isn't likely the girl helped him out and made her time suit his convenience. Placed herself in that house on time to be murdered."

I snorted at that. It was a stupid statement. Yet I was sure that Haydon had killed her—himself.

THAT NIGHT WHEN I was doing a steak in the Chelsia Steak House, Haydon had the nerve to buzz me on the phone. "I'm sorry Race," he said, "that you didn't take my advice and stay away from Vickey Carr."

"What do you want?" I slammed in on him.

"Just want to tell you that I'm giving that little friend of yours—Cissy Madden is it—a chance in the show. I thought you'd like that. Come around and see her." And when I started to say something, "No thanks, boy—no thanks. I'm in debt to you. Vickey Carr's father was my friend. Her death you know—brings me a bit of money."

"Harry," I fairly gasped. "You—you are looking for a showdown."

"Why—I don't know what you mean Race. I—I'm sorry about that kid dying, of course; but it was nice to think that she died in your arms."

He hung up then. Had he simply wanted to get under my skin? And if that was it—well, fair is fair; he certainly had.

I jammed up the recover like to tear the instrument off the wall of the little booth, then stamped back to my dinner—back to it but I didn't eat any more. I couldn't.

It was then that I pulled myself together and made up my mind—that I wouldn't kill Harry Haydon. I'd put the finger on him, though. A dose of lead was too good for him. I set my lips grimly. I'd let him sit for months up in the death house—with the smell of burning flesh in his nostrils. His flesh.

I KNEW THAT I was followed as soon as I left the eating house. I must have been followed there for Haydon to locate me that quickly. I could have ducked the lad easily enough—but I didn't want it easy—at least not easy for one of Haydon's boys.

I took my little lamb down a dark side street, found the empty building I knew was there. Went down the alley beside it, turned at the back and waited crouched against the wall. My shadow came—very lightly, but I heard him. A hand gripped the stone first, then his head came around for a peek. I brought my gun down hard; he dropped like a log.

I stepped over his unconscious body and went back to the street. I felt better.

A voice spoke close beside me. I swung—gun out. It was Riley—carnation, spats, and all, and a cane over his arm. "Easy does it Race." Riley gripped my arm and led me down the street. "I saw you go in that alley. Saw the man follow you—and saw you come out alone. That's more like you. Not dead, I trust. But of course not; I heard no shot—simply a love tap in that playful way of yours. I was wondering, Race, what you thought of our little talk the other night."

"Maybe I should have listened to you then, Riley. Now it is too late. Don't you read the papers?"

"Sure—sure, Race. I read the papers. You're not doing too well. Have you thought about that five-thousand dollar proposition I made you."

"No, no—" and with half a laugh and not a good half one at that. "Nothing for you there now, Riley; Vickey Carr is dead."

"There is still the money. Now, now Race—if I can fix it—so that your client gets that money will you push for that fee for me?"

"I thought," I said, "Haydon gets the money. He's hardly my client."

"We might arrange it so that Haydon wouldn't get it, Race. What then?"

I TOOK THE hand that sought mine. "Right—Riley. I'll push it—hard—for your five grand if I have a client."

"Good boy," he said. "Now listen, Race. I knew Forrester Carr. Knew his sister, too, but not what became of her, though she did get married. Married a lad called—Madison. She took the kid—Vickey Carr—when her brother died."

"Is she alive; is this sister entitled to the money?"

"Hold everything, Race; not so fast. I bounced Vickey Carr on my knees when she was four—just before her father died. There was a birthmark, Race, small you know—but plain to see if you looked for it."

"So?" I asked.

"So—" he said. "Did that girl—that girl who died in your arms, have a birthmark shaped like a leaf? No larger than a dime, under her left shoulder-blade."

"How would I know?"

"Well," he said, "if she didn't—she's not Vickey Carr."

For a moment I had hope. Then it died. "But Haydon killed her; it was Vickey Carr." And when Riley said nothing, "Have you been to the morgue?"

"No—no. Not in it. One of Haydon's boys is checking up on all visitors. I wouldn't want to be checked on. But Haydon is still looking for Vickey. Then, Race, I never heard of a client dying in your arms. A girl who trusted you and put her faith in you, and placed her life in your hands, tush, tush boy. I have more confidence in you than you have in yourself. It just isn't possible; it couldn't happen—not with you."

"It *did* happen," I told him.

"I can't believe it; I *don't* believe it. Suppose, Race, that woman threw herself at you to prevent you shooting at the man behind the drapes; suppose she jumped at you to save his life."

"But why? Talk sense."

"Why—Haydon could have paid her to impersonate Vickey Carr. Any papers she showed you could have been forged; how could you check? She was nervous and in a panic you say. Why? Because she

394   CARROLL JOHN DALY

was paid to lure you to your death. She knew about you and wondered—and was scared. I'd be frightened myself, Race, if I were trapping you to death." He spread his yellow-gloved hands out. "She sprang at you to knock down your gun."

"Yes—yes—" and then because I wanted to think that, "No Riley—Haydon shot her, not me."

"Sure—" Riley nodded. "You'd be his proof that Vickey Carr was dead. And you'd stop looking for Vickey, and give him a chance to find her, kill her, and collect."

"But the girl—she wouldn't offer her life to aid Haydon."

"Not knowingly, Race. But she didn't know. And Haydon—would he mind killing a woman if it helped him? Probably had a reason to get rid of her. Come, come Race—he wanted people to think Vickey was dead—you mostly. Better take a look at that body in the morgue."

I left him—hailed a taxi and was giving directions to the morgue when he climbed in beside me.

"You can let me know when you come out," he told me. "Besides—I may have information for you. I know who the lawyer is who is handling the money." When I stared down at him. "I always earn my fee. You know that."

THE OLD GUY at the morgue knew me. "Vickey Carr, eh Mr. Williams?" He took the bill I gave him and pocketed it. "Hasn't caused much interest. That's the dame got it with you, didn't she? Let me see. Down this way. Not dolled up in all her finery now. Ah—here we are." He

pulled out the draw and I grabbed at the sheet.

He helped me turn the body over.

"Don't look bad," he said. "Drilled in the back—two neat holes—and one through the back of the head. Any shot of the three would have done for her. Nice back she had—not a mark on it but for that lead," and as I took out my torch. "What—with these lights we got. Regular Sherlock Holmes, aren't you?"

One thing was certain. I knew when I raised from peering closely down at the body that there was no birthmark on that back, leaf or anything else. So—the dead girl was *not* Vickey Carr.

I STRAIGHTENED AND pulled down my vest, felt pretty good. I was my own man again. For if Riley hadn't lied to me—and Riley never had—the dead girl was not Vickey Carr.

I was whistling when I left the morgue. I went right down the dark side street where I was to meet Riley. He came like a shadow again. "Worth a lad's life to be seen with you now—mine anyway. Well?"

I told him. But he didn't know now and never had any idea who Vickey was, or where she was. He said, "Haydon was looking for her; you were looking for her. So I entered the picture. She's alive though, Race; you can bet on that."

Then Riley gave me the tip off. "You better find out, Race, just what is in it for you—and for me, and for Vickey. Go see Sam Seed, the lawyer."

I couldn't place Sam Seed; I didn't know him, didn't know his office.

Riley said, "His office is in his hat. He

does a little real estate—a little investment business. Is as honest in a crooked way as you are Race."

"What do you mean by that?" I demanded.

"No offense," Riley said easily. "I mean if he takes a case he sticks to his clients. He's getting old. Has desk space for mail some place or other. But here's his home address."

Riley slipped it to me. I read it as I lit a butt. A Greenwich Village apartment house.

Late—sure it was late for a business call—or any other kind on a stranger. But I decided that Sam Seed and I were no longer going to be strangers; I taxied to his apartment.

I caught him in. That is in bed. He was old, all right. I could see the long white of the night-shirt beneath his bathrobe after I climbed the three flights of stairs. He was waiting for me there by his door, was putting his teeth in. If I didn't know him, he knew me all right. If he was surprised he didn't show it; he said simply, "Come in Mr. Williams. I never thought you'd have the brains to find me. But here you are. What do you want?"

I followed his bare feet down the hall. A shabby apartment house but Sam Seed had done himself proud inside. It was comfortable and expensive—both. I came right to the point. "The girl at the morgue," I said, "is not Vickey Carr."

"So what?" he shoved his feet into slippers, sat down and jerked his elbow—that's right—his elbow at a chair for me. Then he began to stuff his pipe.

"Well—" I said. "You haven't given the money to Haydon?"

"What money?"

"Listen, Seed," I told him. "I'm in this thing to stick. I—I don't know why."

"Why should you?" he pointed the stem of the pipe at me and then lit it. "You weren't hired for your brains—but for your beef—your quick eye and your ready finger."

"I haven't been hired at all," I told him.

"No," he said. "Is it possible that she is dead?"

"Listen." I went and stood over him. "Is there money coming to Vickey Carr? I'm not in a mood to kid." I put a hand on his shoulder. "There is crooked work going on. If you're in it—"

HE CAME TO his feet with remarkable speed. My hand slipped off his shoulder. He flashed out the words. "I'm *not* in it. There is money in trust. The trust expires next week. If the girl comes for the money—she gets it; the principal, all of it. If she doesn't come—the—the other claimant gets it."

"How did you know she'd come to me?" I asked.

"I told her to; at least I wrote her guardian."

"Mr. Madison?" my hands dropped to my side.

"That's right—Mr. Madison. Why did I tell her to engage you? Well, I have wondered about that. It has bothered me that I may have broken my trust with—the dead Forrester Carr. But I guess, like you, I don't like Harry Haydon. I didn't like him bothering me or threatening me; he's a killer."

"But you'd give the money to a killer."

"My dear Williams, I turned over money, once, to a man on the very eye of his execution for the brutal murder of an elderly couple—got out of sick bed to do it too. And there wasn't a nickel in it for me, either. I've got ethics like you have ethics. Not good ethics maybe—but ethics."

"You can identify Vickey Carr—though you have never seen her."

"Yes," he said. "I can identify her." And when I waited, "by her back."

"Does Haydon know about—about the birthmark on her back?"

"So you know," he let his eyes narrow. "And you haven't seen her. Well—well—" he shook his head as if it worked on a wire. "Yes—Haydon knows."

When I just stood and looked at him he went on, "Williams—I'm glad I don't know anything that can help you—for if I did—by gad I'm afraid I'd tell you. It isn't that my heart is touched, or I've taken a fancy for the girl—I don't know her. I guess it's age creeping on and I've taken a powerful dislike to Mr. Harry Haydon. Not simply a dislike for killers, but a personal dislike. Yet—I'll give him the money—on proof of death. Anyway the courts would make me."

He smacked his lips. "I told Haydon Vickey had hired you; I hoped it would scare him."

"This is honest money?" I asked.

"Honest money—and lucky money," he said. "A foolish man, Forrester Carr, a gambler of the worst kind. A sucker for any get-rich-quick scheme. He bought gold mine stock, oil stock—anything that was cheap and promised a fortune.

And—what he left wasn't worth much at the time." He chuckled, then. "Well, suckers have to win sometimes to encourage other suckers. Oil came in—and there is close to four hundred thousand dollars in trust now—for the girl, or for Haydon." A moment's pause. "And you stand there glaring at an old man—when a young girl may need you—if she is still alive."

I turned to the door. Hesitated, then without a word walked into the hall, down the stairs and out into the night.

The shots came from at least two directions, maybe three. Ahead and both sides. Fast—chain lightning with a gun. Maybe I am. But I was hit before I had my gun out.

I was not only hit. I was falling sideways—against the stone balustrade that protected people on the front steps from falling into hard paved areaway ten—fifteen feet below.

That balustrade protected me, too; it steadied me—steadied me as the man came from the right, running toward the steps with a gun in his hand. I wasn't too pleased, but I certainly was a little grim and did feel a certain satisfaction, when I fired. He went down. He wouldn't get up again; he went down hard—very hard. Was dead—very dead.

I was swaying there when the second man stopped, looked at his dead friend, turned and fled. Fled as I squeezed lead again. I saw him stumble, go to one knee, and come up again and keep running. Then things spun. A car motor raced, wheels screeched and I went over the balustrade.

Out. No—I wasn't out then. Sort of dizzy. I knew what was happening; I had a hazy recollection of grabbing at the stone rail, twisting my body around. Then I was dropping—dropping feet first.

I was shooting, too; that is what I was told afterwards; shooting at a car that was speeding away. Nice work, that; I took credit for it. At least I didn't deny it. Certainly I don't recall it. My last conscious thought was of bending my knees to break my fall.

Then—perhaps blackness. I don't even remember the blackness. I just remember a voice saying—and the voice of Inspector Nelson at that, "Shot in the head. No wonder he isn't dead." A pause, then, "Just creased him, eh?"

And another voice: "It will be as near to death as he'll ever come. The danger of concussion is great. Nonsense. You can't talk to him now."

I took a look. White bed, white walls, white nurse, white doctor—and—ruddy unpleasant-looking Inspector Nelson. Then a sudden prick in the arm and I was out cold—again. The last words I heard was the doctor saying, "He'll be lucky if he's out of here in a week." And my last thought was, *do you want to bet on that?* and—the bet. Well, I might have won it—or I might have lost it. You tell me.

CHAPTER 4

THE NEXT DAY, Thursday, I felt a little wobbly on my pins maybe as I took a gander about the room when I was alone.

I thought I should go home; the nurse said I was suffering from shock.

Yes; the shock of being such an idiot. She caught me on my feet so she called in the doctor.

"Listen Doc," I told him. "I've been dropped out of two-story windows, shot in the stomach—had the daylights beaten out of me. I know what shock is, and I haven't got it."

He tasted that one around a bit; decided not to force shock on me and said, "To be perfectly frank you might leave here and be all right—that is with rest and quiet. Again you might drop dead on the street—half a block from the hospital. It's concussion we fear. You're confused and—"

"I've been confused for a month, now; in fact, my mind has never worked well. But I can't stick here; I got to get out. Understand?"

"Quite," he said. "We'll see how you feel tomorrow and discuss it then—eh?"

There was a polite question in his words—but none in his manner. It was as if he had spoken and that ended it. He walked out. I sat in bed and smoked—mostly because it annoyed the nurse; I didn't like her. And, peculiarly, my head was working better than it had in a long time. Maybe a bit of concussion was what I needed. I had a good thought—I think a bright thought. That is bright as far as it went. Then it struck a dead-end street. It seemed like I knew who Vickey was—but I couldn't quite get it out.

The hospital and I were at odds. They wouldn't let me leave; I was going to leave. Why argue the point? When I got ready to leave I'd walk out. It would be that night. This was Thursday. I had promised to see Cissy Madden do her stuff; I was going to see Cissy Madden do her stuff. I liked the girl.

It was after supper I got a look at the paper. I liked the headlines. *Ace Detective shot through the head.* That is, I liked the Ace part. Another—*Race Williams near death from gangland bullets.*

The guy I had smeared was dead, all right. I didn't know him; I liked that, too. So Haydon had to import out-of-town talent for that little crack at me.

I LEFT THE hospital before nine o'clock, in time for the first show at the *101 Club.* I felt pretty good. I went out with the visitors who were being ejected—five minutes ahead of time by the way. I was all dressed—yet, I felt undressed. I had looked all over that room but no guns. Had the hospital taken them or had Nelson?

My head seemed remarkably clear. I didn't worry about my guns—or the absence of guns; I felt sort of cockey. The first show must have been just about over when I reached the side entrance of the *101 Club*—employees entrance. I tapped on the narrow door and it swung open. The lad had a folded newspaper in his hand. He looked at me—started to speak—then said, "It says you're dying?"

I raised my right hand in my jacket pocket and extending a finger at him stepped through the door. He fell back—his eyes wide. "What's the trouble Mr. Williams?" he was genuinely shaken.

"Hand over your gun." I told him.

"Gun—" he squeaked. "I don't have no gun. I just keep out the Johnnies. I ain't even got a blackjack—nor brass knuckles nor a knife—what are you staring at me like that for?"

"I'll kill you," I said, "if you've lied to me, or try to stop me. I'll—"

"Nix—Mr. Williams. I won't stop you—not me. I got orders no one goes in," he ran his eyes down at my pocket but looked at my eyes again. "Now what would be the sense in killing me? And—what's the matter with you? You look wild."

"Where's Miss Madden?" I said.

"Inside—I guess. She did good; I looked at her act. But she's not going on again. Don't point that thing at me—and don't look at me like that."

He didn't have a gun. His hands went up and I frisked him. Then I waved him aside and went in warning him not to peep to a soul.

What was in my mind? I don't know. To get Cissy Madden out of there. To get Vickey Carr; too; it was a strange feeling.

I LIFTED THE key from the door I went through, stuck it in the other side and locked it. I put the key in my pocket, thought somehow that was pretty clever. I turned a corner. Not many lights. Then I walked into a room with mirrors; jerked up my pocket, stepped forward and looked again. It was me all right in the mirror. But the eyes. They were big and bright and glary. I heard a voice—turned around and bumped into a hefty dame, half dressed. She brushed me aside, said. "The kid did all right. I personally trained her. Harry pulled her out of the act and—Who are you? Oh—you're her cutie?"

"Who?" I didn't get it.

"Cissy Madden," she said. "She leaves a hole in the front row. He took her down there; down that hall."

"Who?" I said again.

"Haydon—" she said. "Harry Haydon." She put her hands on her hips now and took a good look at me. "You're drunk," she told me nodding her head as if she'd take no denial. "Go down there. That's right." She ignored my right hand in my coat pocket and pushed me toward a long hall. "The room to the left. Talk to Harry. The kid was good. Make a smell and he'll put her back in the chorus; he always does."

I went down the hall. I didn't feel drunk; I felt particularly sober. I was going to take Cissy away with me. We'd get married. She'd get my slippers at night. Bring the evening papers—maybe she'd read poetry aloud to me. I shook my head. I didn't think I'd go that far, though the picture seemed good—very good. It was like walking on air. I felt funny. Oh, I felt fine—but funny.

The hall got darker as I went down it. I turned at the end. A short narrower hall, darker still. A light at the end from a partly open door. I went down to it. Looked in. A hanging light, wooden cases, beer and liquor I guess. A door down at the end that gave out into the night. It was open.

Then I saw the girl. Her eyes were wide—her head turning as if she sought a way to run for it. There was doubt and a growing uncertainty in her face—not exactly fear. Not yet anyway. She wore some sort of a robe that hung down to her knees—loosely open. I could see the shorts of her costume—she was certainly class. It was Cissy Madden.

I spotted Haydon. He was sidewise to me but watching the girl. He was talking into a phone chin high against the wall. I heard him say.

"That's right. The sedan. Alley door. Here, where I'm talking by the storeroom. Right now—you fool."

He banged up the receiver, turned his back on me and faced the girl; said, "You did very well my dear—very well indeed. Too bad Williams wasn't here to see you. Too bad for you—good for me. So he doesn't know."

"Doesn't know? Doesn't know what?" she asked.

"Take off that robe," he ignored her questions and demanded roughly. "You fooled me until I saw you in the floor show. Take it off."

She pulled the robe tightly about her, held it with her two small hands. Fear was beginning to show, now. She half-turned as if to seek the alley door. Harry Haydon moved quickly. He took her arm—swung her around—grabbed at the robe—tore it down from her shoulders—her bare shoulders. Then he swung her around. Her back was to him; to me, too. We saw it together, Harry and I; we cried out together. We spoke the name together. The name we both knew. He, because he had seen her so out there on the dance floor—and me—because that was the thought that led to the dead-end street back in the hospital. But it was a through street now.

Plainly I saw the birthmark—small but clear—a tiny leaf no bigger than your finger nail there beneath her left shoulder blade. The name we both spoke together was, *"Vickey Carr."*

Harry Haydon spoke the name aloud and I quite evidently didn't. Or, if I did he didn't hear me and the girl didn't hear me. Haydon was talking and I was moving into the room. Just one thought. Cissy Madden was Vickey Carr.

Harry was saying, "Smart, weren't you? Hiding out right under my nose. Madden, eh—Madison of course—your aunt's married name—your father's sister. And played Williams along so as to have him around when you needed him. Well, you need him, now—"

That was my line, my cue; no actor ever had a better entrance. Sure—I like a touch of drama as well as the next fellow. I stepped forward, stuck my finger in Haydon's back and said. "Race Williams, Harry. This is a gun."

Of course he would expect to die, and I was going to scare him half to death. I'd have him down on his knees pleading for his life. That was my mistake. I should have crashed him with something. Action is my meat—not conversation. If he was more of a man than I thought he was— or if he felt that death was sure anyway, I don't know.

Certainly Harry must have thought there was a gun in his back. But he didn't fall to his knees; he didn't cry out for mercy. He swung and drew, and his gun was in his right hand when I grabbed for the wrist.

He was a big man, was Haydon. He was a strong man, was Harry. He was a rough man too. But they don't come rougher than I am. But now—my false strength betrayed me. He was stronger than I was and his left hand was tearing at my right wrist and pulling his gun hand free. Then he saw my eyes.

"Ah—" his mouth popped open and his eyes bulged. "Full of dope or I'm a Dutchman. Hopped up."

His left hand left my right and fastened on my throat, on my neck. Fastened with a strength that was—well not unbelievable because he was doing it; no two ways about that.

I forced his gun up again as my breathing stopped—with a sudden swish of air as if it was the last I'd ever suck in.

Blackness? Almost blackness. I'm not sure *how* I did it, but I'm sure *what* I did and what I was trying to do. No luck there, no luck in a death struggle. There never is. The man who counts on it is lost—and dead—dead.

And I—my right hand was there on his finger. His hand was tightening on my neck and I did it. Thrust his arm back and put everything I had into the grip of the fingers of my right hands. A single shot—a single shot, only. But it was a blast that rocked the room.

It was a big gun. It was a heavy gun. My fingers had tightened on his, on at least one of his. And that finger of his tightened on the trigger of his gun. *No, I thought, I hadn't killed him. I didn't kill him. He had done it himself.*

Nelson was willing to argue the point with me, and the papers never mentioned

Haydon's participation in his own death. And me—I lost my bet if you want to be technical about it. I was back at the hospital again. Sure, I passed out like a young schoolgirl and came to in the same little white bed. *How cute,* I thought.

EVEN NELSON SMILED at me the next day back in the hospital. He disliked me, but he disliked Haydon more. He said, "Worse than I figured him—Race." He gulped. It was the first time he ever called me Race. "Haydon talked a bit before he went over. Died hard, he did. Delirious talk that we couldn't have used in evidence if he lived. And the woman he killed in your arms—she was a girl he had liked in Chicago. No reason for killing, though—except she was getting in his hair—and he wanted you to think that Vickey Carr was dead. So—the time element was all right; he knew exactly when she'd be there."

And Cissy Madden, alias Cissy Madison—alias Vickey Carr. No—she didn't bring me the evening papers or my slippers—but she brought herself and a check.

Her father had trusted Haydon, but her Aunt—Mrs. Madison—hadn't. Haydon, they felt, had tried to kill her as a small child—right after her father's death. Anyway, they disappeared, suddenly, and changed their name to Madden; Vickey, of course, took the Madden name. Where the Cissy came from—your guess is as good as mine.

"My uncle," Cissy said, referring to Madden, as she smiled down at me, "wanted to be sure of you, Race, for he had looked up Harry Haydon and was

greatly in fear for my life. So I met you; that's why I got mixed up in that other trouble. Then—" she paused, "I liked you, Race—decided not to risk your life in case Haydon didn't find out who I was."

"But why take such a chance—and take that job in the floor show?"

"I thought it would be safest close to Haydon," she said. "And—I liked the idea of it—the thrill of it. I never thought he knew of the birthmark. In fact I never think of the birthmark—never want to. He must have seen it out on the floor— guessed what it was and who I was. And—that's all."

The thrill of it. Yes, I could understand that. Some people like to live dangerously—foolishly, too. I should know; I'm one of those people. But the girl was talking—sitting on the edge of the bed saying, "My uncle came to New York today. He gave me this check to give you. Take it Race—I'm to receive a whole lot of money."

"No," I said, "no money." And I was surprised at my own voice but was more surprised at the words that voice spoke. I even sat up in bed and repeated them to be sure I wasn't delirious.

"I messed this thing up," I went on; "I should have known. I should—"

"Come, come, Race." A voice spoke from the foot of the bed. I looked up and saw the white carnation—the whole elegance of Riley. He went on. "I wouldn't say that, Race. Besides, there is the little point of my fee; surely you don't intend to pay that out of your own pocket."

I didn't; I told the girl and she nodded approval, shook hands with Riley and her eyes admired his splendor. Which Riley liked. Riley went on—pompously, "You should take the check, Race. Danger is the way you make your living. As for messing it up. Come, boy—Harry Haydon is dead and you are alive; what could be more complete and satisfying—to your client." And he bowed and waved an arm across his chest at Vickey Carr.

I guess Riley was right and I was wrong. But I was a sick man and in no condition to judge. So—since the check was still in her hand and the hand was still held out to me—I took it.

For the moment then I forgot that I had not killed Harry Haydon—but that he had killed himself. And by the time I remembered it the check was in the bank.

Anyway truth is truth. As Riley said when we were alone and I was still doubtful, "After ail Race—you need the money—and she doesn't."

I like Riley; he is a smart man.

This Corpse Is Free!

Maybe I didn't like Lieutenant McClane. I did, however, admire him. Like Inspector Nelson, McClane was down on private detectives—but unlike Inspector Nelson, it was private dicks in general and not me in particular.

Lieutenant McClane didn't play politics; he ran roughshod over sacred feet, and raised bunions where he shouldn't. A crook was a crook to him, no matter what friends he had.

McClane was in Homicide for a while, but he raised so much trouble there that they took him off that detail. If it hadn't been that Chief Inspector Miller was such a high-class cop, McClane would have been pounding a beat out in Staten Island. Inspector Miller put him on special duty; if he couldn't trust to McClane's good judgment, he could trust his honesty and loyalty absolutely.

Miller must have known that McClane was working a side-issue. I knew it; a lot of cops knew it, and a bunch of the boys in the rackets knew that McClane was out to put the skids under Clancy Toome—an up-and-coming boss in the city.

Certainly McClane was making it hot for some of the lads who had Toome's protection and tagging many of them.

You know as well as I know that a lad who carries the shield of the metropolitan police in his pocket is not often marked for death by the underworld. It is not good business to kill a cop. It hurts the shady clubs; it kills the gambling; it tags a guy for some small crime he has forgotten, and it knocks all the rackets cockeyed for a time. It even closes down the bookmakers—and makes the legitimate night-clubs suffer.

Understand, it isn't done *often,* but it's done now and then. And it was on a Thursday night I had my hunch that this was "then."

Nothing you can lay your finger on, understand. I missed the usual faces around the bars; there were mostly strange faces and honest faces. The *Hot Spot,* one of the shadiest night-clubs in town that catered to the boys on the underside of the city, was practically deserted. In plain words, the grapevine of the underworld had sent out its warning. *Lay low. Get yourself an alibi. Something big is going to break. You'll be dragged in and asked about it. Your past will be raked up.*

I've been around the city a long time. I can remember such situations before— and every time, some big shot took a dose of lead. Gunmen, racketeers, crooked gamblers—even the common pickpockets seem to know, and run to cover.

Anyway I felt it. The cop on the beat must have felt it; dicks on the Broadway detail must have felt it. But if they did, they all ignored it. Why not? It would

break; they'd get a stiff—and the city would be well-rid of a notorious character they hadn't been able to put the finger on. They should worry.

But it bothered me; I had ideas. I gave my friend Sergeant O'Rourke a buzz. Couldn't get hold of him. I had a couple of beers in a low dive that called itself a tavern—was amazed at the lack of patronage—and went to the phone and tried Chief Inspector Miller.

THAT LAD WHO answered the phone gulped a bit when I threw my moniker, Race Williams, at him. He wanted to know what it was about. I said it was important. He wanted to know if anyone else would do; I shook my head and remembering the booth didn't have television, told him "no."

"Okay, Williams," he said, finally, "come over and the—the inspector will be here to talk to you." He seemed to gulp over the "inspector" part but anyway I went downtown.

I was shoved around a bit by the men in blue and finally got into Inspector Miller's office. I drew up sharp; there, sitting behind the desk was Inspector Nelson. I didn't like Nelson. He was a good cop— he wouldn't have been an inspector if he wasn't—but he hated my guts, so why should I admire his.

"Well—Williams," he said. "What's on your chest? Come on—spill it; you'll get no favors here. What did you pull off now?" and mean and low, "Found a body I suppose. A client of yours."

"No," I said. "I want to prevent the finding of a body; I was to see Miller."

"He's not here; I'm in charge." When I shook my head and told him I'd wait for Miller, Nelson added. "He won't be back tonight, Williams. Better tell me—for if anything happens, and you held back information from the police, why—"

I took a grin at that—but it wasn't a very good grin. I kicked myself for coming around. Then I didn't; I was doing the right thing. I said, "Okay, Nelson. I'm a good citizen doing his duty. I've got a hunch a big knock-over is coming off. A hunch—nothing more."

"Nothing more," he looked up at me.

"Well," I said, "the grapevine of the underworld is working overtime this afternoon and this evening. You must have had a report on it; the cops must have noticed it. The old familiar faces are not in the old familiar places."

"You mean business is dull?"

"The lull," I said, "that precedes a storm. I've seen it happen over and over, and so have you."

"And that's all."

"What do you mean. 'And that's all?'"

"A hunch—something any rookie would have. And you walk in here in hopes of ingratiating yourself with Chief Inspector Miller. So I should ring up every known criminal, and suspected killer in the city, and offer them police protection." He lifted the pencil and pointed it at me as if he was playing darts. "We could do with the body of one or two racketeers I could name."

I shook my head. "That's the trouble; there isn't a big feud on in the underworld. A guy here and there gunning for someone—but not big enough to make

the exodus from the spots so apparent. There isn't a crook on the list marked for death that's that big…. But there might be an honest man that big. I was thinking of one man—one name important enough to scare the pants off so many boys. One lad whose death would make a lot of crooks breathe easier."

He straightened suddenly and I thought he had it—caught the significance of it himself. But he hadn't; he said, "Good Lord—you don't think you're that important. You're not asking for Police protection."

"Not me," I told him seriously; "I was thinking of McClane."

"McClane." He frowned, then laughed. "Lieutenant McClane. George McClane. A cop. Sure—there's lots who'd like to see him dead, but not a crook around with guts enough to kill a cop. So you had a tip, eh? Some stoolie shook you down for a few bucks. And you run to me with the story. McClane, or any other cop on the force, can take care of himself—and we don't need any lousy, four-flushing private dick to lend a hand. McClane will laugh when he hears this."

McClane didn't laugh—but then, McClane never heard the story; they fished him out of the East River at eleven o'clock the next morning. His hands and feet were bound together, and someone had poured five shots into his body.

I heard it over the radio. Before one o'clock, it seemed as if half the cops of New York City were in my hair.

They nearly had to break down the door to get me, for I was at the typewriter before I had fully digested the news that came over the radio. Before the cops got in, Jerry—my assistant—had my instructions in writing. I knew what to expect.

They dragged me downtown. I didn't strut my stuff and I didn't talk big; I knew how they felt. Lieutenant George McClane wasn't liked, even on the force, but he was a cop. I knew they were out combing the city, knew they were dragging in lads by the dozens, and I knew they were handling them rough.

The cops who questioned me were strangers. I had been threatened many times before, but I was never shoved around—at least never like this. I didn't see Inspector Miller; I didn't see O'Rourke; I didn't see Nelson. That was bad.

I had a swollen eye and a cut lip before I ever got downstairs in that cop house. They threw questions at me. There were only four of them; I wasn't booked.

The main thing was they kept tossing the same question at me. "You knew that McClane was going to get it… How? Who told you?"

You've only met your cops on the street or behind a desk. Fine, clear-eyed men out to protect you and the city. They were different now: a colleague had been killed—brutally; they were cock-eyed with fury. I didn't blame them, but I didn't like it.

I didn't deny anything—nor I didn't admit anything. I was about the only one that held my head. Finally, I *did* get in my warning. I said, "I've got something to tell Inspector Miller that's important—and it won't wait. Better have him see me."

I worked that over and over as they threw the same question at me. I didn't say that what I had to tell would solve the murder, but maybe I gave the boys that impression. They weren't really rough, yet, and I didn't want them to be.

At last, they got the idea that it might be worth their jobs not to tell Miller or Nelson. I told them that time was short—that it meant a lot to Nelson, too. Which was true. I'm not a fool; I saw what was coming the moment the radio clicked out the news.

If I could get to Miller or Nelson, I could walk out of that cop house a free man in ten minutes.

I GOT TO both of them. Sergeant O'Rourke was there, also. Two cops shoved me in as O'Rourke was saying to Chief Inspector Miller, "I know Williams. He'll make it hotter for the department than the department can—"

He stopped. Nelson glared at me. O'Rourke looked very serious, and Chief Miller quite severe—and greatly worried. It was Miller who spoke.

"We've brought you down here," Miller said, "to find out who gave you the tip off that Lieutenant McClane was to be killed. I don't feel that you will hesitate a moment to give it to us; we appreciate that some stool pigeon gave you—"

"No," I cut in, "it was a hunch; a logical hunch. I explained it to Nelson last night." I went into it again.

When I finished, Miller said, "Are you trying to tell me that, with the millions of persons in this city, you were able—through a hunch—to lay your finger on the one man who was to be killed."

"It's impossible," said Nelson.

"It seems to me," said O'Rourke, "that it was logical. And from the way it turned out, the only solution to the feeling among the criminals of the city. Don't they all say—all we've dragged in—that it was in the air—a killing?"

"But none of them said that they expected it to be Lieutenant McClane." Nelson came in with the crack.

I said, "As if they would," and when Nelson grabbed my arm I shook myself free and faced him. "All right Nelson," I told him, "we'll let the public decide. I came in here last night and gave you the results of my reasoning—and what did you do? Nothing. McClane was killed; you laughed at the idea. We'll see if the newspapers think it's so funny."

"By the time you talk to the papers," Nelson grated, "the murderer will be caught—maybe even convicted."

"So that's it," I told him. "You'd bury me away, eh? I figured that, Nelson." I looked at the clock on the wall; it was ten minutes to three. "If I'm not out of here by four o'clock, it will go to the papers. I wrote it out in detail—expecting something like this."

It tossed him all right; it tossed the Chief Inspector, too. O'Rourke ran a hand across his mouth, and I sort of thought he was hiding a grin. I went on. "Nice reading. Inspector Nelson laughs while cop is shot to death. Where is Race Williams? Hidden away so he won't talk about the—"

"That's enough," Inspector Miller cut in. "So that is what you intend to spread through the papers."

"That is what Inspector Nelson is keeping me from *stopping* being spread by holding me here." I got that one over with the thread out of my voice and some honey into it.

Nelson looked worried, but I'll give him credit for not even asking me to keep quiet about my hunch when Chief Inspector Miller decided I was to be let go. Now you might think I had something on the cops. But the cops are not so dumb—certainly not Miller. He shook hands with me in parting, and said, "Of course, Williams, you appreciate Inspector Nelson's position. Your guess—a wild guess, though unfortunately right—was hardly one that he could consider. But he *did* try to get in touch with Lieutenant McClane as soon as you left, last night. We thank you for your interest in coming to us. The police always expect that of good citizens—their cooperation and their silence. Good-day."

He shook hands with me. Had he said, in effect— "You pull this story on the press and we'll deny it?" Maybe he had; maybe he hadn't—maybe he wasn't thinking any such thing. But I was; you can be sure of that. I'd keep my trap closed.

CHAPTER 2

CLANCY TOOME WAS probably the first one out with a statement. He deplored the death of a "noble" officer. There should be more like him; crime should be driven from the city; everyone who knew Toome, knew he was doing all in his power to rid the city of evil; he welcomed investigation—his life was an open book. He was a man of the people—for the people. And the subtle hint that Lieutenant McClane's attempt to get him was personal.

One could not put the finger on Toome; his alibi was good. Clancy had enough of the right or wrong kind of friends to alibi him, even if he had gone out personally and pumped the lead into McClane. But it must have been a relief to Toome to have the persistent McClane out of his hair; the man had been undermining Clancy's generalship by picking off his army, one by one.

I enjoyed the excitement in the city. I liked seeing the favorite racketeers, who were used to being handled with kid-gloves by the cops, now walking the streets with mouses under their eyes—or a tooth or two missing. And the big mouth-pieces, the fixers, finding their going tough; and their big "influences" not even answering the telephone to their frantic calls.

The police hunt went on, relentlessly. It wasn't my funeral; I stayed out of it. Not that I wouldn't be glad to stick the finger on the lad who bumped a cop. That was bad business—real bad business. But what could I do, that over twenty thousand cops couldn't do? Besides, it was a good thing to keep out of, and I was determined to stay out of it.

The underworld behaved well, practically put a stop to its business. They knew—as I knew—that this could have happened for one reason only: It was someone's life or Lieutenant McClane's life; there were no two ways about that.

I saw O'Rourke on several occasions.

The police were at a standstill. "It's bad business, Race." He shook his head. "If it was any other cop but McClane, we'd have his killer now. But McClane was a secretive man, a lone wolf, and that's not good in any police department. He was always working toward and against Clancy Toome."

"You don't think Toome did it—or had it done."

"Not unless he had to; it's hurt him more than helped him. But what about some of these friends of his? McClane was out to get them. Suppose he was looking for small fry in lowly places, and came across a murder in high places."

I waited until O'Rourke came to it himself. O'Rourke said: "We've looked into McClane's private life; it's what we thought. Unmarried. Lived uptown with a maiden aunt who kept house for him. Had few friends—no women. Ate, slept and lived crime. No bad habits; never took a dishonest nickle, even. A stickler for duty. Spent his last vacation hunting criminals. What do you think of that?"

I shrugged.

O'Rourke permitted himself a dry sort of grin. "Getting diplomatic, eh? Not like you, Race. But you've got good sense. Bad—very bad. Hands and feet tied—gagged—and then shot to death. Gangster stuff all right. Hear anything?"

"Not a thing."

"And you don't want to."

"I shouldn't want to," I told O'Rourke. "As you say, I'm trying to be a diplomat—keep my nose clean."

"Right boy," O'Rourke said. "Stay that way." And then, just before he went, "If you hear anything, see anything, get any hint and can run it down—let me know."

So you see how hard it hit Sergeant O'Rourke; it wasn't often that he talked through both sides of his mouth at the same time.

THE KILLING OF McClane was the topic of general conversation in the offices, and the homes, and the better shops. But not in the places where the wise boys hung out; they spoke of it only in whispers.

But I had other business—at least I thought I had. Jerry, my boy, gave me the tip off when I got to my apartment that night. He met me in the hall and jerked his thumb back at the living-room. "Dame," he said. "I didn't want to let her in, but she said she didn't dare see you at your office and—"

"And," I encouraged.

"And you wouldn't want to miss this number. A looker. Why when you see that face of hers, you won't even want to look at her legs. But you better look; they're worth it."

I got my eye-full a minute later. Legs and all. No ordinary doll this. Slim but built right. Like a speedboat. Real character in her face—eyes that could look you over and size you up—and she was doing it now. Not too much warpaint, but enough. Young or not, she had seen life, taken its kicks, braced herself, held her ground—and, no doubt, struck back. The legs were there, but she wasn't making capital out of them. She said, "Race Williams—" and when I nodded, "I want to talk to you alone. It's business, and I haven't much time."

I took her into the little room that Jerry likes to call the library, because we have some books in there. She waited until I closed the door and I asked, "Client?"

"Well…" She parted lips and showed nice teeth. "If you take clients that haven't any money… Still, I can pay; if not in legal tender, maybe something else. My name is Betty Lou Pierce— I work in the show at the *Hot Spot*—just stepped out of the chorus and doing a solo now. I might pay you by saving your life."

"Sit down," I said; "that's a good start. And in return, you want?"

"I'll want you maybe to save mine." She sat down then, leaned forward and said, "I don't want promises; I've had a lot of them in my day. Look," she pulled it suddenly, "do you know who killed Lieutenant George McClane?"

"Good Lord, no—" it was jerked out of me.

"Is it true you were dragged in with the police net and questioned? Is it true that you were in to see Inspector Miller the night before McClane was killed and gave him a tip? Is it?"

And when I said, "Where did you hear all that?"

"It *is* true, then." She nodded vigorously. "So you haven't heard any such gossip about yourself in the wrong quarters. What is that worth to you? I mean my telling you."

"I don't know," I said, "and that's a fact."

"So no one has tried to put the heat on you—and you do not know why."

"No," I said; "no one has." I was studying the girl, trying to digest what she told me, and not doing so well with it. She did better.

"Well," she said, "if someone tried to put the heat on you, now—you'd guess why—if you were still alive." And leaning forward she threw it at me. "You'd guess maybe it was the lad who bumped McClane. Right?"

"Yes," I told her, "it could be figured that way."

SHE NODDED HER head vigorously. "I'm glad; and I hope you see that you wouldn't have figured out what a stray bit of lead meant unless I had told you. Now—I want something in return; is my information worth that?"

"What do you want?"

"I don't know, yet. I had thought of jockeying you into position where you'd have to kill to save my life; but now that I've had a look at you, I don't fancy that. But suppose—through this information I brought you tonight—you turned up the killer of McClane, for the police. Would you protect my life?"

"I couldn't," I said slowly, "be jockeyed into a position of shooting someone for you. But if you were a client of mine—I would protect your life."

"That client business," she said, "sounds like a hint for some folding money. The kind I haven't got."

"What's your trouble?" I asked her. "We might work out something."

"Oh," she said it airily but her eyes were fastened on mine—green and tense. "There's a man who likes me. Likes me too much and has wanted me to do things I wouldn't do. I simply laughed at him.

Now—he's in a position to press the matter; I'm not laughing. In fact, he could open his mouth in a certain direction— and I'd be dead. Like that." She snapped her fingers.

"I see," I said. "Let me know who he is—what you've done."

"No," she said, "you don't see; you couldn't see." She came to her feet and walked toward the door—swung around. "I wanted to get a look at you. Then think."

"Like what you see?"

She looked at me a long time, very serious. She said, finally, "Yes—I do. I do very much. Take a trip down to the *Hot Spot* and—and a look around. But don't greet me unless I send for you. And if I send for you—I'll—the pay will be bigger than most clients can afford. At least in advertising."

I let her open the door, go down the living-room and pass out the front and disappear. I picked up the evening paper. Already there was a reward offered. Ten thousand dollars for the killer of Lieutenant McClane—dead or alive.

THE GIRL'S INFORMATION was alarming. Not simply that a desperate man would take a shot at me, but that it would get back to the cops and they'd start on me again. I'd better find out how bad it was, how many knew. So I went out and visited the night places. I hit the *Hot Spot*, of course.

I got an unwanted table in the back, and to one side, and decided to see who the girl associated with—if anyone. I wasn't there long before the owner found me. Nat Greer.

He leaned over, offered to buy me a drink, then wanted to know if it was pleasure or business that brought me there.

"Business bad?" I looked the room over.

He leaned close but still he didn't mention the shooting of McClane. "There's been a slump," he said. "You know how it is. I'm doing better than the other places. Costing me a little over a grand a night." And after a bit, "Interested in any of my acts?"

"Not especially; should I be?"

That tossed him, put him on the defensive. He forgot to question me any more, and spent the next five minutes before he left telling me what high-class talent he had.

When *he* left, Muggs Avil came over to see me. He wasn't a bad-looking man. He got his name from mugging, had to illustrate everything he said or did with his face—all of it, his eyes, his mouth. He was a product of the lower city. Ran with the gangs as a kid, but he had fancied himself as an actor and was in vaudeville for a bit. That was where he got the name Muggs. Then he got fouled up with Ed Logan—a known killer—over a woman. Logan threatened to shoot Avil on sight; friends warned Muggs out of town. But not Muggs—instead he walked into a tavern where Logan was, beat him on the draw and left Logan dead on the floor.

Muggs beat that rap. The killing of Logan made him in the city; he dropped all pretense of working, was making real dough—until Clancy Toome started pushing him down. It was a feud of long standing.

It was more than a rumor that if Muggs wanted to open his mouth he could get Toome a long term up the river. The sentimental hearts put it down to the code of the night; hard-boiled gentry put it down to the fact that if Clancy wanted to talk, he could return the compliment and send Muggs up the river for the big burn.

I was surprised to see such a well-known gunman as Muggs floating around the city, surprised more when he opened up with the subject that was taboo along the Avenue. He flopped down beside me, said, "I hear talk, Race, that they dragged you in on the George McClane knock-over."

"I guess they dragged everyone in," I told him lightly.

"Not me." Muggs shook his head. "They came to me. But no threats—pleading like. I'm not a guy to talk to the cops—not me. In a way McClane was my friend." And when I showed surprise, "He was picking off a lot of Clancy Toome's boys, and I took that as a friendly act." His eyes blinked and his mouth twisted. "Of course, I wouldn't talk—but McClane thought I might—and he thought he'd pick up something. They should guess where the kill came from."

"Yeah." I wasn't going to be quoted.

"That's right. Yeah—. Whose hair was McClane in? Whose scalp was he after? Who did George McClane swear to rid the city of? He must have been getting pretty close to someone—" he shook his head, "to rub a copper out." He twisted his face up and twirled his head indicating the sparsely-filled tables. "I'm one of the few lads with guts enough to come out—and get around. I know my rights."

"And being friendly with McClane helps."

"Too many don't know that," he grinned. "The cops know it. It'll make Toome feel pretty big."

"Hurt him more than help him," I said.

He shook his head. "Not with the mob; he'll be a big lad later. I'm not saying he did it, but you know what the boys will think. A lad that fools with Clancy Toome isn't safe. Not no one—not even a cop."

If MUGGS FANCIED himself a psychologist, that was his business. But I couldn't see it that way. So far, every lad who had associated with Clancy had been picked up and put through the wringer. Personally, I wouldn't have been seen having a small beer with Toome for a thousand dollars—well, ten bucks maybe.

"Nice floor show," Muggs nodded. "Nice-looking girls. Nat wanted to know if you came down to take a look at one of the Janes?"

"Me—no. Why?" I was getting bored, but then I might hear something and quite evidently Muggs wanted to talk.

"All business, Nat is; that's what made him. Now, he's gone overboard for a dame who was in the chorus. She does a single, now; good, too."

"Likes her—does he?"

"Cow-eyed over her. Why she wouldn't spit in his eye last week. This week—." He shook his head, looked over at me; his eyelids blinked up and down like a kid playing with Venetian blinds. "What some girls will do for a song—a single song and a bit of dance in this dive." He paused and then, "Dive—yes; I wonder what you'd be doing here, Race, unless Nat sent for you."

"No one sends for me, Muggs," I told him.

"Cops rough with you?" he asked suddenly.

"No—" I grinned now, "nice—like they were with you; I get around, you know."

"Yeah—" he came to his feet. "I heard you got around to the cop house before McClane was blown over," and when I stiffened, but said nothing, he leaned forward and half whispered, "What's in it for me—if I could give you a guess on the killer of McClane?"

"Not a guess." I shook my head, and, before he could leave, "Where you hear I was questioned?"

"It's around," he told me. "You know how those things are. You're smart, Race—to keep your nose clean. Say—I could use a couple of century notes and in return I'd pass the word around that you know nothing, don't want to know anything, and won't know anything. And I'll make it stick. It might be good for your health."

"I'll pass my own around—and I'll take care of my own health," I told him coldly. "And I'm not afraid of any cheap hood—who ties a cop up and then shoots him."

"That'a boy, Race," he put a heavy hand on my shoulder and gave it a squeeze. "A lad as yellow as they come pulled that shooting—and you know who breeds them yellow in this city. Clancy Toome. Take care of yourself."

CHAPTER 3

I DIDN'T LIKE it; I didn't like it at all. I got up, and sauntered out to the bar. In a hazy way I was wondering what Muggs Avil was doing in Nat Greer's place. Not that he wouldn't visit the *Hot Spot*, but Greer was a Toome man—or had been. Maybe Greer was leaving the sinking ship—and Muggs was good for a bit of protection.

I ran into Greer again. I put it to him straight this time—low, but straight. "Listen," I said, "what do you know about my being called in by the police and questioned." When he stalled, and hemmed, I added, "I'm serious; had you heard any such story?"

"Well now, Race— I—I might of at that."

"Where?"

"Oh—around. A rumor. Not that I believe it."

"Who did you tell?"

"No one. Why should I?"

"Everyone was dragged in."

"I wasn't," he said quickly.

"They questioned you?"

"They were here—the police, yes. They questioned everyone. That is what happened with you, I suppose... You know how rumors are; I didn't repeat it about you—if that is what you mean."

"I heard different."

"It may have been discussed. You know how it is; everyone is talking about it."

"I thought the opposite. That it was taboo."

"In private, I mean—a few of the boys." And when I waited. "Lord, Race, it's no secret."

"Okay, Nat." I grinned at him now. "Thanks. Muggs was telling me about it."

That line, I figured, would stop him from thinking that Betty Lou Pierce had told me; it looked as if I might be in for a bit of excitement.

I didn't think things would come as fast as they did. But they came. I saw the play the minute I left the *Hot Spot;* three men changed positions almost at once. One engaged the doorman in conversation so that he put his back to me. The other two crowded me; two guns clamped hard, one on each side of me. A nervous voice said, "In that car, Mr. Williams—take it easy."

The "Mr. Williams" saved one gun-toter's life—and maybe mine, too. For the guns weren't more than against my side before my gun buried itself in the speaker's chest.

"Wait—" the man with my gun on him fairly gasped the words out. "I'm not going to kill you—shoot you even."

And the lad on the other side said, "Take it easy, Mr. Williams; I don't want to shoot, either."

"Want to see your friend dead?" I asked.

"It wouldn't hurt me," the man on the safe side said, as we crowded together on the sidewalk.

The one whose rib my gat was tickling chirped—and really chirped, for there was a bird-like shrill note to his voice, "Show some sense—Mack. Mr. Toome wants to see you, Mr. Williams. Clancy Toome. We won't harm you."

"You won't, that's certain," I agreed.

I said, "We've reached a dead-end street, boys—park your guns!"

414   CARROLL JOHN DALY

"Park them—yes," a new voice spoke coming out of the darkness. This was a brown fedora, a white muffler, a neat dark blue top coat and a cane over an arm. "I'm surprised at you boys, but I did want to speak to you Williams. I'm Clancy Toome."

I knew that. All guns disappeared as a car drew to the curb and landed four customers.

"Nice way you have of making appointments, Toome," I said.

His voice was very smooth. "Nerves on edge, Williams; my fault, I assure you. I said 'Bring Race Williams to me;' they misunderstood. Will you favor me with a visit?"

"What's the matter with my apartment?"

"I think," Toome said very evenly, "that such a meeting might be misunderstood by the authorities, and would bounce back to the disadvantage of both of us. However—there is a taxi. Shall we cruise around a bit?"

"Just the two of us—yes."

He nodded and we walked down the block and on mutual consent flagged a passing cab.

We did an Alphonse and Gaston act but I had my way and Toome got into the cab first. He said to the driver, "A fine night. A lovely night. A bit of air, driver; would you suggest going very slowly through the park?"

The driver did and off we went.

Toome was little more than a common racket-fixer and ward-heeler, but he liked to fancy himself a politician. He talked as if he had read it out of the congressional record and not remembered it very well. He went right to work now.

"Mr. Williams," he said, "I abhor the use of duress, but you are now talking to a man whose whole career is at stake. When a public figure falls, he does not fall alone; he takes with him friends—tried and true and loyal friends. He takes with him the confidence of the people. The little people who trusted him and believed in him, and gave him his incentive to go on, despite the criticism of a hostile press."

"Oh Lord, Toome," I said. "Spare me that. What gives?"

"Lieutenant McClane, a noble officer of the law—a misguided one, certainly, but nonetheless a sincere and honest servant of—"

I stopped him flat now. "Look; are you going to turn my stomach—or tell me what's on your chest?"

"Well…" he snapped out of it. "Do you know who killed McClane?"

"No," I told him. "If I did I'd tell the cops, the same as you would. Or would you?"

"I—" he said, "would handle it in my own way. Look here," he leaned close to me. "If I knew, I'd see that the cops know; I'd certainly see that justice is done. It's playing merry hell with my organization; you know that. Anyone but a fool would know I wouldn't have anything to do with it."

"Unless—" I said, "it meant complete ruin if McClane lived."

"Talk sense man; how do I stand now?"

"Partial ruin; it will be forgotten and you can pick up the pieces. What makes you think I know anything?"

He told me. He knew that I had been questioned. He knew, too, that I had gone to Nelson the night before the killing. "Look, Williams, I'll give you a grand for any information of any kind. What hint you had; who it came from. A thousand dollars for anything you know."

"I don't know anything," I told him. And then, "Suppose it was one of your boys; have you thought of that?"

"Thought of that?" he said and it sounded like he meant it. But then I guess he was sounding like he meant things all his life, when he didn't mean them at all. "Thought of that? I've thought of nothing else. But it can't be; can't because I'd know if it was."

"And if it *was* one of your boys?"

"I'd turn him over to the cops. I've got to clear this thing up; it means ruin." That I could believe, I told him, then added, "Would you turn him over if he could talk—talk about you?"

"I'd turn him over," he said, "so he couldn't talk."

"Couldn't talk?"

"I'd turn him over dead."

O'ROURKE CAME IN to see me. He was very serious. He was on his way to his home up in Kingsbridge—the first time he'd slept in his own bed in over a week.

"I understand the D.A. will want to talk to you, Race," he said. "And the Commissioner wanted to know about your coming to see the police the night before McClane was murdered. I know, Race; I know you don't know who did it. But—would you like to make a guess?"

I looked at O'Rourke, astounded. He was my friend; he knew me. Yet there was doubt in his voice. A certain amount of confusion, too. The killing had gotten under his skin. I went over it all again with him. He shook his head—looked very much disturbed.

"Yes, yes, I know," he said. "This comes from the underworld, Race. I don't say it couldn't easily have leaked out, for anyone could have seen you visit Nelson. You have always played straight with the law—but you played straight with the crooks, too. You've built your reputation on that; you've built your reputation on never betraying the confidence of a client. Nelson was thinking that maybe a client told you something. That would be bad—bad for you. The boys—all of them—over twenty thousand of them wouldn't like that."

"O'Rourke," I told him. "No one has told me who killed McClane; no one even hinted that McClane was to die—nor that anyone else was to die."

"Better do something," he shook his head and left me.

Not a word about his daughters, of whom he was so proud; no little family talk as was his custom. It looked as if I wouldn't be able to keep my nose clean; it looked as if I would have to stick it in police business—yes, and maybe lose it.

IT WAS EARLY evening when the phone call came. It was the girl, Betty Lou Pierce. "Race," she said, "can I count on you? The need may come sooner than you think."

Maybe I was a little sharp with her. I said, "I'm in other things up to my neck, Betty Lou. If you are afraid of some lad, why not drop from under for a bit."

"But the information I gave you."

"Is common gossip through the night."

"That you know who killed McClane?"

"That I was questioned about it," I snapped, "not that I know. I don't know; haven't any idea."

"Okay," she said. "Come down to the *Hot Spot,* now, and I'll give you an idea." There was an intake of breath, then silence.

I thought there was a man's voice over the phone. I wondered if Betty Lou had hung up herself, or if someone had leaned over her shoulder and taken the phone from her hand and gently closed the connection. I wondered, also—was it the man who had killed McClane?

ALL THIS WONDERING went on as I grabbed hat and coat and raced for the street.

Suspense—plenty of it. I had about convinced myself that I would never see Betty Lou again—that is, alive. I came through the bar entrance of the *Hot Spot* and nearly knocked a lad over. There was a curse—a rough hand on my shoulder—then the curse changed as a face mugged before me.

"Easy does it, Race," Muggs Avil said. "You look as if you know something—something big."

"I will," I said, then stopped and shook Muggs off. Muggs was a lad who always wanted to know what was going on; he was curious as an old maid. But then being full of knowledge kept a guy like Muggs from being full of lead.

I sat down at the same undesirable table. The suspense was over; Betty Lou

Pierce came. It was like a little Red Riding Hood story without any wolf. Maybe I felt relief—but I know I felt stupid.

The girl was white; her lips trembled, but her voice was steady and so were her eyes.

"It's been a burden to carry, Race," she let those eyes flash about the room to make sure we couldn't be heard. "And now the reaction when I'm ready to tell you."

"Let it shoot, kid," I told her, "if it's on the level. It will have to be convincing, because—why didn't you go to the police?"

"That's a laugh," she nodded across at me. "The police. I was born and raised among the warped minds of crime; an aunt brought me up when she was sober enough. Have you ever seen a dead squealer?"

"I'm not the cops," I told her. "I'll give you protection. Come on—spill it."

"Sure. The morgue can ring you up if I'm dead—and you can seek vengeance. I don't want vengeance; I want to live. I want to know what you'll do with the information if I give it to you. That's right. The name of the—the one who killed McClane. Will you keep me out of it?"

"Of course, if I can."

"No—your word that you'll keep me out of it. No 'if you can.'"

I thought of O'Rourke, thought of the dead McClane, thought of my license. I stalled around, then said. "Look, Betty Lou. I'll certainly think of your best interests—and so will the police for that matter. Why, you could even hide out— Nat Greer could help you there."

"Nat—" she scoffed. "Do you know any

more jokes?" She leaned forward. "He's my greatest danger; don't you understand—that?"

I thought back, tried to link up Nat with McClane but couldn't. But I could link Nat up with Clancy Toome—and certainly I could link Clancy up with McClane. Therefore, I could link Nat up with McClane.

"Betty Lou—" I said. "You were in the chorus here; you got a spot to sing. Did you get that after McClane was killed?"

"I got it," she said slowly, "the day his body was found."

I gulped and put it to her straight. "You are playing a dangerous game; a very dangerous game. Did you blackmail Nat Greer?"

"Blackmail him," she gasped. "He's in love with me; he wants to marry me. He—" she paused, let her tongue come out and go over her lips. Then she said, "There's an old warehouse down by the river. There was a trunk there. Nice costumes in it. A girl in the show pulled out—married a guy; she gave the stuff to the first one of us who wanted it. I went down there, after the show. The warehouse was empty, the street deserted. I saw it plainly. The body was dragged along the alley—dumped—dumped—" she stopped—her eyes were wide. "I saw McClane dumped into the river—and the man who dumped him. Saw him plainly. I knew him, of course." She straightened—stopped dead; I turned my head.

CHAPTER 4

NAT GREER WAS coming across the room; Muggs was pointing us out to him. Not that Greer couldn't have found us himself, but it would have taken him a few minutes longer. Maybe a minute longer—enough time for me to get the name of the lad who murdered Lieutenant George McClane. The name every cop in the city would give his right arm to know.

Nat was a smooth customer, but he wasn't so smooth now. He was worried; his face was playing tricks like Muggs. He ignored me, said to the girl. "What have you told him? You didn't tell him. You didn't—"

And he knew she hadn't told me. He turned to me. He was himself—smooth as a skating rink and his voice as soft as the hum of a skater upon the ice. "All right—Betty. I'll tell him; I'm proud of it. Race—the little girl here is going to—going to be my wife."

The girl said, her voice strained this, but clear enough, "No, I'm not going through with it."

"Nonsense," he ran a hand through her hair. "I hadn't announced our marriage yet, but I did tell Muggs Avil—there at the door. If you don't marry me—why," he spread his hands far apart, "I better tell Muggs that, too. You are going upstairs—and going to think it over; you'll do that—won't you?"

"Yes—" she was on her feet. "Yes—Nat— I'm going—now. And—and I'll think it over."

She seemed sort of dazed. I reached for her wrist, but she was gone, running down the room—disappearing behind thick curtains.

"Lovely girl," Nat said to me. "Temperamental, too; blows hot and cold. A good actress, a very good actress," and then with a laugh, "I'll bet you a century note she changes her mind and marries me."

I suppose there was a signal; most clubs have them in case of trouble. I didn't see any, though, but a half dozen waiters were suddenly busy about my table—and close to Greer.

What would I have done if the waiters hadn't piled around. I don't know; probably have made a monkey of myself. Grabbed Nat and demanded that the girl return. But she went of her own free will.

Greer left me then. I waited around, looked at the floor show. Betty didn't appear; one of the girls told me she had gone home with a headache. No one bothered me. I could wander about as I pleased. I tried to find Greer; no luck.

The head-waiter said Nat had gone for the night. "Things are so dull at the club, now," he explained.

And what had Betty Lou told me? I could imagine she had told me a lot of things. But truth is truth—she hadn't told me anything.

It was still fairly early. I went home. There might be a call from Betty Lou.

Jerry told me there had been no call from the girl. But O'Rourke had been buzzing me. Also Nelson. O'Rourke got me on the wire a few minutes after I came in. Things were hot in the police department. The D.A.'s office too.

"Look, Race," O'Rourke was greatly disturbed. "There was a telephone call came in—that you were hiding a witness in the McClane killing. Now, now, wait a minute. I know—lots of people would like to see you in trouble. But beside that—a dozen different cops heard around that you know too much, that there is trouble brewing for you. I want to see it this way: maybe you know something and would like to clean it up alone. That won't do, boy; I'm going home for a sleep. Call me there if—you know anything."

"I don't know a thing," I fairly shouted.

"Are you hiding a witness who does know?"

"I'm not hiding anyone; I don't know who killed McClane. Haven't any idea who killed McClane—" and when he was coming hard, "but I got a clue— I'm working on it."

I hung up. He was pushing too close. O'Rourke tried to get me back; Jerry told him I had grabbed my hat and coat and gone out. But the calls got worse. Nelson twice in half an hour. And then—believe it or not—the Commissioner called and I ducked them all.

My license. My reputation—maybe my freedom was at stake. I cursed the girl and the whole police force.

And the moral of it all was: If you want to kill someone in the city of New York, and then have peace and quiet—don't kill a cop; they don't like it.

The doorbell rang. Jerry raised his head—sniffed. "Cops," he said.

"Cops" I thought was right. I couldn't chin with them; I had to be out doing things. Going places. Where? Your guess is good as mine. But the cops—no.

"Okay, Jerry," I told him. "I'll slip up the fire-escape to the roof. Say I'm out; I'll hang close to the window to be sure it isn't someone else."

I climbed out on the fire-escape—waited. Jerry came back. It wasn't the cops; it was Muggs Avil. I slipped back through the curtains. Muggs half-turned, reached for a gun, then grinned. "Little Bo-Peep," he said. "What's the matter, Race? You look wild-eyed."

"So—" I said. "What do you want?"

"What you been doing?" he grinned. "The place is watched; had to slip in through the basement. Cops—real live flat-feet."

"Again, what do you want?"

"The cops," he nodded, "think you know who bumped—McClane."

"I wish I did."

"Oh."

And then he busted out, "How much do you wish it?"

"Why?"

"I might," he said, "have ideas."

"You can't convict on ideas, Muggs."

He sat down and looked at me, his working overtime. "Look, Race—McClane was out to get Clancy Toome. McClane was a thorough man. He talked to me; he knew how I felt about Clancy. And from his talk, I got the idea that he was trying to put a big rap on Toome—an old rap. A murder rap."

"Are you trying to tell me that McClane confided in a—in you?"

"In a guy like me," Muggs bobbed his head up and down. He wasn't insulted.

"McClane," he said, "would confide in anyone to get Clancy Toome."

Which was true enough, I guess.

"Now," he said. "Toome and me never were pals—hated each other's guts, we did. McClane was picking off Toome's boys—pulling down his prestige. Nat Greer and Clancy were pretty close."

"Come to the point," I snapped.

"Nat knocked over McClane. Maybe I can't put my finger on the exact reason, but I exploded his alibi for that night."

"I didn't know he had one—needed one."

"Listen, Race." His hands came far apart—wrinkles ran in and out of his forehead. "Nat has a dame in his chorus, Betty Lou Pierce; she gets a solo spot in the floor show the night after McClane kicks over. And tonight—Nat said he was going to marry her; told me that. Told you, too, didn't he?"

"But she doesn't want to marry him."

"That's what she said, maybe; I got a grand says she marries him—why he's dough-heavy. McClane was close to me; you know that. He died. Nat asked me over to see him, hinted there might be a truce; he is willing to drop from under with Toome. Now, what is on his mind? Perhaps, before he died, McClane said something to Greer, gave him an idea I was going to talk. Nat is out to shove me over—like McClane."

"Far-fetched," I told him. But I was thinking; I had Nat down pretty well for the job myself.

"Yeah," Muggs shrugged and his jaw came up. "I nearly stopped a dose of lead after leaving his club tonight."

"Lads have been shooting at you for a long time." When he only grinned, I said, "What has that to do with the girl?"

Muggs went on, "Well—where was the girl when McClane took the dose. She wasn't at the *Hot Spot*. I talked to some of the girls. Elsa Height—ran out on the show to marry—and she told the girls they could divide up her things. In a trunk at a warehouse. The girls—at least three of them—were around there early the next morning. But the star costume was gone; Betty Lou wore it the next night at the show. So—" he leaned forward now, "she could have been at the warehouse when McClane was killed. She could have seen him killed, or at least seen some part of it, and recognized the killer. So she put the heat on Nat for a better job—and a wife don't testify against her husband. Neat, ain't it?"

My eyes were getting wide. Anyway my brain was expanding. It didn't all fit, but it fitted pretty good. "You're some detective," I told him. "I happened to be with the girl tonight—and she didn't tell me anything."

He nodded. "I know; I saw you. Nat saw you, too, and the minute he saw you he told me he was going to marry Betty Lou. She was playing him against you—threatening him."

"No, no—" I tried to shake it off. "If he killed McClane he would kill her, too."

"He is nuts about the girl; anyone can tell you that. And if you don't believe that—maybe he's killing her now." His eyes narrowed, his lips working. "Why don't you ask her?"

"Because—" and trying to be indifferent, "maybe I will."

"You don't ask her," he said in triumph, "because you don't know where she is. Well— I know."

We did it together, I guess. I had heard Muggs was quick—but I didn't know he was that quick. We were standing facing each other. My gun was pounded against his chest, and I was asking, "Where is she, Muggs?" and it wasn't until I sprung the question that I realized his gun was against my chest too.

We eyed each other a moment, looked silly, then parked the guns. Muggs said, "Interested, aren't you?"

"And you?"

"It wouldn't be too bad for me if this whole mess was wrapped around the Clancy Toome outfit; it would settle Clancy for good. I was interested enough in the shot at me, Race, to double back to the *Hot Spot*, watch the private entrance, and tail Greer and the little lady. There's ten-grand reward. You can take the credit—and give me the money; is it a deal?"

"Provided," I said, "you're right."

"I'm right," he told me. "But I didn't like the eyes you put on the doll. She'll have to be a witness. Look. I'll take you to where they both are hiding out. A quiet marriage—a honeymoon and a return when it's all blown over. That is—unless he intends to come back without the girl; then a bellyful of lead for her. Is it a deal, Race?"

"It's a deal, Muggs," I told him. "If I get the money, it's yours; how do you want to work it?"

"They're alone in the house. Nat has killed once, and he'll kill again. If the cops get hold of the girl, she'll tell the truth; you should handle it easy. Slip the cuffs on him and call the cops. I know the house. I'll get you in—and wait in the cellar. If it goes through as planned—I'll fade. Shake."

He held out his hand and I shook. I never had liked Muggs; I liked him better, then. And the girl. She had had her chance; I had made her no promise. I had to think of myself, first, and think fast. But I was thinking of her—of her life—or her death.

WE LEFT BY the fire-escape. Up over the roof, out the back of an apartment three or four down, close to the corner.

"Up Kingsbridge way," Muggs told me; "you better rent a car."

I knew the ropes on that, okay. Five minutes later we were shooting uptown in a late model. The engine purred.

"I'm not a bad detective, Race," he told me as we drove uptown. "I worked it out pretty well. My only worry was about you—and what you thought of the girl. It wasn't like you not to get the truth out of her. Or did you?" And when I ignored that, "Look at it this way; you can't leave her out of it—not even if Nat signed a full confession. He'd involve the girl, anyway; he'd think she squealed."

"Don't worry," I told him and meant it. "Are you sure they're alone?"

"Sure they *were* alone," he said. "No man can say more than that. But look. If the party is rough, I'll come out of that cellar—and come out of it shooting; no man could be fairer than that."

I'll say this for Muggs. He wasn't nervous; he was smug, if anything. He talked on, felt pretty good. And why not? It could be the easiest ten grand he ever made. I was surprised that he came with me—but he wanted to protect his interest in the money, I guess.

Of course, the idea of a trap did go through my mind: That Muggs might be trapping me for Nat Greer. But that didn't hold water. All he told me fitted it too well what the girl, Betty Lou, had said. Nevertheless, I watched him.

IT WAS A small house; it stood alone. I parked the car some distance away and we walked. One thing was certain: Muggs was not too familiar with the place. At least, he didn't go right to a cellar window. I let him precede me and my hand was on my gun.

"It looks dark and deserted." For the first time, there was a nervous ring in Muggs' voice. "You don't suppose he did the girl in and left."

"I thought he was stuck on her."

"But panic, Race; it gets a guy at times. After all, she stands between him and the hot squat; that takes a lot of love. Better let me open the window. I've had more practice."

I didn't even hear the tinkle of glass, but there was Muggs crouched in the dark by the long narrow cellar window.

"I'll go in first," I said. "I'll take the chances."

I DID GO in first. Things seemed quiet enough in the cellar. I slid in feet first sort of flat on my stomach. It let me face

Muggs—and Muggs could plainly see the gun in my hand—pointed right at him. We were conspirators—pals, if you want—so I didn't say any threatening words. But Muggs had looked down the nose of guns too often not to know the words they spoke.

Muggs grinned pleasantly at me. "Cute—you are. I'm glad I haven't got your suspicious nature."

He showed no gun when he followed me into the cellar.

I stood close to Muggs Avil as my flash searched the cellar. I spotted the wooden steps that led above, measured them with my eyes—the door at the top. My flash played along it and clicked out. I knew that the door above was not locked. Indeed it was open—ajar an inch. A nice invitation, that—maybe an invitation to death. I said, "Okay, Muggs—you stay here. Don't show a light; don't flash one. I've got a nervous trigger finger. Wait here."

No time to waste. There was the girl above, there was Muggs behind me—but he was in the dark, and so was I. What's more, I was going to stay in the dark—no flash was going to guide my footsteps up those wooden stairs. No flash was going to guide Muggs, either—for a shot at me.

I have a good sense of direction. I made the wooden steps in the blackness. No cause for fear; I wasn't afraid. No cause for alarm and I—well, yes, I was alarmed. I didn't like it. And my feet unerringly hit those steps—and unerringly pounded up them. Another minute—thirty seconds, less even, and I'd be out of Muggs' range. I'd have the girl

safe—and—my lips smacked. I'd have the murderer of McClane—the cop-killer. The man all New York was looking for and I—clutched my gun tighter in my right hand.

Things happened then. I don't know which was first but I think it must have been the busted step. The step turned on me—half-swung me. The second thing was the light from back in the cellar. The third thing was the roar of a gun—a flash of flame—and a sharp pain along my right side. It was just above the hip, and helped spin me around.

CHAPTER 5

I WAS FIRING even as I tumbled backwards and sat down on the steps, firing at the light that must have been in a man's hand—the man who was behind me in that cellar. The light went out. Quiet—quiet above and quiet from below. I was cursing the busted step—then thankful for the spin saved my life.

Where was Muggs? Had Muggs done the shooting? If so, why had he stopped? Had I hit him? I sat there on the steps, my gun in my right hand, my flash in my left. But I showed no light.

Whose move was it? It was mine, because I was alone there. Muggs below—and Nat above. Between two fires. I held my flash far out, snapped it on. The shot came.

I saw Muggs. He was leaning against the wall, gun in his left hand. There was blood dripping from his right hand—running down it. There was a wild bright look in his eyes. I said, "Drop the gun, Muggs. Drop it—now."

Muggs cursed and fired; he wasn't a lad to talk himself to death. My finger tightened, my heavy gun belched flame. There was nothing else to do—Muggs was squeezing lead—maybe wildly but certainly viciously.

I saw Muggs' head go back, red appear on his neck just above his coat collar. He jarred and did a little dance like a doll on wires, wires that had gotten twisted. Muggs' knees gave; his gun fell from his hand first, then he went down. He died hard, did Muggs—that is, if he was dead, I didn't know.

I went on up the steps, slammed open the kitchen door. I had come a long way. There was the murderer of a cop somewhere above in the house. And Muggs was working with him—or had been.

Only silence now. I chanced my flash. There was a shot from the room beyond. I ducked out my light. Waited. Listened.

Feet beating across the floor—running feet—a whispered voice and finally one in fear—panic. A man's voice—loud.

"It's Muggs Avil. You talked—and he's come."

Nat Greer; I was sure of it. He was scared, now. He was accusing someone of telling that he had killed McClane—of telling Muggs. And who was he accusing? Only one person—Betty Lou Pierce.

The girl screamed and I was in the next room. My flash found him; he was in the hall by the stairs, one foot on them—backing up. It was Greer all right; my light was smack on his face. His eyes were big and wide—and his face was a pasty

white. The hand that held the gun shook. *Cop-killer,* I thought. The man was mad with terror.

I raised my gun, when the girl jumped forward into the light and knocked down his gun arm. "Don't—don't," she cried. "Don't kill him, Race."

I stepped forward, lifted my gun and cracked it down on Greer's head. He hit the bottom step like a ton of brick, rolled over once and lay still. "Race—Race—" the girl said. "Was that—necessary?"

"Necessary?" I laughed. "He'd be better off dead."

"No—" she clicked a switch and flooded the hall with the light and I saw the phone. "He really loved me; he didn't harm me."

"Phone connected?" I asked.

"Yes—yes," she said. She was staring down at Nat. I was calling O'Rourke. I'd get some action, too, I thought with a little satisfaction. He lived up Kingsbridge way. I was a little disappointed in the girl, too. Hard. I hadn't thought she was that hard; she actually seemed sorry for this killer.

I took the sleep out of O'Rourke's voice.

"Race Williams—O'Rourke," I told him, as offhandidly as I could. "I'm here in Kingsbridge. I've got the killer of McClane. That's right, the murderer of Lieutenant McClane," and after he came to, "Who is he? Come over and have a look; you'll be surprised." And I told him where I was.

The girl was across to me—had me by the arm. "Is he dead—dead?" she gasped.

"Dead—" I looked down at Nat Greer. "What do you care?"

"If he's dead—I won't have to—you won't bring me into it."

"You're in it, sister," I said. "He's not dead—far from it. Look." Nat was beginning to stir—half sit up. I went over and lifted the gun that was there on the floor near his hand—too near his hand.

"Look!" The girl was looking from me to Nat. "Oh—" she moved toward the kitchen. "Is he in the cellar—Muggs Avil?" And when I nodded, "Race, you didn't leave him there alive. I'm glad it's over, now; don't let him escape."

"Who?" I was getting a little bewildered, Yet it wasn't my wound; that wasn't bad. It wasn't even bleeding. At least not much.

The girl was acting funny and I'd have to give Nat some attention. I watched her and knelt down by Greer. His eyes were open; they were rolling. I went through him for another gun, but there wasn't any. He was looking at me and trying to talk. Finally, he said: "He followed us here tonight. I'm sorry Williams; I thought he had come back. I thought you were Muggs Avil."

"He's in the cellar," I said. "Cashing in—or getting ready to cash in; you didn't fool him much."

"No, no—I was a fool," Greer said. "I thought he followed us here. I felt sure I saw Muggs looking up at the window. Later the shots in the cellar. I thought he had come back. I wouldn't have shot at you; Muggs intended to kill all three of us—Betty Lou, me—you!"

O'ROURKE CAME THEN with two cops. He fairly burst in the door as the girl opened it. He said, "Where is he? Where is he?"

The girl said, "In the cellar. Race shot him—I think. He's—down there."

The stamping of feet. I stood up. I looked from Greer to the girl. Nat said, "Will you ever forgive me Betty Lou. I was mad, but I loved you and wanted you and—"

BETTY LOU'S VOICE was low. "Nat, I told you I saw the murderer because I had to trust someone. And—you threatened me. My life wouldn't be worth anything if you let it out that I knew. Then you sent for Muggs Avil—just so he would be there, and I would see him and be afraid—that you—that—Nat—I can't believe it now. And you thought that would make me—love you—marry you."

"I never would have told," Nat pleaded with her. "Don't you see Betty Lou. It would have meant my death, too. I—wanted to frighten you. What will you do now?"

"I'll do what I should have done—tell. It was a terrible crime; Muggs Avil can't harm me now—nor you."

I didn't hear any more, and was glad that I had not mentioned the name of the killer over the phone. I went along the hall, through the dining-room into the kitchen and down the cellar steps. What's more I just missed pitching on my face from the bad step, too.

The cellar was brilliantly lighted. I saw O'Rourke come to his feet, saw him drop the head of Muggs Avil down with a thud on the hard cement floor.

"Is he dead?"

"Yeah—dead," O'Rourke nodded. "But he talked first, Race. Jenson took it down," he jerked a thumb at the uniformed cop. "I'd of bashed his head in if he didn't talk. It seems McClane was playing him against Clancy Toome—and found out about a killing that Muggs pulled off, years back. McClane wanted information from Muggs, so he kept secret what he had discovered—or he thought he did. But Muggs knew—and he killed McClane. It was his life or McClane's—he told me before he died. He was smart, Race, but not as smart as you."

"That's right," I admitted and talked fast to hide my confusion. "He brought me here to kill me—and it didn't work."

"I know," O'Rourke put a hand on my shoulder. His big blue eyes shone in admiration. "And all the time you knew—and tonight you came here to protect a client?"

"We won't go in to that, O'Rourke. Confidence of a client." I tried looking very grave; I was the light-haired boy, now. "But I wasn't sure of Muggs—not fully sure. Muggs, as you say was sharp." I looked down at the dead hoodlum. "Sharp and dead."

Maybe I felt like an idiot, but I hoped I didn't look like one. Betty Lou didn't have to testify; she was my client and I had delivered a cop-killer. Even Nat Greer came in for a smile from the police.

What did Betty Lou get out of it? She got the star billing at the *Hot Spot*—and no talk of marriage, either. Another break for Greer; she was a sensation. I saw her last night and she was packing them in.

What did I get? Well—as long as I had been such an idiot, I went on playing it that way across the board. I turned over my ten grand reward to the police fund. Truth is truth, though; I didn't want any money for laying out a cop-killer. Not me.

Gas

CHAPTER 1

IT WAS AN old fashioned four-story house in the low nineties not far from Central Park; worn stone steps, red brick front and, despite its fresh paint, shabby in appearance. It was like a thousand or ten thousand others in the city of New York that had turned into rooming houses or apartments; relics of a bygone day.

A few had remained private dwellings. This was one of the few and I changed my opinion about the shabbiness as soon as the girl let me in. The carpet was soft and thick on the hall floor. The paintings good; furnishings and knicknacks could have been antiques and probably were.

The hall light was dim but I got a good look at the girl. She wouldn't hurt your eyes but she was no raving beauty. The nervous twitch to her lips and the circles under her eyes didn't help any. There was worry. I thought more than fear back of those glims.

"Mr. Williams," the grip on my hand was friendly and warm but the hand itself was cold. "I'm so glad you came. Father did telephone for you then. You'll take care of him, won't you, Mr. Williams—he is so helpless."

"Sure, sure," I tossed confidence around and spread good cheer. "What seems to be the trouble?"

"Well," she said, "that's it. He doesn't appreciate trouble. If one of his chemicals got lost he'd go on as if it was a major catastrophe. Yet, if someone should empty a machine gun at him he might consider it a small annoyance not worth mentioning."

"Has anybody been emptying machine guns at him?" I smiled with that one. She didn't smile back.

"No," she said. "And I don't want them to, I'm afraid. The trouble—"

A door opened and a voice spoke.

"Troubles," said the low voice, "are hallucinations, creations of our own wrong thinking."

I looked at the little man. I almost said little old man. He wasn't old. He lent a little and cocked his head and gave the appearance of age. His long unruly hair was black, or seemed black in the dim light. I saw the tall young man behind him. Twenty-eight or thirty—broad of shoulders, good face, and a determined if not pugnacious chin. He said half laughing.

"And how do we get rid of these hallucinations, Professor Eslam?"

"We correct our thinking," the older man said quickly. "All right, Edward, you run along with Constance—Mr. Williams and I will talk."

"But," said the young man. "I might be able to help." And then when the professor was insistent, Edward came over and shook hands with me. "Eddie Reynolds, Mr. Williams," he said. "I've read about you and know about you."

He had a good, strong face. His eyes were blue and his hair was blond. He looked me right in the eyes like any upright honest citizen—but so do confidence men for that matter.

Professor Eslam led me at once to the back of the house—through the kitchen and straight to the basement.

"We'll eliminate this trouble, eh, Mr. Williams?" he squeezed my arm. At the foot of the cellar stairs the professor fumbled for keys, found them, stuck one in the lock of a heavy door—had difficulty in pulling its weight back. We walked into a sort of Rube Goldberg room.

"My laboratory," the Professor nodded. "Not as orderly as one might wish. But new things come in and old things go out—as my investments and my endowment policies fall due. Or, at times, as Constance contributes to what she calls the hodge podge."

I looked the room over. There were glass jars. Silver, brass and, I guess, copper pipes—all sizes right up to stovepipe size. It was, I suppose, what a chemistry laboratory in the model would look like.

I DID NOTICE a couple of packing cases—one in particular, in a corner of the room. It must have just arrived from the tags on it and there were more warning and cautions and red lettering on it than you'd find on a government form. There was, entirely out of place, a Japanese screen bent in on itself at both sides as if it concealed something.

Professor Eslam was saying, "You will see. Mr. Williams, how much confidence I have in you—and how much I depend upon you. It is a great country, this country of yours and mine. I owe it much—far more than I can ever repay. But do I owe it the peace of the world?"

I tried to look profound on that one. I finally tossed off an answer that I hoped fitted the solemn occasion.

"I guess," I said with what I thought was not much point, "we all owe everyone the peace of the world."

"Exactly," he turned and beamed on me. "Great discoveries," he went on, "great scientific achievements arise with war. We have the atom bomb. But that is nothing compared to bacteria. Germs delivered upon us from an enemy can lay waste our fields—destroy our wheat, clear the grass from the meadows and starve the cattle. It can wipe out all vegetation and animal life. Mr. Williams, that is the great fear in war today. So—so," he licked at his lips, "I have perfected a chemical that, sprayed upon the fields, will counteract all that—render this bacteria er—these germs useless.

"Do you know," he asked then, "what this government of ours offered me for it?"

"No," I said. "But not anything like it was worth—or what you expect."

He seemed surprised. He stared at me in wonder. Then he said:

"I expect nothing. I do not want one country, but all the world to have it, so germ warfare may no longer cause the sleepless nights of millions—that the talk even of germ warfare may be dead forever."

"You've got something there, professor," was the best I could do on that. My business is saving one human life from a killer on the loose most times—not millions.

"So—" professor Eslam rolled on, "those who would like to make war and are planning germs as the answer to our atom bomb, would like to have this little formula of mine—or even destroy the work I have done—or," he smacked his lips, "or even know what I am doing." He leaned close to me then. "They think I work upon a gas to destroy man, not a chemical to preserve man—to preserve, I hope I can say with all modesty, the human race."

I didn't know about the modesty. He seemed a little wild-eyed like—like—well maybe what he was—a scientist.

I'm for my country. I'm for peace for the whole world. I also work for a living. I didn't like to put it to him; "What's in it for me." I compromised.

"How can I help you?" I asked. "I know everything, now—have seen everything, now."

"No," he walked behind me and stood by the little Japanese screen. "You do not know everything; you have not seen everything. Look!"

After being in on the saving of the entire world, you would expect that anything else would be anti-climactic and so would I. But—we both would have been wrong. Professor Eslam moved the screen suddenly and the fantastic was out of the picture. Reality came in. It came in with a bang and a crash.

On the floor lay a man. In the middle of his back stuck a knife. You didn't have to be a doctor or an undertaker to know that he was dead—very dead indeed.

"Dead," I said stupidly and knelt down by the body. Almost at once I was on my feet. The professor was looking at me out of bird-like eyes, his head cocked, and when he still regarded me without speaking, "Did you call the police?"

"No," the professor's head shook violently. "We can't have the police here. We can't have the newspapers here. We can't let anyone know what I am doing here. This," he waved his hand, "vast array of equipment may mean nothing to your untrained eyes. But to the trained mind! No we can't have the body found here."

"How are you going to prevent that?"

"I don't know, Mr. Williams. That is why I sent for you. I thought you would take care of that little item for me."

"Little item." I'm not thrown easily. "You expect me to juggle that corpse and plant it some place else? Why?"

"For the good of our country. For the good of the world—the little people—the millions of the world. And—a substantial fee for yourself."

You've got to admit that the professor came down to earth with that "fee" crack.

He talked on, then. He covered the world and the futility of wars and had foreign spies tramping through his laboratory in droves, some dressed up like reporters, some like policemen and detectives—and the newspaper publicity.

I got it out of him finally. He denied knowing the dead man. That he had ever seen him before. He tapped his head and kept telling me that the formula couldn't have been stolen. It wasn't hidden in the laboratory. But his work would be ruined, his secret discovered, and always back to my fee.

I'll admit I saw the weakness of his argument. But I saw the strength in it, too, and the truth that I thought he hid, maybe subconsciously. Certainly it would disturb his peace of mind—interfere greatly with his work—maybe knock it all to hell and gone. Guys like Professor Eslam don't like notoriety and excitement. He'd get plenty of that. Never once did it enter his head, or if it did he didn't mention it, that he might be accused of killing this lad. When I brought it up, it didn't throw him. He seemed to think it clenched his argument.

"There," he said with emphasis. "Now do you think going through all that in the newspaper would affect my work. And my prestige—my standing in the scientific world. Why they might even incarcerate me up over night and I can't—can't stand small, closed spaces."

That he could be seriously suspected seemed silly to him.

"Did you kill him?" I finally put it to him straight and when he shook his head and simply grinned at me, "How do I know you didn't?"

"You have a head," he said a little annoyed—nothing more. "If I killed him, would I send for you—of all people—to cart him away for me?"

Not a bad argument that.

I threw questions at him. Did he keep the laboratory doors locked?

"Always," he said. He seemed sure of that, as sure as he was of anything.

"Then how did the body get in here?"

If I was a detective trying to trip him

up, I failed miserably. He said at once and simply. "I must have left it unlocked; I'm preoccupied at times."

He could not remember leaving the door open but he might have. He never left the keys out of his possession—or didn't think he did. At times he had given the keys to his daughter to get something for him. There was a door from the cellar to the alleyway. That he kept locked too, he thought. Then that disarming smile.

"But there is no secret information to be found here. As I said—it is in my head—and written down and hidden away."

"I wasn't," I explained to him, "thinking of your formula. I was thinking of the body. How it get here."

"Oh," he said, "does it matter? The thing I wish, Mr. Williams, is to get rid of it."

"Does anyone else know about it?"

He was sure no one did.

"We keep no servants now," he told me. "No one could know but my daughter, Constance. And she'd tell me about it. Why a woman couldn't keep that to herself."

"But she's worried about something."

"Oh, yes—yes, indeed," he nodded. "That made me think of you. I am watched, you know, and my place in the country has been searched—a little retreat we have. Constance is sure she saw a man in the airy way one night, and a car down the street. Perhaps she did. I want to—to—well—Mr. Williams—solicit your interest in my work. I thought—I hoped to leave you this secret formula if I should

die—be killed you know. There is risk in removing the body I suppose. I thought of a thousand dollars—" and when I stared at him, "but Constance would let me have another thousand without questioning me. Shall we say two thousand to remove the—the unpleasantness?"

"But—your daughter. What of her inheritance? This formula against germs should be a very valuable inheritance."

"She is well provided for. Her mother, you know. Not a great fortune, but enough. And you—I doubt If anyone would kill me so you could obtain the formula. Preposterous idea that."

"You think someone might kill you so that your daughter would inherit it? Is she engaged to this Reynolds?"

"Reynolds?" He seemed to have difficulty with the name and then it came to him. "Edward, you mean. Well now—" and as if the idea just struck him. "she may be, may be at that. A fine boy—I understand. So she tells me."

"Has she any other relatives?"

"She—or me?"

"Both of you?" He was confusing.

"No—not me. She has. Cousins in the South. Alabama or Georgia, I think."

I took on the job—for the two thousand dollars. Foolish you think. No, not foolish. Dangerous I'll admit. But I cut corners; even cut through the middle of the block at times. Stop and think. Private detectives don't draw down dough like I pull in. Sure, I could lose my license—maybe worse. But if I didn't take chances I'd be chasing divorce evidence at twenty-five bucks a day and expenses and staying up nights trying to figure how to do a client out of a few extra dollars on the swindle sheet.

I'm not in this business because I like danger. I'm in it for the money I make. I reckon in dollars and cents. I've juggled bodies before. Less money and more danger, too—or so I thought then.

Edward had gone when we went up to what the professor called the study. Constance came at once. He was simple and direct.

"My dear," he said. "Mr. Williams has kindly offered to ease my trouble," his teeth showed, his gray eyes sparkled. "It is not, in my opinion, expensive—but I find myself somewhat short of ready funds. I have commitments coming in that will—"

"How much do you need, father?" she broke in.

As simple as that. When I left I had his check for two thousand berries—and the admonition not to present it at the bank before noon the next day as he worked late at night and "abhorred" early rising. I also had made arrangements privately with him for that night's work—namely, getting rid of one undesirable body.

CHAPTER 2

That evening I had a visitor. It was Edward Reynolds. Smiling at first, but not later, when he didn't get what he wanted.

"Look here, Mr. Williams," he finally put it straight to me. "I'm in love with Connie Fowler, and—"

"Fowler?"

"Yes, Fowler—Professor Eslam's step-daughter. He didn't tell you that? He wouldn't think of it, I suppose—but that's why she has the money. Her mother left it to her. I want to know what's going on and what her danger is. I'm worried about Constance. People watching the house— she thinks."

"A tall order," I told him. "You'd hardly expect me to betray the confidence of a client." And when he looked at me, "You don't think the old man is using up her money on her. Gypping her out of it—or do you?"

He reddened a bit on that last crack. I wanted him to. I couldn't afford to step down hard on him until after I got rid of the body.

"No," he said. "He's not getting rid of her money. He has no use for money. That isn't it. I—he's not exactly reliable."

"You mean he's off his trolley?" And when he denied that, "Well, then—a few wires disconnected. A shaky antenna maybe?"

"I don't mean any such thing." I had him on the defensive now. "He's the absent-minded professor of books and movies; he's got a good brain, but he's not worldly."

"I can agree with that," I nodded. "Now what is it you want to know."

"Well—" he said. "I'd just like to know if it—your visiting him had anything to do with Madame Paloria."

"Is that," I couldn't help saying, "a woman or a germ?"

"Both," he said with emphasis, "A woman and a pest. Beautiful and snake-like."

I gave that thought. Since there seemed no harm in it, I said, "My visit had nothing to do with Madame Pest."

He kept on talking. His interest seemed to center entirely on Connie Fowler. He gave out with the opinion that Professor Eslam was working on some sort of gas; that outsiders were interested, and that if he needed protection why didn't he get it from the government.

"I don't know," I told him. "Why don't you ask him?"

"You can't get anything out of him. He goes whimsical like a child—he says Madame Paloria understands chemistry. But don't think he hasn't got brains. He was in Washington with the government during the war. Worked on gas."

He left after a bit and I told Jerry what was on the boards for the night.

"I thought you were through with that business," Jerry sniffed. "Not nice you said. What do we do? Go up in the dead wagon—or walk him out like a drunk."

"The drunk act will do."

WE DROVE BY the red brick front about two that morning, and kept on driving. Both Jerry and I saw the man. He was on the steps across the street from the professor's house, pressed hard against the stone balustrade trying but not quite merging with the blackness of the night.

"Watcher?" Jerry asked. "Difficult?"

"Watcher, yes," I agreed. "And I think not too difficult, Jerry."

"We won't be coming that way then. Not the front?"

"Not the front," I told him. "I don't think he's watching for us, Jerry—or even

for a body," for I thought it must be Eddie Reynolds. Then again I wondered about who ever had planted the body on the professor. Was one of that gang watching for results—wondering why nothing had happened. Why the police hadn't showed up. Again the professor could have been wrong. It might have been an attempt to find his formula, two men, a row—and one stabbed the other. Far-fetched? Sure, it is far-fetched. But then a corpse in your basement is far-fetched—any way you look at it.

We drove along the block behind the professor's house. Clear there. I parked the car and covered the street, and Jerry being small and quick, did the casing. He always does a good job and a fast job. He was long, about—ten minutes. He came back pleased though.

"No iron fence with spikes," he rubbed his hands together. "Just a wooden fence between this back yard and the professor's house. No loose boards and the nails are hard and firm. It would screech to high heaven if you pried a board loose. So the body will have to go over the fence. I took so long because I found a knot hole right at the alley by the Eslam dump. I peered through it until my eyes got used to it. The jerk on the steps across the street don't cover our entrance or exit unless he moves. I couldn't even see him."

One last look up and down the deserted street and we went to work. Everything depended on speed. Cops cover side streets you know, but not as fast as we'd be—I hoped.

We skirted down the alley beside the house on rubber soled feet, paused in the darkness while Jerry put a sharp eye to the knot hole. With his "all clear" we went over the six foot fence, dropped noiselessly to the other side in the professor's yard, and cat-footed it to the alley door.

It was unlocked. We went in. Almost at once the voice spoke from the darkness.

"I'll go above now," the professor whispered. "The door will lock itself when you come out. Good luck."

This time there was a change in his voice. Not that rambling indifference of the afternoon—but clearly an anxious note—a nervous tone. Absent-minded he may have been, but he hadn't forgotten the body.

There was a light in the laboratory and I moved the screen and we got an eye-full. The knife was gone. I knelt down and turned the body over. Sightless eyes stared up at the light. He was not a pretty picture. An evil sinister face, thin lips, slightly bald—in the early forties I'd say. His clothes were well tailored and expensive. I gave Jerry a look. He had been around the lower city all his life.

Jerry shook his head. He didn't know this character. He was a stranger to me, too. We worked fast. The longer the body was in our possession, the greater the danger.

Jerry didn't need any instructions. We bent down together and had the corpse swung up between us, an arm over each of our shoulders. With us it was like a three legged race; easy after you do it together a few times.

Jerry took a gander out the alley door— gave the nod. Thirty seconds later we had the corpse draped over the fence. Another thirty and he was on the other side propped against the fence. Then we swung him again and were down the other alley behind the professor's house and toward the back street.

I took over there, while Jerry went out and got the car. He parked it by the alley, was out of it fast, the rear door open, the engine running silently. Then the body was between us again. To any householder who may have been looking from a window, or to any late home comer who happened along—it would be simply a drunk being escorted home.

Another minute and the corpse was on the floor in the back of the car and we were off. We didn't hurry and we didn't loiter. Things were safe now if we weren't stopped and searched. Uptown, then cross to the Bronx side for I wanted to leave the body as far from its original place as possible.

A quiet street, an empty lot, a cut curb where trucks went up and we swung into that lot. Close to a walk-up apartment, we dumped our load. Then a turn and back downtown. I looked at my watch. It was exactly four minutes of three.

I'm not saying it isn't a creepy job, and I don't recommend it as a business tor a young man. At three-thirty-five I hit my bed. Two thousand, you may think, was not too much money for the chance I took. Yet, it was ample pay. My inheritance I dismissed with a grin. I never was one for secret formulas—gold mining shares and oil wells.

THE PROFESSOR. ADDLE-PATED lad all

right. If he wasn't, I wouldn't have taken on the job at all. His childlike trust in me appealed—so did the money, I guess.

Next morning Jerry showed me the item in the paper. An unidentified man had been found up in the Bronx. No papers were on the body but the police were trying to trace him.

Curiosity and an idea of protecting myself later, if anything untoward happened, made me call up my friend Sergeant O'Rourke at Homicide. I often checked on morgue stuff.

O'Rourke didn't know yet who the dead man was. He'd give me a buzz if anything turned up later.

Something did turn up. It was about noon. Jerry brought the man in. For once Jerry wasn't holding his nose to signify that the law had called on me. Jerry was fooled completely. The stranger looked a banker, lawyer, salesman; any high type business man. He shook hands—grinned and said.

"Never had the pleasure of meeting you, Mr. Williams, but we know all about you down in Washington. Good stuff, too. I'm Mel Brandon, government agent. I was wondering what your interest was in the knived body picked up in the Bronx this morning."

I didn't like it. I didn't like it at all. I fool with the politicians. I fool with the racketeers and I fool with the police. But I don't like fooling with government men. I didn't show it. I said simply.

"Probably nothing. I check on all misplaced persons—dead ones. Can't tell when I might pick up an honest penny."

"So Sergeant O'Rourke told me." Mel Brandon nodded. "His name was Carl Fieze. Here's a picture—mean anything to you?"

I looked at the picture. It was my stiff all right. I shook my head; chose my words carefully, gave the picture back to him.

"Never heard the name. Means nothing to me. Foreigner?"

"No—American citizen." Brandon put the picture carefully back in the long bill folder. "Interested in chemistry?"

"Not since high school." I grinned. "H²S—I think it was. We called them stink bombs." I took a sheet of paper and started to write down the name, Carl Fieze.

"No." Mel Brandon leaned across the desk and put a hand on mine. "Forget about him. If he's called to your attention, give us a buzz. O'Rourke will find me." He hadn't sat down and he turned now toward the door; paused and came back. "Carl Fieze was interested in gas during the war—would sell stolen or bribed information any place to the highest bidder."

"You want to know if I have a client interested in—gas." I asked lightly, I hope lightly.

"No," he grinned. "Fieze isn't interested in gas now. Simply a routine call, Mr. Williams. I'm not interested in gas either. Nice to see you in the flesh."

A hearty hand grip and he was gone. I wished I had never buzzed O'Rourke. Yet it substantiated the professor's story; someone was after his formula all right. That made it very real indeed. Brandon had said he wasn't interested in gas—after bringing it up, too. I gulped over that one.

But government men always want to tell you nothing and learn everything from you. Even the police find them that way—and don't like it.

Why it should worry me I don't know. It wasn't the first government man who had come in to see me. Every now and then I'd have a visit. Always wanting to know something—never giving out with anything. Always pleasant—easy-going—cordial, but I don't know any more efficient, nor dangerous men.

I lifted the phone to buzz O'Rourke and ask him how he happened to send that lad around to see me. Then I didn't. That would draw too much attention to me. I knew what happened. Government looked at the corpse, identified it—and dug every bit of detail out of O'Rourke. I was part of that detail. It didn't mean anything.

THE TWO-GRAND CHECK was good all right. That evening I blew up to see Professor Eslam. It didn't seem like anyone was home and I was about to give up when he opened the door a bit on the chain and looked out.

At first he didn't seem to recognize me. I almost said: "You know me. I took a body out for you last night." I didn't say it. Not because I didn't think he wouldn't appreciate my humor, but because I was in no mood to appreciate it myself.

"I was in the laboratory," he told me after he cleaned up his glasses and shook hands. "Williams, isn't it—of course, Mr. Williams. Dear me, you'll have to come downstairs. A burner on, you know. I quite forgot I sent for you. I'm alone—Constance went off, some place."

I went down to the laboratory with him and watched him do tricks with blue lights and what I used to call test tubes. I didn't tell him he hadn't sent for me. I let that ride. Finally he folded up his bag of tricks, took off his rubber gloves, washed his hands in the sink and we went upstairs again.

"Constance worries me," he told me. "Went out with young Edward I presume. Dear me—I can't think what I wanted you for. Let me see," he began looking in a little book he took from his desk.

"I came to tell you that things went off satisfactory last night."

"Yes—" he said sort of doubtfully and when I was beginning to get a little sore. "You mean the body. I—I—" he began to pat his pockets and then exclaimed. "Don't tell me I forgot to deposit Constance's check—for I was at the bank."

"That was all right," I said. "But there was a disturbing circumstance. A government man came in to see me—wanted to know what I knew about Fieze—" and when he looked oddly at me, "That was the tag of the body—the name of your stiff."

"Really," he seemed interested now. "I don't recall the name."

"Well," I said, "this Fieze—this body of yours—was interested in gas during the war."

"Ah—as I suspected. They know then—" and suddenly it hit him. "But what, Mr. Williams, made this man approach you—this F.B.I. man—did you say?"

"I didn't say," I told him. "And he didn't say. Just a government man. Not very communicative you know. Just routine—I always ring up the police about unidentified bodies—would look odd if I didn't this time." Not exactly true that. But near enough. "You haven't been questioned?"

"No—no I haven't. Routine, you said. I wonder. Last night, Mr. Williams, when I left you below. I came upstairs and looked out the front window. Curious to see how you progressed. There was someone across the street."

"I know that," I told him. "It was, I believe, Edward Reynolds. He couldn't have seen anything. If he had—why they'd of been here to question you. He'd of told them where I came from."

"No, no—I think not," he said. "You see he is going to marry my daughter. Why was he watching? I caught him down by my laboratory once and he said—" and suddenly breaking off. "Mr. Williams. I paid you for last night's work—you did well. If you feel that this may embarrass you, endanger you, I will go right to the government man now and tell him the truth. I have some influence there. If it is true that this man was after my formula, I would receive consideration."

"Why," I asked him, "the sudden change? If it meant such catastrophe yesterday to call in the police, why is it different today?"

HE STRAIGHTENED AND looked directly at me. "Mr. Williams," he said. "Yesterday it was my burden; my trouble. I have no right to make you a victim of my—apprehension. I must protect you if danger threatens. The law might be severe with you."

A strange lad the professor. If he had asked my advice yesterday instead of dealing out the high talk and cash fee, I'd of told him to buzz the cops. Today it was different. I had monkeyed with that body. Not that they mightn't come down as hard on Professor Eslam as they did on me. But I never was much for that stuff that misery loves company. Maybe it's true—but I prefer not to have misery.

"Sit tight." I told him. "You paid me—keep thinking of the good humanity, all of it—and your fear of small spaces." I hoped that last would get him.

It did. But not in the way I thought. He seemed pleased with it, more than frightened. He said:

"Very well, Mr. Williams. I will let things rest in your more experienced hands. Any time it becomes necessary, feel assured that I will bear the brunt of our little conspiracy and admit—no—insist that you moved the body at my request."

I guess he meant well. But a lot of good that would do. I could see the cops caring why I moved it.

He got up suddenly; ran for the door calling back.

"The number three tube. It's lit—wait here for me."

I heard his feet beat through the hall; clatter down the cellar stairs. It was a good ten minutes before he was back. He sat down and beamed on me.

"I had to let it cool slowly," he explained his absence. Then he was off on a lecture. For the best part of half an hour I listened to him wipe out again all possibilities of germ warfare. Right in the middle of a sentence the phone rang.

Professor Eslam stopped talking, looked at the phone, then with an apology for interrupting me, he lifted it and said:

"Professor Eslam—yes?"

That very expressive face of his played more tricks than a ham actor on television. He gasped, tried to talk, at last said: "I'm still here. Don't hang up. When? I—I—"

He put the phone down on the desk and started to jiggle the connection. I took it out of his hand—listened, then replaced it in its cradle. He was breathing heavily. He half lifted himself from his chair, fell back, pointed to a silver bottle on the mantle.

"Water—" he gulped. "They have Constance. They are going to kill her unless—unless I give them the formula."

CHAPTER 3

THE WATER WAS cold. Some of it he got down and a lot of it he poured over him. At length I got a coherent story out of him.

"When did they get her?" I asked. "What arrangements do they want to make."

"I don't know. The man said he would call back—after I had time to think—about her death."

"It sounded like a woman," I told him.

"A woman?" he seemed surprised. "No a man, with a hushed voice. As if he talked through something."

"A handkerchief." I guessed for that is the oldest and steadiest trick to disguise a voice on the phone.

At first he was for calling the police—and then no. He said:

"They would kill her. My formula is worth a fortune. The man's name was Fieze as you said. The voice on the phone told me that Fieze would have sold out to me—so he was killed and left in my laboratory. What is my duty?"

"You've got to decide that." I told him. "Which comes first with you—Constance, or the formula?"

He didn't hesitate a moment. "Constance," he said. "No child of my own could have been closer to me," and his head went down on his arms on the desk.

He was an odd bird certainly. He was in serious trouble. No doubt about that. If the government was interested in these lads, they were formidable indeed—and would go a long way for what they wanted—to murder surely. I finally asked him.

"Do these people know what the formula is? I mean exactly what it can do?"

He straightened suddenly.

"No—of course not. Otherwise—" and suddenly he threw back his head and started to laugh. I thought first it was hysteria. It wasn't. He said at last. "Look, Mr. Williams—I lose nothing. Our government loses nothing. I give them this formula—they let Constance go unharmed. Perhaps they sell it to a foreign power. What of it? I still know the secret and I want the world to have it."

I waited with him for the call he was to receive. I told him that I often worked between racketeers and honest citizens. That I was known in the underside of the city as the halfway house between the cops and crime. He would suggest that I act for him. I'd make a deal with them. If he wanted to give up the formula for the girl, why that is the way it would be. First we'd have to be assured that they had the girl. Second, that she was safe. Third, that she would be returned.

"They'll trust me," I told him. "All crooks do. That's how I make my living."

He jumped at the idea.

"It won't matter," he said. "In the long run the whole world will have the formula. My purpose will be accomplished. Constance will be saved," his head began to nod, a faraway look came into his eyes. "Man too often spends his energies and his brains destroying things. Germs, yes. That was good. Now—I will build things. I will make crops grow where nothing grew before. I'll reclaim thousands—millions of acres of lost land."

He was off on another world shaking achievement. He had saved man from being destroyed. Now he would preserve man. On and on. I sure thought he was a good little guy. How he could talk. I was bored, but I honestly did wish I knew what he was talking about. Gas was his line all right— I got plenty of it then.

WE SET UP our strategy. That is, as much as we could with as little as we knew. The idea was that I was to listen in on the extension phone upstairs. He took me to his bedroom and went downstairs and called up a friend at the University to be sure it was working okay.

"The switch is here on my desk," he told me when I had returned to the study.

"I generally have it on, but turn it off for privacy when I pick up the phone. If it is off then there is no connection."

It was dusk when the phone rang. I motioned to Professor Eslam to delay things and I hot-footed it up to his bedroom. I grabbed the phone. Not a sound. Not a buzz. Not even a crackle. The phone seemed dead. I waited and held my breath. Nothing happened. It must be working. It had been all right before. Now—nothing.

I went downstairs. I went easy and quietly. The study door was open a little as I had left it. I could see Professor Eslam. He was holding the phone and talking.

"Very well. I will come alone. Yes, at once," and he hung up.

"You heard—" he started and stopped when I shook my head. Then he looked down at the switch at the side of his desk. His eyes widened—his cheeks bulged. "I—habit is a terrible thing," he said. "I turned the switch off when I lifted the phone— I must have."

Too much is enough and sometimes plenty. I think that was the time it was enough but not plenty yet. Then he said: "I'm to go alone, Mr. Williams. They won't have anyone come with me; they never heard of you."

"Never heard of me?" I wasn't flattered—and I don't think I was conceited either in my surprise. All first-class crooks know me.

Professor Eslam broke in on my thoughts. He was over to the bookcase removing books, fooling with the door to a small safe that had been concealed behind them. He was saying.

"I may have misunderstood about you. But her voice. Constance—cried out over the phone. They—must have hurt her. It is possible they said they'd have none of you. I must meet them alone at my little cottage up in the Westchester Hills."

He turned with a folder in his hands. He laid it on the flat desk, opened it disclosing numerous sheets of papers.

"The formula," he said.

"All that?"

"Oh yes—yes—all that. It has been worked out in detail. Cheap to manufacture and almost ready to be produced in great quantities."

"Professor," I told him seriously, "you have what it takes inside; but these lads would make a monkey out of you. You can't go alone."

"I have to," he said simply. "There's Constance—her life. You didn't hear her voice, Mr. Williams."

"Suppose they kill you?"

"It doesn't matter: I must go for her sake."

"It may not matter to you if you are dead—but what about her. If they have the formula—what about her?"

"Yes—" he clutched at the desk and looked at me blankly. "What about her? Mr. Williams—what—what am I to do?"

I DON'T THINK I ever liked the little guy more than I did right then. I gave it to him straight. I talked turkey to him. I knew these sort of lads and he didn't. He should turn the formula over to me. I'd give it to them for the girl.

"But—" he looked at the clock on the mantle. "If I'm not there by nine o'clock,

they'll kill her. It's a long drive. I've got to go."

"You go," I said laying my hand down on the papers on his desk. "But I'll take these papers. Tell them I have your formula, that I will give it to them for the girl—alive and well. They don't want the girl. They want this. They'll have to do business with me."

"I don't know. I don't know. This keen mind of mine. Where is it, now when I need it most?" He gripped at my hand. "Mr. Williams, I'm simply a baffled, confused old man."

"Look," I said to him. "You go to this cottage of yours in your car. I'll take mine and wait some place—a mile say from the cottage. Some gas station—some lunch room," and when he just looked at me, "You'll meet these people. You'll tell them I have what they want. That you are to telephone me. That I'll meet them any place—any place within reason. At your cottage if they wish."

"Call you—yes—yes. There is Grogan's Place. Gas station and lunch room—open all night. A mile from my cottage. But you, surely you won't use your own name there. It would excite suspicion and—"

"Your head isn't working so bad," I tried to cheer him. "I'll use the name Case—just call up Grogan's Place then and ask for Mr. Case." He seemed uncertain. "They'll agree." I said. "They'll have to agree."

"Yes—yes—" he was still hesitant. "If you think it best. I leave it in your hands. Constance's life in your hands. With me—it doesn't matter. You are right. It is my work they want—not my child."

And coming down to earth with one of those crashes of his. "I have little money, Mr. Williams—but Constance will not be ungrateful—be sure of that."

My line I suppose was to dismiss the money. I didn't. After all. I work for a living. Romance is all right. The sex interest is swell. But the girl was engaged to another man—all I had from her was a handshake, a cold hand at that.

We worked it out my way. I wrote down the name Case for him so he couldn't forget it. I had him give me directions to Grogan's Place and repeat it over and over so I could be sure he wasn't talking about two other lunch rooms. I wrote it all down. I had him give me instructions even on how to reach his cottage if things went wrong. He seemed vague on that. He did much better with Grogan's Place.

"I could find my little two-story stone-house blindfolded," he told me. "But directions," he went over it again, "off the main road, so secluded, so restful. I wonder if I will ever enjoy its quietude again."

"For years and years," I told him. "With Constance, too. Don't worry; I've worked things like this over and over—between clients and crooks. I know the ropes."

It didn't seem to make much difference now but I had him give me all that was said over the phone. It was a lot for such a short talk. They didn't want a third party mixed up in it. They didn't give him time to insist. He was to drive to his cottage in the Westchester Hills. They would watch him arrive. If he made a false move or did not come alone, Constance would die.

That was all. It wasn't much to go on. But I had done business on less—a lot less.

We made our arrangements. I'd give him a few minutes start. He was to drive his way. I would drive mine. I wouldn't follow him. His departure might be watched.

I saw him leave the house. A pitiful little figure. His clothes expensive—well made but hanging on him—his head cocked to one side. I watched him go up the street in his car.

No one covered the house. I left then. His formula clutched tightly under my left arm in a manila envelope. My right hand rested easily in my jacket pocket. It held a gun—a finger was wrapped around the trigger of that gun. The document was important. At least one murder had been committed because of it—and more might be in the planning. Not the making. I'd see to that. In that envelope could very easily lie the girl's life. Professor Eslam's life. And if you want to get personal—my life.

CHAPTER 4

IT WAS A nice early spring night when I headed the car in against the wooden fence that said *Grogan's Place*. "Place" was right. A lunch counter by the gas station—three tables in the back. A dumpy woman was behind the counter. A truck driver was drinking coffee and dunking bread in it—great slabs of bread. I took a table in the semi-dark—ordered coffee and slipped the dumpy dame a dollar.

"A call for Mr. Case is coming in. That's me. Watch it, will you?"

She looked at the buck, looked at me, said without expression.

"Coffee. Case—C-a-s-e," spelled out the name.

I nodded, said "Right" and waited.

It was longer than I thought. I got nervous. I watched the clock on the wall—my own watch. It was ten o'clock when the call came.

"It worked—it worked." Professor Eslam's voice was shrill, excited. "He'll do business with you. Come right up here to the cottage."

"All right. I'm on my way."

He hollered me down before I could leave. Wanted to know if I knew the way. I told him I had the directions as he gave them to me but he made me repeat them to him—and seemed surprised. Then he corrected me. Gave me different directions. I didn't hear any other voice—but there seemed to be a rumble in the background. Maybe someone was listening in behind him.

"I must have been confused before," he said; "I'm right now. They will watch you arrive. It's a left turn at the fork—not right one."

I was on my way. Strange country, little used back roads—but my sense of direction is good. This time the professor's directions were excellent.

The house itself was not far from the road. It was a two-story stone affair. I could make it out in the shadows among the trees. There was a circular driveway. It was risky. One murdered, a girl and her stepfather facing death—and a fortune on the seat beside me.

Blackness in the house as I pulled up before the front door. Not a sound, not a figure as I stepped from the car and pressed my back hard against it, the envelope held across my stomach in my left hand, my right with the gun in it behind the envelope.

The door suddenly opened. Light shone. I saw Professor Eslam. He was alone. He came quickly down the steps to me.

"Mr. Williams—Mr. Williams," he gripped at the envelope. "I am alone inside—quite alone. They—are watching I think. Two of them. Let me hide this inside. They will return as soon as they are assured you came alone. One of them talked to me. An evil-looking man."

We were inside. He slammed the door shut. I heard the chain rasp home.

"Upstairs," he cried. "Quick. I must hide this."

I tried to grab his arm but he was on the stairs— I called to him to take it easy.

"No, no—" he was excited. "They were here when I arrived, Mr. Williams. They kept me from going upstairs. I heard a noise and I think—could Constance be up there?"

I HAD OVERTAKEN him. He was trembling. The manila envelope clutched tightly to him.

"She wouldn't be there," I tried to quiet him. He leaned heavily on my arm as we reached the landing. I had to steady him from falling.

He raised a hand, both it and his arm shook. He pointed down the hail, toward the front.

"That room. I often work there. I can hide this there—then you talk to them."

I held him then. His arm was hard, felt surprisingly muscular.

"I can't see a thing," I told him; "where is the light-switch?"

He stretched out a hand. There was a click. A dim light went on. I saw the closed door at the end of the hall. He seemed steady now. I went to the door. He was behind me. I could hear his breathing. He was not doing so well.

Professor Eslam was close against me when I opened the door. Blackness. His hand pushed by me. I heard again the click of a switch. Two lamps showed light. I only saw one. It was over a chair. The light glowed down brightly but not on the chair. Rather on what was sitting in the chair. It was a man all right. He was slumped, his head to one side as if he suddenly fell asleep. In the center of his forehead was a hole. There was a line of red down his face—over the bridge of his nose. He was not nice to look at; he was dead.

"Know him?" I asked the professor.

"Him—him," the professor gasped. "Her—the woman. Is she—is she all right, Mr. Williams?"

I saw her then; she was on the floor. The black dress, the nylon legs. The rest of her disappeared or rather was hidden by the end of a big couch.

I don't know why it came to me then.

"Madame—Madame Pest," I gasped.

I walked to the end of the couch. The woman was lying on her face. One arm folded under her, the other up over her head as if to ward off a blow. It looked as if she was struck down from behind. I knelt beside her. There was a knife-wound in her back. And she wasn't all right; she was dead!

Even then it was dawning in my mind. What was wrong with the picture. Someone who didn't know me. Who had so little respect for me that he didn't mind my walking in and finding a couple of dead bodies.

Too much is enough and sometimes plenty. I had had the *enough*. Now I had the final cue. I had *plenty*; I knew.

I had been dumb. I admit that. But it wasn't luck that saved my life. For I knew—knew maybe only a split second before I was to die. I knew as I turned—and because I knew, I saved my life.

I swung and threw up my left hand and took the knife through my sleeve and through my arm—deep and hard and vicious the blow was. I heard the knife hit bone—scrape and strike my chest.

Hit bone. A bad break that you think. No, a good one. For otherwise it would have buried itself in my chest. For it was long and sharp and cruel and driven with surprising strength. I could have killed him then. But I didn't.

Not that I thought that he was little and weak and no match for me. No—nothing high-minded like that. It was simply a case of even though I knew—I didn't quite believe—couldn't believe. I couldn't accept the truth of what I knew.

I knew. But it didn't make sense. When it did make sense, I was falling backwards tripping over the dead woman's legs; then I went down.

There I sat with my back against the couch, blood pouring from my left arm—my chest. I was looking into the bird-like eyes of Professor Eslam. I was looking, too, at the knife in his hand. He was bearing down on me—ready for the kill.

I RAISED MY right hand with the gun in it, said. "One more step, Professor Eslam, and I'll blow you across the room."

I think that was the first time he saw the gun. Or maybe the first time he realized that I was able to lift the hand that held the gun. There was surprise in his face—a hurt sort of surprise.

It stopped him. He staggered back as if I had struck him. Then his left hand suddenly flashed up. It held a small bottle.

"Shoot, Mr. Williams," he said, "and I'll drop this on the floor; much more powerful than nitroglycerin—far more devastating than what you call T.N.T. I am a chemist you know. It will, as you so expressively put it, blow both of us across the room."

I stirred, drawing up one foot. I kept my gun steady. I was wondering what a shot would do. Not what it would do to the professor but what it would do to the bottle—to me.

"It is very delicate glass," Professor Eslam said as if he read my mind. "The least jar will send it off. You can't shoot without ending life for both of us. Don't get up—even if you are able. I am a nervous, absent-minded man. So you guessed, a little late, but you guessed."

"Not too late," I said with satisfaction.

"Ah well," he moved over to a chair and stood by it and at least paid me the compliment of putting it between us. "I abhorred the necessity of killing you. I rather liked you. Your conceit. Your assurance. I will leave here. If you do not try and follow me—you can live."

"Take a step toward the door and I'll plug you," I told him and meant it. He could walk out that door, toss his explosive back and blow me up alone. I added, as I thought I saw a speculative look in his bright snapping eyes, "I could shoot before that bottle reached me—and will if you toss it."

He looked at me long and hard but he didn't go toward the door. I had won that point. I tried another. I said:

"Now professor, put that bottle down on the table. Put it down now or—I'll shoot." I held the gun steady—lightened my trigger finger.

"Shoot," he said and held the bottle out at arms length.

There you are. He knew what was in the bottle, and I didn't. He knew if it would go off by simply falling to the floor, and I didn't. If he was bluffing, it was a swell bluff. If I was bluffing—well he had called that now. He was right. I didn't shoot.

"Let us talk it over," I tried.

"Good," he nodded at me and sat down in the chair. "You think, Mr. Williams, time is on your side. I am quite willing to talk. For I think when you realize that I have killed two people—no. I did not kill the man there. The dead woman did that for me. She thought I was infatuated with her—and see the result." He waved the hand with the bottle in it and my stomach turned over. "Time will convince you that life can be pleasant. I am willing to let you live if you give me a start. Say twenty-four hours. If you will let me tie you up—then I—I will give you my word—that I will not harm you."

"Did the dead man in your laboratory have your word?" I asked him. "Did this woman Madame Palodia, or something, have your word?"

"Madam Paloria," he corrected me. "So you heard of her. Edward, no doubt. Ah, well—we may reach an agreement. I think time favors me—you think time favors you. What would you like to know?"

"All of it," I said and when he cocked his head and put those bird-like eyes on me, "You might start with the dead woman there—why you killed her."

HE ACTUALLY SMILED then, said, "Shall we say because my family did not quite approve of her. Or, because I wanted all the money."

"For that formula against germs?"

Remarkable man, the professor. He actually laughed. "There is no formula, Mr. Williams, none whatever. The stuff in the manila envelope is a jumbled mass of chemical notes, simply thrown together. For Constance and Edward who never got a look at them—except from a distance—and you later. Germs indeed! There is no money in germs. And you were right to curry favor with the government man. He will forgive then any little delinquency about disposing of the body. I had one ambition—to be rich. To have a great fortune—to play with chemicals—not work with them. Certainly I pretended I didn't care for money. Certainly with a vast fortune within my grasp—actually in my laboratory, I even made Constance think I was always short of money.

"Those three people—Fieze—Fielding and Madame Paloria, whose name I believe is simply Emily Krause, were in Washington during the war. They sold information to the highest bidder. I made some money through them but the real money was to be made in one product. It was too difficult during the hostilities. What these three people needed was an outlet. A New York City outlet. Easy of access and free from suspicion. My house was the place. I was a respected citizen—a university professor. This product could be kept in my place in large quantities. It was a product that was worth little at its source of supply—worth little in passage. Yet—a few pounds of it would be worth more than an average man earns in a life time. Worth it—once it was safe in my house."

"Dope," I guessed it.

"Narcotics," he nodded. "We kept it in my laboratory. And lately we have kept the money there. The money—right close to my hands. A fortune—a dozen fortunes, and yet they were not satisfied. And I was known as the house of drugs to but three people. Three live people then. Three dead people now. Every one of them were already suspected. Fieze even known. But the government wanted the place of supply—my place. They did not have it yet. So—I eliminated two of them—Emily Krause killed Fielding. It was planned that she and I would split the money between us. She—" he looked at me almost coyly, "she was in love with me, Mr. Williams. If you can believe that."

"I can believe anything of you now," I admitted. "But this place here of yours. They would find the bodies here and—

recognize Madame Paloria as a visitor at your house."

"But this," he said, "is not my place, it was Ficzc's place. I misled you on that. A little chemical I have, and Emily Krause would not be recognizable as Madame Paloria. No indeed." He shook his head. "I would have been very rich," and after a pause, "will be very rich."

"But me—why bring me into it?"

"You *did* move the body of Fieze for me. But Constance was suspicious. Not of my doing anything wrong, but others harming me for my secret—the bogus formula against germs," he chuckled then. "Only that very morning, with the dead man in the laboratory, she threatened to call you. So I told her I would send for you. There was no other way. She is very determined."

"And suppose," I said, "I had refused to touch the body?"

"I had money—plenty of it," he said and added simply, "I would have paid you much more."

Not a fine commentary on me—but—true, I suppose.

CHAPTER 5

There was nothing mad about the professor. A ruthless, cold-blooded, shrewd man. I wasn't thinking of the dead Fieze in his laboratory or the dead woman there on the floor. I was thinking of the others—the thousands—tens of thousands of others he had helped reduce to slavery with dope.

I know the results of drugs. I've seen enough of it. The woman with a knife in her back was better off than these other victims.

The blood ran down my arm and down my chest—but if the professor hoped I'd bleed to death or pass out from loss of blood, he'd be disappointed. Not that I mightn't. I felt weak enough. But I felt strong enough to press my right index finger home on a trigger. If I passed out it wouldn't mean his life—it would mean his death. My last act would be to close my finger—once.

Professor Eslam talked on. Money was his only motive. The others were going to double cross him. They even kept the money at his house. He knew and struck first. As for the woman. He seemed mostly to resent her insistence that she take the name Madame Paloria and come to his home openly.

They had made use of him. He gave them what they needed more than anything else, "respectability." That was himself, of course.

We played our game together. I encouraged him to talk. He encouraged me to listen. What time could do for either one of us, I didn't know. He sat in the chair, the bottle in his hand. I leaned against the wall on the floor—and the blood dripped more slowly, I thought—and my gun was held against my leg, always pointing upward, always pointing at Professor Eslam. He was saying.

"You must not feel too chagrined, Mr. Williams, that I took you in so completely. Really—I was quite a character—quite myself all the time. You are used to dealing with big-time criminals, blustering known racketeers with the stamp of crime heavy upon their features. The best government men never suspected me—never would have known. They would have found me only through these others. Things came to my house and left there so easily. I paid you the compliment of finding it necessary to kill you."

"Why bring me here? Why kill me? I knew nothing."

"You would have in time—just as you did know a second too soon. Once you ceased to protect me—to watch over me—to have my honest scattered brain little ways before you. But mainly you had to die quickly because you talked with the government man. That was getting too close. No, Mr. Williams, my plans for these other two were already made. I had to fit you in quickly and I did. You live on excitement. I had to furnish you with excitement—not give you time to think. Offer you danger and adventure," and cocking his head in that odd little way, "and money, of course."

"But what of Constance? Is she dead?" I asked.

"Dead?" he jarred erect. "I wouldn't harm Constance. I love her very much. My dear, dear, Mr. Williams—you are so naïve. Constance is away spending a few days with friends in Greenwich, Connecticut. Edward has taken her there."

"Then this kidnaping, the phone call, was all a fake. But the phone did ring, and you did talk to someone."

Oh, yes—Emily—Madame Paloria here. It was all to keep you keyed up—excited. Little time for you to think. I called her from the laboratory and you fell so nicely into my plans. Almost as if they were your own."

"If things went wrong—" I started but he cut in.

Things do not go wrong with me. They have not gone wrong now." He came to his feet then, "You want to live don't you? Very well. I will go. If you shoot—you get this bottle."

He turned and walked straight toward the door—the bottle held high in his hand.

I CRIED OUT for him to stop. I drew a bead on his head. He kept walking. Thoughts? Plenty of them. If it was a bluff and the bottle contained nothing harmful, what then. Why he could leave the room—get a gun. I—I was terribly weak. I didn't know if I could follow him or not. I had lost plenty of blood.

He was at the door. Now—or—or—

I dropped the nose of my gun and pulled the trigger. The bullet caught him in the right leg below the knee. He sat down like a fat lady with the chair pulled from under her. He turned, too, and I saw his face, his eyes, but I saw the bottle—the bottle still in his hand. I made the effort and came to my feet. I could stand. I could walk— I was walking toward him. The bottle was still in his hand. He was tearing at the cork and I was weaving, staggering toward him. My stomach turned over.

Could I reach him before he pulled the cork for that seemed to be what he wanted to do. I couldn't make it in time. The cork was out—and— I lurched forward. He put the bottle to his mouth and drank the contents.

"You surprised me, Mr. Williams," he said thickly. "I didn't think you would do it. You can stand the loss of a great deal of blood. I had hoped you would keel over while I was talking to you. Do not distress yourself that I am in pain from your shot. The bottle contained a sedative," and with an almost whimsical twist to his lips, "a rather powerful sleeping drought—for I will sleep forever. No, no—nothing so melodramatic as nitroglycerin," he paused and coughed.

I didn't say anything. Stood there—wavering and looking down at him.

"A few minutes—hardly more than a minute, Mr. Williams." He didn't talk so well now. "There is a phone below—better have your wounds attended to," and his mind beginning to go I suppose. "Yes, yes, I know—you are young and strong but there is the danger of infection. I tell you what. If you don't tell Constance what I did—about—these people—these dead—people—then I won't tell the government man about your moving the body."

He never did tell. He slumped forward then—sort of doubled up on himself and died very quietly—very easily.

As for me—I staggered down the stairs—found the phone and lifted it.

Head Over Homicide

IT WAS NO use hashing it over; it was no use telling myself that if it was anybody but R. Riley I wouldn't be there. It was no use recalling that Riley was well past seventy, favored spats, sported a cane and wore a posy in his lapel. The worst was the sudden recollection that someone had told me the R stood for Reginald.

The truth was that it was a cold, bitter night. The wind blew up the deserted street; the black hulks of cars parked along the curb that were such a welcome sight an hour or two ago suddenly took on the appearances of hearses. I had crouched in that narrow, ill-smelling alley for two solid, frozen solid, hours. It was now after one o'clock. One in the morning, understand, and cold enough to freeze a brass spittoon in case I didn't mention the weather before—or even if I did mention it, for that matter.

You may say that such thoughts come from an overactive imagination, or thyroid if you are medically inclined. Maybe the smell did, for it was too cold for any real odor to get through—though the filth was there.

I thought of Jerry, my boy—anyway my assistant if you are one to quibble over calling a forty-one year old "boy"— parked in the car around the corner all wrapped up in the heavy blankets from the back of the car. I wondered idly if he had fallen asleep—and if he had, what difference would it make? But if—

I slunk back; drew in a deep breath that like to put icicles on my lungs, and pressed myself hard against the grimy brick walls of the house—right beside the worn stone steps that led up to the front door. For the black sedan that slid to the curb looked more like a hearse than any of the other cars. It had come—silently and shadowy—and crept into the picture.

A heavy-set man in a black top coat and gray slouch hat, whose face was a blob of white in the night, came from behind the wheel and out the open door, his rubber soled shoes hitting the sidewalk with no sound. He then opened the rear door of the long sleek boat, stuck his head inside, then looking up at the red brick of the house, waited.

For the first time I heard the purr of the engine—no more than a gentle hum across the fifteen or twenty feet of sidewalk between us. Nice motor tuneup. I decided then if I met this lad socially—I mean otherwise than at his funeral— I'd ask him where he got the motor job done.

After running his eyes up and down the house, he covered the block carefully both ways, slowly turning his head. He evidently found the emptiness satisfactory, for he left the car and walked close to where I crouched hidden from his view by the projecting stone railing of the steps.

Standing beneath the first floor windows, he raised his left hand slowly. It was some sort of signal to whomever was watching behind the heavy drawn curtains above.

His right hand never left his coat pocket and it didn't take any imagination, or overactive thyroid, to picture that hand gripping a gun and a finger caressing a trigger. Having done his duty and announced in pantomime, "The car awaits, my lord," he turned from the window and backed up beside the steps close to where I was crouching behind the cans that smelled so—in theory anyway.

He kept coming back on me slowly and the softly purring car could hardly be heard at all above the slithering rubber soled feet. He was protecting the front steps of that house and whoever was to come down them—or thought he was. As a matter of fact, he wasn't protecting anyone—least of all himself.

IF WE HAD rehearsed it for hours, it couldn't have worked better. I straightened to receive him, stepped clear of the cans and let him back into my gun. Odd, isn't it, how instinct or intuition warns us of danger. I hadn't made a sound; I hadn't cast a shadow; and yet he knew. Somehow he knew before he actually contacted my gun—and I knew that he knew. It was the way he teetered on his heels before he took that final backward step—a step he couldn't control, for he was off-balance; a step he would have given anything to have not taken. Stiff—he was as hard as a board, his whole body tense. And his right arm jerked, hesitated—but his hand didn't come out of his pocket.

At that very moment of full awareness of danger, his instinct paid him off in fact. He laid his spine right smack against the nose of my gun.

"All right, Charlie," I told him. "You're not kidding yourself; it is a gun." And when his right arm moved, perhaps convulsively, I remembered my promise to Riley, cursed the promise, too, and said, "If you want your friends to picture you a hero, and read in the papers how you died gun in hand, why draw it."

He wasn't a publicity-seeker, so he didn't make a move. I leaned over, stuck my hand deep in his right overcoat pocket, and removed his gun. No trouble there; this boy was a professional, and the professionals know that the man with the gun talks and the man without listens. That's the reason today that there are so many old-time professional criminals— only the fresh young punks die young.

I dropped his gun easily into a trash can—no tossing it—no noise. I lifted off Charlie's hat with my left hand and cracked him behind the ear with my rod. It was hard—maybe you might call it vicious—certainly there was a reasonable possibility that I had fractured his skull. Okay, you are gentle folks and particular how you crash a skull. So what—we all have our little peculiarities, and I don't overadmire lads who mess around with young and innocent girls—no, nor even with old and uninnocent ones.

Charlie went as cold as an Eskimo's feet. And believe me, it was not with any sense of the niceties of life that I caught him as he fell; it was just that I thought that head of his might open up and rattle when it hit the cement, and I was all for retaining the peaceful quiet of the winter night.

I didn't tie him up; I'm not a lad who gilds the lily. I didn't think about his freezing to death there—unless it was for a moment of pleasant contemplation. He had made his alley—let him lie in it. I stretched him out for a long winter's nap, straightened, and watched the stone steps that led up to the front door of the old house.

A minute later—certainly no more—and the heavy door above opened, squeaked, and closed. Then figures came down the steps. There were two men in heavy overcoats. My liver came up in my throat, dropped back and kept my heart where it belonged. That was when I saw the tiny shape between the men—the slim figure of the girl. A girl whose head was bare and whose hair streamed down her back, and twisted around front too. I saw also the flimsy garment that might have been a nightdress—and was—and the bare feet that half dragged, half walked between the two men.

Two men—strong men—at least strong enough to hold up the body of a young girl and drag her through the bitter cold of that winter night. Two men in heavy warm coats, with collars turned up, hats pulled down—warm hands hidden in thick fur-lined gloves—well thick gloves, anyway. The fur-lined part I ran in to make me feel better, if I had to slip up on my promise to Riley and shoot both of them to death.

I moved then. Stepped forward, jerked

up my gun, but my opening line was spoiled as the man nearest me on the right of the girl said to his pal. "Hurry, you fool; get in behind that wheel."

That was my cue so I came in. "All right, Charlie," I said. "Drop the lady." I stuck my gun into the side of his cheek and added, "This is your obit, Charlie."

I admit to lack of originality. Maybe it was just my night for "Charlie's" or perhaps my creative genius got frozen in that alley. And now for the first time the show didn't go according to rehearsal. Charlie dropped the girl—ducked his head from under my rod—hollered something to his friend that sounded like "cop," though I'm not sure and hope it wasn't as offensive as that. Anyway he ran for the open front door of the car; his friend simply hurled the girl in my direction and followed.

Because they muffed their lines was no reason I should let the whole show fold up at the climax. I caught the girl, grabbing her under the knees, and tossing her over my shoulder took it on the run myself— but toward the corner and my car and Jerry parked around it.

The car was there. Jerry was behind the wheel and, of all things, awake—and we were moving almost before I plunged through the open rear door with the girl. If the rest of the cast let me down, Jerry didn't. He had the right lines and correct amount of humor mixed in with the surprise in his voice. "Gawd," he gaped, "you might have put some clothes on her before you brought her out."

As I slammed the door, peeled off my overcoat and slipped her into it, Jerry threw his punch line at me before I got the blankets off the floor. "A half naked girl—" disgust was in his voice. "Ain't we getting just like the dicks in the racy fiction?" Then he asked where to and when I told him the Landsgrove residence, he swallowed his next smart crack and blurted out.

"No. No, Boss. Not her. Not Becky Landsgrove—the missing heiress—who was kidnaped, or eloped, or ran away from home—or had amnesia—or got drunk or—or—whichever paper you read. But Boss—Boss—not the ten thousand dollar reward for whoever—whoever—"

"All of it, Jerry." Maybe I gloated a little. You got to admit it was a good haul. Harland D. Landsgrove's daughter Rebecca—of the front pages—and the ten grand for her return. I put the two blankets around her, all wool, and pulled her close to me for warmth. Her warmth, understand—not mine. However, it was nice to feel that much money in my arms. Still, it wasn't all mine—not by a good sight, it wasn't—damn little of it mine.

Ten thousand; and out of that Riley was to get eight—and his soft crack, "At that, Race, I'm not making as much as you are." Meaning to leave me with the impression that it had cost him plenty for the information he passed on to me— but really leaving me with the impression that he was a bigger liar than I thought he was. The headlines would be worth a fortune to me. Newspapers-radio-TV. Maybe newsreels—why, I'd be right up in the Hooper rating, with tooth paste even, Riley had raved.

So you see I wasn't such a bad guy hold-

CARROLL JOHN DALY

ing the girl close to me with only a two thousand dollar interest in her. You can forget that night-shirt business—already there was my overcoat and two blankets between me and the night-shirt. If she was a nice armful or not—who could tell?

SHE WAS SOBBING and clinging to me. I said: "Easy does it—you're going home, and—"

Fingers bit through the blanket into my arm—a wet, cold mouth against my ear opened and lips moved and words came. "No—no—please."

Sure, I held her tight then. I ran a hand through her hair—no treat that—it wasn't silky and electric to the touch. If there was any emotion caused by it, it was that grand passion one feels when ringing out a mop. But the poor kid—the poor, rich kid. And I thought then, after I get her home I'll go back and lift up Charlie's head—that is my first Charlie—and put it back on the pavement again in a way that he would remember. Damn Riley, and my promise not to shoot unless I had to save her life. I felt mad about the kid. It was like holding a terror-stricken child in your arms; and if you never held one, don't tell me I'm sentimental.

"It's Race Williams, Honey-bun," I told her. "It's the U.S. Cavalry in the last reel—it's the Marines landing," I laughed lightly at my own cleverness if she didn't. "In plain words, you're safe—and you're going home; going to your father and your own room and your—"

Hell I forgot how old she was and didn't know whether to say she was going home to her dolls, or her fifth of scotch.

Things broke then—and the convulsive moans stopped and she began to cry—softly and steadily which, I suppose, was better for her if not for me. I never did know what to do with crying women, outside of slapping them around and that didn't seem to be the answer. I called her Honey-bun again which was a sort of steal—you know, a feminine "Charlie" act—as I poured out my whispered instructions to Jerry at the wheel. I told him to make it fast and get to the phone as soon as Becky and I left the car at the Landsgrove house.

CHAPTER 2

ANY IDEA I had of getting Becky into her father's house unseen was dissipated, but it wasn't much of a dissipation for I wasn't too set on the idea. There was a police car right smack in front of the house.

The shades were drawn and darkness hung over that dreary big house in the exclusive neighborhood. But a faint light could be seen through, or under, or on, the shades of most every room. No figures walked the street and maybe I was wrong in thinking there were half a dozen cops hidden about. The set-up though was as it should be if a distracted and grief-stricken father waited for a ransom note.

The newspapers themselves were torn between a romance with a sociably-undesirable suitor and an out-and-out professional snatch. Both stories were good for circulation, and a few years back the romance one might have been the best;

but since the laws on kidnaping had reached the cold meat stage, most of the boys in that line had migrated to other fields. So now a kidnaping job had a touch of originality to the public. Of course, any story that Rebecca Landsgrove had met with an accident, or even sudden and violent death, lacked the suspense of illicit romance in high finance, or the socially-prominent being held for ransom; besides, the morgue and hospitals had been covered.

Becky made the distance from the car to the flight of steps leading to her front door half walking and half being carried on my right arm—with my left holding her, and trying to keep the blankets from staying on the sidewalk. As for Jerry, he had slipped from the car and into an alleyway between the houses, leaving the car at the curb. We are not children in this business, and where the police left the way open for anyone to get into the house, they sure had made arrangements so you wouldn't leave unnoticed.

Things broke before we hit the top step. The door opened, voices spoke. A low husky one said: "It looks like—by gawd, it *is* the girl."

Then we were inside. There were running feet and a cop in uniform came out of a side room with a cup of coffee in his hand looking for a place to set it down—and finally put it on the floor. Sergeant O'Rourke opened a door and let more light into the hall as he stuck his head out—turned and said something to a man inside. That was the big moment— or should have been.

Harland Landsgrove shot out of the library in a dark flowing dressing gown— he called it later—though it looked like a bathrobe; his gray hair was rumpled, he needed a shave, and his eyes were bloodshot. He hollered, "Becky—Becky—my own little girl," and ran toward us with arms outstretched.

So far the play proceeded according to the script and this time the leading lady hashed it up. Instead of dashing from me and meeting her old man half-way, she threw up both arms, lost her blankets—or mine if you are a sticker for accuracy— then turned and threw her arms around me and shrieked: "No—no— I can't. I'm afraid. I'm afraid."

THAT STOPPED THE loving father act cold unless he wanted to take both of us in his arms—which he evidently didn't. It pulled him up short. He skidded a bit on the highly polished floor and sort of jarred into us, regained what he thought was his dignity, and said: "Becky—Becky. Who is this man?"

"It's your daughter, Mr. Landsgrove," I said, as if he didn't know. "I've brought her home." Which if not much in the dramatic was, at least, fact and better than anything I had heard.

Landsgrove tried to pry Becky loose from me, so she clung the tighter. Sergeant O'Rourke made cooing noises but I finally saved the day—or the night—by picking the girl up in my arms and getting things back in order. I was thinking of that ten grand—or at least my piece of it.

"Becky is inclined to be a little hysterical, Mr. Landsgrove," I told him, and by great will power refrained from adding, *and so are you.* "I'll carry her up to her room—then you can get the doctor to look at her."

"Doctor? Doctor?" he ran a hand through what passed for his hair. "Yes— to be sure. Nevins. Where is Nevins? Ah, yes, Doctor Hillman, Nevins—at once, please."

"At once, sir." This crack came from a portly gent who looked so dignified and important that I knew he must be the butler. A heavy woman floated into the picture like a giant tug ready to berth an ocean liner—no nonsense about her. She cleared the path to the wide stairway— and spoke to me. "This way, sir. The poor dear. We'll get her to bed with a nice hot drink and a bag."

What kind of a bag she didn't state.

We made a parade of it up the stairs and even though Becky tried to shut off my windpipe, it would have been easy-going if Mr. Landsgrove hadn't been jumping in and out. Sometimes ahead for me to bump into; sometimes on the side to squeeze us against the wall: then behind treading on my heels as I swung from side to side like a greedy road hog in Sunday traffic. Finally we reached the hall above and the housekeeper, in pink robe and curlers that bristled like tiny machine guns, was holding open a bedroom door. "There, Miss Becky. She'll do all right, sir, in her own little room—in her own little bed."

So I carted Becky across that half acre room and deposited her on her own massive little bed and, bending over, tried to remember what you did to break a head lock. At last I slipped from under. Her eyes were wide and frightened, and the coat was open, and the condition of her nightdress a censorable item. I pulled the coat around Becky as the big woman, who someone addressed as Mrs. Horton, started tossing blankets over her—not mine.

Landsgrove spoke to me: "What— what did you do with her clothes?" When I turned and looked at him, not having a fast return for that one, he said with less accusation: "But—but she isn't dressed, you know."

The girl started to cry then and held out her hands locked together. Her mouth was twisted up and her eyes pin-points of fire. I took her hands, and separated them and held one of them, and the other came over and gripped mine.

I think it was then the doctor came. If it was, he must have been sitting by his door with his bag in his hand. The sound effects had gone dead and outside the girl's occasional sob, the spoken drama had deteriorated into a pantomime.

THE DOCTOR KNEW his business and he knew his Landsgrove, too—at least the old man—for he talked to Harland soothingly, as if he was the one who had the real shock. Then we were all crowding out in the hall.

Sergeant O'Rourke smiled at me—a knowing smile—and said: "The name is Williams, Mr. Landsgrove. Race Williams—he's a detective. Private kind."

"Oh—oh, yes—to be sure." Landsgrove nodded. "Called me up this afternoon— about—yes, about Becky."

"That's right," I smiled. "Wanted to

know if she was still missing and if the reward was authentic as stated in the papers."

When he nodded but said nothing: "You told me it was—and there is your daughter." I pointed at the closed bedroom door.

"Yes—yes—"Landsgrove started in on that to-be-sure line again, caught himself up and said, "Inspector Nelson—I—I don't see him about."

"The inspector," O'Rourke said. "Oh—I'll get in touch with him. I suppose, Mr. Landsgrove, you may wish to talk to Mr. Williams alone—in the privacy of your library." He nodded at Landsgrove and winked at me and repeated "in privacy."

Now O'Rourke was my friend. He was a good lad. He was, of course, a cop first and my friend afterward. But I liked the old coot and I know he liked me; and maybe if he didn't entirely approve of some of my methods, he envied them— being tied up with red-white-and-blue tape. You know a search warrant for this— no tapping of telephones for that—and stepping on the wrong toes of the right people. It wasn't like him to deal himself out on the first break of the case; then again maybe it was. If the whole thing had a fishy taste to it, it might be better for a cop not to know too much—at least have it blurted out to him before witnesses. Maybe he wanted to see what kind of a story Landsgrove came up with after he talked to me and the girl—who now was under the doctor's care and not subject to police questioning. Then again, there was O'Rourke's wink to consider.

Inspector Nelson. I hadn't known he was on the case; but, of course, he would be. Big money—big pull—big-shot Nelson. We saw little to like nor anything to admire in each other. Nelson didn't like private operators in general, and me in particular; in fact, he was after my license because he couldn't keep me in line. But don't get the idea that he wasn't a good cop—and a mighty shrewd one, too. He was all of that. Also, he was unreasonable and arrogant and—oh well, let us say that in my opinion he was an all around stinker; to be fair, he held about the same opinion of me—that is, the stinker part. In simple words, we didn't sort of take to each other.

CHAPTER 3

Down in the spacious library with its walls of books, fireplace, great windows with heavy curtains—that I suppose were called drapes—Mr. Landsgrove made himself comfortable behind the huge flat desk that next summer he would probably rent out as a roller skating rink.

Maybe Landsgrove didn't make himself comfortable but that was the impression he gave—at least in words, and I was supposed to be in on it. After I was seated opposite him, he pushed over a humidor of cigars. I nixed them—said something about cigarettes, but he never produced any. So I didn't either. When I'm sitting down with a guy who has made his pile, I don't like to study him through a smoke screen—at least one of my own making.

"Now, Mr. er—Mr. Williams, that we are comfortable, that you have excused the loss of—er—complete stability of a man of the world and recognized, yes, and readily understood er—er—" he looked toward the ceiling and let that go and said simply, "of a father, shall we talk."

"What of a father?" I wasn't willing to let it go at that. I was looking the place over. Sure, it was sweet of O'Rourke to let me alone with this bird and put the bite on him for the ten grand; but O'Rourke was hardly in charge. And there was that wink—that decidedly friendly wink. I was looking the room over when Landsgrove came out of the father act and said abruptly: "Well, Mr. Williams—suppose you tell me all about it."

I heard him all right but I was looking at the alleged drapes by the windows—the ones on my left. Maybe I don't know much about the way society furnish their houses and I am certainly no authority on drapes; but I've been around and—what with Television commercials and one thing and another—it was the first time I had ever seen drapes wearing shoes.

I looked over at Harland Landsgrove and said: "Very little to tell. I went looking for your daughter—found her and returned her." When he shook his head with a "that won't quite do" attitude, I added, "Two men brought her out of a house." I gave him the location and, after looking at my watch, added, "It was one eleven. I stuck a gun in one of them and he tossed your daughter to me. They jumped in a car and drove away; I brought her here."

"I see, I see—" he nodded. "You let the—these men—get away."

"Why, yes—" I gave him a wide-eyed, innocent look and, thinking this as a good time to mention money, said, "After all, Mr. Landsgrove, I work for a living and the ten thousand you offered was only for the return of your daughter. If you had—"

"Come, come, Mr. Williams," he broke in. "It is not as simple as all that; we are both men of the world. You called me yesterday afternoon, verified the reward, and twelve hours later produced my daughter." He leaned forward, "After all, we are alone here and—you may talk freely."

"Since you brought it up, and made the point of your own integrity—or lack of it—we are alone except for the big ape behind the curtain—the one to your right, my left!"

THE LAD BEHIND the curtain stepped out. I can't say I had expected him, but I was pleased; it was one of my moments. I liked embarrassing Inspector Nelson and this was it. Inspectors are not often hidden behind even expensive drapes; or if they are, they are not often discovered there. Nelson didn't like it. "So—so, Race Williams—" he spluttered. "You called me—me—a big ape."

See the point? He avoided the issue; he left out his slinking behind the curtain. He covered his embarrassment with an accusation—what I had called him. So—being a fair-minded man and seeing the justification of his complaint, I defended myself with the truth. I said quite honestly, "I didn't know you were the big ape who was behind the curtain; how could I?"

Poor Nelson. That was his weakness; no humor, no imagination. It may have been his strength as a cop, but as a human being—well as a being of any kind, for I never quite saw the human part in Nelson—it was a weakness.

He seemed to take my crack as an apology. "No matter—no matter." He shook his head and feeling that I had defended my position went on to defend himself. "Williams," he said to Landsgrove, "operates a one man detective agency," which was a reflection on Jerry he would resent when I told him—and I would tell him all right. "Such men are often apt to tell one story to the police and one to the client." He turned on me. "Come, Williams; I want the truth—all of it."

"That's it." I shrugged. "I was at the right place at the right time—"

"Yes, I believe that." Nelson stood glowering down on me. He was of the old school in that respect, and I'm not saying it's bad—but I'm not saying it's good either. If he was on the juvenile detail it would have been a riot. "Come now. How did you happen to be in the right place at the right time. Remember, this is a serious offense—perhaps."

Get the "perhaps?" I certainly did.

I still kidded around with my choice of words, but not with what those words added up to. As Nelson said, it was a serious offense, perhaps, and he could make plenty out of it. I gave him a story that I couldn't prove—but then he couldn't disprove it either.

"Well, yes," I grinned up at him. "It was a break. Two women in the subway. Just talk—you know how they have to holler to hear each other above the roar of the trains. I got enough to know one thought something queer was going on—a young girl in a house. Thought she screamed once—you know the talk. This woman was walking by the place—that sort of stuff, and there you are—she put the finger on the house."

"I see," Nelson nodded. "Quite a coincidence. You heard that right after you telephoned Mr. Landsgrove and got his—"

"Oh, no," I cut in, "I heard that first; didn't think anything of it. Then I read the papers about the reward and wondered—and called Mr. Landsgrove. A long shot, you know. Then went up and laid around the house. Never thought there would be—"

"And she walked out of that house, and you grabbed her, and let the two men get away. Is that what you want me to believe, after hearing two women—that you can't identify—talking about a girl acting oddly?"

"You make me sound awfully lucky," I grinned. "Personally, I had put it down to patience. I was there in the cold for hours. But what's the matter with my story? You've heard worst that didn't turn out so fortunate."

That last crack should hold him. Why the police must have had hundreds of calls from people who claimed they had seen Becky; and after the reward notice, why half the cops in New York must have been chasing down stuff that the department knew was as phony—yet they had to run it down anyway.

CARROLL JOHN DALY

WHILE NELSON JUGGLED it around and tried to think of cutting remarks with that dead imagination of his, I turned to Landsgrove. "You want to beef about my story? You have your daughter." Not liking the curtain act with Nelson, I continued. "And now, Mr. Landsgrove, there is the little matter of ten thousand dollars—I believe you used the words *immediate payment* when I spoke to you on the phone."

"Well—" he pulled at his chin. "I'd like to know a little more—and—there isn't any hurry, is there? I mean—"

"Wait?" Nelson said. "These men—two of them you say. You had a gun, Williams, and yet—"

"I'm sorry, Inspector," I came in. "I was thinking of Mr. Landsgrove's daughter; she was more or less hurled at me—the men were running, coat collars up, hat brims down. By the time I had drawn her back out of danger—" I spread my hands apart. "I didn't know how many others might be in the house."

"And you are trying to tell me—you, of all people, couldn't have shot them."

"Yes—" I nodded; "I could have. To be perfectly frank, Inspector, it wasn't because of your threat to get me for open gun-play—or was it flagrant gun-play? Very expressive; I remember at the time I thought you should write for the little magazines." I turned to Landsgrove, "Such a choice of words—such—"

"Never mind that." Humor or not, Nelson knew this wasn't simple, whole-hearted praise. "All right—you weren't thinking of me when you didn't shoot; then who were you thinking of?"

I didn't tell him the truth—that I was thinking of Riley, and cursing him, for I'll admit I would have been a pleasure to run a bit of lead up or down those boys' spines. But I had a good story. I used it. "I was," I said, "thinking of the girl; one shot might have brought others—and in the mêlée—" I turned to Landsgrove, "That's what I mean by the nice use of words— mêlée— well, I didn't want to risk her life in a gun battle which, since you were not paying for it, would have come entirely under the head of pleasure."

"I see—" Nelson said. "I suppose you can go for now. Mr. Landsgrove is at liberty, of course, to do what he wishes. But if I were in his place, I'd— I'd wish to know a little more before parting with any large sum of money."

I WAS ON my feet now. Maybe Nelson couldn't think up wisecracks—and what's more, I didn't think it was funny.

"Why you brass fixtures—"

I started in on Nelson and stopped dead. All right, score one for him. Score one for me, too, for shutting up.

"Go on." Nelson licked at his lips and looked over at Landsgrove. I couldn't think of anything funny to say—that is anything I'd be liable to laugh at for any length of time afterwards. I turned to Landsgrove and tried. "Look nice in the papers, won't it? Father welches on reward for missing daughter."

Nelson said: "It would seem to me the most natural thing in the world for Mr. Landsgrove to wish to question his daughter before paying any reward. Hear her story—"

"Yes—yes—to be sure," Landsgrove said and I couldn't tell if he thought that reasonable or an excuse to hang onto his dough. Don't tell me because he had a million he wouldn't miss ten thousand; the more people have, the harder it is to pry them loose from any fraction of it. Then Landsgrove went on. "It's after two, Mr. Williams. Say this afternoon or later this morning, Mr. Williams—you do not find that unreasonable to wait for the—the reward."

I did but perhaps no one else would—that is, no one but Riley.

Nelson stuck his jaw in again. "And I don't think, Mr. Landsgrove, that you will care for the publicity that Mr. Williams might give out—that is before you hear your daughter's story of events."

Another one below the belt, but this time it didn't hurt. What I was getting out of it after Riley had his cut didn't amount to so much—but the publicity would be worth plenty. I said: "You can't keep these things from the press. They'll know she's back. A house full of servants, Mr. Landsgrove, and I was seen coming in with her. It would be too much to hope—"

"Of course—of course—" Nelson nodded. "Look at it like this, Mr. Landsgrove. If it all came out now—this story as Williams tells it—before we hear what the girl has to say, why, poor Williams, a man known to shun publicity for his clients, naturally not knowing him you might suspect that he talked." Nelson laid a hand on my shoulder, "Why not spend the rest of the night here, Race; then if the servants talked to newspaper men—one could hardly suspect you."

I thought it over—or pretended to. Naturally I wanted to stay near my investment. I tossed in one. "Well," I shook my head. "Servants here—servants there—an hysterical girl—and of course, the cops around. Yes—I'll stay," and with a shake of my head, "though I hardly look on Mr. Landsgrove as a client."

Nelson nodded. Certainly a confused story would reach the press through Nelson; and certainly I would gain nothing by that story, and the police would lose little.

"Very sensible," Nelson nodded. "We'll go over your story again—and the girl's story when we get it. If the truth—er your story came out now, it might interfere with the police. And knowing you, Race, I know you wouldn't want to hamper justice. Besides—after Mr. Landsgrove talks with his daughter he might—just might want to edit the whole story for the press and—"

Then came what Nelson considered a friendly smile, which was known to throw young women into convulsions. "Well, if you don't see the reporters, Race, you can hardly be blamed if they garble up the yarn—and these servants whom you seem to think have special methods of communication."

The grin widened to more of a grimace. "And these talking cops. No, Race—if you are here we can't blame you for—" he turned toward the door where a cop now stood. "How's that—ah—" he turned back to Landsgrove. "Doctor Hillman sees no reason why we can't talk to her for a few minutes."

"But I thought," Landsgrove said, "that

is, I understood Doctor Hillman has given Becky a sedative."

"To be sure—to be sure—" Nelson spoke to the money Landsgrove represented. "But I had a word with the doctor and he understood the necessity for police questioning."

"Yes, yes" Landsgrove said. "I'll go right up and—"

"No—no—that won't be necessary—not at all necessary." Nelson was being almost coy. "You've had a hard time, Mr. Landsgrove; little sleep, worry—I can't understand how you bore up as well as you did."

"Well—I think," Landsgrove ran a hand through his hair. "I suppose I should—as her father."

"And quite right," I came in. "She'll need you, Mr. Landsgrove, after such an ordeal—facing strangers, even though Inspector Nelson is—"

"Come on then," Nelson snapped. "Not you, Williams; you wait here."

CHAPTER 4

NELSON SLAMMED OUT of the room with Landsgrove crowding him as he had me on the stairs. The door closed. I grinned and wandered around a bit. The books were good—that is, the bindings were. Maybe the pages weren't cut—maybe they were; I wasn't that much interested.

It wasn't hard to detect what business Landsgrove was in. Books on oil. Maps and charts and a lot of reports by the Federation Oil Industries—whatever that

was. They were bound in leather covers with gilt letters on them. I took a smell and it was real leather. I wondered, then, if they were that important to Landsgrove—or if they were something for visiting oil men to see. The paintings on the wall were nice—that is if you are interested in derricks and oil wells. There were some of plain desert land with hills in the background and I guess if things broke right, the artist would come back and paint in the oil. Some of them had figures up in the corner—and I guess it was how many barrels came in a day. Some had dates—and I guess that was when they first blew. Sure, sure, it might be when they ran dry—but I didn't think Landsgrove would be pleased enough about that to hang a painting of it. Besides—

I swung around and saw my visitor. He had closed the door softly—very softly. "Sorry," he said. "Sorry I startled you—I'm Walker, Carter Walker." He waved a hand toward the pin up oil display on the wall. "The secretary you know."

I didn't know but I let it go at that. If he was Landsgrove's secretary that might explain the pussy-footing entrance and the silent door closing. At least that's how I pictured butlers and secretaries for millionaires. Don't tell me different; I go to the movies.

This bird was about right for his job—dark hair with a touch of gray in it along the temples. He had sharp eyes too, and took me in with a couple of quick keen looks. Age, thirty-five or so; I wouldn't go higher than forty—even if I was pushed. He said: "You're Williams—Race Williams the detective fellow. Read a lot about you in the papers." He lowered his voice, "So you brought her in—I mean Becky. Is she, was she harmed? I mean—she's quite all right, eh?"

"She's as good as could be expected." I gave him the hospital fluff-off. "Why the hush-hush? It wasn't her fault she was kidnaped," and when he simply looked at me, "or was it?"

"Her fault—really, my dear fellow—how absurd. One doesn't—I don't understand."

"Me neither," I told him. "But keep it out of the papers—or make a good story for the papers. Too bad that reward didn't have a no questions asked clause."

"Well," Walker said, "What does she—what does Becky say?"

"Search me," I shrugged. "She was pretty well shot—might have been drugged. How does she get along with her father?"

"He adores her," and when I didn't show too much enthusiasm, "in his way. Not a demonstrative man you know—hardly a sentimentalist." And suddenly, "I wouldn't worry about the money—not at all. It's been a horrible time the last few days—horrible you know."

He sat down then, leaned over and lifted a cigar from the humidor, unwrapped it carefully, examined it critically, rolled it around a bit in his fingers; then digging a tiny knife from his pocket, he cut the end off slowly and carefully. Walker put the cigar on the edge of the table—a most unsatisfactory climax I thought. He got up and went to a cabinet—a Chinese one, I suppose—opened it, and disclosed bottles and glasses. No ice.

"Drink?" he asked and when I admitted it was possible, he took out a bottle, a couple of shot glasses, two larger glasses and finding a magazine—two in fact—set them on the table first, then placed the glasses and bottles on the magazines. "Help yourself," he said.

I poured a drink in the shot glass, watched him lean into the cabinet and produce a bottle of spring water. He poured himself one—found it wasn't enough and added a little more whiskey. He poured that into the tumbler—added water, a little more. Held it up, seemed satisfied—lifted his glass said: "Well."

I lifted mine, not bothering with the water, and tried. "How."

He set down his glass without drinking from it; looked at me a moment and said: "How did she look?"

I let my glass join the tumbler and the cigar on the table having a rule never to drink with strangers—when they don't drink. I said: "She looked awful."

"Poor kid," he said, "poor frightened little kid." He thought that over a minute—decided he could improve on it and added, "Poor foolish little kid."

After that he shook his head, shivered like a man who had just downed a drink, left the cigar and liquor on the table, said with a nod, "Nice knowing you," and turning walked out of the room closing the door.

The butler came in fully dressed and looking more distinguished. He brought sandwiches and coffee. "I am sure Miss Becky would want you to have something," he told me, letting me know it was his own idea. He waited then and tried. "She's very much like her mother—her dead mother, sir."

I nodded, looked very solemn.

"I've put you in the small room on the third floor, sir; not exactly a guestroom—not the room Mr. Landsgrove or Mrs. Halstead, that's the housekeeper, would have chosen, but—" he leaned forward—"it's directly over Miss Becky's room, sir—directly over it." And before I could make a crack he came very close and hardly breathed the three terrible words, "No bath, sir."

I shook my head and I hope showed horror, smiled and nodded showing that, under the circumstances, I would bear up with fortitude and understanding. I didn't question him. I know when to keep my trap closed—at least sometimes I do. When you get that conspiratorial approach from someone who feels you are in on the know, you can kill everything by letting on that you are not in on it. That is, if there is a know.

He waited and I tried a sandwich. Thin bread—crusts cut off; sliced white chicken with just the semblance of a piece of lettuce—as if the head of lettuce had stuck to the bread. Butter. I suppose it was butter and not oleo. They say there are palates that can tell the difference: maybe—but I can't. I simply guessed that butter went with a housekeeper and butler—and even the oil paintings.

I thought something was coming the way he waited around—unless Landsgrove had told him to watch the plates. But he stood there and I ate the sandwiches—peeking under each piece of bread for a thick white substance that denoted too much salt but was really arsenic.

Butts remained silent, then said: "The reporters have been calling, sir, constantly the last few minutes. They seem to know a great deal. I heard one of the officers, that is a police officer, sir, say the inspector would be furious—though furious wasn't the word. May I show you to the room now?"

I looked at the shot of whiskey—half reached for it and then lifted the bottle.

"A little drink never did anyone any harm." I smiled at Butts and when he agreed with me, "Well—a short snort for you, eh?"

"Oh no, sir—not that." He put so much enthusiasm into his refusal that my hand half-way to the shot glass, stopped dead and jumped back. Maybe he was simply a conscientious butler—I don't know. Anyway I left with him, liquorless.

He proceeded me through a door at the far end of the room—down a small hallway, into the dining-room, through a swing door to a pantry, and so to an empty kitchen.

"The reporters are actually clamoring at the front door. It was suggested to me by Inspector Nelson that you would not wish to meet the press. The servants stairs, sir; I hope you won't mind."

I said I thought I'd make it. We went up two flights of wooden stairs in semi-darkness. Even as we turned on the landings of the first floor it was plain I was seeing how the other half lived—no carpets or rugs. Then right by the head of the narrow stairs, my room. A rug there but I've seen better. A bed— I've seen better; let it all go—I've seen better.

Butts said: "If we had turned left instead of right on the landing below, you'd of been at Miss Becky's door. I hope, sir, you'll understand that this room is my suggestion, sir—entirely on my own responsibility."

He paused then and suddenly opened his left hand. Two white pills lay in the palm. "Miss Becky sent you these," he pushed them into my hand, turned quickly—at least quickly for his ample girth—and was gone. The climax then had been good. It didn't mean much as I sat there with the two pills in my hand— staring down at them. Yet, they must mean something. I lit a butt and stared at the pills. Ten minutes later I got up and looked out into the hall—then I decided that a trip below wasn't to my best interests. So I hit the hay—but didn't lock the door. The reason was simple; it had no key.

CHAPTER 5

THE DOOR CLOSED. I heard the click of the latch—and was wide awake when the key turned; the key that hadn't been there the night before. The feet were very soft crossing the floor but I had my gun out from under the pillow and pointed upward through the sheet before the feet had reached the bed. You wonder about that? Why I had a gun under the pillow in such a respectable house?

The answer is I have a gun under my pillow in my own bedroom, in my own apartment. The nervous neurotic type, you'll say—perhaps. And you admire the indifferent devil-may-care boys who are in my business. Sure—I admire them too—I always liked their light laughter at my old maid ways. I respect them, too, for their great courage, their raucous laughter at danger, and the indifferent way they fall asleep any place, and open strange doors with a hearty jerk and empty hands.

Why, I've shown my respect for them over and over. I've stood beside their graves while the dirt was chucked in, head bowed—my hat in my left hand—and, of all things, my right hand up under a left armpit. You said it. I'm the nervous type—the living type.

My left hand was ready and when the weight came on the bed, I pulled the chain and let the light go on. It had not been a heavy hand on the bed—rather a light fanny. The girl was pretty—more than pretty—the low back, thin black nightdress was plainly visible between the open folds of the outer garment, whatever that was. The dark eyes and half-closed lids and the sharp but well-formed nose; and I looked at the hair. A little wild but only wild in the way it hung down over her shoulders—brushed and combed and shining. I put up my left hand and ran a hand through it and thought. *No mop— not anything like a mop.* Then I spoke: "You're—but you are Becky—the girl—"

She laughed. It was low and deep and nice and she took my hand and held it; then put the other hand around it.

"Nice, huh?" she said; "not the frump you carried into the house. I came to, to— well you did so much and risked your life. That's what the pills meant; the dope I didn't take." She hesitated and then, "I thought you'd come to me; but maybe this is better, safer."

So that was what the pills meant. I nodded in understanding. I said: "Yeah—I know—you came to thank me." I sat up straighter in the bed and put my gun back under the pillow. I got a good look at her and decided a fifth of gin would fit better than dolls.

"Yes, of course." Her hands tightened and I noticed they weren't hot now— not even warm—rather a little cold; and I looked her over more carefully. Her face—her half-closed lids—her red, red lips, the shadows under the eyes—the dark pencil. All in all there was an unnatural look about her.

She repeated: "Yes, of course, I came to thank you, but—" After a pause, she said suddenly, "Don't you want to hold me and, and—and—" her two hands tightened on my left hand—and held tight.

HER EYES MUST have watched mine for she let go my hands and pulled her négligée tightly about her. I raised my eyes and looked at her again—her too-red lips—her so-made-up eyes—and I dropped the gin for a coke; or maybe a tall lemonade with a cherry on top of it; or, at a pinch maybe, a small glass of sherry. I knew what she was then—or what she was supposed to be—she was playing a part. You know, as if an angel in the Christmas play had suddenly been yanked out to play the part of a slinking woman of evil. At least that would be her name for it. And very slowly she began to cry.

"Nix, kid—" I told her. "You tried to sell me a bill of goods—why?"

"I—I—I've read detective stories and—I'm not that bad, am I—I mean—" and suddenly. "Oh no—you can't think that. I came—I wanted you to marry me," and when I smiled, "Why not—lots of men would—lots. I'll have money when I am twenty-one. I could make it worth your while," and when I grinned, "I know about you, Race Williams—I do. Mrs. Halstead, our housekeeper, said you'd do anything—absolutely anything. For money, of course."

"Did she," I guess I bristled and then trying to be fair. "She meant most anything. What's the matter with you? How old are you anyway—seventeen?"

"Seventeen?" she gasped. "I'm almost twenty-one now, another three months— less than four. I know you must think me an awful child—everyone does—but I'm not really. I'm through school—just through—and father, well I've been at school almost steadily; that, and a girls' camp in summer."

"What?" I gasped. "You are to have a lot of dough of your own when you are twenty-one. And your father keeps you jailed in girls' schools—girls' camps most of the time—then—"

"Yes—I know. Anyone would marry me for the money. I thought of that when I was lying there in bed. Then I got thinking of you and at least I'd know it was for the money. But after I was twenty-one I could have the money and could pay you off. Father isn't to blame. When I was seventeen I—I ran away and got married; he was a foreign count—or said he was. Father had the marriage annulled. It never came out. Then father kept me at schools—here and there; I shouldn't blame him."

"Okay, okay," I interrupted. "So your old man was right; he was too busy to give you any attention, or find you friends, or see that you were entertained at the right places. So he kept you locked up—in girls' schools—and now you'll be twenty-one and have money; and the vultures will descend in droves dressed up like eagles and robins and even doves, I suppose." I looked at my watch, "It will be dawn soon. What did you tell the police?"

"Oh," she perked up almost gaily at that, "that I was on the corner and a car drew up and a man leaned out and asked if I was Rebecca Landsgrove and I said I was; and he said he was a doctor and my father had met with an accident and I got in the car and—and—well I didn't remember much after that, except I was some place in the city. That house I came out of." She paused and then, "Well?"

"It is not too bad—if you can make it stick and don't change it. It's been done that way—mostly with children. You read it, I guess."

"If it's been done—what's wrong with it?"

"Nothing." I finally told her, "If you stick to it. I mean if—if—if the police don't find your clothes in that house, and you add to the story to make it better. All right, Honey-bun, you—"

"Honey-bun," she clutched at my hand and brightened all up. "Honey-bun—that was what you called me in the car. I've been trying to remember ever since—to see if it was true."

"Your father's wealthy. You will have money of your own. Stick to your story; maybe they'll disprove it—maybe they simply won't believe it, but they won't badger you too much."

"But you don't believe it—do you?"

"No," I said, "I don't." And when she waited, "No ransom note, no money demanded—at least that I've heard of. And you didn't want to come home. You—"

"But the police won't care," she seemed to be thinking aloud. "Father's money— and position and influence," she paused, and then, "So money is worth something. If you have enough, you can get away with anything."

"Just about," I agreed. "Pretty near anything—except murder."

Her eyes opened wide—her lips began to tremble, the color went out of her face.

"Murder," she mumbled and tumbled off the bed in a dead faint—no fake faint that one. You could see it coming and she hit the floor like a thousand brick.

I was out of the bed, had Becky up on it and her head hanging off it, I cussed out my former laugh on the absence of a bath; no water for a fainting female.

CHAPTER 6

BECKY CAME AROUND and our positions were reversed. She was lying on the bed and I was sitting on the side of it holding her hands. The color came slowly back into her face—and she began to smile.

After a bit, she said: "It's all right—I

faint easy. I'll be fine in a minute. But why did I—did I—?" The color started to go and I thought, *here we go again,* and then the lips tightened and she sat up and gave it to me quick. "That's why I wanted you to marry me," she said. "Then you couldn't testify against me."

"Testify against you—what for—why?" I was a little confused. The word *murder* had hit her and dropped her over.

"I mean after you move the body—" she told me. "You will move it, won't you—?" And her arms suddenly shot around me and she was pouring it out and holding me tight. "Someone will go there and find the body—and my clothes—my things will be there—and my handbag and—they'll identify him even if it wasn't his right name. They'll identify him through me—because of my bag and the gun, too." Tears were on my face as well as hers—though not my tears. "I didn't mean to kill him—that is, I didn't want to kill him—I—I—I couldn't bear to have him touch me."

She was confused now, for it seemed—and rightly seemed, I soon found out—that she thought she had told me all this before she keeled over and I might as well hear the rest of it. I finally tried. "Who was he—and where was it? Better tell me everything, Becky."

Becky let go of me. She looked sort of wild. She shook her head; I mean really shook it as if to clear out the cobwebs. Then it hit her too.

"I thought I told you but I didn't—did I? He was Victor LeRue. That was never his real name; he made it up to impress me." She paused. "I guess it did at that.

It was on our marriage license; I married him when I was seventeen. I forgot him quickly enough after father found out and separated us. He was no good—really no good. Then he waited for me that day and—"

"What day? The one you—disappeared?" She was going too fast for me.

"NO—before that—" She hesitated and the color came back into her face; in fact it lit up like high noon on the desert for a few seconds, then was gone. "But I was with him when I—when they thought I was kidnaped—or something. We were married and father found out, got the marriage annulled and sent me abroad to schools at first—then other schools, girls' schools, back here in this country. I was never really anywhere with anyone, except Carter Walker. Well, Victor had been waiting and watching for me that day and fed me a line. That I still loved him, and was afraid to be alone with him because I did love him; and partly to convince him, but more to convince myself that it was all dead and over—yes, and revolting—I—I said I'd meet him again and take a ride with him."

"And you did?"

"Yes, I did and I was—well practically a prisoner up at the lake; the cabin by the lake, Carter Walker's cabin. You see I knew that cabin and could get in. It was unoccupied and I thought—I could talk and be through with Victor and laugh at him—and know I hated even the sight of him."

So THE TRUTH was coming out. "Poor kid" was right. She had made a mistake in her marriage and her father had sentenced her to solitary confinement for years; at least what amounted to that for a young girl. She had nothing but female companionship and—Carter Walker, the secretary. She told me about him. How he came to see her in Switzerland and later at the other schools and camps—and took her around a little.

"Like a jailer," I nodded.

"I suppose father thought of it like that—but not Carter, or not me when I was with Carter. He was very kind—very understanding, and I'm sure my final liberty was brought about through him—his influence with father."

She stopped a bit as if she was thinking it over.

"Maybe I resented Carter but I shouldn't have. He was too good—and considerate—and put up with a lot from me. I don't know why."

"He got paid for it," I said; "and after all, it was better than hanging around oil wells."

She blushed. At least she flushed up, for they say girls don't blush today.

"No," she was emphatic. "Carter didn't get paid for it—" and with a twisted sort of smile at the corner of her lips, "and I don't know if I was better than the oil wells. Though he certainly must be very fond of me—very—"

"Enough to marry you, I'll bet."

"Why, yes—" she seemed surprised. "I can't figure out why— I've tried and tried and I can't figure why—unless it is the reason he told me."

"It might," I didn't put too much heavy irony in my voice; I didn't think I needed to. "It might," I repeated, "be the money you'll get when you are twenty-one."

"Oh, no—" She shook her head. "It couldn't be that. Carter wouldn't be interested in my money—not at all."

There you are. You place her; I couldn't. One moment all innocent and childlike; and the next—well there she was at a cabin some place with an ex-husband she didn't think much of; and in between that a switch in character where she just shot Victor because—well, because she had to shoot him. And the crack that her father's secretary Carter Walker wasn't interested in the money she'd get.

In the long run, it all boiled down to what she wanted me to do. She wanted me to go to that cabin and remove her clothes, and her gun, and her bag, and any other evidence that might "embarrass her" if the body was found there.

"For it will be found, won't it? You see, it's a summer cabin really—but sometimes, of course, someone will go there and find the body." She looked at me shyly then. "I don't suppose anything really has to be done about the body yet—but if you went there for my things you would see it and wonder. That's why I told you I had to—to shoot him."

Truth is truth; she was right about that, I might—indeed I just might have wondered a little bit if I walked into a cabin and stumbled over a dead man. She was sure he never could be connected with her for he had only used that phony alias—Victor LeRue—just for her and the marriage license. And since she had been found in that old house in the city, the police never would connect her with him; his real name was Richard Larsen.

DON'T GET THE idea that this was all the simple cold-blooded telling of the killing of a man, for it wasn't. She broke down and cried occasionally and she would brush her hand over her eyes and run it up into her hair too, and wonder out loud if it was all real.

"Victor made me drink," she said. "He made me—but it happened— I know it happened. I can see him lunging at me, and my lifting the gun from under the blanket on the bed—you see there was no lock on the door—and then I was firing. That's the whole story."

"Not exactly," I tried. "That's all for the cabin in Connecticut, maybe. But it was a cold winter night, and there is thirty-five or forty miles to go— How did you make the switch to the house here in New York?"

"Oh," she said, "that. I'm not sure. I fainted, I know—or maybe I didn't then. Anyway I ran out of the cabin. I—I—" she paused, "I had to step over him in the doorway. Yes, I suppose it was cold. I don't remember that; I didn't feel it. They picked me up in a car—some men— two—maybe three—and well—there was the reward, I guess. Anyway, that is all blurry. Then you came."

"How long were you at that house?"

"I don't know, exactly. Not long I think; I slept. I don't know them. I don't know anything about them." Suddenly she was out of the bed and standing there and her voice was raised and she was saying, "Why do you question me like this— why? Don't you understand what I have gone through. Why do you—?"

I held her then—standing there in the center of the room. She wasn't a bad armful when you got the full impact. I didn't try to show her the absurdity of her accusing me of bullying her; I didn't even mention she had come to me and spilled the works. I guess it was true— colored a bit—maybe even most of it was true. I suppose I could even understand her going with the jerk ex-husband—to find out what was on his mind, and what trouble he could make for her. I could understand her confusion of time, for certainly she was a mess when I grabbed her outside of that house. That was no act.

No—I don't pretend to understand women. Not any of them, any time, any age, for that matter. But before I saw her back to her room, I wanted to know one thing. "Where did you get the gun?"

"Oh that," she said. "I swiped it out of Carter Walker's apartment one day." I wanted to know if he didn't miss it. "Oh, yes—" she said. "But he couldn't prove I took it; at least he couldn't get it back from me."

"He didn't give it to you?" I tried.

"Oh, no." She really smiled now. "In fact, the other day I found him in my room looking for it. That's why I had it in my bag that day—that day I met—" Her head was coming up now, "It's terrible, but I know now I had to kill him or—or be killed. I told him I'd tell—tell father— the police—everyone, that he had held me against my will and that was when— when I shot him."

I'm not saying there weren't a lot of

loose holes in the story; and I'm not saying I bothered too much about clearing them up. After all, she should pay a good price if I cleaned her stuff out of that cabin—and in three months she would be able to do just that. I even thought for a moment about marrying her, but decided against that. In the first place I don't fancy gals who decide to pop off their ex-husbands. In the second place I've heard a lot of talk about heiresses that turned out to get a load of bum stock. But she'd have money; otherwise, why did her father's secretary want to marry her.

Becky was back in her own giant bed and had gobbled up the couple of pills she had held out on the doctor, and tossed her arms at me like a child to be kissed—and what's more, I kissed her like a child. But before she passed out, I got the location of the "cabin by the lake" and then put my question before her flickering eyelids closed. "What was the reason Carter Walker gave for wanting to marry you?" I asked.

She smiled—a sleepy, pretty, damn it, a childish smile. Her lips hung open a moment and the end of her tongue came out, it licked at her lips and her eyes opened—but not too wide—and she said: "Carter said it was because he loved me—had always loved me ever since I was a little girl. He said—he said—he didn't care what I did—ever did—he loved me anyway. He—he—"

I leaned down to get the end and she mumbled: "Carter is cute—real cute."

"Yeah." And as long as I had taken the trouble to bend over, I tried. "Sure—he's cute. What did he say?"

"He said—he said it was his gun—and if necessary he'd take the blame and say he shot—him."

She sort of sighed and turned on her side and damn it, if she wasn't asleep. I straightened and went back to my own room through the dimly lit hall. I was grinning to myself. Carter was sure pretty cute at that.

I CLOSED MY door and stiffened, really stiffened. If you had plastered me in the kisser with a ton of coal, it wouldn't have hit me harder. So Carter Walker would take the rap for murder, would he. But how did Walker know about it? When had she seen him? How—how—but could she have seen him before she saw me? Would she—

It was possible. She was a girl who got around. But would she tell Walker—and why—why— What the hell? Was she going to marry him, too, so he wouldn't be able to testify against her.

Footsteps were pounding up the stairs—heavy feet, cops' feet. I got into bed, jerked out the light and the door burst open. It was Inspector Nelson and he was cock-eyed.

"All right, Williams," he said, "how did you do it—when?" He popped on the lights from the switch at the door. "You double-crosser; the papers are already on the street and they have the story just as—just as—you told—told—"

"I know." I tried to act sleepy; "just as I told the police— Oh well, I suppose they left my name out of it."

"Your name out of it?" he tossed a newspaper over on the bed. "Name out of it! They've got your picture all over the front page."

That brought me up, but it wasn't true; it was a small picture—but a good one. It should have been. I had planted it with a couple of boys that afternoon in case the story broke right—and Jerry, of course, had telephoned the dope in at the first all-night drug store he found after leaving us at the Landsgrove house.

"Sorry, Nelson," I yawned. "My apologies to you and the police—and to think all this time you have kept a picture of me hidden in your wallet. I—honestly, I never thought you cared."

I fell back on the pillow as he banged out of the room. Then I was up and reading it. It was good—very good; it did me justice for once. Not the heading exactly, but the sub-heading was fine: *"Race Williams sweeps Heiress From Arms of Death."* That would be Eddie Regan on the News; I always liked Eddie. I liked him a lot better now.

I was up early that morning; I nosed around and was pretty well convinced that Carter Walker hadn't been upstairs to the girl's room. Indeed, he had left the house as soon as he left me. Now—what and WHAT AND WHAT?

CHAPTER 7

I DIDN'T SEE Becky again that morning. But I saw Carter Walker— I saw him while I was cooling my heels waiting to go into the library to talk to Harland Landsgrove. The police had thinned out; indeed, if they were in the house, they were well hidden from view. Carter Walker came out of Harland Landsgrove's office a little flushed, and with a brief-case under his arm. I heard Landsgrove say: "Carter—Carter—I'm surprised and shocked. Surprised and shocked—but perhaps—perhaps—"

Walker stopped and looked at me.

"Race Williams—" he said. "Ah yes—Mr. Williams—I've talked with Mr. Landsgrove and—and—I believe he has your check ready." He looked at me steadily then and after a fairly long scrutiny, "Very fine work on your part—very opportune—"

He smiled then. "A great deal of money, Mr. Williams. Ten thousand dollars. I feel sure you will earn it—yes—yes—I understand you are very discreet—I did say *will earn it by*—by remaining discreet. Good-day, Mr. Williams."

Half-way to the front door he stopped and came back. "If your further interest is aroused, please—please call on me—I will make it worth your while."

Mr. Landsgrove did not ask me to sit down. He stood behind his desk waving a check in his hand though the ink must have been long dry. He said: "We feel—that is Rebecca and I—and—and—" he seemed to hesitate, then laid great emphasis on the name "Carter Walker, now that the unfortunate incident is over—and you have been duly compensated—we think it is for the child's best interest to forget the incident."

"The incident." I took the check and got a look at the amount, pocketed it, and then, "And the police are willing to forget it?"

"The police," he said and reddened slightly. "I presume they will perform their duty as they see—see it. Good-day, Mr. Williams." He didn't hold out his hand but before I went he couldn't refrain from the final crack. "It's a great deal of money, isn't it—and I assure you it won't come out of my pocket."

There you are. There was something fishy. I bought an early afternoon paper; outside of one paper, Becky was shoved to the second section and there were no pictures. That one paper had a feature story on the front page. It was not a nice article, but it wasn't too bad either—that is if you weren't the girl or her father or her friends. It was a bit of whimsy written with tongue in cheek I suppose—but on occasion the writer's mouth opened, and her tongue stuck out and there were barbs on the end of it.

It wondered if a certain young society girl was kidnaped, or did she kidnap someone herself; and it asked if the rumors that Becky had in her short trip from home been secretly married come from close friends. Maybe, the whimsy went on with a bit of vitriol as a chaser, *"when the rumor of that secret marriage is confirmed we'll try hard to believe that it took place in those dear lost days—and not in the five hours proceeding the announcement to the press."*

Landsgrove felt he was a sucker for paying out that reward money and his pride wouldn't let him have me believe it came out of his pocket. I suppose the girl would pay for it in the long run.

WHEN I REACHED my office the tele-phone wire had been burning up—Eddie Regan of the *News*. He came around to see me. He was full of complaints and abuse and what guys will do for a little newspaper notoriety, and what his editor thought of him and he of me.

I quieted him down—admitted someone might have made a fool out of me but certainly the story I gave to him was true. I did admit that there was no fight in the kidnapers, and explained that by the simple conceit that when Race Williams sticks a gun against a lad there never is much fight. Sure I tried to ignore the fact that maybe they didn't know who I was. But guns are guns—so what.

Sergeant O'Rourke dropped in too, and shook his head and clucked over the check I got and smiled over my story.

Then he leaned forward and said: "Listen, Race—I wouldn't peddle that story of yours any longer. The girl's story has changed. It went from kidnaping to amnesia; then to partial amnesia; and finally to a yarn that she had a row with her father and to punish him just went to friends. You know that childlike reasoning—'you'll be sorry when I'm dead' stuff. She wanted to worry her old man. Get even with him for being shut up so long in schools. Then she got scared of what he might do when she came home and—well, sort of staged a comeback in her nightdress—an escape from her captives—and you horned in and frightened her friends."

"Go on," I said.

"That made her ridiculous, and she got hysterical, and there you are," O'Rourke grinned and spread his hands.

"And the police swallowed that?"

"The police," O'Rourke said, "don't have to believe it. The girl is nearly twenty-one; it has now become a voluntary absence from home. There is no complaint against anyone—including parties or party unknown. It was a nuisance. It was far more than that." He shrugged his shoulders.

"But what good would it do to prove that she was off with some guy? What charge could we make? And if we made one, what one could we make stick? Her father was convinced she was absent involuntarily, so his panic was genuine. The girl never requested any protection. No law has been violated except the law of good taste which any lawyer would point out, isn't found on the statute books. And besides—"

"There is a lot of money involved."

"Oh, yes—quite a lot of money," he hesitated, "all the way around, and the hush-hush is being felt."

He started to talk about his daughters. The youngest of them would be graduating from high school and entering Vassar.

"Next May," he said when he was leaving, "I'll be a grandfather again. I will be a grandfather four times over." He hesitated. "You know, Race, it's a little harder than being a father." He frowned. "Hard to understand that. Doctor Henderson—that's one of the psychology professors at Columbia—says that isn't true." He shrugged. "But what the hell, he's never been a grandfather."

What did I gather from O'Rourke's visit. A hint that I fold up on my talk? Information he hoped to get out of me?

Or—what was more likely the truth—he was in the neighborhood and dropped in. A naïve attitude that last, you think. With any cop but O'Rourke it might have been.

I CALLED UP to see how Becky was—and got her old man. She was still sleeping. He appreciated my interest. Becky appreciated it, but he was sure that it was better for her if she didn't see anyone connected with the case. She was quite "contrite" he said. What did he mean? Your guess is as good as mine—maybe better.

Moving bodies around is not my business. I've done it, of course; I'm not one of these detectives who think of their licenses all the time. Those birds—outside the lads who own the few big agencies never average more than sixty or so bucks a week—if they average that. So if that's all a license is worth to a guy—why, defense plants are better. I know an expert mechanic who gets—but so do you.

I thought I'd go up and look the ground over in Connecticut and see how the land and the body lay. First though, I had to pay off Riley. Riley is quite a character. He spent seven out of his first ten years of manhood in jails—and hasn't been on the inside of one since. Riley passes out information; he says he is just a jobber of criminal news.

Other lads buy up products and sell them. Riley buys up information and peddles it. Sometimes the information is given to him and there is some sort of a split after it pays off… lots of guys on the underside of a great city have information to sell and do, and die. Not Riley.

He's sure of his stuff. And he's clever; he never sells a bad steer.

Riley met me in a crowded bar where I couldn't demand answers or threaten him. His clothes were immaculate—his carnation fresh—his cane swung under his arm, his little white mustache well waxed. He twisted the black ribbon on his glasses. He sipped his drink and, with his hat pushed back in a rakish angle, eyed me from his tonsorial splendor.

"The boys," he said as he pocketed the money without counting it, "or at least one of the boys, is annoyed at the head-ache you gave him. However, the money should help." I started to crab a bit about my small share.

"There, Race, it was nip and tuck with them if they would chance bringing the girl in themselves and grabbin' off the whole reward." He shook his head. "I advised against that, of course—the police wouldn't have liked it."

"You didn't tell me," I tried to get my information by being clever, "that they were in on the show and shouldn't be handled rough—just—not to shoot."

"Perhaps," he smiled at me, "I didn't know they were in on the show. As for the cracked head—I rather enjoyed that. He drove a hard bargain with me."

"The girl," I said, "was going home anyway? They collected at both ends, eh?"

"Perhaps," he took another sip. "I am interested only in the business end of my transactions—not the moral end of it." He finished his drink and bid me good-day. "No kidding, Race, they left us only two thousand each." The word grand would never pass Riley's lips. "I wanted

you to know they drove a hard bargain—a very hard bargain for our work."

And he was gone.

Our work. I liked that. He got a tele-phone call; he made one to me. We met in a bar where I paid for his drink—and he got two thousand dollars for it.

I finished my drink and since it was still early, took the long drive to Connecticut. Not long as the crow flies—nor long as the happy motorist takes his family on Sunday. Say forty or fifty miles—it wasn't so far out of Stamford, but more inland.

CHAPTER 8

I FOUND THE side road—the little dirt lane as the girl described it—where the cottage was. I drove easily by it—went another good mile and discovered that there was an out on a main highway on the other side too. I turned, went back and parked off the road, backing in on hard ground well hidden from the lane but in position for a quick get-away.

I left the car and cut across the fields—if you can call them fields. The frozen ground was hard—there was no grass, but twisted growth still stuck out of the ground. I know it would have been easy to drive straight up to the cottage. But not me. If a body was there—I wouldn't like them to see me.

I could always back out of the girl's story with the simple statement that she never told me or that I thought it was hysterical wandering—that is, I could if I wasn't found there.

The house was ideal for an entrance.

One could slip around to a side window and let himself in without being seen from any direction, and—

I saw the car—big expensive dark blue affair. It was not a police car—if a cop owned it for his private use, he had other income besides what the county or state paid him. The car was expensive without being gaudy. It was more a big executive car, such as Harland Landsgrove might have, and should be chauffeur driven—though on an errand like this not likely.

There was a window; there were closed shutters. There was a bent blind and being easily tempted I peered through. There was a light in that room. A broad-shouldered well-dressed man in fedora hat and top coat was busy. It was a bedroom, and a bedside lamp was lit. What was the big executive type doing—you'd never guess it. He was making the bed; that's right—he was finishing, fluffing up the pillows—not with a practical hand but doing a fair job at it.

He stood back and looked it over. He walked around the bed; he tucked it in a bit here, a bit there. Then he turned, jerked a rag off the table and began to dust things. That's right—table, head and foot of bed. My first thought was that he was destroying fingerprints—then I saw the gloves he wore. I watched him go to the door and wipe first the knob on the inside, then the outside. My second thought was the same as the first—except now that the fingerprints he was removing were not his own, or if they were he had left them on another visit. He turned and faced the window and I pulled back—before he had seen me, if he could see me, but not before I had seen him.

You guessed it, or had you? I hadn't. It was not the girl's father. It was the secretary, Carter Walker. Okay, so I slipped around behind the house, found the back door not only unlocked but a little "ajar," and walked in. Had the girl sent him? Had the father sent him? Or, had he come on his own?

There was a cozy little living-room with an open fire place and burned logs in it; soft easy leather chairs; a couch; a huge rug and a few throw rugs—I know because one of them right by the kitchen door nearly tossed me. There was a bear rug before the fireplace and an antlered animal above it. I say antlered because I'm not a big game hunter and have hurt lads' feelings by calling a moose a deer, or an elk, or even once a stag, which you would think would cover about any male of the species. I sat down in a comfortable leather chair and waited. I had nothing to hide; that is, nothing from Carter Walker.

I COULD HEAR Walker moving around in the bedroom—I could see the door which was partly closed. It opened and I grinned; this was going to be good. I'd sure fix our secretary's little red wagon. He came out. He didn't see me; he couldn't. He came out backwards having a last look at the room—stretched forth a hand and gripping the knob pulled the door gently to—tried it to see that the latch had caught, then turned slowly and faced me.

Would he faint? Would he go for a gun? Would he— And do you know what he did? He looked straight at me. He bent a little and peered at me—interested, maybe only mildly interested.

He took a step forward and looked closer. He said, and his voice was even and calm, "It's—you're the detective fellow, aren't you? Er—Mr. Williams." In a relieved voice, not because I was I, but because he was proud of remembering names, "Mr. Race Williams, of course. Very clever—very clever indeed. You followed me here."

"We'll let it go at that?" I said and when he waited. "Which room is the body in?"

"Ah," he seemed pleased. "So that's it. Then you didn't follow me; Becky told you."

He shook his head. "I saw her this morning, but she never mentioned you. Dear Becky—dear, sweet, uncertain, confused Becky. I suppose she thought you'd make a better job of it. She did tell you, didn't she?"

He leaned forward and took a step. "Mr. Williams, there is nothing I wouldn't do for Becky—nothing at all; we're going to be married."

"Yeah," I got up and stretched. "But she can't marry a lot of people so they won't have to testify against her."

I left him with that jolt and took a tour around the bungalow. It wasn't a very long tour. The bedroom he had been in—another bedroom—one bath—kitchen, and what might be described as a lean-to—only it didn't lean. The cottage was a rather nice little job. The closets were small, but plenty of them; and though a body could have fitted nicely into one or two, and be jammed into a couple of others, it wasn't.

No body; no sign of any body. Could Carter Walker have moved the body. He could have, but he hadn't. How did I know he didn't. Well, I was playing detective now—just like they do in books. All this stuff about me isn't true—at least right then, I didn't believe it was true. Race Williams all mouth and beef and gun. Not a bad combination either. The mouth tells guys what I will do—and the beef and the gun do it. A guy doesn't need much more in my business—but if his mind gets working, there is no reason why he shouldn't use it just so as he doesn't overdo it.

Most times I find that when I get on this deducing—with two and two making four business, it generally makes six. Most times I'm satisfied to let someone else tell me what the score is. They do a much better job than I do—especially when they have a gun coming out of their mouths dragging a few teeth with it. But now—

I CAME BACK to the living-room and said to Carter, "You own this place?"

"So you know that," he nodded. "Yes."

"Did you know the guy—Becky married, years back?"

He hesitated and then, "Yes—I did; I arranged the settlement. It was quite generous. He spent it though. He went to jail later; he was no good. Poor kid—poor adorable child."

"And you met him again maybe—lately."

"Look here," he said. "I understand you are on our side. Why the questions?"

"Don't worry. I'm on Becky's side all right," and when he cheered at that; "and that don't mean your side."

"Oh, but it does," he said. "There is nothing you could do for her benefit that wouldn't please me."

"Even break up her marriage—to you?"

"But that," he shook his head, "wouldn't be for her benefit. It couldn't be. She needs someone—needs someone very much now—with her mind mixed up like it is. This—this—"

"Killing a guy, eh?"

"Killing someone—" he paused. "I won't enter into a discussion of anything like that, no matter what she told you. You don't know Becky; you don't understand her. She will need someone now more than ever, someone who doesn't care what she did—whose—whose every thought is for her, about her. She needs the faith—the real faith—that she did only what she had to do from someone who believes it, believes in her enough to live with her always."

"And her money?"

"Oh," he said, "that; it isn't as much as she thinks it is."

"Still a good sum of money."

"Well—not when you expect more—" and with a shrug. "But it won't matter; she'll have me."

That one tossed me a bit, so I changed cars.

"You didn't have time to move the body, did you?"

"Body?" he said. "I don't recognize the fact of a body."

"Of course you don't," I nodded. "Because there wasn't any." And when his eyes opened wide, "Poor Becky—confused Becky. Do you want to tell me about it,"—and like the high class detective I was I threw in, "or will I tell you."

"Suppose you tell me."

THAT WAS WHAT I wanted and that was what I did. I let him have it.

"Your cottage, your gun, you arranging to pay off the unwanted husband. You keeping tabs on him, knowing that he was in jail. You figuring Becky—poor confused Becky wouldn't be too hard to handle. Becky who was in girls' schools for the last three—maybe four years. Okay. Becky finds you a little on the old side perhaps, and the father doesn't approve. So you make a plan.

"The former husband comes out of prison. You brace him; you give him a few hundred out of your savings, promise him more from Becky's inheritance, get him to lure, or drag, or coax her to this cottage. Becky—with your gun in her handbag—the gun you made sure she had by hunting in her room for it, after she took it—took it to protect herself from this husband."

"Good Lord!" he said. "You mean I wanted her to kill him—shoot him dead?"

"No. You didn't want that—nor neither would the ex-husband. The gun, you see, was loaded with blanks. This former husband promised her something to come here, made a play for her here, or threatened her in some way—forced her into grabbing the gun. Maybe she was doped up; maybe she had a snoutful; maybe—but she fired and he fell, and she thought he was dead. Then—then—"

His easy "nothing-throws-me" pose was gone. He had stepped back and sort of flopped into a chair. His hat was off and on the floor, and he was running a handkerchief across his forehead; and his mouth was hanging open and his eyes were bulging. "Go on; go on," he said. "Go on."

"Sure, I'll go on." I was feeling pretty good. "So you were down the road with a couple of strong armed guys you hired—maybe private detectives. Maybe you carried her out of this cottage; maybe you found her on the road. Maybe you pointed her out to the boys—and they drove her to that house and got frightened and—well figure the rest out for yourself." I went closer then. My case was complete.

He was staring at me now. Bewilderment—no other word for it.

"Well," I said, "not bad—eh? About perfect. And now Becky has such a confused story that her father might even smile on your marriage to Becky. A husband who can't testify against his wife. Anything to add?"

"No—no." He put both his hands on the chair and tried to rise but didn't make it. "No," he repeated. "There is nothing to add—nothing." His head bobbed up and down. "Remarkable—remarkable." Then he smiled or tried to. "You—you—are you going to take that story to the police?"

"No," I said, "I'm not."

"Good—good." He was recovering quickly. "Let me know the amount of your fee—a generous amount, Mr. Williams. You are—a remarkable—a very remarkable man." He fumbled around in his coat but if he was looking for a checkbook he did not produce it.

I said: "My fee? Wait till you hear the payoff."

He waited. I lit a butt and turned toward the door, or half-turned. He didn't look like a killer but one never knows. "You see, I'm going to tell Becky the truth—that you didn't dispose of any body for her, because there wasn't any body. And I'll let her know that your love for her was so great that you would saddle her mind for the rest of her life with the horror that she had shot her ex-husband dead."

"And now—now—" he said slowly, "she'll know she didn't kill him, believe she didn't kill him." He thought for a moment. "I wonder—but no, if you go to her with that story, I'll have to admit it." He nodded then. "But of course—of course—of course—"

CHAPTER 9

THAT'S THE WAY it was when I strolled out the door. I paused to drink in the cold winter air, threw back my shoulders and hummed as I found the lane and strutted up it to my car. What the hell. No body—no cops—no crime, even. I felt pretty good; why wouldn't I. So I'm a detective whose cases don't require headwork. Maybe. But when headwork was required, I sure used it.

I saw the thing in all its simplicity. Carter Walker—close to big money and never a chance to get his hands on it. And then—a small down payment on a cheap summer place way off in the woods. A few bucks to a fortune hunter and the promise of more when he married the heiress. A slight threat of the former husband and on top of that Becky spots Walker's gun—and takes it. Then to be sure she'll be carrying it, she finds him in her room looking for it.

Were the blanks in it then or did the ex-husband put them in up in the cottage? Did it matter? And the men hired to pick her up—detectives or cheap hoods—and of course, they didn't know the racket, but seeing a chance to cash in on the reward, they spilled they had the girl to Riley. And Riley tipped me off—smart guy, Walker, or so he thought.

That evening I saw Becky Landsgrove. She was young and frightened now. She came into the room, quickly, closing the door—looking back over her shoulder, then running to me.

"You—you—the body is gone." She was on me, clutching me by the shoulders—big eyes on me—frightened—wide eyes.

"Listen." I held her. "I've got good news for you, Becky, very good news," and when she came in with that if the body was found some other place it wouldn't make any difference because no one would know the name he had married her under.

"Yeah—you told me that." Then I asked, "Have you seen Carter Walker?"

"Yes, oh yes."

"What did he tell you?"

"Nothing—nothing. He seemed stunned and—he said you would tell me something."

"And not to believe it. Not to—"

"No—no—he said I was to believe it. It was all true. Something about not worrying; that if I heard it from him I wouldn't believe it, but it was true."

It threw me, but only for a moment. Then I saw it. The game was up; Walker was going to make the best of it. Becky couldn't tell her father without admitting her meeting with her ex and—so Carter might keep his job. Though I doubted that. But he could get another if the truth was not known.

I TOLD HER. Gave it to her in detail. So she'd see how each part of it was worked. She was stunned. I had to go over it twice—three times, some of it. She couldn't seem to believe. I started over it again.

"Oh, it isn't that," she told me. "Carter would have the head for it. But you see—it's so unconventional, and Carter couldn't—never has done anything unconventional."

"I suppose," I said, "it would be conventional to keep still about a killing, maybe remove the body."

"But that wasn't planned by him. It was something thrust on him. Something he had to do because—because he loved me. This—this—" her eyes widened; her lips parted. Her smile was beautiful. "Wonderful," she breathed, "but why—why didn't he tell me himself—before, I mean and—"

"Tell you," I laid it out for her. "Because he wanted your money, wanted to marry you. I—I," and I puffed a little there. "I saw it all and forced the truth out of him. He admitted it—all of it."

"I can't—can't—" and then her head began to bob up and down. "Yes—of course, I see it clearly now. Victor didn't fall right away when I shot. He sort of stared at me, grinned at me, then he clutched at his chest. It was so—so melodramatic. I see it now; I was confused or I'd have known. How could I be such a fool? It was so corny, so terribly corny. Then I ran—and—yes—they brought me to that house.

"Carter was there—and—he said he'd dispose of the body but not to let the other men know. He said—they only knew he was looking for me—and that they didn't know about the cottage at all and—and—he'd go and dispose of the body—"

Then she began to talk as if to herself. How clever it was of me to find out the truth, and she supposed Carter would have told her after they were married.

"I see now," she said. "He didn't tell me because—because he knew I wouldn't believe it. I'd think he just made it up to—to—to ease my mind. But Carter Walker of all people—to do that—to jeopardize his position with—with the company—with society. Carter who prides himself on—on—on—"

The door opened and Carter Walker was in the room and the girl was across to him. She was in his arms and he was holding her like—well like he had never held a girl before and didn't know exactly what to do with her. Becky was laughing and crying and saying: "Carter—Carter. It is true. You wanted me that much; loved me that much and—and I never killed anyone—never—"

You want to know what happened after that? I didn't. I turned and picked up my hat and walked out and smacked right into Harland Landsgrove coming in. Maybe I shouldn't have done it. Maybe it was none of my business. But it popped out of me. I said: "If you don't do something, Carter Walker is going to marry your daughter," and when he stared at me, "they are in the library in a clinch."

That was the first time I had seen relief, even pleasure, in his face. He actually beamed. He laid a hand on my shoulder. "I hoped; yet I couldn't believe that Carter would—could be such an idiot—and that Becky had sense enough."

He laughed and clapped me on the back. "By Jove, Mr. Williams, come in and have a drink with me. I do believe this is the happiest moment of my life—certainly the first happy one I've had about Becky since her mother died."

I could have gone a drink right then. I needed one; at the same time I felt if there was a toast with it, I'd have choked over it. I left Harland Landsgrove laughing happily on the steps. I of the room—across the hall and went down the street. All right, all right. Maybe Becky deserved what she was getting—at least her father thought so, but it didn't strike me as particularly funny.

They were married suddenly and secretly a week later and left for Palm Beach. Sure I got a notice of the marriage, undated, and the papers must have got one, too, for it was more than hinted they had been married a month earlier, which would cover the time of Becky's "disappearance."

I don't know where they got the money for the trip—probably from her old man. Her old man sent me a check for five thousand dollars—for services rendered. Now, I like money as well as the next fellow—probably better—but I sent it back. It was all something I didn't want to be a party to. I stuck it in an envelope and, without explanation, sent it back.

Six weeks more and things began to happen. It happened first right by my garbage pail. I was putting some stuff in an old newspaper. I looked at the date. The paper was ten days old. It was a small item. The body of a man had been found half a mile from Proctor Lane—up in Connecticut. His fingerprints disclosed a prison record. He was easily identified as Richard Larsen.

The ex-convict, the short paragraph concluded, *had evidently been killed some place else. He had been shot twice through the chest—one bullet entering the heart. Doctor Walton said because of the severe cold it was difficult to place the time of death—perhaps ten weeks—certainly not less than a month.*

Do you get it? Good—I didn't; that is, I didn't get all of it. Not right away, I didn't. Sure, in time it drifted through that brain of mine that I hadn't quite used my head as I thought I had. Becky Landsgrove *had* killed her ex-husband all right, and Carter Walker had gone back to the cottage and disposed of the body. When I found him there he was simply checking up to see that there was no trace of the dead man's presence left behind.

No wonder he was startled and confused and bewildered at my beautiful recital as to what had really taken place. And he jumped at it because it gave him an out as being an accessory after the fact of—of—well, it was homicide no matter how you looked at it.

The bell rang then, and I went to the door—and jerked back. It was Sergeant O'Rourke. Had he seen the item, too? Was it coming out now? O'Rourke was my friend. Sure, he was my friend but he was a cop first and he'd want to know about— Boy, he sure was dressed up.

"Just dropped in to see you, Race," he beamed all over, and when I asked him to have a drink, "Not yet, thanks." He came into the living-room, started to sit down, thought better of it, stuck a hand under his stiff collar, grinned sheepishly, "Mary Margaret wouldn't like it," he shook his head, "not liquor on my breath," and then, "and since I've kept the crease in my trousers I might as well—"

"Mary Margaret," I gasped. "Who is—"

He wasn't listening to me. He was unwrapping the square parcel he had under his arm and finally produced a portrait photograph of—of course—his youngest girl Mary Margaret.

"She won the scholarship," he said proudly. "It's being presented tonight— It's all written on that card there clipped to the picture. I was wondering if that friend of yours on the News couldn't get it in—tomorrow or the day after. My wife said to see that the picture is returned. Mary Margaret—it's spelled out there at the bottom."

I was taking the photograph and nodding and thinking, of course, it wasn't about finding the body—for that was over a week ago. Then I blurted it out. "What—what—" I asked, "did you think of the secretary marrying his boss's daughter?"

"What secretary?" his eyes widened. "What boss's daughter?"

"Why Landsgrove's daughter, Becky, of course—and Carter Walker, Landsgrove's secretary."

"Oh," he grinned and rubbed at his nose. "The cops always figured she was with Walker—sort of a premature honeymoon." Then he laughed. "Landsgrove's secretary, eh—that's a good one. Carter Walker would enjoy being called that—I don't bet." And then as it struck me in a sort of haze, "The catch of society, Carter Walker—he could buy and sell Landsgrove over and over."

There was more talk and it came out. Carter Walker was secretary of the Landsgrove National Oil Company. O'Rourke was saying: "Secretary and Treasurer, no less—and holding the controlling interest in the company; very wealthy man; shrewd man, too—one of the best brains in the industry, I am told."

"Money—brains—then what did he want to marry that girl for—Becky Landsgrove? She's—she's goofy!"

O'Rourke laughed and laid a hand on my shoulder. "They're all goofy, Race," he said. "But—but we marry them anyway, God love 'em."

He was gone. I knew now why Carter Walker married Becky. Why—why—he would have been willing to give her up to free her mind from the awful load that she had killed a man, no matter how or why. And—yes, he had married her for the reason she gave me. He—he—well, he loved her.

The next hour I spent composing a short note. In the end it read simply.

Mr. Harland Landsgrove.
Dear Mr. Landsgrove:
Through some error in this office—a check made out to me by you was returned to you.
Will you please, if you still have the check, send it to me at your convenience—or if destroyed—make out another.
Thanking you—etc.—etc.

There you are. After all, from what Landsgrove had said at the time—Carter Walker must have put up the ten grand reward—and I had kept quiet about the body, even if I thought there wasn't any. Also, there is no doubt that I did give Carter Walker—Secretary and Treasurer of the Landsgrove Oil Company—the idea that—that gave him a happy (hic) care-free (hic) bride. And who am I to criticize if a guy wants a (hic) bride.

I have always said my business is a rough business, no place for clever thinking and keen character analysis.

CARROLL JOHN DALY